The Trail of the Rainbow

By

Helen Makinster

ISBN: 1-4033-2838-2 (e-book)
ISBN: 1-4033-2839-0 (Paperback)
ISBN: 1-4033-2840-4 (Hardcover)

This book is printed on acid free paper.

1st Books - rev. 07/23/02

<u>Dedication</u>

For my husband Robert, whose support, love, and guidance go without measure.

For Lila Bertino, my mother, for her loving faith in me.

For Clara Bo Whiteman, my beloved friend, who said it would be done.

For Judith Royer who made this book a reality with her hard work typing and editing it.

For Stephen Strickland, thank you for the follow-up editing, God bless.

Introduction

Self-discovery ripens and comes to full fruition for Ken Ferries in the autumn of his life. The events that lead him into the realization of his powerful psychic awareness are often poignant and highly charged emotionally. Ken will encounter the prickly emotions and the suspicions of a small town caught up in the gripping murder of a wealthy rancher's wife.

Loss of laid back rural innocence has made its claim on the lives of the people of Rosewood, Texas. It has forever changed the life of Ken Ferries, who will never view the course of life the same again. In this small community, he will come to understand fully the old expression that there are more things in heaven and on earth than this world dream's possible.

Forward

Dreams come mostly to us in a jumble of nonsensical short reels. However, those dreams may sometimes have a meaning that we may interpret abstractly. They indubitably have a message for us. However, those dreams are more like visions. · They are powerful and we cannot overlook them. I do believe that our super-conscious beckons to us prophetically to clearly search for their meanings. Such a dream led me to write this novel "The Trail of the Rainbow". It compelled me to get up one morning from my bed and write of this vision/dream. As I wrote, an unseen presence came to me with a clear message. I realized that the message held power and greatness for everyday life. This power is more far-reaching than most of us comprehend. While I wrote, I came to regard life with yet deeper significance than ever before.

We are all in a state of Grace in our boundlessness to learn, no matter what life we have chosen. Life is the powerful teacher that allows us, through our errors and stumbling blocks, to come to our river's deepest depths. This then is a truth that ultimately each soul is led to. Our journeys are our own free choice. Would we wish it to be any other? My attempt here, as I write this down, is to explain my own reality arrived at over the years. As you seek your own, may you have peaceful journeys.

Chapter____1

"Nadine Rogers? Yeah, I knew her," answered the man with the steel gray eyes solemnly. For a moment, Ken Ferries, former newspaper reporter, thought he saw a flicker of pure anguish in the eyes of this man, yet he noted at the same time, the crease of his strong jaw hardened. He sat quietly for some time before he finally spoke again. He had a deep voice and a slow Texas drawl, which sounded almost reverent as he went on.

"Prettiest woman in these parts, I reckon, and there was more than one man would of liked to call her his own. But Nadine was Will Rogers' woman from the time they laid eyes on each other, and everyone knew it." He paused a moment and then went on. "They just came together from that night they first saw each other at the dance there at Windom Hall. That's the town's gathering spot and about everyone around here takes in the dance on Saturday night."

"Will hadn't been home long, a few days maybe, after a 4-year hitch in the Marines. While he was gone overseas, Nadine and her folks moved here from Oklahoma. Her folks bought the old Willard place and set it to rights again. Place had been run down some years after Gus Willard went to the local old folk's home. Gus had a no account son and his Mrs. died when the kid was in his late teens. Right after she passed, the son took off and nobody's heard of him again. Stole what money Gus had in the house and headed off in that old pickup truck with the dented up fenders that he drove like the mill-tails of Hell. Probably good riddance, but I felt bad for Gus. Seemed like he aged fast after the Mrs. died and the only kid they had turned out no account."

"Say, mister...?" Jeff turned now to the bespectacled Ken, who had removed them and taken out his handkerchief to mop the sweat off his broad brow. "Why would you be so interested in the Rogers family?" He held a steely gaze on the man like he was looking clear through him. It was the way Jeff sized up a person, never wavering that clear penetrating gaze. He was a rugged man, due to his work in the outdoor elements all of his life, but also roughly handsome.

Ken had met Jeff earlier coming out of the country grocery store carrying a sack under one arm and holding a Coca-Cola in the other. He'd held the screen door ajar for Ken and nodded as Ken's big frame entered the store. Ken had noted the name of the grocery store as he'd pulled his car up in front of it— Wieses Country Store. Upon entering, he'd noticed the elderly man behind the counter, tidying up the shelves with a feather duster. At the cash register was a plump, pleasant-looking white-haired lady tallying up the day's cash flow. He introduced himself to the elderly man, handing him his business card and explaining the nature of his visit to Rosewood.

"Oh, sure, we know the Rogers family, but I reckon Jeff, the fella that just went out of the store, is the one you ought to talk to. He can tell you more than the Mrs. and me. You see, he used to go with Nadine Rogers before she took up with Will and married him. Jeff and Will grew up together and are closer than some brothers, and so if he's a mind to, he can tell you the information you're asking about." He paused as though to gain his composure. "Certainly the worst possible thing we've seen here," the elderly man said, shaking his white head. "That sweet young woman was loved by everyone who knew her and we still can't believe it."

Mrs. Wiese turned away from the cash register now and, addressing Ken, said, "We're just country folks here, mister, and like Don's a-telling you, there's nothing like this that's ever happened, least not here in Rosewood. Nothing that would equal the horrible thing that happened to that sweet child Nadine." Her eyes held unshed tears and she fought for control as she went on. But her voice broke as she spoke again. "Don here and me," she gestured to her husband, "are in our eighties and we've watched most of these folks grow up, and seen some die off. But I can tell you, it's hit this community with a sick and hurtful thud." She placed a clenched fist to her breast.

"Yes, ma'am," Ken murmured in reply. He felt obliged to explain why it had so greatly impacted him, though he was a long-time veteran of many such news copies.

"I grew up on a ranch in a close-knit community like Rosewood," he reflected aloud. "So I guess it's reasonable I felt such a pull toward this particular case." He could sense that they relaxed when he shared his background and expressed keen insight for their grief. They could hopefully see that he wasn't just another case-hardened news reporter gone freelance out to hustle a story.

"Well now, it has been my pleasure to talk with you good folks," Ken said, "but if I'm going to speak with Jeff out there, I best do it before he takes off." Ken had noticed Jeff put the grocery sack in his pickup truck and then settle onto the wooden porch step to drink the Coke. Ken opened the screen door and found Jeff with his long legs stretched out before him. He had leaned back with his elbows resting on the porch. He squinted up at Ken as Ken slowly lowered his husky frame down on the porch and extended his hand in greeting.

Thus had ensued the conversation regarding Nadine Rogers and her family until Jeff suddenly became aware that he had spoken more than he customarily did to anyone, let alone a stranger. And especially about this particular and all too painful matter. He had been caught up in a quiet moment as he often was at these times, thinking about Nadine. The love he had for her burned like a torch inside him even now, and had from the first evening he met her at that Christmas party at Pace and Marilyn Allard's home.

Pace, a fellow attorney, and Marilyn held an annual Christmas open house for the whole community to express their goodwill and appreciation to the people of Rosewood. Sometimes Jeff felt there was a hint of ruthlessness in Pace since he had ambitions that reached beyond his career as a small-town lawyer. Jeff couldn't quite establish the nature of his uneasy feelings, but they would appear every time he was in the presence of Pace.

He had always liked Marilyn Allard, a pretty woman who had gone to school with him. Marilyn came from a prosperous family of landowners, the only child of Abe and Lillie Falzone. Abe was a real estate broker and had done very well. Several people over the years had been heard to say that he probably had more money than God. Marilyn was unspoiled, though greatly privileged, as the Falzones made special efforts to see that their daughter kept her modest and unpretentious nature while growing up. She had gone to study law at an elite school in Boston, but met Pace and decided to leave that career to her husband. Sometimes Jeff detected an underlying sadness in Marilyn and felt she put on a brave front.

That year, Jeff had brought Muriel Jacob, a long-time friend, to the party. Muriel had asked him if he was going to the Allard's open house, and though reluctant to go, he knew Muriel would like him to take her. When they arrived, Jeff had seen the girl sitting by the fireplace in the large wing-back chair, a golden girl with a saucy little smile. She was the most beautiful girl he had ever seen and she made his heart thump like a runaway horse in his chest.

He remembered asking Muriel with halted breath, "My God, who is that? She... why, she...." And he sucked in his breath. "She's so beautiful." He had flushed beyond his golden tan when Muriel smiled at him, her eyebrows raised, amusement playing in her eyes. She asked, "Would you like to meet her?"

He was usually a quiet man and was flustered by having expressed that much out loud. "Well now, I reckon I would," he'd told Muriel.

She had tucked his arm under hers, saying, "Well, come on, cowboy. I'll introduce you." And she had teased Jeff, chuckling aloud "I have never seen you so flustered."

Nadine had placed her slim hand in Jeff's heavily-callused, work-worn one as Muriel introduced them and so had ensued their relationship. Jeff had been careful not to pressure Nadine, who had expressed her plans for a teaching career. She had gone to a community college in Oklahoma before moving to Rosewood and planned to resume school in nearby Tyler soon after the holidays. How many times he had cursed himself since for not asking Nadine to marry him. They had dated awhile, long enough that he felt he should have proposed.

5

Ken asked Jeff, as they sat there on the porch, if he had been satisfied with all of the specifics of the trial, if he felt there might have been some things that had not been brought to light. "Guess maybe I never thought about it," Jeff drawled. "'Cept those three privy rats got sent up where they belonged."

Ken arose slowly from the porch, feeling his sixty years, and handed his business card to Jeff. He explained the research he was doing in the Rogers' case since retiring as a journalist and going freelance. He extended his hand to Jeff once more and bid him good afternoon.

It was a hot, humid day for early spring and he needed to relax in an air-conditioned building and enjoy a good supper. He hoped the café would have both. Ken walked toward his gray sedan with a big-man's gait, leisurely, never hurrying. His large frame and easy manner often belied his strong intellect and unwavering sense of purpose. Those only became apparent as one came to know Ken Ferries. He'd always been noted by other journalists as a man with bulldog tenacity and honesty who would never resort to any form of yellow journalism, a man who wanted to get to the guts of a story. Yet he was adventurous and quietly aggressive too.

Ken possessed a near psi ability which at times was uncanny even to him. He felt compelled, in fact almost driven, to the Nadine Rogers case. He had seen her picture staring up at him from a news story and, even in that black and white photo, he had noted a woman so lovely and sensitive it was like she spoke to him. Why would anyone harm her, he'd pondered at the time? She was a busy rancher's wife, a mother of three grown children, and a grandmother, although one would not have know this to look at her. She was of notable splendor, the way some women are even in advancing mid-years. She looked ten or more years younger than the forty-six she was at the time the photo was taken.

Several things about this case just didn't add up right and the curiosity of Ken Ferries was whetted. He had made a careful list of the many people involved directly or indirectly in Nadine Rogers' murder case. It became a near obsession to Ken to vindicate this sad chapter of a beautiful woman's untimely demise. He knew within reason it would never be completely resolved, because a soul leaving is never easy for those left behind. But, in the case of murder, the healing is slower and closure is practically impossible. Ken knew the Rogers family was to be dominated with a sad and terrible shadow for the rest of their lives.

With a purpose, Ken drove to the café he had seen in Rosewood, looking forward to what he hoped would be a good meal. It was a lengthy drive to his home in the suburbs of Waco and he had advised Sarita that he would not be home that night until late. He shared his home with Maggie, a 4-year old Golden Retriever, and his live-in elderly housekeeper Sarita. She was a spirited, lovely woman nearing her mid-seventies with a commanding presence and she fussed over Ken like a mother hen over a baby chick. A smile lit up his broad features thinking of her. Her black eyes would bore into him while she pulled up her short, squat figure to scold him about not eating on time. "Aw, Sarita," he mused. Such a good caretaker, a good woman. Sarita was born in Mexico and had come to work for Ken and Gloria so many years ago it seemed like a lifetime now.

Gloria— God, how he missed her. She had been gone five years now and it had not gotten any easier for Ken in her absence. The cancer, when they found it, took her so fast. Within three months she was gone. Ken was deeply grateful that Sarita was there and he felt that, if she had not been, he would have possibly sunk into extreme depression or much worse after Gloria's passing.

Gloria, a freelance writer, hired Sarita while she was expecting their first child, a bright-eyed and perky little girl they named Holly. Holly favored her mother, with the same gray-blue eyes that would turn violet at times. She had that silky dark brown hair like Gloria's and always the same ready smile. She was Ken's pride and joy. It had seemed only natural for Sarita to stay on helping the family. After all, to the Ferries, she was family.

Two years after Holly was born, Carter arrived, a husky young man even at birth. "Little sober-sides" his mother would say, smiling softly as she'd lightly pinch his nose. Sarita would sometimes pantomime as Carter grew into a toddler, mocking his sober little face. "Aw, so serious, Señor Carter," she would coo lovingly to the boy. Carter would try to hide his face but not before his bright blue eyes glowed and a quick smile could be detected melting the last vestiges of his reserve. Like Holly, he adored Sarita.

They were a happy family, but children grow up before one realizes it. Soon came a day when Ken and Gloria watched somewhat sadly as their Holly went away to begin nurse's training. There she met and became engaged to Bart, a tall blond young man with a sunshine nature that matched hers. He was but a short time out of medical school. They married after a rather short engagement and Bart, a general practitioner, hung out his shingle in San Antonio. Theirs was a joyful union, their love and affection apparent to all.

Carter spent two years in the Special Forces division of the Rangers and later, after mustering out of the service, entered college for police science in Houston. Carter had not been in a hurry about a career and debated for some while before deciding, while Holly had known since she was a girl that a healing profession was to be her vocation. Ken had felt no concern, knowing Carter to be a person who weighed choices. Ken had great admiration for both of his grown children and their vast personality differences.

It gave him pause on a deeper level to ponder these two souls, both from the same family but so different. And yet they always held each other in the highest regard, having a special love-filled brother/sister relationship. They were indeed kindred souls, these children of his and Gloria's, and he basked warmly in thinking of them.

Carter had surprised everyone last Easter when he brought Lila home, a beautiful young student teacher with a mound of auburn hair and flirtatious cat-green eyes. She was nearly as tall as the six-foot three Carter. Her warmth and humor quickly captured the entire family's heart, as Ken was certain she had already totally captured Carter's big heart. Carter was never easily flustered, but he would redden with a slow smile on his wide features while Lila openly flirted and teased him outrageously. She was as mischievous as Holly and with that same sparkle for life. Ken smiled now thinking of Holly, who had winked at him over

Easter dinner and said, "I think Lila is just what our Mr. Sober-sides here needs to lighten him up. Eh, Dad?" Sarita had nodded crisply, expressing her agreement.

Yes, life had been good and full, Ken mused as he slid into a booth at Dolly's Café. Mostly good but a bit lonely at times, he decided as he picked up the menu. A slender blond woman, with her hair caught back in a barrette, approached with a pad and pencil poised to take Ken's order. After a brief greeting, she pointed towards the counter and said, "Our specials are there, if you're interested." There was a wall-length mirror where someone had written in red letters the heading "The Specials of the Day".

"Well," Ken drawled, "how about that catfish supper? Nice and fresh, is it?"

"You bet," the waitress answered in a husky voice, while Ken noted her nametag reading Muriel. After writing up Ken's order and walking a few steps away, she turned around to face him again.

"Sorry," she said, "I forgot to ask what you want to drink."

"Black coffee and a tall, cold glass of water will do fine," Ken smiled. He looked aimlessly around the café, noting the décor was homey with crisp red and white country curtains at the windows. The spic-and-span look was favorable to him.

He continued to take a survey of his surroundings, a habit he had developed as a result of his years of observation as a journalist. There was one lean cowboy sitting at the counter laboring over a piece of pie. He had nodded briefly at Ken when he'd entered the café. A young couple sat in the booth in front of Ken, engaged in a heavy conversation and focused completely on each other. He noticed no one else. Then he realized what he had done and grinned to himself. "News hawks, just can't break the habit."

Muriel brought Ken a mug of coffee and a tall, ice-filled frosty glass of water. Ken realized suddenly how thirsty he was as he reached for it. He also felt a different draft of coolness shift toward him which seemed to penetrate his whole body, and he involuntarily shivered. Looking back toward the counter, he saw a deeply weathered man with black eyes like coals bearing down on him. It gave Ken a start, as just seconds before he had looked toward the counter where one lone cowboy had been sitting eating his dessert and drinking his coffee. Ken noticed this man was an Indian and his thick gray hair hung down to his shoulders like a heavy mane. He was adorned with a gourd that appeared to be some kind of jewelry suspended on a piece of rawhide.

Ken nodded politely at the man but he sat there with a watchful, unblinking stare boring down on him. Ken turned back to his coffee in an effort to break the discomfort he felt crawling up and down his spine. When he looked up again shortly, the man had disappeared.

When Muriel brought his order, he asked her, "Did you see the Indian man at the counter?"

"Oh, him." Muriel shrugged. "He gives me goose bumps. You never know when he'll pop up. That's Nathan Tom, the old goat and sheep rancher. He is a weird one, all right." She went on, "But some folks claim he has supernatural powers and is a shaman. I don't know how much of that I believe, but you gotta wonder the way he seems to appear out of the woodwork and then just as readily disappear."

Well," Ken chuckled, more relaxed now, "he sure gave me a start." He then further engaged Muriel in light conversation, asking her how well she knew the Rogers family.

"Sure, I know them. You've probably heard about Nadine Rogers," she commented while she openly studied Ken.

He noticed her features were almost feline in appearance, a pretty woman with those chiseled features he found very striking. "Well, yes, I followed that case closely while I was a reporter for the *Waco Centennial*. But I retired a while back and began a new career as a freelance writer and I've been researching that case in depth." He handed her his card and she examined it.

"That's interesting, but why this particular case?" She then put the card in her apron pocket and held a questioning gaze on Ken, her eyebrows arched.

"I suppose mainly because some things I've come across just don't add up right to me. When I read the coverage on the case, I was just drawn into it."

"How so?" she asked him, her interest clearly sparked now.

"Oh, regarding some of it, I really can't say. I guess you might call it a hunch."

He watched the lean cowboy stand up and dig into his jeans pocket to fish out several coins which he laid on the counter. Then, he turned to Muriel, tipped his hat and bid her good evening.

"Good night, Cole," she smiled, "and thanks. Be seeing you."

"Maybe you can shed more light on some things for me," Ken said, regarding her closely now. She hesitated a moment and then shrugged.

"Well, why not. Well, that is to say, if I can I will. I 'll tell you what," she went on, "if you have some time, I can meet you across the street in, say, an hour and a half?" She looked at her watch and pointed at the front window. "Do you see the sign that says Bailey's Lounge there across the street?" He turned to look and then nodded. "You could wash that catfish down over a drink while we talk," and she smiled at him.

She had a face that was open and honest, a kind of homey personality. She now flashed an even brighter smile at Ken as she waited for his response. The cool green uniform she wore gave credence to a shapely, slender figure and Ken decided he liked this self-assured woman. She offered a friendly, easy-going manner in an off-hand way which put most anyone at ease. She might be direct, but that was to Ken's liking. She waited expectantly for Ken to answer and he smiled, nodded, and said, "Well, all right. I will be waiting at the Lounge, Muriel."

"Great," she smiled back at him and he noticed her eyes matched the green of her uniform.

Ken had lingered over his good meal and then paid Muriel his bill. He made a mental note to return to Dolly's Cafe as he concluded the food was excellent. He leisurely walked across the street to Bailey's Lounge. It was twilight now and he took notice of the evening star overhead, the only one he could see so far. Entering the lounge, he stood for a moment to adjust his eyes to the diffused lighting and then noticed a circular booth toward the mid-section of the lounge. He made his way to it, then seated himself, making certain he would be facing the entrance. He could hear strains of a soft Mexican melody in the background from a stereo somewhere. It gave way to a relaxed atmosphere.

He checked his watch and realized it would be less than an hour before Muriel would meet him. A candle burned softly in the center of his table. A Mexican man of middle age behind the bar motioned to a young woman coming from the back of the lounge, pointing in Ken's direction.

"Hello and good evening, sir. My name is Pearl. May I take your order?" She beamed at Ken with a dazzle of perfect white teeth.

"A gin and tonic," he answered, returning the smile to the pretty girl he figured was about Holly's age. "Pearl, a lady will be meeting me here in less than an hour, so I won't need anything more until she gets here. All right?"

"Very good, sir," replied the young woman as she turned towards the bar to place Ken's order.

A Southwestern flavor, Ken noticed of the lounge interior, as his eyes became more accustomed to the lowered lighting. A man entered the lounge, made his way to a bar stool and sat astraddle it, leaving his somewhat battered Western hat on. He flicked a glance at Ken when once seated, then turned to the bartender and ordered a glass of draft beer. Ken idly noticed that the man was probably fifty years old and looked as if he hadn't shaved in a few days, as evidenced by the black stubble on his face. He had a hard look about him, Ken silently deduced, as he watched him dig into his Western shirt pocket for a pack of cigarettes and lay them on the bar. He wore jeans and well-worn riding boots and propped his elbows on the bar surface as he lit one of his cigarettes. He then watched Pearl bring Ken his drink. Something in his eyes was especially cold as he regarded Pearl and Ken felt uneasy at that coldness emitting from him. Ken sensed a darkness surrounding this man, so thick that he could almost see it visually. The man took a slow sip of the beer Pearl had placed before him, and with a cool deliberation, gave Ken a sardonic, icy sneer. Ken hoped Pearl would watch carefully when her shift ended at the lounge. He felt a sudden protective, fatherly instinct toward her.

The man turned back to his beer, with the cigarette poised in front of his mouth. After a length swallow, he pulled a long deliberate drag on the cigarette and blew a great gray cloud of smoke which circled his wide-brimmed hat. Ken took another slow drink of his gin and tonic in an effort to make it last until Muriel arrived.

He checked his watch and wondered if he should call Sarita to tell her he had made up his mind to get a motel room somewhere, since it would be too late to drive home that night. Better to start early in the morning, he decided. As he sat there, he thought about Nadine Rogers and went over again in his mind the reported circumstances in regards to her death. The accounts on television and the news copies said she had been killed in her spacious ranch home and the three men had been her killers. The reports also stated that they had entered the ranch home, catching her unaware and thinking no one would be home that day. They had come with the intention of robbing the home.

Nadine owned and operated the Arts and Crafts store in Rosewood, and on certain days during the week, she herself worked in the store. On the other days,

Rosie Wilson, their friend and neighboring rancher, operated the store for Nadine, helped some days by another friend, Sissy Conway.

The time estimated for Nadine's death had been registered at around 7:00am on Friday, July 5th by the Coroner's report. The instrument which bludgeoned her to death was a heavy, long-handled poker from the home's wall-length fireplace in the living room. Apparently, Nadine had not noticed the trio's pickup coming toward the ranch house from the gravel road. She had probably not been sitting in her customary chair which faced the dominant bay window where she could have easily seen the roadway. She may have been painting one of her well-known portraits in another room. She was building acclaim in her own right as a unique and talented artist of the Southwest.

Ken thought it odd that she would not have at least heard the truck pull in, if indeed she had been taken by surprise. These curious facts kept prickling away at him regarding this whole case, among some other unlikely elements.

Still engrossed in deep thought, he had not seen Muriel as she made her entrance. She slid into the booth and teased, "Penny for your thoughts". A pleasant smile dimpled her face.

"Oh, Muriel, sorry, I really was in deep depths, I guess," he said as Pearl approached their booth.

"Hi Muriel, what will it be?" Pearl addressed her.

"Oh, you know, my usual, Pearl—a whiskey sour and Ken here could use more of whatever he was drinking."

"How's Angie, Muriel?" Pearl asked before she left their booth to order their drinks.

"Well now, she will be coming home from Waco for a few days and I suppose you know she attends Bailor College?" Muriel said with a note of pride. "Anyway, she's just doing real fine," she drawled.

"Terrific" Pearl smiled, "Perhaps I will get to see her while she's home. I know you are proud of that girl and you should be too. She is a great kid."

"Sure am, honey. She's truly the joy of my life and was right from the first day she came into this world," Muriel stated with resolve.

Pearl smiled at Muriel with an obvious fondness and then went to the bar to order for them. As she did, Ken noticed the man sitting at the bar got up in haste and headed to the lounge's door to depart.

"Pearl used to sit with Angie for me some when Angie was tadpole size and so, of course, those two are close. That Pearl is a fine young lady," Muriel noted, her attention drawn to Pearl talking with Sal. Muriel looked over at the bartender then, waved at him and called out, "Hi, Sal."

He addressed her with, "How's it going these days, Muriel?"

"Oh, pretty good," she said and then turned her full attention to Ken.

Ken noticed that she had released her shoulder-length dark blond hair from the barrette which had held it back in Dolly's Café. In that easy manner of hers, she began with "So, all right, Ken, let's get at those questions and I will see if I can fill you in on anything you don't already know."

He liked her precise way of getting right into the matter at hand and he told her that whatever she could relate, he would appreciate.

"Well, now, let's see," Muriel began, as she leaned her face into her open hand, with her elbow propped on the table. "I met Nadine a short time after she came here from Oklahoma with her parents. She was just twenty years old. Of course I knew Will all the way through school. Used to go out with him some but nothing serious. We were just good friends. When Nadine moved here, Will was still away in the Marines. You know, it is a tight-knit community and it doesn't take long to get to know people, even if they move here from someplace else." She went on, "Of course, there's an influx of drifter cowboys—well, you know, range hands and crop followers too. And you don't really know some of them unless they are the regulars who return.

"What kind of man is Will?" Ken asked.

"Rock solid. A good man, deeply in love with his wife, and was from the first time he saw her. That was at the local dance hall, just a few days after he got home from a four-year hitch in the Marines. He joined right after he graduated high school.

"So, you would say their marriage was solid?" Ken said in conclusion.

"They were in love, both of them, as much if not more than the first time they laid eyes on each other. They had everything going for them—three beautiful kids. Phyl first—well, her first name is Phyllis, named after Nadine's mother. She's married to Chance Bennett, a local rancher, and they have a little girl Bree Carolyn. The middle name comes from Will's mother's name. She is a tiny doll and looks like her mother, who is a carbon copy of her own mother. I think little Bree is three-years old now. Phyl and Chance have another baby girl a couple month's old and, of course, her name is Nadine Darnell. Then there is Will Earl, the oldest son of Will and Nadine's. He looks just like his Dad, very handsome. And then there's that cutie Ty, his given name is Tyler Eugene. Ty's mainly a combination of his mother and dad, with a break-your-heart smile," she said tenderly.

"Phyl is a darling young woman and so close to her mother that it breaks my heart whenever I see her. You knew, didn't you, Ken, that she is the one who found her mother? My God, bad enough she lost her mother but to find her like that!" Muriel suddenly shivered. "Little Bree was two-years old at that time and was with her mama but, of course, she probably does not remember. But that trauma will be with Phyl for life. The whole family has changed so much and no wonder. I can tell you, Ken, it has changed this community I grew up in."

"Tell me, Muriel, in what way?" Ken encouraged her.

"Well, you tend to be more suspicious of others and especially a new face, I guess. You know the acceptance people always showed to anyone who came here is guarded now and it will be for a long time, I'm afraid."

"You trusted me, Muriel, enough to join me this evening," he said and smiled at her warmly.

"Ken, you offered information about who you are and there's a congenial manner you express that is to my liking." She smiled to confirm her appraisal of him.

"By the way," she said, "my last name is Jacob. Meeting you at the café came about quickly and I never thought to properly introduce myself."

He took her hand to shake it. "Muriel Jacob, it is a pleasure that is all mine." He noticed that she did not wear a wedding ring when she placed her left hand on the table top. He had purposely looked. It had been so long, Ken realized, since he had spent time talking with an attractive woman in a relaxed, conversational manner. He found it comforting and again realized he was lonely, and had been far too long since Gloria had passed away.

"How long have you lived here, Muriel? Or did I understand you to say all of your life?"

She chuckled. "That's correct and bet you're wondering about that, right?" she quipped, amusement playing on her face.

"No, not really. You see, I grew up on a ranch near a small town like Rosewood and those were some of the best years of my life. But when I was ready to graduate high school, I decided to go for a journalism career. I went to the university in Houston. Tom, my brother, went to agriculture school and helped our folks with their ranch. Then later, after he married, he and Robin bought a ranch of their own a few miles from our folks. It's just a few miles out of Snyder, Texas. Do you know where that is?"

"Yes, I do," she nodded. "Been there once or twice a few years ago."

"Well, now, it has grown a fair bit since Tommy and I were lads," and he smiled broadly, revealing even white teeth, Muriel noticed.

She wondered how old Ken was, because he was a ruggedly handsome man with slight touches of silver at his temples. But that only distinguished him to great advantage. His eyes were almost intense blue and, but for the silver at his temples, his hair was black with a bit of a wave to it. Muriel found she was enjoying this man's company in a way she had not enjoyed male company in a long time. She listened now to Ken relaying his background.

"My folks are in their eighties and they sold off their ranch a few years ago and moved to Snyder. They fully enjoy their freedom and they are both in great health, thank God. I don't believe I could keep up with either one of them. They seldom miss a dance at the Senior Resource Center and they bowl with a tidy average beyond most people half their ages." He chuckled. "They are avid walkers and Mom's a terrific cook. I tell you, Dad's flowers that he enters in flower shows always take top honors, and of course, Mom never fails to win awards for her canned foods and pastries." He smacked his lips for emphasis.

"Now," Ken paused, "tell me about you, Muriel."

"There isn't too much to tell, Ken. My parents own the country grocery store. You can't miss it the way you come into Rosewood."

"So, that's your parents, the Wieses. Yes, I met them today and they are a very nice couple" Ken said. "I chatted awhile with them after giving them my card and telling them the nature of my business here. They suggested that a friend of Will's, Jeff Colter, might tell me more about the Rogers family. I had met him on his way out of the store as I came in. He held the screen door open for me and then I saw him sit down on the porch step to drink a Coke. Trouble was, Jeff didn't feel much like talking about it. Seems he is very close to the Rogers family, but then I guess you're aware of that, Muriel."

"Jeff went through school with me and Will. My folks probably told you about them being best friends all of their lives?"

Ken nodded that they had, letting Muriel go ahead with her account.

"You know poor Jeff had it written all over him, the way he felt about Nadine, but he never acted on it once he knew Will and Nadine were in love. He just stepped aside and I know it hurt him real deep. It's too bad he never married. Oh, he dated some but just never found anyone that he felt measured up to Nadine.

"I got married awhile after I graduated junior college from Tyler, and Bill, my husband, got killed shortly after Angie was born. He was in a freak accident on a ranch we had leased…" She paused and Ken noticed her swallow hard before she resumed. "We'd been married a few years before we got Angie girl. She is one of the principal reasons I kept my sanity because I got real close to the edge when I lost Bill. My brothers and sisters are some years older than me, six of us. I was the last of the Wiese crop for my folks," she said and smiled widely, then chewed lightly at her bottom lip. Her eyes held a hint of humor.

"What?" Ken prompted her with a quizzical smile.

Still smiling, she related, "Well heck, after Mavis came, my dad crowed that the Wiese clan was complete and I've heard that his cronies gave him little peace with their off-color jokes, as only old cronies can do." And she chuckled in that deep husky voice that Ken found so earthy and appealing.

"As a matter of fact, Nadine Rogers, being a couple years younger than me, became a close friend of mine and she kept me afloat. She would literally drag me out of what was developing into a severe depression."

Ken listened attentively as Muriel went on. "She would not allow me to stay in bed where I would try to hide out if I could. I would let Mavis, my sis seven years older, take Angie to her home where Angie would be surrounded by Mavis and John's lively household of four children. That usually included half the neighborhood kids too. Mavis was always a mother figure and God bless her caring for Angie when I couldn't. Nadine would march in and command me to get up, go shower, and put on my face, as she called it. She would push me into the bathroom, scolding me at my protests while rummaging in the closet for something cheery for me to wear." Muriel smiled, her eyes a bit misty now.

"After a shower, she would pounce on me with comb and brush in hand and shove me down at my dressing table to arrange my hair to her liking. And with a saucy smile, would tilt my chin up for me to look squarely at myself, commenting, 'There honey, now aren't you pretty.' She was the light at the end of the tunnel, Ken, and the energy that girl had was boundless. She would say, 'Now call that sweet sis of yours and tell her we're on our way to pick up your sugar pie Angie. Then we are going to Mt. Pleasant to buy us all new dresses. Oh, now it's all right.' And she would wave her dainty little hand above her blond hair, wiggling her fingers, 'It's already taken care of. Rosie has agreed to see after my Phyl and Will Earl and Ty. And my big lovable hunk Will knows we'll be home sometime later so you go on now and call Mavis.'

"She'd call me every morning by at least 9 to see that I was not still in bed. And all that time talking about a picnic she had arranged for the children and us. Or it would be Sunday dinner—'Noon, straight up. And, honey, you must wear that soft lemon-colored dress we found for you over at Nicole's Classy Lady when we shopped in Mt. Pleasant.' And always ending, 'And don't forget to put on a face, Sweetie.'"

"Ken, I just didn't have time to grieve my life away because Nadine just took over and helped give me back my life." Her voice caught and Ken saw her swallow hard but she finally went on after a pause, "But you know, the key words she said that brought me around most was when she pointed at Angie asleep one day and said, 'Honey, don't make that little girl lose both her mommy and her daddy.' Well, something just pulled me up and out on the road to life again when she said that. Damn those bastards," she said and her eyes widened with tears as she clenched her teeth.

Ken reached for her hands, cupping them in his big ones. He felt his heart go out to this spunky woman as he watched the naked grief in her eyes. Her voice choked with emotion when she spoke again.

"I've tried to be there for all of them, the whole family, like Nadine and Will were for me when Bill died. But I feel so damned helpless." And tears were coursing down her cheeks. Ken produced his handkerchief and she dabbed her eyes quickly.

"Oh, well, maybe I better have one more of these," and she smiled with effort, holding up her drink, "then I can tell you more." She waved Pearl over to their table.

"Say, sweetie, we'll have one more of these before we call it a night. Ken here has quite a drive to go home yet." She looked around like she had only just realized and said, "Is this place dead or what?" Then she added, "Oh hell, it's Monday night so not unusual."

Ken realized she was being blunt in an effort to override her emotions and changing the subject was another tactic.

"Say, Muriel, when you came in here, did you notice the guy at the bar?" he asked her, as she seemed more settled.

"No, can't say that I did. Why?"

"Oh, I just thought somehow that he didn't fit in a community like Rosewood, looked kinda mean and scruffy."

"He's probably hired out on a ranch around here and not one of the locals. A drifter more than likely, like the ones I mentioned," she said.

Ken recalled that Nadine's parents had bought a ranch and he asked Muriel if they still lived on it.

"No, you know, Ken, they were killed in a car accident going to visit relatives in Hugo, Oklahoma not more than four years after they bought that ranch. Awful for Nadine—she was their only child. She inherited the ranch, of course. She was married to Will by then and Will told her he would help her with whatever she wanted to do with it but to leave it in her name. So she leased it out to a young couple that's worked it and kept it real nice. They run several head of cattle on it too. It's been very profitable.

The Conways, Bud and Sissy, haven't approached Will yet but Sissy did tell me that, awhile before Nadine was killed, she and Bud had arrived at an agreement with Nadine to buy the ranch. They put their hearts and souls into that ranch and raised their son Barry and daughter Kathy on the place. It's home to the Conway family. The Conways weren't more than nineteen and twenty-one years old when they leased that ranch right after they were married. Bud worked for Will Rogers Senior when he was a kid in high school. Hard workers, both of them, and I admire them. They waited on their family some years and saved and scrimped so they could build equity. And then, of course, when they could buy, it would give them bigger equity in the place. They are busy with the ranch and yet stay involved with their growing children too. Sissy even fills in now and then at Nadine's Arts and Crafts Store here in town.

"Say," Ken said, "this is perhaps off the subject but I'm curious about Will's name—same as the famous poet-humorist and yarn-spinner Will Rogers. You know."

"Well, now," Muriel smiled, "you see, Will Senior was named for 'the' Will Rogers" and she emphasized the latter.

"Just an old reporter's habit of wondering, I guess," he replied with a grin.

Muriel went on to explain that Will's father was born in Oklahoma and his father, Will's grandfather, was from a long generation of settlers in that state. But

Will's dad came to Texas with his bride Carolyn shortly after they married. They worked hard and, in time, bought property and began putting a ranch together. Will Senior became a sharp businessman and, over the years, made sound investments here and there. He's now worth a hunk of change.

Muriel went on, "Will is a chip off the block and he and Nadine built up their ranch to a high success too. He also made some very wise investments that haven't hurt them, rest assured."

Ken had heard of Will Senior from the market reports on livestock as well as several other far-reaching investments around the state. He knew him to be in control of various land developments and, of course, active in the cattlemen's association.

"Will's dad is in his early seventies and looks like he could pass for sixty or so," Muriel said. "Carolyn is a beauty, a lovely woman, and, like her husband, belies her age. They are just terrific people and that about sums it up."

Ken was enjoying the conversation and company so well that, when he glanced at his watch, he was startled to see that it was nearing 9:30.

"Say, Muriel, I'd better call Sarita and tell her I have decided to get a motel tonight and come home in the morning."

Muriel's eyes widened and she asked, "Who's Sarita? Your wife?"

Ken could see she appeared a bit flustered and he couldn't help but grin sagely.

"As a matter of fact, she's an elderly lady who has been like a family member since before my oldest child was born. She is my live-in housekeeper and she stayed on after Gloria, my wife, passed away five years ago."

"Oh," Muriel said, while working out this piece of information. "Oh," she said again thoughtfully, "for some reason, it just had not occurred to me to ask if you were married. We've discussed a great deal tonight and never got around to that," she said trying to seem off-handed about it.

"Well, yes, I was, and to a fine lady for a great many years. We had our daughter Holly and then two years later, Carter, our son. Holly's married now, no children yet. She's a registered nurse and Carter will soon graduate. He was a late bloomer on a career choice but spent some years in the Rangers, a special division of the Army. Now he is taking police science. Seemed he didn't know what he wanted career-wise for awhile there but both of them are great kids," Ken said with obvious pride. "Holly's husband is a doctor, a general practitioner, and I like him. He's a fine young man."

"Ken" Muriel said softly, "it sounds to me like you have a very special family but it must get lonely for you now that your children are grown and your wife is gone too."

"You know, Muriel, Gloria and I had a better-than-good marriage and we were very happy and, yes, I have been lonely since Gloria passed away. Frankly, I never allowed myself to realize just how lonely. But tonight, sitting here and talking one-on-one with a lady who is…." and he paused to search for the right words, "great to be talking to, a warm and vital woman who is so full of life…." His voice trailed off and, feeling his face color, he hoped she had not thought he was making advances.

Muriel reached for his hand. "Ken, you are a special person, do you know that?" Still holding his big hand in hers, she held him with a clear gaze and went on with deep seriousness in her husky voice. "You know, I have never believed in pure coincidence myself. I do believe there is a deeper meaning that brought you to Rosewood. Perhaps it is not quite clear yet but I do believe it is meant that you be the one who researches Nadine's murder." She drew her breath in sharply on that last statement and her voice shook when she went on. "It has to be a strong guidance from perhaps— who knows, only God knows why we take the roads we travel because, after all, it is a mystery. But there's ever a purpose, I know there is."

Now she smiled at him and said, "And by the way, Mr. Ken Ferries, the pleasure has been mine. Now go call Sarita. You did say Sarita?"

Ken nodded and then asked her where to find the public phone.

"Over there" and she pointed. "That is the direction to the restrooms and there is the public phone in the hallway."

"I will call Sarita and then escort you to your car, Muriel. And I want to thank you. You are a very charming lady and I assure you that I have greatly appreciated this whole evening with you."

Muriel thought the depth of his smile was a strong measure of his character. She returned the smile with that stealthy grace and feminine allure she held for Ken.

Ken made his way to the men's room first and then returned to the public phone to call Sarita. He knew she would be watching the 10pm news, as was her habit before retiring for the night. After the first ring, Sarita answered the phone, speaking in her prominent accent.

"Bueno, this is the Ferries residence. Who is speaking, please?"

"Sarita, hello, Ken here. Say, I will get an early start in the morning since it is late. I don't want to drive the distance to Waco tonight."

"Señor Ken, I know you well, big man. You like to talk mucho aplenty and the clock goes on tick tock," she snorted. "But is wise you stay where you are this night."

"Good," Ken responded with a wide grin spreading on his face. He'd known almost by heart what Sarita's response would be. "So, hasta la vista, Sarita and I will see you sometime mañana."

"Be careful now, Señor Ken, and watch for all the fools on the highway. O-key?" She had a certain emphasis on the word okay, simple and very literal. The way Sarita could illuminate words Ken never ceased to enjoy.

"Yes, Sarita. Goodnight and not to worry now."

He returned to Muriel and found her engaged in conversation with Pearl. "Ladies, if I may interrupt," Ken smiled at them. "Perhaps you can tell me, is there a motel close by?"

"Oh, certainly," Muriel spoke first. "That would be Larkins' Motel just on the outskirts of town. I can lead you right to it on my way home."

"Great, then I can get a good start in the morning. And, by the way, is the café open early?"

"Sure is. Six o'clock every morning," she assured him.

"Well, then, good evening, Pearl," Ken said and then hesitated. "Young lady, I don't want to be an alarmist but I noticed that man at the bar earlier when I came in."

"Yes," she said, with an inquiring look on her face.

"I just got a feeling about him for some reason. I do hope you are parked close by or that someone will see you to your car?" Ken left it posed as a question.

"Oh, yes sir," Pearl smiled and pointed at Sal behind the bar. "Sal always watches out for me and makes certain I am safely in my car. So good of you to be concerned and thank you for that." She smiled brightly at him.

"Good night, honey girl Pearl," Muriel said as she hugged her and waved to Sal.

"See you, Muriel," Sal called after them as they walked to the exit, "and tell Angie I said hello."

"Will do, Sal. Good night now."

"That was a very nice thing you did there, Ken," Muriel said as they stepped out into the still, cool evening air.

"Just a fatherly concern," he smiled down at Muriel. "My Holly is about Pearl's age."

Ken thought he saw a figure standing in the dim light of a street lamp, as though someone was observing them. He had caught it more from his peripheral vision but, when he looked directly, there was no one there. He walked Muriel to her car, a red Toyota Celica, parked in front of Dolly's Café, and then moved on to his silver gray Lincoln Town Car parked a few feet ahead. The car was comfortable for a big man and, while he had given some thought to trading it in since acquiring several miles on it, he found he was reluctant. It was somehow still a link with Gloria. They had selected it together and agreed that the combination of silver gray exterior and red wine interior was to their shared liking. Besides, Ken had pointed out to Gloria, it had all the bells and whistles. They had been in a jovial mood that day, a feeling of light-heartedness had enfolded their spirits. The day was into the glory of Indian summer, with touches of golds and reds on the trees and shrubbery. Gloria had suggested they take their new car and go sightseeing to celebrate all of fall's splendors.

They had discovered a quaint country inn later on that perfect day and, after a sumptuous meal, they had danced to a string quartet. Gloria teased and flirted the way she always did with Ken when she was feeling especially buoyant. She loved to banter in good humor and her jubilance for life kept her younger than her years. She had a sweet laughter like the tinkle of tiny bells and a sparkle of mischief in her eyes. He'd often reflected how good she had been for him. She had kept him lighter, knowing how to smooth out the bumps in life. Her spirit was radiant and infectious for anyone fortunate enough to be in her company. Her loss still hurt him deeply clear through to his inner being, even though the time she was gone had stretched into years now.

Ken watched as Muriel pulled out slowly and drove in front of him. He followed behind to Larkins' Motel. He pulled up beside her at the entrance and they rolled down their car windows.

"Ken, I will see you at Dolly's in the morning. Sleep well and thanks for a good evening."

"Likewise, Muriel, and good night. I will see you early in the morning."

She held her hand up in a brief wave and drove off.

Ken stepped inside the lobby of the motel office and, seeing no one, pushed the service bell on the counter. An Asian man in his early thirties stepped from a room on the other side of the register counter and greeted Ken with a wide smile.

"Sir," Ken inquired, "do you have a non-smoking room?"

"Why, yes sir, we sure do," the man replied politely. "And will it be for one night?"

"Yes, one night."

The motel was small but well maintained. After Ken registered, he returned to his car. Fatigue assailed him as he slid in behind the steering wheel. He was glad he was prepared, an old habit of bringing a change of clothing plus toiletries. He was anticipating a good night's rest after a very long day.

He suddenly felt an overpowering sense of awareness which prickled into the same chill he had experienced earlier in Dolly's Café. A voice spoke to him in a strange, obscure way, in a pitch Ken was certain he had never heard before. It was unearthly —and yet like that of the elder reservation Indians. Ken swung around to peer into the staring black eyes of the Indian man that he had seen at Dolly's. The man sat straight and unblinking for some moments until he spoke.

"I have come with a message. I arrive to tell you of the reason you have come to this place."

Ken realized that, due to his alarm, he had not understood what the man said to him when he first spoke.

"What do you want?" Ken said, and though he seldom swore, he said, "You scared the hell out of me!"

The man raised a brown-skinned hand the color of deeply tanned leather as though to silence Ken. "You are the Redeemer, it has been foretold. You will see in your dreams and a rainbow will guide you to the trail's end. Ho." And the man raised his hand up again. "Go in peace, big man, and find now the trail of the rainbow."

With that, he exited the car so hastily that Ken wondered if he had really been there. He shook his head to clear it and started up the engine. He found the motel room and parked in front of the amply lighted entrance. He gathered up the items to bring in with him. He opened the door to a lighted room and put down all that he carried onto a chair, then hastily locked the lock and deadbolt.

"What an infringement on the nervous system," he thought. "Why that old Indian is sure inharmonious to one's physiological state." Then he released a deep breath that he hadn't realized he had been holding. He chuckled out loud in relief.

He made certain once more that the door was double-locked and then took his clothes to hang in the closet. He arranged his accessory kit at the bathroom sink. He disrobed, took a shower and quickly got into bed. Though he had suffered a shock just a few minutes earlier, he easily drifted off in that state of pre-sleep. It had proven to be quite a day, was his last conscious thought as he lapsed into sleep.

Ken was dreaming and he saw Gloria the way she'd appeared to him the very first time he saw her. She had stood hesitating at the wide doorway into the El Rincon ballroom. The El Rincon Manor was a dinner spot and cocktail lounge which housed an upscale, ample-sized ballroom. Gloria was standing there like a breath of fresh air with a soft white eyelet dress that nipped in at her tiny hand-span

34

waist. It had flowed down into a cascade length at her knees. The sleeveless dress had shown off her creamy white shoulders and high-set breasts to great advantage. Her dark silky hair was caught up on one side with a cluster of rose-colored bougainvillea. She was the loveliest girl Ken had ever seen. He'd felt a sharp intake of breath when he saw her standing there as though searching for someone in the large ballroom.

Ken had arrived earlier solo to meet his friends and to enjoy dancing with the various young ladies. Many of them frequented the El Rincon ballroom regularly on Saturday nights. He was sitting at one of the tables off to the side of the dance floor with Floyd Cavlo and Buddy Squire, two favorite college friends. He had been facing the entranceway where he could observe who came in, as he was hoping Misty Summers would appear. She was a willowy blond girl he dated some. They were good friends and both loved to dance, gliding easily around the dance floor. Misty was witty, full of fun, and chatty with the usual entourage of college students. The group would enter with enthusiastic laughter, waving to others and anticipating a fun-filled evening.

As Ken sat staring at the lovely girl in the entrance, he noticed her turn to leave just as Misty and two other young women walked up to her. He saw them exchange greetings and hugs. Misty spotted Ken as he arose from his chair and he waved them a greeting and then motioned for them to join their table.

"Well, hi you all," Misty exclaimed, flashing her brightest smile. "Now, you know Megan and Julie but I want you all to meet Gloria Pillard. We all had to gang up on her because our Gloria here is a real book-worm," Misty said, hugging Gloria around her trim waist.

Ken felt himself blush deeply as he realized he had been standing there stupefied, staring at Gloria. Misty grinned and then winked broadly at him.

"What's the matter, Mr. Ferries, cat got your tongue?" she had quipped.

Ken mumbled something he hoped was appropriate and smiled as Frank asked Julie to dance. Misty pulled Buddy to the dance floor. A young man drew up to Gloria from the next table but Ken interjected, "She already has this dance." He smiled warily down into her lovely face with its incredible blue-gray eyes that appeared to have a violet hue. The young man politely asked Megan to dance and they whirled away to the strains of a Tommy Dorsey number.

Ken was a tall, big-boned man but light on his feet, a ruggedly handsome man. Gloria was a small woman in stature but, nonetheless, the two of them were sensational on the dance floor. People often pulled back to watch them. They were both gifted and could dance to almost any style of music. They had laughed and talked that evening, getting acquainted. Ken knew beyond a doubt that this lovely girl was the one for him. He felt that, in some way, he knew her from some long ago past and he could not understand it. He had silently chided himself for his bizarre thoughts.

"Gloria," Ken murmured in his sleep as he dreamed of seeing the girl in the white cotton eyelet dress smiling up at him. They were once again dancing the night away while falling deeply in love. As they danced in Ken's dream, he held her out at arm's length but it was not Gloria who was smiling back but Nadine Rogers. She spoke, conveying a message, "I am the trail of the rainbow. Follow me."

Ken's eyes flew open wildly and he sat up in bed quickly, reaching for the light switch next to the bed. "Jeeze!" he said aloud. "Must be the gin and tonic and that old Indian unraveled me. Whew!" He expelled his breath heavily as he arose from the bed to get a drink of water. His mouth felt extremely dry. "Probably that gin," he decided while he downed a whole glass. It took him awhile to get back to sleep as he lay there reflecting on the dream.

At six, he awoke to the alarm clock on the nightstand and quickly arose to go shower. He gathered his belongings and put them in his car, then dropped the key at the desk and headed off to Dolly's. It was a pleasant morning—the heat of the day hadn't set in yet. Ken found he was hungry when the aromas of breakfast assailed him as he entered the café. Several people were seated at the counter, tables, and booths.

"Hi there, Ken," Muriel greeted him with a wave. Ken slid into the one available booth and she came over promptly with a menu in one hand and a coffeepot in the other.

"Oh yes, ma'am, coffee!" He beamed at her, then looked around, "Say, you are really busy in here this morning."

"Always are in the mornings," she said as she poured a steaming mug of coffee for him. "How was your night, Ken? Sleep good?"

"Well, yes, pretty good," he cocked a sideways grin up at Muriel, "but after we parted at the motel, I had a rather unsettling experience." He shook his head as though still in disbelief.

"Oh?" Muriel said, her eyebrows raised in question.

"When I returned to my car after I had registered, I had a visitor in my car."

"Yes, go on, tell me about it," Muriel prompted as she quickly scanned the customers.

"Tell you what. I will give you a run-down on what transpired when I'm in town again. Then we will have time to talk," Ken assured her.

"When will you be back again, Ken? I would like to see you any time," she said, sitting the coffee pot down on the table, "because if you uncover anything more regarding Nadine's death, I want to help you any way I can."

"Things are pretty flexible for me," he said as he reached inside his shirt pocket producing a memo pad. He checked it and said, "I'm free this weekend."

"This weekend would be great, Ken. I'm off work Saturdays and Sundays so it's a date then?" She added, "You know, I can introduce you to the locals around here." And she flashed that smile that had such an impact on him.

"Sure," he responded quickly, then warmly asked, "only on the condition you'll give me the honor of squiring you, my good lady, out to dine while I am in town." He then followed up with "And since you are in Dolly's Café five days a week, is there a nice dinner house close by?"

"Oh, yes, that would be Jillies out south of town about three miles. They have excellent steaks, or whatever delights your pallet. Ken, do you like to dance?" she said, as though it was an afterthought.

He resisted a grin and softly said, "Well now, I have been known to cut a few capers on the dance floor, but it's been awhile," he added.

"Every Saturday night at Windom Hall here in Rosewood there's a dance and always a good time to be had. Most everyone from here shows up."

Flirting openly, Ken said, "Sounds like fun and I would enjoy it, especially with a pretty lady."

"I haven't been flattered in awhile by a man of such noble character. It is sincerely appreciated," and Muriel's face took on a soft appearance. She grinned impishly and winked at him in an effort to lighten the moment.

Ken felt light of heart when he left Rosewood and it dawned on him once more that it had been a long time since he had felt quite this way. Muriel had a low and husky woman's voice that Ken found very sexy. She was a Lauren Bacall type, the screen star he had always admired. He wondered why she had not remarried after the death of her husband. She certainly was a woman one would not have expected to remain single for long. She was witty, keenly sensitive, and very striking.

As he drove towards Waco and home, he thought about the good-natured rousing that had gone on in Dolly's Café. An assortment of ranch hands, a few truckers, store and shop workers had gathered to enjoy breakfast and linger awhile over their morning coffee before beginning the business of the day. Ken overheard the loud guffaws, good-natured kidding, and usual fish tales about who had caught the biggest catfish. Some of their heckling, of course, had been directed at Muriel but it was obvious she could hold her own and outranked them with her quick wit.

Ken knew and understood these country folks so well and they were to his liking. His roots ran deep with theirs. It was another reason why the murder of a popular and well-known citizen less than a year ago didn't total up in his mind. He thought it ludicrous, as he sat there observing these homey and kindly people. He knew they were kind and hard-working, open and honest with giving hearts, just good souls in the main.

"Say Muriel," one of the cowboys had chortled, his straw Western hat pushed back on his head. He'd cupped his face into his open hands while resting both elbows on the table. "Well, now honey," he'd grinned broadly up at her as she poured coffee for him, "now hows come you never bought that Pinto for Angie? Here I was thinking we had us a deal."

"Well, Rex," she drawled lazily, "I always though if you buy a dead horse, you ought to at least have a hog to eat him but I don't have a hog, Sweetie. And since you do, I figured maybe you'd want to keep him."

After the laughter had died down, Rex said, with a wide flirtatious grin, "Now, you wouldn't slam an outhouse door that hard, honey, but boy howdy, you can sure hurt a guy." His face expressed exaggerated suffering.

"Rex," another cowboy hooted, "you know you ain't gonna get ahead of Muriel. Why, hell, she's too feisty and quick for ya." And there followed more hoots of good-natured laughter.

Muriel returned to Ken's table and rolled her eyes. Loud enough to be heard, she proclaimed, "You know, it's just routine and a skill I've acquired after putting in enough time here." Then she turned and broadly winked at Rex, who held his coffee mug on high in salute to her. "These guys would rather jaybird than eat any day but, heck, it fills in my days. Especially since Angie is off to college now, it gets kinda lonely, you know."

Ken saw the loneliness in Muriel as he had come to know it too well within himself. Again, he was glad that she had agreed to have dinner with him on Saturday and then attend the dance. She was a comfortable person to be with and had nothing pretentious about her. He saw a sharp-witted lady with womanly allure who was seasoned by life. She did not put up with a fake coyness, Ken mused.

When Ken had stepped up to the cash register to pay for his breakfast, the cowhand Rex was standing beside him. He leaned over the counter as Ken pocketed the change Muriel gave him.

"Say Muriel, did you hear the one about the lady from New York City?"

Muriel answered, "No, I haven't, Rex, but I bet you are going to tell me." And she grinned widely at him.

"Well, now, seems this lady got her first hunting license and she came to Texas, went out in the country and shot her first animal. This cowpuncher came walking up and the lady says, 'Now see here, that's my animal. I shot him and you can't have him.' The cowpuncher says, 'Yes, Ma'am, but could I have the saddle off of him?'"

Ken was unable to stifle his laughter and Muriel chuckled, covering her mouth. She said, "Rex, pay me for your breakfast and get out of here and go to work!"

He did so and then took Muriel's hand, kissing her palm as she swatted at him playfully. "Ain't she the cutest, sassiest little filly you ever did see?" He winked at Ken.

Chapter____2

Ken reached home, a welcome sight after the lengthy drive. Home, a tidy, cheerful yellow house trimmed in a mellow white with a varicolored red brick wall almost halfway up the sides. A long winding terracotta-tiled walkway led up to the front porch which was graced the full length by the same tiles. The driveway to the house boasted a colorful row of Texas yellow roses all the way to the end. The attached garage housed a workshop area as well as ample space for two cars. Sarita maintained an abundance of flowers in the front of the home. Wisteria hung in a cascade like a garland around the porch.

The back yard was equally spacious. Ken had installed a gas barbecue pit and put in a Colorado flagstone patio with an umbrella table and several chairs for entertaining friends. The fish pond, with a fountain that Ken and Gloria had built, was a joy to them. They had marveled at their novice talents since it had turned out so well. Over the years, they had held festive and fun-filled gatherings with their good friends, their neighbors, and family out in that backyard.

A large pecan tree graced the east side where Holly and Carter had spent many fun hours with their swing set and sandbox, a child's paradise. Shrubbery was in abundance where they could crawl under and behind, playing hide and seek. Ken still heard their laughter ring out when he would sit on the bench by the fish pond, eyes closed in quiet meditation. Such happy children, as children should be, and he felt that he and Gloria had done well with them. He knew it was mainly their own great strength of love that was the reason for the two well-adjusted young people.

Ken and Gloria had wanted children but it had taken some years for their first child to arrive. Ken and Gloria had married shortly after Gloria graduated from college. Ken was a cub reporter by then and they shared a one-bedroom apartment. They swore that no couple was ever more in love. They had been gleeful in their love for each other and seldom quarreled, but were quick to make up when they did. Gloria was devout to her writing and began to build more than a little notice in the publishing world and readers audience. As Gloria's acknowledgements grew as a serious writer, Ken's own career did as well. His bulldog tenacity to follow a story and get the facts gave way to highly deserved respect. They had shared a love of writing, though in different fields, and respect for the other's achievements. Miss Holly, as Ken fondly called her, was born when Ken was thirty-four and Gloria a year younger. Then Master Carter, his affectionate title for his beloved blue-eyed son, arrived two years later.

When Ken stepped into the kitchen from the garage, Maggie assailed him with great affection. "Here, now, Maggie girl. Yes, I'm home." He chuckled as he kneeled down to receive her doggy kisses while he hugged her squirming body.

"Where's Sarita, Maggie?" he asked as Maggie twirled round and round in front of him. He rose from his kneeling position and then saw the note on the counter bar next to a pot of recently perked coffee. He read Sarita's large scrawl: "Have gone to market. Lunch awaits you in the refrigerator, Mr. Ken. I will see you PRONTO!"

Ken opened the door of the refrigerator to find a sandwich and fresh slice of melon covered neatly in plastic wrap. He gave Maggie a doggie biscuit to satisfy her while he settled at the kitchen table to enjoy lunch. "Good to be home," he thought as he took in the cheerful kitchen. A sliding glass door led from the kitchen to the patio and he watched the residents of the birdhouse right next to it. Milky, the white Persian cat, sat longingly peering up at the chattering wrens who had taken up residence in the blue birdhouse Carter had made in wood shop.

Ken decided to take his coffee to the bench by the fish pond and enjoy this peaceful setting. Here he could reflect quietly and just enjoy the fragrance of the honeysuckle vine that climbed up a trellis behind the fountain. It was alive with various birds singing their joyous songs and he recalled how much he and Gloria had loved to listen to them. They would try to distinguish the many feathered visitors. They had put hummingbird feeders at the kitchen window and near the patio door so they could study them. They had boastfully claimed that there were more hummers at their feeders than anywhere in the neighborhood. Gloria would smile with that special twinkle in her eyes and tell Ken that God's creatures knew when they were especially loved. Ken would sagely agree and hug her to him.

He sat now sipping his coffee in great relaxation and once again though about Gloria and her powerful, determined strength. He remembered the courage she had displayed to him and their children, while knowing that those last days were going to be short. She had tried to cram in to them all her thoughts and revelations. She had encouraged her husband and children not to remember the ravages the cancer had taken but to remember her with love. She wanted them to carry on her wisdom for living life fully and ever seeking it out. She implored Ken not to immortalize their great love so much that he gave up loving someone special again.

"It needs to be, Ken," she pleaded. "You are a very loving and warm-hearted soul and it is not something one should ever do, stop loving. We all have sorrows and losses. Do you hear me, Ken Ferries?" she admonished while holding him and intently looking deeply into his eyes. "You do know that we gain all that we seek in joy," she had said softly, "and my dear, we have gained so many joys, now haven't we?"

Ken had kissed her warmly and whispered her name as tears coursed his cheeks. He had assured her that they had. He had declared to her that she was and always would be one of the best parts of his life and he loved her deeply. Then he thanked her for the gifts she had given him—of love, their children, and just plain every day joy. She had lingered on three days after that special talk but slipped away early on the third morning. He had felt her Spirit leaving like a soft whisper and, though he had slept very little, he had been dozing lightly. His heart had throbbed as his eyes opened wide and he arose from the cot that he had placed in their bedroom weeks before. He had wanted to be close but not disturb Gloria for she could scarcely rest as the cancer invaded her small body progressively.

She had wanted to be home to die and they had both agreed on it, as they had always done on major issues. He had sat on the bed and cradled her in his big arms, letting his tears fall while telling her in a tormented hoarse whisper of the love he had for her. Finally, with his big gentle hands, he had laid her back on the pillows and arranged her bed jacket softly. His heart had constricted with grief.

"Gloria, Gloria, my life," he whispered softly. "I will see you again one beautiful time somewhere," as he had strangled on heavy tears. Then he had picked up the telephone receiver on the nightstand and called his children. Holly's husband answered the phone and had instinctively known when he heard Ken speak. He had said quietly, "Wait, Ken, and I will wake Holly." Ken noted the husky tone in his son-in-law's voice and knew he would reach out in comfort to share his young wife's grief.

"Daddy," Holly said, "it's Momma, isn't it. She's gone, isn't she." Her voice had broken on a sob.

"Yes," Ken had answered, his voice heavy with grief. "About... ten minutes ago maybe." By then, he was nearly numb with grief.

"Daddy, oh Daddy, I can't hardly stand it," she had cried, "but Bart and I will come now. We can leave in a few minutes."

"Just be careful," Ken had said, "and don't hurry now. I'm okay. I love you, sweet girl," he had said with a strangled sob.

Holly's voice was shattered in grief when she had answered, "I love you, Daddy. I will be there soon."

Carter had answered the phone on half a ring and, before his father had spoken, he had said, "Dad, it's Mother. I know already...... I know because she came to me tonight just before you called." And then Ken heard his son choke on a heavy sob.

Ken said, "Carter, I love you, son."

Carter had answered, "I know, Dad. I know you do and I love you. Dad, I will be there before noon as I bought a ticket awhile ago to be prepared for this." He hesitated and said, "If you are ever prepared for this." And once again, he said, "Dad, I really love you so much."

"Carter, I love you and I'm here for you, son."

They said goodbye and then Ken hung up the phone. He made his way to Sarita's bedroom door and knocked softly.

"Si, Senor Ken, is that you?"

"Sarita," Ken said, "It's Gloria. Can you come, please?"

The door opened quickly and, as Sarita looked up at Ken's sorrow-filled face, she crossed herself and her dark eyes filled with tears. "Oh, si, señor. Mi señora Gloria." Sarita said and clasped her heart.

It was Sarita who had thankfully taken over and called the funeral home and Gloria's physician. She made all the pre-arranged details finalized. Ken was so grateful to her for he found he had little strength or energy to sustain him. He had gone through the motions much like a robot with others at the controls.

The funeral had been like a dream, a terrible and tragic dream from which he felt he would never awaken. He saw his children in their grief and Connie, his mother-in-law, who appeared numb and wax-like as well. He could not offer to console for he was inconsolable.

He thought for a moment that he could see Gloria standing there in the Chapel with her Dad, looking out at the loved ones gathered there. Frank, his father-in-law, had passed away some years ago. The vision startled him and he wiped his eyes to clear them. When he looked at the same place again, he seemed to see an etheric glow where the two figures had been.

He reached out to take his mother-in-law's hand next to him and smiled down at her, saying, "Connie, she's with Frank."

Connie answered in a soft whisper, "Yes, Ken, I know." Then she rested her beautiful halo of gray hair against his broad shoulder.

At eighty-three, Connie was a bastion of great strength. She displayed a kind of loveliness which was more apparent now even with the loss of her beloved daughter and husband. As Ken silently observed this, he felt a rush of awareness which moved him to tighten his grip on her slender hand.

It was Sarita's way to deal with this painful time by serving others, much as she always had. While the many friends and family had gathered at Ken and Gloria's home after the service, Sarita ministered to everyone like a patron saint. How blessed they all were, Ken thought that day, for this gracious and spunky lady who had come to him and his family so many wonderful years ago. Ken had been caught up in his past review and hadn't heard her approach. Her words pulled him from the past back into the present.

"Ah, Señor, I find you," Sarita smiled, as she joined him on the bench. "How was your travel? You are tired after a long trip, eh?"

"Yes, Sarita, it was an eventful trip and I have met some interesting and fine people. I do believe now, more than ever, that there is much more to this set of events than was ever brought to light. And yes, I am a bit tired," he sighed.

"Well, my dear amigo, I do believe you are the one who will resolve this if there is more to resolve, but now you must siesta, then I fix you fine dinner."

"I will certainly take you up on the siesta, Sarita, but please light on the supper. I will need full concentration to sit at the computer and keep my mind on matters at hand. As you are aware, I tend to over-indulge on your marvelous cuisine."

"Oh, si," Sarita nodded her head briskly, "then I fix for you quesadilla and a fine green salad with plenty of my fresh vegetables." And as an afterthought, as she stood up, "and maybe a little vino, then later you sleep better, eh?"

"A small glass of wine," Ken smiled, while measuring off a token amount.

"Si," Sarita smiled in ready agreement as Ken followed her short strides to the sliding glass door. He was grateful for the suggestion of a nap and went to his bedroom. Then settling in the overstuffed chair in his amply-sized room, he removed his shoes and enjoyed the cushioned comfort of the deep pile carpet beneath his feet.

Cozy and cheerful, this bedroom, and yet not so feminine that it excluded either the feminine or masculine gender. Gloria had been selective and articulate with her efforts to create comforts they could both enjoy. Ken often felt that, had Gloria not been a freelance writer, she could well have gone into interior design. She had displayed great talent in both fields.

He carefully removed the bedspread and placed it on a quilt rack, then pulled a light cover over himself and quickly drifted into a deep slumber. It was dinner hour when Sarita lightly tapped on his door and Ken was surprised at the length of time he had slept.

"Yes, Sarita, I will be right there," he called out to her. The wonderful aroma of Sarita's cooking assailed him as he joined her in the dining room.

"Come, Señor Ken, is caliente and ready. Now we eat."

He easily devoured three helpings of quesadilla and a hearty salad, followed by a half glass of red wine.

"You do see, dear lady, that I am a total pushover for your fine cooking," and he beamed at Sarita.

Light conversation followed regarding the events of his trip to Rosewood, along with his announcement that he would be returning there on Friday morning and would not return again until possibly Monday.

"A word of caution, Señor Ken." Sarita's face took on a serious countenance. "Since you have questions of this foul deed, I would pray you, my amigo, to watch closely your back side."

"Sarita, my tendency toward natural snooping from the reporter side has instilled in these old bones a keen desire to be ever cautious, even while seeking out the deeper causes. You know the real Ken Ferries," he added and winked at her broadly. He patted her hand in reassurance and said, "You are a dear lady, Sarita, for being concerned and I truly appreciate it. But I would not want to play the reckless fool and irrationally get into something serious as this without common sense or caution."

"Oh, si, Señor Ken, this I do know of you. My concerns are only for one who has become most dear as my special amigo. You go now, go and busy yourself," she admonished him with mock scolding to break the serious cord of the conversation.

Ken gathered up his silverware and dishes, carrying them into the kitchen but Sarita intercepted. "You have mucho copy to put on that machine, I know, so bamanos now, pronto." And she jabbed playfully into Ken's ribs with her fist.

He pretended to lose his breath with an exaggerated whoosh but carried the plates and silver to the sink. "All right Sarita, you win. I'm off to the computer and thank you for another of your perfect gourmet dinners."

"Oh, is nothing," she shrugged indifferently. "I am always happy to please, but gracias," she added modestly.

Ken knew that it made Sarita feel very effective to be acknowledged, as he had always been conscious of the fact that everyone needs encouragement. Although Sarita, in her typical manner, would wave aside any compliments. Ken had arrived at the conclusion long ago that Sarita was not one who wanted to appear conspicuous or in bad taste. So appearing to enjoy a compliment might attract attention and be a violation of what she considered proper behavior.

Gloria and Ken had given up long ago trying to dissuade Sarita of this notion. She was just being herself, as Ken often remarked. They learned to find her absolutes humorous rather than annoying. After all, who of the populace on the planet did not have their own private agenda and wasn't that the sum total of whatever one's life experience had conditioned them to be? With that conclusion came the deeper communion of minds and hearts between them all. They had developed more than a servant-employee relationship. Sarita was family and they loved her unconditionally.

Ken worked at the copy he had from his notations and meetings with the principal people involved. These personalities needed to be included and that would involve collectiveness and conciseness to give readers a clear-cut picture of all the characters involved. Being descriptive and yet basic while cutting through the chaff would be a lengthy process but Ken had never been a man who wavered once he set his course of direction.

He had undertaken a study of each of the men imprisoned in the Rogers case. There was Galin Harmond, a man he knew had served time for auto theft and then been on probation. At thirty-eight years old, he was a lean-muscled, trim man with a towering 6 foot 6 inch frame. He had been no stranger to trouble, as evidenced by the obvious knife slash scar on his left cheek. Born in Nebraska and raised on a cattle ranch in the Panhandle, he was known locally as a hard-working ranch hand. In his early twenties, he had gone awry, falling into certain company that hung below the law. He had paid his dues and led an exemplary life since, said his attorney. He had maintained his innocence all through the trial, saying that the three of them stumbled onto the murder scene and then fled out of fear.

Larry Gomez was nineteen, a local youth with family still in the area, and flashy-looking with his Hispanic good looks. His previous run-ins with the law had amounted to driving too fast and being a bit hot-tempered with his fists. During the trial, he had trembled and appeared hapless. Tears often coursed his handsome face.

Jyp Donohue was a range hand and, like Larry, was quiet throughout the trial. He had appeared in perpetual shock, according to the reports Ken had read. He was a big raw-boned man in his mid-fifties, a nondescript kind of man, with eyes that appeared like two hollowed-out sockets. No one knew much about his background, except that he came from Sweetwater, Texas. He had drifted from one ranch to another, until settling on the Rogers ranch four years earlier. During the trial, he had seemed incensed and much like he was watching a horror movie. The reports said he had swallowed hard and often as he listened to testimony.

The climate in the courtroom was one of stoic, suppressed anger, the kind that Ken had seen occasionally explode into an out-of-control mob scene. Ken knew this was the main reason such cases were often tried away from the local area. Many of the locals attended the Rogers trial, as they were a well-known and highly respected family. The spectators sat through as the whole sad drama played out and showed their unified support for the Rogers family.

When the verdict was read, reports said that Larry Gomez had literally collapsed and Galin Harmond sat down as though falling with the breath knocked out of him. Jyp Donohue had looked from one face to another in an effort to grasp what he had heard the foreman of the jury say.

The television and newspaper reports had portrayed Jyp Donohue as a man without emotions and Galin Harmond as a hardened man who thought of little else than saving his own skin. As for Larry Gomez, he was described as a juvenile gone wrong, falling in with corrupt company. Galin, a handsome man, was known to be a Casanova of sorts and had created some ill feelings among the locals for a reported affair with a rancher's wife. Galin had been heard to make frequent references to Nadine. All of it was pure supposition but it had played heavily into the weightiness of the whole case against Galin. Ken knew that, all too often, the sensational could easily overshadow the facts in cases such as this one.

Getting the facts, as he had learned from past experience, was laborious but it was the only direction he had ever used in his journalism career. He intended to apply it as a freelance writer as well. He knew it would entail extensive hours of note-taking, interview, travel, and just plain sleuthing. He had a thumbs up attitude, for reasons he could not fully access, but he had known from some inner sensitivity that there was a root not completely dug out on this case.

Friday morning came and, after a lengthy shower to awaken himself, he sat down to enjoy one of Sarita's ample breakfasts. "Fit for a king," he assured her, and then made playful commands to Maggie to watch out for Sarita and the household while he was gone. Maggie cocked her head as though she could certainly comprehend every word Ken said to her. Ken was not at all certain that she didn't understand. He promised himself, that upon his return home, he would take her up to a nearby lake so Maggie could swim and chase after sticks he would throw for her. She loved to race after squirrels too and bark playfully at them. It always refreshed the two of them, those outings.

Chapter_____3

Rosewood came into view after some hours of driving and Ken went straight to Larkins Motel to register. He inquired of the same Asian man if he knew where to find the sheriff's office and the man complied with directions. Ken set out to visit the sheriff and found the office easily.

"Yes, may I help you?" asked a rather portly man with a heavy thatch of graying black hair. He stood as Ken entered the office.

"Well, now I suppose you, sir, are the sheriff," Ken said as he extended his hand to the man.

"That would be me," he smiled, exposing two gold front teeth. He shook Ken's hand firmly.

Ken handed the man his business card while he explained the nature of his visit.

"Well, I reckon there won't be a whole lot to follow up on, Mr. Ferries," the sheriff said, as he scratched behind one ear while studying Ken's card.

"Perhaps," Ken agreed, "but I'm willing to establish if there was more involved and how each of the accused fit into this murder."

"Well, now frankly, it puzzled me some, and especially where Jyp Donohue was concerned and that Gomez kid," the sheriff related while Ken noticed the name slate on his desk read Sheriff Bruster Hernado.

"Why is that?" Ken asked.

"Well, sir, I just couldn't figure old Jyp for that type and the Gomez kid had a wild hair but he just wasn't cut out to be a killer, least ways sure never figured it of him. I knew Larry Gomez' family before Larry was born and they are good people, hard workers. Larry was too. He should of worn off some of that youthful energy in amateur boxing but Rosewood is small and I couldn't get much assistance to set up that mission." After some careful thought, the sheriff said, "Say, Mr. Ferries," and he paused before he spoke again, "I was thinking I would go down to Dolly's Café since it's about dinner time. Why don't you and I just stroll on down there? I will get Katie to mind the office for me."

"All right with me but please just call me Ken. And, as a matter of fact, I had that plan myself after leaving here."

"Well, good then, we can talk over dinner," and he called out, "Say Katie." An adjoining door opened and a middle-aged red-haired lady came into the office smiling and looking inquisitively at Ken.

"Katie, this here is Ken Ferries and he's a freelance writer. Now he's asking about that Rogers case. Maybe I can fill him in on some of it, don't know, but I'll try anyway." He shrugged. "We're going down to Dolly's and have some dinner now so would you be so kind to see after the office?"

"Sure would, Sheriff," and then she addressed Ken and extended her hand. "Say, Mr. Ferries, didn't you used to be a journalist for the Waco Centennial?"

"Yes, I was up until a few months ago," he smiled as he clasped Katie's hand in a friendly greeting.

"I used to read your column regularly," she said, "and it is such a pleasure to meet you."

"The pleasure is all mine, Katie," Ken assured her.

"Well, I do recall your name now, thought for some reason it wanted to come to me," the sheriff said with a new assessment of Ken. "I recall seeing your picture with your column several times and I don't fail too often to remember a face," he related.

Ken had noted the Spanish name of the sheriff but he was sure that he was not fully Spanish as his features portrayed Anglo heritage with his clear blue eyes. The sheriff placed his hat on and they left the office, walking to Dolly's Café a short distance down the street. Ken stood several inches taller than the man he accompanied. He judged the sheriff to be a few years his junior as well.

Ken thought, "Well, at least he isn't hard-nosed and is open to discussion. That's a favorable sign." From his past experience as a reporter, Ken knew the law could be very uninformative. But then, in some cases, he readily agreed that they should be, that they were just doing their job.

Ken saw Muriel as they entered the café and she turned from the cash register in surprise when she saw him.

"Well, hello, Ken. I didn't think I would see you until tomorrow."

"Oh, you know our Muriel," the sheriff smiled at her as she greeted him.

"Hi there, Bruster. Yes, Ken and I have met."

Ken smiled warmly at Muriel, "Well, I figured I had better get back here and talk with Sheriff Hernado before the weekend."

"That's great. It's so good to see you again. And say, I forgot to tell you how to get out to my place, Ken," she smiled with that special cheer she had. She wrote the directions and phone number down and handed it to him. He put it in his shirt pocket.

As Ken and Bruster made their way to a table, Bruster said, "How long have you known Muriel, Ken?"

"Not long. I was here a few days ago and came in here for dinner. We struck up a friendship while I was having supper and then we got together over a couple drinks at Bailey's Lounge after she got off work. She's a fine lady," Ken said as they sat down at the table.

"None better," Bruster agreed, "and life hasn't been real easy for Muriel, raising that sweet little girl Angie alone after losing her husband. Just a young woman when Bill got killed. I always felt like she held off ever marrying again because she was concerned maybe some other fella wouldn't be the father figure she wanted for Angie. I don't know that for sure but she is a mighty pretty woman. There was plenty young bucks would of jumped at the chance to have her," Bruster went on, " and there are still some of them that would."

"I'll bet there are," Ken said as he smiled at Muriel coming toward their table with menus in one hand and a coffee pot in the other. He felt a rush of pure warmth and joy at seeing her again. He noticed Muriel's cheeks had high color as she handed Ken a menu and her green eyes sparkled with a kind of radiance.

"What will it be, gentlemen?" she said in that husky voice Ken found so enticing.

"Oh, I think one of those California Garden Burgers and fries for me," Bruster said. "And a cup of coffee," he added.

"Make that a pair all the way, Muriel, except maybe we better leave the bill open for some dessert. And that will be one check, please, and give it to me," Ken said.

Bruster started to protest but Ken raised his hand, "Next time you can do the honors."

"All right, then," Bruster agreed and smiled at Ken while placing his hat on the chair next to him.

"How long have you been sheriff, Bruster?" Ken inquired, opening up further conversation.

"Well, this is my second term," Bruster drawled as he reached for the sugar container and poured a generous portion into his coffee.

Ken liked this man and sensed a goodness of character here. "Got a family, Bruster?" Ken opted for more conversation while sipping his coffee.

"Yes, sir, a fine wife, my Sadie. We have thirty-five years to our credit and two terrific kids, grown, of course. And they have made us grandparents plus we recently arrived at that estimable position of great grandparents," he chuckled as he shook his head. "Sure makes a man feel his mortality, eh?"

Ken agreed. "Well, sir, you are mightily blessed, it sounds like to me."

"How about you, Ken? Got a wife and children?" Bruster prompted.

"I lost Gloria, my wife, to cancer five years ago," Ken said quietly.

"Oh, that's a damn shame, Ken," Bruster said, stirring his coffee. His clear blue eyes took on a sad expression.

"Yes, it was. She was a wonderful woman in every way and together we raised two bright and special children. There are no grandchildren yet. I expect Holly, my daughter, and her husband, Bart will be surprising me one day though, since Bart is well established in his medical practice now. Holly has been at her nursing career for some time too, so the time is probably just about right for them to bring on a new generation." Ken felt suddenly upbeat at the idea of being a grandfather.

"Now, it does say something to a person," Bruster elected, "in that finally one has reached that long sought-out executive position of the council, so to speak," he chuckled. "Sort of like the honored position that the seniors in high standing of the company have acquired, you know." He chuckled again. "There is a certain status within a family, a hierarchy if you will, that one usually acquires for just having lived long enough and experienced those big and small tribulations on that old journey of life. You see, it is one that a grandparent can celebrate, that is if they have arrived along with some common sense and, hopefully, a smattering of wisdom." Bruster added the latter almost abstractedly as he stared down into his coffee cup.

"I like that," Ken nodded. "It gives me a whole new dimension about one day becoming a grandparent." He openly admired Bruster's keen insights and his breadth of wisdom. He observed that Bruster had reached an effectiveness about people and who they really are.

Muriel came, bringing more refills of coffee and she touched Ken's shoulder lightly. "Ken, what are your plans for today?"

"Well, Muriel, I thought I would see the attorney Pace Allard sometime today for a brief audience. Otherwise, I have no definite plans. What's up? Is there something special you have in mind when your shift is over?"

"Angie is home and I thought perhaps you would come by after I'm out of here. You could follow me to my place and meet my daughter. Besides, I made a three-layer German chocolate cake in honor of Angie's brief visit home."

Ken leaned back and looked appreciatively up at Muriel. He smiled a broad, teasing grin. "That sounds like a great plan, my dear lady, and you can rest assured there will be no foot dragging on my part. That is my favorite cake and the bonus of two lovely ladies company—I ask you, how could a fella be crazy enough to decline?"

"Good then. It's a date. So will I see you here this evening for supper?"

"Yes, I will be back here to dine and then wait for you to finish your shift," Ken assured her.

Bruster quietly observed Muriel's retreat to go pick up their order, then looked at Ken squarely. With a broad wink, he said, "You do know you are wise not to hesitate where that lady is concerned. It does appear that she is attracted to you, and like I told you earlier, she is mighty selective. There's plenty of these hombres around here would sure like to rope that pretty woman. Why, hell, any one of them would if they thought they could." He chuckled in good humor, a casual communicative way that Ken was understanding concealed a shrewd mind. In many ways, Ken observed, the longer he was in the company of Bruster, the more he realized how much they were alike. He realized there was a far greater depth to

Bruster than first met the eye. He traded on a good old boy façade and Ken wagered that was why he had been elected to two terms as sheriff of the county.

"There's plenty of perks in a job like this," Bruster went on. "As well as a downside, of course. But mainly, you gotta relax some and not get all perplexed or you will get yourself a big ulcer." He gave forth another chuckle. On that note, Muriel returned to their table with their meals.

"Here, gentlemen. Do keep some room for pie. It's Dutch apple, made fresh this morning," Muriel said, tantalizing them further by smacking her lips.

"Well, now, Bruster. This temptress can stop right there, can't she?"

Bruster agreed, "No argument because I never could use a lot of opposition against apple pie." He chuckled again exposing those two gold teeth.

Muriel later returned with more coffee and two generous slices of pie. She left their bill on the table and Ken reached for it. Muriel placed her hand on top of his and looked deeply into his eyes. "Ken, I will see you later this evening."

Ken felt a warmth fill him and a fervency of feeling flourished in his heart at her touch. Bruster, he knew well enough by now, missed very little with his laid-back vigilance. It amused Ken that anyone less observant did not fully appreciate Bruster's mien and thought of the man as aimless. He would be in for a rude awakening, he deduced as he smiled knowingly at Bruster.

There was a sudden shift of attention from Bruster as he glanced toward the entrance of the café. A good-looking young man with blond hair made his way toward the table. Ken took him to be nineteen or twenty years old.

"Hello there, Ty," Bruster greeted him. "So, you've been away, son. Haven't seen you in some time." The youth came over to Ken and Bruster's table. Muriel turned toward him, set the coffee pot down, and embraced him.

"Hello, sweetie," she said tenderly. "I've missed you."

"Missed you too, Aunt Muriel," he drawled as he smiled fondly at her. He turned to Bruster. "Bruster, it's good to see you again, sir."

"Ty, this here is Ken Ferries. He hails from Waco. Ken, meet Tyler Rogers," Bruster said, introducing them.

Ken shook the young man's extended hand while he was evaluating Ken with an open curiosity.

"Ken here is a freelance writer, Ty, and a recently retired journalist."

"Is that right?" Ty said, still studying Ken. "What paper did you work with, sir?"

"The Waco Centennial," Ken answered.

"You look like someone I've seen before," Ty said as he smiled openly at Ken. "I expect I have seen your picture in the paper with your news column."

"No doubt," Ken said as he looked keenly at this young man. He saw the strong resemblance to his mother, the same blond hair and Nordic good looks.

"Are you going to be here awhile?" Bruster asked.

"That depends," Ty said in obvious hesitation. "That is to say, if Dad and Will Earl could use an extra hand right now."

"Oh, son, I figure on a spread like your daddy's, he would welcome an extra helping hand any time," Bruster said as he carefully studied Ty.

"We'll see, I reckon," Ty said with a slow, rather sad smile pursing his lips.

"Say, Ty, why don't you stop by this evening. Angie is home and she'd be glad to see you. Like I was just bragging to Mr. Ferries here, I have a big three layer German chocolate cake," Muriel said in an enticing voice, then hugged Tyler once again.

"Aunt Muriel, I am not about to pass up one of your special cakes and I have missed Angie. I guess last time I saw her was…" and he stopped before proceeding on, "well, at the services." And his voice took on a husky note.

Muriel spoke up with bright and brimming accounts of Angie's accomplishments in college. Ken knew it was to detour Tyler's thoughts and bring him into center.

"You know, Ty, what about that Angie girl? She made the Dean's list!" And Muriel went on in glowing accounts.

"No stuff" Ty said, a wide smile spreading on his handsome youthful face. "Heck, she will get so smartie I can't stand her. And I can't put any more frogs down her back like I did when we were ten, now can I, Aunt Muriel?"

"Now see here, I happen to recall that you two could both hold your own and I still remember it was an even toss-up as to who could think up the most mischief," Muriel related with a chuckle.

"Yeah, for a girl, she was all right," Ty grinned scampishly but with clear affection in his voice. "So," he drawled, "I think a big juicy hamburger and fries topped off with a malt ought to fortify me awhile, Aunt Muriel."

"Ought to do it," Muriel smiled at him.

"Say, Ty," Bruster addressed the young man, "where have you been, son?"

"Oh, here and there," the boy drawled in a ho-hum manner and shrugged his well-formed shoulders. Ken noticed he was lean and muscled, no stranger to working hard. "I worked at different things to get some experience besides ranch work and I've sorta drifted around the state these past few months." Ty sounded somewhat evasive.

"Why, son, I kinda thought you'd get back to college," Bruster elected.

Before he could respond to Bruster's question, Muriel said, "I'll get your order put in, Ty boy."

"Okay, thanks, Aunt Muriel." Then he pulled up a chair and sat down at Bruster and Ken's table. "Sheriff, I just took a time-out, a sort of sabbatical, you could say," and the grin he used was forced.

Bruster looked deeply into Ty's face, reading the young man's inner space and Ken knew he was seeing the torment in his eyes as well.

"Why don't you drop around out to the house, Ty, and visit with the family and me. We'd like to have your company any time and I got a new young stud ready to be broke. I know you're a natural with horses."

"Sounds like a plan to me," Ty grinned loosely. "How's tomorrow morning look?"

"Now, that would be fine and you can join the Mrs. and me for breakfast about 7." Bruster took out his chain length watch and said, "I better be moseying on back to the office." He put his watch back into his watch pocket and addressed Ken,

"Never could wear one of them wrist watches. They always quit on me. If you are ready, Ken, you can walk along with me and I will point out Pace Allard's office."

"Yes," Ken agreed, "that would be helpful. I am ready to get an interview if Mr. Allard will permit me the time. Ty, once again a pleasure to meet you. It seems we are both invited for some cake this evening so I will see you tonight," Ken trailed off, waiting for Ty's response.

"Yes, sir, I will see you at Aunt Muriel's and it was nice to meet you, Mr. Ferries."

As they readied to leave, Muriel came with Ty's malt and Ken turned to her. "See you for supper hour, lady."

"Yes, Ken. About six, then?

"Six o'clock it is, Muriel." he agreed.

He heard Muriel tell Ty that his burger and fries were coming up right away as he and Bruster were leaving.

"That Ty is a fine lad," Bruster was saying, almost as though he was talking to himself. "But I'm concerned about him because his Daddy has all but stopped living. It's like Ty is totally orphaned and he is still a kid really." He hesitated and then went on, "Will Earl is young too, and well...." He paused again. "Well, it's like with the tragic horror of all that has befallen that family, they have shut down, even with each other. You know, Ken, that's a road sign for real problems. Now, you take Ty for instance. I heard some unsettling things when that boy was gone and I made it my business to keep tabs on him long distance. Of course he wasn't aware of it. Oh, well, I'm just glad he is home again and I will try to keep him interested in staying, then getting back into school."

"Well, Bruster, the way it was when Gloria passed away was the most heart-breaking episode in our family's life but God only knows the unspeakable mourning in the Rogers family the way that came about," Ken declared.

"Yes, sir, I couldn't agree more and I don't imagine I could even fantasize the moment to moment of inordinate grief that's within their family. Anyway, I just pray that God will bring them closer in time, as there is a great measure of healing that way," Bruster expressed with the deepest of emotions. Ken knew by the way his voice was strained.

They walked in the direction of the Sheriff's office, caught up in their own thoughts. Then Bruster stopped and pointed at a yellow colonial house which had been converted into a series of professional offices.

"That is where you can reach Pace Allard. He's in the office to your left as you go in the front door. Good luck, Ken, and stop in any time. I will be glad to help you any way I can. Oh, and I'm much obliged to you for dinner and the next time's on me," he said as he took Ken's hand in a hearty grip and shook it.

"The pleasure's been all mine, Bruster. I will certainly see you again, no doubt soon. Thank you for the information too, as well as your good company."

Bruster smiled that gold tooth display and tipped his hat to Ken as he walked the short distance to his office. Ken watched this rather portly man walking away and felt a deepened regard and respect for this man. His stately bearing showed clearly in the caring he had expressed about Muriel and the Rogers family.

Ken entered the tidy foyer of the office building and looked to the left at the door. It read in black letters, "Pace A. Allard, Attorney of Law." Before Ken went into that office, he took note of the office to his immediate right, an insurance firm. He opened the attorney's door and a dark-haired woman in her thirties looked up from where she sat at her desk. She asked if she could help him.

"Yes, ma'am. I don't have an appointment, but, if possible, I would like to speak with Mr. Allard," and he handed her his business card.

"As it happens, Mr. Allard just returned from dinner and, if he has time, he will see you. Meanwhile, if you will wait, sir," and she motioned toward a couch and some comfortable-looking chairs among some tastefully arranged potted plants.

Ken idly picked up a Sports and Field magazine to leaf through as he sat down on the couch. The secretary opened the door to the left of her desk and went in with Ken's card. She returned briefly and said, "Mr. Ferries, Mr. Allard said he has a few minutes before his next appointment is due."

Ken thanked her and strode through the door into Pace Allard's office. He saw an impressive man with a neatly trimmed mustache which matched his dark hair tinged with gray. The hair color set off his almost pearl-gray eyes. He was probably in his early fifties and, though quite slim, he was not underweight. Ken decided that he probably worked out with weights. Ken extended his hand and Pace responded quickly with a firm handshake.

"Mr. Ferries, I believe you are the Ken Ferries with the Waco Centennial, correct?"

"Yes, sir, I was until a few months ago. I retired and am into freelance writing now."

"That is interesting. What would bring you to a place like Rosewood? Are you doing some research here?"

"As a matter of fact, I am, sir. The Rogers case," Ken said and watched Pace Allard as he appeared to close down the earlier friendly expression.

"Now, why would that case draw you into a lengthy trip to an ordinary small town like this?" Pace pressed on, watching Ken with those pearl gray eyes.

Typical lawyer, Ken thought, as he suppressed a smile. "Maybe it's because it is a small town and not the ordinary occurrence for a small community, sir," Ken said.

"Is that right?" Pace said, still trying to correlate the reason behind what Ken was presenting to him as he held Ken's unblinking gaze.

"You were the Prosecutor, weren't you, Mr. Allard? And therefore, I should imagine that you would have a lot of insight you can share with me on the Rogers case, on what evidence would precipitate such a grizzly act on a very small-framed woman by three men. She had not been sexually violated, if some accounts I have read are correct?" Ken left it hanging there as a question. Ken pressed on since Pace still continued to say nothing. "Now, would it not have been a more tactical move on the part of these three men, after finding Mrs. Rogers at home, merely to ask her for the checks that Mr. Rogers said he had made out for them and then return another time when the home was unoccupied?"

Pace had watched Ken with a veiled expression but he finally spoke. "Well, sir, if you have covered this case through the media, then I should imagine that you do know that one of these men was an ex-con and also that he was attracted to the late Nadine Rogers. And she would have spurned even a suggestive remark, let alone an overt advance." He went on while Ken listened and he had a feeling that the man was merely circuitous, saying no more than Ken knew already. He seemed to take the position of a man in an arena attempting to keep an opponent from scoring instead of trying to exercise a possible hypothetical view.

Ken was thinking, "The Attorney at Law, on all the time, and every minute with a counter-attack." He worked to keep an amused glimmer from his eyes.

"I've known the Rogers family on a social basis and, like most people around here, they had an open door policy to their home. At least they did until this happened. Now, why, Mr. Ferries, would you want to re-open wounds with this pursuit?" Ken noticed that a muscle jerked on his cheek and he felt aversion clearly coming toward him from this man.

"Mr. Allard, to be quite frank with you, I've felt that there was a possibility that some of the information may have been erroneous or perhaps not presented. Yes, I did follow the case and have been researching it. I mean no disregard or lack of respect for your very astute abilities as a Prosecutor but I would be less than prudent if I did not express myself frankly." Ken went on, "After reading all of the accounts of this case and researching a great many other crimes during my career, I came up with some missing pieces. As severe as it is for these three men, who I add may be the ones who committed this horrific crime, I still find room for some questions."

Pace colored ever so slightly and said, "Mr. Ferries, without a shred of doubt, they did commit this crime."

"Well, now sir, I've taken a great deal of your time and I do thank you for giving me this audience," Ken smiled, not taking the bait to ignite this man farther.

Pace seemed a bit surprised that Ken was the one to close the meeting, as it was never his countenance to be one-upped on any issue. He showed an undercurrent of anger towards this formidable figure standing here with hand outstretched but he was skillful at concealing it. He was well-practiced at hiding his emotions so he forced a congenial smile and shook Ken's big hand.

"All the best to you on your pursuit. I'm sorry I couldn't be of more help to you, Mr. Ferries." By now Pace felt that his face had frozen into a grimace but he added, "Since you will be here quite a lengthy amount of time, I am certain I will see you again."

Ken bid him good day and made his way out of Pace's office. He knew he would receive no cooperation there. This man, Ken knew, saw himself as one of superior stock and, if crossed, would be a predacious adversary. He figured Pace was apt at systematic investigation and a force to reckon with in a courtroom. The man was obviously bright and certainly no fool. There was, however, an austere, detached, and cold aura Ken felt the moment he first came into his presence. He was also aware that Pace had been quick to see who and what he truly was and not the unassuming man he was usually taken for. He knew that Pace did not misjudge him but he had not misjudged Pace either.

Ken felt a slight sudden breeze on him and took notice of the soft scent of roses blooming close by. He did not trace where they were growing as he looked around. The fragrance became headier as he closed his eyes and breathed deeper of the nectar.

"Hm, someone has a lovely rose garden," he thought as he walked with that easy gait on past the office building. He decided to explore the town of Rosewood. As he walked on, he came to a small playground park and sat down on a bench, thinking of the events that had transpired earlier. He wished he had a cup of coffee while he relaxed, taking in the serenity of this tidy small town. There was nothing gross or unstable in the neat and tasteful appearance of Rosewood. The manicured lush lawns and picture perfect homes graced the scene everywhere Ken looked. A small blue bird swirled down at close proximity and alighted near Ken. The small feathered creature was observing him and Ken wished he had some bread crumbs to toss out to it.

"Well, little fella, guess I will stroll around and give Rosewood a look over but I have enjoyed your company. Sorry I didn't have a treat for you though." And the little bird cocked its head as though it understood.

Ken walked out of the park and, in another half block, he again caught the fragrance of roses just as he was reading the sign over the doorway of a charming little shop. It had been converted into an arts and crafts store, this rustic simple house with its cedar shingle siding. The sign, reading "Nadine's Arts and Crafts", had bright blue birds and butterflies in flight and a garland of colorful rosebuds. It held a beckoning promise of what was inside, for it literally said cheer. The house had bright blue shutters at the windows and a matching blue door. There was a stained glass arch of rainbow inset in the door. The tidy little house gave off such a "set free" feeling, like stepping into a wondrous fantasy world, Ken thought as he opened the door.

As he stepped inside, he felt a momentary jolt as he saw a golden girl sitting on a stool behind the counter. It was Nadine Rogers! He frantically sought to clear his head for a few seconds as he realized this lovely young woman must be Nadine's daughter. She was smiling at him now the same way her mother had in the dream where he had seen her. Though still a trifle unsettled, he returned her smile while searching for something appropriate to say.

"Why, I was just strolling about when I saw this attractive little shop and decided to come in and look around a bit," Ken smiled warmly back at her.

Her voice was soft and girl-like with a melodious tone. "Please, do look and enjoy," she said and then paused. "Would there be something of special interest that I can help you find, sir?"

"No, I don't believe so at the moment but I will perhaps find something that I simply must have," he chuckled with the air of the holiday mood that had just captured him. This shop was conducive to that kind of congeniality. There was a very special ambiance that enraptured Ken as he took in the whole environment of this lovely setting.

As though drawn automatically, Ken moved on to an arched door at the end of the store that had a calligraphy caption saying "The Gallery". He again caught the heady fragrance of roses as he stepped into the gallery where one of the paintings held him spellbound. It was of Nathan Tom sitting cross-legged with a rainbow and monarch butterflies surrounding him. The butterflies had alighted on his raised arms and around this ancient man's long gray mane of hair. They were flitting about him as well, as beautiful as the colorful rainbow. The ancient man staring at him from the painting seemed to bore into him with those unflinching black eyes, just as they had on the two encounters Ken had had with him. As he stared mesmerized by the beauty of the painting and the message it was giving him, he had not heard the young woman speak to him.

"That was my mother's last painting," the girl said in a wistful small voice.

Ken realized that she must have been standing beside him for a few moments before her voice had penetrated his awareness.

"Oh, I am sorry. I was so taken with this exquisite painting that I didn't realize you were standing here," he said. "Now, what was it you were saying, miss?"

"This painting," she said as she gestured toward it, "was the last painting my mother did. I see that you appreciate fine art," the petite young woman said as she studied Ken's face.

"Yes, I do," he assured her, "and I don't suppose that this lovely piece is for sale since it is the last one that your mother did?"

"I am sorry, sir, but no it isn't. However, I do have some smaller prints of it if you are interested."

"Yes, I am. If you will show me, I will purchase one as I would be so honored to have one of your mother's finest works to grace my home."

The young woman smiled and it jolted Ken's big heart as she was the portrait of her mother.

The print was as lovely as the larger painting and Ken felt such a sense of comfort that he was able to have this. He wanted to express this to the beautiful young woman so like her mother. Instead he found that he was asking her if she noticed the lovely fragrance of roses in the gallery.

She smiled with a great tenderness and said, "Yes, I do sometimes. I have asked others if they smell it but they never have. You are the only one who ever has except for me." She paused and then went on, "My mother's favorite perfume was a rose scent." Ken could see that she was fighting hard for control.

How strange this was, he thought, and yet so many of these occurrences were decidedly beautiful, like Nadine herself was beckoning from beyond the veil.

"I should introduce myself," Ken said, as they walked over to the counter so that he could pay for the print. "I am Ken Ferries from Waco" and the woman reached across the counter to place her small hand in Ken's large one.

"Phyllis Bennett," she said while she regarded him with a hint of curiosity.

Ken felt somewhat hesitant to express the true reason for his visit to Rosewood to this young woman due to the nature of it. He knew, of course, that in a small community it would not be long before everyone knew he was researching the Rogers case. "I am a freelance writer," he volunteered, "doing research here for a story I've been putting together." He searched the small heart-shaped face looking up at him.

"Oh my, that is very impressive," she said as her eyes took on a bright look.

"Well, I suppose one could say it has merits," he agreed. "My wife was a freelance writer as well and I would like to tell you she was one of excellence" Ken said proudly.

"Perhaps I know of her," Phyllis said. "Oh, now I don't mean personally but her writing as I read as much as I'm allowed with two tiny children." Her eyes twinkled now as she spoke of her little ones.

"I lost Gloria five years ago but I should imagine that you may very well have read some of her work since you read a fair amount. That is if you read her type of literature."

"Hm," she paused in thought. "Let me think now. Gloria Ferries. It is a familiar name so I am certain I have read some of her books." Suddenly she brightened. "Oh, why yes, I certainly have as she was one of my mother's favorite writers. She wrote mystical novels and I have all her books. You know, we never could wait until she wrote another of her wonderful stories" she stopped suddenly. "Oh, dear me. I am so sorry about your wife. You must miss her so terribly."

"Yes, I do, very much," he smiled at her softly, "but she would have been pleased that you and your mother enjoyed her through her writing."

"I am sorry that I never met her in person," Phyllis said, "but it is such a pleasure to meet you, Mr. Ferries."

"I can assure you the pleasure has been mine, young lady. And now, if you wouldn't mind, I'd like to ask you about the Indian man in the beautiful painting of your mother's."

"That's Nathan Tom. He is rather elusive as he is very, well, I would say mystical. Some say he is a true shaman. For his own reasons, he was drawn to my mother. My lovely mother had her special ways with people. That is why I still cannot grasp how anyone could have harmed her." The girl's voice choked but, with effort, she went on. "Nathan allowed my mother to come to his modest residence and do that wondrous painting of him. He is a gentle old soul really, though most folks here think him weird. He has a great grandchild he calls Moonbeam who is about fourteen. He has raised her since she was very small and her parents were both killed in an auto accident. His grandson Stran, the father to the little girl, was the last of Nathan's family except for this girl. Stran's wife, Willie May, would not have let the child go to any of her family because they were a wild bunch. Moonbeam's given name is Monda and, at school, that is the name she goes by. She is a lovely girl but very studious and keeps to herself. She helps her great grandfather with the goats and sheep that they raise. I would not be surprised if this girl is not as mystical and wise as the elder Nathan for she has the same kind of presence and bearing.

"How would I find this man's residence to ask if he would see me?" Ken inquired of her.

"I can't guarantee that he will see you, of course, but I would be happy to draw a map for you to his place." Then she hesitated, "If you don't have a four-wheeler, I would not take my car there since the road has major potholes and big chuckholes. It is ten miles out to Nathan's ranch after you turn off the main road but it seems more like twenty," and she laughed lightly in that merry lilt.

Ken was liking this young woman the more he came to know her. He could see that she was a highly spirited person, not much more than a girl, and yet he felt the presence of an old soul residing within.

"Most certainly I had better rent a four-wheeler then but that shouldn't be a problem. I will just run up to Longview and do that before it gets any later. And say, Phyllis, you've been ever so helpful. Now, one more thing, is it possible I can get this print framed here?"

"Oh, most assuredly. There is a lady who will be here shortly and Rosie does a very good job on borders and framing."

"I will trust her judgment on both then and return after I have come back from Longview."

"All right, Mr. Ferries. We'll see you later. I'm so glad you are pleased with the print."

He raised his hand. "Please, do call me Ken. Yes, I am delighted with the print, Phyllis."

"Wonderful then," she smiled, "and I hope Nathan will see you and you don't have to make that rough ride out there for nothing."

He nodded and returned her smile. He stepped out the door and then breathed deeply of the outside air. He could not shake the feeling that he had talked to Nadine herself and he thought that, in a way, Phyllis was a clone of her mother. Yet it was more than the sensation that Nadine had been standing and watching close by while he and Phyllis had been conversing—it was like a true presence.

He checked his watch and decided to go talk to Muriel about renting a four-wheeler. Then he hoped he could see old Nathan and get back in time for dinner at Dolly's Café. When he walked into Dolly's, Muriel was engaged in a conversation with one of the prettiest girls he had ever seen. And he saw the likeness of Muriel in this striking young lady. He was certain it had to be Angie.

"Oh, hi Ken. I want you to meet my daughter, Angie," Muriel said, her face alight with obvious pride.

"I suspected right off that this lovely lady had to be Angie. You look a lot like your mother."

Angie smiled at Ken and, in the same husky voice as her mother's, said hello. She was slender like her mother, with the same green eyes but her hair was a lustrous brown with highlights of copper. She was a girl who would make heads turn wherever she went.

"Angie, this is Ken Ferries and he is from Waco. He came here to do some research."

"What kind of research, Mr. Ferries?" Angie pressed as she extended her slender hand in greeting.

Muriel quickly intervened with an enthusiastic pitch. "Ken is a freelance writer, Angie," and she smiled at Ken with an unspoken message. Ken was quickly able to translate that Muriel hadn't had the time to talk to Angie about this painful subject alone.

"Your area is very nice here," Ken said as he sidestepped any further questions she might pose about his research.

"Yes, it is homey and I miss it when I'm away at school but, of course, I miss Mom even more," and she smiled lovingly at her mother. Muriel put her arm around her daughter's tiny waist.

"Muriel, I have to run over to Longview and rent a four-wheeler as I plan to explore some rough road. However, I hope to be back here at six o'clock for dinner."

"That's fine, and, if you are a bit later, don't be concerned since I won't be able to leave here until at least eight anyway.

"All right then. I'd best get going. Angie, I will see you again before I return to Waco since your good mother has invited me out to your home to help you enjoy yours and my favorite cake." He smiled and winked good-naturedly at Angie.

"Say now, Mom, that's great," Angie smiled with a bright cheer that made her even prettier. "It's so nice that you will be joining us, Mr. Ferries. I am looking forward to it."

"Please call me Ken, Angie, as I am sure that I will be seeing you and your mother often," he said, as he watched Muriel's face color slightly. She expressed a demure look. It struck an amused cord in Ken as he had not seen this side of Muriel. She was usually forthright and not the least bit subdued.

"Well, then Ken, I certainly hope that is the case and we see you often," Angie chuckled as she glanced at her mother. There was a hint of mischief in her green eyes.

Angie had a stately bearing about her that Ken had not seen in a girl her age. It usually didn't develop until later in life, if at all. He knew he was going to like Angie even more as he came to know her better.

"So then, you both have a great day and I will see you later this evening." He was making his way out the door as they both bid him good day. He checked his watch again as he climbed into his car and then headed off for Longview. The day was pleasant and not too hot, for which Ken was appreciative. As he drove along, he noticed the pink and purple larkspur in abundance growing in the pastures and along the roadway. There were some wooded areas and the rolling hills were a generous sea of green. A scattering of farm and ranch homes were in view and some had private catfish ponds on them. The setting was one that Ken liked and he sighed, feeling relaxed as he thought over the day's events. It seemed that all was moving along rather well, almost effortlessly, as though some force was propelling him.

Longview came into view, an attractive mid-size city and he drove along the business section until he spotted a large auto dealership. He pulled into their parking lot and took notice of the sign, "Bradley's New and Used Auto World".

He noticed an array of four-wheelers on the used auto side. He entered the showroom and made his way to the counter where two ladies sat at their desks. From the side, a salesman about Ken's age approached him.

"Sir, may I help you?" he asked as he walked toward him.

"Well, now, I expect you can," Ken said, returning a smile. "I need a four-wheeler to rent for a couple of days."

"All right, sir. Any particular four-wheeler you had in mind?"

"I should expect that a Jeep would be fine since I understand I will be encountering quite a rough road."

Ken was led to a fire engine red Jeep after he had completed the paperwork. He had been assured that his car would be safe to leave until Monday the following week. As he started the engine, it turned over quickly, then slowed down to a purr. Ken was comforted that it seemed to be in good condition, that it was no more than five years old. As he drove back to Rosewood, he remembered that he needed to stop at Nadine's Arts and Crafts to pick up his print. He drove straight to the shop and met Phyllis just as she was coming out the door.

"Hello, Ken. I see that you took my advice and got an appropriate vehicle to drive our rough country roads."

"Yes, ma'am, I sure did. This Jeep handles well. I haven't driven one in years, not since my few years in the Army, but I must tell you the comfort of one has vastly improved," he chuckled.

"Ken, I will go in with you and introduce you to Rosie. Then I will run along as a friend is minding my two little girls for me. I just fill in here on occasion if Rosie or Sissy get tied up."

"I was fortunate to meet you then, Phyllis," he smiled a generous smile at her.

"I was in luck too," she agreed happily.

They entered the shop where a silver-haired round-faced lady looked up from her project, her glasses perched on her small round nose. She reminded Ken of Mrs. Santa Claus with her round short body and features. She had bright snappy blue eyes and a waggish merry smile of greeting as she said in an unmistakable Irish brogue, "Well, now Miss Phyll, that was indeed a short trip."

"Oh Rosie, this is Ken Ferries. Ken, meet my second mother, Rosie Wilson."

"Aw, go on with you, lass. I could never fill your dear Mum's shoes. But I love this child like she is my own and that's a fact." She reached over the counter and took Phyllis' hand in her own. "Mr. Ferries, it is indeed a grand pleasure to meet you, sir. You have such fine taste in paintings. That one is my favorite of Nadine's paintings too." Her eyes took on a moist look.

"Thank you, Mrs. Wilson," Ken said. "It is a pleasure to meet you."

"Aw, go on now with the formality," she chirped lightly. "Call me Rosie, everybody does, you know.

"Only on the condition that you call me Ken." He smiled at this chipper short lady who had to hold her head back some as she peered up at him over the top of her wire frame glasses.

"Yes, sir, Mr. Ken. Then it is done. Would you like to see the border and frame that Phyllis and I selected for the print?"

Ken nodded and Rosie walked to a table behind the counter. "Well, step around the counter and come see what you think. I'm just putting the finishing touches on it."

Ken was delighted with the whole project and could see that Rosie was a pro at her craft. The border picked up the beauty of colors in the print and the frame was rustic and ever so suitable for that type of scene. Too perfect. Rosie had completely captured the mystery as well as the mystical that Nadine conveyed in this beautiful piece of art.

"Nadine titled this 'The Mystic', you know, Mr. Ken. Would you care to have a gold metal plate with that title inscribed on the bottom of the frame?" she said as she played those blue eyes on him.

"But of course," he quickly agreed, as he came out of a near hypnotic stare at the painting. It was so deeply captivating that he had found it hard to draw his eyes away.

"Rosie, how about if I stop in on Monday and pick this up. I have something to do this afternoon and this weekend is full for me too."

"Why, most assuredly, Mr. Ken. That will give me time to have the metal plate finished and put on the frame."

"Then you are pleased?" said Phyllis, as she waited for a sign from Ken. Rosie also waited for his reply with polite expectancy.

"How could I not be greatly pleased," Ken said as his face spread into a warm smile. He addressed Rosie, "My dear lady, you are quite apt at your business and a credit to the finishing of beautiful art, I must say."

"You see there, Rosie. I told you that Ken would love it. And he is so correct, you do have a wonderful gift," Phyllis assured her fondly.

"Aw, go on now with the two of you," Rosie sniffed. "You will be putting this old lady's head to full with all that fine poetry you are blustering on about." She dabbed quickly at the corner of each eye, while Phyllis gave Ken a broad wink. She reminded Ken a bit of Sarita with her seeming off-handed way of receiving a compliment. Ken liked this fine lady and could easily see why Phyllis was so deeply drawn to her.

"I had best be heading out to Nathan's before the afternoon is gone," Ken said, "and with luck, I will get to talk to him."

"Oh, he is very selective of his company, Mr. Ken, as I am sure Phyl has told you. Don't be offended if he just clams up, as he has a way of doing."

"Yes, thank you, Rosie. Phyllis has also warned me," he laughed with good nature. He walked to the entrance and bid them good day, then departed for the hot red Jeep waiting for him. The Jeep made him smile as it gave him the feeling of unbounded youth and high spirits. He climbed in and started the engine. "Well, little classy Jeep, you and I are off on a high adventure," he said softly to himself just as Phyllis came out of the shop.

"See you again soon, Ken," she said, "and have a good day."

He gave her a thumbs up and a wide smile as he pulled away and drove down the street. He turned at a corner and went out onto the main highway with high spirits. He knew the road would be rough out to old Nathan's but that did not dampen his peppy mood. He traveled along at a reasonable speed so he could still enjoy looking at the countryside. He came to a road crossing and pulled over to check the map Phyllis had drawn for him. He realized after a brief study that he would need to turn right from the main highway.

Chapter_____4

The road on the other side of the highway was in good condition and Ken supposed it led to a ranch back a few miles. The name on the mailbox read "Will T. Rogers Ranch" and it was decorated with stencils of wildflowers in an array of bright colors. Suddenly, a deep feeling of indescribable sorrow welled up from his solar plexus. It was as though he had picked up on a terrible anguish and overwhelming grief wafting through the very ethers. His throat constricted and he felt a rush of unbridled hot tears scalding his cheeks. He had had a similar experience when Gloria died.

"Ohhh," he wailed aloud, as though in great physical pain. He fumbled for his handkerchief. "My God," he said aloud, "what's come over me?" He heard the sound of whippoorwills in a lovely cadence off in the distance. He mopped his face on his handkerchief, blew his nose, and turned off down the rough road.

"This is all just too weird," he thought as he avoided the first chuckhole. As he drove on, he noticed a large red-tailed hawk a hundred or so yards ahead. It landed on a rough and crudely built fence a few feet from the roadway. The hawk seemed to be watching Ken as it sat on the fence.

"Say, fella, you are the biggest red-tail I have ever seen," Ken said as he pulled even with the big bird. The great hawk faced him squarely as he passed by. For some reason, Ken felt the same downdraft chill he had experienced in the two sudden appearances of the elder Nathan.

"Weird," he muttered to himself as he hit a sizeable pothole. "Uh-oh, little Jeep, we are being put to the test. I think you'll hang in there just fine, but I'm not so sure about me," he chuckled. He noticed a cloud of pure white in front of him in the clear blue sky and wondered why he hadn't seen it earlier. It was the only one in the sky in his view. As he drove on watching for the worst of the chuckholes, he took notice of the cloud again. It had scattered into what looked like large letters and he read them aloud. "Why, I'll be damned. It spells out 'redeemer,'" he mumbled in amazement.

Ken shook his head and pondered, "What else am I going to encounter?" He again had a powerful sense of something looming just out of sight, like a great force pulling at him. It had been thus ever since he had stared at Nadine's picture that first time, as though she was calling out to him, compelling him to undertake this vigilant search. He was not in total clarity of it, even though he had felt there were some gaping holes in the case and the evidence. He had just considered it a veteran newsman's hunch, but all these events had extended to far more reaching circumstances than the typical cases of his career. It was as though Ken was being brought to fore to hasten an awareness he had let lay fallow, a pressing pursuit of energies intervening that would not allow him to deny these bizarre events.

"Sometimes it does seem that we so-called rational folks get thrown a curve ball," he said aloud. "But I wonder what's going on," he mused as he picked up the fragrance of sweet clover wafting through his open window. He noticed a colorful array of sweet briar which his parents had called pasture roses. He heard the trill of a meadowlark and the lonely, yet lovely, call of the turtle dove and took comfort in these familiar sights and sounds. He reached for the bottled water he had propped in the seat, grateful that he had purchased this from the car dealer's vending machine before he left. He took a refreshing swig.

"How much farther, little Jeep, before we are at the elder sheep and goat man's abode?" he said aloud, as he lightly patted the steering wheel. A soft wind arose quite suddenly, rippling the clover and grass in the pastures. A raven flew low and, as it began to ascend with the wind, it maneuvered like a well-balanced acrobat. The sky seemed to be deepening into a soft color of pink, and as Ken watched, deepened farther into a darker shade of mauve. The first drop of rain fell on the windshield, running slowly down like a gentle tear.

"Oh, great. Now you and I, little pal, will probably get mired down here in the mud unless you've got the grit it takes to haul us out," he addressed the Jeep. "Maybe I've gone round the bend. What am I doing, anyway?" he said to no one in particular as more rain drops splashed lightly on the windshield. He could see a hillside off in the distance that seemed to jut higher than the others in the area and it appeared that he was heading straight toward it. As he drove on, the rain began to spatter down in earnest-sized drops and he rolled up his window and found the windshield wipers. The little Jeep purred onward as though it had a will of its own. For such a rough road, the Jeep rode fairly smoothly and Ken wagered it could no doubt pull out of a mudhole easily. He silently commended its abilities.

"Well," he said out loud, "I could sure use one of Muriel's steaming cups of coffee about now and I am reasonably sure I will not get the offer of one from old Nathan," he lamented with a sardonic, half-amused snort. The rain was pelting down heavier now and still Ken moved forward in the direction of the great mound of hill in front of him. As he was reaching the hill covered in a sea of green and various wildflowers, he saw a rainbow arching over the whole expanse of this massive hill.

The little Jeep came to a cattle guard crossing and then Ken saw that the road rose upward all the way to the crest of the hill. He hoped that by then he should have reached the end of this journey. The rain was slowing down and the air from the open window held a sweet and freshly cleaned pungent aroma. He breathed deeply.

He then saw Nathan's white wooly fat sheep contentedly eating of the plentiful grass. As he drove on up this hill that had just missed being a small mountain, he thought for a moment that he'd seen a brilliant shaft of light from his peripheral vision on the right. It was as though moonlight had suddenly appeared up over a mountain in a darkened starless sky.

All that he saw when he quickly turned his head that direction was a small-framed girl with a stick prompting a herd of goats along. She had in her company a large white dog that Ken was certain had to be part wolf with its massive shoulders and head. It was one of the most beautiful animals Ken had ever seen. The girl, Ken decided, must be old Nathan's great grandchild. She had allowed her shiny long black hair to hang down her back and she wore a bright blue loose shirt with a long print skirt of many colors. She appeared to be little more than a child of twelve or less and yet Ken knew that she was a teenager, from what Phyllis had said.

Ken brought the Jeep to a halt and hoped the girl would talk to him since she was approaching within a few feet of the road. As Ken got out of the Jeep and walked around it, the girl was there in front of him. It surprised Ken that she had moved so quickly to that place. Before he uttered a greeting, the girl spoke. Peering deeply into his eyes, she said, "Grandfather awaits you."

Her own eyes were black pools just like her grandfather's. Her skin was a warm brown and she had delicate features, high cheekbones and large dark almond-shaped eyes. Her mouth was sensuous for one so young, full and lightly pink with a slightly taunting pout. She regarded Ken in the way a much older person would and Ken knew he was in the company of a very wise and ancient soul. It was, in a way, a soul awareness, for he felt a chill course through him from head to foot. He recalled that Sarita once told him that was the soul's way of knowing. He had accepted that from Sarita as valid, as he knew that her wisdom often exceeded his logic.

"How did you grandfather know that I was paying him a visit?" Ken asked the girl, who was watching him with those enormous dark eyes.

As he held his eyes with her own, she answered, "He has his ways." Her voice was as crystal clear as a soft running brook.

"Yes, I certainly have come to see that," Ken smiled at this elfin girl. He decided he would attempt further conversation with her and remarked on her dog who was sitting close by. He seemed aloof but Ken knew he could move with lightning speed.

"That is quite a fine dog you have there, miss. Does he happen to have some wolf in him?"

The girl gave a brief nod, still regarding him with those all-seeing eyes that knew the depths of his soul.

"Well, apparently you've trained him well since he is around your sheep and goats."

Again she merely nodded and then said to the large animal, "Chacato, come." And the big dog came and sat by the girl, looking up at Ken much as the girl did, as if looking into the depths of his soul. "We have taught Chacato well, Grandfather and I. Yet he is a free spirit and we allow him that. Therefore he respects us as we do him."

The first hint of a smile came as she said, "You may call me Moonbeam as my elder grandfather does. Now you must go. He awaits you." And she turned her back to him and went along with her goat herd.

Ken knew that she regarded the conversation closed, so he walked around the Jeep, climbed in and started the engine. As he drove away a short distance and adjusted the rearview mirror, he looked back for the girl and her dog but saw nothing but grass with dots of wildflowers scattered in it. He pulled the Jeep to a stop and got out to look fully at the place where he had been in her company.

"Come now, what kind of wizardry is this?" he said aloud and felt a tingle up and down his spine. The girl had not had time to disappear with that giant dog and a whole herd of goats. It was as though they were a fog, and a breeze had blown in and dissipated them away.

"Do I really feel I am up to all of this weird sorcery?" He found that he was talking to himself again, much to his vexation. "Oh, well, I've come this far, so I may as well see it through. I can't get past the feeling that old Nathan knows a lot more about what happened to Nadine Rogers than anyone has ever suspected." He went on, "They think, at least most of them, that he is just a strange old fool who has been out in the hills too long." With no one better to direct his conversation to, he said, "Well, little red Jeep, we will see, eh?"

He had the window rolled down and felt a warm spatter of rain on his arm just as he crested the hill. Looking down, he saw a modest cabin, some out-buildings, and a corral with two horses inside. As suddenly as the rain had started, it stopped now as Ken moved in the direction of the little homestead. As he pulled in front of the cabin, he noticed the black and white goatskin stretched out to the left of the entrance and a window with 6 small panes on the other side. He knocked on the rough crossbar wooden door and listened for a response. The two horses stood watching and began to whinny gently at him.

"Well, hello there. At least the two of you are greeting me," he said good-naturedly, as he walked toward the corral. He admired them both, the one dappled gray and the other a pinto. They were both well-cared for and each one had good confirmation.

Sometimes when he saw good horses such as these, he missed the time he had spent growing up on his parents' ranch. He had ridden all the time as a youth. Sometimes, he and his brother Tommy had helped their Dad round up the beef cattle when their father needed every available hand. As boys will be, he and Tommy had slipped off to swim in their neighbor Jake's pond when they could. They would catch the biggest bullfrogs just at dusk. They put them in a bucket with a lid on it so as not to lose their catch. Then off they would go to Jakes to see if he would fix the three of them fried frogs legs. Old Jake explained to them that there was a certain way to prepare them or else they would hop right out of the skillet. Tommy, nicknamed "doubting Thomas", tested out Jake's theory one evening just to make sure his instructions were right. Jake floured the frog legs after showing the boys how to ready them. He placed them in a very hot cast iron skillet with hot bacon fat and fried them to a golden crispness. Tommy decided to try it himself. He was busy at the task when he suddenly jumped back, his face filled with horror as two sets of frog legs sprang out of the skillet, narrowly missing one "doubting Thomas". Ken thought of this long ago saga as he patted the big gray's neck and he laughed out loud.

He noticed a large rainbow again and, as though drawn in that direction unmindful, he walked around the corral and beyond it. He noticed a hillside that the rainbow seemed to arch over. As he came closer to it, he stopped short as there appeared to be someone sitting on top. A soft breeze had picked up as he made his way to the hill. He had not realized how warm he was feeling until this refreshing cool appeared.

"Say there," he called to the figure on the hillside. The person did not respond. The figure of what he thought must be a man seemed to have his arms lifted up and out toward the sky. "Hm, perhaps it is the elder Nathan and he is in prayer," Ken deduced.

As he came closer, he could see that it was Nathan Tom and that he was facing him. He approached a few more feet and then froze, staring in shocked amazement. The old man sat cross-legged with butterflies that numbered in the hundreds on him and around him, all in a blaze of beautiful colors, though mostly large Monarchs.

The rainbow colors were more vivid than Ken had ever seen and it was as though everything in sight took on the brilliance of its cascading and luminous luster.

He thought of the painting he had been drawn to at the arts and crafts shop and stood speechless as he realized he was staring at the same scene Nadine had painted. The elder Nathan's black eyes stayed fixed on him, as though he was in a hypnotic state. To further amaze Ken, the butterflies began to leave Nathan and circle him, then alight upon him as if on command. Suddenly the scent of roses was heavy in the air. It was as though he was dreaming all this and yet somehow he knew he wasn't. He could hear Nathan speaking to him now.

"Once you pass the thorns of doubt, big man, you step into the world of unexpected visions and there the truth awaits."

A picture like a movie began to form up above Nathan and he spoke again in that strange unearthly way he had the night by the motel. He saw three men bending over and looking down at a figure on the floor. He saw it was a woman and she looked like a broken doll. A sea of red was on the walls and on the ceiling. This bright red was a swirl around the figure on the floor and the three men were transfixed with utter horror on their faces. The men had no such red on their clothes and, though Ken stared in shock, it registered like a bright beacon within the confines of his senses. In a fascinated horror, he watched it play out like a macabre theater drama.

Another picture came into view as the first one faded away, of the three men running and clambering into a truck and driving away at great speed. That scene shifted to the vivid picture of a young woman, her body great with child and carrying a small girl in her arms. He could hear the shrill screams from the woman and the child, then he saw the woman lose her footing and pitch forward as a large man's arms encircled them to prevent them from falling. He lifted the woman and child together in his sturdy arms and carried them to a pickup to put them inside. He came around to the other side and got in. Ken could see that he was driving with one hand on the steering wheel and holding Phyllis close to him with the other. He was talking to the young woman, who Ken realized was Phyllis. He could see the terror on the man's face, as on the child's and her mother's.

The scene abruptly changed and he could just make out the shadowed figure of a man in a pasture off at a distance running to a vehicle partially hidden in some tall trees. He could see the man reach the vehicle, a dull green older model Jeep. The man drove off rapidly with a great cloud of dust billowing out behind the Jeep.

All of this faded away and Ken found that he was sitting in the little red Jeep as though he had never stepped from it. He felt as though he had just awakened from a slumber and he removed his glasses and rubbed his eyes. He looked around but all he saw were the two horses calmly swatting flies with their tails. There was no sign of Nathan on the hill where he had seen him sitting before all of this bizarre vision. He saw a shadow over his head and looked up to see again a larger-than-usual red-tailed hawk flying low just above him.

"Well, I do believe this is about enough to fill a whole book but I don't know who would believe it," he said out loud and shook his head. He felt more overwhelmed now that he had glimpsed another world. As he started the Jeep and was pulling away, his mind was a whirl of all that he had experienced. He wondered if he had been under hypnosis, which was why he didn't remember walking back from the hill to his Jeep.

"Am I being led?" he was thinking as he pulled away from Nathan's yard. "I suppose it is obvious that I am, at least for me it is. But is it by this elderly Indian or the spirit of Nadine Rogers or perhaps all of the above?" he thought as he drove along slowly. He noticed it was getting close to five-thirty.

"Yes, and what of this strange old Indian?" As crazy as it seemed to him, he wondered if he had experienced a type of psychosis, except that Nathan was fully capable of transforming back into human form. He had been aroused by something extraordinary that allowed him to speculate on such an astonishing possibility. He had absorbed a great amount of reading over his lifetime and knew that many cultures readily accepted these things as the norm, such as Native Americans who had not pulled too far away from their cultures. He knew that it was an established knowledge and practice of people in India too. Western cultures have closed their eyes to this higher frequency but sometimes it smacks us soundly in the chops when we are feeling superior. You might say we get a curve ball thrown at us.

"Whew, I have been getting them faster than I can catch them!" he laughed now and it felt good. "Well, looks like I can get back to the motel and shower before going to the café to relax with a good dinner," he murmured to himself, checking his watch once again. He was too keyed up by all of the mystique to feel tired. He felt like he was on alert for any other event out of the ordinary, another curve ball maybe. He smiled warily as he entertained these thoughts.

It was a slow drive back to Rosewood as it had been to drive the ten miles out to Nathan's but he didn't mind as it gave him time to ponder all of the day's startling events. He pulled in at the motel and quickly made his way out of the Jeep. He went into his room and checked to see if he had any messages. He had told Sarita the name of the motel in the event that she needed to get in touch with him. The phone system registered no calls so he headed for the shower, hoping he could unwind.

After his shower, he was greatly refreshed and more than ready to head to Dolly's for a steaming cup of coffee while waiting for his supper.

"Aw, you're back," Muriel smiled a sunshine smile for him.

He felt such warmth and pleasure at seeing her that he boldly took her hand and said, "Yes, and what a day I've had, lady. I can't wait to just sit and admire you, you wonderful sane person."

"Wow, you must have had quite a day," she laughed.

"Let me tell you, quite a day is putting it mildly," he assured her.

"Ken, sit down and I'll bring you a cup of coffee. You look like you could really use one," she said earnestly as she searched his face with concern.

A few people were seated in the café and three more entered as Ken slid into a booth and picked up the newspaper someone had left. Muriel arrived with the coffee pot and poured a mug full for him.

"Ken, the lasagna is on special and I can vouch for it being excellent."

"Then so be it, my good lady. And maybe a salad with that and I think I'll be in great shape," and he winked teasingly at her.

"All right, Ken. Do you want the house dressing for that salad?" she said while writing up his order.

"Again, I will trust your judgment, Muriel," he said as he picked up the coffee mug.

"Bet you will like it too," she smiled with a cocky little grin spreading across her face.

"Now that I am nearly salivating just thinking about the sumptuous food awaiting me, I must tell you that I have already got things better collected," and he sighed deeply.

"Ken, when you come out to the house this evening, I want us to sit down and really have a talk, okay?" she inquired. "Angie and Ty will probably take off to go see friends after we have dessert and then we can talk in private, just us," and she let the latter hang.

"Muriel, I haven't had a better offer than that for longer than I care to remember. I really do enjoy your wonderful company, pretty lady."

She smiled happily at him and said, "Thanks, Ken. I haven't had such a nice compliment for a long time either. Now I will go put in your order, kind sir," and she returned the earlier wink Ken had given her.

As she turned to walk away to place Ken's order, she stopped to speak to a handsome young man attired in Western dress clothes who had just entered the café.

"Well, hello, Will Earl," she said as she hugged him to her.

"Auntie Muriel, how are you doing?" he drawled with a soft affectionate smile, as Muriel pulled back from the hug.

"I am fine, young man, but I do have a bone to pick with you. How come you haven't stopped by? I have missed you."

"Well, as a matter of fact, other than getting knee deep with work out at the ranch, I reckon I don't have a good excuse," he chuckled, looking down at her. He was probably twenty-two or three, Ken thought, as he took in this very impressive looking man who easily stood six foot four. One could say he was movie star handsome and he was rock hard from hard work.

"You know Angie's home?" Muriel said as she studied Will Earl's face and waited for his response.

"So I hear," he grinned with a hint of mischief playing in his eyes.

"Listen, you big lug, why don't you drop by this evening and see her. And, by the way, have you seen Ty yet? You know, your wandering little brother is back?"

"Yeah, I saw him today and he said he was gonna go see Aunt Muriel and Ang and that he was also having some of Aunt Muriel's top-of-the-line cake. So I guess I'm invited too?"

"Honey, you kids never need an invitation and you know that," Muriel said and reached up to pat him lovingly on his tan cheek.

"Say, come on over here, Will Earl. I want you to meet a friend of mine," Ken heard Muriel say and she put her arm around his and led him to Ken.

"Meet Ken Ferries, Will Earl. Ken, meet Will Earl Rogers. You met his brother Tyler earlier today."

Ken started to get up but Will Earl said, "Oh no sir, please don't get up." And he extended his hand, which Ken shook, feeling the strength of this young man.

"Listen, you two get acquainted while I put in Ken's order. Oh well, I just as well take your order now too, Will Earl."

"All right, tell me what will fill me up good, Auntie, because this cowboy's feeling lean in the mid-section," and he flashed a warm smile up at Muriel.

"Ken's having the lasagna with salad and house dressing. How does that sound, my hungry cowpoke?" she said smiling with affection down at him.

"Sounds good to me, so just make it a pair, except if you have that great peach ice tea, I'd rather have that than coffee."

"Sure do, sweetie. Now you and Ken just visit and I will place your orders and check on some of the other customers."

"So, how long have you known Aunt Muriel?" Will Earl asked Ken, as he directly looked into Ken's eyes. He had an open directness that Ken instantly liked.

Ken made an appraisement closer now that Will Earl had slid into the booth across from him. He thought he must favor his father. His eyes were of a color that made it hard to say what their base color was because they were green-blue and yet had some brown flecks in them. Ken thought they were probably the type of eyes that changed with whatever color he wore. As he sat down to join Ken, he had removed the black Stetson hat and placed it carefully down beside him. He had crisp deep brown hair with reddish highlights that he smoothed with his broad strong hands as he waited for Ken to respond to his question.

"Well, to tell you the truth, Will Earl, I haven't known Muriel very long. You see, I am a writer and I'm doing some research for material I'm working on. I live down in Waco."

"Well now, sir, that is interesting. If you are going to be around here awhile, maybe you would like to come to the local rodeo Sunday. That is, if you like rodeo?"

"Why yes, I would enjoy that. As a matter of fact, I haven't been to one in some time," Ken said, feeling that he was going to like this young man a great deal.

"I ride some of them spirited broncos, mainly for the heck of it," and a slow grin spread over his young face. "My mom never liked us boys to ride those wild Cayuse but, shucks, I reckon fellas got so much vinegar they got to get out of their systems," and he shrugged.

Ken noticed that a shadow passed over Will Earl's face and he knew that the mention of his mother had put a real hurt upon the young man's demeanor.

"Say, Mr. Ferries, what do you write about? I don't believe you said, else I forgot to ask."

"First of all, Will Earl, please call me Ken," and Ken was relieved that this young man quickly got on another subject. He knew that he had to in order to step around any painful discussion of his mother.

"I was a newsman for many years, up until some months ago. I knew one day I would get into freelance writing once I retired, so I write whatever I am especially drawn to, about most any subject," he elected for an attentive Will Earl, who seemed greatly interested.

"What a good feeling, I would imagine, to pick what you really enjoy. It does sound like you've had the drive to get where you are at in life," Will Earl said thoughtfully as he searched Ken's face.

"Have you gone to college, Will Earl?"

"Yes, sir. I took business and agriculture, plus some animal husbandry. I figured I'd better be sharp on all those since I am naturally geared in that direction," he grinned that winsome grin of his and Ken thought in quiet amusement that he probably had several young ladies clamoring for him.

Muriel came with their supper and Will Earl gave a resounding, "Yippee, now would you look at these lavish digs. Boy, have I got a home for them," and he rubbed his stomach.

"Now that is a man after my heart who appreciates good food," Muriel laughed and ruffled Will Earl's perfectly groomed hair.

"Here now, Auntie, you don't mess me all up. I'm heading out to see that pretty daughter of yours and I know I have some stiff competition with all those college dandies after her."

He was in a happy mood, Ken could see, and he knew that Muriel gave this young man a lot of comfort that he surely needed. He had seen the same interaction with young Tyler. They had lost their mother at far too early a time in their lives and that in itself was extremely sad, but the way it came about was unspeakable. The impacted magnitude of it was beyond comprehension on these young siblings of Nadine's. He felt a growing lump in his throat and an overwhelming compassion. He reached for his water, taking a liberal long drink in an effort to still this emotion building up suddenly in him. It was one thing to read about these people and look at them in news copy or television, but to meet them and see the human spirits of them was a disturbance indescribable at times. Yet he reasoned that they would have to move on with their lives. He felt almost as though Nadine was close around him, that she herself was prompting him to help them with some sort of closure. He was coming more and more into that mode of thought since he had been drawn to this case.

"Are you all right, Ken?" Muriel was saying. He had been unaware that she was observing him so closely.

"Oh, sure. I just didn't realize I was so thirsty," and his short laugh came out somewhat strangled.

"Well, you two, dig in now and then later we'll all head out of here and get into that cake that's waiting for us."

Ken knew that she had not been fooled by his off-handed statement about being thirsty. He had come to realize that her wisdom ran deep. He was so attracted to this woman that he had known for such a short time but she felt like someone he had known for a very long time. Ken knew that the feeling was mutual. He thought that if something came of it, then it would probably be good for the two of them. He reasoned that he would not rush into a relationship but they could coast along with a good friendship and then see how it would develop.

Muriel was the first woman since Gloria had passed away whom he had some stirrings about, yet he didn't know if it was quite the same way he had felt when he first saw Gloria. He had the passion of youth then and perhaps was more able to throw caution to the wind. He had not one whit of caution the first time he had seen Gloria and knew that he wanted her for his own. He was extremely comfortable with Muriel and she made him feel a certain refreshment for life that he had lost after Gloria died. He thought, as he sat there and watched this handsome youth eat with such gusto, that everything was that way when one was the age of Will Earl. Always unbridled passion with whatever they did. Maybe the sweetest part of age was that you slowed down to pause for introspection before you thrust into things. So he comforted himself with these quiet revelations and watched Will Earl polish off the hearty supper Muriel had placed before him a scant few minutes earlier. He could recall Carter's near insatiable appetite and how Gloria would marvel at their husky son's love of food. She used to tease Ken too, in their early days of marriage, about his hollow legs, as she was certain that was where so much that he ate had to go.

Ken sat there and pondered deeper into his own private world of thought. He had never felt old and didn't feel that he ever would, no matter what his age, because he had always felt so connected to his own Spirit. He loved young people, being around them and their great enthusiasm kept him fresh in his outlook. It was just that he had learned to pace himself but always stay in movement, mind-wise and body-wise. It was one of the things he found that he admired so in Muriel. She kept busy and was full of sparkle for life. From all he had noticed of her, she appeared to meet things head on. "Yes, lady, I think we could grow into a beautiful dream world with some great quality time," he decided, as Muriel approached with the coffee pot and a smile as big as Texas.

He felt Will Earl's observation of him and Muriel and knew this sharp young man had not missed the growing attraction between them. Muriel poured more coffee for Ken and sat a pitcher from her other hand down on the table.

"Will Earl, honey child, be my guest. This is full of peach tea just for you from Auntie Muriel."

"Can I have your hand in marriage, sweet lady?" Will Earl said, and took her hand to kiss it.

"I bet that would create quite a stir, but I will give it some thought," she purred in that husky voice and then she winked at Will Earl. She turned to look at the clock and said, "I think we can get out of here in less than an hour, okay?"

Ken and Will Earl both agreed that was fine, as Ken noticed the last customer stood at the register to pay for his supper. That would leave just him and Will Earl.

"What do you think of Aunt Muriel, Ken? She's kinda terrific, isn't she?"

"I can't disagree with you one whit, Will Earl. I would add to that, she is a stunning woman."

"Well, do you think you might be interested in her, Ken?" And then he blushed but went on. "I may be over-stepping myself, and if I am, please excuse me, but I never could figure out why Aunt Muriel never married again. She is not only a looker but she is one great woman and a guy would be doing himself proud to have a lady like her." He paused. "Whoops, there I go again, letting my motor mouth get my big foot in there. I do apologize, Ken."

"As a matter of fact, I do find Muriel very lovely, and since my wife passed away, I haven't thought about another woman until I met Muriel a short time ago. Since you brought this up, I will tell you something. We are going out for supper tomorrow evening and to a dance after that. Then, from there on, who knows if she can stand me afterwards," he laughed good-naturedly.

"That is about the best news I've heard in a long time. Let me tell you, she likes you a lot because I have known that sweet lady all my life and believe me, I can tell." He went on, "Ken, I think I am a good judge of character and you are a nice guy or I would never have said a word to you about seeing Aunt Muriel. I feel like she is a second mother to me."

"Thanks, Will Earl. That is one of the best things anyone has ever said to me. I find it an honor that you bestowed it on me." Ken held Will Earl's eyes and he said, "You do know that you are wise for your years, don't you?"

A serious expression crossed Will Earl's handsome face. "Sometimes, Ken, life slaps you a hard one and you either revert or grow up overnight. Reckon I figured I would die on the vine in my twenties if I didn't pull myself up by the boot straps." Ken nodded, not wanting to press him any because he knew it was too much for Will Earl to get into.

They talked about ranching and Ken's days as a reporter until Muriel said, "Okay, fellas, let's go see about that cake waiting for us. I don't think Angie and Ty ate it all but you never know," she teased Will Earl and tucked her arm through his. Ken saw Muriel to her car and then walked over to the Jeep. As he did, he saw Will Earl climb into a late model red and white pickup. As he pulled past Ken, he gave the horn a toot. Muriel pulled out behind him and Ken followed behind her. They drove out of Rosewood less than two miles where both Muriel and Will Earl pulled into a long driveway by a tidy-looking home. Ken could see it clearly since the porch light was on at the entrance. A brighter light came on as Muriel went around Will Earl to the top of the driveway.

Ken parked the Jeep in front of the house and then walked to the driveway entrance. Will Earl motioned and called out to him, "Come on, Ken. Aunt Muriel just put her car in the garage and we can come in the house through this side door." Muriel joined them by the time Ken reached Will Earl and they made their way through a laundry center into a bright cheerful kitchen.

Angie and Tyler appeared from what Ken supposed was the living room, with Angie smiling at them in welcome. Tyler greeted them with, "Hi, you all. We been waiting on you and we are ready for that cake, Auntie." He had such boyish charm that Ken had to chuckle at his eagerness.

"Hello, Mr. Ferries. It's good to see you again," Angie smiled a bright greeting.

"Angie, it's good to see you. And please, call me Ken."

Ken watched Will Earl as he played a teasing smile on Angie and he noticed Angie's face turn a soft pink as she looked at him.

"Angie, I've missed you, pretty woman. Come here," and he held out his arms to her. She walked to him and he hugged her and lightly kissed her as Muriel watched the two of them with a misty look on her face.

"Okay, enough mush, you two. Let's have at that cake," Tyler said, reaching over and untying Angie's crisp white apron bow as she turned around and swiped at a ducking Tyler.

"Come, sit down, all of you. Angie will help me cut the cake and serve it. Good, Angie honey, I see you made the coffee." Muriel reached over to embrace her daughter.

"Aunt Muriel, if you have some milk, I would rather have that than coffee," Tyler said as he reached out and put his hard worked hand on her arm.

"I am way ahead of you, Tyler, you sweet boy. I know you so well," and she patted his husky shoulder as she retrieved a large glass tumbler from the cupboard.

Ken felt such warmth spread through him as he looked at these good people, glancing from one face to another. Again, he thought of how much he missed the few times when his family could get together.

"What are you thinking so deeply about, Ken," Will Earl prompted.

"Just that you are all so warm and friendly and it does my heart good. I don't see my family as much as I would like to, not since my kids moved so far away.

"Do they live in other states?" Tyler asked, as Muriel sat a large glass of milk down in front of him.

"No, my daughter Holly and her husband Bart live down in San Antonio and my son is in Houston. They, of course, have busy lives, what with both Holly and Bart in medical professions and my son taking Police Science to become a police officer. Carter is about your age, Will Earl. I had the pleasure of meeting your sister today at the Arts and Crafts Store and my Holly is about the same age as Phyllis."

"Well, now, by gosh, you have almost met the whole clan except for our Dad and those two little baby doll nieces of ours and their Daddy Chance," Will Earl smiled broadly at Ken.

"Speaking of your Dad, how is he doing? I haven't seen him for weeks," . Muriel said to Will Earl.

"He isn't doing well, Aunt Muriel. I am concerned—well, all of us are—but what to do about it is the question," and there was such a sad note in his eyes and a heaviness in his tone.

Muriel shook her head sadly and reached across the table, taking Will Earl's broad hand in hers and squeezing it. She looked at Tyler who kept his face downcast. She reached for his hand and he took hers first. Ken saw the unshed tears in the boy's eyes as he looked at Muriel.

"I love you all so much," she said in a near whisper, "and you know that I will always be around for you." He saw Angie put down the fork she'd been holding and encircle Will Earl's waist.

Ken cleared his throat to relieve the tightening in it and Muriel said with a forced brightness, "Okay, who is ready for more cake and how about some more milk, Ty." She got up quickly and went to get the coffee to refill Ken's cup and he saw her dab swiftly at her eyes.

"Aunt Muriel, I still have some milk but I sure would take another piece of that fine cake," Ty said as he collected himself into a lighter vein. Everyone else said they didn't want any more dessert but took refills on coffee. The mood began to smooth out into one of long-time friends and family again. Ken could feel himself relax and join in the spirit of their camaraderie.

They chatted aimlessly for another half hour and then Ty stood up with his dessert plate, glass, and fork to take them to the sink. "I better head on home and get to bed. Gotta get up early to be over to Bruster's."

"That's a switch, little bro. You going to bed early on a Saturday night," Will Earl grinned at his brother.

"Well, Bruster collared me today when I dropped in at Dolly's for lunch and asked me to start breaking in a stud for him. I'm joining him and the missus for breakfast too."

"Hey, bro, stay loose, okay?" and Will Earl stood up and took him by one arm and shook his other hand.

"I'll do just that. And Ang girl, it was good seeing you. It's been awhile," and he bent down to hug her, then did the same to Muriel. He reached out his hand to Ken and said, "Sir, it has been a pleasure to see you again and I hope to see you again soon."

"Ty, you can count on it," Ken assured him.

After Tyler left, Muriel said how concerned she had been when he was gone because no one heard from him. They worried because he was still not more than a youngster.

Will Earl spoke up, saying, "He's a good kid, Aunt Muriel, and I figured him just to be off somewhere trying to handle things the best way he could. I knew he would come home one day before too long." He paused and then went on, "Reckon I wasn't there for him and Dad hasn't been either. But I am going to be from now on," he said with a determined note.

"I know you will, Will Earl, but you've had your own wounds to handle, honey. You kids need each other. Just hang on to your Dad because, even if he isn't present right now, he is going to need all the love and understanding you can give him." She smiled softly at Will Earl as he reached out to clasp her hand and kiss it, then place it to his cheek.

"I know, and I love you. Well, just thank you, good lady, for being here for all of us," and his voice was thick with emotion. "Now," he said as he looked at his watch, "can I steal away with your daughter awhile and take her out for a late movie?"

"That is up to Angie. She's a big girl now," Muriel smiled at her daughter.

"Then, come on Ang, we can make that late movie if we hustle over to Longview," and he stopped short, "that is, if you will be honoring this old cowboy with your lovely company?"

"I think that, since I haven't got a better offer, Will Earl, you may escort me to the movies," and she winked at her mother.

"That ought to remove any smug over-fried notions I might have had about how indispensable this cowpoke is," and he placed his hand on his chest and grinned in that teasing way he had.

Angie stood up and hooked her arm through Will Earl's. "Lead the way, cowboy. And listen, Mom, that was a good dessert but then I've never had a poor one you've made," and she came over to kiss her mother. "Ken, I have enjoyed visiting with you so much and it is great that we will be seeing you often."

"The feeling is certainly mutual, Angie. You and Will Earl enjoy the movie now."

The young couple departed and Muriel started to clear the table. Ken got up to assist her. She started to protest but he held his hand up, "I have always done this and it is not any more than showing a lady how you appreciate her. By the way, that cake was to die for."

After they had finished the kitchen chores, Muriel said, "All right, Ken, let's go have that talk. We'll get comfortable in the living room."

"You have a nice home, Muriel. It is like you, warm and vibrant," Ken said as he appraised the setting of the living room with its cottage style brushed cotton drapes in soft plaid colors. Various bric-a-brac complimented the comfortable furniture and Ken noticed that it was a place a man of his size could find cozy.

She sat down on the sofa and said, "Ken, sit where you are comfy."

He chose an ivory high-backed swivel rocker that was of leather so he could be directly facing Muriel. "Muriel, before we get too heavy into all of the events I want to talk to you about, would you like to run over to Longview with me in the morning and have breakfast? I want to return the Jeep and get my car."

"Sounds like a great plan to me, Ken," she said brightly.

"All right, then, what about eight-thirty or whatever time would work best for you, Muriel."

"Eight-thirty is fine with me. I am open to whatever time works well for you," she assured him.

"Good then, it is settled. Now, first off, I was going to tell you about the strange visit I had after I left Bailey's and went to that motel you told me about."

"Oh, yes, I remember. Dolly's was packed that morning and I got so busy you said you would tell me when you returned from Waco."

"Well, Muriel, I went in to register after you pulled away and, when I came out of the motel office, I got in my car to turn on the ignition and I just felt like I wasn't alone. I had a weird chill course through me, the darndest feeling like nothing I've ever had, except the time in Dolly's when the elderly Indian appeared so suddenly. So, I hear this strange voice in the back seat of the car and whirl around to see old Nathan Tom's piercing black eyes. Muriel, how he got into my car, I will never know because I am a creature of habit and always lock my car doors when I get out."

As he progressed, Muriel's eyes grew wider and wider but she still said nothing, allowing Ken to continue.

"He said to me, 'I have come with a message.' And he said that he could tell me the reason I had come here. He said I was the Redeemer who had been foretold and I would see dreams and a rainbow would guide me to the trail's end. Then, in closing, he said as he raised his hand, 'Ho, go in peace, big man, and find the trail of the rainbow', then he got out of the car so quickly I wondered if I had really seen him."

He went on, "Of course, you can imagine my nerves were more than a little choppy after all of that." And Ken couldn't help but chuckle, "but it still gets weirder yet. Because after I lapsed into sleep, I saw in a dream that Gloria and I were dancing just like we did when we first met in college. Muriel, we were dancing and it was so real. Then when I looked down at Gloria, it wasn't her any more but Nadine Rogers! She spoke to me as she smiled and said, 'I am the trail of the rainbow. Follow me.'"

"My God, Ken, that would be enough to keep you awake the rest of the night!" Muriel said as she looked at Ken in dismay.

"I did have a time getting back to sleep but I lay the dream off to the earlier events and the gin and tonic from Bailey's. Anyway, that is just a small portion of what's occurred since my return to Rosewood."

"Please do go on, Ken. Oh, first, would you care for some more coffee or perhaps a soda?"

"No, thank you Muriel, but go and get whatever you want."

"No, no," she said, holding up her hand, "I am anxious to have you continue."

He went on and touched briefly on his meeting with Pace Allard and how he smelled the scent of roses when he left Pace's office. Then he told how he had ended up at Nadine's Arts and Crafts and how he had been stunned when Phyllis was sitting there behind the counter because she looked so like her mother.

Muriel nodded and said, "Yes, now you know what I meant about her being a clone of Nadine."

"It was as though I was literally directed to the Gallery where Nadine's paintings are hanging and I just stood there gaping at the one of Nathan Tom with those butterflies on him. And there's that large brilliant rainbow in the back of him where he sits on the hill. Muriel, it is so beautiful and I smelled the fragrance of roses again as I studied that masterpiece of art."

Muriel's eyes held a misty look but she said nothing, allowing Ken to go on. "Phyllis had startled me because I was so caught up looking at the painting that I hadn't seen her walk up by me. She said that was the last painting her mother had ever done. Of course, she couldn't sell it but I bought a nice-sized print of it and it's being framed at the store. I ask Phyllis if if she could smell the fragrance of roses and she said she could. Then she told me she did often but that others did not. She said that a rose perfume was what her mother always wore."

"Oh, Ken," Muriel cried, and tears were running freely down her cheeks.

"Muriel, aw Muriel, I am so sorry," and he pulled himself up from the swivel rocker and went to sit beside her as he pulled out his handkerchief for her. He locked his arms around her and she lay her head down on his shoulder, still weeping softly. Ken let her cry, but soon she raised her head and dabbed at her face, brushing the tears away.

"Muriel, perhaps I should tell you no more," he said consolingly.

"Oh, no, Ken, please do go on. I think it is so beautiful that you and Phyl could experience this. I just feel Nadine's presence is around and I know even more that it is after you've told me this."

"You know, Muriel, when Gloria died, I saw her at the service. She was in the church standing with her father who had died some while before. I told Gloria's mother but never anyone else until now."

"Ken, you have given me such a large measure of comfort," then she reached up and pulled his face down to hers and kissed him. He was surprised at his eager response and found he was kissing her back while he felt the fire catch between them. They both pulled back suddenly and stared deeply into each other's eyes.

"Now, I guess I'm pretty impulsive, Ken. I'm sorry."

"I believe it was spontaneous for us both, Muriel. And, by the way, lady, I haven't felt like that in a long time."

Her face was flushed and she stood up. "Neither have I, Ken."

"It's okay, Muriel, if we coast for awhile," and he smiled up at her, then checked his watch. "Listen, it's ten o'clock and I am going to share the rest of these staggering events with you on our way to Longview in the morning, okay?"

"You may do that," she said, her voice even huskier now. He reached for her slender hand and stood to face her. He drew her into his arms and kissed her hungrily, while she responded the same way.

"Lady, I have got to leave now or else we'll be farther along than we'd planned and I don't want us to move too fast. We need to know each other awhile."

She placed a slender finger to his lips to hush him and whispered, "It's all right, Ken, we don't have to hurry." She stepped to the living room entrance door that led out onto the porch. "I'll see you in the morning."

He stepped out into the night and went to the Jeep. He felt lighter than he had in some years. "My God, Ken Ferries, you are really taken with this lady," he said out loud as he spun the Jeep around to head back to Rosewood. The night sky was ablaze with stars and he felt a lingering passion. It was hard not to turn the Jeep around and go back to Muriel. As he was passing Bailey's Lounge, he saw a man get into an older Jeep. A thought flickered through his mind that it looked like the man he had seen at Bailey's the last time when he had been waiting for Muriel to join him.

He drove to the motel and decided to shower before scribbling off a few notes. But first he checked to see if there were any messages for him. Sarita had called to assure him all was well and, of course, he knew it was more that she was concerned about him. He chuckled and decided it was best to call her and let her know he was all right. He would let her know he would be home either Monday evening or sometime Tuesday. She would be watching the news or just getting ready to retire, he noted as he checked the time.

"Sarita, Ken here. Say, I just received your message and, if I don't see you Monday evening, I will on Tuesday. And, by the way, everything is going fine here." He shared with her that he had met the Rogers' children and was very taken with all three of them. He neglected to pass on information about Muriel because he felt that was just too intimate a subject yet, one he wanted to savor before he discussed these new-found feelings with family. He considered Sarita very much family.

He took a shower and sat down at the desk to make some notes to transpose to his computer later at home. He thought, at one point, that he heard an unusual noise and sat alert for a moment. Then he went back to his notes after deciding it was probably the tabby cat he had noticed earlier prowling about the motel office.

He checked his watch and decided that it was time to retire, as it was eleven-thirty. He felt good as he settled into bed and once more he thought of Muriel. She was a woman to think about and she had stirred him from the first time they met. He was certain that he was falling in love with this radiant impressive lady but the time was still too brief and he said aloud, "Don't cannonball this, Ken old boy. Easy does it."

He turned on his side, fluffing his pillow, and saw the silhouette of a man standing outside his window. The soft lights from outside cast his shadowed form on the closed loose-textured drapes, allowing Ken to clearly make out a male form with a Western hat on. The figure was standing squarely facing the window and then started to walk on. Ken heard the sound of a doorknob being turned. He waited a moment, then eased out of bed to pull back the drapes slightly. He could just see the shoulder of someone as they walked away from his door. He did not hear any further noise but he lay awake and suddenly, chillingly, remembered the man who had climbed into the Jeep he had passed at Bailey's Lounge earlier. It was the same man he had seen that night in the lounge and the Jeep was the same dull green! It was also the same older Jeep he had seen in his vision at Nathan Tom's!! The man in that vision, though he had not seen his face then, had to be the same man who ran to the Jeep. And was the same one he had seen at Bailey's the night he'd met Muriel there.

"He walks in the shadows, this guy," Ken thought, "and he does not want to be seen that much. I wonder why?"

He delved deeper in thought. It was strange that, after seeing him again, he'd had a prowler at his motel room. Who else could it have been and what is he up to? "Seems to me the guy is trying to scare me off," he decided quietly. "Well, I'm not that easily scared and this just provokes my curiosity more, if indeed you are trying to run me off, mister," and he drifted off to sleep.

His alarm jarred him from a sound sleep and he prepared to go pick up Muriel. He felt rested and was looking forward to seeing her again, actually very eager to see her. He arrived a little before eight-thirty and noticed in the daylight how cheerful her home was. Anyone would be drawn to it. "How this all suits Muriel," he thought as he noticed the row of shade trees running along the fence line next to the driveway. Some horses were on the other side of the fence, calmly munching away at the grasses in the pasture.

Muriel opened the door to the side entrance and called out, "Good morning, Ken."

He noticed the sweet peas that climbed up a stringed lattice by the side door. "Muriel, that is so pretty and the fragrance is heavenly," he said, pausing at the door.

"I see you like flowers too," she nodded and smiled warmly at him. The heady fragrance of the sweet peas just added to his high spirits. "I've always loved flowers, Ken, and I'm glad you do too. Come on in and say hi to Angie and I'll go grab my purse."

Ken followed her into the kitchen where Angie sat clad in blue jeans and a Western style cotton blouse. She wore riding boots too, all to the advantage of her good looks.

"Well, young lady, you look like you are going for a ride," Ken greeted her with a broad smile.

"Oh, hello, Ken. I don't get to ride while I'm away at school so I take advantage of it the few times I'm home. We have three horses— you may have noticed the barn out back of the garage?" She paused— "Do you like to ride, Ken?" Angie asked politely as she regarded him openly. So much like her mother, Ken thought.

"Sure do, Angie, but it has been quite awhile, I'm afraid. But when I was growing up as a ranch kid, I was on a horse all the time."

"Well, then, you can relate," and she smiled with a deepened appreciation, "because I grew up on horses too."

"Funny, isn't it Angie, how you really get a sense of freedom from riding," Ken answered.

Angie smiled brightly and shook her head in agreement. Ken knew that she was happy to relate to someone who shared her enthusiasm for horses and riding.

"Listen, Angie, do you want to go have breakfast with your mother and me? I do feel like I am interfering with your time together."

Angie smiled at Ken and said, "No, but I do thank you. And, trust me, you are not interfering at all. I am glad that Mom is getting out for a fun day. You know, she works and then keeps this place up too. So, you two, go and enjoy, please."

"Angie, you are a good daughter and a thoughtful, caring young lady," Ken said resolutely.

"Why, thank you, Ken. Now, tell you what would be a great thing that we three could do sometime when I am home again and you are back here— that would be go riding. Would you like that?"

"Say now, you can count on that, Angie. It sounds like a great plan to me."

"Then it is settled," she grinned as her mother came in.

"What's settled?" Muriel questioned, looking from one to the other.

"Muriel, Angie and I have a plan. The three of us will all go riding next time she is home. Angie, here's my card. You let me know when you will be home again, all right?"

"Well, you two are quick," Muriel laughed in that husky deep way she had.

"Heck, why mess around, Mom? Haven't you always told me that one may delay but time will not?"

Ken chuckled and Muriel grinned, shaking her head as her lovely spirited girl stood up and hugged her mother. They were so affectionate towards each other. Ken felt a deepened glow of warmth for this mother and daughter as he stood back and watched the two of them.

"Now, scoot, you two, and have a great day," Angie said as she took her mother by the arm and led her over to Ken.

"Angie, you have a great one too," Ken told her.

"Honey, we will see you later. Oh, are you going to the dance tonight?" Muriel asked as she paused at the door.

"Yes, Will Earl asked me to go so guess I will see you two there, huh?"

"Yes, and Ken and I will go out for supper first though," she said to her daughter. "Honey, do be careful while you are off by yourself on the horse."

"Oh, count on it, Mom," she said and wrinkled her pert little nose at her mother.

"So, we are off," Ken smiled at Angie and tucked Muriel's arm under his as they told Angie goodbye and she waved them on. When they climbed into the Jeep,

Muriel laughingly told Ken that she had not felt so young and carefree in a long time. Climbing aboard a bright red Jeep expressed it for her.

"Know what you mean," Ken gave a short chuckle, remembering how it had affected him the day before when he had driven it out to Nathan's. Muriel looked so relaxed and happy sitting there beside him and he felt in total union with her.

"So, where do you suggest we have breakfast, Muriel, since I know so little of Longview?"

"Well, Cedar Ridge is excellent and the prices are do-able. It has a nice mellow appeal too."

"That sounds perfect since I want to relax with you over a good breakfast and be able to discuss the events of yesterday as well as talk about us too." He reached for her hand and squeezed it lightly. He noticed that Muriel had brushed her hair down into a soft cascade to her shoulders and that the sunlight created a luster that gave off reddish highlights. Muriel's features had such a special kind of grace and beauty, a soft maturity that only added to her overall attractiveness. She had a sensuous mouth and Ken knew after kissing her that she was a responsive woman who would be ardent with love-making. He knew that she would never go there with a man unless she trusted him and loved him. He had known that from the tenor of her character, her theme and essence picked up from their first meeting. He reasoned that she was as lonely as he was for the company of a good relationship but, like him, she had been hesitant. He could understand it too, after being widowed with a young child to raise.

"Okay, lady. We are here at this car rental and I will return the Jeep. So, come on in with me and I will settle up on the rental fee and then we are off to breakfast." She slipped out of the Jeep easily before he had gone to open the door for her.

"Whoops, I forgot, Ken. It has been too long, I guess, since I have played the role of lady," and her husky laughter followed. Ken took her by the arm and pulled her close to him. He openly flirted with her, "You are a lady, believe me." And he locked deeply into those cool green eyes with their teasing note. She turned to the red Jeep in a moment of play and patted it, saying, "Thank you for all the exhilaration, little red Jeep. There for awhile, I was Angie's age again." She turned back to Ken and winked.

Ken chuckled and they walked arm in arm into the auto dealership. The exchange of business was quickly concluded and they left in Ken's car, with Muriel pointing out directions to the Cedar Ridge Restaurant. They walked in to a pleasantly attractive establishment and Ken could readily see why Muriel had said it held mellow appeal. A white-haired lady with merry blue eyes escorted them to a table by a window with a large expansive view. Flowers of every hue graced the garden next door.

"That is a gardener's dream, Muriel," Ken said as he looked out at the wide variety of flowers. "And I might add, you are a sweet lady of unparalleled refinement and judgment," Ken said as he held Muriel's chair for her.

"I am so pleased that you approve," and she sat down. She took the rosebud vase on the table and moved the single red rose to the side. The white-haired lady in her frilly pink and white uniform returned with the water pitcher and filled their glasses, asking if they wanted coffee.

"Oh, yes, we both do," Muriel said and smiled cheerfully at this very handsome woman. The lady left and shortly returned with a carafe filled with coffee. After setting it on the table, she lit the candle in the warmer beneath it.

"I will give you some time to decide on your order," she said with a hospitable smile, and retreated.

"Muriel, what is your favorite breakfast here?" Ken asked as he scanned the menu.

"Well, frankly, everything is to die for, but my personal favorite is the Eggs Benedict."

"Then Eggs Benedict it is for me," Ken said, "and especially since I trust your good judgment.' He smiled at her.

"So that is all settled," Muriel said and placed her hand on her neck for a moment. Ken wondered if it was an unconscious habit she had when she let her hair hang free to her shoulders. He was anxious to learn so many things about her. The waitress returned and took their orders while Ken fully appraised the restaurant and all of the tasteful ornamental garnishments. He knew that the food would be the same, one of embellishment, and, of course, most certainly every bit as tasty as Muriel said it was to be.

"Ken, what month were you born?" Muriel asked him.

"Why, in May. Why do you ask?" and he searched her face with quizzical eyes.

"Well, I study a little astrology and you sure do fit the pattern of those born under the sign of Taurus, though I don't know what date your birthday falls on in May." She waited expectantly for his answer.

"It is the tenth of May. Now I am eagerly awaiting your reading of me. Do I measure up?" he said in jest.

"Well, sir, if you haven't figured out by now how you measure up with me, then you must have missed the boat somehow," and she muffled a short giggle with her hand to her mouth. "You are one deeply appreciative of the arts and fine surroundings," and she waved her hand as she looked about the restaurant to express one of her examples.

"I suppose I've treated astrology as," and he paused, "perhaps a bit of a lark, like something people do to amuse themselves. I really haven't thought about it one way or the other."

"The waters run deep, Ken, and though I am mostly a novice, I have uncovered aspects that were right on regarding people I have charted for. They were surprised to find out it fit to a capital T."

"Well, sweet lady, you have now piqued my interest. Do please go on."

"OK. You do not give up once you begin something," and he grinned and nodded. "You have the ability for psychodynamics and are meticulous in the scrutiny of details, as well as of people." She grinned and then winked at him. "How am I doing so far?" He nodded again. "Your family and roots are an indigenous part of you, and as natural as flora and fauna in your overall bearing. Should I go on?" she said with those cool green mischievous eyes searching him.

Ken nodded and she continued, "You are what some might say stubborn but I would be more inclined to say determined." At that he chuckled and then related how often he had been called a maverick in the newspaper days. At age sixty, he thought that perhaps he had mellowed some and developed more caution. She grinned at him and reached for his hand, "But don't you see, Ken, that you still have bulldog tenacity which has just tendered and smoothed with the years? You have embraced changes most assuredly, dear man, but I do not think that it has escaped scaring the hell out of you at times." He looked at her and realized that this bright, rather bold lady had him pegged to a gnat's eyebrow.

"I can assuredly relate to all of it, Muriel, and let me tell you what I do see about you, in return. My turn now," he smiled engagingly at her. "I would say effervescence would largely characterize you and a knowledge far exceeding the average that sometimes surprises those who haven't bothered to look past the surface. Plus, pretty woman, you are very tantalizing and you aren't aware of it." Muriel blushed at the last observation Ken shared. That amused him and he thought it only proved his point.

The lady who had seated them returned now with their breakfast.

"Say now, this is as ravishing as I expected," Ken said as he looked at the tastefully done breakfast.

The waitress smiled and asked if there was anything else she could bring. They both declined and she left them to dine alone.

"So, now dear lady, since I have unwittingly revealed so much about myself, it is only fair that you tell me what month and day your birthday falls on."

"I am a Capricorn and January 15th is my birthday. From what I have observed from the reading I've done for myself, it seems that Taurus and Capricorn do seem to hit it off." She smiled off-handedly and raised her eyebrows the way she often did when she was trying to suppress amusement.

"Well, it seems that we've tested that pretty tried and true, wouldn't you agree?" She smiled in a sensuous way while biting down softly on her lower lip. It was clearly a non-verbal communication and Ken needed no further assurance.

"All right now, Ken, please tell me about all of your experiences since you came back from Waco. What happened when you went to Nathan Tom's ranch?"

"I must tell you Muriel, that I have had some strange things happen in my life but I've always come up with some kind of answer. However, the incidences that have gone on ever since I first began this research on the Rogers case are like nothing I've ever experienced and, believe me, are sometimes darn near chilling! I rented that Jeep because I knew the trip out to Nathan's would be on bad roads. Phyllis had cautioned me on what to expect and it was just as she said. At the risk of your thinking I have gone round the bend, I must tell you that, when I came to the Rogers mailbox and read the name, a force I cannot describe reduced me to such an onslaught of grief that I literally wept like a child. I had to wait until it lifted before I could proceed on down the road to Nathan's."

Chapter_____5

Muriel said nothing but reached out and patted Ken's hand. Her face held such affection for him.

"Well, as I went on my way to Nathan's, I ran across his great granddaughter— but first let me back-track to the way I reacted when I read the name on the Rogers mailbox. It was a grief like I experienced when Gloria passed away and the only time that I had ever had that kind of extreme grief. It was as though I had picked up on that family's grief. Do you understand, Muriel?" She nodded earnestly.

Ken went on. "I know that, in my way, I have grieved for Nadine and have been incensed over that vital woman's death. But it was like she spoke to me and let me understand how tragic her family felt."

Muriel spoke softly now. "Ken, she undoubtedly was," and her eyes held brightness in them which Ken knew to be unshed tears.

"So," he pressed on in a lighter vein, "I got into some off and on rain showers which didn't last long and then the sun would peek out. I saw this red-tailed hawk sitting on a fence, and Muriel, he was unusually large for a red tail and he sat facing me, which was odd too. Not sitting in a regular position but standing kind of side-saddle face on, if you will. That would be awkward for a bird of his size and I have never encountered such behavior in that kind of big bird. You could see it in a small bird and never notice but it would be easier for a big bird to balance gripping his talons into the fence. Of course, that was but a mild aspect of my journey that day," and he could not resist a nervous chuckle.

"As I picked my way along as carefully as I could, I came to some hills and saw a young Indian girl that I supposed was Nathan's great granddaughter who Phyllis had mentioned to me. She was taking a herd of goats to pasture and I stopped the Jeep in the hope that she would talk to me. She was in the company of the biggest dog I've seen, a real beauty of an animal. I asked her if he was part wolf, which she affirmed. She also told me that her grandfather awaited me and that struck me as strange since I hadn't told him I was coming to visit. She would only tell me that he had his ways. She did not give me a chance to question but went back to leading her goats away. I watched her for a moment and then climbed back into the Jeep. When I looked in the rearview mirror, there was no sign of the girl, the dog, or the goats! I stopped and got out to look and, so help me, Muriel, they had literally vanished into thin air!"

Muriel's eyes were wide and then she spoke, "Ken, now if this had come from just anyone, I would question it. But I know a few people in this world who are so trustworthy you can take what they say to the bank. My friend, you are one of them."

"Thanks for the vote of confidence, Muriel, because you don't know how much I need it." Her smile warmed him and he proceeded with his story. "I came to this hill that was practically a small mountain. As I wound upward, it crested and I could see this humble little cabin below with a couple horses in a corral close by. I made my way down to the cabin, parked in front of it and got out. I went to the door and knocked and no one responded. Then I called out and asked if anyone was home. Again, no response so I walked over to admire the horses and pet them.

"When I turned around, I could see someone on what appeared to be the top of a small hill so I took the worn trail that led to that hillside. As I approached, I could see that it was Nathan Tom and he was literally surrounded with butterflies of various sizes, mostly those large monarchs. They were on him as well as around · him. And then a rainbow formed all around him as he sat there cross-legged on that hill. My God, Muriel, it was exactly as the painting Nadine had done. Then the butterflies began to surround and alight on me! Old Nathan's black eyes stayed fixed on me and, Muriel, I believe I was in a trance because I could feel but I couldn't move. I suddenly smelled the scent of roses and it was especially heady in the air. All of it was like a dream and yet I knew it was not a dream, that I was wide awake. Then, Nathan finally spoke and he said, 'Once you pass the thorns of doubt, big man, you step into the world of unexpected visions and there the truth awaits.'"

Muriel seemed to be transfixed as she listened and Ken had a fleeting thought that she had decided he was surely crazy. Naturally, he reasoned, she would be in utter astonishment but she had earlier expressed her trust in him.

"Muriel, this picture like a movie began to form up above Nathan and, at that time, he spoke again in that strange voice. I can't describe it because I've never heard anything like it before. Now, here I am telling you this, and until this moment, I had not remembered what he said to me next because I suppose I was so totally shook to the depths. After these pictures formed, he said, 'A bird of paradise as blatant and stirring as a rainbow will co-mate with him who has arrived The Redeemer.'"

"And then was a resounding echo as loud as thunder ringing in my ears and I clasped my hands over them. I stared in horror at that which played out before me on that screen, for lack of a better description. I saw three men bending over a figure so broken and there was bright red blood all over. It was on the walls and the ceiling as well as on and around the figure on the floor. But none on the three men who appeared to be just frozen in horror as they looked."

"Ken, don't you see what has happened to you?" Muriel suddenly exclaimed, her voice shaking.

"Why no, I don't know. Well, I don't know for certain," he said and reached for his glass of water. His hand was shaking.

"Ken Ferries, you have what," and she paused as she searched for the words, "what I believe is called retro something. I know, it is retro-cognition and it means knowing the past."

"Well, Muriel, there is more I have to tell you. I am not easily shaken but this had really taken all the composure that I could muster."

"I can certainly see why, Ken," and once more she reached for his hand and clasped it in both of her own.

He went on. "The picture changed and I saw the three men jump into a truck and drive away fast. As quick as a flash, another picture started, one of a young woman in an advanced state of pregnancy and carrying a small child in her arms. The young child was screaming at the top of her lungs and they nearly fell as this big man caught them. The man lifted this woman and child together and carried them to his pickup. He put them in it and ran to the driver's side and got in. He was driving with one hand and talking to the young woman trying to calm her and the child. But I could see that he was greatly shocked too. The young woman was clearly Phyllis," Ken said. He saw the horror on Muriel's face as she put her fist to her mouth in an effort to keep from screaming.

"Hell," Ken muttered, "why didn't I pick another time and place to tell you this, if at all." And he clenched his jaws tightly.

"Ken, you hear me," Muriel's voice was ragged with heavy emotion. "I thank God that you told me, and yes that was Phyl. It had to be because what you saw was what happened. The big man was Ham Wilson, his given name is Hamilton. He and his wife Rosie are the Rogers' neighbors."

"Yes, I remember that he was one of the witnesses in the trial," Ken said as he felt himself begin to calm some. Muriel had also gained some control. "I met Rosie Wilson at the Arts and Crafts Shop and found her to be a delightful person," Ken related.

"They are two of the best people in this world and thank God that Ham happened there when he did or I don't know what would have happened to Phyl and little Bree", and she shuddered.

"Since I have gone this far, Muriel, I will tell you the rest but it isn't so, well— awful, as what I've related already."

"Ken, I know this has been hard for you to tell me because it would take a great deal of courage to tell what you have. And then, aside from that, to tell someone whom you know was close as a sister to Nadine. I want you to know that I am deeply honored that you care enough for me and trust me as you do to have related all of these episodes," and she smiled in such a profound way that he knew she meant every word. He reached for the carafe and poured more coffee for them, then began anew to share the rest of these strange events.

"In one of the pictures, I saw a man run across a pasture to an older dull green Jeep hidden partially out of view in a grove of trees. Now, Muriel, after I left your home last night, I passed by Bailey's Lounge and saw a man come out of the lounge and get into an older Jeep. Never thought much about it but he did look like the man that was in the lounge the night I was waiting for you. I got to my room at the motel and decided to shower. Then I noticed that Sarita had left a message so I called her. After the shower, I wrote a few notes and then turned in. I had heard a noise while I was writing notes but decided it was the motel cat out on the prowl. But when I shut off the light and settled into bed, I rolled over and saw the form of a man with a Western hat on outlined on the drapes. I eased out of bed to look and then I heard the door knob being tried. I was peeking out one end of the drapes but by then all I could see was the guy's shoulder as he walked away. I got back into bed, and as I lay there, it hit me like a clap of thunder that it was the same man I saw getting into the older Jeep at Bailey's <u>and</u> the same one in the vision!"

Muriel's eyes grew large now with fright. "Oh, Ken, that scares me because I am afraid for you. It could very well mean that this man killed Nadine and those three other men happened on it only moments afterwards. The man may have found out you are researching this crime and is afraid that you will come up with something."

"Muriel, I have thought of that and I feel that this guy is probably trying to scare me. But I don't scare easily. However, as Sarita would say, I do need to watch my backside." His laugh was tense.

"Ken, I am the only one that you have mentioned the research to and Jeff Colter and my parents. That's all, isn't it?"

"No, I have talked to that attorney Pace Allard and I haven't really tried to be secretive except that I didn't want to mention it to the Rogers family as it is far too painful to discuss with them. It's hard enough on you, Muriel."

"Yes, it is but, if there are things that haven't been brought out, I want to know. And besides, if the three men are in prison for a crime they didn't commit, it needs to be brought to light."

Their cheery waitress came over to the table and asked if she could get anything else for them. They thanked her and told her no so she put their bill on the table. Ken reached into his wallet and put his card down on the check after signing it. He handed it all to the waitress.

"Very good, sir. Was everything all right?" she asked. Ken noticed that her nametag read Violet.

"Everything was perfect, Violet," Ken assured her. Muriel nodded in agreement.

"Well, now, you both have a lovely day," Violet said, smiling with that gracious way she had. Ken thought how her name suited her. They assured her they would and bid her the same. She left and returned with Ken's card.

Ken then suggested to Muriel that they go sightseeing around Longview, if she would like to, because he had never been there.

"That is a great idea, Ken. I know some neat places here to show you that I just bet you will enjoy."

"Well, you know, all work and no play has made old Ken here a dull boy for too long. All of the things I've shared last night and this morning deserve some balance. The two of us deserve some plain old fun now."

"Your experiences really aren't off balance, just not the established patterns of life." She stood up as Ken stepped around the table to take her arm. She continued, "Most of us don't have that kind of psychic connection because we don't connect with Universal Consciousness so easily."

"And are you saying that I do, Muriel?"

"It certainly seems so, from all that you have said and encountered," she said as they made their way out the door of the restaurant.

"I never thought that of myself, although I have always seemed to pick up on events rather quickly. I have never encountered such tumultuous events as the ones I've had since I began researching this case."

"Have you thought that you probably had this ability all along but shut it down because so many people are jaded about such abilities?"

They reached Ken's car and he opened the door for Muriel. He looked down at her, an earnest searching look, then scratched his chin thoughtfully. "I think at times I did wonder, Muriel. I remember that my parents would wonder how I would know that someone was coming for a visit when they didn't know. There were other things over the years too but I didn't consider them unusual. Perhaps it was because it was always the way I was and therefore I didn't perceive it as different."

"Well, you probably didn't until something with such magnitude as this hits you, then you can hardly think of it as commonplace."

"I guess so because, let me tell you, I have always felt that I operated from a totally old-fashioned perspective and yet I have always been drawn to the esoteric. I felt that it stemmed from this forever inquisitive mind, the natural reporter's mind."

"Yet, some well-known authors today were also reporters and many of them had extremely profound esoteric experiences and their lives changed dramatically. I'm sure you have heard of Ruth Montgomery and Jess Stern."

"Yes, as a matter of fact, I have," he said and shook his head as he smiled at Muriel. Suddenly he felt a great uplifting sense of joy that she had shared this information with him. Impulsively he bent down and kissed her, then drew back slightly as he looked into those sea green eyes. "Pretty lady, thank you. I think I am in love with you and it is just like that."

"Ken Ferries," she said in that husky voice, "I think I am in love with you and it is just like that." She snapped her fingers for emphasis, stood on tiptoes and pulled his mouth down to hers. She kissed him with a lingering passion until a car horn blew. They looked around to see a red convertible with three young people giving them the V sign. They laughed and waved at the teenagers. Ken gave them a snappy salute as he walked around the car to get in.

"Okay, lady, where to? I am open to anything that you decide."

"We can go check out a museum or are you interested in that sort of thing?" Muriel volunteered.

"I am interested in anything that you are, so point the way."

They went to a museum and spent an hour. Then they found out there was a flower show and decided that was a mutual interest. They spent time enjoying all of the various horticulture displays of wonder. They found a booth at the flower show that sold cappuccinos and strolled through the gardens to a bench beneath a weeping willow tree. They sat down there to watch the waterfowl in a nearby pond. A white peacock approached them and Ken openly admired him.

"I don't recall seeing a pure white peafowl before," he said in awe of the lovely bird.

"I can't say that I have myself but he is a beauty. He seems to have singled us out." She chuckled and said, "Mr. Peacock, you are indeed a humdinger."

The feathered creature cocked his head as though he understood and puffed his feathers out in yet grander fashion. He strutted proudly by, it seemed on their behalf.

"I think he knows something about the two of us. He is expressing a kind of insight that we will enjoy the wondrous beauty he possesses in his carriage and adornment in our life together."

"Ken, you are a romantic, I see, and I think that is something special in a man. It is probably why I have stayed single for so long because I haven't experienced this for a long time," and her eyes held unshed tears.

"You know that I want to kiss you, Muriel, and I don't give two hoots in hell who is watching," and he pulled her into his arms and kissed her. He felt her firm breasts heave against him. They pulled apart and noticed two very elderly ladies adorned in flowered wide hats watching them a few feet away. Both were seeing two lovers and it set memories in motion for them. Ken looked at them, smiled and waved. Muriel followed suit as the two women waved back. Then they turned to cast some food down for the waterfowl swimming in the pond.

"Are you hungry, Muriel?" Ken said as he checked his watch.

"Not starved because that big breakfast is still hanging on. However, something light would be fine with me."

"Tell you what, why don't we go have some ice cream, my pretty lady?"

"That sounds great and I know just the place where I used to take Angie for a treat. They have every kind of ice cream there is and more besides."

They made their way to Ken's car and headed for "Harley's Delights— The Best Ice Cream", which Muriel attested it really was.

"You know, I feel like I'm eighteen again and I'm having a ball. How about you, Ken?" Muriel's face was radiant.

"Ditto," Ken laughed as he encircled Muriel's waist and they walked into the ice cream parlor. "Okay, what's your favorite, my lady?" Ken said as they looked at the assorted ice creams in the glass-enclosed counter.

"The peach cream with pecans has been one of my occasional sins and a favorite of mine."

"I will try that too, so make it two of the peach cream with pecans," Ken told the young man. He looked to be about sixteen and the hair visible beneath his little cap was so red Ken thought it would bleed if it was cut. He had a smile as big as the state of Texas and hardly a patch of skin that showed was missing a freckle.

"Coming right up," the boy said as he dug deeply into a carton of ice cream. "Now will that be a dish or cone?"

"How about two sugar cones and make them double dips," Ken said and Muriel laughed.

"Ken, I will be as rotund as a ball if you keep treating me this good," she chuckled and poked him in his stomach lightly. They chose a table with pink and white striped cushions on the chairs and giggled over a story Muriel related to him about a half-grown pup she had when she was a child. The pup had found its way into the home-made ice cream bucket her father had momentarily left unattended one Sunday afternoon. The puppy had climbed to the top of the picnic table and, when Muriel followed her father outside, there sat her wirehaired terrier Spankie with ice cream dribbling off his whiskers. Muriel laughed and said that at first she hadn't known if Spankie had so overstepped the rules that he would be sent away. But her dad was a man of moderate temper and, after scolding the dog, he dished him up a bowl, set it on the ground, and sat the dog in front of it.

"I imagine that you and your big family had a lot of good times and plenty of experiences. It is great that you grew up that way, Muriel."

"Well, we never lacked for too much, not the important things anyway. We had a real love for each other and that is partly why I like being here, especially after Bill died. I felt no place could be better for raising Angie."

"Now, on the subject of Angie, I must tell you that you've raised a fine young lady there and I can see why you are so proud of her, Muriel."

"She is the light of my life, Ken. And she has such a good head on those little shoulders. I have never had problems with Angie, not even in those turbulent teen years. She is in love with Will Earl, though she hasn't told me right out yet and maybe not even him. I suspect that she wants to be a bit cautious since she is still in college and he is having to deal with so much. You know the loss of his mother and then his dad..." and she paused as though searching, "well, he is in a complete emotional plummet. Will Earl is having to deal with so much."

"And that just increases my admiration for a very savvy young lady. But then I am getting to know her mother and I suspect that she is a great deal like her," and he smiled engagingly at Muriel as he licked a dribble of ice cream making it's way down his cone.

Muriel regarded him now with a loving tenderness and could see for a fleeting moment the boy that had been masked by the man. He was certainly this mature man sitting there across from her and yet with every man she knew, sometimes that mask slipped and the boy was still there. She found it was especially endearing in Ken now.

"Do you know what I wish?" Muriel asked and smiled slightly as she poised her question.

"What do you wish, pretty lady?" Ken returned the smile.

"I wish it had been a few years back that you had come into my life, Ken, because, as terrific as my relationship to Angie is, she really needed a father figure."

"I know that is important but sometimes life hands us a whole different ball game and, honey, you have done a super job with raising that child alone. Besides, Angie has so much going for her—number one, she has such good common sense. Second, she was blessed with a deeply caring, loving mother. So you have always put that girl first in your life and now, my lovely lady, it is time for you. I know that Angie wants that for you too because you have raised an insightful, caring young woman."

"Yes, you're right, Ken, but it is just that when you are a parent, you always want to be and do all that you can for your child."

"Of course and you are right on because, when you are a good parent in every sense of the word, I think it means that you've truly learned to honor your own Spirit. Because you do that, you honor this child whom a Higher Power entrusted to you. Now, if you will permit me to go on?" Ken said and Muriel nodded. "You do know that, in some cases, parents have given all that they can in love and the young people will still take the wrong road, regardless. I feel we've all been given the choice to choose our own paths. So, now Muriel, on the flip side of that, there are those who have gone through total hell and they keep right in there helping others. In a lot of ways, it is rather like a crap-shoot. All anyone raising children can do is their best with the information they have and hope for the best. At the risk of boring you, I say this, Muriel—it is hard for some people to see that there is cause and effect, or as some say karma, but it is the law and rules out every time."

"You aren't boring me at all, Ken. I do believe that is a good analogy and I happen to agree with you."

He smiled at her and said, "By the way, this peach ice cream is delectable and I am a peach and pecan fan for all time now."

"Good, then we will have to come here now and again, just not too often unless you like portly ladies," and she raised her eyebrows in mock question.

"I would love every pound regardless," Ken said and winked at her.

"Yes, somehow I believe you would," she smirked and wrinkled her nose.

"You know, Muriel, just before Gloria passed away, she said something very profound that I would like to share with you. It shows that she really loved in a way that was so giving right to the last," and he reached for her hand, placing it on his cheek. "She begged me not to immortalize the love we had together but to love again. She didn't want me to be alone." And his voice caught ever so slightly as he worked at his emotions. "Of course, at the time, I was so crushed that I could only agree dumbly because I couldn't imagine life without her. I know now more than ever that life goes on and the human spirit is so capable of ever loving. She knew that better at the time than I did. Just maybe, in some way, she led me to you."

Muriel's eyes held unshed tears and her throat tightened but finally she spoke. "Oh, Ken we were both so very blessed with true loves and now we are again. It is so—well, beautiful, and thank you for sharing that with me."

"Thought you would want to know that somehow, because I feel in some ways you are rather like Gloria. You have that same depth of character. I realize it now the more I am around you, pretty lady. Yet you are different too, with a quality I am so drawn to. I hope you have not minded my comparing you to Gloria," and his voice trailed off.

"I am honored, Ken, because she sounds like an aces kind of person. I think she was extremely wise and understood what loving someone truly was."

"Well, sometimes we had our spats but we had this inside track that always let the other one keep their dignity. I think we valued each other's individual aspects and never failed to honor that."

"Bill and I never had as many years together as you and Gloria did but I believe ours was the same kind of marriage. Until now, I just never found that in someone else, not enough anyway, so I didn't get involved in a heavy relationship." She went on as she wiped a water spot with her napkin. "You see, I dated and had fun but always kept it light. If they wanted more, I pulled back."

"I guess we were both waiting to find each other, huh?" Ken smiled at her, keeping his eyes fully fixed into those sea green pools. He could see the passion for him there and he felt the same stirrings. He reasoned that he must not press but he wanted this woman. It was more than passion, it was a deep longing to hold a woman tightly in his arms again. It had been too long. He knew it was the same for her and that it would complete their pleasure and enchantment in each other. The stirrings inside him were such a combination of joy and love that he felt he could literally climb on top of the ice cream parlor chair and announce it to everyone.

He chuckled out loud and Muriel raised her eyebrows, "What?" When he told her, they both giggled like adolescents on a first love adventure. Ken noticed the red-haired boy with the million freckles observing them with his wide smile. Ken waved to him and winked. The boy nodded and winked back in good spirits, seeing the obvious joy in the couple.

"All right, my fair lady, where to next, since I know nothing of the attractions here?"

Muriel looked at her watch and then said, "Do you like zoos?"

"I like anything you do and I am open to whatever you suggest. Besides, I haven't been to a zoo in years, not since Holly and Carter were pre-teens."

"Good. Then I think you will like this one. We can wind up the day and then get back home to freshen up for dinner at Jillie's Steak House. Then, after dinner, we can make it perfect for the dance."

"So, lead the way," and Ken tucked her arm under his and they settled into his car. Muriel directed him to the city zoo.

"Perhaps it sounds strange to you to suggest a date at the zoo. But some of my best times with Angie, Nadine, and her kids were at this zoo."

"It doesn't sound strange to me because you've probably guessed that I was ever the family man, so this brings back some good times Gloria and I had with our kids too. Besides, it keeps me young. It's been too long since I've had a fun day at a zoo." He suddenly laughed as he recalled Carter at four years old staring down an enclosed orangutan with a solemn angry glare. The ape had its tongue pushed out and stared fixedly at a silent seething Carter. Ken had almost dropped to his knees in unabashed hilarity when his small son stretched up onto his toes and poked out his tongue, giving forth a resounding raspberry. The big ape, feeling outdone, reeled backward and began to screech. Carter stuck up his nose and proudly turned his back on the ape. Ken shared this story with Muriel and they laughed together over the polished justice with which a four year old had handled such an improper insult in an impromptu fashion.

As Ken parked the car close to the zoo entrance, Muriel said, "Ken, that was a delightful story about Carter and I can't wait to meet your family."

"I am anxious for you to meet them, Muriel, and Angie too. I would like to set that up when I have them all home. We'll work on setting up that date, all right?"

"Angie will be out of college for the summer soon so it would be fine any time with us. It depends on what works best for you. I can always get someone to fill in for me at Dolly's."

"Then it is a done deal. When I return home, I will call my crew and start making arrangements for a major family gathering." Ken felt himself speed into a heightened heartiness at the prospects of his family meeting Muriel and Angie.

"Well, I just hope they will approve of me, Ken," and she paused. "I guess I am sort of nervous, you know?" She lowered her head, giving him a nervous smile.

"They will love you, Muriel, and Angie too. I can tell you that my children are so all together and they love their old dad. They have expressed concerns for me and told me I should have a social life."

"Well, sure, Ken, a social life, but honey, a...." and she trailed off.

Ken was grinning now with that teasing way he had and he finished for her, "You mean a wife?"

Muriel felt her face grow hot to the roots of her scalp but she stood there with her eyes cast down not able to respond.

"Honey girl, don't you think they would more easily accept a wife than a casual fling?" and he laughed.

"Oh, Ken, you know darn well what I mean. I put myself in a presumptuous role and didn't have the least intentions of that."

"Don't get so upset, my lady, we do not have to be coy like bashful twelve year olds who found out they have a crush on each other. You know I am playing for keeps. Now, how about you?" He still had that twinkle of amusement and reached for her, pulling her close. He kissed her emotively, feeling the passion fill him again with her lips pressed to his.

"Now," she breathed heavily, her hands pressed to his chest, "we had better take in that animal kingdom show."

"Yes, we had better," Ken said, his breathing heavy, holding a look at Muriel which conveyed the heated arousal within him. They walked through the gate that led onto a garden walkway. The various animal enclosures were a short walk away on a lightly pebbled trail.

"Did you know that, at one time, I seriously considered becoming a zoologist? I decided maybe it wasn't in vogue for a girl after I mentioned it to some of my friends. Rule number one, I learned since, is to listen to your own heart on career choices and not to your friends," Muriel said somewhat dourly. "Of course, on the other hand, if I had been truly dedicated, nothing would have swerved my course from that goal, I suppose." And she pointed out a colorful butterfly that seemed to make it's way straight for them. "Oh, look Ken, it's landed on my arm," and her voice was almost girl-like in delight. The colors were like the brightness of a celestial body and Ken could hear the intake of Muriel's breath as she stared enraptured at the beautiful winged creature. "Ken, I almost feel this is a good omen, like a sign from heaven," and he noticed her eyes were misty with unshed tears.

"And, do you know what?" he said softly, "I just believe you are right." He slid his arm around her slender waist.

Suddenly, the butterfly lifted in a dazzle of colorful splendor and circled around them. Then it lifted higher and beyond their heads in a flight pattern as if to bid them farewell.

"Good-bye, lovely creature," Muriel said and smiled at the rainbow of colors leaving them now. They watched its ascent until it appeared but a speck in the blue of sky. They walked down the pathway and watched the antics of the spider monkeys and the apparent boredom of the giant cats. They stood by the aviary which housed exotic birds and it held them fascinated until Ken spoke.

"Muriel, you fill me with wonder."

"Why is that, Ken?" She regarded him with a sideways expression, a teasing look he had noticed before. It was almost like she had a secret.

"I would never have guessed your desire for a career in zoology."

"Why not?" And she turned to face him fully.

"I don't know, but had you said a model, I wouldn't have been surprised. You have certain characteristics that modeling agencies look for."

"Well, that is very flattering, Ken, but it would have bored me to tears," and she laughed that husky resonance that never failed to speak expansively to those inner male stirrings of his.

"You are truly a wonder, Muriel. Maybe that is part of my great attraction to you."

"Oh, please do go on, tell me more," she purred, looking at him through her lashes.

"Okay. For one thing, I see the warmth of a very loving woman and yet also, a certain acquired toughness, the kind of toughness that speaks volumes. It says, don't try and tread on me, for one thing. And, I know who I am and where I'm going. You have virtue, a certain moral excellence," he went on. "There is also this ladylike quality that shines through but you have a strength that I'm wagering could see you through anything life deals you."

"I think so now, Ken but it was probably acquired when I finally took a long hard look at that little girl who suddenly just had one parent to take care of her."

"You had it all along, Muriel honey, because you know God doesn't make mistakes. We just suppose he does," and he took her arm, moving on to watch the adult bears lying languidly by a large water pool. The three young exuberant cubs were joyously wrestling and tumbling about. Ken and Muriel laughed aloud at their antics and then moved on to admire the elephants. Ken always felt a kind of kinship to them, in an obscure way.

"Did you ever feel that animals have some human characteristics when you watch them, Muriel?

"Sure. Nadine and I used to comment on that every time we came to this zoo. We would laugh about it but agreed that it was fitting just the same."

"Say now, I'm thinking we should get back to Rosewood and give ourselves some time to get ready for supper," Ken suggested after checking his watch.

"I don't know where the time has gone but, when you are having fun and in wonderful company, time does fly," she sighed.

"Dear lady, we are going to keep on having fun because we have embarked on a beautiful adventure together," he assured her as he put his arm around her waist.

"Ken, I love you so," and her eyes were aglow with a genuine emotion that came from a deep source in her heart. Ken could feel himself tremble with emotion. He took her hands in his own and lifted them to his lips, kissing them.

"Muriel, I love you. Oh, God girl, I have been so lonely. Where have you been?" he breathed heavily.

"Where have you been, Ken Ferries?" she whispered. Her eyes filled with tears and she said, "I thought you would never come."

They made their way to Ken's car just holding each other close, not talking. They were each in their own private thoughts about the rapture between them. There was no need for talk because they each knew their souls had come to experience that mystical knowledge of divineness people know when they have fallen in love. Ken opened the car door for Muriel and she slid into the seat. He walked around to settle into the driver's side and then reached for Muriel and kissed her with a hunger he had held too long. He felt the same response from her. When he released her and started the car engine, she sat close to him and put her head on his shoulder.

Finally Ken spoke. "Honey, we have so many things we will need to discuss but we'll get to all that in time. It will just fall into place, I think, because there are some heavy forces at work directing us on."

"I think so, Ken, I really do, because the events that have taken place are not just happenstance," and she trailed her fingers along his ear. He took her hand and kissed it, nodding his head in agreement. They reached Muriel's home and he walked around the car to open the door for her.

"Listen, hon, I will come back about quarter to six to pick you up for supper. All right?"

"All right. I do want to freshen up and I'll be ready when you come," she said, smiling up at him. He gathered her up in his arms again and put her lips to his in a lingering kiss.

"Wow," he breathed out loud, "you do make me sizzle, and baby, it's not from the heat."

"Go, right now, Ken," she chuckled with that husky depth she had and smiled alluringly. Ken never failed to catch his breath when she did that.

"Gotta go," he said and pulled back from her. He got in the car. "I'll see you in awhile then, baby."

"Love you," she said and Ken answered, "Ditto."

As he pulled out of the driveway, he noticed the sky held a dark gathering of storm clouds to the east. By the time he reached the motel, the clouds had formed into a full-scale cloudburst. As he sat outside his motel room waiting out the giant-sized raindrops, he thought of Muriel. He could feel a high level of energy from this storm and thought how like his own feelings of wild energy, the likes of which he had not experienced in a long time.

"You're like a high school boy, old fella," he silently mused. "Here you are, sixty years old, and you can't wait to make love to that lady," he thought as his heart pounded at the prospect of holding her while their passion mounted into dizzying heights. He knew that he was playing for keeps and that this wasn't just two people involved in a short hot fling. He sat there and reflected on the whole sequence of events of this short time. From somewhere, he heard a voice within—or was it without. He couldn't be certain. Nonetheless, he heard, "To thine own self be true, Ken Ferries." He looked around toward the back seat but saw no one. With a sudden awareness, he realized that youth had not cornered the market on deep passion and love between two people.

The rain finally slacked off so he got out his motel room key and made his way to his room. As always, he checked for messages and found none so he began to disrobe and head for the shower. As he turned on the water and started to step in, he heard the phone ring. He turned the shower off and went to answer it, sitting down on the bed.

"Hello?" he said.

"Ken Ferries?" a male voice said.

"Yes, speaking. Who is this?"

"If you don't back off, you better watch your ass," the deep male voice threatened.

"Who is this?" Ken said with an angry edge in his voice, only to hear a click and the phone resumed its usual tone.

"All right, now I know for certain that somebody intends to play hard ball," he said aloud. For a fleeting moment, he felt a chill up his spine. While he showered, he thought about the best plan of action and knew he needed to see Sheriff Hernado to tell him about the threatening phone call.

He dressed, selecting a white Western shirt and finely tailored black Western suit. He put on his horse hair bolo, a prized gift from an elegant old Choctaw chief. Ken had spent a few days interviewing a large gathering of Indian tribes from all over the country and then wrote at length about the various ceremonies and rituals. He had always been greatly interested in the cultures of Indian peoples and held a deep affinity for them. He pulled on a pair of highly polished black Laredo boots and a handsome black Stetson. He added a red wine handkerchief to his jacket and then tipped his hat in a gallant gesture to the man who looked back at him with a teasing glint.

"I reckon you'll do to please a mighty pretty woman," he chuckled. He went to his car but looked around to see if anyone suspicious was watching him. He saw no one but the marmalade cat sleeping on a mat at the entrance to the room next door. The sky, he noticed, had pretty well cleared other than a few clouds. He unlocked his car and decided to swing by the Sheriff's office, though he doubted that Bruster would be there since it was Saturday evening. But one of the deputies probably would be and he could relate the message to Bruster so at least it would be on file.

When he entered the Sheriff's office, a young blonde man in an officer's uniform and badge greeted Ken with a "Howdy. What may I do for you, sir?"

"I am Ken Ferries. I don't suppose the Sheriff is here?"

"No sir, he isn't, but I can help you. Do you need to file a report?"

"As a matter of fact, I do" and he related to the deputy the call he had just received.

"Mr. Ferries, do you have any idea why you would have received a call like that? Or any idea who it was?"

"Not a clue, other than I am a freelance writer and have been gathering information on the Rogers case from some local people," Ken stated. He felt he knew a possible caller but did not want to detail this to anyone other than the Sheriff. The young man regarded Ken with an open curiosity and knew that he wondered why this nicely attired stranger would be threatened by any of the locals. He was pondering it and Ken could understand why he would.

"So, I will stop by Monday and talk to the Sheriff. Meanwhile, if anything else transpires, I will call. I do thank you for your assistance," and Ken extended his hand to the deputy.

"Yes, sir, that is what we are here for and glad to oblige," the young man said.

Ken returned to his car and noticed that it was time to go out to Muriel's. He drove by Bailey's Lounge and looked to see if the older dull green Jeep might be parked there but it wasn't. In a way, he felt a sense of relief but he intended to keep a watchful vigil from now on.

Angie met him at the door, attired in an Aztec design blouse and vest with full skirt. The blue green color and summer white blouse accented her beauty dramatically.

"Wow, young woman, you are drop dead gorgeous! I should imagine that Will Earl better be on alert or some young rascal will steal away with you," Ken asserted.

Angie tilted her head sideways and smiled, exposing perfect white teeth. "Well now, Ken, you are looking mighty fine yourself. But I do thank you. Every lady needs assurance, you know." She stepped back and said, "Come in. Mom will be out in a minute."

He removed his Stetson and stepped into the living room. Angie invited him to sit down and she motioned toward the comfortable big swivel rocker he had sat in the night before. He settled his large frame into the deep comfortable contours of the chair and Angie asked if he would like a glass of lemonade.

"Say, that sounds refreshing. Yes, I would, Angie. Thanks."

When Angie retreated to get Ken's refreshment, he noticed a photograph of a handsome dark-haired man sitting up on a shelf. He supposed it was Bill, Muriel's deceased husband. He had reached that conclusion as he could see a slight resemblance to Angie. Angie returned with the lemonade, along with one for herself, and settled on the couch across from Ken.

"Is that photograph of your father, Angie?" Ken gestured to the picture.

"Yes, it is, but sadly, I never knew him. He died when I was a baby."

"That is sad, Angie, but I can see that you resemble him some. He's a handsome man."

"Oh, do you think I favor him, really?"

Ken nodded and then replied, "Yes, I do. But I think that you favor your Mom too."

"Yes, I can see my mother every time I look in a mirror," she smiled with warmth at Ken. "I think Mom's class reunion is coming up pretty soon and I believe that my Dad was a grade ahead of Mom," Angie said. She picked up a book from the coffee table. "Here. Want to look at this? Mom had it out last night showing me pictures in her high school year book."

"Sure would," Ken replied and reached for the book Angie held out to him. "Oh, now, here your Mom is a cheerleader, I see," and Ken could see even more that Angie favored her mother. "You know, had I just picked up this book and saw this picture, I would certainly have thought the girl with the pompoms was you."

"Everyone says that when they see pictures of Mom taken awhile back. It's fun sometimes to let them think it is me," and she chuckled with amusement at the fun she'd had fooling people. Ken noticed that she had that same sparkle of mischief in her eyes that he had seen in her mother.

"Now here is one of your daddy and he played football, I see. He was a husky, good-looking young man."

"He was, wasn't he. I guess that was the year my father graduated and so the book for the year Mom graduated must be here somewhere." She lifted up a Sears catalog that was sitting on another book on the coffee table. "Yes, here we go," she said and brought the book over to Ken.

Her finger was placed beside a picture of a younger Muriel but Ken thought she was still as pretty. He thumbed through the album as he sipped the lemonade and saw a picture of Jeff Colter. He had his arm slung casually over another boy's shoulder and they both held football helmets. The other boy resembled someone he felt he knew but he couldn't quite recall. Then it hit him—it had to be Will Earl's father. He confirmed it when he read the name.

He came across another young man's picture and stared at it with a flicker of recognition. The name rang a bell but he didn't think he knew him. The last name was Willard and the first name was Catlin. He noted that the youth had written something under the picture, something inscribed to Muriel: "To the sexiest girl in the whole class with those cat green eyes and what a figure- wow! Good luck, little Kitten, from the Cat man, Cat Willard."

Muriel came out to the living room then and proclaimed, "Sorry, Ken. I was tracking down a pair of pantyhose without a runner," and she stared at Ken as he stood up. "Say, cowboy, you are a real hunk" and she whistled.

Ken felt the breath leave him at the sight of Muriel clad in a clingy black and white stunning Western three piece ensemble. The long-sleeved blouse was a beaded floral lace with appliqués on the collar. The elegant black denim shawl and skirt were beaded and fringed in white. Her high-heeled boots were white lace-up leather with the same lace design on the side of the boots. Her hair cascaded down to her shoulders like spun silk and looked the color of golden honey in the lamp light.

"Cat got your tongue, big man?" she teased with that saucy look. She knew he was befuddled and at a loss for words.

"Muriel, you are so beautiful, I am just speechless," and he felt his heart thud with sudden emotion so powerful that he fought inwardly for control. He knew that he was head over heels in love with this stunning woman.

"Mama, you are just beautiful, like Ken said," and Angie went over to her mother and embraced her.

"Pussy cat, you are too," Muriel said and held her daughter close.

"Mom, I have film in my camera so let's get pictures," and she went to retrieve her camera.

"Come over here, Ken, so Angie can get our picture. I promise I won't bite," she teased.

He went to her and kissed her quickly before Angie returned.

"All right, you two, just like that be looking at each other," Angie instructed. "Now, one more and then Ken can get a couple of Mom and me, okay?" So they posed for another picture and then Ken took some of mother and daughter.

"Mom, you take one of Ken and me now," Angie said as she handed the camera to her mother.

"Say, am I a lucky man or what, getting my picture taken with two beauties," Ken boasted good-naturedly.

Angie looped her arm through Ken's as Muriel snapped their picture. The doorbell rang and Angie opened the door to a handsome smiling Will Earl.

"Come on in and get your picture taken," Angie said and pulled him in by the arm. "See Mom and Ken—aren't they both simply photogenic?"

"Well, I reckon," Will Earl said as he took in the two standing side by side. "You two are going to turn some heads tonight, you can bet on it. And Angie girl, my forever gorgeous one, you are especially radiant this evening," he said and quickly tipped her head back and kissed her soundly.

"Oh now, here, here," she gasped, "in front of Mom and Ken?"

Ken could see that she liked that kiss more than a little, regardless of her pretence.

"All right, fire away," Will Earl said as he hugged Angie tight to him. Muriel took a couple pictures of them and said, "Will Earl, you are ever the handsome hunk. But that navy sport coat with the Aztec blanket design topped off with your white Stetson is perfect for you. And Angie is right on target with her attire too."

"It figures," Will Earl teased Angie. "Now we go together like a hot fudge sundae. And one of these days, she will believe me." He kissed her again and she blushed prettily.

"Well, if we are going to go, we had better do it before they roll up the streets," Muriel said as she retrieved her fringed black and white denim purse off the coffee table.

"Want to join us at the steakhouse for supper, you two young folks? My treat," Ken invited.

159

"Say, that is mighty nice of you, Ken, but Ang and I are invited over to a couple's who went to high school with us. They asked us over to a little supper party and then we will all go to the dance. So, see you there." He winked teasingly, "Now you two, have fun but stay out of trouble."

"Heck, Will Earl, that's no fun," Muriel said, poking him softly in the ribs. They all laughed and headed for their vehicles. When Ken and Muriel settled into Ken's car, Muriel turned to Ken, "Aren't they a cute couple?"

"They are indeed and I think they will become a couple on a permanent basis one of these days," he agreed.

"I am hoping that is the way it turns out, Ken, because I know that they are in love. I think that anyone around them can see that in five minutes or less."

There was a sudden and definite fragrance of roses in the air and Muriel turned to Ken, her eyes wide with surprise. "Ken, do you smell that?" Her voice reached an upward pitch and Ken nodded. "Is that the fragrance you have told me that you and Phyllis have smelled so many times?" Her voice was quaking with emotion.

"Yes, it is Muriel," and he reached for her hand and placed it to his cheek.

"Oh, Ken, I would recognize that rose perfume anywhere. I know Nadine is present," and the tears ran down her cheeks.

Ken reached for tissue in the console beneath the glove compartment and dabbed at the tears on her cheeks.

"Oh, I have such a mix of emotion, Ken. One that she is gone and yet she is here."

"I know, sweetheart, but what a gift she is sending us. Muriel, she is here, honey. It is just that most of us mortals can't see through the veil."

The fragrance began to fade and Muriel unzipped her purse and took out a compact. She opened the makeup mirror to retouch her tear-stained face. As she put the compact back in her purse, she spoke in a hushed voice. "Ken, I prayed so hard that she would somehow come to me and let me know if she is all right. I know now that she was giving me that confirmation. I really feel it."

"Yes, she did," and he pulled her close to him and kissed her lips as he slid his hand behind her neck. "Oh, baby, let's go to Jillie's Steakhouse now or I will take advantage of the fact that Angie is not home."

"We better go now," she whispered to him, "because I am on shaky ground myself." Muriel directed the way to Jillie's and Ken noticed that several other people had the same idea, judging by the number of cars already parked at the establishment.

"They are packed here tonight, but then it isn't unusual for a Saturday night. With the rodeo tomorrow, this is about normal," Muriel said.

"Well, I have worked up quite an appetite by now," he laughed lightly.

"I would imagine that the ice cream cone you had for lunch has worn pretty thin," she said as Ken got out of the car to go around and open the door for her.

"A good steak is going to fix that," he said and helped her from the car. They walked up a rustic deck to enter the front door.

"Say, this is nice," Ken said as he took in the interior of the place. The bar where they entered had a grand rock fireplace at one end of the room. A massive pair of longhorns was mounted above the mantle and an old-fashioned juke box sat in one corner playing a country ballad. Ken hadn't heard it in a long time. The smell of cigarette smoke assailed them from the various patrons at the bar and the tables scattered around the room. Everyone turned to look at them and some called out hellos to Muriel, which she returned with an acknowledged smile and friendly wave.

"Ken, let's go right to the dining area," she suggested. "If we want a drink, we can order from the dining room."

"Fine with me, honey. You just point the way."

Suddenly, Muriel stopped short and Ken said, "Muriel, what is it?"

"Oh, nothing. Come on, I'll tell you when we get to a table in the dining room."

The dining room was graced by another stone fireplace but it wasn't quite as large as the one in the bar. The overall setting of the room was done in a Western flavor, a real Texas collection that spoke volumes about the home state with ropes, saddles, and, of course, the state flag draped by the fireplace. A young Mexican woman with a soft accent led them to a table which was clad with a red and white checked tablecloth. In the center was a metal bucking horse holding a burning votive candle. Ken noticed that each table had these candle-holders but some were Texas Longhorn bulls and others were cowboys. The checkered tablecloths also varied, being reds, greens, or blues.

The Mexican lady took their order. Then Ken reached across the table and said, "All right, lady, what brought you up so short when we made our way through the bar?"

"You didn't see Jeff Colter there, did you? He was sitting at a table to the right of the fireplace. It is kind of shadowed back there so I just happened to see him."

"No, I didn't see him and, if I did, I just didn't notice that it was Jeff since I just met him that one time."

"Well, it kind of surprised me when I saw him because he was sitting there with Marilyn Allard. But then maybe Pace is here too and I just didn't see him. After all, that bar is packed in there."

"Shouldn't we have stopped at their table to say hello, honey?"

"Maybe. I don't know," she hedged and her voice trailed off. The Mexican lady with a name tag that read Lola returned with an old style blue enamel coffee pot that she set down on a brass trivet shaped like a horse shoe. The handle of the pot was modernized with a durable rubberized handle grip, freeing the server from burns. She lifted from the serving tray two glasses of water, some salsa and chips. Then she filled two hefty mugs with steaming black coffee. Once finished, she smiled and retreated from their table.

"Ken, I don't like to pass on rumors," Muriel hesitated, "but you know working at Dolly's I hear everything that is going around." Her face colored some but she went on, "You know Marilyn Allard was in school with me. And well, she was a couple grades below me."

"Yes, go on," Ken prompted.

"Well, you met Pace and he comes across as 'Mr. Sociability' but I always felt like there was an icy side to him. And I felt that Marilyn was not the happiest person. I mean, she seemed to change after she and Pace were married. She was always such a sweet person and it just hit me that she got sorta stiff and, well, not the same Marilyn."

"Do you think that she and Jeff are having an affair?"

"You know, I don't, not really. But, of course, that has been hinted at by some. I have overheard it in the café. But Jeff was so broken up over Nadine, of course we all were, but I know Jeff was in love with her. He never tried to come between her and Will though. He thinks so highly of Will, you know, and it just isn't Jeff's style to try and cut in on someone that way." She went on, "I just have an idea that Jeff is someone who Marilyn trusts and she probably needs a trusted friend's ear. She and Jeff dated some in high school but they were mainly just buddies, like Jeff and me—or so I thought at the time."

"Do Marilyn and Pace have any children, Muriel?"

"Yes, their son Thor is away at law school and their daughter Katie got married a year and a half ago to a Navy lieutenant. They are overseas somewhere now. I'm sure Marilyn was really lost when Katie left because they were especially close. Thor tended to be a bit like his father, pretty much all business, but I didn't get that he was quite as driven as Pace is. So, that's about it," she said and Ken knew she didn't want to discuss it further.

"Aren't those three men in Huntsville Prison, Muriel?"

"Yes, Ken. Why do you ask?"

"Well, I need to talk to Bruster about a matter and I thought maybe I could get some clearance to visit those men soon." He went on, "I want to talk to the defending attorney too and possibly the judge, if they will see me."

"Well, the defending attorney was Con Womack and the Judge is an old hard-liner who is up to retire soon, so I have heard," Muriel said. "In fact, both of those men are termed 'old-liners' and I've felt that they both had some questions about the case. I am sure of it or else Judge Bullard would have given the death penalty."

"Now, that just whets my curiosity all the more. I will try to get an audience with these men," Ken said with a note of certainty. "Now, which of these salsas is the hottest?" and he had a corn chip poised over the green salsa.

"Um, not that one, sweetie, unless you want to breathe fire like a Chinese dragon," Muriel chirped in amusement.

"The only fire I am interested in breathing is over one pretty woman I am presently in the company of," and he winked suggestively at her.

She smiled seductively at him and then looked up at a tall figure that had just arrived at their table.

"Well, hi Jeff, old buddy. Sit down and join us," Muriel said to a smiling Jeff Colter.

"Oh, just for a minute, Muriel," Jeff said. "I got somebody waiting," and he pulled up a chair from an empty table and sat down.

"Jeff, you've met Ken Ferries, haven't you?"

Jeff turned those steel gray eyes on Ken. "Yep, sure did, as a matter of fact, back at your folks' grocery store," and he extended his rough work-worn hand to Ken.

"Good to see you again, Jeff," Ken offered and Jeff, who wasn't long on words, nodded politely.

"So, how you been, Muriel?" Jeff ventured.

"I've been doing a lot better, Jeff. And yourself?"

"Oh, coming along," he mused.

"Haven't seen you in Dolly's for a long time. Where have you been?"

"Keeping right busy out on the spread. You know how that is, Muriel."

"I do, Jeff. But give yourself a break now and again, cowboy, and keep in touch with old friends."

"Well, I just reckon that I needed to do that so I'm taking in the dance tonight."

"Hey now, that is great. Ken and I will see you there because that is where our next stop will be."

"That's mighty fine. And, by the way, Muriel, you are looking great, but then you always were one of the prettiest gals in Rosewood," and his eyes took on a sparkle that added to his rough good looks. He stood up, "So I will see you two later. And, pretty country girl, save a dance or two for this old cowpoke." He leaned down and kissed Muriel on her cheek and nodded to Ken as he made his way back in the direction of the bar.

"So, I guess Jeff saw us when we were coming to the dining room," Muriel said thoughtfully.

"He has probably heard the rumors, Muriel, and realized that you have too. He figured you were in a position of not knowing what to do, and being a friend, didn't want to embarrass him or Mrs. Allard."

"I'm sure you are correct, Ken, and I know that whatever is going on between Jeff and Marilyn is their business. They are both good people— that is the bottom line."

"You are a good person yourself, Muriel, and it doesn't surprise me that you take that attitude."

She smiled at Ken and said, "Well, thank you, Ken. I just see two very lonely people there who have found solace together and I honestly believe that is it." She did that little habit she had, placing her hand underneath her hair on her neck in a rubbing motion. He smiled softly at her. "What?" she looked questioningly at him.

"Oh, nothing. It is just that I see all of these little things I love about you, like what you just did."

"What was that? What did I just do?" and she was looking at him with her eyebrows arched in question and a half smile with her lips closed.

"You know, that little thing you do with your hand underneath your hair, when you are thinking heavily or are a bit perplexed."

"I know. It's like that with me too. I drink in everything about you, mentally record all the details."

He smiled at her lovingly and then looked up at the waitress. "Oh, boy, here comes supper," Ken said as Lola set down the steaks, Western beans, and all of the trimmings.

"We are going to need the exercise we'll get from dancing after we put this away," Muriel giggled.

"Well, honey, like Will Earl said the other evening, 'Have I got a home for this'" and he laughed as he thought again how much young men like Will Earl and Tyler could eat.

Someone from the bar let forth a resounding "yippee" and Muriel frowned and looked in that direction. "If I didn't know any better, I would swear that sounded like Will Rogers," and she trained her ear toward the direction of the bar. Ken asked why she thought it was him. "I've known him all my life and I know his voice as well as my own. Listen, I'm going to take a peek but I'll be right back. Okay?"

"Sure, Muriel. That's fine with me."

She clasped his hand firmly as she walked by. Ken watched her make her way toward the bar entrance and saw her scan the room. He saw her figure stiffen and she turned around to come back to their table.

"Ken, that is Will out there and he is drunker than Cooter Hill. He's in the company of one Tess Roberts so I didn't want him to see me under these circumstances."

Ken wanted to laugh at her description of Will being drunker than Cooter Hill. The last time he had heard that was from his father who was a very descriptive man, in a colorful sense. He knew that the sight of Will being toasted had upset Muriel and so he confined himself to expressing a measure of concern, which he did, in truth, feel.

"Oh, Muriel," he said, reaching for her trembling hand.

She was biting down on her lower lip in an effort to keep from shedding the tears Ken could see in her eyes. "That damned fool. What's he doing anyway?" she cried and the tears came now unchecked.

"Muriel, he needs to go for some help, honey, because this is bigger than even his friends can help with. By the way, who is Tess Roberts?"

"About the biggest tart in the county," she sniffed and dabbed at her eyes with her dinner napkin.

"Muriel, listen to me, baby. You can't let this crush you. I know that Nadine doesn't want you to do that to yourself."

"You're right. I think she was letting me know in the car earlier. So maybe when Will's grief has kindled down from a raging fire, she can come to him easier like she has to me and to Phyllis." She took a drink from her water glass. "I feel that you are the catalyst for bringing her to me. She came to you, knowing you would be the one who would distribute all these things from her through you." She looked more relaxed now and then said, "Ken, do you follow me?"

"Yes, honey, I follow you. Because I think more now than ever that she is one of the forces, along with a Higher Power, who brought me into this case."

"Yes, and I believe she has even played matchmaker with us," Muriel smiled at him with a deep expression of love in her eyes.

"I have a very strong suspicion that is the case," he agreed in a tender voice that came from the deepest resources of his big heart. "Eat that steak, pretty woman, before it gets cold," he ordered with gentle prompting.

She cut a piece of the steak and exclaimed, "Now this is real steak and so tender."

Ken took a bite of his steak and said, "The kingdom of Heaven has certainly received us. This is delicacy beyond belief." Ken felt ravenous but made him self eat slowly and savor every bite. "I was hungry as a grizzly bear. I know that if their steak is this terrific, the dessert is too. We will need to make room for some."

"Well, we will see, because, when I make my way around this steak and the extra trimmings, I may be too full. But, hon, don't let me stop you from having some."

"I never need much of an excuse for treating myself to goodies, as my Holly used to call dessert when she was a tyke." It had been a standing joke in his family. "I must tell you that Holly could literally charm her poor old father out of his eye teeth, Muriel. The way it went was that she had to at least clean up a decent portion of her plate before she got dessert. However, when the time came for that, there would be little Holly with one elbow resting on the table, her hand placed to her head, and the other hand stirring the contents of her plate in a casual way but eying everyone as they had their dessert. She could evoke the most pitiful little sounds I have ever heard. Of course, after a few minutes of this, Carter would reach over and pat her, telling us, 'Sissy can have my goodies.' Then, of course, I would prevail on Gloria that perhaps we could give her dessert this time and next time cut her main portion down. It worked every time." Ken laughed at the memory.

"Why, Ken Ferries, you were a real enabler," she laughed.

"Guilty as charged," he chuckled.

"The memories of our children are so precious. They are like collectibles we can summon up when things seem too heavy for us to handle." She went on, "I remember when Angie thought that we ought to move Toby, this big black Newfoundland dog, into her bedroom at night because he might get cold outside. He was as big as a Shetland pony and as crazy over her as she was over him. Never did I have to worry with Toby around because he was like the whole National Guard," and she chuckled. Her face softened into a tender smile as she sat for a moment in quiet reflection before going on. "I got up one morning extra early and, like always, went to Angie's room to peek in at her. Here was Toby, asleep on Angie's bed with just his head showing since Angie had covered him tenderly with her comforter. She was on a pallet on the floor and both were sound asleep. So, in essence, we do these things to allow our children to be children, even when it doesn't, for all practical purposes, follow the guidelines," she said almost meditatively.

"Yes, I believe so, Muriel. But these are things that are ever recalled as the pure joys of parenting. I think the real important part is seeing these little people in the light of the true love and enjoyment they give us."

Muriel just smiled and nodded her agreement. The waitress returned and asked if they wanted dessert. Ken asked what the special was for the evening and she replied, "Fresh-baked apple pie." He pursed his lips and said, "Say now, I am ready for that. How about you, my lady?"

"All right. I did make room for goodies," she laughed lightly and winked at Ken.

The waitress left their table to get the pie as Ken filled first Muriel's coffee mug and then his own. Muriel sat stiffly as they heard a loud male voice call out, "Okay, Will, you son of a gun, hang in there. And don't you go doing any old thing I wouldn't," and it was followed by boisterous guffaws.

Ken reached for her hand and smiled in tender understanding in an effort to ease the strained look on her face. "Honey," he prompted, for she had her head down now with her eyes fixed on the pattern of the tablecloth. The soft flickering candlelight shimmered in the highlights of her hair. She was so lost in thought that she hadn't heard Ken speak so he repeated the endearment.

"Oh, Ken, I am so sorry. What were you saying?"

"I just want to ask you something," and her face was fully alert now with her attention focused on him. "Muriel, after what I have shared with you, do you accept that I have..." and he hesitated, seeking the right words, "well, I guess one might term it unusual abilities, for lack of a better description."

"I certainly do believe that you are very clairvoyant."

"Now, if you accept that, and I have only recently begun to myself, will you trust me with something else that I will share with you?"

"Certainly, Ken. What is it?"

"As I sat here and watched you, Muriel, I just picked up on something regarding Will. It came to me so clear and strong that I know it is pure truth. Will is going to pull out of this. I know he will never get over the loss of his wife but he will heal and go on living. Now here is the wondrous part of this message. Nadine's own spirit will be instrumental in his healing."

"Since you are the one telling me this, I am filled with relief. I fully accept what you have told me," and her eyes held the shine of joy along with tears.

As the waitress returned with their dessert and the bill, Muriel wiped away her tears. Lola thanked them and asked if everything was all right. They both assured her it was wonderful. Lola's eyes filled with pleasure and her soft features became even lovelier. In a gentle Spanish voice, she said, "Gracias."

Ken placed a sizable tip on the money tray and said to Muriel, "Are you ready, lindo señora?"

"I am, señor." She offered her extended hand and they made their way to the bar. Just as they entered, a pretty Mexican lady walked up to them and spoke to Muriel.

"Muriel, hello. How are you?" she said as she looked openly at Ken, not concealing her curiosity.

"Oh, hello, Margarita," Muriel said and embraced her. "How are you doing?"

The woman shrugged. "Some days are better than others, you know. But Carlos and Bonita, they are not so good most of the time."

"I know, I know, Margarita. Please tell them hello for me and give them my blessings," Muriel said and then added, "Oh, this is Margarita Gomez. Ken, this lady is my friend and she is the one who gets credit for that scrumptious pie we had with supper. Margarita, meet my friend, Ken Ferries."

Ken smiled at the lady and said, "You are truly an artist, for you do have a gift at pie making. It is a pleasure to meet you."

Margarita's face took on an appreciative glow for a moment but Ken could see the sadness that dominated her overall demeanor.

"I am pleased and I thank you, sir," she said as she looked directly into Ken's eyes.

Suddenly, Ken felt a thrill course through his heart while he stood smiling at Margarita. Just over her head glowed the faintness of a lady with fair skin and unearthly beauty. She was dressed in a light blue gown with a flowing hood loose over her golden hair. A bright aura surrounded her in a dazzle of shimmering lights. Ken, unabashed, reached for Margarita's hand and said, "Please, señora, trust me that all will be well. You have a special angel who surrounds you."

"Señor, what do you know? What have you seen?" Margarita asked.

Ken held still, transfixed as the image of the lady in blue began to flow into yet finer mist, a powder of blue. Then Ken saw her no longer, yet the presence of her energy lingered. Margarita looked ever more intently at Ken, her deep dark eyes filled with a bright radiance and sudden awareness.

"You have seen my Lady, my Madonna, my Holy One," and sudden tears came down her gentle face as she made the sign of the cross on her forehead. She enclosed both of Ken's big sturdy hands in her own and raised them to her lips and kissed them. "You are mistico. Oh, I mean a mystic. I am sorry. You maybe do not speak Spanish?"

Ken found his voice again after being speechless at the vision. "Some, yes, some Spanish I know." When he spoke, he noticed that his voice was deeply husky.

He became fully aware of Muriel now. She stood there as though in a trance, with the wonder of a child who had witnessed something incredible.

Margarita took Muriel's hand now in her own and said in a voice not much more than a whisper, "This man, he is a messenger sent from God. He is an Earth Angel. I too have seen my Lady one time for she came to me at my worst hour, when my son was sent away." Her voice caught with a heavy sob that came from the depths of her soul.

"Yes, Ken is a wondrous man, Margarita. You can fully trust him. I think there are some things that you must know in time so I would like you to call on me soon. Come to my home and we three can have a talk." Muriel reached up and stroked Margarita's shiny black hair that trailed down her back.

"Oh, yes, yes. That would be good. I am so, how you say, anxious to talk with you, Muriel, and this fine man, your friend," and she smiled at Ken. He noticed how truly pretty she was with the lines of sorrow eased now from her face.

"So then it is done," Muriel said and hugged her friend once again. "We will get together soon."

"Gracias, Mr. Ferries and my friend here," and she patted Muriel's arm.

"Please call me Ken. I must say that I feel it has been such a beautiful message for the three of us. I am deeply overcome, to put it mildly."

On an impulse, Margarita hugged this towering man and then stepped back while still holding her dark eyes to his. "Mr. Ken, go with God."

Ken and Muriel made their way to the outside, stepping into a chorus of crickets while coyotes, off in the distance, held a critical discussion. They walked to

Ken's car which took on a silver sheen from the full luminous moon overhead. They both felt the magic of this magnetism and shared it in silence, an unspoken awareness that needed no speech. Ken opened the door for Muriel and she slid inside, not wanting to break this feeling of serenity. The weight of Ken's big body settling into the car beside her was the only observation that momentarily shifted her from the feeling that she was in a spellbound state. They just sat there for some moments before Ken spoke.

"Muriel, if I had the faintest doubt before of the innocence of those three men, it is completely erased now. The problem is getting the attention of the appropriate people who won't give us the brush-off to work on this case."

"The word is being given to us, Ken, from a power greater than all others. Now if we can just get to the sources that will help us gain the concrete proof we will need."

"Well, it seems to me, with the help we have been getting, we will be led to the right earthly sources too," Ken said and he felt a tug of lightness in his heart.

Muriel drew Ken into her arms and kissed him with a lovingness that was deeply maternal, like one would kiss a child. They held each other quietly and reflected each in their own thoughts about the powerful experiences they had been subject to and that they knew were limitless.

Chapter____6

Ken spoke now, "All right, I guess that we had better get to that dance and see if I have developed rusty legs." He chuckled at the thought of being clumsy since he hadn't been on a dance floor in five years. Muriel snuggled up close to Ken as he started up the car and she remained that way as they drove to Windom Hall. When they arrived, Muriel commented that everyone from Rosewood and surrounding area must be there. The parking lot was full of vehicles but, with some scouting, Ken found a space to park.

They entered the spacious dance hall and a band was playing a Country Western song. People were either on the dance floor swaying to the music or in clusters at tables that lined the room.

"Ken, let's find a table," Muriel said, taking his hand and pushing through the throng of bodies at the entrance.

"Well, hello, Muriel," came from a burly man with a colorful Western vest on. He took her arm, stopping her, and she replied, "Well, hello there, you."

She turned and said, "Ken, this is Ham Wilson. Ham, meet Ken Ferries." The man extended his hand to Ken and they both acknowledged the pleasure of meeting. Ken had an awareness of the man's identity before Muriel introduced them. He looked like the man he had seen who lifted Phyllis and her tiny child in his stout arms and placed them in a pickup truck. The vision still came to him as keenly as the day he'd witnessed it.

"Say, Rosie is sitting over there, Muriel. Why don't you stop by our table and say hello?"

"Sure will, Ham. Listen now, you better be saving one dance for me," she teased.

"Now, you can count on that, honey child," and he winked at Ken. The man wasn't quite as tall as Ken but he was more massive through his shoulders He had a roughness of outer appearance but Ken sensed a very strong character emitting from this powerful man with the iron gray hair.

"That is one fine man and his wife Rosie is as solid as a person can be," Muriel said as she led them to the table where Rosie and an elderly gentleman sat visiting and watching the dancers.

"Dag gone," the old fellow said, "if it ain't that pretty gal who I been pining away for. I was just hopin' she would show up and make the evening perfect for an old cowpoke by dancing one with me."

"Sage Murdock, it sure wouldn't be the same if I didn't get a dance with the best looking cowboy in this crowd," and she bent down to hug the small sturdy old gent. His lined weather-beaten face spread into a wide grin.

"Muriel, you and Ken draw up some chairs and sit down."

Muriel introduced the craggy old rancher Sage to Ken and he extended a gnarled rock-hard hand to Ken while his keen brown eyes fixed on him. Ken felt Sage was seeing clear through him but the spark of mischief was unmistakable.

"I reckon you ought to know, mister, if I was twenty-five or thirty years younger, I would be giving you a run for this pretty woman," and he chuckled.

"Yes, and I bet that you sure would have been some tough competition, Mr. Murdock," Ken related good-naturedly.

"Oh, now you flatter me, Sage," Muriel winked at the elderly man.

"They tell me that flattery wins out about every time," Sage assured Muriel and then laughed in his crackled old voice which held the powers of a vital man regardless of his years.

"Sage Murdock, you old rascal. Now you behave yourself. The way you go on with the lassies is scandalous," Rosie snorted, but her cheery Irish blue eyes held amusement.

"Yes, indeed, and it has kept me from drying up and blowing away. So I reckon I will be sparkin' the ladies till they cover these old bones up in the sod," and he leaned over and gave Rosie a kiss.

"Here now, Sage Murdock, you old tease. I am a woman spoken for long ago and with a brand on too," and she held up her left hand and wiggled her ring finger.

"Har, har," old Sage roared. "I always figured I would meet my demise at the · hands of a jealous husband anyway, Rosie."

"Humpf," Rosie snorted and shook her head. "Well, now, that print you bought, Ken, is all ready any time you want to pick it up. I know you will enjoy it so much. Now, while I've my mind on that, I must tell you that Phyllis and I are holding an art showing of her mother's paintings at the gallery in Longview a week from Monday. Some other artists from the local area will be showing too. I have a brochure here in my bag with the location and time."

"Oh say, that is wonderful, Rosie. I will arrange for that day off at work so I can attend. I would not want to miss it for anything," Muriel assured Rosie.

"I want to attend too, because I have a lot more business to conduct within the area here. A week from Monday would be perfect," Ken said as he and Muriel studied the brochure.

A voice came out over the microphone as the music stopped and people were making their way to tables. A lean good-looking man from the band called out, "This is a request, special for Sissy and Bud Conway for their twenty-fifth wedding anniversary."

A petite dark-haired woman and a husky red-haired man entered the dance floor, just the two of them, as people stood and clapped. The young singer sang "Dreamin' Again", one of the great Jim Croce's renditions. The woman locked her slender arms around her husky husband's neck as they swayed to the strains of the music, He held her slender waist while they gazed into each other's eyes. People were now joining them and Ken reached for Muriel's hand and pulled her to her feet. They glided out onto the dance floor as smoothly as though they had danced together forever. They became oblivious to everyone but each other as the lights softened the room. The shining crystal ball hanging from the ceiling rafters made hundreds of colorful prisms. Near the close of the dance, Muriel's attention was suddenly caught by something. Ken felt her body tense as he trailed her glance.

There standing at the table was a dark-haired man dressed in a white Western shirt and a Stetson pushed back on his crisp dark hair. He was the handsomest man Ken had ever seen, even with his face now constricted with terrible grief.

"Oh, God, Ken, that's Will. Come on, I need to talk to him." It was easy to see that the man was drunk as he tottered on long jean-clad legs. A woman stood beside him, her arm around his waist in an effort to steady him. Ken supposed it was Tess Roberts, the woman Muriel had seen in his company earlier at Jillie's Steak House.

"Will" Muriel called his name as she approached him, Ken following behind her.

"Oh, Muriel." Will's voice cracked on an anguished slur. "What's you doing here? I mean, did you hear that song, huh?"

"Come on, Will. Please come outside with me, honey. I want to talk to you, okay?" Ken saw the strong resemblance of Will Earl's features to his father's.

"I was tellin' Tess here that I would make it up to her and we was gonna dance. But that song, did you hear that song, Muriel?" he lamented as tears made their way down his face.

"Listen now, Will. Tess won't mind if we go outside and get some fresh air." She turned to Tess and looked at her imploringly. "You won't mind, will you, Tess?"

Ken noticed that the woman was pretty but in a hard way. With her black hair pulled back to one side and caught up in a silver barrette, she looked like she might be part Indian. She wore a great deal of eye makeup and had a white beaded leather vest on with nothing under it. Her voluptuous figure sported a pair of tight black velvet jeans finished off with fancy high-heeled boots. The jeans were tucked inside the boots so the fringed leather up the sides was visible. Ken supposed she was about forty years old.

She was glaring now at Muriel but finally shrugged, "Oh, what the hell. He sure ain't in any condition to dance, let alone anything else."

181

"Ken, would you give me a hand here with Will?" Muriel asked and her face was pale, even in the dim light.

"Sure thing," Ken said as he went to Will and looped one of his arms over his neck. Ken then placed his arm around Will's trim waist. Together they made their way to the entrance, Will limply hanging between them and Tess following behind. They reached the outside and Will said, in a slurred drawl, "I think I am gonna be sick as an old hound dog that got himself a rotten dead rabbit."

"Come on with me to that stretch of grass across the parking lot, Will. Just hold on now, sweetie," Muriel urged him.

Ken nearly carried Will to the grassy area where he let spray a stench of overloaded whiskey. The man's shoulders heaved from the wretching of his stomach. "Oh, God, what did I do this for," he said as he reached into his hip pocket and produced a handkerchief to mop his mouth. Tess had maintained her position at the entrance of the dance hall, arms crossed under her well-defined, nearly exposed breasts. The look she sent to the three people across the parking lot was full of irritation.

"Well now, Tess old girl, I surely am sorry for ruining our party," Will pleaded across the space between them.

"Hell, what party, Will. Seems you can't hold your liquor or nothing else," she huffed and strode back into the dance hall.

"Now I went and messed up. I reckon Tessie girl is just plain fed up with me."

"Will, listen honey, it's all right now. Why don't you let Ken and me take you home?"

"I don't wanna go home, Muriel," he slurred. "Can't take it out there no more. I am alone and it just isn't the same like before, you know?"

"Yeah, I do, baby," she crooned as she put her hand to his face. "You aren't alone. You've got your boys with you, and Phyllis is close by with those two lovely granddaughters."

"It just hurts so bad, Muriel, and I can't find anything that eases it. It's like pure hell every day," and his voice caught on a heavy sob. Ken looked at this broken man and his stomach caught in a tight knot as he witnessed Will's naked grief.

"Now, I am imposing my stuff on you, hon, and your friend here," Will said, as he seemed to fully notice Ken for the first time.

"No, no," Ken protested. "Any friend of Muriel's is a friend of mine," Ken protested. "Ken Ferries," he said as he shook Will's work worn hand.

"Sure am obliged to you, Mr. Ferries. I am not always this obnoxious."

"You're all right, Will. Please just call me Ken."

"It's done, Ken," Will agreed.

A pickup pulled up with two people inside and parked in front of them. Jeff Colter came around the truck and said something to the woman passenger inside, then turned to them.

"Will, Muriel, what's happening?" he said as he nodded to Ken.

Muriel answered, "Oh, our Will here just overdone it and got sick so we brought him out to get some fresh air. He'll be all right."

"Listen, Will," Jeff said, "why don't you let me take you home?"

"Oh, Jeff, Ken and I were going to take him home but he isn't ready to go yet," Muriel said, still steadying Will.

"Is that right," Jeff said and stepped toward Will. "Well now, Muriel, you and Ken here just go on in there and dance. Will and me will go out to the ranch and, if he don't want to head out there tonight, he can come bunk with me." Ken noticed that Jeff had a determined stance as he stood squarely in front of an unsteady Will. "Come on now, Will. You get in the truck and we can go out to my spread tonight," and he took Will by the arm. Will brought his other arm up with a raised fist, trying to put it to Jeff's jaw. Jeff easily avoided the blow.

"Don't wanna go," Will lisped. "I gotta stay here. I can't stand it to go to bed. I just want my wife and she—oh, oh God—she's gone, Jeff and I want to die. I ain't no good any more for nothing."

"Jesus, Will, you can't do this and she wouldn't want you to," Jeff's voice rose with a terrible half sob. "God, man, I loved her too."

Will seemed to slump. "Okay, Jeff, I will go with you. Jeez, I'm sorry," Will's voice, though slurred, sounded like an obedient child's. "Good night, Muriel, Ken. Guess I am going home with Jeff here. Sure do thank you two."

"Good night, Will," Ken echoed the same.

Muriel reached up on an impulse and kissed his cheek. "Listen, handsome, you start keeping in touch now, you hear?"

"I promise, Muriel, sure enough." He seemed more sober now.

"Thank you, Jeff. I love you two cowboys," and she stepped to Jeff and hugged him tightly.

"Yep, me too, Muriel. Just don't worry. It's all gonna be okay," Jeff assured her.

"So, you keep in touch too, Jeff. Haven't seen you in some time, you know," Muriel said as Jeff was leading Will to his pickup.

He tipped his hat and briefly turned around. "I'll stop by before long, Muriel, and we can have a cup of java. I want to discuss something with you so I'll be calling soon to set up a time to get together." He bid Muriel and Ken both a good evening again and then opened the door of his truck for Will. The woman passenger moved over to make room for him.

"Say, Ken, I think that was Marilyn Allard in there with Jeff but he was probably taking her home and just saw us here in the parking lot. He probably wondered what was going on with all of us."

"Probably so," Ken agreed, "because he is bound to know Will is out there on the edge."

"Now that Will is safely in Jeff's care, that is a relief, at least for now. So we can get back in there," and she pointed to the dance hall. "And we are going to enjoy this evening because I think that you and I make a darn good pair on the dance floor."

Ken laughed as the earlier tensions began to leave and he tucked his arm through Muriel's. "Pretty woman, lead the way." They made their way through the crowd to Ham and Rosie Wilson and old Sage Murdock.

"Well, howdy, you two. Mom and me was wondering if you'd left," Ham drawled.

"Had a little meeting with Will Rogers. He had over-indulged and we took him outside. Then Jeff came by and took him out to his place," Muriel said.

"Damn shame about that man. Mom here and me, we've been real concerned about him. You feel so helpless, you know. God knows there sure aren't any better people agoing than Will." Ham put his head down and shook it from side to side.

"We just put that whole family in our prayers every day," Rosie said and her face took on a sad countenance.

Sage shook his white head sadly and cleared his throat loudly. As they stood there, a woman's voice from behind Muriel said, "Muriel, hi there."

Muriel turned toward the voice. "Well, Sissy, happy anniversary, girl."

"Why, thank you, Muriel." She smiled warmly at her and glanced at Ken.

"Oh, Sissy, this is my friend, Ken Ferries. Sissy Conway, Ken. That big redhead with the freckles is her husband. He's sneaking up on me to give me a big kiss because he likes to hear me squeal when he scares the daylights out of me. Stalking up from behind the way he has since he was ten years old," and she giggled.

"This girl's got eyes in the back of her head," the rugged but clean-cut man said as he hugged Muriel and kissed her lightly on the cheek.

Muriel introduced Ken and Bud Conway, and Ken noticed that they could both look directly into each other's eyes from the same level of height. Ken noted that the man had hands close to the size of hams and they were rock hard. He thought that, in the case of Sissy and Bud Conway, opposites did indeed attract, as the old saying went. Sissy was a tiny person, standing no more than five feet if even that tall since she had on high-heeled dress boots. Ken decided that he liked this couple on the spot.

"You know, Ken, Muriel used to babysit me and my brother, Abe. I had this hot crush on her and all she saw was this pesky brat kid," and he laughed good-naturedly.

"Yeah, and you are still that pesky kid," Muriel teased and then said, "Hey, happy anniversary, redhead, to you two. And you are a perfect couple, by the way." A Kenny Rodgers song "For the Good Times", accompanied by the band's vocalist, floated through the room. Muriel whispered in Ken's ear and he smiled at her and nodded. She reached for the elder Sage's hand and took him to the dance floor. The old man knew his way on the dance floor, Ken could see, as he glided with Muriel through the number. Ken asked Rosie to dance and she smiled at Ham. He grinned at them and nodded his approval.

"So, Mr. Ken, Phyllis tells me that your wife was a writer and that she and her darling mother loved her books. Now, she is such a dear, my little Phyl, and has loaned them to me to read."

"Yes, Gloria had developed a highly respected career as a writer. I was extremely proud of her, but above that, she was a wonderful wife and mother, a very lovely warm human being."

"Well, I do believe, my good man, that if she could, she would tell me she had a fine husband and father for her children."

"I believe she would, Rosie," and Ken smiled down at this perky saucy lady with the merry blue eyes.

"Now, the likes of that fine woman you are sporting here this evening would be a fine catch, if I may be so bold," Rosie said in her heavy Irish brogue, never wavering those keen blue eyes from his.

"Rosie, I am tending to believe that you are right. And since you are spoken for already, I think that Muriel is probably the next best catch." Though his eyes were full of amusement, he kept his face deeply serious.

"Ah, now, be going on with you and your blarney, Mr. Ken. But do you know what they say? Matchmakers come straight out of heaven." She laughed lightly and suddenly reached up and gave Ken a slight tweak to his cheek.

"You, Rosie, are a marvel and I am thinking that big fine man you're married to is deeply appreciative of that fact."

"Well, now, there's as fine a man as you would ever encounter, my Hamilton. I would be testifying to that fact. We've been together now going on fifty-one years."

"Rosie, you must have been a girl when you were married," Ken smiled at her.

"Not much more," she chirped. "I was a lass just coming twenty with the finest red hair that you ever did see and a quick temper to match. But, when Hamilton smiled at me standin' there on the village green in his uniform, I knew he was to be my husband indeed. It was love at first sight with the two of us." She looked so soft as she reminisced. In her eyes was a shine of deep love that Ken knew she had shared for better than half a century. "Of course, now what with that temper, we could get into some donnybrooks now and again, but then Hamilton knew all the right things to say and do," and she chuckled while her eyes danced with merriment.

"I just bet that he did, but the two of you must have done the right things that made a marriage sail for all those years."

"That is a fact plain to see. Maybe because, in my mind, even when there were those tough times, Ireland was a might bit far away so I would say to meself, 'now you see here Rosie McAllister Wilson, you'll be sticking to that man like corned beef and cabbage.'"

Ken tossed back his head and laughed heartily. He liked this sharp-witted white-haired woman and saw a flash of the girl with the flame-colored hair that hung down her back. The wind was lifting and twirling it around as she clutched desperately to keep a floppy straw hat on her head.

"I just bet you were quite the colleen and there was many a sad Irish lad when Ham took you away."

"Well now, there mighta been a couple," she grinned slyly and winked.

Ken walked her back to her husband who greeted them with "Well now, did my Rosie tell you some of her fairy tales straight out of Ireland? She has a ton of Irish lore, you know."

"Not a word did I peep because you know Mr. Ken here might well think old Rosie has a studdle in her noodle," and she wrinkled her little round nose and chuckled.

"Rosie, I would love to have you share some of the stories you know some day. I'm serious," he proclaimed while she waved a hand in protest, still chuckling.

"Oh, all right then. You bring Muriel out to the ranch one day and I will reward you with a fine Irish stew topped off with apple cobbler. Then we will sit down to as many old Irish tales as you can stand."

"You are going to have guests one day, dear lady, for that is an offer I am not about to refuse. Would it be all right if I tape the stories that you share with me?"

"Why, certainly, Mr. Ken. I would be quite honored if you transposed them into a book," and she beamed with pleasure.

"Yes, it could be titled something like Fairy Tales from Ireland and might be a book for all age groups," Ken said. "We could co-author it, if you like. I think it would prove to be a great book, not to mention the fun of putting it together," Ken said as Muriel and Sage joined them.

"Well, now I am truly blown away, Mr. Ken. If you think, after hearing all these tales, that they would merit being put down in a book, then you bet I think it would be a fine idea meself. Muriel, your man friend here wants to listen to the prattles of an old Irish woman tell the many tales of me homeland. Now what do you think of that?" Rosie was aglow with pleasure.

"Why Rosie, I think that would be wonderful. I have always felt that you should compile all of those marvelous stories into a book," Muriel said, sitting down across from Rosie and reaching for Ken's hand. She gave it a squeeze to show her joy. She felt such delight that Ken would bestow such a gift on her long-time dear friend.

"Ken, would you mind if I steal away with this sweet pretty woman for a dance?" Ham asked.

"Not at all," Ken assured him as Muriel stood up to join Ham for a slow dance. A young female singer with the band was singing in company with the male singer. The Randy Travis rendition was a favorite of Ken's and he was especially proud of his own collection of country music tapes. He knew that it was something else he had in common with this pretty woman he had fallen so deeply in love with. He watched her glide through the steps with Ham on the dance floor and felt such a mixture of exhilaration and over-the-moon joy that it was as bracing as a tonic. He was not aware of anyone else in that dance hall at that moment or he would have seen Angie and Will Earl come up to the table.

Angie touched his arm and smiled at him. "Penny for your thoughts," she purred, her green eyes so like her mother's looking teasingly at him.

"Hello, Angie, Will Earl," Ken said, starting to get up.

"No, no," they both protested. "We are here with some friends but we just saw you all over here and wanted to say hi," Angie said. Will Earl went over and hugged Rosie and then shook hands with Sage.

"Rosie, how are you?" Angie said. "Haven't seen you in a while," and she bent down to kiss the older woman on the cheek.

"Well, child, it has been a spell indeed. I must say that you are just getting prettier every time I see you."

"Thank you, Rosie. Mr. Murdock, how are you?" she said and walked around the table to hug the elderly man.

"Why, I'm as fit as a brand new fiddle, child. And you, I reckon, are more and more the picture of that pretty mother of yours every time I see you. This young rooster here better be on his toes now or some buckaroo will be trottin' off with you before Will Earl gets a rope on ya," and he gave a deep guffaw.

Will Earl pulled Angie's slim body close with one long arm and said, "Well, now, a man's gotta treat a pretty girl right, Mr. Murdock, else he shore enough will lose her so that's why I don't get any opposition," and his handsome face broke into a good-spirited grin.

"Atta boy, that there's usin' the old noggin, son," and the old fella nodded his approval.

Muriel and Ham returned and Angie lightly hugged her mother and greeted Ham. Will Earl walked over to the husky-framed Ham and shook his big hand.

"Well, I guess we'd better get back to our friends over there" and Will Earl nodded in the direction of the young couple sitting at a table close by.

"Have fun," Muriel called after them as they walked to the table where the couple sat. As they were getting ready to sit down, a pretty young woman walked up to their table with another young woman. Ken noticed that Will Earl looked uncomfortable but Angie smiled at the two girls, whom he supposed were around Angie's age.

"Oh, boy, here comes trouble," Muriel said and was shaking her head.

"Is that right?" Ken said searching Muriel's face quizzically.

"Yeah, I'm afraid so," she said low enough for just him to hear her.

As Ken followed Muriel's watchful gaze, he saw Angie say something to Will Earl, who looked uncomfortable. Then the pretty Hispanic girl pulled Will Earl out onto the dance floor. As they danced, Ken noticed that the girl had curly black hair and a rather fair complexion. She had an off-the-shoulder lacy blouse cut low that exposed a portion of her full and well-defined breasts. The full street-length skirt she wore showed off perfect shapely legs with extreme high-heeled shoes which did not in any way impair her easy sexy grace on the dance floor. She was a sensuous Latin beauty and Ken wagered a man would be hard put to resist her. Angie's beauty was classic, and though they were extreme opposites, they were both beautiful. The Hispanic girl was provocative while Angie was immutable and serene.

Ken asked Muriel to dance and they went to the floor. Muriel snuggled her head on Ken's shoulder and he sensed that her eyes were closed so he was certain that she did not see the Hispanic girl reach up to Will Earl and pull his face to hers. She held him there in a tight embrace, crushing her mouth to his. Her body was so close they were hardly moving as her sexy young hips swayed, getting the most mileage out of the close clinch. Will Earl reached upward and pulled her arms down, locking them behind her waist. Ken saw her sultry pout, but her wide eyes held an open invitation and stayed fixed on the handsome Will Earl. Ken could see that the young man was beset with frustration and arousal but he led the Latin beauty off the dance floor to her girl friend. She was engaged in a conversation with a young man sporting a wild-colored Western shirt. Another young man walked up to the couple as Will Earl and the girl were approaching them. He was part Indian and wore a fine Western hat decorated with conchos. His black leather vest with a white Western shirt served to accentuate his dark good looks. He smiled broadly at the girl with Will Earl and his eyebrows raised while he pursed his lips into a whistle. As Ken and Muriel danced by, Ken heard the man ask Will Earl, "Do you mind?" Will Earl shrugged, "Be my guest" and walked quickly away as the man asked the girl to dance.

Muriel was watching now too and Ken asked her who the wild beauty was.

"That's Carmen Muñoz and she's wild all right, at least over Will Earl. She uses every angle in the book to try and snare him."

"I sorta gathered that," Ken chuckled.

"Ticks me off," Muriel huffed, and Ken knew that her protective mother's instincts were on full raise.

"Oh, honey, I think that little Angie knows just how to handle that situation, so don't you fret now, Mama." He pulled her closer and kissed her there on the dance floor, caring little for the reactions of the on-lookers.

"You're right," she replied. "I think that daughter of mine is as wildly in love with Will Eaarl as her mom is over a Mr. Ferries. I would like to see anyone steal away with the men in our lives," and her face held pure passion while she looked into his eyes. Angie and Will Earl danced by now as Will tugged on Ken's jacket and said, "Howdy, you all." The young couple whirled away and Angie puckered her lips at her mother in the form of a kiss.

"They are going to be all right, Muriel. I think they are too deeply in love to let anything distance them," Ken said as he watched them dance over to the other young people in their company.

"Well, Carmen's mother Lupe is a good woman and she has worked as a part-time housekeeper for the Rogers family for some years. Billy, her father, and kid brother, Bobby, work out on the Rogers ranch. Carmen has helped her mother with a catering business since she was knee-high and so they are no strangers to hard work. Larry Gomez was real taken with Carmen and they dated some but Carmen's head has always been in a whirl over Will Earl, ever since she was a little kid. I used to shrug it off because lots of girls were ga-ga over him. I figured it was a kid's crush she would get over."

"Did Will Earl ever date Carmen?" Ken asked.

"No, not really like a date, just a whole group of kids all together with no special pairing off. Tyler did date her some but I think she scared Will Earl with her determined pursuit of him. Besides, he was always drawn to Angie. That seemed to escalate as they got older as it was always mutual. Lots of rodeo cowboys here tonight," Muriel pointed out to Ken as she looked around. "Maybe one or two of them will keep Carmen so busy she won't try to stir things up tonight."

"Sometimes I think it is more of an obsession than it is love when someone doesn't move on. Normally people come to realize that they need to get over it, you know." They stood there talking at the edge of the dance floor until Ken suggested that they go to the bar for a drink. The bar was in an extended area of the large dance hall.

"They don't serve hard liquor here, Ken, but they have soft drinks and coffee. Is that all right?"

"Sure, it's what I had in mind anyway. So let me get something for us and we'll sit down in there and talk a little while and catch our breath."

"Sounds good to me. I am thirsty so, hon, get me a ginger ale and I will just sit down here. My feet need a break." She clutched at his arm and smiled up at him. She strode to a table in a corner of the bar area and sat down.

"Here we go, a cool refresher," and he sat down beside Muriel. They faced the dance floor so they could watch the dancers.

"Ken, you are a darn good dancer," Muriel said as she picked up the glass of soda and took a lengthy swallow. "Whew, that is so refreshing."

"Thank you for the compliment, my lady, but you are a great dancer too so that makes it easy for me to look good," and he smiled with tenderness at this stunning woman.

"You, my dear, are such a flatterer and you gratify this lady's vanity to the max." She smiled in that deeply passionate way she reserved just for him.

"I think I am a good judge of dancing. Well, I should be because I practically lived in the dance hall when I was in college."

"Ken, is that how you met Gloria?" Muriel asked, watching his expression.

"Yes, it was. She had arrived alone and I looked up at the entrance of this big ballroom and I could see that she was looking for someone. Well, she was. As it happened, she was waiting for some other girls, one of them being a girl I kept watch for because we dated some and danced a lot together. We were just pals who shared a common interest in dancing. Anyway, when the other girls arrived, Gloria was just getting ready to leave. They caught up with her and they all came over to our table. Naturally, I cut right in before someone else made off with Gloria," he grinned at Muriel.

"Well, you two shared a good life together and I am so glad for you, Ken." And she added wistfully, "Mine and Bill's time was wonderful too, just too short though. I would love to have him see Angie growing up."

Ken reached for her hand and brought her fingers to his lips to kiss them tenderly. "Muriel, let's make every moment count because we both know that one never knows how long we have. I know we have something together that is as beautiful as what we both had in the past."

"Yes, we really do, don't we. I couldn't agree with you more. We will always celebrate our love and time together." Her voice was deeply husky and there was a dreamy look in her eyes as though she was remembering a time from long ago. "Ken, I want to ask you something, at the risk of perhaps sounding strange."

"Please ask. You know that I am far from being close-minded. You should know that by now, Muriel," he laughed lightly.

"Okay, so now I will just throw this out to you. Have you ever wondered if, in another time and place, you have known someone you recently met?"

"Well, maybe not quite the same way but yes, I have had occasions where I was either drawn to someone and had a feeling that I'd known the person forever. Or, by the same token, I've seen or met someone casually and had an instant aversion to them."

"Well, last night, I had this strange dream about you and we were dressed in clothes that looked like the Revolutionary Era. We were in a massive ballroom dancing. We were younger people than we are now but still it was us."

"I have at times since getting to know you felt like I have always known you. I did with Gloria and my children too. Of course, we can't really prove something like past lives because that is what it amounts to. But, on the other hand, I believe a powerful soul awareness surfaces every so often and speaks to us. Of course, so often people brush it off or try to search for another explanation," Ken said as he caressed her slender hand.

"I don't ever recall having a more vivid and clear dream. Between you and me, I think it was the two of us in that time span together." She went on, "I've never really thought too much about it, you know, the possibility of past lives, but I have dealt in astrology some just for the diversion."

"I am coming to realize more and more that everything we experience is for a reason, Muriel and so I would say that you were given a definite message. You have the wisdom not to just push it aside. After all, it would not have been so vivid a dream if it had not been meant to convey a message for you."

"There, you see, I just knew you would feel that way. I knew you would offer me some good logic and not brush it off as weird. After all, I've had my share of totally scattered dreams, as everyone does. But this one wasn't like that at all."

"It is in all probability that you, my sweet lady, are beginning to open to things unseen, just as I have. Maybe it is because we operate from the same type of internal rhythm that we came together at this time yet again."

"Gotcha, honey," she smiled, feeling total rapport with Ken's statement. "I would wager that we have just started on a blow-your-mind journey together."

"You can count on it," Ken assured her with an assurance he could feel in the deepest source of his being. "Are you ready to try another whirl on the dance floor?" Ken offered.

"Never turn down a dance, especially when it is proposed by a good-looking man," she flirted teasingly.

"Then, lady, lead the way," and he cupped his hand under her arm as they made their way back to the dance floor. They danced almost every dance together for the rest of that evening or sat with Sage Murdock and the Wilsons at their table. Ken engaged Sage in a conversation about his ranch while Muriel was dancing with Bud Conway.

"Have you lived here all your life, Mr. Murdock?" Ken ventured in friendly conversation with the old rancher.

"Well now son, you just call me Sage. Yep, been here all my life and watched a big share of these folks grow up," he laughed. "Guess that about makes me dang near as old as these hills, I reckon. My grandpappy come here, now that was a spell back. He settled this area and I am on the same old homestead he started clean back in the mid 1800s."

"Sage, I would fully enjoy it if you would share some of you and your family's experiences with me. I expect you know the whole Rogers family quite well since they have been here for a number of years."

"Right as rain," the old man said. "Young Will's parents came here soon after they were married. Good people to the core. I watched them spring from meager conditions to some of the biggest ranchers in the state." He went on, "Now, there are two folks who prospered from back-breaking work. I tell you, that was tough times but they honed out a fortune and part of it was that Will Senior had plenty of foresight. Now I don't reckon that anything has ever happened to that fine family with all the hard times that was anything compared to the loss of young Will's wife. Losing her life at the hands of them people… but there, I suppose now I shouldn't have mentioned that." He bowed his craggy white head, then suddenly lifted it as though from some inner prompting. He focused his keen brown eyes on Ken and said, "You know, it was a bit strange the day that terrible thing came about."

He stopped so Ken said, "Sage, please go on."

"Well, sir, I live about two miles down the road from Will's spread and I tell you old Tatter was raising cane the morning they found that pretty wife of Will's. Now Tatter, he is my dog, a fine Border collie." Sage looked down at his folded hands and steadied them a moment before going on. "I was having a cup of java before taking my usual mosey around the place. Tatter was raising cane. Now mind, he ain't given to that, well not to excess. Oh, now, he'll bark when someone drives up, all right, but it just weren't the same, you know? That dog had spotted something that clearly unsettled him, so naturally I stepped out on my side porch off the kitchen to take me a look see. I called to Tatter and he comes right over. He's a good dog. I look in the direction of the barn and he is growling low in his throat. I just figure maybe I ought to fetch my firearm. So I go and retrieve my rifle and I can still hear that dog barking, just having fits. I'm thinking that maybe it's an animal of some kind after the calves or maybe after the chickens. I got some calves behind the barn's back entrance and a big chicken pen on one side of the barn."

"Well, now Tatter and me head on down towards the barn and he is keen enough, he has stopped the barking. But he is still growling and the hairs bristled up on his neck and back. We step in the barn and I see that nothing is disturbing the chickens. But I tell you, just when we stepped in there, a man tore out of there like he was on fire. Law, he startled me so bad. All I made out was he had on some of them jogging shorts and jogging shoes. Now mind, I never did see what way he took off because Tatter was after him in a flash. By the time I got to the back entrance, the man had cleared the corral fence and was off like a shot into the brush and trees. Now, what he was doin' there, I'll be switched if I know. But it was a might unsettling and all after I heard about Nadine Rogers."

"Sage, do you happen to remember the time it was that morning when it took place?" Ken prompted the man.

"Roughly around eight a.m. or shortly after because, you see, I rise early and go feed the stock and chickens. Then I cook up a little grub. It's been my way for so long I reckon I can't recall when it weren't." He narrowed his eyes in a squint trying to recall the details. "Well, sir, I take my second cup of java and sip it slow whilst I listen to the eight o'clock morning news. Then I go make my rounds on the spread. I got a catfish pond on the place and I usually fry up some fresh cat for breakfast. That's what I was havin' that morning and I ain't even sure why that stands out in my mind. But I recall I had just set my plate in the sink and poured me some java, then I turned on the radio for the news and old Tatter commenced to set up a clatter."

"Sage, did you notice anything else about the man you saw?" Ken asked when Sage didn't say any more. He hadn't wanted to interrupt Sage's train of thought.

"Hmm," Sage said thoughtfully as he rubbed his throat. "Seemed he was well-built, not out of the ordinary for size but in good condition. Now, by cracky, I do recall that he had one of them there bands around his head, sure enough."

"Like maybe a sweat band, Sage?" Ken asked him.

"Yep. Sorta like them hippy fellas is fond of wearin'. I can't tell you rightly what color his hair was but I do remember how he was dressed. He had on some sorta sleeveless shirt, like them t-shirts them joggers wear."

"Did you ever mention this to anyone besides me, Sage?" Ken waited for the elderly man to respond as he studied this spry old rancher.

"Well, no, can't say as I did. 'Cause you see, at the time, I just figured maybe it was one of them joggers that was takin' himself a rest from the heat in the barn and old Tatter didn't take kindly to him. Rightly now that came to mind after I had gone back in the house and thought some on it."

"Are there many joggers you see out that way, Sage?"

"Oh, not a lot but every now and then a few of them fool-hardy folks are out on the main road that passes my place. They go early of a morning afore it gets too hot in the day. I spot 'em now and again 'cause I ain't set back too far off the main road. Law, I reckon now I am just clean out of step with all that. Beats me why anybody would want to get out there a draggin' their keisters up and down the roadway huffin' and puffin', sweatin' their brains out." He shook his white head and snorted at his statement.

Ken smiled at the elderly man. "Well, Sage, it truly is a different world and I know what you mean, all right," he said in a philosophical reasoning spirit. Ken found this aging and historical man to his liking. He looked around to see if he could spot Muriel and, as he did, the Wilsons were walking back to their table.

"Say now, Ken, Muriel will be here in a minute. She is talking to Sissy and Bud Conway at their table." Rosie was looking flushed from dancing as Ham helped seat her at the table.

"Oh, well, that's find, Rosie. Sage here and I have been having a good visit."

"Sure as hootin'" the old man agreed. And I would enjoy the pleasure of your company any time you can stop in. I always got a pot of java on for my friends."

"Why, that's right good of you, Sage. I aim to take you up on that in the near future," and Ken shook hands with the man as he stood up.

"I am countin' on it, Ken. You bring that pretty lady with you now, sure enough. I got so many eggs from my old biddy hens I can't get them all sold. I can't eat that many so you plan on the two of you takin' some off my hands. Well, it's gettin' way past an old man's bedtime so I will tell you all good night. I have enjoyed the evening with you find folk."

"Well, sir, the pleasure's been mine." Ken stood up and shook Sage's hand as he clasped his shoulder in a friendly gesture.

"You be careful now going home," Rosie instructed the lean old fella. He picked up his Western hat and Ken couldn't help admiring the slender hard body of this man who had to be at least eighty years old.

"Oh now, Rosie, don't you fret. I reckon I could drive that route blindfolded I been over it so many times." Those keen brown eyes held cheerfulness, for that was what held the resiliency of this sturdy kindly soul. As earlier with Rosie, Ken now saw momentarily the remaining essence of a younger Sage, a stately slender cowboy with keen brown eyes and wind-tanned skin with rakish good looks. Ken shook his head slightly and the vision cleared as Muriel walked up and put her arm around Sage.

"Are you leaving us, Sage?"

"Yep, gotta hit the hay. But it has been right fine being in the company of you all. I'll be meetin' up with ya soon, if the good Lord's willin'." He tipped his hat at them and made his way toward the dance hall entrance.

Ham chuckled as Ken settled Muriel at the table. "That old gent never ceases to amaze me. Why, he has got more stamina than a lot of these cowboys half his age. Up until about three years ago, he was bustin' broncos. I don't think he would have quit when he did but Dottie, his sister, raised cane with him. Like he told me, he'd about as soon go through fire and brimstone when Dot's got her hat squared on a matter."

"Well, he is an admirable man, all right," Ken agreed.

"Ken, I got caught up talking to Bud and Sissy. You probably wondered if I'd forgotten you," Muriel said touching his arm.

"No, I was enjoying Sage's and my conversation. I figured that you had probably run across some other friends."

"I usually do when I come here because I know just about every person here and we get long-winded." She laughed lightly.

"I'd say that is good for you, lady," he smiled lovingly into her pretty eyes.

Angie walked up to their table with Will Earl trailing behind. She placed her slender young hand on Ken's shoulder. "Want to glide a college girl around the floor, Ken?" Her eyes so like her mother's smiled down at him.

"Why, Angie, you bet. I am honored, honey." He rose to take her smoothly to the dance floor as Will Earl and Muriel went to the dance floor too.

"Ken, my mom looks happier than I have seen her in quite awhile. You know, that really took a toll on her when we lost Nadine." Angie bit her upper lip as her eyes grew large with unshed tears. "Oh, Lord, I guess because they were so close and all and it was bad enough the way it was. Just such a terrible thing, you know. You are a good person, Ken Ferries, and I like you a lot. I just want you to know that whatever happens with you and Mom, you've given her joy that she's surely been lacking for some time."

"Your mother is a beautiful woman, inside and out, Angie. I guess since you have told me what you have, I want to tell you that I am in love with your mother."

Angie stopped dead still on the dance floor and squealed softly. Then she reached up standing on her tiptoes and kissed Ken soundly on his cheek. Ken chuckled and felt his heart spring with the total joy of acceptance from this lovely young woman.

"Ken, is it okay if I tell Will Earl?" Angie asked shyly, looking up at him with such a happy radiance on her face.

"I just don't mind at all, young lady, because I haven't tried to cover it up and certainly not from that pretty mother of yours."

"Ken, this is the best thing that has happened for our family in a long time. Now if I could just see some healing for Will Earl's family so that family can draw together again. It has about destroyed all of them," Angie said wistfully.

"Well, honey, with folks like you and your mother and other people here, I think in time they will have some healing. Granted, there will always be scars but life is on-going and the process will be a healing one for each of them in their own way. See, Angie, there is no set time on the grief process, I mean the heaviest of it. But, in a case like this, it will take great effort on everyone's part to glean some much-needed healing so all of them can embrace life once more."

"You are so right on, Ken, and I feel better just talking about it with you. Say, your daughter and son lucked out having a father like you." Her smile was warm and engaging.

"Sweet child, your mother was blessed by all that is Holy getting a daughter like you. Trust me, she knows it too. And Angie, thank you for the compliment."

"Likewise," she said as he led her back to the table to be joined by Muriel and Will Earl.

As they stood there, Will Earl suddenly took Angie's arm and cupped his hand under her elbow, saying, "Well now, you all, reckon we will be running along but we'll see you later." He thanked Muriel for the dance and then, rather hastily, pulled Angie away. Angie appeared surprised but then Ken noticed Carmen approaching their table.

"Well, that was fast foot work," Muriel said, arching her eyebrows in question.

Ken noticed that Carmen was standing there looking after the retreating couple. He didn't tell Muriel that he had noticed what precipitated Will Earl's abrupt departure. Apparently, Carmen was of the mindset that it's a jungle out there and all's fair in love and war. It was a mystery that Ken had found difficult to understand because he reasoned that a girl with such extraordinary attractiveness didn't have one shred of trouble drawing men to her like bees to honey. Of course, Will Earl was not showing her the same attention. Angie was the kind of girl who had that inner light some women possess. Her mother had that same magnetism. Ken knew that was one of the reasons Will Earl was in love with Angie.

In order to draw Muriel's attention away from the couple's hasty exit, he pulled her to him and they danced. While he held her close, he whispered, "I love you, Muriel." And he kissed her ear.

"I love you, Ken," she responded and he could feel her heart beat against his broad chest. They danced until the last dance was called and Ken felt more alive that he could remember with this woman he loved so hopelessly.

They told the Wilsons good night and walked out into the night to be greeted by a full silver moon. It looked like some precious metallic element that had outdone itself with stupendous and preposterous overhang.

"Muriel, did you ever see a moon like that? That is something to behold! One for the record books, I'd say."

"It is just especially for us, Ken—a grand flourish on our behalf. It's our moon this night," and she snuggled closer to him as they made their way to the car.

He wanted to take her to his motel room where they could unleash the passion they both felt and make love all night. Yet he knew that it was not the time, not yet, even though it was what they both wanted pressingly. He knew that Angie was home for a visit and he felt that it was just not the "above board" thing for them to do. After all, the girl had hardly gotten to know him, he reasoned, and to keep her mother out all night with him did not set good in his mind. He wanted to get off on a good footing with Angie and, when he and Muriel did come together fully, he wanted it to be a beautiful expression of their total surrender with nothing to depreciate it in any way.

Angie was so in love with Will Earl, it was obvious. And yet she used a level head, knowing she had college to finish and Will Earl needed time to go through the hardest throws of grieving. So, he reasoned, in view of that kind of maturity in one so young, he and Muriel could certainly express as much maturity as Angie was showing.

They reached the car and Ken opened the door for Muriel. As he walked to the driver's side, he sensed rather than saw that he was being regarded by someone or something. He felt a sudden prickle up his back. He looked around and saw at the farthest end of the parking lot, in an area of shade trees and flowering shrubs, the glow from a cigarette. It was an instinct he had long ago learned to pay attention to from his years as a journalist and his training in the military. He recalled that, hours earlier, he had received a threat at his motel room and knew that it was tactical to be a bit paranoid and keep his guard up.

The cigarette glow suddenly went out and Ken climbed into the car, saying nothing to Muriel as he put the key into the ignition.

"Ken, is something wrong?" she questioned.

He did not want to alarm her so he passed it off as just taking another look at the night's enormous moon. She snuggled up to him and they made their way to her home, not talking, just basking in their own thoughts. They reached Muriel's home, and by the light in the living room, Ken knew that Angie was home already.

"Will you come in and have some coffee,Ken?" Muriel suggested.

"Sweetheart, it is late but I will come for you in the morning. We will go have breakfast and then take in that rodeo, if that is agreeable to you." He searched her face to see if she wondered why they hadn't gone ahead to his room. If that was the case, she gave no indication of it from her manner.

Ken saw her to the door. They kissed lingeringly until she pulled away and opened the door. "Is eight thirty all right then?"

"That is fine with me," he assured her and took her hand, palm up, and kissed it. "Love you, pretty lady," he whispered. "Sleep well, honey."

"Yes, I will certainly try, and you too." Her voice was extra husky.

"Muriel, is everything all right?" he asked.

"Sure is. I love you too, it is just…." And she hesitated, "well, it is hard to let you go. I know why and I am even more in love with you for that kind of insight because it expresses that special kind of character you have. Thank you for that."

"I should have known that you would realize why I didn't just take you straight to my room because, God knows, I wanted to. Oh, baby, it is not easy for either one of us, I know."

"Well, now, our time is coming soon," she crooned softly. It will be even better this way."

He didn't say anything, just kissed her hungrily and almost roughly, then turned to bound from the porch to his car. She opened the door to her house and the light silhouetted her hair. He ached to run back and take what they both longed for. Instead, he drove straight to the motel with his mind clambering about Muriel. He knew it would not be long until they made love and it gave him near breathless heaviness in his chest, the deep stirrings of a man in love.

Chapter_____7

At the motel, before exiting his car, he made certain that no one stood in some shadowed area to take him by surprise. Sarita had been right when she had cautioned him to watch his backside. Again, he was grateful for the lights posted at each door of the motel rooms.

When he got inside his room, he checked to see if there were messages. When there were none, he began to disrobe and head for the shower. He let the water run down upon him for some time after he had bathed, allowing himself to enjoy the full flow of stinging pellets that massaged him. He knew this would not only refresh him but, hopefully, relax him enough that he could get to sleep.

When he stepped from the shower, he heard the phone ring and went to answer it after a quick rub with the towel. He picked up the receiver and said nothing but he knew someone was on the line. Finally, the same male voice that had called earlier spoke.

"Ken Ferries, you'd be wise to move on and mind your business." Ken still didn't speak. "Do you get my drift?" And then he hung up.

Ken could feel the ire more than fear build up within him. He made a silent vow that he would dig as deep as he could to find out who took Nadine Roger's life. He finished drying off with a vigorous rubdown and then decided he would crawl into bed with just the sheet over him. The air seemed somewhat heavy so he surmised that a storm was about to set in. He lay there awhile, mulling over the phone call, and thought that the man who had called him was growing more alarmed by the simple fact that Ken was asking questions about the case. And the questions were indicative of the speculations regarding the murder case and they were being asked by a well-known former news reporter. Apparently, the man had concluded that a well-known reporter, one who had investigated numerous crimes, was apt to stumble onto some concrete evidence.

"Well now mister, whoever you are, don't look for me to take a swan song any time soon," he said aloud. Ken reasoned that, if this man made too much of a statement, if he overstepped certain boundaries, he would give cause for an all-out investigation. Ken doubted that he would press that much. Therefore, he concluded, he was trying to scare him off but had too much to lose if he made an attempt at violence. However, he was not foolhardy either. He knew enough of human nature to fully understand that a person of that ilk, when cornered, is capable of anything to escape retribution.

As he lay awake, the sound of the wind came clearly. It seemed to pick up exuberance rather quickly and lightning flashed suddenly, giving off an eerie glow in the room. A thunderous blast followed that shook the window. The thunder sounded as though it must have been directly overhead. He could then hear the rain coming down like the rupture of a dam. He arose to open the drapes and take a look at nature's grand and dramatic performance. He could feel the hair on his body raise and thought how much a part of this we are too, even this magnificent display of wild energy.

The storm lessened its ferocity after another half hour and the rain became a gentle pattern, after having liberated its oppression. The land sorely needed this rain, Ken thought as he drifted away into sleep. He dreamt of an enormous red-tailed hawk flying toward him which suddenly turned into old Nathan Tom Nathan's fierce black eyes staring into his as he stood on the grassy green hill. He slept on with such wild and scattered dreams, seeing an Indian girl with a white half-wolf dog standing on yet another high hill. Then she pointed to the arch of rainbow that was as colorful as the one he had seen over Nathan earlier at his ranch.

He awoke feeling refreshed even though he had dreamed sequential dreams that had remained in continuous order. He showered again to become centered and ready for the day as he thought of the dreams and the messages they contained. He had time, after he dressed, to put down some notes so when he returned home, he would be able to transcribe them onto the computer. He checked the time and decided to call Sarita to give her mind some ease. He knew she would be concerned about him if he didn't call.

"Sarita, Ken here." She answered the phone on the second ring.

"Ah, yes, and how are you, my hombre. I listen to the news this morning and the reports say you have a storm?" She went on before he could respond. "I was going to call you this very evening, amigo, if you had not called." Ken suppressed a chuckle as he thought of his earlier reasoning. Yes, he knew Sarita so well.

"Well, yes Sarita, I am fine. And yes, that was a wild storm for a good half hour but then it petered out into a nice steady rain. It's all gone now though. How are you, Sarita?" he questioned.

"Oh, seguro que si (of course) not to worry, señor, but Maggie misses you mucho."

Ken again suppressed a chuckle. "Well, now Sarita, I miss Maggie and you, dear Señora," he added. Then, before she could protest her independence, he went on. "Yes, I know you are doing fine, Sarita, but I do enjoy our eventful conversations. I will be home no later than Tuesday, sometime that day."

"Then I will see you on Tuesday, my amigo," she responded. They both said adios.

It was getting close to the time that he was to pick up Muriel for breakfast. He double-checked the door to his room as he went out, making certain it was locked. He reasoned that it locked the minute he closed it but he still felt the effects of the two phone calls from the threatening stranger. The marmalade cat walked up to wind itself around Ken's pant legs, calling out in soft meowing friendship.

"Hello there, kitty cat," Ken said and bent down to run his hand lightly down the length of the cat's soft furry back. He thought of Milky, his white long-haired cat who kept vigil at the foot of the birdhouse most of the time. He liked animals great and small and had often felt he had been fortunate to grow up as a country boy.

The cat's attention was suddenly diverted by a white miller and he crouched low while stealing toward the unsuspecting prey. Then, in one grand leap, he caught the miller in both paws and proceeded to make a tiny meal of it.

Ken opened the door of his car and climbed in, but his attention was caught by a piece of paper on the windshield, held fast by the wiper blade. He reached for the paper and noticed that the message had been hand printed. The paper was dry so he knew it had been put on the car sometime this morning. Ken studied the contents closely as he read it. He had seen no one at the motel save for the young Hispanic woman who was pushing along a service cart of cleaning agents and linens. He put the note inside his shirt pocket and got out of the car. He walked over to the young woman.

"Good morning, ma'am," and she regarded him with a slight smile as she nodded her acknowledgment. "Ma'am, someone left a note on my car this morning. I was wondering if perhaps you saw them leave it?"

"Si," she said and nodded her head.

"Was it a man?" And again she nodded her head.

"Was he in a vehicle?" Ken pressed on.

The girl shook her head and explained in broken English that he was on foot. She had met him as she came out with the supply cart about an hour earlier. She described him as wearing jeans, boots, and a well-worn Western hat. He looked like he was maybe in his late forties.

"I do thank you. Gracias," Ken said, smiling down at the small-figured woman who was not much more than a girl.

"De nada," (don't mention it, you're welcome) and the girl smiled and shrugged her slender shoulders.

Ken returned to his car and climbed in, then started it up and vowed to watch even closer from now on. As he drove out to Muriel's, he went over in his mind the contents of the note. It wasn't so much the content but the script, Ken thought. Why, he didn't understand, but it somehow seemed familiar to him. It was certainly a man's writing and the tone of the note seemed a male design. The note was very explicit and to the point. It stated that time was running out and "If you don't heed this and get the hell back to Waco where you belong, you are going to get hurt!!!" Ken had received some threats over the years but never to this extreme significance. It occurred to him that perhaps he had already unknowingly hit upon something that was unraveling for this person.

"Well, I am not going mention this to anyone except Bruster," he said aloud, while he noticed the fresh look to everything a good rain always issues. When he arrived in the driveway at the side entrance of Murials home Angie was picking sweetpeas. She waved with her free hand while smelling the sweetpeas that she held up close to her face.

"Hi there, young lady," Ken greeted her as he got out of the car.

"Hi back at you, Ken. Just come here and smell this delightful fragrance." She smiled and held the bountiful colors out for him to inhale.

"Oh my, they do smell heavenly, Angie," he attested.

"Come on in. Mom's about ready," she said as she slipped her slender arm through his. As they entered the laundry room, she stepped ahead of him into the kitchen.

"Sit down, Ken, please," and she indicated a chair at the kitchen table. "I will just fetch a vase for these." She stood on tiptoes to reach for one in the cupboard. She filled the vase with water and expertly arranged the flowers, then stood back to appraise her work. "Pretty, huh?" She placed them on the kitchen table.

Ken agreed that they were but said, "They are not one whit prettier than the young lady who picked them."

"I do thank you for that, kind sir," she gushed modestly and reached for the coffee pot and filled a mug.

"Here you go, Ken," and she placed it in front of him at the table.

"Thank you, but I probably won't finish it all before your Mom is ready to go."

"That's OK," she shrugged. "If you are like my mother, she has got to head for the coffee pot first thing of a morning. Besides, I'll bet you haven't had a cup of coffee yet this morning."

"No, ma'am, I sure haven't. I do appreciate it too. By the way, do you want to have breakfast with your mother and me because you are certainly welcome."

She pondered that a moment and then said, "Tell you what. Will Earl is on his way here to pick me up and I will ask him if we can't join you and Mom."

"Very good, Angie, because we would like that, your mother and I," he assured her. They heard a vehicle pull into the driveway and Angie's face lighted.

"That's probably Will Earl now." She went to the laundry room entrance to see him in and Ken heard Will Earl's deep voice say, "Howdy, honey bear."

He heard them giggling and he guessed what had transpired out in the laundry room. He judged that there was some fun-loving horse play in progress. He had no doubt of it when they returned to the kitchen with Angie's flushed cheeks and Will Earl's eyes full of spark and mischief.

Muriel walked into the kitchen then and bent down to place a warm kiss on Ken while Angie and Will Earl looked on. Then she smiled at her daughter and Will Earl, who in turn were looking knowingly at each other, their young faces both grinning broadly.

"Now, Auntie, I just don't reckon I had better even go there, huh," and his eyes held a teasing note.

Muriel pointed a long finger at him and put out a mock threat in her eyes. Will's smile just grew even broader and he winked boldly at her.

"Say, Will Earl, Ken has invited us to go to breakfast with him and Mom. So, how's about it?" Angie purred up at him playfully, batting her eyes.

"Why sure, Ang," he smiled at Ken. "Now tell me, just how can a man refuse? Would you take a look at little miss splendiferous here and tell me that I could logically refuse her anything?" and he hugged her closely to him. "So, sure, you bet we will, Ken. Thank you for asking us. Angie has to leave late this afternoon to get back to school so it would be great to spend that time with you and Aunt Muriel over breakfast."

"All right, that is settled. Now, may I suggest that we go to Dolly's since it is the only breakfast place in town?" Muriel ventured. They all chorused agreement and then made their way out to their vehicles.

"Muriel, that is a great outfit you have on, honey," Ken said as he held the car door open for her.

"Thank you. I'm glad you like it. Everyone tells me that this is a good color for me because this shade of green brings out my eyes.

"Yes," he said and then grinned in flirtation at her, "and, baby, it brings my eyes out too."

"Here, here, that kind of flattery can get you anywhere, you know, so watch out," she smiled at him. "Ken, you look terrific yourself."

"Honey, I am terrific, just you wait," he told her in an enticing sexy manner, giving way to a lighthearted frivolity that this beautiful woman brought out in him.

"Ken Ferries, I do believe you are leading me astray," and she giggled self-consciously.

Ken liked that about her and he looked with such tenderness while she placed her hand under her hair and rubbed her neck. It was just one of the endearing habits she had that he had filed away in his heart.

They met Angie and Will Earl at the entrance to Dolly's Café and Will Earl held the door open for them to enter. There was a free booth at the end and they made their way to it.

"This place is really full this morning, what with that rodeo going on today. We are lucky to get this booth and not have to wait," Muriel commented as she looked around.

The waitress brought menus and the coffee pot over, then smiled at Muriel. "Well, good morning, Muriel, Angie, Will Earl. How you all doing?" She looked at Ken, still smiling.

Muriel said, "Hi Annie. We are all just right as rain. Say, meet Ken Ferries here. He's a friend of ours from Waco."

"Now, it is a pleasure to meet you," the woman said and Ken thought she was probably about Muriel's age.

"It's nice to meet you, ma'am," Ken said while she was filling the coffee mugs.

"Oh now, shoot. Just call me Annie like everyone does around here," she said still smiling down at him with large chocolate brown eyes and an abundance of dark hair piled high. She had an instant likeableness about her that sprang from a happy disposition. "Angie, you home for awhile now?" she asked.

"No, Annie, I just got away for the weekend. Have to head back late this afternoon but wish I could hang around longer. Can't though as the books await me."

"Will Earl, you riding today on one of them bronco horses at the rodeo?" Annie asked.

"Aw, not this time. I want to spend all the time I can with Ang here." He added, "But I think Tyler is signed up for it. How about your son Joe Jr? Is he signed up to be in it today?"

"Against his mother's better judgment, like always. Yes, he is," and she shook her head. "You young buckaroos have iron in your hind end instead of hide, I reckon. Oh well, cowboys will be cowboys and so mothers just have to tend to their bruises and pray."

Ken watched Will Earl swallow hard and he knew that it was just a chance remark on Annie's part.

"Say, those buckwheat cakes are the special this morning with side orders of a couple eggs and bacon," she said with her order pad poised.

They all agreed on the buckwheat cakes all the way around. Ken watched Will Earl and, in an effort to remove him from the place he knew he was in, he began light conversation.

"Say, Will Earl, do you raise any crops on your father's ranch? I know it is a beef cattle ranch and your father has a lot of cattle."

Will Earl cleared his throat before responding. "Well, yes, as a matter of fact, we do. Alfalfa, mainly, and it is top grade. This neck of the woods just seems to have the right soil for raising it."

"Howdy, you all," a smiling Tyler said as he approached their table.

"Well, little brother, howdy right back at you," Will Earl visibly brightened at the sight of his brother. Angie slid over closer to Will Earl and patted the seat beside her.

Tyler was dressed in a blazing red and white bold-striped Western shirt, blue jeans, and tennis shoes. The color of the shirt did justice to his yellow-white hair. His gray Stetson hung down between his shoulder blades tethered by a braided leather cord with a horse hair fringe. He could cinch it with a clip on the braid to seat it firmly on his head.

"You gonna ride today, aren't you, Ty?" Will Earl asked.

"Sure enough. I guess I am pure glutton for punishment 'cause if I wasn't, after working on training that stud for Sheriff Bruster yesterday, then I guess I got a little streak of pure crazy in me." He grinned and his face took on a more boyish appearance.

"It is the testosterone, trust me," Muriel crooned as she reached across the table and patted his hand. The color rose in Tyler's cheeks while Angie smothered a giggle. Will Earl chuckled and reached over Angie to give a playful pat to the top of Tyler's head.

Auntie, you be good now," Tyler protested while trying to escape Angie's attempt to tousle his hair. He grabbed her small wrist and said, "Help, help," in jest.

Ken noticed for the first time the array of freckles across Tyler's slightly turned-up nose. He favored his sister Phyllis more than he did his brother.

"Hey, bro, you are gonna shed the tennis shoes before you climb aboard one of them cayuses since I reckon you'll need all the protection you can muster," Will Earl cautioned him.

"Oh, ya, got my riding boots in my truck. I learned my lesson when I got my big toe broke a couple years ago." He whistled low, "That one made me take some notice."

"Well, ride 'em, cowboy but come back to us put together like you went in there, Ty." Angie smiled at him with fondness.

"Say, Tyler, how about some breakfast?" Ken offered.

"Oh, don't reckon I better since I will be getting tossed from here to kingdom hill, but I would take a glass of orange juice. Much obliged, Ken."

"All right then, a glass of o.j. it is," and he motioned to Annie.

"This young man could use a tall chilled glass of orange juice, Annie," and he indicated Tyler.

"Coming right up," she said. "And how's Ty these days?"

"Doing good and reckon I'll be seeing Joe Jr. at the rodeo today."

"Oh, yes. You know Joe, Jr. He wouldn't miss being in the whole shootin' match, just like Joe Sr. always was until he decided he better stop riding them mean critters. When you hit fifty, your bones don't take right kindly to that kind of mistreatment."

"Well now Annie, I guess Joe Jr. and me has got a few good years then, that is if we hang loose," and he grinned up at her.

She patted his shoulder and retreated to get his juice.

The good-natured ribbing continued throughout breakfast and once again Ken thought how much he had missed family camaraderie in the past five years. The gatherings of his clan were too few and far between due to the distances of his adult children.

"Well, I best be moseying over to the rodeo grounds to get signed in," and Tyler stood up and thanked Ken. "Be seeing you all later."

Ken watched him as he made his way to the door. He suddenly felt that cold downdraft he had experienced before. Tyler paused at the door, then turned to give them a quick smile and wave. The chill coursed through him and he visibly shivered. He felt as though every nerve within his body was filled with a strange awareness. He had watched young Tyler leave and could see every person in the café from his vantage point except the other booths behind where they were seated. However seated at the counter was old Nathan Tom.

Ken knew he had not been there until that very second. Black eyes the color of coal held fast upon Ken for the old Indian was turned in his direction. It was strange because it occurred to Ken that no other person except himself seemed to be aware of this ancient, imposing man. People walking right by him or seated next to him took no notice of his presence.

"Ken, is something wrong?" Muriel said.

223

Ken kept his eyes straight on Nathan and did not turn to look at Muriel as he answered. "Muriel, look straight ahead at the counter closest to the door and tell me who you see."

"Well, there's old Dade Cameron, Billy Swarts, and young Freddie McCoy. Why?"

"You don't see anyone else then," he said feeling himself pressed with an anxiety in the pit of his stomach.

"Honey, no, not at that end of the counter. I see one empty chair between a couple guys I don't know. Why?"

Ken realized that Muriel's voice had taken on a note of concern and he sensed that Will Earl and Angie were regarding him.

"Oh, nothing. I just thought that I saw someone I met the other day and I was just trying to recall his name," he lied.

Ken looked momentarily at Will Earl and Angie. He could see the questions he knew they had left their faces at his answer. Then he quickly looked back to Nathan and found he had completely vanished! Ken knew the man could not have humanly vanished in that few seconds he had glanced at Will Earl and Angie.

"Say, it is getting time to think about heading on out to the rodeo grounds," Will Earl said as he checked his watch.

"All right, I will just take care of this check and we'll get going," Ken agreed as they all made their way out of the booth.

"Hey, Ken, I've got the tip," Will Earl said as Ken was reaching in his vest pocket for his billfold.

Angie reached up to Ken and gave him a hug. "Thank you for breakfast and everything," she smiled at him and he knew she was referring to the conversation they had had at the dance.

"Yeah, Ken, thanks. But now the next time is on me." Will Earl reached for his hand and shook it.

"Mom, love you. We'll see you and Ken at the rodeo." She hugged her mother to her.

As the young couple made their way to the door, Ken and Muriel paused to pay the bill. When that was done, they walked to Ken's car parked a short distance form the café. Once they were both inside, Muriel turned to Ken.

"All right now, Ken. What was that all about?" she said as he turned to focus fully on her.

"Oh, you didn't buy my little white lie, I see," and he laughed lightly.

"I do feel, Mr. Ferries, that I am coming to know you pretty well with all that we have shared so far," she said pointedly and grinned tauntingly at him.

"You are one sexy woman, Muriel Jacob, and I am ever a human male. It has not been easy to hold off," he picked up her hand, drew it to him palm up and ran his tongue lightly on it. Then he kissed her hand top and bottom. He could hear the intake of Muriel's breath and he winked at her.

"Okay, hon. I saw old Nathan Tom as plain as day sitting there between the two guys that you said were strangers to you. I kept my eyes fixed right on him when I noticed him and I do not know how I could see him as plainly as I see you right now." He went on, "You see, when you asked me if there was something wrong, I answered but I did not look at you. Then I asked you who all you could see closest to the door at the counter. You indicated that there was a vacant seat at the counter between the two fellas that you didn't know, right?"

Muriel nodded her head in agreement and Ken proceeded, "Now, you could not see Nathan but I did plainly. I am certain that no one else saw him either. When you sounded a bit alarmed, I looked for less than two seconds at you all and then right back to where that old Indian was staring at me with those black eyes that burned holes in me. And so help me, that old man was gone. I mean, like two seconds tops! Initially, I got this chill that I've had the other times right before I've encountered him. Now, let me tell you, this is just too damned weird for words, this whole thing!"

"Ken, you are a sensitive and you pick up on things that other people don't. That in itself is clearly why you were brought into this whole thing. You see, you had probably pushed these awarenesses down for the most part but they were always there, just beneath the surface. Now trust me, there are no accidents. Like my daddy used to say, 'Everything is in divine order and we humans just don't always get it.' I've always felt like my quiet little father was a very advanced soul. He is not a man of many words but what he says is so often deeply profound." She followed up with, "Now, you take my mother, she's feisty but she would do anything in the world to help anyone. However, she does speak her mind," and Muriel chuckled.

"I kind of gathered that when I met them at their store that first day here. But I think I did win her over when I told her and your dad about my country boy background," and he smiled at her.

She put him at ease and he could feel himself mellow out with her down-to-earth explanations. It was just another of the many things he thought as he again realized how much he loved her.

"Another thing about my parents," Muriel said. "Whenever one of us kids got caught red-handed doing some kind of a no-no, our mother would put her hands on her hips and look at us like the dog had just peed on the floor, or worse. You knew where you stood with her." And she laughed heartily, as did Ken. "Now Daddy handled it another way. He would look at us silently awhile and say, 'All right, what should we do about this?' Then he would let us decide on the proper punishment that fit the crime. We learned that we had best not set it too low because we had to rethink it if we did. So, either way, they both quite effectively raised a whole passel of young'uns because we all turned out pretty much all right."

"Well, I can certainly attest to at least the one I know." Ken leaned over and kissed her.

Chapter____8

"So, all right, sweet man, let's roll and go watch those cowboys." Ken started the car and pulled out into the traffic, which for Rosewood, was unusually heavy, especially for a Sunday morning.

"By the way," Ken said, "I really wonder why old Nathan showed up just for me to see him, because I have noticed, when he shows up, it is not by happenstance. Is it to have me confronted with another of the strange clues he seems to be pointing out?"

"Well, of course, we will probably be finding out fairly soon," Muriel said, "and you can take that bet to the bank."

Ken just nodded his agreement and wondered, in a rather abstract way, if old Nathan was aware of the threats he had been getting at the motel. He seemed to be aware of everything somehow.

"You know, Ken, I heard that Nathan Toms is a full-blooded Kiowa and that no one is certain of his age. As I mentioned before, several people have said he is a shaman. I didn't really buy that, just thought he was a reserved backward strange old Indian, but now I have to take it back because I know for certain that you have nothing to gain by telling me the things that you've encountered in reference to old Nathan. Besides, Ken, I trust you and have such respect for you, not to mention loving you, no holds barred." She moved over closer to him. "Oh, boy, would you look at all the trucks and car's here. I bet we'll have to walk a ways," Muriel said as she looked around, trying to help spot an empty parking space.

"That's all right if we have to walk. At least for me it is, since I need the exercise. I usually take my dog Maggie out for a walk every day and I have been remiss since being here." As an afterthought, he added, "However, you are on a dead run, Muriel, working in that café, so you get more than enough exercise, honey."

"Heck, I don't mind, Ken. In fact, it feels good to get out in the fresh air and walk."

They did have to park some distance from the entrance gate where Ken purchased tickets for the rodeo.

"Do these rodeos always have this large a turnout?" Ken asked Muriel as they looked up at a sea of faces in the bleachers.

"Sure do and you should see it when the fair is going on and a rodeo too. People thick as fleas on a hound dog's back," Muriel accounted. Ken chuckled heartily at this colorful description.

"Mom, Ken," Angie called out. She was standing up not quite mid-way up a section of bleachers. She motioned for them to come up to where she and Will Earl were seated. Ken tucked his hand under Muriel's arm and they made their way up to the pair.

"Come on, you two. We saved a couple places for you," Angie said and scooted closer to Will Earl as Muriel sat down beside her. Ken sat down by Muriel after excusing himself to the lady he passed who was holding a curly-haired tot on her lap. The little girl shyly peeked at Ken as he settled himself down on the hard seat.

"Say there, where did you get all those pretty curls and big blue eyes?" Ken said, smiling down at the child. He thought she looked no older than three.

"From my mommy," she said, then announced, "My name is Samantha and I got three years old yesterday." She was holding three small fingers up to show him.

"Well, now, happy birthday, Samantha. Did you have a nice birthday with cake and ice cream?" Ken happily engaged her in conversation while her pretty young mother smiled at him.

"Uh huh. Daddy, he is in the rodeo today so Mommy and me come to watch him ride."

"Which one is your Daddy? Would you tell me his name?"

The little girl proudly announced, after looking at her mother for confirmation, "Daddy's name is Wesley Stratton and his number is eight."

"Then I will be looking for your daddy," and he smiled down at the bright-faced child. The young mother cheerfully smiled over at Ken and said, "Since everyone is getting acquainted, my name is Sue Stratton." She held her hand out to Ken over the top of her daughter's curly golden head.

"Ken Ferries. I'm pleased to meet you, ma'am. Now this lady sitting next to me is Muriel Jacob, then her daughter Angie and our friend Will Earl Rogers." All of them acknowledge the introductions just as Tyler Rogers was being introduced over the loudspeaker by a voice with a heavy Texas drawl.

"Now, you all, here's a hometown lad, twenty year old Tyler Rogers, number three. Been ridin' reckon before he could walk. Now Ty took the purse home when he was just seventeen for ropin' and tyin' in twelve and a half seconds. Now let's see if this cowboy can hold on to that record."

When the shoot flew open, Tyler sped out in pursuit of a big black half-grown calf. Will Earl leapt to his feet, twirling his Stetson wildly over his head while yelling encouragement to his plucky young brother.

Ken was swept up in the excitement as he watched Tyler spring on his horse like a fireball after the calf and swiftly pull him down with one wide swing of his rope. His long legs dropped from the horse to the ground with the sureness of a trapeze artist. He ran down the length of the rope and tossed the calf to the ground, tying him with such hast that all of his movements appeared as one. Kneeling beside the defeated calf, Ty quickly threw his strong muscled young arms above his head to show his time.

The crowd exploded into a fevered pitch of excitement and loudly cheered as the announcer screamed into the microphone, "Way to go, Ty. Folks, this cowboy just broke his own record at eleven and a half seconds."

"Hot damn," Will Earl shouted. "If that little bro' of mine didn't just top his own record." His handsome face was alight with pride as he lifted Angie off her feet, gleeful with exuberance. Ken watched Ty as the young man sat astride his fine mount and easily rode out of the rodeo arena, waving his wide-brimmed hat at the crowd. Ken thought what a dashing young man he was. Tyler turned his horse in a short circle with one final gesture, his young face afire with happy affirmation. Ken saw the rainbow but closed his eyes tightly after staring at it above Tyler's blonde head, hoping to clear his vision. When he looked again, the colors had deepened more intensely and there was no mistaking the spectrum around the young man.

"Nadine, you are here, aren't you," he mused to himself while he felt the deepened emotion flood his heart for this mother who was taken so savagely in the prime of her life. He felt Muriel looking at him as she reached for his hand and squeezed it in her own. He knew that the naked emotion he was feeling was clearly discernable to her. She leaned over and impulsively kissed his cheek as the announcer drawled out the next contestant's name.

The events went on, with the barrel racing next. Which involved several young women contestants, one of whom he recognized as Carmen Munoz. She placed first in that division, as Tyler had in his.

"Say now, folks, here is a young man, twenty years old, right here from Rosewood— Joe Ferral Jr. number five. And he's taking on that bull, Hillbilly. I reckon Hillbilly comes by that name 'cause, when he gets a bull rider on him, he'll loop to one side like he's been hangin' on side hills, sorta like one set of legs is shorter than the other." The announcer chuckled at the humor he found in that. "Now, Joe, Jr, hang onto him 'cause old Hillbilly's known for that scam."

"Oh, lands, Annie would flip if she knew Joe Jr. was courtin' bulls!" Muriel said. Ken heard her draw her breath in sharply.

"You mean the Annie that waited on us at Dolly's this morning?" Ken asked.

"One and the same," Muriel said and shook her head.

The bull with the young man astride him exploded out of the gate when it was swung open and rodeo cowboys in the arena bolted over the high fence. The snorting beast Hillbilly twisted to one side round and round like a giant top. The left legs looked like they were hardly touching the ground, while the right side of the sorrel-colored massive animal appeared to be nearly touching the ground.

"Oh, God," Muriel almost screamed, "he's going to fall and pin Joe Jr. down with him!"

Angie reached for her mother, clutching her around the waist as they both stood up. A rodeo clown reached Joe Jr., pulling him away as the hefty critter fell heavily down onto his right side, bawling in rage. Two rodeo clowns illustrated their talent, skillfully using their ploy to lure the angry beast into an open gate and out of the arena.

"Now that was one lucky cowboy. He hung right onto old Hillbilly and gained a score of eighty. Say now, Joe Jr., not bad for your first time around." The announcer drawled on, "Joe Jr. cottons to it sorta natural like though 'cause his dad Joe Sr. took home some fine buckles for bull ridin' in his day. Okay folks, next is number eight. That would be Wesley Stratton, a young man of twenty-four years old. He's been at this bull ridin' since he was eighteen and he's got the buckles to prove his skill too. He hails from Idabel, Oklahoma. Drawed a bull today called Old Sandy. Now folks, Sandy got that handle by the pure honest fact that he's keen on pullin' ever sandy in the book to heft a bull rider off of him. He's got his work cut out for him if he can pitch Wes, 'cause I've seen this boy ride before and he gets a tight rein and an easy seat."

"See, that's my daddy," Samantha said proudly as she tugged on Ken's shirt sleeve. Ken smiled at the child and nodded his head at her, silently sending a blessing out for the Stratton family.

The rider and bull tore out of the opened gate and the thick-bodied bull moved like a freight train that had gone awry from the tracks. He quickly hitched sideways in a yet wilder gyration that would dizzy the most astute and capable of bull riders. The long-legged Wes appeared to be one with the brute and rolled with ease at the bull's every trick to dislodge him. In the midst of one vicious twist, the bull suddenly flipped the other way in his efforts to rid himself of the determined rider. The dung-colored bull roared his indignation and heaved straight up, arched his great back, and came down like a descending rocket. He twisted wildly as he defecated, slinging it full bore on the rider and the two clowns who were drawing closer. A sharp whistle blew and the rodeo clowns inched closer, giving Wes the opportunity to bail out from this powerful force while it was still in the middle of a spasmodic rage.

Sue Stratton was on her feet now and, for the first time, Ken saw that her young body was thick with child. "Wes, get off him before he kills you," she screamed and the cords in her neck stood out like taut ropes.

Like a movie turned down to slow motion, Ken watched as Wes heaved his long legs over the animal and sprang cat-like in one bounce away from him. The clowns had already fired up the bull's attention and he centered on them as Wes was lifted to the high fence by reaching hands. As the bull charged one of the clowns, he safely dove into a nearby barrel. The bull gave the barrel a pitch as the other clown began to toy with him. He ran a zigzag comical trot toward the open gate, taunting and luring the bull into the gate as he out-maneuvered the beast's deadly charges.

"Hey now, that Oklahoma bull rider got a score of ninety. How that cowboy can hang in there! It's gotta take pure grit and brawn, not to mention plenty of savvy," the announcer commented, his voice huskier from his hours of commentary.

Ken turned his full attention towards Sue Stratton now and noted that her face was ashen. "Mrs. Stratton, are you all right?"

The girl turned to stare at Ken, as though she was struck dumb. Ken repeated the question. "I think so." She hesitated before going on, Yes, I believe that I am." She suddenly gripped at her stomach and her pallor was plain to see.

Ken reached for Samantha and said, "Honey, would you change places with me. Sit over here by this nice lady." He indicated Muriel, who by now was regarding the little girl and her mother. Muriel reached for the tot as she walked in front of Ken. She lifted the child onto her lap, smiling and cooing friendly conversation to distract her.

Now, Mrs. Stratton," Ken said as he scooted over to the young woman, "you just let us help you. It's going to be just fine now."

The young woman relaxed momentarily and smiled with effort. "Please, just call me Sue. Could you send someone to page my husband? I think maybe the baby is coming but it's too early. I'm not due for a month yet!" Her face held alarm.

"Now, now Sue, don't you fret. I'll just have Will Earl go fetch your husband," Ken assured the distraught woman.

Angie, who had been leaning forward, watching this drama unfold, now leaned toward Will Earl and whispered to him. Will Earl stood up hastily, saying, "I'll go get her husband. We'll meet you at the entrance gate."

Ken reached carefully for Sue Stratton, steadying her to her feet, and began the slow descent of the bleachers. Muriel and Angie led the little girl between them, following Ken and Sue. They made it to the gate just as Will Earl and Wesley Stratton bounded up to them.

"Honey, what's wrong?" a wild-eyed young man said.

She could not answer for she was gasping in a deep contraction. Wes scooped her up in his arms, walking quickly to the parking lot as the rest of them followed.

"Do you folks know where I can find the hospital?" Wes' face was fearful. Then for the first time, his attention turned to Samantha. "Sammy, you come on here to Daddy 'cause Mommy needs us to go right now."

"Listen, Wes, why don't you let me ride along and I will show you how to get your wife to the hospital. Angie, you follow and you can pick me up," Will Earl suggested as he handed her his truck keys.

"All right. Say now," Wes said, "we surely do thank you good folks. We're much obliged but you will pardon us, 'cause we gotta get Sue here to the hospital. Don't reckon we have a lot of time."

"That's fine. You just go along now. Bless you, folks," Ken said as Wes put his wife into the pickup. Will Earl climbed in beside Sue and settled Samantha on his lap.

Ken and Muriel watched Wes scoot quickly from the dirt parking lot until they were out of sight. "Wow, I sure hope that little girl is going to be all right, her and that baby pecking at the door," Muriel said as she took Ken's arm. "The rodeo is about to wind up, Ken, so do you want to go back and finish watching the rest of it?"

"We may as well, and then later, we can call the hospital to find out how Sue Stratton is doing. Maybe Angie and Will Earl will still be there and then we can find out. But, if they aren't, we could just run over to the hospital and get hold of Wes. That poor man really was shook. Can't say as I blame him," Ken elected.

As they walked back to the gate, Muriel asked, "Ken, when Tyler was finished in his event, I looked at you and you had such emotion on your face, honey."

Ken stopped and regarded her. "You know, his mother was right there with him, Muriel. I know she was because I saw the rainbow colors that encircled Ty when he'd finished his event. They were as clear and vivid as the ones I had seen surrounding old Nathan Tom."

Muriel's lips quivered and she bit down on them in an effort to forestall the tears filling her green eyes. "My sweet man, sent straight from Heaven, I love you so." She stood on her toes, pulling his head down. He met her lips fully as she kissed him with touching tenderness. "She was truly a rose, Ken, so lovely she took your breath away. There was nothing mean-spirited about Nadine. And, honey, I just cannot see why that beautiful woman had to go like that," and Muriel's voice caught on a heavy sob.

237

"Listen to me, sweetheart," Ken said soothingly while he held her close. "Maybe, just maybe, she came here for the soul purpose of lending God's light to the world, perhaps even through the way she died. Muriel, doesn't it have a clear message to us all that we as God's children need to look at what we take away from ourselves through violence, greed, and all unloving, uncaring acts? You see, honey, I think she speaks volumes, even in her death, that we all need to realized we are the Absolutes, the Angels in human forms."

"You mean she chose to do this?" Muriel said as her eyes widened.

"Not on a conscious level, no, but before she ever came here. Because, Muriel, the origin or creation of this world, the cosmogony, if you will, is in complete and divine order. Even if we don't get that fully, it is still true.

"Then, my God, what a sacrifice Nadine chose," and Muriel expelled her breath shakily.

"Yes, but haven't we all in various ways? Didn't a young man a couple thousand years ago?"

"Yes, he did that, didn't he." Muriel breathed in deeply as she held Ken's eyes with her own.

"And Muriel, you will always remember Nadine as the rose she was. And she always will be because her life is forever. She'll always be a beautiful Spirit who is the trail of the rainbow, bright and perfect, leading us on a trail of what true spiritual love is. I believe we were all given more of a shining, clearer journey in our own lives in coming to understand the essence of hers. I feel that she has given a more loving power to every life she has touched and I intend to see that she will have touched many more lives in my endeavor to write her story."

"So then, what you are saying is that Nadine's life was not in vain after all," Muriel softly persisted.

"No, her life was not in vain because this precious rose chose to be here for forty-six years. Dearest Muriel, you can see the many gifts she gave and is still giving."

"Ken, I want you to know that you have helped me more than anything else in finding inner solace and a larger measure of peace since Nadine was taken away," and she brushed her tears away quickly.

"Well, honey, I'm glad that I have been of help, some comfort for you," he said and kissed her once again. "So, now, shall we proceed, pretty lady, and watch the rest of these rough and ready rodeo cowboys perform their incredulous feats?" He grinned boyishly at her.

"Lead the way," Muriel smiled up at him, her eyes still bright from tears. He tucked her arm and they made their way back to their seats in the bleachers.

Just as they were seated, the announcer drawled, "Now folks, here is a fella who most of you will recognize from a few years ago. He happens to be the possessor of many hard-earned buckles and he's taken home some hefty purses in the past. He's a local man— number ten, one Will Travis Rogers. He has drawn one rip-snorter of a bull who has clearly earned the name Tilt-a-Whirl. So, good luck, Will, and hang darned tough." He quipped, "Now, none of us is getting younger but then, neither is Tilt-a-Whirl."

"Oh, Ken, what the hell is he doing? Is he out to commit suicide?" Muriel swooned and Ken grabbed her as she pitched forward.

Almost dream-like, Ken watched Tyler race up onto the fence just as the gate flew open with Will astride Tilt-a-Whirl. The wild beast leaped and twisted in every freaky movement he could design to rid himself of this rider. Even before the gate had opened, Ken had stared in fascinated horror at the power of this animal. The bull's rage was clear as he tried to stomp and thrust his way out of the narrow chute. All the while, he was bellowing with more intensity and rage than the bulls preceding him. The massive bullet-gray bull twisted around and around, as sprays of saliva coursed from him and flew in a wide whirling pattern.

Ken sat transfixed as he saw Tyler climb part way over the fence. Just as he prepared to drop into the arena, Jeff Colter grabbed Ty around his hips and pulled him backwards. Ty fell on Jeff as they hit the ground but he was safely out of harm's way.

Ken glanced at Muriel who appeared frozen into a state of shock. He held her close in a firm clasp around her waist.

Just as the whistle blew, the bull gave one extra wide tilt and threw Will like a projectile high into the air. Ken saw once again the array of rainbow colors curved around Will as they had been around Tyler. This time, the sweet scent of roses was so powerful that their heavy fragrance was unmistakable.

The rodeo clowns were desperate to gain the bull's attention away from Will, who was lying in an extremely awkward position. One of his legs was twisted at the knee in a freakish posture and he appeared to be unconscious. As the announcer yelled into the microphone, the two clowns managed to divert the bull as he was headed toward Will with his head lowered. The angry bull now kept a vigil on one clown and suddenly made murderous haste toward him. The clown made a hasty beeline for the opened gate. Even in this chilling moment, Ken could not help silently applauding the miraculous skills and mercurial pace of these fearless rodeo clowns.

"Folks, I think Will caught a horn to the head and that leg don't look good but the ambulance is here. That would be Will's son, Tyler, out there with his Dad and I believe Jeff Colter is with him to make sure Will don't stir around. I reckon some of you remember Jeff as a former rodeo contender. Darn good one too. Well now, I think Will is responding but Jeff is making sure he don't stir. Folks, let's just hope and pray that this cowboy's all right. He hung right in there and put up a darn good fracas and plenty of bravado. He chalked up an eighty-nine and that ain't shabby."

The ambulance attendants were squatting down by Will now and checking his vital signs. They carefully put his head and neck in a brace and placed him onto a gurney. After putting him in the ambulance, Ken watched Tyler start to climb in too, but one of the paramedics restrained him.

As Muriel got to her feet, Ken stood up with her, still supporting her at the waist. Jeff was now leading Tyler away and Ken knew they were going to Jeff's car and then the hospital.

"Ken, let's go to the hospital," Muriel said while taking the stairs two at a time down the bleachers. Ken lifted her partially to keep her from falling in her haste.

They reached the parking lot and made it quickly to Ken's car. Muriel slid in but then held the door ajar so Ken couldn't close it. She started climbing out with one leg poised on the ground and reached around for a note on the windshield.

"Oh, here Ken. Someone left a note for you." Ken took it quickly from her hand.

"Let's just hurry now, hon. I will read it later." He slipped it into his shirt pocket. Muriel was out of the car before Ken had time to go around. He quickly pushed the locks shut as he was getting out. He hurried after Muriel as she made a dash for the hospital door and they entered at the same time. At the front desk, Muriel inquired after Will. The pert little nurse, about five feet tall and with deep chocolate brown eyes, appeared to be in control of any situation. She appraised Muriel now and, with cool diplomacy, said that she would call the second floor to inquire of his status.

"Please, nurse, where is his family? I would like to be with them," Muriel pleaded.

"Well, miss, are you family?" the nurse ventured.

Muriel shot a look at Ken and then, without hesitation, said, "Yes, I'm his sister."

Ken felt worked to suppress a grin and once again marveled at the strength of this woman he loved. "She'd have been one hell of a reporter," he mused, "with her break-down-the-doors decisive purpose."

The nurse frowned, "They are on the second floor, Miss. You will find them in the waiting room."

"Thank you," Muriel answered as she went swiftly to the elevator. Ken followed.

"Ken, sorry about that," she said, her green eyes holding his. "I am sorta his sister, you know," and her voice trailed off as she searched his face for a sign of disapproval.

"Yes, I should say that you certainly are, and you do not need to apologize to me at all," he assured her. They made their way to the sitting room where they found Jeff and Tyler.

"Oh, Aunt Muriel!" Tyler's voice shook and his deep blue eyes were wide with fear as Muriel held him close.

"Are Angie and Will Earl still here at the hospital?" Muriel asked Jeff.

"Yeah, and we just got here ahead of you. I had them paged so they will be here any second," Jeff confirmed.

At that moment, Will Earl strode into the room with Angie close behind him. His eyes were wide with alarm as he looked from one to the other of them.

"What's going on, Ty? Aunt Muriel?" He looked bewildered, while glancing at Jeff and Ken too.

"It's Dad, Will Earl. He got hurt at the rodeo," Tyler said, now fighting to hold his tears in check.

"Jeez, how did that happen?" Will Earl asked and the color drained from his face.

Jeff went to him and took the young man's arm while Angie held him by his other.

"Listen, Will Earl, it's gonna be okay. Your Dad has probably got a broken leg. They got him up in surgery right now," Jeff said as he held onto the young man a little firmer. Ken noticed that Jeff had not mentioned that Will had taken a blow to his head from the bull's horn. Jeff went on, "Now, boy, you just hold it steady like, okay? Your Dad's one tough horse and he will be fine. He just sorta went off half cocked, rode a mean old bull and took a hell of a rough fall." Jeff's eyes were wide and Ken saw the fear there but his demeanor never betrayed him.

"Oh, God, what was he doing riding a bull?" Will Earl had by now gone chalk white and became unsteady on his feet. Jeff and Angie led him to a chair. Jeff pushed him firmly into it as Angie sat down beside him.

"Listen, Mom, I am not going back to Waco now. Okay?" Angie asked. "I will call the university and tell them it is a family emergency. And, while I do that, I will call Phyllis too."

"Oh, honey, yes. That is a good idea," Muriel said as Angie stood up. She kissed Will Earl on his cheek and made her way to the phone.

"Mrs. Stratton is having hard labor but they seem to think she and the baby are doing okay," Will Earl said and his throat was working hard.

"Oh, Will Earl, that's good. Are her husband and little girl okay too?" Muriel asked. He nodded yes.

"Angie and me kept an eye on the little girl while Wes went out to his truck and got him a clean shirt." Ken could see that Will Earl was working at diverting his thoughts.

Angie returned and told them that Phyllis and her husband were on their way to the hospital after dropping the children off at the Conways first. A half hour passed and Phyllis and her husband arrived. Phyllis went straight to her brothers, who had both stood up. The three of them locked their arms tightly around each other. Chance, Phyllis' husband, a tall handsome man about thirty years old, stood turning his Western hat in his big hands. His somber eyes held a deep concern as he watched his wife and her brothers holding each other tight. The man clenched his jaws and swallowed hard.

"What happened to Dad? How did he get hurt?" Phyllis asked as she pulled back to look up at her brothers.

"He probably has a broken leg," Tyler answered while continuing to hold her close. "Sis, he took on a bull at the rodeo and God why, I don't know. But you know he has been really out of it," and the tears finally surfaced.

Will Earl reached up almost angrily to brush away the tears that came now unheeded. Phyllis put her fist to her mouth in an effort to stop a hysterical sob. Ken could feel his heart roll over at the sight of these three adult children standing there encircled in their grief and fear for their father. Jeff hung back, his head down, and Muriel was looking at the trio with pure anguish on her face while twisting her hands in helplessness.

Angie walked over to her mother and whispered to her, then left the waiting room. Muriel and Ken were the only ones aware that she had gone. When she returned shortly and spoke to Will Earl, she told him she had called his grandparents. "Lucky they were both home. I thought you would want them to know." She searched their faces as she spoke.

Will Earl put his arms around her. "Oh, gosh hon, I am so glad you did, I just clean forgot."

"Angie, thank you. With all the shock over hearing about Dad, I forgot to call Grandma and Grandpa," Phyllis exclaimed as she wiped her tear-stained cheeks. She reached over to hug Angie.

"Yeah, thanks, little half-pint. Shows how much we need you, Ang," Tyler said as he bent down to kiss her cheek.

"Hey, you all, what are friends for, right Chance?" Angie stated as Chance seemed to come out of his shocked stupor for the first time since he arrived.

"Sure as heck, Angie, and girl, we are mighty proud we have friends like you and your Mom and Jeff."

Muriel walked over to Chance. "I want you to meet Ken Ferries, Chance. He is a good friend of ours."

"Well now, sir, it's a pleasure to meet you." He turned to fully face Ken and took his hand in a firm grip. He regarded Ken with an open friendliness. Ken got a sense of the man's overall presence as he looked into Chance's deep blue eyes. He saw there a man who was forthright and plainly a good person.

"Mr. Ferries, anyone who's a friend of Muriel's and Angie's is a friend of mine too," Chance related.

"Well, thank you, Chance, but just call me Ken. I am glad to meet you. I have met your lovely wife and her brothers and Jeff there before."

"Ken, my goodness, I am sorry I didn't acknowledge you when I got here. I was so scared and just wasn't aware of anything else," Phyllis said as she came over to Ken and took his hand in greeting.

"That is certainly understandable, Phyllis. Now, my dear, do not fret one whit," and he patted the young woman's shoulder.

Shortly, a handsome older man and an equally impressive, very striking woman entered the waiting room. Ken could immediately determine the relationship of these two to the three grandchildren. Will was tailor-made to his father, Mr Rogers Sr. They both had the silver hair at their temples and shoulders that were wide and firm. He stood easily at six foot five and his eyes were a deep gold brown. He was extremely impressive, even with the deeply etched look of concern on his face. Mrs. Rogers hair was silver white yet she had the face of a woman who was younger by at least fifteen years. She was quite beautiful, with a slender tall carriage. Ken could see where Will Earl and his father came by the multi-colored eyes. Carolyn Rogers' eyes were wide now with an obvious fear in them, yet she and her husband were clearly the two strong figureheads of the family and otherwise centered and calm. Ken knew they were making every effort to remain calm for these grandchildren who had already been robbed of their mother. And now, here they wre in the throws of great fear for their father's well-being.

"Granddad, Gram," Will Earl said, reaching them first as Phyllis and Tyler drew up behind. They all hugged the couple close to them.

"Now here, boy, what's this all about," Mr. Rogers said as he stepped back from Will Earl. Mrs. Rogers was holding Phyllis and Tyler around their waists while Will Earl related the incident. The older man's face filled with a deepened despair and anger and Mrs. Rogers seemed to swoon momentarily. Her breath came out ragged so Phyllis and Tyler led her to a chair and Muriel slid into the chair beside her.

"My great aunt Jessie, what in the name of all the saints was he doing at damned near fifty years old riding a bull?" Mr. Rogers roared.

Carolyn rose swiftly to go to her husband. "Now, now, Will Justin Rogers. You just take yourself in hand. We can't get all up in arms about how this happened to Will. We have to keep our heads and pray that he is going to be all right. We will deal with what we have to, now please." She looked up at her husband imploringly, then reached up tenderly and touched his cheek.

Ken watched as Will Senior took her hand and kissed it. "Oh, all right, Carolyn. Of course you are right. Now I don't suppose there is any point in asking at the desk what's going on now," Will Senior said to no one in particular.

"I will go see, dear," Carolyn said. "Muriel, please go with me. Will Earl, you and Tyler take your grandfather over there and sit him down while Chance fetches him a cup of black coffee. He certainly needs one."

Chance was obvious in his gratitude to be called upon to be helpful. He went quickly to get the coffee from a vending machine in the hall. Ken joined Jeff as the two ladies departed and Angie sat down with Phyllis, talking soothingly to her. Jeff, who had been quiet for the most part, now seemed glad for Ken's company.

"I don't know but it sure appears to me that Will is bent on total destruction. He ain't too concerned how he does it, just so he gets the job done." He kept his voice low so that the others didn't hear him.

"Yes, it would appear as such, Ken agreed. "God willing, he will be all right. Just maybe this will be a wake up call for him, Jeff."

'Well, by Jaspers, I hope you are right, Ken, because if anything happens to him, I don't know what those three good kids would do. I been dang near sick over their Pa so I can't reckon what it's doing to them." His steel gray eyes held pure sorrow as he looked at Will's children and his father. He went on, "Carolyn is a right cool head in a crisis, which you probably noticed. She's a real feisty woman under all that glamour. And W.J., he's a mighty shrewd man and cool as a cucumber when it comes to business. But he gets pretty shook up when his family is hurt in any way."

This exchange surprised Ken, as he knew Jeff was usually extremely quiet. Ken was glad to have this rare opportunity to talk with Jeff, and besides, it helped to lift some of the tensions. Jeff suddenly placed his hands to his knees and leaned forward, turning slightly to make eye contact with Ken.

"Ken, you're seeing a lot of Muriel. I don't believe in beating around the bush so I'll just ask you straight out how you really feel about her."

This didn't surprise Ken because he had already arrived at the fact that Jeff, though quiet, was a straight-to-the-point kind of character.

"Well, since you don't know me, Jeff, and I drifted into Rosewood with the intention of researching the Rogers case, I can very well see how you might wonder about me and my feelings about Muriel. I am glad you asked me because it tells me how much Muriel means to you as a good friend."

"Well, I couldn't have a sister who meant any more to me than Muriel," Jeff related.

"I was certain of that, Jeff. Yes, I will tell you that I am in love with Muriel and, if she will have me, she is going to be my wife." He smiled at Jeff, whose face took on a lively pleasure.

"Now, glory be, that is the best thing I have heard for so danged long, Ken, especially with all the purely miserable crap that 's been going on here for almost a year now. I would like to know why you have some questions about…well, about that crime," he finally said, unable to make direct reference to Nadine's death.

"I just came across several things after researching some news copy, Jeff, so I decided to delve deeper. I can't tell you without sounding strange but I will try to explain. You see, it was almost like Nadine beckoned to me every time I would see her picture, like she was trying to tell me something."

Jeff's eyes never wavered as he watched Ken and listened to him carefully.

Ken went on, "I am an old veteran with a lot of years as a newsman. I'm no stranger to crimes, having done in-depth investigations on many, much to the vexation of more than a few people. But I have to tell you something about this—it was as though I was totally compelled to dig deeply into this particular case. I tried to reason that it was because I was a rural person myself, being raised on a ranch, and it was particularly strange to me that a crime like this would happen here. It seemed highly inordinate."

Muriel and Carolyn now returned but they went to talk to Will J. and the others so Jeff took the opportunity to ask Ken more questions.

"Well, sir, have you had reason to feel that you might have some additional information since you've been here and checked around?" Ken looked keenly at Jeff and decided that he could safely confide in this man. He reached in his shirt pocket and retrieved the note Muriel had found on the windshield of his car. He quickly read it before handing it to Jeff.

"Now Jeff, Muriel doesn't know about this so don't mention it to her or anyone else, please. I have filed a report with the sheriff's office as this is the second note plus some threatening phone calls too."

Jeff looked down at the note and when he looked back up at Ken, his eyes held shock. "Say man, you were right on because this looks like you have rattled the hell out of somebody's cage. Jeez, this has got to mean that that case wasn't cut and dried." He shook his head. "Ken, you really have opened up a hornet's nest, I'm wagering. You'd better be careful."

"Oh, you bet. That is why, first thing in the morning, I am dropping by the sheriff's office to talk to him personally. When I stopped in Saturday, he wasn't in and I filed a report with his deputy. But I didn't relate anything much to him, other than I had gotten this threatening phone call. Figured it would be better to talk to Sheriff Hernado since I had discussed my purpose here with him over lunch awhile back."

"I think you're pointed in the right direction there, Ken, because old Bruster is pretty sharp. A lot of people here have underestimated him."

251

"So you could see that about Bruster too, eh Jeff?" Ken grinned knowingly at him.

"It has been my experience that too many folks check out the top layers of a person and don't bother to delve any deeper. It don't pay to make snap judgments and, like the old saying goes, appearances are deceptive."

"Well, on that point, I could not agree with you more, especially with forty years experience in the news business. I've learned never to judge a book by its cover, Jeff."

Muriel walked up to them and said they should be bringing Will out of surgery within a few minutes and then the doctor would come talk to the family.

"So, how about you and Jeff and I going to the cafeteria to have a round of coffee after they let the family in to see Will?" Ken suggested.

"Sounds like a plan to me," Jeff agreed. Muriel nodded her head and tucked her arm around Ken.

"Ken, come with me to meet Will's parents. Jeff, you come too and you can say hello to them, okay?"

"I'd like to do that, Muriel. I haven't talked to them for longer than I can recall. Wish it was under better conditions though," Jeff said as he put his arm through Muriel's free one. The trio went over to Will's family and Angie, who was holding Will Sr.'s hand.

"Carolyn, W.J., I want you to meet a close friend, Ken Ferries. We were at the rodeo when Will was hurt and came right over here."

"Why, it is our pleasure to meet you," Carolyn said and started to stand up.

Ken protested, "Oh, no, please," and put his hand out as she placed her slender hand in his as a greeting.

Will Sr. was on his feet now and said heartily, "Sir, you would not happen to be the Ken Ferries with the Waco Centennial, would you?"

"Yes, sir, I was up until a few months ago," he said as the two men shook hands.

Mr. Rogers then turned to Jeff, "Now look here, mother, see who's here?"

Carolyn's face spread into a smile, as Jeff bent down to kiss her softly.

"Hello there, sweet lady. And how's the best looking lady in the county doing? Well, other than currently... Jeff gazed with a deep fondness at the older woman.

"I have been well, Jeff, but Will J. and I miss you. You haven't been by for so long, dear," she said and put her hand to his cheek.

"Now, I promise, Mom Carolyn, that I will do better on that if you will promise me some of those wonderful Toll House cookies you can make better than anyone else's mother. If you promise that, you will for certain see me and my old truck out your way soon."

Will J. grinned widely at Ken and said, as he nodded in Jeff's direction, "That boy there and Will Jr. could put away two dozen cookies faster than Wyatt Earp was known to draw a side-arm." He grabbed Jeff and hugged him in a bear hug with obvious affection.

A young man attired in surgical scrubs appeared and a hush fell in the waiting room as every face turned toward him.

"Hello. I am Dr. Ellis. Is this the Rogers family?"

Carolyn Rogers stood up and announced, as spokesperson for everyone present, "Yes, Doctor, we are Will Rogers' family."

"Well, now," the pleasant young man smiled, and Ken felt an instant peace settle around his heart, "though Mr. Rogers took a hard blow to his head and suffered a mild concussion, he is in no danger but we are monitoring him closely. Now, he did fracture his left leg and fortunately, it was a closed break just below his knee. We put in some screws to stabilize the break and, with some physical therapy, I do feel the prognosis for Mr. Rogers is very good."

Carolyn's face took on the radiance of pure relief and Will J. noisily cleared his throat, shifting his weight from one foot to the other.

"When may we see our father, Dr. Ellis?" Phyllis asked, her voice slightly trembling. Her brothers stood by, listening carefully.

"Oh, I should think just as soon as your father is not quite so groggy. That may be another forty-five minutes to an hour." He started for the hall and then turned around to address them again. "I will have a nurse drop by and tell you when he has come around, all right?"

"Oh yes. We do thank you, doctor." Phyllis smiled with obvious relief on her lovely face.

The young doctor Ellis raised his hand in a gesture of agreement, smiled and made a quick exit from the waiting room as he was being paged on the intercom.

"Say, while we are waiting for Dad to wake up, Angie and I will go see how the Stratton family is doing. We'll be right back." He briefly explained how they got involved with that family.

"I don't think that ought to surprise anyone that the poor lady went into an early labor," Will J. snorted and shook his head.

Will Earl clutched for Angie's hand and began to move out of the waiting room, clearly not wanting to respond to his grandfather's remark.

"Say, what do you all think of going to the cafeteria and I'll buy everyone some coffee? It's going to be awhile before Will comes around," Ken ventured.

"Why, yes, Ken, that would be a bit of a relief from all of this anxiety," Will J. sighed gratefully.

"Yes, thank you, Ken. Phyl, hon, would you go out to the desk and tell them we will all be in the cafeteria if they want to find us?" Carolyn asked.

"Sure will, Grandma. I will leave word at the desk for Will Earl and Angie too." She left to go to the nurses' station. She rejoined them halfway down the hallway and put her arm through Chance's. The two of them looked at each other with relief on their faces.

"Oh, Chance, better call Sissy and Bud to let them know how Dad is. Let's go back to the nurses' station. You all go ahead and we'll join you pretty soon, okay?" Phyllis smiled at all of them.

"Sweetheart, you just go on and do that," her grandfather said as he bent his tall frame down to hug the girl to him. Carolyn led the way to the cafeteria and they all settled at a long table after Ken paid for their coffee.

"This is so thoughtful of you, Ken," Carolyn smiled at him. Ken noticed how ever more beautiful she was with the edge of tension eased from her face.

"Oh, I am just happy to be able to be of some comfort, though it is small." He smiled at the imposing lady.

"Ken, what brings you to Rosewood?" Will J. inquired.

"I took up freelance writing recently and I like to cover various areas for information for my writings," he answered, bypassing an in-depth discussion.

"Yes, Ken's wife, who passed away a few years ago, was also a freelance writer. Perhaps you happen to recall some of her books—Gloria Ferries?" Muriel skillfully introduced them to another subject deliberately.

Carolyn's fine features creased into a tiny frown while making an effort to recall any of Gloria's literature. Phyllis then returned with Chance.

"Say, Phyl, you have read Gloria Ferries books. Tell your Grandma about some of them. She is trying to recall if she has read any," Muriel interjected before Ken could reply. As Phyllis sat down, she related some of the titles of Gloria's books.

"Oh, my yes, dear. She was a wonderful writer, one of my favorites. W.J., you have read some of her books, don't you recall now?" Carolyn turned to her husband.

"Say, by golly, I sure do. Why, she wrote one that I was especially taken with. It was pure genius and I couldn't put it down until I had read it from cover to cover." Will J. smiled at Ken.

"Now what one was that, Grandpa?" Phyllis inquired.

"I believe it was titled 'Wings of Angels' and it really captured the human spirit," Will J. answered. Ken could feel his throat constrict as it had been one of Gloria's best masterpieces and was his favorite too.

"Ken," Carolyn said. He looked quickly up at her and noted her searching eyes as they held his own. "I am certain this bothers you because here we are so freely discussing your wife."

"Oh, no please Carolyn. I am very proud that you all recall Gloria and her literary talent. I was just going to say that that was my favorite of her many books too. It was written just a short time before Gloria passed away."

Muriel's eyes were fixed on Ken and he knew she felt his mixture of emotions. He clearly saw the understanding in her eyes. He was grateful for her wisdom as she too had experienced shared love and memories with a mate who had passed away. He was grateful that she allowed him the natural onslaught of feelings that were bound to come over him at times. It was just one more comfort that they could share between them, part of the deepening love they were coming to express more and more.

"Say now, here they are," Jeff said as Angie and Will Earl came in.

"Well, what's the word with Sue Stratton, Angie?" Muriel asked.

"Wes and Sue have a little boy and Samantha was the first to tell us that she 'gots' a new baby brother," Angie tittered happily.

"Yeah, and he is doing okay, Wes told us. But he is just a bit little because he came a month early. They feel he will be just fine though." The relief showed on Will Earl and it spread around the table to all of them.

"Now, how about that! By gosh, it seems that everything is going good finally, after all the shake-ups that has gone on today. Now we have some triumphal feats to sing about," Tyler said and jumped from his chair. It was plain that the young man was almost giddy with a near hysterical release. He went around the table and hugged all the ladies and shook hands with all the men, shaking their arms heartily.

"Tyler Rogers, I sure hope that you are this excited when you become a father one day," Angie teased.

"Well, I just hope, when that day comes, Half Pint, that it won't be so full of chaotic upheavals."

"Amen to that," Will Earl agreed, letting out his breath heavily.

"This is the nurses' station on the second floor, calling the Rogers family," a female voice broke in over the intercom.

"Guess we best be heading up there and see your Dad," Will J. said as he helped his wife up. "Thank God and homemade biscuits now, this day just may have turned out to be a top of the heap one after all," Will J. said, his voice raspy with emotion.

Muriel took hold of Carolyn's hand. "Listen, dear lady, you and W.J. and Will's children go see him now. Then later the rest of us will." When Carolyn started to protest, Muriel put her arm around her. "It's important that you all have this time with him, Carolyn. Besides, we couldn't all go in together anyway. Just tell him we are here and will see him later." She smiled at her reassuringly.

"You are so sweet, Muriel. And Will is so blessed to have friends like all of you." For the first time, tears streamed down her cheeks. Will Earl and Tyler shuffled their feet while Chance looked down at the floor. W.J. bent down and kissed his wife, then retrieved his handkerchief to blot her tears. When they all departed, W.J. was supporting his wife carefully around her waist while Chance and

Phyllis twined their arms around each other. Tyler walked a few steps ahead and then turned to wait for Will Earl.

"Ang, come with me, honey," Will Earl said and took her small hand in his.

"It's okay, Will Earl. You just go on now with Ty and the others," she said softly, looking up at him with reassurance.

"Come on, Ang. Will Earl needs you and so do I," Tyler said and sniffed while straining to keep his composure.

Angie turned to Muriel who put her hand on the girl's shoulder. "Go on, hon. Go with them."

Angie nodded to her mother and walked away between Will Earl and Tyler. Muriel looked after them and finally sat down heavily as though her legs could no longer support her.

"Say now, must be about supper time, from the looks of folks filing into this cafeteria. I am suggesting that we all have a bite to eat. Besides, it will probably be awhile before the three of us can go see Will." He looked at Muriel, concerned by her look of extreme fatigue.

"That sounds like a good idea, Ken, but only if you will allow me to buy dinner for you and Muriel," Jeff suggested.

"Well, all right. I am open to that, because it has been awhile since breakfast," Ken agreed. "We do thank you for the offer, Jeff."

"Oh, yes, thank you, Jeff. But please, I want you both to go ahead and get something to eat but I will just sit here and drink my coffee," Muriel said, as if she was only partially present.

"No way, lady. I won't take no for an answer so you just as well hop up from there and join us in that line forming over there," Jeff demanded.

"Yes, Muriel. You need something to eat. I want you to keep your pretty figure but starving yourself isn't the way to do it." Ken's eyes crinkled with mischief at her.

"Oh, very well. I guess I'm outnumbered," and she got up slowly, managing a chuckle at Ken's remark. Jeff gave her a slow easy knowing smile.

Jeff followed behind Ken and Muriel, insisting that he pay for the three meals.

They made their way back to the table.

Two of the medical staff were seated at the ample table now, one of them Dr. Ellis who recognized them. He was eating a generous piece of pie heaped with ice cream. He grinned and pointed boyishly to the pie with his fork. "How's this for a good staple diet? However, it will get me through the next several hours, I think." And the nurse sitting across from him smiled at his remark and shook her head.

"Well, Dr. Ellis, it ought to at least put you on a sugar high for a few hours," Muriel smiled and sat down beside him. Ken sat down on the other side of her and Jeff walked around the table to face them and nodded politely at Dr. Ellis.

"Say, about Mr. Rogers," Dr. Ellis said, turning his full attention to Muriel. "I have noted what appears to be a state of heavy depression and apathy in the man."

Muriel related the events to this young doctor, stopping now and again to swallow the growing lump in her throat. Jeff kept his face downcast and Ken rubbed Muriel's back in an effort to comfort her through the commentary. Dr. Ellis removed his wire-rimmed glasses while he still focused on Muriel and systematically polished each of the lenses with a napkin.

"Well now, I shouldn't wonder that he is heavily depressed." He placed the glasses carefully back on and Ken could see that, beyond his very professional manner, he was deeply moved. The nurse, a woman in her mid-fifties, carefully kept her eyes averted, her attention on her meal.

"I would suggest that Mr. Rogers get into some grief counseling and the sooner, the better. As it happens, we have an excellent group meeting here one day a week with grief therapists on staff. The therapists are always available at any time to the group members."

"I hope that some of us can reach Will and get him to seek help, but so far his family and friends have been unsuccessful, Dr. Ellis," Muriel said, fighting for control.

Young Dr. Ellis' face took on full compassion as he regarded Muriel. "Well, since Mr. Rogers will be here for a few days, I will bring one of the grief counselors with me on my routine rounds. But first, I will ask Mr. Rogers some questions regarding his apparent state of mind." He continued, "Perhaps this injury was for the best, since he was fortunate that he wasn't hurt more severely. You see, so often people such as Mr. Rogers who have been so horribly traumatized become extremely self-destructive. They shut everything else out because their personal pain is intensely acute."

Muriel nodded her head in understanding, and for the first time, Jeff looked up and made eye contact with the doctor. Ken could see that a chord of understanding had struck him, that Jeff realized how he himself had not been fully able to reach his arms around his own grief nor find a glimmer of peace in his own Spirit. Dr. Ellis stood up and looked at a clock on the wall above the table. He thanked Muriel and made a retreat from the cafeteria. He appeared always rushed, as was the usual condition of doctors, Ken thought.

Muriel turned now to Ken and sighed, "Do you think that Dr. Ellis will have a breakthrough with Will?"

"I do, yes. I believe the possibilities of it are stronger now since he will not be as apt to walk away. A well-trained therapist knows just how to approach these matters, Muriel."

"I think so too, for some reason," Jeff agreed, finally speaking up. "It's clear the man isn't listening to his family or friends. That is plain to see."

The nurse made ready to leave and Ken noted that her name tag read Midge Maples. She smiled softly at them and said, "Godspeed to your friend or family member."

Muriel regarded her. "Will is a dear friend and we thank you so much for expressing that to us." Her voice had a catch in it.

The lady put her hand on Muriel's shoulder and said, "I do believe that he will be helped a great deal and I will say blessings and prayers for him."

Muriel thanked her again and, as the nurse left their table, said, "People as a whole are so good, aren't they?"

Jeff nodded, not saying anything, while Ken just took her hand in his own and squeezed it lightly.

Carolyn returned to the cafeteria and again Ken was struck by this lovely woman's bearing.

"Oh good, you have all had something to eat," she said and took her place beside Muriel.

"I just spoke with Dr. Ellis a moment ago and he told me that he had talked with you, Muriel, regarding Will getting some counseling. I ventured a bit farther and said that I thought the children should too. He's agreed with me that they certainly should."

Muriel ventured, "I do think that, since they are so concerned over their father, that the three of them will agree more readily to counseling."

"I agree with that. I intend to speak with them about it over supper while you and Jeff and Ken are visiting with Will," she confirmed with a determined tone.

"Very good, Carolyn." Muriel leaned toward her and hugged her. "Lord knows, they all would benefit and it is sorely overdue." Her voice held a note of relief.

"Oh, here they all are now," Carolyn smiled in greeting to her approaching family and Angie.

"Carolyn, will we be allowed to see Will or would it be better to wait until tomorrow?" Muriel asked.

"I think there will be no problem getting in to see him now. Besides, he is expecting all three of you, dear. It's important that he is in contact with friends and family, Dr. Ellis told me."

"Very well, then we will go now and ask if we might get it for at least a few minutes." Muriel stood up while Ken and Jeff also got to their feet.

"Mom, I will see you at home later if Will Earl and I are gone when you come back here. Or will you be coming back to the cafeteria?" Angie searched her mother's face while she waited for an answer.

"Oh, honey, I think we have all had about enough for one day. I think I'll just have Ken take me home after we have seen Will."

Carolyn smiled up at Muriel, Ken, and Jeff while she clasped Muriel's hand in both of hers. "Thank you, Muriel. Thank you to all three of you. Muriel, I will call you soon, all right?"

"Oh yes, please do, Carolyn." Muriel bent down to kiss the older woman, as did Jeff. Ken shook her hand warmly and smiled with a warm reassurance at this exceedingly charming woman.

Will J. had been very quiet since they had returned from their visit with their son but he stood now. Ken noted that he looked heavily fatigued after seeing Will Jr.

"Now, Muriel, I hope that maybe you and Jeff can get through to that boy of ours so he will come back to us." His voice seemed to crack with heavy emotion as he spoke. He took Muriel in his long arms and held her close. Muriel patted his back as she laid her head against his chest. Will J. then released Muriel and hugged Jeff roughly around his shoulders. His face contorted with such emotion that it was painful to witness. Ken knew this man was not used to allowing his emotions to be seen so nakedly but his deep despair was obvious.

"I know… I know, W.J." Jeff said, conveying a message they both understood without further commentary. He stepped back and took the older man's hand in both of his own while they held each other's gaze.

The grandchildren had seated themselves at the table and were deep into their own thoughts, as were the others. Chance Bennett appeared to be greatly concerned for his wife, whom he studied with the eyes of a man weighted down with helplessness. He had no idea how to console her broken heart over the mother she lost nor the father she couldn't reach. Angie was in the midst of deepened thoughts and torment as she glanced from one to the other and then back to Will Earl. Will Earl appeared to have aged prematurely as his shoulders drooped like an old man. Tyler appeared the picture of near collapse and Ken knew that inside he was feeling like a child who had been suddenly orphaned by both parents. The air in the room felt so close and thickened by sorrows that Ken felt he was struggling to breathe.

Now Muriel and Jeff were moving toward the exit of the cafeteria so Ken shook W.J.'s hand and patted him soundly on his solid shoulder.

"Hope to see you again, Ken, and once again, thank you," the older man said, his voice gruff but in more control.

"No thanks needed, sir. I am certain that we will meet again." He left to join Muriel and Jeff outside the glass entrance doors.

Muriel clung to Ken as though she needed his support and Jeff helped brace her about the waist. They moved down the wide hallway and toward Will's room. When they stopped at the nurses' station to ask if they might see Will, Midge who had been at their table in the cafeteria smiled warmly at them.

"Why yes, that would be fine if you don't stay over ten minutes. Mr. Rogers is getting somewhat restless now."

"Thank you, nurse. We won't stay long," Muriel said.

"Muriel, I am going to stay here and wait for you and Jeff. The two of you need this few minutes alone with Will.

Muriel met his eyes and nodded. She was fully aware of this decision of Ken's as being the right one for the moment.

Ken went into the waiting room and idly reached for the first magazine he saw on the stand by the chairs. A pretty woman looked back at him from the front cover and he absently leafed through the pages. He realized with a rush how tired he was.

Chapter____9

"It has been quite a day," he thought and went back over the events. He silently gave thanks that it hadn't turned out any worse. "Maybe, just maybe now Will is going to start recovering. That is certainly going to help the whole family come together once again," he mused, not really seeing the pictures in the magazine he held. He reached inside his shirt pocket, remembering the note and stared at it. He studied the handwriting more than the message and could not shake the feeling that the writing was somehow familiar. It was deeply perplexing to wonder why the script seemed to be one that he knew. He hoped he would unravel this nagging question soon. He had always been articulate, a stickler for details, when he was a reporter and he was no less so with any other issue of importance. He knew his own psyche well and knew he would always search for the smoking gun. He knew he would worry over this script like a dog chewing on a bone until he was satisfied with his answers. His mind was awhirl now so he leaned back and closed his eyes to rest. A form began to take shape in his mind's eye, a whirling crimson color and inside it a large red-tailed hawk that seemed poised with talons outstretched to attack its prey. His eyes flew open and he shook his head to clear it from the startling image.

He chose to treat the vision he had just experienced as a reaction to the stress of the day, to being overly tired. He rose to his feet, restless now, and looked out the window behind the row of chairs. He was surprised to see that the sky color outside ws a bright crimson with a slightly purple hue mixed in with it. He had little time to ponder this thought when he heard Muriel softly call his name.

He turned to greet her and Jeff now and pointed wordlessly to the display of heavenly colors outside the window. Muriel gave a sharp intake of breath and Jeff whistled softly.

"Man, I don't believe I have ever seen anything quite like that," he proclaimed and shook his head in wonder.

While they looked, a towhee landed on the window ledge and regarded them with curiosity, twisting his head.

"Shall we go to the nurses' station and tell them to get a look out this window? I hate for anyone to miss a lovely sight like this," Muriel suggested.

They made their way out of the waiting room and stopped to tell the two nurses at the desk about the hue of color outside. Each nurse took a turn to go see it as Dr. Ellis came down the hall. They asked him if he had seen the unusual sky and he said he hadn't. But he went to the waiting room window to witness it too.

"That, as my young daughter Jolea, would say is super outrageous," and he smiled with that boyish wide grin. Ken thought that if anyone could get Will to seek help, it would be this young doctor. He had a very winsome personality and a friendly spirited humor. They bid him all good evening and made their way outside. The sky color had taken on even more definition.

"Ken, what do you think this means?" Muriel asked as they stood somewhat spellbound by the sight.

"I don't really know, but I think that it sends a clear message to appreciate the joy of sights like this. I would say it is just another of God's many splendors, pretty lady," and he hugged her to him.

Jeff stood there, his hands jammed into his jeans pockets, leaning slightly forward watching the spectacle before him. Ken thought that, on the way to Muriel's, he would tell her of the vision he had seen in the waiting room before seeing this beauteous vision outside the window.

"Say, I gotta get back to the spread, Muriel, Ken, but I'll see you folks soon. Oh, say Muriel," Jeff paused, "when is a good time for me to come talk to you?" Ken could tell that Jeff felt suddenly awkward.

"Listen, Jeff, why don't I just stroll over to my car and then you walk Muriel over when you are both ready." Ken saw the instant relief and gratitude in Jeff's face as he took Ken's hand and shook it.

"Ken, thanks. And listen, this won't take long. It's just that I have a rather pressing matter to deal with and I could use an old buddy's savvy on the matter." Ken noticed that Jeff had agreeable good looks in a very masculine and virile way to which most women would be easily drawn. As he looked keenly at Jeff, he centered on a scene that suddenly ventured forth with stark clarity.

"Why am I seeing this?" he silently questioned. It was a personal revelation and Ken felt like an intruder who was spying on people, a prowler on the watch. He collected himself and once again shook Jeff's hand. He walked to his car a short distance away in the lot. The revealed scene had startled him and he hoped that Muriel and Jeff hadn't noticed.

He had seen Jeff and a woman together and they were disrobed, standing a few feet apart. She was not someone Ken had ever seen. Her hair had cool copper highlights though it was black. Her skin was a tawny color, a light tawny though.

She had a slender figure and well-rounded high breasts. Her overall body structure was quite voluptuous with long well-shaped legs. Ken could see her face and her eyes were half closed as she watched Jeff. Her full shapely lips were parted seductively. Ken saw the passion on the face of the man as he took one step toward the woman and kissed her almost savagely. Ken had felt the loneliness, anguish, and starved passions leaping like flames from both of these Souls' Spirits. The scene had left in a matter of a few seconds but it had been so intense that Ken had picked up on the arousal of emotion between this couple.

"My God, where is this all taking me? Now I feel like a damned peeping Tom," he said out loud but softly as he unlocked the car and slid in.

He had only been there for about five minutes when Jeff opened the door for Muriel and she slid in beside him. Jeff bent his head down and looked in at Ken before closing the door. "Be seeing you, Ken, and Muriel, I will be over in a couple evenings. I will give you a call first and thanks again, lady." He walked away in the direction of his pickup and they could hear the click of his boots on the pavement.

Ken started the car and they made their way out of the parking lot. Muriel was quiet and thoughtful but she finally spoke. "Something's got Jeff in a grip of some kind and it isn't like him because, frankly, he has always been one cool dude, as the kids would say." She chuckled low in her throat and continued, "I just hope that whatever it is, I can make him feel better about it."

"Muriel, you can just by hearing him out, by just being there for him as the friend that he knows you are."

"Yes, of course you are right, Ken. After I get home from work Tuesday, he will come out and we'll talk. I told him we will as long as he needs to."

"He couldn't ask for a better assurance of a good friend than that, I don't believe. Now tell me about Will."

"Well, like Dr. Ellis said, he is in a serious state of depression. Therefore, he had little to say to us. We could see that he was extremely tired but, you know, Ken, for some reason, I feel that things will start to turn for the better, even in light of all this heaviness now."

"I do believe you are right, honey. I must tell you that, when I was waiting for you and Jeff there in the waiting room, I just closed my eyes a bit and saw this pretty color. That was before I had seen it outside from the window. And I saw this red-tailed hawk, hon. He was enormous and had his talons outstretched like he was about to spring on his prey. It was as though I was experiencing a vision more than just an idle daydream. Anyway, I opened my eyes and stood up, then turned to look out the window and there was all this breath-taking color....but no red-tailed hawk."

Muriel locked her arms around herself and shivered. "Ken, I literally have goose bumps. What in the world does that mean?"

"I'm not certain at this point but, after all the things we have experienced, I have a strong feeling that it is some kind of sign, an omen if you will."

"I just hope it is a good omen, if that is indeed what it means. But something that lovely sure has to be," she sighed and settled back in comfort. Ken could see that she was in need of some much-needed rest.

"Listen, Muriel, I will come to Dolly's in the morning for breakfast and then I have some people I want to see, like that defending attorney for the three men. After that, if possible, I would like to speak with the judge too."

"Ken, I will get off work early tomorrow evening, so if you want to come out to the house…?" she hesitated, leaving the question hanging. "Well, it would just be me there because Angie is leaving early in the morning."

Ken pulled the car over and turned the key off. He turned to look into those green eyes which were turned up at him.

"Are you sure, Muriel? Because, if you are, it's what I want too, babe. That's for certain."

"Yes, it is, Ken. And you can take it to the bank." And she reached up to pull his face to hers and kissed him in a way that she had not before. She pressed her tongue lightly onto his lips. He felt like he would melt, that he was aflame with passion. He knew he was shaking with this heady desire for the woman in his arms. She pulled back and smiled provocatively up at him, then placed a slender finger to his lips.

"We better pull back now, honey, and just ride this out until tomorrow evening."

Ken blew out his breath heavily, then slowly bit down on his lower lip. He looked at her and, then with great effort, started the engine of the car.

"God, girl!" he breathed heavily. "You are like a life force with me. It is not going to be easy when I leave for Waco."

"You'll be back," she answered, her voice like a deep purr.

"You can take that to the bank, too." He looked at her for a moment and smiled teasingly. He eyes filled with a tantalizing gaze that was especially for her own arousal.

"There are some things that are right in this old world, Ken, and I know that we, are for each other. Honey, it's gonna be a great one all the way for us." She placed her head onto his shoulder. Her breathing became shallow and he realized that she was asleep. They pulled up in the driveway to Muriel's home and, as the car stopped, Muriel sat up straight.

"Whew, I dozed off, I guess," she said with a note of surprise.

"Yes, you did. And now I am going to see my dream girl to her door and tell you good night." He kissed her warmly and then opened the car door to walk around to Muriel's door. He walked her to the porch and she opened the door, but then reached up soundly and kissed Ken. He held her in his arms and kissed her lips, her eyelids, her forehead, and her lips once more. Then he raised one of her hands, palm up, and pressed his tongue lightly on her palm.

"Good night, pretty lady. I will see you in the morning." He turned around and went to his car. He turned back to see her standing halfway inside the doorway, a halo of light around her head.

"I love you, Muriel," he whispered aloud. His whole being hurt with a sweet ache at the powerful feelings inside him. While he made he way back to Rosewood, he whispered his thanks as a prayer for this love that had come to him. When he passed Bailey's Lounge, he did not see the green Jeep and he breathed in deeply, feeling a certain relief.

"Maybe I can get a decent night's sleep without this tormentor calling me with one of his cheery messages," he thought with jaded humor. He parked the car, being careful to scan the whole area before getting out. He made his way to the motel room with his key ready to put into the lock. The marmalade cat lay on the mat at entrance and he stood now to wind himself around Ken's trouser legs, purring lovingly and staring up at him.

"Well, old friend, how have you been today? Catch any more millers for a little snack?"

The cat purred louder in response as Ken bent down and stroked its furry back and down to the end of its fluffy tail. When Ken rose from the bending position, the cat turned to stare into the shadows intently and then suddenly arched its back and hissed.

"Well now, tabby, what do you see? Another cat on your turf or, heaven forbid, a dog?" He chuckled at the cat's alert stance of defense.

Ken opened the door and withdrew his key but, for some reason he could not understand, he felt the hair prickle on his neck. The cat growled with a snarl and vacated the mat just as Ken put one foot in his room. He hastily shut the door and checked to make certain that it had locked behind him.

"I think that I must be over-reacting," he chided himself thoughtfully. Nonetheless, he turned the lamp off in his room and stepped to view the outside entrance from his post at the end of the drapes. His stomach turned as he clearly saw a man emerge into the light and stare for several minutes at the door, then reach out and try the doorknob. It was the man Ken had seen in Bailey's Lounge, he was certain, and the same body structure as the man he had seen in the vision running across the pasture. While he stared, the man seemed intent on opening the door and Ken sensed that he was skilled at breaking and entering, and that a motel room break-in would be a piece of cake for him. Ken suddenly felt an unnatural calm course throughout him as he stood transfixed watching this man. He heard the distinct, unmistakable roar of hundreds of large birds flying down to rest in feeding areas. He recalled that sound from childhood when he and Tommy would watch with their father as thousands of grand Canadian geese would alight.

Everything took on a crimson color and he heard the screech of a winged creature like a hawk. He had no more heard it, and the arguing going on in his head, when he saw it! He felt like he was staring at such an outlandish and bizarre event that his mind could not begin to comprehend and yet it happened as fast as the click of a camera shutter.

An actual red-tailed hawk had landed on the man's shoulders and somewhere the scream of the man penetrated Ken's mind while he stood there in fascinated horror. The crimson color deepened as blood from the man's shoulders coursed down his shirt where the talons of the hawk held fast. The hawk suddenly lifted from its shoulder perch and, when it did, the man ran like one being pursued by a lunatic with a weapon.

Ken slumped back from the window and sat down on a chair at a nearby table. He leaned his head down onto his hands, with his elbows resting on the tabletop. The jumble of his nerves at what he had witnessed gave into spasms of uncontrollable shaking. He sat there for some time in the darkened room trying to correlate what he had seen and yet keep his sanity in perspective.

"Well, Ken, old boy, you have certainly arrived in an overwhelming, ludicrous, and not to mention, bizarre state of affairs. Any science fiction writer would be hard-pressed to equal this," he said out loud. He wondered if his mind had gone and if he had imagined what he had just witnessed. Yet an inner sense prevailed and he knew that, from the beginning, this quest was to be a labyrinth of strange and unusual circumstances. While he sat there starting to calm down, he knew that he was the focus of an evil and dangerous foe and that a strange supernatural power had interceded on his behalf.

Another thought invaded him out of the blue. "There are more things in heaven and earth that we do not understand." On that note, he got to his feet, checked the door once again, and decided that he would shower in the morning because he was suddenly exhausted.

Though he slept heavily, he dreamed deeply vivid dreams. He saw a hazy crimson background which would then deepen in color as a giant hawk appeared. While he watched in wonder, the hawk took on the form of a man, an ancient Indian man with the face of Nathan Tom!

When he awoke and looked at the clock radio's glowing red numbers, he saw that it was almost 7 a.m. He lay back for a while and thought about the dream. He decided that it was certainly no more bizarre than what had occurred the night before, or for that matter, what had been occurring ever since he had first been drawn to that picture of Nadine Rogers smiling up at him from the newspaper. She was luring him then as she had continued to do. Interesting that she had selected someone with a media career who had a nose for unanswered questions and unusual ideas. How unusual he could not have dreamed, he thought as he lay there reflecting on the past couple weeks.

"If you make it through all of this in one piece and with your sanity intact, you can survive anything that comes your way, Ken Ferries," he thought with sardonic humor.

He got up and made his way to the bathroom, stretching his arms above his head in repetitive circles to loosen the tensions from the night before. He allowed the sting of the cold jet spray needles of water to hit him for some minutes before adjusting it to warm. Then, slowly, he soaped his body before finishing his shower.

"Ah, boy," he groaned as he briskly rubbed his body dry. "I think just maybe you are back among the living now."

He felt hungry suddenly so he quickly shaved, brushed his teeth, and selected his clothes. While putting on his shoes, the phone rang and he felt himself tense before reaching for it.

"Hello?" he said, feeling guarded and ready for the voice of the threatening stranger.

"Ken, Sheriff Bruster Hernado here."

"Well, good morning, Bruster. I was planning to stop by and talk to you this morning."

"My deputy told me that you had been in to file a report, Ken. I thought maybe you'd be stopping by this morning. Say, I will buy us some breakfast after we talk in my office."

"Say now, that sound all right, Bruster. Just give me a few minutes and I will be there."

"Good enough, Ken. I'll see you in a few minutes."

After he hung up the phone, he made certain that he had the note which had been placed on his car. When he started for his car, he double-checked the door to make certain it was locked. Then the Asian man from the motel called out to him.

"Ah, Mr. Ferries, I would like to speak with you this morning." He was smiling in greeting.

"Why, yes sir, what can I do for you?" Ken regarded the man questioningly.

"Mr. Ferries, my wife is a light sleeper and, last night before 9 o'clock, she had retired. I had gone into the shower about that time when she called me very alarmed. I ran to her to see what had brought about such a fearful tone and she told me not to turn on the light. She motioned for me to join her at the bedroom window where she was looking at something outside. Then, Mr. Ferries, I heard it. This man was standing at your door screaming and trying to fight off some great bird that was ripping his shirt away. We could see the blood from his shoulders where the bird had sunk its talons. Ah, Mr. Ferries, I do hope that you heard this or perhaps you saw it?" He was almost pleading and Ken could see the fear in his eyes.

"Yes, sir, I not only heard it, I stood at the end of the drapes and watched. The man was trying to open the door to my room just before this large bird attacked him."

"Oh, thank you, thank you, Mr. Ferries. We were afraid that we had taken leave of our senses."

Ken thought to himself that he could certainly relate to the man on that.

"Mr. Ferries, should we not summon the sheriff's department on this matter?"

"As it happens, I am meeting with the sheriff this morning, sir. Trust me, I don't believe that there will be further trouble from this individual," Ken offered.

"Well, I should not wonder, after his experience. But I do not believe that my wife nor I shall easily recover from the unbelievable sight that we witnessed." Ken could tell that the man was still bewildered and on edge from the aftermath of such a strange enigma.

"I certainly understand where you are coming from because it was shocking and freakish, to put it mildly. But I am glad that someone besides myself did see the whole thing," Ken said, hoping he had given the man some comfort by the fact that three people had been subjected to the phenomenon.

"Well, it is a relief that you saw it too and I will tell my wife that our minds are intact," the man said with a nervous laugh.

Ken bid him good morning and unlocked his car door. He noted that there was no message on the windshield this time. As he made his way to the Sheriff's office, he wondered how this phantom stalker was doing. He concluded that he would certainly have a sore set of shoulders and probably a fevered brain as well after such an otherworldly experience.

"I should hope that perhaps this will stop him, or at least slow him down for awhile. I want to get to the bottom of this case first." He had spoken aloud as he parked in front of the Sheriff's office.

"Good morning, Ken. Grab yourself a cup of coffee out of the coffee pot over there and come join me in my office. Katie always makes sure she has the coffee on, by golly." Bruster smiled at the red-haired lady.

"Good morning, Mr. Ferries. Good to see you again," Katie smiled pleasantly at him.

"Good morning, ma'am. Good to see you again. And say, I am glad that you had coffee ready." He held up his cup in a salute of thanks and smiled engagingly at her. She smiled warmly back at him as he turned to follow Bruster into his office. Bruster motioned to a chair on the other side of his desk and, as he sat down, reached for a pad and prepared to write up a report.

"Bruster, here are the notes left on my car windshield," and Ken handed them to the Sheriff. Bruster read them, studying their content as Ken sipped his coffee. Finally, Bruster looked up and fixed his eyes on Ken. Ken could see that they were filled with questions.

"I believe this would more than indicate that someone is not taking kindly to your investigating the Rogers case. They are afraid that you are breathing down a neck or two, eh?"

"It would seem so, yes. There would be no other reason for anyone to threaten me on the phone and in these handwritten messages." Ken watched Bruster as he looked once more at the notes.

"Ken, has the person given you a specific reason at any time as to why they want you to leave Rosewood?"

"Not one," Ken said with assurance.

Sheriff Bruster picked up a pencil and scribbled something on the pad, then drummed the pencil lightly on the surface of the blotter on his desk top.

"I see you have made notes of the days that you found these notes and the phone calls. That's good, Ken. It all helps, you know."

"Bruster, this will sound insane, I know but, thank God, I have two witnesses who will confirm what I am going to relate to you.

Bruster reached for his coffee mug and leaned back in his swivel chair. "Go ahead, Ken. I believe I have lived long enough that nothing would surprise me." He grinned, showing his gold-filled front teeth.

"I had quite a day of it yesterday, Bruster. You probably know that Will Rogers rode a bull at the rodeo yesterday and ended up in the hospital with a broken leg and concussion?"

"Jeez cripes. No, I didn't know. What in tarnation was the man thinking?" Bruster looked dismayed and shook his head.

"I couldn't say but it appears the man has got one go-to-hell attitude on life," Ken said.

Bruster nodded solemnly and looked down into his coffee mug, studying its contents.

"Anyway, I had taken Muriel to the rodeo, so naturally when they loaded Will into the ambulance, we got up and headed off to the hospital. When we got to the car, Muriel spotted this latest note on the windshield. I practically snatched it out of her hand. I haven't wanted her to know about these notes or phone calls. With all that happened, she didn't even remember the note that I stuffed in my shirt pocket. We just went to the hospital where we met Tyler and Jeff Colter. Angie and Will Earl were already at the hospital because the wife of one of the bull riders sitting by us went into labor. The young folks had seen them to the hospital. From the hospital, they called Phyllis and Chance and Will's parents. Well, Bruster, after all was said and done, finally Muriel and Jeff were allowed to see Will for a few minutes. Afterwards I took Muriel home since she was beat by then.

I was too, and in fact, so much so that I decided I was just going to forego a shower until morning and just go to bed. Probably a good thing or I wouldn't have seen this guy standing at my door. I heard a noise like someone was trying to open the doorknob so I got out of bed to look. There was this guy standing at the door working at breaking in. I could see him from the end of the drapes and I didn't have to move them to look out. I knew instinctively that this guy would be able to break in easily enough but, Bruster, all of a sudden, there was a roaring noise. Then, what looked like a hawk, the biggest hawk I've ever seen, came down and landed its talons right into this guy's shoulders. The man started screaming and I just stood there. Guess I was sorta frozen to the spot. Bruster, the man's shirt was ripped near off of him and he had blood running down his arms. He took off screaming and flailing his arms. I just plopped down in a chair then and sat in a daze for some time before going to bed."

Bruster's eyes widened and he seemed to be at a loss for words. "Mother Mary," he finally gasped. "You did say there are others who saw this?"

"Yes, the motel manager and his wife saw it too."

"Well, Ken, I got to tell you that is the damnedest story I have ever heard, and believe me, I have heard some doozies. If it was coming from anyone else, I would be hard put to believe it."

"As Muriel would say, Bruster, you can take it to the bank," Ken chuckled.

"I will get over and talk to the—I believe the name is Chan—after we've had breakfast. I'll get a statement from them too. Now, is there more you want to relate to me before we go on over to Dolly's?"

"The only thing I can't understand, Bruster, is that the handwriting on these notes looks like one I have seen before and that has me in a quandary."

"You don't say. Hmm, now that is interesting, something we will both think on." Bruster stood up and reached for his hat on the hat rack just behind his desk. "Like you say, Ken, I don't think you will need to be concerned about this man for a while but I will beef up security none the less. Are you going to be in town awhile longer, by the way?"

"No, I thought maybe tomorrow I would go home for a few days and then come Sunday, head back here. There is going to be an art show next Monday with the main theme being Nadine Rogers' works of art. I told Muriel I would take her to that in Longview. She plans on switching work days with one of the other waitresses."

"You and Muriel have become quite an item, haven't you, Ken—if you don't mind a nosey old lawman saying so." His broad face was spread in a courteous grin.

As they made their way out of Bruster's office, Ken shared that they were indeed an item and "If that lady will have me, we will be a permanent item." He could feel his heart rejoice at the mere mention of it.

"Say now, Ken, That's about the best news I have been privy to in a long time." He took Ken's hand in his own and shook it warmly.

The morning was pleasant and the birds set up a noisy chatter as the two men strolled to the café. It gave Ken back a feeling that this world was settled within him, a reassurance after the chilling events of the night before.

"You know, Ken, this pretty well establishes for me that gut feeling I've had all along about the Rogers case."

"How's that, Bruster?"

"Like I told you, I just couldn't quite feel that those three men fit the profile of cold brutal killers from what I had observed. Like I said, Larry Gomez was a wild kid but not mean-spirited. I tend to believe it was all pretty hasty, the whole trial. There wasn't enough uncovered, in my personal opinion. I believe others felt like I did, Ken. For sure you have, mainly from researching into it. This puts the capper on it because someone is certainly shook over your research. If there wasn't something to hide, why then all the extreme measures?"

"That is my contention, Bruster. Either the guy is scared stiff or utterly stupid in showing his hand like this. It has to be one or the other." Ken summed up as he reached to open the door of the café.

"Hello, hello, you two charming gentlemen." Muriel bustled up to the two of them and motioned for them to follow her to a booth in the far corner where they could have some privacy. After Ken was seated, he pulled her lightly down by her arm and then kissed her.

"How's my pretty lady?" Muriel blushed slightly.

"Walking high on happiness now that you are here, Ken Ferries." Her eyes held a special message for him. He winked at her as he took the menu she offered. Bruster sat there with a Cheshire cat smile, gold teeth exposed.

"Now, darned if it don't look like I'm about to lose my favorite waitress, Muriel. But then I reckon, if I got to, at least it's to a top of the line sort of guy like Ken here."

She smiled happily at Bruster and he noted a lightness in her that he realized he had not see for years. She handed him a menu, still smiling, and said, "I will be right back with the coffee and to take your orders, fellas."

"Ken, that girl is in love and walking in high clover," he said to a beaming Ken.

"Well, so is this old retired reporter, who isn't feeling so old theses days." He smiled warmly at Bruster.

"Say, back to this strange set of events, Ken. You know, before you came into the office, I got a visit from Bud Conway. He's a local rancher in these parts."

"Yes, I met Sissy and Bud Saturday night at the dance. They were celebrating their twenty-fifth wedding anniversary."

"As a matter of fact, that evening when they were at the dance, their two youngsters Kathy and Barry were scared out of their wits. It seems that the dogs got to raising a ruckus and Barry went outside to see what the commotion was all about. He figured maybe a stray dog had wandered up so he called the dogs. They came but they acted spooked and kept looking toward some outbuildings. The boy turned a high-powered flashlight on and shone it toward the buildings but he didn't see anything. So he brought the dogs in to an enclosed porch to settle them down. Later he told his folks that he figured it was a coon or some other varmint but he said he had never heard them act like that before. They had been extra spooked, the way the young man described it. Well, the kids watched some television and the dogs seemed to settle down. Then Kathy told Barry she would go out to the kitchen and fix them some cocoa while a commercial was on. She was out there preparing the cocoa but started feeling kind of funny, like someone was watching her. She just suddenly sensed it. She said she looked up above the sink and there stood a man staring in at her. Well, the poor kid almost fainted and she ran out of the kitchen screaming for her brother. Luckily, their folks came home within fifteen minutes or so but they were two frightened youngsters. It does seem rather strange to me, Ken, because you know that ranch belongs to Will now that Nadine is gone. It was hers, belonged to her parents and she inherited it after they were killed in an accident."

"Yes, Muriel has told me about that."

"You know, this all seems to settle around Nadine somehow. I mean, don't it strike a chord with you?"

"Now that you mention it, it is a bit odd that it involves the Rogers in an abstract way. Especially with the two incidents, it does make you wonder."

"May not be anything but a coincidence but I am filing it away here" he pointed to his head, "and will see what else turns up before I am fully settled on that connection."

Muriel returned with the coffee pot and Ken shoved their coffee mugs to the edge of the table for her to fill.

"Gentlemen, we have a Texas omelet on special this morning, with either biscuits or your choice of toast."

"Tell me, pretty lady, what all is in a Texas omelet?" Ken grinned up at her.

"Just about everything except the kitchen sink," she teased. "Seriously, Ken, they are good and very filling, I might add. I think that we make a tasty omelet here too."

"I can vouch for that, Ken," Bruster added.

"Sounds good to me then, because I am hungry this morning." As Muriel wrote it down, Bruster told her to make it a pair. They ordered toast to go with it and then settled back to resume conversation as Muriel went to place their order. Bruster reached for the sugar and poured his usual generous portion into his coffee, then stirred it thoroughly before he spoke.

"You know, Ken, the morning that Nadine was killed, I got the call and was heading out to the Rogers' spread when I met up with a pickup truck going like a bat out of hell. I met up with another one with some men in the back of it armed to the teeth so I made a bootleggers turn and got in as close as I could behind the men in the tailing pickup. We hadn't gone far when the one I was behind gave a helluva burst of speed and rammed the other truck off into the ditch. I thought one of them cowboys was gonna be thrown out of the bed of that truck, rifle and all. Bobby Munoz was danged near pitched out and it surely would have killed him if his Pa hadn't made a grab for him. Well, now, quicker than you could spit, two men jumped out of the cab of that truck to be followed by the three in the back of it. I tell you now, I was having to do some fancy footwork and get my gun drawn to get to those men before the shooting began. I drew down on the lot of them and told them I would drop the first man who didn't take me serious. I tell you what, the adrenaline was really pumping in this old boy's system!"

Ken could see that, even now, it was extremely unsettling for Bruster to talk about it. "The men in the truck they had been pursuing were plenty scared and young Larry Gomez almost fell down when I ordered them out of the pickup. I thought he was going to faint. I have never seen a man's eyes as big as old Jyp Donohue's before nor since. And Galin Harmond was shaking so hard he could hardly climb from behind the steering wheel. I had told the other men to heave those rifles across the road and be doing it pronto. They all complied, I gotta say, but the passion on everyone's face was high. I mean, there was pure hate etched on those boys. I was just damned glad I had got to them when I did because I know three men would have been dead and five on their way to prison. I got a couple of my deputies out there pretty fast because I needed backup pronto. It sure was an explosive situation." He shook his head at the recollection.

"How did these men happen to take after the three men, Bruster?"

"Well, everyone in these parts has a radio in their rigs, you know. Phyllis had seen Galin's truck with Jyp and Larry roaring out of the yard when she drove up with her little girl. Then Ham Wilson met them on the Rogers driveway because he was not far behind Phyl. Thank God he got there when he did too, because he had hardly driven up when here came Phyl holding that tiny girl in her arms and screaming in total hysteria at finding her mother. Ham called me while he was bringing Phyl and little Bree with him. At first I couldn't understand him and had to get kind of cross with him to make some sense of him. I could hear the baby girl wailing and crying in the background. Sweet Jesus, it was terrible. I could hear Phyllis literally screaming and Ham himself in near hysterics trying to calm her."

As he talked, Ken noticed that Bruster's jaw clenched now and then as he felt the strong emotions from reliving that day. "You know, Ken, Galin Harmond said that he picked up that long-handled poker, the weapon there, where it had been dropped before they ever saw Nadine's body lying in the hallway. He said he reached down after entering the kitchen as Larry Gomez called out for Mrs. Rogers. He never realized there was blood all over it. He remembered saying to the other two men, 'Well what you reckon this is thrown out here for?' by that time, Larry and Jyp had gone into the living room right off the kitchen. Galin said he was the first to hear Larry scream and Jyp strangle out, 'Oh, my God.' Then he ran into the room to see what had happened. He said it was pure carnage, the most chilling sight he had ever witnessed. He literally panicked, as did the other two men, so they just ran from the house and fled in their pickup. You know, Larry Gomez was just like a part of the family here and the Rogers boys were friends of his. He and Ty Rogers graduated together from high school. My point is, he is like all these folks around there—had an open door policy of just calling out to somebody and letting them know they were there. Most often, people just came inside the residence. I mean, we're just country folks here and nobody thought anything about it—well, up until now, that is. Now, on top of folks having the jitters about this, the Conways got their wits scared out of them with this wacko prowler, not to mention the encounters you've had."

"Bruster, thank you for sharing this with me because it gives me more understanding of how this could have all come about." Muriel came up to their table now with their breakfast and refilled their coffee mugs. "Say, lady, that looks delicious, and I don't mean the food alone." He flirted with her outright, knowing she would blush and smile in front of Bruster. Bruster chuckled, catching the teasing humor, and gave Muriel a wink.

"Ken Ferries, you know you are an outright flirt," she feigned disapproval with a stern look and her hands on her hips.

"But I never lie to a pretty woman," he teased her and winked.

"Then I will be seeing you, Mr. Honesty, later on," and she grinned softly at him with the hinted suggestion that only they knew what lay between them.

"Count on it, pretty lady," he said and his eyes held the message of promise.

Bruster chose that moment to be seemingly unaware of what was transpiring between the two people. Muriel smiled and walked away to tend to other customers while Ken's eyes followed her retreat. He turned to look straight into Bruster's clear gaze and felt himself color slightly, then shrugged. "That lady has got me, hook, line and sinker." Then he laughed almost boyishly.

"Well, I told you before that a man could count himself lucky to win over a woman like Muriel. You are one lucky man, Ken."

"Thanks, Bruster. You are dead right about that. Now I want to ask you if you think I would need a special dispensation to talk to those three men."

"You might, Ken, but I can fix that for you. You just let me know enough ahead of time so that I can place a call to the warden."

"I would appreciate it, Bruster. I will figure out when it would work best for me and then get some time in with my son too. He is in Houston, you know, going to the police academy there."

"Why, Ken, that's right fine. I know you are proud of him and you ought to be."

"Yes, he is a good lad, that Carter."

"My son is one of the deputies here and you will have to meet him one day, Ken. He is taller than his old Dad but he always told me it was all right because he will always look up to his old Daddy." Bruster's smile expressed the good nature that Ken had liked right from the start.

"That says it all in volumes, Bruster, when you get that kind of regard from your grown son."

"We're mighty appreciative of our children and of each other, Sadie and me."

"That helps, because most youngsters will grow up solid when there is good rapport between the parents." Bruster nodded to show his agreement.

"So, what do you have planned today, Ken? Anything special?

"For one thing, I want to stop in and pick up a print that I had framed at Nadine's Arts and Crafts. Then I was hoping I might get to see both Con Womack and Judge Sam Bullard."

"Well, good luck with that testy old judge. Those two are a pair of shrewd foxes but you can add rude on top of that for old Sam Bullard, especially if he don't take to you right off," Bruster warned. "I think he is due to retire right soon but I believe Con will hang in there a few more years. He lives for challenge and loves playing devil's advocate. Told me one time he was Irish so if you are for it, he's against it." Bruster laughed heartily.

"In my line of work, I've had to meet all kinds of hard cases like those two so you might say my hide has gotten toughened," he chuckled but silently was glad that Bruster had given him some information on what to expect from those two old salty dogs. He just hoped he would be able to see them both.

"You check at the courthouse in Longview and you might be able to see the judge. Part of the time Con Womack is there too but he has also an office on the same street as the courthouse."

"I am mighty obliged to you, Bruster. I don't know if I will get anything out of them but don't you think it might be a good idea to discuss with them some of the events that have taken place since I started researching this case?"

"I surely do, because, as I've told you, I've felt that there was a great deal more to this case. All of these recent developments will certainly whet their appetitie for more follow-up. I know for certain that Judge Bullard would have imposed the death penalty on Galin Harmond if he hadn't had some feeling that things weren't quite right with that case. He is one hard-liner, Ken."

"So I have heard," Ken agreed.

They left the café after Ken told Muriel he would see her later that evening. They walked back to the Sheriff's office, arriving just as a young man in a deputy's uniform was coming out.

"Say, this is my son, Ken. Come on over here, Tony, and meet a friend of mine," Bruster called to the young man. He was a taller version of Bruster and had the same affable presence as his father. He walked toward them smiling with his hand outstretched to Ken.

"Now I'll bet you are Mr. Ken Ferries. Katie said that you and Dad had gone to breakfast. It is a pleasure to meet you, sir."

"Tony, the pleasure is mine." Ken shook hands with him.

"Your father was just telling me about you," Ken said, as he measured this man in closer scrutiny.

"Oh boy. I hope it was good stuff." His chuckle sounded just like his father's, hearty and resounding.

"Sure was, Tony. He is as proud of you as I am of my son Carter, who, by the way, is taking police science in Houston. About ready to graduate now, too."

"Say, that is great. Sounds like you and my Dad share some things in common."

"Yeah, Tony, I think that we do," Bruster said, smiling appreciatively at his son.

"Yes, except I haven't as yet been blessed with grandchildren, so your Dad's ahead of me there."

"Well, that does seem to come around in due time," Tony chuckled brightly.

"Listen, Dad, I better go. I've got a call from out at the Conway's while you were gone about a young bull that somebody killed on their spread."

"How's that, Tony? Why, Bud Conway was in here earlier on another matter." Bruster looked perplexed and reached up to the back of his head, just beneath his hat, and scratched.

"Yes, I know, Dad. But after he was here and placed that report, he went out with his horse to look over the stock. That's when he found the bull."

Bruster shook his head. "Tony, you best be getting on out there then."

"I will see you later then, Dad. Once again, Mr. Ferries, it was good to meet you."

"Call me Ken, Tony. Glad to meet you too. I will be seeing you again."

The young man gave a short wave and then walked to his cruiser parked in front of the Sheriff's office. After he pulled away, Bruster stood watching after him thoughtfully. Finally, he spoke to Ken, "Now that is damned strange in view of the incident Bud reported out there earlier."

"Yes, I agree with that, Bruster. Naturally, you can't help but wonder if they aren't related incidences."

"Well, I've got this unsettled feeling that they are, Ken. Anyway, good luck to you on your trip to Longview and let me know how that turns out."

"Sure will. I will swing by tomorrow morning and let you know before I head back to Waco."

"Good enough then, Ken."

"Thanks again for breakfast, Bruster." He spoke as he walked around his car and unlocked it. Bruster waved and smiled, then walked into his office.

As Ken drove toward Longview, he mulled over the events that seemed to be piling up faster than his mind could handle. However, it was a day he felt might prove productive, even overriding the possibly virulent attitude of the old judge Sam Bullard. Ken had to inwardly smile at Bruster's descriptive colorful picture of the two men, judge and attorney. He decided that he would try the judge for an audience first.

He also thought of Will Rogers and wondered if young Dr. Ellis would have any luck getting past the massive depression of the man. He needed help to get him to start handling his life again, to cease the self-destructive behavior. He said a prayer aloud for the Rogers family as he drove. He hoped that goodness could and would prevail once more for that family and draw them close together again.

He thought of Muriel and his heart was so full of love for her that he felt almost dizzy with its effect on him. He laughed out loud and chided himself for being such a wreck, just like a twenty year old.

He drove up to the courthouse and parked some distance from the entrance under a large acacia tree with yellow flowers. He admired the array of well-tended flowers that graced the median between the street and sidewalk.

"Flowers are a good omen," he decided promptly as he mounted the courthouse steps. Inside he paused to admire a life-size bronze sculpture of a fallen policeman with another officer bent down on one knee supporting his fallen comrade. The artist had clearly captured the distress of the man holding his comrade and the horrific pain etched on the injured officer's face. He felt a sudden tearing at his heart as he thought of the good officers, both men and women, he had known who had died in the line of duty. He thought of his son, of Bruster and Tony, of all the law enforcement people, and he whispered a prayer for them.

He turned and made his way to an information desk where a pretty black girl in her twenties smiled a greeting at him.

"May I help you, sir?"

"Yes, I hope that you can. I wonder if perhaps Judge Bullard is here in the courthouse. And if not, how might I reach him?"

"As it happens, he passed this way no more than five minutes ago on his way to his chambers." She smiled and her eyes took on a glow of mischief as she held up some pink carnations in a white milk glass vase.

"You see these lovely flowers? Well, every other day, Judge Bullard brings me some from his garden, different ones depending on the season of the year. The first year I worked here, I was scared of him because he acted purely peeved at everyone. Do you know the judge?" Her smile was teasing now.

"No, young lady, I haven't had the pleasure but hopefully I will today.

"Well, his bark isn't at all who he is, trust me. He does have a heart, but after my first few encounters with him, I couldn't do anything but stammer and shake. One day, he walked up behind me and tapped me on the shoulder. I turned around and he was holding three of the prettiest red roses out to me. He just waved my thank yous aside and strode off with his usual bearish look." She had a delightful young girl laugh and Ken found himself laughing along with her. "So hopefully, he will take time to see you but you have now been forewarned and forearmed."

"Why thank you, young lady. It has been such a pleasure to talk with you. It does seem that the honorable judge presents different facets to everyone."

"Well, only until they get to know him," she smiled broadly.

He made his way along the corridor in the direction the young woman had given him. He breathed deeply as he entered an office where an older woman looked up at him over ornate half glasses.

"Yes, may I help you?" she said and tucked a stray piece of hair back into the bun at the nape of her neck. She watched Ken with a coolness that he was sure had been acquired to ward off annoying time-wasters. He made a mental note that this sixtyish stern lady was the perfect counterpart for Judge Bullard.

"I will start by introducing myself," and he handed her his card.

"Hm," she said as she studied the card, then looked up at him with just a hint less of coolness.

Quickly before she could interject anything, Ken continued, "I am doing research on the Nadine Rogers case as a freelance writer. I retired a short time ago as a journalist with the Waco Centennial."

"Yes, Mr. Ferries, I read your column for years but now I assume you are here to discuss aspects of that murder trial with Judge Bullard?"

"Yes, I am, if the judge will spare a few minutes."

She sat there for a few moments and then rose, pulling briskly at her skirt which fit over a rather attractive figure. The figure did not seem to comply with the lady's severe demeanor nor the old maid hair style. She reminded Ken of a teacher he had had in sixth grade. Miss Ethel Pickett had greatly intimidated him for the first half of the school year. However, he fondly recalled her now as the person who had been largely instrumental in encouraging him to get into the field of writing. She had also been one of the prime characters in his life who had given him insights into the whole package of people, not just the covers, so to speak.

"I will see, Mr. Ferries, if the judge will see you. Please take a seat," and she motioned to a chair at the front of her desk. She returned in a short time, saying, "Mr. Ferries, Judge Bullard will see you."

She stood aside as Ken entered the judge's chambers. A craggy man sat behind a massive oval desk in a swivel chair staring out a side window. He was watching a honeybee flitting from one tall flaming red canna lily to another.

"Damnedest insects, aren't they? The sting hurts like hell but they are also the honeymakers. Go figure, humph!" he growled.

"Well, sir, I never thought much about that but you have a point, I would say. No pun intended."

'Har har," he laughed harshly. "I like that. Shows you are on your toes. I should not wager as to why you were a journalist." His old face seemed to crinkle deeper with the laugh lines like pinched dry prunes.

"Well, get on with it. Maude tells me that you are researching the murder case I presided over some several months ago, regarding Nadine Rogers."

"Yes, Judge Bullard. While I was still a newsman, I was drawn to that case, and frankly, I felt that some key points in the case weren't—well, weren't fully presented during the trial."

"Yes, yes, go on." The growth on his white eyebrows almost covered his steely blue eyes, giving him even more of a dour look.

"It seems to me that a lot of circumstantial evidence was presented without much follow-up."

Judge Bullard pulled on his lengthy earlobe and studied Ken, his eyes unflinching. Ken decided to go on with his hypothesis distilled from news accounts before coming to Rosewood. He then related some of the sinister events shortly after he arrived in Rosewood and started asking questions. He carefully avoided the metaphysical aspects but knew that he had more than enough other information to perk this old judge's legal juices to the full. When Ken abated, the judge leaned back in his swivel chair and folded his hands across his stomach. He said nothing for some time while he stared above Ken's head.

Finally he spoke and it was almost as though he was talking to himself after pondering quietly. "You know, Mr. Ferries, there is nothing more limiting or pathetic than a self-imposed blind fool. In all the years that I have sat on this bench, I have seen many of these kinds of fools. Now, I am known as a damned old hard-liner and have been put under siege by the general public for most of my career but I could give a damn about those wring-your-hands liberals as well as the blood drinkers who think nothing of extermination. I do not make statements of this kind, and certainly not to the press or to freelance writers, but I did not feel that the death penalty was in order for this case. I did, however, feel for the brutal way Nadine Rogers was snuffed out."

"So then, Judge, you did feel that there were some questions regarding these three men as the murderers of Mrs. Rogers?"

"Hell, you don't jump the gun when a person's life is in the balance. I happen to know that you, Mr. Ken Ferries, followed that format throughout your journalistic career. That was why I knew that what I read in your column was researched and not a bunch of crap just for a story." He continued, "As you know, there was not enough evidence presented on those men's behalf so I just couldn't let them walk either. But I think maybe you have started to unearth some facts and I hope you will keep me updated on this. In case you haven't already been warned, I would caution you to watch yourself carefully."

"I certainly will, Judge. I have appreciated your taking time from your busy schedule to discuss this with me."

"Now, good day to you, sir." And with that, he turned his attention back onto the hovering bee that was still infatuated with the cannas.

"Well, Con Womack ought to be a piece of cake," Ken thought as he walked from the Judge's chambers.

"Thank you, ma'am," Ken said as he passed Maude at her desk.

"Oh, you're quite welcome," and she smiled, which achieved a magic transformation. She had lovely features, a good bone structure, and china blue eyes that held a note of cheer in them with an undercurrent of amusement. "Well, now what do you think of our dear and illustrious Judge Sam Bullard, Mr. Ferries?"

"Well, he is pertinent and gets right to the point, but I can't fault him for that. Certainly I felt that he had a respect on my behalf and I didn't get that he is easily impressed with the majority of the population." Ken kept his face from betraying his amusement as he gave his opinion to Maude.

"Mr. Ferries, Judge Bullard never missed reading your accounts and he would never outright betray the fact that he holds you in high esteem. He roars over what he terms complete dribble and hackneyed ill-informed trash put out by the vast community of the press."

"I must say that I am highly honored indeed, because I did take into account that he is not easily impressed."

Maude stood up and stretched out her hand to Ken. "It has been a pleasure to meet you, Mr. Ferries. And, for the record, I too have been a fan of yours." Her smile was warming.

"That is certainly nice to hear," Ken smiled, looking deep into her eyes. He saw a woman who had taken life on at full tilt and he knew that she had struggled to get to where she was now. Like a film unfolding before him, he saw a pretty young woman, not much more than a girl, with a little boy held on her hip. She was reading a telegram that said "missing in action" and he knew that she had been widowed and left with a child to raise alone.

"When I get this book written, I will give you a copy and one for Judge Bullard too."

Her eyes filled with pleasure and she answered, "My name is Maude English and I thank you. Please have a good day."

"I will and you as well. Now, might I inquire of you where I can find the attorney Connie Womack's office?" She reached for a pad, wrote down the address and handed it to Ken. He thanked her and made his way out of the courthouse, first waving to the young lady at the information station. He gave her a victory sign and she smiled broadly at him, clasped her hands together and shook them to show Ken her pleasure.

The office of the defending attorney was easy to find since it was a few doors down the street from the courthouse. Ken looked at the black lettering on the woodsy green door and admired the attractive etched glass scene of wild waterfowl around the edge of the frosted glass. The scene warmed Ken's spirits as he went inside to find a large potted fern in the foyer. Just beyond the foyer, Ken could see a young blonde woman busily typing at her desk. As he came into the office, the woman looked up.

"Yes, sir, may I help you?"

"Yes, I hope you can. I would like to speak with attorney Connie Womack," and he handed her his business card.

"As it happens, sir, he should be back," and she looked up at the clock above her desk, "any time now. Perhaps you would care to wait?"

"I am willing to wait," Ken assured her and she pointed to some comfortable chairs across the room. She resumed typing as Ken took a seat and picked up a magazine from an end table that also held a brass candlestick lamp. He leafed through the magazine and was surprised to come across a section that portrayed one of his assignments on the culture of Native Americans in Texas.

"Hm," he said aloud, not realizing that he had spoken.

The blonde secretary turned around from her typing. "I'm sorry, sir. Were you talking to me?"

"Oh, excuse me. I must have been talking out loud and I didn't realize that I had."

She smiled and turned her attention back to her typing. Ken marveled at her astute hearing above the furious high-speed clattering of the typewriter. He quietly reminded himself to buy a copy of the magazine with his article in it.

A man entered the office who Ken recognized from television coverage of the trial. He was almost gaunt and his navy suit hung on his lanky frame like it had been carelessly thrown on him. He brushed aimlessly at a strand of hair which had lost its way down his high forehead. His hair was not an indication of his age, which was probably close to seventy. He had a full head of jet black hair, combed casually in keeping with his overall appearance. He could have been bedecked in a designer suit and still given the impression of a hard-working Georgia dirt farmer from the 1920s.

The secretary handed him Ken's card after he asked if he had received any messages while he was gone. He had not seen Ken when he walked in and now he turned to look at him.

"Well, hello, Ken Ferries," Con Womack said, turning large owlish eyes onto him, taking full appraisal of him as he walked towards him. Ken stood up to take his outstretched hand. "You are the Ken Ferries who was a reporter and now gone freelance writer?"

"One and the same," Ken smiled at this big raw-boned man and shook his hand firmly.

"I do have some time so please come on into my office. Ellen, if I receive calls, tell them to call back in half an hour, that I am in a conference."

"Certainly, Con," his secretary agreed and nodded to Ken.

Ken noticed that she was an attractive woman with warm brown eyes, probably in her mid- to late thirties.

"Ellen is my daughter-in-law and a darned good secretary too. I had a deuce of a time finding anyone who would put up with me as long as Ellen has." His fondness for the woman showed clearly on his homely but kind face. Ellen just smiled at Con and Ken could see that she had a deep respect and fondness for her father-in-law.

The walls in Con's office were lined with law books, enough to fill a modest library, Ken deduced. His desk was of massive proportions with a large leather swivel chair to hold his angular Abe Lincoln frame.

"Would you care for coffee?" he asked as he strode to a coffee urn on a cart.

"Yes, sir if you are having some too."

"Never pass it up, especially if I can get someone to join me. Makes it taste better, you know, to converse over a cup of good coffee. Ellen out there has just the right touch with it." He smiled at Ken as he poured two mugs full.

"Take cream and sugar?" he offered.

"Just black, thank you." Ken settled back into the depths of the large leather winged back chair as Con handed him the steaming mug.

"You know, Mr. Ferries, I am noted as disagreeable and I probably am. My wife tells me that I have a streak of pure cussedness in me but I can't abide pretentious or highhanded bullies. I can spot it in one's makeup before they open their mouths. I fully support ameliorism, a doctrine that purports the world might be better through human effort if we could all just knuckle down a bit more and not just let a few higher-minded people handle it all. I do see the efforts in some but it is kind of like keeping the trash cleared. You know how it goes—you can go and do it all alone. So, what I am saying to you, sir, is that I do salute you because you were part of the media for years and you are one of those high-minded souls who has made some difference in your own way."

"Sir, I do thank you for that. It has completely made my day because, before coming here, I spoke with the honorable Sam Bullard and, in his own off-handed way, he paid tribute to me as you have. I am greatly honored."

Con Womack threw back his head and laughed heartily. "You damned sure can be honored if old Sam even bothered to see you, let alone passed out some semblance of a compliment."

"I did gather that from a source or two beforehand," Ken chuckled. "Now, what I stopped by for was to share with you some developments which have come about since I started researching the murder case of Nadine Rogers."

Con Womack's owlish faded blue eyes centered fully on Ken. "Yes, please proceed. You have aroused my interest."

"First I would like to ask you a question, Mr. Womack."

"You may and I will answer it if I can." He still held the same owlish look on Ken.

"Did you feel that those three men committed the murder of Mrs. Rogers?"

Con Womack stared at Ken even more intently, as though he was weighing his words fully before he spoke. "Mr. Ferries, I have presided at some cases during my career where I have had more than a few questions and some I knew outright from common sense were as guilty as hell. Yet as a defending attorney, I had to present their case in accordance with our justice system. However, I did not do more than that. Where I knew or had questions, I poured forth every conceivable law tactic in the book to present the best defense that I could. I interviewed all three of those men, showing no mercy with my in-depth interrogations. After looking into all aspects of the questions and holding lengthy debates in that courtroom, I believe that people neglected to weigh all the possibilities of that case because their furor got in the way. The horrific demise of such a well-known citizen set people off like a powder keg. Add to that an ambitious prosecuting attorney like Pace Allard with his cunning courtroom intellect who had little trouble manipulating the jury."

"So, what do you think of Pace Allard overall?" Ken smiled, feeling that he had pretty well gotten his answer.

"My personal opinion is not to malign the man's reputation. As I said, he is very skillful at his work, but on a good day, I would find it hard to like the man and not just because we are on opposite sides of the pole. I have dealt with Pace before in a courtroom and I do admire him as an above average attorney. However, as a fellow human being, I feel like I have bitten into a sour lemon, frankly. He can be charming, as you have probably heard, but don't oppose the man, for God's sake."

"Yes, I myself have had privy to both sides of Pace Allard on a recent visit to his office," Ken offered. "Now, sir, I am taking a lengthy amount of your time but I do want to share with you that, since beginning my research in Rosewood, I have received numerous threats. Plain and simple, I was told to get out of town."

Con Womack let forth with a whistle and looked startled.

Ken added, "Now, I have filed a report with Sheriff Bruster Hernado."

"Yes, I know Bruster. Good man," Con said, nodding his head.

"So naturally, I am certain that I have opened up a can of worms and somebody is scared of what I may uncover."

Chapter____10

"Good God, man, be careful. I just think this only tends to prove what I felt right along. It was all too cut and dried and too many loose ends left hanging. By jove, I hope that you are taking every precaution because it is for certain that somebody's tail is caught in the wringer, and so is your safety." Con went on, "Now, I believe you should get a permit for a gun if you don't have one already."

"I did think some on that but, on the other hand, I have reason to think that I will be all right." He hoped that Con would not ask him why he thought so.

"None the less, you take care at all times and I hope that you will keep in touch, keep me informed."

"Yes, of course. I also told the judge that I would do so with him."

"You know," Con said thoughtfully, "I always knew that old Sam Bullard had some major questions himself or else he would have handed down a death sentence."

Ken agreed, nodding his head. "Sir, it has been helpful to talk to you and I do appreciate it."

"Call me Con, and now I hope that soon this thing will break wide open. If those men are innocent, I hope they will be out of prison soon. Now more than ever, I do believe they are innocent."

"Well, Con, it might be that a special investigation will have to be called in on this in due time."

"Yes, Ken, that very well may be the only recourse."

Ken added, "Like I said, Con, I will let you know all that develops." They both stood up and shook hands. "Good day to you, Con. It has been a pleasure."

"The pleasure's been mine, Ken. I will be hearing from you."

Ellen looked up from her typing as Ken entered the outer office. "Have a good day now, Mr. Ferries," and she smiled politely at him.

"Yes, ma'am and good day to you." He thought that she had a charming smile with deep dimples and a gentle expressive look in her eyes. Ken could see why Con liked this young woman so well because Ken sensed her caring soul and the pink aura around her. He felt that she operated with people from a deeply caring and supportive communicative approach.

He went out of the building and walked back down the street past the courthouse and to his car. He stood for a moment before walking to the driver's side and breathed deeply of the clean fragrant air which the various flowers and flowering trees provided. After he opened the car door and slid in behind the wheel, he jotted down a few notes in the notebook from the seat beside him. It was a habit he had developed in high school.

He started the car and pulled away form the curb. While he drove, he ran over his meetings with the judge and Con. He had taken a fancy to both of them, even in view of old Sam Bullard's barbed wire personality. He had looked past the outer covers and seen the soul of the real man. Con Womack was a straight-down-the-line sort of man himself, except perhaps 50¢ more tolerant than the judge. Ken smiled as he thought of the two men—both powerfully strong personalities but deep down-to-the-core good people.

"Oh, boy, I am as hungry as a bear," he said aloud as he checked the time on the car's clock. It was after twelve noon and he was looking forward to a good lunch at Dolly's served by one pretty waitress. His smile deepened as he thought of Muriel. His mind ran down so many different avenues while he made his way back to Rosewood.

He thought of what must have happened the day Nadine died and he had a flash of the tiny woman sitting in her favorite chair working on a colorful paper flower. A shrouded figure seemed to approach her. She was smiling at whoever it was but Ken could not get a clear picture. He shook his head and frowned, wondering why he was seeing this. He saw her get up from the chair, laying aside the flower. The shadow figure moved closer to her and the smile she had earlier was replaced by a look of surprise and shock. Two arms reached for her and pulled her close. As she struggled away, the arms reached for her again and this time the figure was roughly kissing her and pulling at her blouse.

"Good Lord, why can't I see who it is?" His mind spun and churned like a cyclone. He could literally feel the emotions of both of these figures, the small woman's shock mounted into terror and desperate escape. Ken could see her face and the tears and knew she was pleading with the person who held her captive. He felt the emotions of the other person, crazed and desperate emotions that had been held in too long. He was now out of control like a wild surging river that had broken free from its banks. A primitive savagery had ruptured through by the rejection and a deadly foe now combined with lust and rage overrode sanity.

As Ken saw this in his mind's eye with abject horror, he pulled from the roadway, trying to stop what he saw. He realized that he was sweating profusely and reached for his handkerchief to mop his face. The ugly scene persisted and he felt sickened with nausea washing over him in waves. Nadine broke away somehow while they were by the massive fireplace. She stumbled and attempted to run away but she got just inside the hallway when the first blow hit the back of her head. She crumpled to the carpet. Ken felt faint and weak as he witnessed the total savagery upon this tiny woman. He saw the shadowed figure turn away from the grizzly scene, still carrying the weapon and exit the residence. With his head resting on the headrest, Ken watched while the shadow figure left and he knew that whoever it was had the ability and endurance of a sprinter.

Something just didn't fit and Ken could feel it prickle around him. He kept his head back and his eyes closed thinking when something like a soft breeze suddenly wafted through the air. He opened his eyes and sat up straight while he looked around. He could not account for the breeze as the air was still.

He started up the car and pulled out onto the highway again. He felt a crying in his heart and was surprised to feel that his cheeks were wet with tears.

"God, I pray that this will all come to a head soon," he said as he wiped at his face with the back of his hand. He felt as though he wasn't in the car alone, as if a strong presence was sitting beside him. He knew that the golden spirit of Nadine Rogers was there, confirmed by the sudden fragrance of roses. He spoke aloud to the presence, "Nadine, this unfinished chord will be completed and then you can rest, beautiful spirit." As though in answer, the rose fragrance became more potent.

It stayed with him the rest of the way to Dolly's, then dissipated as he parked the car.

He walked into the café and Murial turned from a customer at the counter to smile a greeting at him. He felt a stilling within him just seeing her, one of peace and quietude. He felt that her presence gave him a grasp on reality and centered him. He walked to a booth and she followed behind him, sat the coffee pot down on the table and slid into the booth across from him. She took his big hands in hers and held his eyes.

"What is it, Ken?" she whispered and brought his hands up to her lips, kissing them softly.

"I saw Nadine the day she died, Muriel. I saw all of the events unfold like a horrible nightmare but, damn it, I couldn't see the face of the person who... who..." and his face jerked with emotion. Muriel reached for a mug sitting upside down on the table and righted it, then poured it full of coffee.

"Ken, it's all right if you want to wait and tell me later." Her green eyes held sorrow for him and such love that he felt calmed again by it.

"Afterwards, I could smell that rose fragrance again, honey. I knew that she was confirming to me what I saw in that vision."

"Oh, honey," Muriel said and clasped his hand to her mouth, squeezing Kens' hand firmly with the other one. Her eyes were glistening with unshed tears.

"I don't know why I wasn't able to see the face of the person who killed her, Muriel."

"I don't know either, Ken, but there is a reason for it, I just feel it. So much has come to light since you've come here that I know all of it will be shown to you when the time is ready. Now, you haven't had lunch, I bet." Her eyes took on a brighter spark in an effort to cheer him.

He felt himself relax more and shook his head no. "Just soup and a sandwich, pretty lady. And a glass of water." He smiled to reassure her that he was all right now.

"How did it go with your trip to Longview, Ken?"

"It went very well, honey, much better than I anticipated. Maybe it is why I was shown more on the way back here as it was a sign that it will soon come to a close."

'Well now, you see there, God is always there in the wings and just working through you over time, big guy," and she blew him a kiss. "I am going to get that soup and sandwich for you," she said, sliding out of the booth. "Oh, Ken, what kind of sandwich? The soup is beef barley."

"I don't care. Surprise me." He grinned happily at her. He took a long drink of water as he realized how thirsty he was. He thought with wry humor that about all he would need now was one of Nathan Tom's incredulous visits.

Muriel returned fairly soon with the soup and a chicken salad sandwich. Ken was greatly pleased since it was a favorite of his.

"I am going to let you relax and eat, my love. Then you might want to go sneak a nap." Her wink was suggestive with a slight naughty smile.

"Now, do you think I need a nap, Miss Muriel?" he teased back. She blushed deeply but her eyes sparkled like that of a mischievous child.

"You just might," she said and walked away with a backward smile and a wink.

"Whew, I haven't had this much pure joy and seductive flirtation from a beautiful woman in so long, I had darned near forgotten how one feels drunk with the intoxicating high of it." He grinned at his pleasurable thoughts almost sheepishly.

He finished lunch and, after lingering over coffee, remembered that he had told Phyllis and Rosie that he would stop by to pick up the framed print. He finished his coffee and strode over to the cash register. He waited for Muriel to finish with another customer to come wait on him.

"Muriel, I will stop back in and have supper around 6:30."

She reached for his hand and held it momentarily, her eyes never leaving his. "Ken, I will see you then, and after I finish up, we will go on to my place. It is fairly slow on Monday night so we can probably get away from here by 7:30."

"Oh, that will be fine. Say, I just as well check out of the motel and, then in the morning, I will take off for Waco." She nodded her head in agreement and he paid his bill, then left for his car. When he climbed in, he thought for a moment about himself and Muriel. He felt not the slightest bit of unease about having a romantic rendezvous with her. He reasoned that they were two grown adults in love and not out for a fling or a one-night stand.

"So, Ken old fella, you better be taking that lady out to find a ring," and he smiled at the thought of Mrs. Muriel Ferries. He remembered that he had told Sheriff Bruster that he would let him know if he got to see the judge and Con so he parked his car just in front of Bruster's patrol car. Katie smiled and raised her red eyebrows at Ken as he entered the office.

"Hello, Ken. Good to see you again. Did you need to see the sheriff?"

"Yes, Katie, as a matter of fact, I do, but just for a few minutes."

"Go right on in. He is in his office," she smiled at him.

"Hey, Ken, I see you are back already. Now how did the trip to Longview go?"

"Couldn't have been better, Bruster. As you suspected, Judge Bullard undoubtably had no other recourse but to sentence those three men. But he is one tough old cookie and I am certain that he would have handed down a death sentence for the one man had he not had some questions as to his guilt. And Con Womack said that he felt certain on that as he has known Judge Bullard for years."

"Did Con express his opinion as to how he perceived those three men?"

"Sure did, Bruster. He had not felt that there was enough presented in that trial and that it was swayed by the strong emotions of the public plus a very powerful prosecutor. From what Con said, he's a real bull in the courtroom."

"That is right enough on all counts. It was sure a factor on how I personally felt about it. Say now, I took a report from the Chans over at Larkins motel and they are still pretty shaken over what they both saw. That is truly the wildest thing that I personally have ever heard."

Ken chuckled aloud but he wondered what Bruster would think if he knew the rest of the story.

"What did you think of those two crusty old gents,Ken?" Bruster's eyes held an amused look.

"I don't think that Judge Bullard would win in a gracious gentleman's popularity contest but he is very shrewd. I got that right off. He did allow me the privilege that he had found me to be an all right reporter. I was especially pleased as his measure of the press in general rates lower than a bunch of aggressive arrogant tabloid hacks."

Bruster let forth with a roar of laughter, holding his stomach. When he stopped laughing and wiped away the tears from his eyes, he said, "That's good, Ken. At least you rated better than lawmen. He thinks they are in a class with Barney Miller."

"Now, you take Con. He is outspoken and that is a fact. But he isn't in the same ballpark as that contrary old judge."

Bruster still gave a rousing chuckle. "No, I have to agree on that."

"Why, Con offered me coffee and we had a good conversation. Mainly, I did listen to what the man had to say, though. Comes from a long acquired habit as a reporter, I suppose."

"Well, Ken, it is a good habit and one that has made you so well established in that part of your career," Bruster reflected with a more serious tone.

"It was an interesting experience meeting with those two official class minds. By the way, old Judge Bullard has a high regard for honeybees and flowers. Now that for certain lends to the man's character, regardless of his many disputatious views," and he laughed lightly. "They both advised me to watch out for myself and to keep them informed. Oh, and by the way, Con spoke well of you, Bruster, noting you as a good man when I told him I had filed a report with you."

"Well, I take that most happily because, as you may have guessed, Con is not one who passes out praise lightly." Ken was glad that he had remembered to pass that comment on to Bruster.

"Now, what's this about Judge Bullard and the bees and flowers?" Ken related the story of the young woman and the flowers the judge brings her every other day and his remark on the honeybees.

"I reckon it just proves that, somewhere, the orneriest of the lot have some goodness. A fella just has to hunt it out in the likes of honorable Sam Bullard." Bruster smiled widely at Ken.

"I do believe you are right, Bruster. Now, I'd better get over to pick up my framed print at Nadine's Arts and Crafts. I told Rosie I would stop by today."

"All right, Ken. I'll see you later. Oh say, I darned near forgot. The way is clear for you to go to the prison and talk to those three men. Now you might want to take at least three days when you do. The warden says that two days would be the minimum to talk to all three of them if you are planning on at least an hour interview with each."

"That isn't a problem. I appreciate your clearing the way for me, Bruster." He shook hands with him and left the office. He bid Katie a good afternoon on his way out.

When he reached the arts and crafts store, he noticed Phyllis' car was parked in front. As he opened the door to the shop, he met Phyllis on her way out.

"Hello, Ken. Did you come by for your print?"

"Yes, I did. It's good to see you, young woman. How is your father doing?"

"I stopped over there this morning and Dad had a discussion with Dr. Ellis, who is very persuasive. I think that between the doctor and Grandma, he will get some help."

"Well, my dear, I will say a prayer that he will. I hope that all of the family will join him in that counseling too."

"Oh, I don't think that will be a problem because my brothers and I have been very concerned over Dad. We will do whatever we can to mend as a family." Her voice trailed off.

On an impulse, Ken hugged her. "It is what is needed, Phyl. Trust me, it is what your mother wants."

"I know you are right about that. Thank you for your comfort."

"Any time that I can be of help in any way, please let me know."

'Oh, I will." She stood up on tiptoe and quickly kissed him on his cheek and then hurried to her car but not before Ken saw the tears in her eyes. He watched with compassion as she drove away and then went into the shop. Rosie smiled at him from behind the counter as he came in.

"Aw, now Mr. Ken, you would be here for the print. It is right here and I believe you will be happy with the results." She reached under the counter and brought it out. She propped it up so he could take in the whole scene.

"Rosie, that is just beautiful. What else can I say?" Rosie stood beaming with gratitude and delight at his pleasure.

"There is a certain feeling that one breathes in when they look at this, Mr. Ken," Rosie mused after she had turned the framed print around to fully appraise it herself.

"Yes, I know what you mean, Rosie. I am anxious for my elderly friend Sarita to see it because she is very sensitive to objects and undoubtedly will like this one. There is no doubt that Mrs. Rogers captured a powerful essence in this lovely piece of art."

'Who, might I ask, is your friend Sarita?"

"Well, she is my housekeeper but, in truth, more of a dear family member since she came to us when Gloria was expecting Holly."

"Aw, now 'tis good that you have had her there with you, Mr. Ken. It would have been terribly lonely for you after your dear wife passed on." She sniffed as she carefully began to wrap the framed picture.

"You are so right about that, Rosie," and he smiled at this charming woman who had the same generous spirit as dear Sarita. He thanked her and told her he would see her at the art show the next week.

After leaving the shop, he climbed into his car and was relieved not to see a note on the windshield. He made his way to the motel and thought about Muriel's seductive remark about taking a nap. He laughed out loud and shook his head. As he approached the motel, he reflected that he might take her suggestion but first he would compile notes so they would be ready to work on at home. He walked over to the motel office before going to his room and was greeted by Mr. Chan.

"Mr. Ferries, you are all right?" His face beamed with friendly light.

"Couldn't be better, Mr. Chan. I hope all is well with you and your wife?"

"Oh, yes, we are fine now. The sheriff came by and talked to both of us, took our statements. He was as mystified by the strange event as we were."

"Yes, he expressed as much to me, Mr. Chan. He said he had never encountered such a strange occurrence."

"My ancient great grandfather, who was born and raised in China, used to share some very strange stories with me when I was a boy. But I thought it was just the old one's superstitions and it was for me quite imponderable. And now I must tell you that I have been greatly humbled and I hope that some way my dear departed wise one knows and forgives me my doubts and inattentiveness."

"Somehow, Mr. Chan, I am sure that he does know, that he has always understood. Now, sir, I will be checking out later on today. However, next week I will return and would appreciate it if you would keep me in mind for the same room, if that is possible."

"Oh, yes, Mr. Ferries, that will be fine. I hope that you have a safe return and we are so happy to accommodate."

"Very good, then. I will bring the key over to you later this evening."

The man nodded and smiled. As Ken went out, the friendly cat walked up and wound himself around Ken's pant legs, purring happily and looking up at him with yellow-green eyes. Ken bent to stroke his glossy fur coat in appreciation of the feline gesture of welcome.

"You stand guard, old buddy, while I am away." The cat meowed as if in compliance.

He walked to his room and, after entering, pulled a chair up to the desk to make his notes. Afterwards, he sat back in the chair and stretched his body out fully into a sloped position. He raised his long arms above his head, twirling them for circulation.

"Well, lady Muriel, I think I will rest now. I hope that you know I am eager for this magnificent celebration of two lovers coming together in body and spirit for the first time." He smiled softly at the rapturous glow that washed over him. He bent to remove his shoes and then walked to the bed where he stretched his long frame out comfortably. He closed his eyes and saw the allure of the woman he loved and he stilled his longing, drifting into a peaceful slumber. He dreamed of his daughter Holly and saw her holding a smiling little girl with hair the same color as her mother's, but her eyes were the deepest blue. She clearly said, "Hello, Grandpapa."

He awoke and pondered the dream. He felt a sense of joy at having a sweet grandchild like that little girl. "Oh, well, sometime maybe." He lay there for a few minutes more and then decided to shower.

He made ready to put his belongings in his car after a lengthy shower. He dropped the key off in the office and decided that he would go by the restaurant and have some coffee, then eat later.

"Hi, Muriel. I took your advice and caught a nap," he grinned widely at her while she blushed deeply. Two cowboys sitting at the counter passed amused knowing glances. Ken acted nonchalant, then walked to a nearby table. She came to him with coffee pot in hand.

"Those two at the counter had better not say one word, and as for you, Mr. Ken Ferries, you have to do penitence to gain my good graces again." She pretended to glare at him.

"Ah now, honey girl, I love you and besides, I want to tell you that I had this wonderful dream about Holly, my daughter. She was holding a cute little tyke on her lap who looked just like Holly when she was little. The little one looked up at me and said, 'Hello, Grandpapa.'"

"Ken, that is precious. Maybe it is going to be for real and your daughter will be expecting soon." Muriel's eyes sparked with a teasing note, then she bent down to whisper in his ear, "I'll bet it will be an adventure to be two sexy grandparents." Her eyes took on a saucy look.

"You will undoubtedly be the prettiest, sexiest grandmother around," Ken whispered back. "Muriel, I just want some coffee for now. Dare you sit down with me for a minute?"

"Sure can," she smiled and sat down to face him. She took his hand and squeezed it lightly.

"Muriel, would you be able to go to Houston and Huntsville with me next week and just take that week off?"

"I am certain I can arrange that, Ken. I am owed some vacation time that I haven't taken. What's up, hon?"

Well, I thought maybe we could go visit with my son and he can meet you. Then, through Bruster's efforts, I have clearance to interview the three men in prison if they will agree to see me."

"Well, Larry Gomez' mother stopped by for a visit. It was brief as she was on her way to work but I did share with her that there was a possibility that her son and those other men may be released. I did caution her to keep it between her and her husband. Is that all right, Ken?"

"Oh, sure it is, Muriel."

"Well, that lady and her family need to have a glimmer of hope. I just felt like it was all right to give her some and, honey, she left here looking like she had dropped ten years off her."

Ken reached for her hand and kissed her fingertips. "God willing, this will all be over soon, pretty lady," he sighed.

"Yes, I pray it is. Say, how were you received by Judge Bullard?"

"Well, that old gent is a curmudgeon and not overly blessed with chivalry but, on the other hand, he is shrewd and sharp-witted. I do not think that much is easily put over on him. He was open to hearing me out and in a back-handed way complimented me on my journalistic career."

"I'd say you did fairly well. Now how about the defending attorney?"

"Again, I was well-received and, in fact, we shared a cup of coffee in his office."

"Goodness, hon, you seem to have the magic touch, even with the unapproachable old pillars of the law. It is no wonder that I am mere putty in your hands."

"Since that is the case, then you won't mind waiting on me and getting me a donut to go along with this mug of coffee."

"I just think that my indulgent nature might be prompted…" and her voice deepened into a sensuous allure. She picked up the coffee pot and gave his cup a warm-up. Then she focused her teasing green eyes on him and smiled before leaving to retrieve the donut.

As Muriel left the table, the café door opened and Pace Allard walked in.

"Hello, Pace," Muriel greeted him.

"So, Muriel, how are you? I haven't seen you in some time." He focused on her with a courteous smile, exposing perfect white teeth.

"Oh, doing tip-top, Pace. And yourself?"

"Very well, thank you," he assured her.

Ken studied him and noted that the man was handsome but there was a rigidity there. He presented a picture-perfect neatness right down to his highly polished brown shoes and seemed to be so perfectly programmed in an odd sort of way. He presented a feeling of unreality to Ken.

Pace became aware of Ken and turned his pearl gray eyes onto him with just the slightest glimmer of annoyance. It was so quick that Ken debated if he had seen it. He returned a brief nod to the crisp one he had received, then sipped his coffee. Pace seemed to emit a feeling like an artificial flume spouting frigid water. Ken felt it pour forth and give him a cold feel in the pit of his stomach.

Pace turned and sat down at the counter by one of the cowhands. He drew both men into casual conversation. Muriel brought Ken his donut and inclined her head slightly in the direction of Pace. She winked at Ken and then turned away, going behind the counter where she got a coffee mug for Pace and filled it. Ken listened to

Pace as he inquired of the two men, "So how's the world been treating you, Gordon? Lance?"

Ken knew that the man secretly found himself high born but one grizzled hard-worked range hand answered. "Well now Mr. Allard, I reckon I'm doing better than a green hand."

"Then Lance, I would say you can't do one bit better than that."

"Now that's a pure fact," the other man agreed. The two men guffawed as Pace smiled broadly at them. He said something to the men that Ken couldn't hear but he looked over in his direction. Then he picked up is coffee mug and made his way to Ken's table. A ready smile creased his mouth but his eyes held the look of a mean boy, Ken noted carefully.

"Well, Mr. Ferries, you are still here in our little community, I see. How is the research coming along?"

"It is coming along, Mr. Allard." Ken motioned to the empty chair at his table and asked Pace to join him. Pace set down his mug and seated himself across from Ken.

"Hm, I am reasonably certain that you have arrived at the conclusion that there is nothing further to add to that case?" Ken didn't know if he was posing it as an absolute or as a question. He could feel Pace measuring him as he waited for a response.

"Let's just say, Mr. Allard, that there are enough questions in my mind to merit further investigation." Ken sat back and watched closely for the man's reaction to that. He noted the muscles in Pace's face jerked but, other than that, the veiled look in his pearl gray eyes gave no indication of the concealed animosity. Ken knew well that this man held contempt for him because he judged him crass enough to dare question his knowledge and competency.

"So Mr. Ferries, I dare say that, though the fingerprints on the murder weapon were Galen Harmond and the three men beat a hasty retreat, you still question this case? Well, I find that most extraordinary." Pace raised his eyebrows at Ken as though confirming his confidence that he was totally clueless and probably daffy to boot. Ken also knew that Pace was shrewd and had perhaps found indications of other evidence leading him to defend himself.

Ken smiled a deliberate knowing smile, holding straight eye contact with Pace who was still smirking. He thought, half in amusement, "Oh, you sly fox you." From the first meeting with Pace, he had known the man was not a fool, in fact was very cagey. It would not have been a cake-walk coming up against this man, an expert at cajoling and calculating his maneuvers.

"Now, that will just have to remain to be seen, sir. As you know, nothing is ever usually cut and dried." Pace stood and smiled wryly at Ken as he realized that Ken could see through the pat hand he played. He knew it was better not to push further tactics on a man like Ken Ferries.

"It was good to see you again. I'm sure we will undoubtedly meet again since you will be in the area for awhile yet."

"Oh, yes, I'm certain that we will cross paths again. A good day to you."

Pace momentarily explored Ken's face for signs of social superiority. He nodded curtly and bid him good day. He spoke briefly to Muriel and left a sizable amount of change on the counter before going out the door.

Muriel came over to Ken's table and smiled down at him. "I wonder what Mr. Spit and Polish wanted?"

"I don't know, Muriel, but I do know that the man is a chameleon with a mania for manipulative measures, an apt con man." Ken did not reveal the thought that crossed his mind next but he had seen sociopathic personalitites with some of the same characteristics as Pace displayed. He wondered if the man didn't practice social democracy so proficiently that most people did not see the underlying layers. "He was curious to know where my research had led me and I didn't give him any information since the man's giant ego for being right is more hefty than any other concerns to him."

"Can you imagine what his wife has endured then, Ken?" Muriel shook her head but kept her voice low even though the two ranch hands were the only others in the café at the moment.

"Yes, I can but maybe she has reached a saturation point now, Muriel."

"What do you mean, hon?" Muriel searched his face.

"Oh, I don't know. That just popped out. Probably nothing other than thinking anyone who lived with a pompous ass like him all those years ought to get a medal."

Muriel threw back her head and gave a throaty deep laugh. Ken chuckled lightly as well. Muriel warmed up his coffee as Phyllis Bennett walked into the café.

"Hi there, you two." Her pretty face was alight and she came over to put her arm around Muriel's waist.

"Honey girl, how are you doing?" Muriel said and kissed her lightly on the cheek.

"Well, Aunt Muriel, I told you I would stop by after I saw Daddy and let you know what's happened to date, especially about counseling. He has finally agreed to it because Grandma got her head set on it and Dr. Ellis got persuasive. So, between the two of them, Daddy's first session has gotten underway."

"Oh, praise God literally, Phyl." Muriel then put her fingers to her lips and her eyes were glassy with tears. "Little girl, that is just so good to hear."

Ken reached out and patted Phyl's hand. "Sit down and join me, Phyllis. Won't you?" Ken urged.

"Oh, Ken, I wish that I could but Sissy Conway has got my two little darlings and, sweet as they are, they are a handful." She gave forth with her tinkling girl laugh that reminded Ken of tiny bells ringing.

"All right then. When you see your Daddy, tell him we all love him and we will see him soon."

"I will, Aunt Muriel." She kissed her lightly and bent down to hug Ken.

"Muriel, listen. Why don't we plan to leave from Longview after we take in the art show? Will it start in the morning that day?"

"From what Rosie told me at the dance, it starts at 9 and closes at 5. But if we need to, we don't have to take in that show, Ken."

328

"We sure don't want to miss it. I feel it is important and imagine how crushed that sweet girl would be if her Mom's best friend wasn't there. So, here is the plan, pretty lady. You have all of your things ready and we will go to Longview to the art show that morning. We'll stay about an hour and then fly to Dallas and then go on to Huntsville. I think we will get good flights. Then, after I see those three men in Huntsville, we will rent a car and drive on to Houston."

"I will get someone to take us to the airport in Longview, Ken. I'll find someone attending the art show that day too and they can ride over with us, then take my car back. We'll leave your car here. How's that?"

"I think that will work just fine. But we will need to clear it with that person to pick us up in Longview on Sunday." He added, "But let's take my car."

"That won't be a problem because I think I can count on Rosie Wilson to do the honors. She is such an old sweetie. I will talk to her right away."

"Since she was prodding me a bit at the dance to gain a firm hold on one Muriel Jacob, we will tell her that we are taking my bride intended to Houston to meet one of my children. That ought to make her burst at the seams having the inside track on that piece of news."

"Oh, you bet it will, God bless her. She is outspoken, that old darling, but all heart. You would not find a more loyal friend."

"She has shades of my dear Sarita, the same kind of personal and the dearest kind of friend," Ken said, shaking his head and smiling as he thought of Sarita.

"How about Sarita? Is she going to be open to a new lady in your life, Ken?" He caught a bit of wistfulness and anxiety in her voice.

"Pretty lady, she will love you. How could she not? I know that we have to discuss so many things in preparing for our life together but, trust me darling, that is just not a big issue. Nor will it be regarding my son and daughter." Ken saw the relief on her face and she smiled tenderly at him. "I guess maybe I better have that special on the board there, hon. I'm ready for it now," he said as he checked his watch.

The evening rolled on and few people came into the café. Ken saw Muriel talk to the cook in the back. Then, she came over to Ken's table.

"Say, Ken, that is Dolly and she owns this place, of course. I have it all worked out with her for next week. Her sister will come take my place. Anyway, I have vacation time coming so it wasn't any problem. Besides, Dolly is a real fine lady and I have worked here a lot of years.

"Well then good now do you think you will be finished in another hour Muriel"?

"Ken you take my key and I should be done here in another hour and a half".

"No, honey, I will just wait for you."

"No, no, just go make yourself at home. Make coffee if you want. There is apple pie in the fridge to go with it." She winked at him in high spirits.

"All right, pretty lady. That is too tempting to pass up."

She reached into her apron and handed him her house key, then bent down to kiss him. "I will see you pretty soon," she whispered, her voice husky.

"I can't wait," he whispered back and held her eyes with his own. All of the emotions of a man in love were nakedly clear for her to see.

Ken made his way to the car and noticed that across the street the dull green Jeep was pulling away from Bailey's lounge. He could see the man driving it but not clearly enough to make out what he looked like. He apparently saw Ken and accelerated the Jeep, rounding a corner and driving out of sight.

"Well, the guy likes to stop in at the watering hole every so often and it seems he picks an evening when it's not very busy," Ken mused as he unlocked his car and slid in behind the wheel. He made his way out to Muriel's home and enjoyed the cadence of the crickets after he got out of his car. The moon was beautiful and so bright that it was almost like daylight. Ken caught sight of the horses close by. One whinnied at Ken and the other two made nickering noises. All came to the fence to observe him closer. He reached across to the closest one and stroked the mare's silky coat.

"Life is good, girl. Plenty to eat and two big fellas there with you," he crooned aloud. She nestled her head on Ken's broad shoulder and blew happily. He stepped away then and made his way up the three steps to the narrow open porch and let himself in through the laundry center. A small nightlight made it easy to find the light switch and he turned it on, making his way into the kitchen. He easily found the coffee and decided to make some. While it perked, he found the apple pie, cut a slice and heated it in the microwave. He took the pie and mug of coffee to the living room to settle into the big comfortable chair he'd taken a fancy to.

He noticed that Muriel's high school yearbook was still on the coffee table. He retrieved it and began to pour over it leisurely, chuckling at some of the inscriptions from her classmates. He remembered some of the silly but fun quotes from his yearbook even though it had been so long ago. He smiled when he came across one of Jeff and Muriel who were obviously engaged in horseplay. Jeff was holding a long-legged Muriel in his arms clad in bobby socks and penny loafers, a slim skirt and high school letter sweater. Jeff was wearing jeans and boots but had on a football helmet. You could see that they were both caught up in the lighthearted exuberance that young people that age fully appreciate.

He turned the page and stopped short when he read a young man's name under a picture of him attired in a basketball jersey and shorts. He had written his name in his own hand and it read "From the Cat Man to one sweet Chick. Best-looking girl in the state of Texas. Love Catlin Willard." Ken flipped through the book again looking at the writing that he had seen when he and Angie scanned it before.

"Jeez!" he mumbled and then whistled aloud. He felt like his head was spinning as he studied the handwriting. He was near certain that it was one and the same as the person writing the notes left on his car window. He would ask Muriel if he could borrow the book and have Sheriff Bruster compare the handwriting.

He put the book aside and pondered the situation he had stumbled onto. His mind went back to the first time that he and Muriel had gotten together at Bailey's Lounge. The man had come in and sat down at the bar, ordering a beer. If this was indeed Catlin Willard, then no wonder he took of that evening as quickly as he had. He hadn't wanted Muriel to recognize him. Of course, he did not appear to bear much resemblance to the 17 or 18 year old youth in the yearbook, but then, Ken reasoned, most of us change as we mature. After all, the man he had seen in the lounge was close to fifty now.

"What was the connection to this case though? Was he a man who had returned after years had gone by to his boyhood roots and gone bad and killed Nadine?" He recalled that Jeff had said Nadine's parents had bought the Willard place when they moved to Rosewood. And Jeff had said that Gus Willard's only child Catlin had taken off. He had not said the youth's first name but Ken reasoned it had to be the one. It just fit too well. Then it hit him fully. He could feel his heart quicken.

"My God, Nadine was the owner of the ranch that Catlin's parents had until her folks bought it from Gus." What had the circumstances been? Maybe Mr. Willard didn't have any kin that he knew how to contact and, being in failing health, put the ranch up to be taken by the state. Or, perhaps before he died, he was approached by Nadine's parents and they bought it from him.

"Just maybe that is the reason Nadine's life was taken. That man may have approached her several times to buy the ranch and she had not wanted to sell it since the Conways were close to buying it." He felt a chill course through him and he shuddered. Again he saw the man running across the pasture, going to an older model dull green Jeep concealed in a grove of trees.

He reached for the coffee mug and swallowed a large sip. Then he put his head back and closed his eyes. Once again, he thought of the incident regarding the Conway family. He felt a sickness come over him when he remembered that Bud Conway had gone to the sheriff's office to report a prowler. Then he had reported finding a bull shot on his property.

He thumbed through the book and looked at the picture of a girl he found to be as striking as Muriel but she was an underclassmen, a junior. She had written a note under her picture: "Muriel, you are ever Aces and always had time to listen even to younger scrubs like me. Best of luck always, your friend, Marilyn Falzone." Ken recalled that Muriel had pointed out she had become Mrs. Pace Allard. And he remembered that Marilyn's family were wealthy; he was aware that they were as notable as the Rogers in the business world. Mr. Falzone was a state representative and had been for many years.

He stared at the face of the pretty girl and, as he did, he saw her face crumple into a massive sorrow so powerful he felt overcome with it. He clenched his eyes closed tightly and when he opened them, the picture was as before. He shook his head and then carefully closed the book and put it back on the coffee table. Strange how the cosmos brought him such awareness since he had become engrossed in Nadine's case. A spark lying just under the surface seemed to have caught fire from the highest realms.

As these thoughts ran through his mind, he heard a car drive up outside and knew it must be Muriel. He heard her come into the kitchen and call, "Hi, Guess who's home?"

"It must be the pretty woman I met one day and fell madly in love with," Ken answered happily. She walked into the living room to Ken and bent to kiss him. She pulled back and held his eyes with her own. Speaking huskily, she said, "Ken, I'm going to get a quick shower first and then I will be back. Will you wait for me that long?" Her eyebrows raised in question but her eyes held a teasing look with promise in them.

"I think I can manage that," he smiled at her.

She reached up to the lamp and turned it to the lowest setting, kissed him again and retreated quickly.

His mind stayed on her while he sat there in the semi-light room. He felt all his senses quicken with joy and arousal, with all the longing he had held in check for her. He sat with his eyes closed until he heard her call his name and, when he looked, she was standing a few feet from him. He sucked in his breath sharply at the sight of the beautiful woman standing there. Every curve of her lovely body showed clearly defined through the filmy gown she wore. Her hair hung loose near her shoulders and gave off a radiance almost like an aura. He was awash with desire for her even more.

His breathing was fast as he stood and went to her. His mouth crushed hers hungrily and he lifted her in his arms. She laughed softly with that deep throaty laugh that so intrigued him. She whispered to him and he followed her directions to the bedroom. A soft pink light from the bedside lamp was all that lit the room.

He laid her down on the bed and disrobed quickly. He heard her gasp sharply at the sight of his body. Ken was a man who had taken care of himself, staying lean and hard though his build was massive. He knew he could be proud of the powerful body he had maintained.

She whispered to him and he moaned with the exotic, intoxicating ecstasy. Her response became moans with little soft cries and later, when Ken rained kisses upon her, he felt her cheeks wet to his lips.

"Muriel, what is it?' he whispered to her softly.

"I'm just so happy to be with you. I can't help thinking how much love I have missed and how lonely I was for someone I could love again."

"I know, Muriel, I felt he same way, my darling. But we are just going to fully embrace every moment together and go forward now." The moonlight came through the window and gilded their bodies as they lay locked in each other's arms.

"Honey, I want to surprise you when we go to Houston," he whispered to her. "And no, you are not getting me to reveal it no matter what you do so that is going to be one tough time for me," he chuckled boyishly.

"Ken, you know that I will give you no peace because I was always a holy terror if someone was keeping a secret from me. Just ask my parents what I put them through before the Christmas packages were finally passed out." His laugh was mirthful. "My mother described me as very meddlesome and nosy."

"Well, my little sexy kitten, you have just met your match," he teased. He pulled her closer to him. "I love you, Muriel." He heard his voice choke with emotion.

"I love you, Ken. Oh, how I love you," she whispered.

Ken realized that they must have slept awhile for he awoke as the first rays of dawn were filtering through the window. He could hear Muriel's soft breathing beside him, sleeping peacefully. He looked at her as she slept, her lips parted slightly soft and pink. Muriel was a very pretty woman with fine bone structure. Her nose turned up just slightly and a tiny array of charcoal freckles were scattered across it. He liked all these little wonders that appeared when two people came together anew. All of it was exciting and mystical. He knew it would never end, this powerful love they shared and he thanked all that was holy that he could know two such loves in this lifetime.

While he observed every little feature of Muriel's peaceful face, she suddenly turned from her back and rolled on her side facing him. His face was level with hers and he continued to watch her for a moment before she opened her eyes. She stared into his and her eyes seemed to take on a deeper green. She smiled with an expression of total well-being. She leaned into him and kissed him with passion. Seeking his lips and finding his tongue with her own, they thrust together almost savagely. Then she screamed but muffled her cries against his massive shoulders. When they were spent, they lay there with Ken kissing her breasts and the hollow in her throat. He whispered her name between kisses.

Again they drifted into sleep. When Ken awoke, he could hear the shower just off the bedroom. He lay there fully enraptured and aflame with love.

"Hi, guy," she said as she came into the bedroom, a towel around her head and a light robe on.

"Hi, pretty lady," he crooned softly, smiling back at her. He got up and they embraced. Then Ken went to the bathroom where a warm shower awaited. He hummed as he had not done since Gloria died. "I have come fully alive again," he mused to himself happily.

When he got out of the shower, the aroma of bacon and coffee aroused a bearish appetite in him. He chuckled out loud and thought it was no wonder due to all the activity he had enjoyed so deliciously. He dried briskly and put on his shirt and slacks, chiding himself for forgetting to bring a change of clothes in from the car. He slipped on his socks and walked into the kitchen, slipped his arms around Muriel's waist while she fried the bacon. She turned in his arms to face him and they kissed with the sensitivity of two people in love.

"Gonna burn that bacon," she said and laughed in that husky way he liked. She smiled up at him and her breathing was heavy.

"Yes, it seems that the two of us are quite befuddled. I forgot to bring in a change of clothes last night."

"You watch this bacon for me and maybe pour yourself some coffee and I will go get your clothes."

Ken started to protest but Muriel had already started for the door. "It's okay, trust me. In case Mrs. Thelma McCarty has happened along, she will have broadcast our night together all over the county. She is the town librarian and the biggest gossip in the whole community. She should be coming along about now on her way into town. She's my closest neighbor just up the road." Her face held satiric humor. "She will literally be salivating that Muriel Jacob finally got laid and she would know, of course, living so close by."

Ken, who was turning the bacon, now turned off the flame and tossed back his head to roar with laughter.

"Muriel, my darling, you are never going to be accused of being sanctimonious," he said, still chuckling.

"Lordy, I hope not. Scandalous maybe but I will be happy to leave sanctimonious to good old Thelma." She dashed out the door. She was back by the time Ken had taken out the bacon and poured the coffee.

"I thought you would want the tote bag too?" she inquired as Ken went to retrieve his clothes draped over her arm.

"Oh, I'm glad you brought that since my underwear is in there along with my shaver."

"It was just as I thought. The widow McCarty passed by and was really craning her neck to see your car. She almost didn't see me she was so intent." Muriel's eyebrows were raised but she had pure mischief in her eyes.

"Well, you did say she is a widow, Muriel. How old is she?"

"Oh, I imagine in her late 60s. Why?"

"Has her husband been deceased quite awhile?" Ken answered Muriel's questions with another.

"I guess Doyle has been gone about eight years now." She was looking at Ken questioningly.

'Well honey, after all that time, maybe she is just frustrated." He kept a straight face while he took a sip of coffee.

"Oh, Ken Ferries! You may be right but that mouth of hers would sidetrack a man faster than a racehorse. I am not so sure that Doyle didn't just cash in a little sooner than he would have otherwise."

Ken just shook his head and grinned. He asked Muriel what time she had to be at work.

"I don't have to be there this morning until 9 o'clock because some days I rotate with one of the other girls. It works out great for all of us. It was perfect for the two of us, wasn't it." She gave him a broad wink as she pulled an egg carton from the refrigerator.

"Yeah," he smiled. "It's like everything for us is headed for perfect, like blessings from a higher place. I don't really know but I'm not going to question it and will happily accept all these great and wonderful tidings."

"I know it is from a heavenly realm, Ken, because it all feels so perfect and so right," and she came to him and kissed him. She looked at the kitchen clock as she dropped eggs in the skillet. "We'd better get started here though because it is almost 8 now." They sat down to breakfast and Ken recalled the high school yearbook with the familiar script in it.

"Muriel, honey, I looked through your high school yearbook while I was waiting for you to come home last evening. I want to ask you if I can borrow it for a short while."

"Well, yes, of course, but why? I mean, are you doing an article of some sort?"

He pondered a moment and then decided to level with her about most of the occurrences.

"Muriel, promise me that you won't get upset now when I tell you this." She stared at him but didn't answer for a moment.

"Go ahead, Ken, but I can't sit here and tell you that I won't be concerned or upset because it depends on what it is about."

"Well, first of all, let me go in the living room and bring back your yearbook. I want to show you something." He left the table to get the book. While he was in the living room, he opened the book and found the picture of Catlin Willard where he had written the inscription. He returned and sat down by Muriel, then placed his forefinger under the photo of the young man.

"Do you remember this man, Muriel?"

"Yes, I do. He graduated with me but I haven't seen Cat Willard since he left here right out of high school. Honey, what is this all about anyway?"

"Well, I have received several threats through notes on my car and some by phone at the motel." Muriel's eyes grew wide with fright.

"Oh, God, Ken. I didn't realize you were in danger." She clutched at her chest.

"Now listen honey, just calm down. It's okay. I have filed a report with Bruster and, besides, I have reason to believe that this guy is laying low at least for awhile. He had an experience very recently that scared him into a cocked hat, if you will pardon the expression. It's one that I borrowed from my colorful Dad." He chuckled to ease the moment.

"I don't care, Ken. This terrifies me. Oh, honey, if anything happens to you, I just couldn't handle it."

"Muriel, I have been in some situation before where I have had to keep my eyes peeled. Now, trust me, darling, it is going to be all right. Besides, I have the feeling that this thing is about to crack wide open." He took her hand and kissed it, then put it to his face and held her eyes lovingly in his own.

"You see the writing under this fellow's picture? It looks like the writing in the notes. I kept wondering why it seemed familiar and then, last night when I was looking at this book, I remembered where I had seen it before. Angie and I had looked at this together while I was waiting for you to finish getting ready for the dance. She had shown me pictures of her Dad and this book of you as a senior. So, I think that Bruster and I need to compare the script. Now, Bruster may want to keep this book for awhile to have a handwriting analyst confirm it one way or the other."

"Sure, Ken, that's all right with me. But I am in a quandary about this. Why would Cat Willard be doing this? From what I've heard, he took off right after his mother died. He was pretty wild when we were kids in high school. He asked me out on a date and I did go with him to a movie and later for a Coke. On the way home, he tried to squeeze the Coke out of me as I recall."

Ken had to chuckle at Muriel's description. He was sure that his Dad would fully appreciate this lovely, down-to-earth woman who had a pattern for word phrases like his own.

"Honey, just think about it. Nadine's parents left that ranch to her and wasn't Gus Willard the one who sold it to her folks?"

"Yes, he did because he was in failing health and knew that he couldn't keep up with it. It was starting to get run down and I think the heart just went out of him after his wife died. Cat up and left and never contacted his Dad. Gus had tried to find Cat, I heard, but to no avail. So he gave up and I expect what money he had from the sale of the ranch was drained by the home care he needed before he passed away. To tell you the truth, everyone just kind of figured maybe Cat wasn't alive either. I just never thought about him and I don't think anyone else did either. He was gone so long and after a while, you don't dwell on it really." Ken nodded his head in agreement.

"Ken, are you thinking that maybe Catlin returned here and wanted to buy the ranch from Nadine and she refused him? And he... oh God!" She crammed her fist to her mouth and her eyes were wild with horror as the possibility hit her fully. "Ken, why wouldn't someone see him and recognize him though?"

"Maybe he is extra careful, Muriel. Another thing, people change and it has been a lot of years since he was here, honey."

"Of course you are right," she agreed.

"One thing puzzles me about all this supposition. If Cat did try to make an offer to Nadine and she refused, why would he do such a horrible thing? If the man had the kind of money to make an offer for that property, he could certainly find another place for sale. The only thing that really did cross my mind is that he might have made advances to Nadine and she fought him and he just ran amuck. I mean, the guy can't be very stable if he is sending out threats to me."

"No, he certainly isn't but there are things about Cat Willard that I just couldn't figure out when he was a kid," Muriel said, then went on. "He was an only child and maybe he just came into this world with a blueprint for pure mean, a contemptible jerk. His parents didn't lavish him with extravagance but he seemed to have this overblown ego, like he needed to outshine the other guys. He was always driving too fast and he could be really competitive and a bit ruthless at basketball. I remember the boys would talk about it at times and couple of the girls he dated, including me, said he wanted to get pretty frisky. Yet he didn't get bad enough that we were afraid of him. I just thought he was a bit of an overheated puppy like a few other guys until they got put in their place." She grinned and winked at Ken.

Ken grinned back at her with a teasing look. "Sweet lady, I can see why some of those boys tried and I can't say that I blame them."

"Well, they found out in a hurry what my attitude was on it." She glanced coyly at him. "Honey, now Cat was ornery but it's hard for me to think that he could ever have been capable of…" She stopped and put her hand to her throat.

"People change sometimes, Muriel. One thing for sure, Sheriff Bruster will run a make on this man and we will find out if he is indeed the guy who has been handing out threats and was involved in that crime. You might ask Will or one of his children if anyone other than Bud and Sissy Conway tried to deal with Nadine on that property."

"Oh, honey, you bet I will. I will ask one of the kids first though and, if they don't know, I will ask their father. He is bound to know. Well, I hope he does anyway." She looked at the kitchen clock and rose quickly.

"Oh say, I've got to get my uniform on, Ken, or I will be late. Now you stop by the café before you leave for Waco, please."

"Muriel, I will go now before I get crazy and keep you right here." His eyes were filled with seductive teasing.

"You make it tough on a girl, Ken Ferries." Her eyes held the promise of still more passion and lovemaking. She left the kitchen quickly, knowing how tempted they both were. He thought it was going to be difficult to be away from this woman for a few days. He stood up and started gathering the dished to carry them to the sink.

344

"Hon, you leave those dishes and I will get them when I come home," she called to him.

"Okay, pretty lady, I hear you," he answered but continued with the task. He carefully wiped and rinsed them, put them in the dishwasher and then was wiping down the range when she returned to the kitchen.

"Honey, you didn't have to do all this," she admonished.

"Why not? I ate breakfast too, didn't I?"

"Okay, I'll accept that. Like love is a two-way street and so are the chores." She giggled lightly.

"You got it, sugar," and he kissed her quickly, then pulled back to smile down at her. "You have an added sparkle, lady. Did you happen to notice?"

"Shows, doesn't it?" and she kissed him. "I guess I'd better scoot. Just lock the door behind you, hon." She blew a kiss and departed.

He made his way into the bedroom, taking the tote bag along with him. He opened it to remove his shaver and went into the bathroom. He stared at himself in the vanity mirror and noticed a definite second self, one that he had not seen for much too long. The beauty of being together intimately with someone was a friendship unparalleled and he had missed it. He finished shaving and then paused at the bedroom, embracing inside the solemn occasion of himself and Muriel coming together for the first time. He would remember the beauty of this forever, he knew. He breathed deeply and expelled his breath slowly. He hefted the tote bag to his shoulder and made his way out of the house, making certain that he had locked the door behind him. He pocketed the house key, thinking he would return it to Muriel .

before leaving for Waco. He then remembered that he had left Muriel's yearbook on the kitchen table so he put his tote bag in the car and returned to the house. He retrieved the book and shook his head for forgetting it. "I think I suffer senior moments from time to time," he chuckled ruefully. "Of course, it could just be the result of being totally giddy over a beautiful woman," he silently chided himself. "At any rate, I would prefer the latter excuse," he spoke aloud as he climbed into his car.

He decided he would first drop by Sheriff Hernado's office and turn the yearbook over to him. Katie greeted him when he came into the outer office.

"Good morning, Ken. How are you this morning?"

"Oh, hello, Katie. Never better and yourself?"

"I am just tip top. I got a call last night from my daughter and son-in-law in Beaumont with the news that I am going to be a grandma for the first time." Her smile was literally amplified.

Ken went to her and took her hand, clasping it with a genuine expression of happiness for her. "Well, Katie, I would surely say that kind of news would make a person be in a tip top frame of mind. Congratulations!"

"Thank you, Ken." She smiled more radiantly. "Now, I imagine you came to see Bruster so I will tell him you are here." She stepped into Bruster's office and announced that Ken was there to see him. Bruster called out to Ken to come on in. He stood up from behind his desk as Ken came in. He could see that the Sheriff had been engrossed in some ledgers that were open on his desk.

"Bruster, I hope this isn't a bad time for you. It looks like you are pretty busy," he said as he indicated the open ledgers atop the desk.

"Aw, just doing some backtracking on some matters from awhile ago. Nothing that won't wait a spell," he smiled exposing his gold front teeth.

"Well, I have some information for you about who has been sending me those threatening notes and visiting me at the motel too."

"You don't say. That's great! What have you got there?" His voice rose slightly with excited expectation.

Ken laid down the yearbook and then sat in one of the chairs in front of the desk. "That's Muriel's high school yearbook from her senior year. I was looking through it last evening out at her place. When Angie was home, she showed me a couple of the yearbooks because Muriel's reunion is coming up. Anyway, last night I realized that was where I had first seen that handwriting from the notes. I was just killing time waiting for Muriel to come home."

Bruster suppressed a knowing smile but not before Ken saw the quick sparkle of awareness. He chose to pretend that he didn't notice and went on with his account. "If you will recall, Bruster, I believe I did mention that the script looked familiar to me."

Bruster nodded and went to his file cabinet. "We will find out soon enough." He pulled a folder from the cabinet and Ken reached for the yearbook, finding the picture of Cat Willard. Bruster put one of the notes next to the picture with the inscription.

"Why, that boy has been gone since his mother May passed on, God rest her soul. That kid high-tailed it to God knows where and just broke the man's heart, I reckon. My lands, that sure enough looks completely comparable with these notes." Bruster reached up to scratch the side of his head. He had a mystified look on his face, as though trying to sort through the implications of this puzzle. "Humph," he said as he continued to study the notes and inscription. Finally, he fixed a blue-eyed stare on Ken.

"Listen here, Ken, I just think that we've got something here. I take it that Muriel gave the okay to hold onto this yearbook awhile?"

"Oh sure, she did, Bruster. She is kind of shook up after finding out about the threats but there was no way that I could keep it from her any longer."

"I appreciate the lady's concern but, after what transpired at Larkin's the other night, I reckon our boy is still pretty shook. Why hell, that kind of unnerves me so can you imagine?" He shook his head and studied Ken as though trying to fully contemplate it all.

"Bruster, Muriel is going to inquire of the Rogers family if anyone other than the Conways were offering to buy Nadine's ranch property. It's the only thing that makes any sense to me, especially if Cat Willard is involved."

"I tell you, that man has been laying darned low if he is back around Rosewood. But, of course, it might be that nobody recognizes him since he was only eighteen when he left. I will run a make on him and see what shows up. Meantime, I 'm going to get a police handwriting expert to give us a definite opinion. Might take awhile to get but we will get to the bottom of it."

"All right then, Bruster. I guess I had better get over to Dolly's and tell Muriel goodbye and then head home to Waco for awhile. But if you want to reach me at any time at home, you have my card."

"Sure will, Ken. We'll be seeing you and thank you. I truly think that we are getting somewhere with all of this. I am eager to follow up on it."

The two men shook hands and Ken made his way out of the office, giving Katie a high sign on the way out. He drove to the cafe and parked just outside. He noted that Tyler's pickup was parked just ahead of him. He walked into the café and Muriel was serving Ty a hot chocolate with whipped cream mounded on top.

"Howdy, Ken." The youth's face spread into an easy smile. "Come on over here now and join me." He indicated the chair in front of him.

Muriel winked at him with a special light in her eyes as he approached the table.

"Hi, guy," she purred in that husky voice that never failed to shake his heart.

"Hi, pretty lady," he said softly. "Say, how's one fine young bronc rider?" he posed to Tyler.

"Good as a top hand, I reckon. Good to see you, Ken. How about some hot chocolate? I'm buying." He grinned boyishly at him.

"Well, all right. That sounds fine to me, Ty. Thank you." Ken sat down to face him. "How's your Dad doing, son?"

"He's coming along. I think he is deciding that maybe we got to do some salvaging with each other family-wise. I reckon we all ganged up on him along with

Dr. Ellis. And then, with Grandma, no one can duck away once she sets her sights on you," he chuckled lightly.

"I am glad to hear that, Tyler. Say, that was some fine rodeoing you did on Sunday."

"Aw well, I been at that a spell. Kind of gets in your blood, but then, I guess I better mosey back into college. I made a pact with my Dad this morning. Told him I would if he'd agree to that counseling like the rest of us Rogers are doing." Ken just nodded his approval as Muriel brought Ken his hot chocolate.

"Ken, Ty here tells me that a man stopped by one time and spoke with his Mom about that property but he said he can't recall the man's name." Muriel studied Tyler's young face anxiously as she spoke. Tyler kept his eyes on the mug of cocoa and sipped it slowly while Muriel relayed this information to Ken. Ty finally leveled a look at Ken as he set his mug down.

"Yeah, what's this all about? Why is that relevant?" The boy shrugged his wide shoulders.

Ken decided to relate some things to Tyler but would ask him to keep the conversation just between the three of them.

"Muriel, can you sit down a minute? I want to explain a few things to Ty that have to remain just with us."

"Yes, sir, I am agreeable to that." Ty was looking from him to Muriel, his eyes holding a question.

"You see, Tyler, Muriel mentioned that the Conways were in the process of closing up a deal to buy your mother's property when..." and his voice trailed off as

Ty nodded slowly. "Well, anyway, son, we've reason to believe that the man you met came to offer to buy that property may be trying to scare Bud and Sissy off that ranch."

"How's that?" Tyler's forehead creased into a frown and he looked confused.

"Well, while Bud and Sissy were at the dance Saturday night, their two youngsters had a prowler. Then the next morning, Bud was out checking his cattle and found a young bull that had been killed."

Tyler sucked in his breath sharply. "Jeez, that is terrible but I can't see why that guy would go out on a limb like that. I mean, if he could afford to buy that ranch, cripes, there's other ones for sale."

"Listen, Ty," Muriel said and reached over to place her hand on top of his. "Hon, does the name Catlin Willard ring a bell with you?"

The boy frowned thoughtfully and then shook his head again.

"You know your Mom's parents bought that ranch from Gus Willard and Gus had a son named Catlin who left here about the time he graduated from high school with me, your Dad and Jeff. Do you think your mother ever mentioned to your father that this man Catlin made her an offer on the property?"

"Well, I don't rightly know, Aunt Muriel, but I can find out. I will just ask my Dad kind of casual like so he won't think too much about it."

"Then you let Muriel know, Ty. It would be much appreciated but just don't let on to anyone at this point. If this is who we think it might be, we don't want to scare him off."

Tyler nodded, then downed the contents of his cup. He laid some change on the table and stood up, reaching for his Western hat and placing it on his head.

"I gotta get out to the spread before Will Earl is sending out scouts to hunt me down. Had to pick up some stuff over at Jessie's Hardware to take out to the ranch." He smiled at Ken and extended his hand which Ken shook warmly.

"See you next time around, Ty, and thanks."

The lad tipped his hat at Ken and smiled at Muriel.

"Aunt Muriel, you take care now. I will find out about that and get the info to you, if there is any to get."

After he departed, Ken reached into his pocket, looking around the cafe to see if anyone was watching them before he handed Muriel her house key. Her eyes sparked with mischief as she slid the key into her apron pocket.

"Come on out and see me again sometime, big boy," she drawled sexily, stealing an old Mae West phrase. She gave him a exaggerated slow wink, then chuckled huskily.

"Count on it," he said and leaned over to kiss her.

"Ken, call me, please," she whispered.

"Every evening, baby," he assured her.

"Gotta get to Waco, honey, but be sure now and get things set up with Rosie, won't you? Then we can take right off from that art show next week."

"Will do, darling. Please be careful," she cautioned him.

"Everything is going to be all right, Muriel. By the way, I am betting that it is Catlin Willard. The handwriting from your yearbook compares with those notes but Bruster is going to have a police handwriting analyst look it over to be certain."

"I am so glad that there are some breaks coming along with this, Ken. I love you so and can't wait until you are back again."

"I love you, pretty lady," and he reached for his hat and made his way to the exit while Muriel watched him. His heart felt heavy to leave her so, just before he went out the door, he blew her a kiss. She smiled a little sadly at him but then blew a kiss back.

After unlocking his car, he removed his lightweight jacket and placed it over the passenger seat. He hit the interstate soon leaving Rosewood behind. He reached for a tape and put it into the stereo, then relaxed as he listened to the soft strains of a favorite Kenny Rogers tune. The traffic so far was light and he was glad. He prepared to ease along at a reasonable speed and think about all that had developed between him and Muriel. His spirits soared as he thought of their lovemaking.

"God, woman, how I love you," he spoke aloud and smiled, feeling arousal and passion to the depths of his being. He forced himself to draw away from these thoughts and, with the great effort, centered on his conversation with Bruster regarding the handwriting on the notes.

The time moved on and he checked his watch, realizing he had made good time and was approaching the outskirts of Waco. He arrived home and drove up the driveway. He felt as though he had been gone a long time because so much had transpired in his life. He wondered for a moment, as he opened the garage, if Muriel would be willing to come here to Waco and make her home here with him. There were so many things they had to discuss but somehow he felt comfortable with it all. He knew they had such an easy rapport between them.

Chapter_____11

He lifted his belongings out of the back seat and the garment bag from the hook and walked into the kitchen where Maggie greeted him. Sarita was at the kitchen sink busily preparing salad greens. She turned a bright smile toward Ken and quickly dried her hands on the towel.

"Ah, señor, you are home at last. We have missed you, Maggie and I." She came to Ken and gave him a resounding pat on his shoulder. Ken reached out to hug her before she could escape. He bent down to Maggie, who could hardly contain her excitement at seeing her master. He ruffled her behind her golden ears and crooned her name over and over as she whined her excited pleasure.

"Sarita, I have missed you, my good lady."

"You come now, Mr. Ken and I will get you a cup of coffee. Then you can tell me all about your adventures while I finish up with these," and she indicated the greens in the colander. She poured the coffee and sat it down on the kitchen table where Ken sat. He took in the warmth of being home once again in his kitchen. While Maggie peered up at him now with adoration, showing in her gentle brown eyes, he asked Sarita if all had been well for her while he was gone.

"Oh, si señor. Maggie, she is good company for an old one, you know. We have our discussions, the two of us, and I do believe she understands my every word." She laughed softly.

"Of course, she does," Ken agreed, "Don't you, Maggie. Because you are a very smart dog." Maggie's ears perked up and she wagged her tail back and forth across the kitchen tile. "I believe, Maggie, that I will get up early in the morning and take you to our old haunt at Brazor's Lake to check out the squirrel population. We haven't done that in a long time, have we, girl?" Maggie had by now gotten to her feet and laid her chin on his leg, looking up at him intently with her same gentle expression.

"Oh, say, I have something to show you, Sarita. I almost forgot it. I will be right back—it's in the car trunk." Maggie followed him to the garage and back into the kitchen. First he handed Sarita a gift he had purchased at Nadine's Arts and Crafts and she carefully opened it. She smiled with pleasure at the music box which played a lovely Mexican tune.

"Aw, now, Señor Ken, gracias. I have mucho felicidad" (much happiness) and her black eyes shone as she watched the twirling señorita atop the frosted green and gold box. A hint of tears shown in her eyes and she looked at Ken and said, "When I was a small niña (girl), my madre would sing this song to me and my hermano (brother) and our two ser hermana (sisters)."

"Sarita, I am so pleased. It would seem that, without knowing it, I happened on a perfect gift for you." Sarita nodded briskly and turned to set the music box down on the table but not before Ken saw her wipe her eyes hastily. She turned around to face him after touching the music box lovingly with one finger.

"Well now, señor, what do you have there?" She pointed to the wrapped package Ken held. He placed it down on the table and removed the wrapping from the print, then held it up for Sarita to see. Her eyes widened and she seemed overcome.

"Oh, señor, it is so…how you say beautiful. The man is." and her voice trailed off. He is a hechicero (shaman) who has great powers, mucho magic!"

"Yes, he does indeed." And for a fleeting moment he wondered if he should tell Sarita about Nathan Tom. He decided he would not at this time but instead he told her it was painted by Nadine Rogers, the woman who was murdered. A sad look came onto Sarita's face as she studied this masterpiece of art work.

"My amigo, this one was special because, you see, she captured the…essencia (essence) of this very old and wise one. How sad such a one has to be taken so cruelly." She bit down on her lip.

"Yes, it is a tragic loss, Sarita. A whole community that was so simple and innocent lost a beautiful loving spirit."

"She was beautiful in spirit as well as in the physical, Mr. Ken. And what of her family?" and she crossed her heart quickly.

"They've come close to being destroyed but I believe this angel, their wife and mother, has reached down from heaven and is healing their hearts in ways that some of them are not aware of."

"There are many things unseen, señor, that come down from heaven but still the effect is there. Some who are wise beyond this world understand it," and she looked keenly at Ken.

Ken just nodded his agreement but, as with many times over the years, he wondered if she didn't know of many mysteries that she did not openly express.

"Well now," and she bustled back to her task of washing salad greens. "Now I will fix for you a good meal. I have it all prepared so soon we sit down to it."

"All right, Sarita. I will just take Maggie out to the fish pond with me and then please call me when you are ready. Oh, may I help you with anything first?"

"No,no. It is all done except for the salad I make and a few minor details."

Ken walked out the sliding glass door off the kitchen and a small hummingbird circled his head anxiously. He noticed Milky, the Persian cat, still holding her usual vigil at the base of the blue birdhouse. She chose to ignore Ken and Maggie after one haughty glance at them.

"Well, at least, Maggie girl, we were noticed if but briefly." He chuckled and sat down on the bench that overlooked the pond and fountain. He watched the colorful goldfish swim and thought of the times that Milky had been highly unsuccessful at her efforts to capture one. After one headlong plunge into the pond, she lost interest except to stare into the water now and then.

"She doesn't have any better luck with the elusive birds in the comfort of their little house, does she, Maggie?" Maggie nuzzled her nose into Ken's big hands and regarded him as though she understood his every word. He and Sarita both thought that she did. She was a highly intelligent dog and Ken had known it when she was a puppy. One day, she had followed him out the door, giving puppy yips. When he turned around and bent down, she hopped into his arms. She snuggled up to him giving him puppy kisses and then fixed him with her brown eyes as if to say, "Don't you get it that we belong together? We are a team."

Friends had urged him to come and select one of the puppies from a litter their Golden Retriever had had awhile after Gloria passed away. He had never been sorry that Maggie had known more than he did how much he needed a pet.

Ken had decided that, over supper, he would talk to Sarita about Muriel. He closed his eyes and considered what he would say to Carter later on tonight after he had talked to Muriel. He was reasonably certain that Carter would give his blessings as would Sarita and Holly and his son-in-law, who was such an affable young man. Ken could easily see why Holly was so enamored with him. Bart was not tough to take and Ken was happy with her choice.

Sarita called to him so he and Maggie made their way back to the kitchen.

"Is it all right that we dine here, Mr. Ken, instead of the dining room this one evening?"

"Sure, Sarita. As a matter of fact, I would much prefer it when it is just the two of us," he said happily. He held a chair out for her to be seated. "So, Sarita, I have some news for you. I hope you will be pleased." He reached for the tumbler of water and took long drink before going on.

"Yes, my dear amigo, please go on," and she sat there watching him closely with an expression of puzzlement. She was quick to pick up on the feelings of others, especially his.

'Well, Sarita, I have met a lady who I am, well, I am in love with her, and you are the first in my family that I have shared this with." He watched her closely. She did not by word or gesture express what was going on with her at this announcement.

"Hmm," she finally allowed and then said no more until it felt to Ken as though an eternity had passed. "I want you to know that I am so honored that you have cared to tell me this news. And I want to say that I know you have selected a fine lady, my amigo. You see, I have asked so many times to all the saints to bring you another love. I know you are a fine man who has been more lonely that you have ever said, my dearest friend." She swallowed hard and Ken could see the heavy emotion on her face. He knew that she was thinking of Gloria at this moment and yet he also knew that Sarita was firm in her belief that life goes on.

"Ah, now, my friend," she said and looked warmly at him, though her eyes were bright with unshed tears. "The past has its memories and is so beautiful but so is the future." She raised her hand and cocked her head down slightly. "I say to you and your lady, go with God and know all the joys of your union."

"My lady, you are so dear to me. You are my friend equal to no other and my wonderful confidante who is ever there for me." He found his throat constricted with his own emotions while he spoke.

"Oh, now we are both so serious and this is a joyous announcement. By the way, what is this lady's name? Come, come, tell me more about her!" She was smiling broadly at him.

"Her name is Muriel and she has been a widow for many years. She has one grown child, a lovely girl of twenty years old. By the way, Angie goes to the university here in Waco."

"How long ago was she widowed? You did say many years, Mr. Ken?"

"Angie was a baby and her father was killed while working on a ranch. It was very hard for Muriel raising her daughter alone. She devoted her life to the child and, though she told me she did date, she was concerned about another man taking the place of Angie's father for various reasons. I think she just didn't happen to find someone who she felt would be right for her or serve as a good father for the girl."

"It was not supposed to be, señor, because you and Muriel were meant to be together."

Ken just smiled softly at her and then took a bite of the tasty Spanish rice on his plate. "Ah, Sarita, you have created another of your masterpieces," he said with his fork poised for another bite.

"You know, señor, I am truly surprised that some lady has not caught you before this time. You are such a one who is adulador (flatterer) and not too bad-looking, I might add." She laughed with her usual high mirth.

"Is that so, my dear señora. You think I could have been a real ladykiller with my charming ways? Now, who is the adulador, I wonder?" He loved this banter they had always enjoyed. It never failed to lift his spirits when they had sagged.

Sarita raised her brown hands with her short fingers splayed and rocked her head from side to side. Playing the comic, she batted her eyes and whistled softly.

Sarita, how he valued this dear woman. She could bring out a smile or laugh from anyone. He thought again how her comic antis had made Carter laugh in spite of himself. He would forget his sober solemn stand and fall into titters which he would try to smother with his hands. As a grown man, she could still prod him with humor and have him chuckling in no time. She was special and had made their lives the better for her loving spirited presence.

"Listen, you must go and give your lady a call now so bamanos as soon as you are finished. She will be concerned for you after your long ride home."

"All right, Sarita, I will take you up on that. Then I am going to call Carter afterwards because I plan to be in Houston next week."

"That is good, Mr. Ken. He will be so happy that his padre is coming to see him." Her eyes sparked with high approval.

He finished his supper and retreated to his bedroom where he called Muriel. She answered on the first ring.

"Hello there, pretty lady. How's my girl?"

"Oh, Ken, never better but missing you already."

"I know. Me too. I love you, honey, and it isn't easy to be away from you but it won't be for long."

"Listen, Ken, Jeff just went out the door when you called. We had a lengthy discussion and I told him we are going to Huntsville and then to Houston to see your son. He is so happy for us, Ken, and he likes you a lot. And trust me, honey, he is a man of few words, as you may have noticed, and he doesn't easily express himself. So you know it really comes from the deepest part of Jeff when he says something."

"Oh, yes, I picked up on that the first time I met the man. Another thing, he is the kind of person who is a loyal friend—once your friend, always your friend," Ken summed up.

"I've always known that and knew I could count on him for anything. I just hope that everything is going to work out for him too, because he is one great man all the way."

Ken knew there had been a heavy discussion between the two and he did not pursue it. He knew Muriel would tell him if she wanted to and also knew that, if Jeff had sought her confidence, it was safe with her.

He told her of Sarita's response to his finding a lady he wanted to share hislife again. Muriel breathed a long sigh of relief at the news.

"I am so thankful, Ken. I know she has invested a lot of her life with you and your family and that she is an important member of your family."

"You will love her, Muriel, just as the rest of us do."

"Somehow, I think you are right," she said huskily.

"Oh, and everything is set for Rosie Wilson to go with us to the art show and then take us to the airport. She and Ham will both come and get us on the condition that we have supper with them." She giggled. "Rosie says its blackmail."

"Tell Rosie I am looking forward to it," he assured her. "I will call and get everything arranged for our flight. It sounds like we are all set, sweet lady." They talked a few more minutes and Muriel finally suggested that he get some sleep after the drive he had made. Then she coyly teased, "After all, we didn't do a lot of sleeping last night, now did we?"

"Not as I recall, you luscious sexy woman." His chuckle was low and husky as he remembered their night together.

"We are going to have a lot of those," she assured him.

"Oh, sweet baby, I hope so," he breathed heavily. They concluded their conversation and, after Ken hung up, he lingered awhile thinking of her and the intensity of their lovemaking. It was with effort that he focused himself back to the business at hand. He reached for the phone again and dialed Carter's number.

Carter sounded sleepy when he answered the phone.

"Hello, son. Did I wake you from a nap?"

"Dad!" His voice came more alive. "I had settled in front of the televisions after putting away more than I needed for supper. Guess I just dozed off. What's up?"

"Are you going to be home this weekend, son?"

"I sure can be. Don't have anything special planned except maybe get together with Lila for supper and possibly a movie. If there's anything you have in mind, she sure would be open to it."

"Hey Carter, how is that girl? I was drawn to her right away.

"She's doing just fine. She took to you too, Dad."

"I am glad for that. Now, tell you what, I'm bringing with me a friend of mine I want you to meet. So, if you aren't tied up, we'd like to get together with you and Lila too, if she can."

Carter's voice rose with expressed cheer. "Why, sure thing, Dad. How's everything been going with you?"

"Never better, Carter. How about you?"

"Good mostly, but we are into the final windup at the Academy and it's some of the toughest part of the training. But then, I figure I can handle it after the tough training I had in that Ranger drill I went through."

"You bet you can, Carter. Son, I am real proud of you." He followed by telling him that he had started researching a murder case and had turned up some information that had not been checked out during the trial. He avoided expounding on the subject at length in an effort not to alarm his son regarding his safety.

"Dad, I have always been proud of you and of Mom too. You have both been my examples in life," and his voice became slightly husky.

"Carter, a parent could never have a higher tribute paid them than that." His own emotions were clear as he spoke. They chatted about mundane subjects that only a father and son who shared an easy bond could appreciate. At last, they bid good evening to each other.

Ken knew that Carter would ponder who he was going to bring with him but he also knew that Carter would never press him for information. His son had that quiet nature of "wait and see" and rested quietly until the right time for a subject to be discussed. On the other hand, Holly was ever bright-eyed and bushy-tailed with unrestrained enthusiasm. Ken chuckled out loud at the exuberance of this tiny dark-haired girl with the pixie features. She could melt anyone's heart with her pleading violet eyes and determined mind. She could cartwheel anyone's heart and he and Carter had been putty in her hands. Gloria had taken the situation in hand on a few accounts but she too could be put under the spell of her winsome daughter. Ken marveled that Holly had never been spoiled for all of it but she was one of the most stable, well-balanced people Ken knew.

It was going to be a beautiful day and Ken gave thanks for the bluebird sky. He and Maggie made their way to the expansive park to enjoy their adventure. Maggie was excited and anxious to explore but she was also well-behaved and stayed by

Ken's side as they walked up one of the trails by the river. The chirps of birds greeted them from the treetops and Maggie stopped now and then to "read" them along the way. They walked at least a half mile when Maggie began to whine. In a clearing sitting alert was a large gray squirrel eying them.

"Oh, all right, Maggie, if you must." Ken knew it was a game of wits and chase and Maggie would not catch the elusive gray coat at her best. Besides, it was great exercise for her, Ken reasoned. She tore off in a great flurry of yellow flags of hair flying in accelerated motion toward the squirrel. He took off in one bound, leaving his sentry post at her hasty approach.

Ken doubled over with laughter at the antics of the squirrel with Maggie in hot pursuit around a pine tree. Then, the squirrel, in one quick motion, flew up the trunk of the tree. Maggie was left at the bottom stopped, looking totally confused, cocking her head from side to side. The squirrel hung from his vantage point staring down at her. He began to scold and chatter as though mocking his tormenter. Maggie barked her contempt at the rancorous squirrel as though admonishing him with, "It was all in fun. Can't you take a joke?" She finally turned her back on the squirrel almost haughtily and sought relief behind a large juniper tree.

"Ah, yes, one of the sacrifices of having a beloved pet," Ken said, fishing some folded paper towels from his pocket and a coffee can from his carrying pack. Undaunted, Maggie ran to the edge of the water to refresh herself with a long lapping drink. Ken joined her to wash his hands at the river's edge.

"Well, let's stroll, old girl," he suggested to Maggie. They walked the wooded pathway, with Ken admiring the way this area was cared for. The flowers were in full bloom and radiant, the trees gave off the fragrance of pine and juniper. Picnic tables were stationed at various sites with a scattering of people seated there, some with thermos and cups, enjoying conversation or a book.

A small terrier leaped wildly and yapped furiously but was tethered to a small pine tree by a leash. Ken and Maggie made their way past him and his mistress, a heavy-set blond lady. She lifted her eyes from her book long enough to give a sharp . command to the terrier to which the pooch paid no heed. Maggie strolled leisurely by with a certain elegance, as though to say, "Some upstarts these days have no manners at all."

They wound their way deeper into the woods, away from the edge of the river. A golden butterfly encircled them both lazily and, as Ken stared, it alighted on Maggie's head. It looked as though Maggie were wearing a colorful ribbon bow. Ken chided himself for not having his camera.

The trail was getting more convoluted as they walked on and they came in sight of the river once again by a marsh area. A coot bird rose in alarm and other aquatic birds followed suit as Maggie took on the pointed bird dog stance.

"Doing what comes natural, hey girl?" Ken said quietly.

They moved on and suddenly Maggie's hair bristled. Ken could hear the low growl in her throat. He caught sight of a group of peccary in some thicket.

"No, girl," he commanded as he walked to her and put his hand on her head. She lifted her velvet brown eyes up at him, looking wistful but making no move.

"Good girl. Those fellows are mean so let them alone," he assured Maggie. The peccary made haste away from them with a few loud grunts and Maggie stood at attention watching them plunge deeper into the thicket.

Ken and Maggie then moved on until Ken saw a clearing with a fallen log. After scaring a small ground squirrel into its confines underneath and inspecting the top, Ken sat down to rest. Maggie took a close tour of the area while Ken reached in his pocket for a handkerchief to wipe the perspiration from his forehead. The weather had warmed up. He reached for his water bottle hooked on his belt loop and took a long swallow. Refreshed now and with Maggie in sight, he let his mind stray to Muriel and could almost feel her softness touching him.

"How many times in one lifetime is a person blessed enough to find two true loves," he thought. He smiled as the joy of it held him in this moment of thankfulness.

Maggie suddenly came to him and sat in front, watching intently. She didn't look directly at him, as though seeing something she was curious about. She moved her head from side to side. Ken looked where she was focused but saw nothing.

"What is it, girl? What do you see, Maggie?"

Maggie paid no heed to Ken, which was unusual. Suddenly he felt a presence sitting beside him yet still he did not see it. He felt a kind of raw energy and the air seemed very stilled. Whatever it was touched him and only then did he notice an ethereal Light taking shape. He stared in awe at these lights, knowing they were not of this earth because the colors were so intense.

"I am in the presence of an angel," he thought, and as he did, he could hear a voice speak to him. The voice sounded in his head for it was not an audible frequency but rather a telepathic awareness.

"You are reaching the truth. The trail of the rainbow leads you and will not fail you." Then the Lights began to ebb and slowly float away. He sat there for several minutes in a state of awe at what he had witnessed and "heard". Finally, he stood up and so did Maggie.

"Well Maggie, I think we were presented with the wonder of a message from the Kingdom and I certainly do not question it. Let's go, girl. We will try this another day before I leave again." He patted Maggie lovingly and they made their way back down the trail on which they had come.

He knew that the visitation had brought him confirmation that this situation was close to being solved. That would bring peace to so many people and Ken felt an uplifting at the thought.

They met the woman with the anxious spotted terrier as they progressed down the trail. Her fanny pack was tucked in at her ample stomach, her book tucked under one arm. She was trying to restrain the terrier who was a humorous sight as he leaped erratically around. Ken kept a straight face as they approached and heard her muttering low obscenities at the terrier, yanking on his leash as he whirled around like a top.

"Stop, you s.o.b." Settle down. You are like the freaking plague, jumping everywhere," she groaned and gave the leash a hefty snap. This pulled the dog into a closer proximity to her and lifted him to his tiptoes as he tried to go after Maggie. Maggie appeared completely oblivious to the pair and walked on past them.

The scene was almost too much for Ken but he nodded politely at the woman, whose face by now was scarlet and sweaty. She paid no heed to Ken's greeting and huffed on up the trail, still cursing and grumbling.

He and Maggie reached the car and climbed in. He suddenly realized it was lunchtime as his stomach growled at him. The morning had been good and Ken reinforced to himself that the two of them would do this again before he left.

"Now it's time to head home, eat a good lunch and then get cracking on the work pile by the computer," he thought as he drove along. They made their way through traffic easily since Ken knew some shortcuts. After reaching home, they made their way into the kitchen where Ken was greeted by the aroma of a favorite dish of rice and green chilies. Sarita was placing the makings of a large fruit salad on the table.

"Ah, Sarita," he breathed in deeply, his head slightly back and his eyes closed. "That, my dear lady, is heaven sent. And I am hungry enough to more than do it justice."

"Well, Mr. Ken, I fix plenty. I know how you like it and it is also a favorite dish for me, too," she beamed her pleasure.

Maggie made her way to her water bowl and, after her drink, sampled a few dog biscuits, which Sarita had deposited in her food dish.

Ken told Sarita of the trek he and Maggie had shared and Sarita laughed heartily at the description of the encounter with the lady and her terrier.

"Our Maggie girl, she is truly a lady," Sarita crooned down at her as she lay stretched out on the floor. The only indication she had heard Sarita was a swish, swish of her silky tail across the tiled floor.

Ken retreated to his office room and worked at his computer, taking a break now and then to refresh his coffee. When he worked he took little notice of the clock above the desk, thus he was surprised when he glanced at it, to notice it was after six o'clock. He found Sarita setting the table with a light supper for which he was grateful.

"For tonight, a little vino, señor, then you sleep good," and she winked at him.

"That sounds good, Sarita. I probably will need to unwind after five hours on that computer."

They enjoyed light conversation and were just finishing supper when the phone rang. Ken reached for it and a youthful female voice spoke, "Ken, hello. This is Angie Jacob."

"Angie, hello, so good to hear from you."

"I thought I would give you a call and ask if you are busy tomorrow evening. I would like to stop in for a visit if you are available."

"Why certainly, Angie. I would be delighted. And you can meet Sarita too."

"What time would be best for me to come over? I mean, I don't want to interrupt your supper or anything you have planned."

"Angie, my dear child, you are welcome to come here any time. Just join us for supper. Can you come around 5?

"Yes. That is so good of you, Ken. But are you sure it will be all right with Sarita?"

"Sarita will be delighted. I tell you what, it will give me a chance to show off my future daughter. How's a barbecue sound? I barbecue a mean steak," he added.

"Golly, Ken, I would really love that. And just for the record, you have sent my heart soaring over you and Mom. I am proud I am receiving the honor of becoming your daughter."

"Angie, honey, I am blessed to be getting another lovely daughter."

Her voice was soft and sincere as she thanked him.

After they ended their conversation, Ken told Sarita that he would do the honors of getting the evening meal the next evening. But he hoped she would put together one of her terrific fresh salads.

"Ah, señor, for you, I do think it can be arranged," she said teasingly. "Now I take it that I will get to meet this young lady you call Angie?"

"Yes, I am so pleased that she called. I thought how perfect a time for you to meet her. You will like her, Sarita, and she is so like her mother.

"Mr. Ken, I have never known you to show bad judgment with anything, let alone with people, so of course I will like her and her Mama too."

He reached out to hug Sarita impulsively and he was surprised that she happily hugged him back.

"Now, you go, my amigo, and call your lady," she ordered in Sarita fashion.

Ken grinned happily, stood at attention and gave her a brisk salute.

"Yes, señora." She swatted at him while he did an exaggerated duck and then left the kitchen to go call Muriel from the privacy of his bedroom. Muriel answered on a ring and a half in that husky voice that always sent a thrill coursing through him.

"Hi, honey. How's my guy?"

'Well, pretty lady, doing well other than missing you. But guess what? Angie called me awhile ago and she's coming over tomorrow evening and I am fixing the three of us barbecue."

"Ken, that is so good. I am so happy to hear that. You know, sweetheart, she has really taken to you."

"I have taken to that little gal too. But how could I not when she is so like her lovely mother?"

"Well, thank you, my adorable sir," she drawled sexily. "Say, Ken, Bruster stopped by for a coffee break this afternoon. Since things were slow, I sat down for a few minutes and chatted with him. He said he has been keeping a watch on Bailey's Lounge to see if the man with that older model Jeep stops in. He has his deputies watch for it too but they haven't seen it yet. Oh, and Ken, can you give Bruster a call? He has some information for you."

"I will do that first thing in the morning, Muriel. And thanks, hon."

"Ken, if I catch sight of that Jeep, I will get hold of Sheriff Bruster even if I have to call him at home."

"That's great, Muriel, because evenings have been the time that I have seen the old Jeep parked at the lounge."

"Something rings a bell with me about that Jeep. For the life of me, I don't know why but maybe it will come to me."

"Yes, sometimes when we try to think so hard on something, it just won't come until we kind of push it away and then, bingo, there it is."

They talked on for a few more minutes and told each other good night. Ken hoped that there would not have to be many more of these partings between them. He decided to go into his office and keep transcribing the notes he had accumulated on his last trip to Rosewood. It was his custom to work late into the night when there were fewer distractions. He could sleep in if he felt like it in the morning. He reasoned that he had built up quite a book on this case as he scanned his notes and the material already transcribed.

At midnight, he decided it was time to stop. He would call Bruster in the morning and wanted his mind fully clear to jot down any information Bruster had to share with him.

He slept soundly and awoke to the aroma of fresh coffee. The clock on the nightstand said a little after seven. He made his way to the bathroom and took a quick shower. As he dressed, he wondered about the information Bruster had for him.

"Bruster, good morning. Ken Ferries here. Muriel told me last night that you have some information for me."

"Good morning, Ken. As a matter of fact, I do, regarding Catlin Willard. I ran a rap sheet on our boy and he has not been a good boy from the information I got here."

"I kind of suspected that if he was alive all these years," Ken drawled.

"He was about eighteen when he left here and he drifted around a lot. Over those first few years, he got into some fracas with the law for fights, broke into a roadhouse down in Louisiana and got arrested before he stole anything. But he was in the slammer for a year down there for breaking and entering." Bruster paused for a moment, then went on. "He left there after he got out of prison and moved on to Arizona awhile. He stayed loose, working on a couple ranches. Then he went on to California where he managed to land a position with a movie company as a stuntman. Seemed he sort of mellowed out after that. Mostly the trouble he got into was for fights and some petty theft but it seems that the one big scrape got his attention and he cooled his heels after that."

"He must have made some pretty good money then, being a stuntman for a movie company in California," Ken elected.

"Yes, sir. I reckon if a person is willing to break his neck for work, then a movie company is going to pay them some pretty fair bucks," Bruster drawled.

"So, what happened to him after he left California or do you have that information?"

"This is the weird part, Ken. The trail just cools on him after he retired from that job as stuntman. He is close to fifty and that kind of work was probably getting pretty rough on him. From what I found, he was a real loner, though one of the best stuntmen in the business."

"It sounds like he decided to come back to this area and take over that ranch from his dad, not thinking that his dad had passed away and the place had been sold."

"Yep, it sure point that way, don't it. But with the kind of money that he had bankrolled, it does seem strange that he would not just scout out some other property instead of getting in deep enough to commit a murder," Bruster gave a lengthy sigh on the other end.

"There is no accounting for the actions of some people, is there, Bruster. Greed is one of the major factors that can get in the way of some folks. I understand from Muriel that ranch the Conways are on has built up into quite a money-maker."

"Well, yes it has and that would be one of the reasons right there if Cat is indeed our man. When Nadine wouldn't cut a deal with him, he just blew his cool."

"We'll find out soon enough. Maybe I better give old Judge Bullard a call this morning, and Con Womack too. I did tell them I would keep them updated on any developments in this case."

"Good idea, Ken. Reckon that's about it for now but meanwhile, I will call you if anything more turns up. A fine morning to you and we'll be talking soon."

"Same to you, Bruster. When I get back from Huntsville and Houston, I'll get together with you over coffee and maybe a piece of pie."

Bruster chuckled. "You know I am always open to that, Ken."

They hung up and Ken made his way to the kitchen where Sarita was fixing the morning meal.

"Good morning, Sarita," Ken said, his voice singing out cheerfully. Sarita turned her chocolate brown eyes on him, showing her happiness at having him home. With the spatula in her hand, she indicated a mug on the counter bar beside the coffee pot.

"Señor, you have a cup of coffee and soon I set this omelet down for you."

Ken sat down at the table and watched several hummingbirds in combative dips and dives trying to jockey for position at the feeding. He and Sarita made light conversation and, after breakfast, Ken went to his office to call Judge Bullard. He was surprisingly affable and genial and told Ken an off-color joke, his old voice cracking in merriment. Ken knew that the craggy old gent liked him and it gave him an inner satisfaction because everyone knew the esteemed judge was not easily taken with his human counterparts.

He called the defending attorney after that and Con's daughter-in-law greeted him first. He returned the greeting and stated the nature of his call.

"Con's just walking in now, so if you will hold a moment, he will take your call in his office," Ellen stated.

"Certainly, Ellen. Thank you."

Con's deep voice rang out in a few moments. "Hello, Ken. Good to hear from you."

"Con, I wanted to update you on some of the things regarding the Rogers case. Sheriff Hernado has sent away a high school yearbook of a friend's that compares with the handwriting in those threatening notes. Now we will have to wait while a police handwriting analysis is done but it is almost certainly the same writing. If it is, the writing is of one Catlin Willard who was born and raised in Rosewood. He left after he graduated from high school and the man is about fifty years old now." Ken went on to explain all of the possibilities and mentioned that there had been a man Tyler Rogers remembered making an offer to buy the ranch. "A couple named Conway have lived on it for years and were about ready to close a deal on it when Nadine was murdered. Since then, Bud and Sissy Conway have had a prowler at the ranch and someone shot a fine young bull of theirs." He went on to fill in the additional information.

"Well, I had felt that there were some gaping holes in this case, Ken. It appears that is going to be confirmed before long."

"I think it will be and more so, once Tyler asks his family the name of the man who stopped by to talk to his mother about the ranch. He didn't pay much attention at the time because it was just a business discussion between his mother and this stranger." He told Con that he would be in touch again as soon as there were more developments.

Ken then turned his attention to the computer and worked steadily until noon. He decided to refresh himself with a cup of coffee and sit down with Sarita for lunch. She had earlier come to the office door and suggested he join her for lunch in five minutes.

They had just finished lunch when the phone rang. Sarita was closest so she picked it up.

"Bueno," she spoke in her soft Spanish. "For you, señor," and handed him the phone.

"Hello, Muriel. What a surprise! What's up, honey?" He listened as Muriel began to tell him.

"Ken, Ty was in here awhile ago. I don't have a lot of time to talk because we're busy at work but I felt that this shouldn't wait. Ty asked both Will Earl and Phyl if they happened to know or remember the man who had asked their mother about selling him the ranch. Will Earl didn't but it seems that Phyl came to the ranch one day just as the man was leaving in the dull green Jeep. Phyl said the man looked kind of scruffy and she had been concerned for her mother since she knew no one else was home. She had expressed that concern to Nadine, but her mother seemed to think the man was harmless, just rough looking. He had made a second sizable offer for that ranch but, of course, Nadine was loyal to the Conways. Naturally she wasn't going to deal them out."

"Muriel, did she happen to mention the man's name to Phyllis?"

"No, Ken she didn't. She probably didn't to Will either but I am going to see him when I get off work. I will ask him but I will just mention that the suspect may have shot one of the Conway's bulls and let it go at that."

"That sounds wise. By the way, how is Will doing?"

"He is having a lot of intensive counseling and it has been hard but he's starting to open up, from what Tyler tells me."

"That's good. I just feel that it will help him so much even though it is naturally tough going, especially right now at the beginning."

Her voice was husky with emotion as she agreed, "Yes, I know. So, gotta go sweet man but we will talk later this evening. Tell that precious girl of mine that I love her."

"Will do, pretty lady. I will call you about nine tonight."

"I love you, Ken," she said softly.

"Double ditto, pretty lady," he relayed back and hung up.

"Sarita, I am going to work again but I will get the steaks ready for our barbecue a little after three. Then we will have it all prepared when Angie gets here at five o'clock."

"But of course, Mr. Ken. You will see I prepare for you the corn when you are ready and the salad."

"Sarita, I didn't think about the corn," and he batted his forehead with his hand in mock reprimand.

"Ah, well, it is why birds fly and Sarita is here," and her black eyes sparkled with amusement.

"Sarita, if I ever take you for granted, please conk me a good one along side my head. Again I am indebted to you," and he bowed low.

"Leave me to my end of this—how you say?—arrangement, amigo. Go on with you now, pronto." She chuckled.

"As instructed, señora," but he smiled warmly at her as he left the kitchen to work on the draft of his book.

He was surprised when 3:30 rolled around and Sarita's soft voice called to him. It had not seemed that he had been working for three hours. He felt good about the draft— it was rolling right along. He smiled to himself as he joined his dear friend who was busily preparing the corn.

"I will go get the steaks ready but first, let me help you with the other preparations," and he did in spite of her protests.

Every detail was in readiness when the front doorbell sang its welcome and Ken opened the door to a smiling Angie. She looked like a flower in a colorful raspberry cotton tank top with matching camp shirt and crisp white denim shorts that showed off slim tanned legs. For a fleeting moment, Ken saw Muriel at this girl's age. They were both stunning, this mother and daughter pair. He reached for her and hugged her in a fatherly embrace and led her to the kitchen to meet Sarita.

"Sarita, see who we have here. This is Angie."

"Aw, señor, she is lovely like your Holly." She came to the girl and enfolded her slender hands in both of her own. "It is my pleasure, young lady."

"Sarita, it is so good to meet you. Thank you for the compliment," Angie smiled in happy response.

"Come now, we will go to the patio." Sarita took Angie's arm and led her to the sliding glass door as Ken followed behind them.

"What a lovely place you have here, Ken," Angie said as she looked around. "Oh, you have a fish pond and fountain. How pretty. I just love it all. It is like stepping into a wonderland."

"Angie, do you think your mother would live here? I mean, she has been there in Rosewood for all of her life and it would be difficult to up and move..." Ken's voice trailed off, waiting for her response. Sarita artfully pretended to get very busy at arranging the already arranged umbrella table as Angie turned to fully face Ken.

"Know what, Ken? She had better or she will hear from me!" and she turned her pert little nose up at him and grinned impishly. She came to him and stood on tiptoes to kiss his cheek. Ken was so overcome that he felt unable to speak for a moment.

"Angie girl, you have just given me the best wedding present anyone could receive." On an impulse, he lifted Angie around her waist, hugging her tight and twirling her around and around. They were laughing wildly. When they stopped after the third swing, Sarita came to the pair and wrapped her arms around them both.

"Of course she will come here, Ken. And I couldn't be happier for Mom and for me too because we are both lucking out. She has got a great guy and I'm getting a second wonderful Dad."

"On that note, lets have a toast to the three of us," Ken proposed as he wiped at his eyes. He filled the tumblers with lemonade and ice and handed one first to Sarita and then to Angie.

"To Sarita, my dear friend who is a part of our family and always will be. I want to tell you that you will have a home wherever this family is because we could not have survived without you. Now, to the joy of gaining another beautiful daughter, one that I have come to love as deeply as I do my two other children. Miss lovely Angie Jacob, may we all celebrate becoming a full family the rest of our lives." Ken smiled with a lingering affection at these two special women as they drank their toast.

"Now listen, dear Ken, Dad, I want to toast you. It's my turn now," and her eyes twinkled up at him. "To a fine man, I give this toast in love and admiration and thanks for offering me a father again. And boy, have I gladly taken him up on the offer!" She winked at him and they drank to the toast.

"Now I want to show you both something that I have in my handbag so please sit down. When you see this, you will need to be seated." After they sat, Angie withdrew a sizable photo pack from her shoulder bag. She sorted some snapshots and spread them on top of the table. Ken reached to pick one up of him and Muriel and felt his jaw drop in shock at what he saw. He noted the same apparition appeared in every single picture. He glanced at Sarita who crossed herself quickly after looking at the photos, then closed her eyes to murmur a prayer in Spanish. Ken finally looked at Angie whose eyes were fixed on him.

"Ken, it is Nadine. I can see that it is," and the girl's eyes grew wide with a kind of fear for a moment.

"Angie, listen carefully to me." He reached for her small hand and concealed it in his larger one. "You do not have to be afraid. Just see this as a beautiful expression of love that she is emitting to us all from heaven. It tells us that she is not really away, just on the other side of a very fine veil. Now, Angie child, it is not one that most of us can see through, just some people who have a second sight. Now and again, when someone is suffering the grief and shock of losing a loved one, those on the other side will reach out and try to help those left behind to deal with their loss."

"Then it really does mean that we don't die, not really." Angie's eyes were shining with tears and her small chin trembled.

"No, we don't. Our bodies do, yes, but our souls don't and that is the very essence of who we truly are, sweet child."

"Ken, you know so much. No wonder my Momma loves you." She got up and came around the table, bent over and kissed him on top of his head as she held her arms around his shoulders.

"Aw, Angie, I'm just a man who has been given so many wonderful gifts of life, honey. You and your mother are two more gifts."

Sarita cleared her throat. "Now, little señorita, come now with me. We will bring out the salad and I have made for us a special pecan pie. You help me retrieve, yes?"

"Oh but yes, Sarita," the girl's vouce was lighter now and she happily went with Sarita to help carry the food.

Ken studied the snapshots a moment more before attending to the steaks which were almost ready to remove from the grill. This enchanting soul had emitted a wavelength like an ultraviolet image to show any mortal that there was a world beyond this one. It humbled Ken as he thought of how this woman, even from where her soul resided, was reaching out to others like a beacon with her love. Once more he vowed to her as he stared at the snapshots that her loved ones would know some measure of peace.

Angie returned carrying the salad and placed it on the table with Sarita behind her carrying the pie in a covered container.

"Ken, those snapshots are for you. I have others," Angie said as she picked them up and stacked them into a pile.

"Thank you, honey. Now, let me just get you a fine old Texas steak, child, and one for Sarita. We will all sit down here and enjoy."

They did enjoy the time spent together and Ken could see that Sarita and Angie were completely taken with each other. Sarita asked her to come and visit any time, "even when the señor is away". Ken realized that it surely must get lonely for Sarita when he was gone.

Maggie came wandering over to Angie and cocked her head in question at the girl. She had been laying out under the cool shelter of the lilac bushes but the aroma of steak had lured her out.

"Well, look at you. Aren't you just so beautiful," Angie exclaimed. "What is your name, pretty one?"

"This is Maggie. Maggie meet Angie," Ken introduced them. As though she understood his every word, Maggie put her paw up for Angie to shake, a trick Ken had taught her as a puppy. After she and Angie had bonded, Ken did allow her a steak bone at which time she happily retreated to her spot at the end of the yard to savor it.

They cleared away the food and took the remains into the kitchen. Ken then guided Angie on a tour of the house.

"Ken, it's time to get back to the dorm. It's eight o'clock and I do have an assignment I need to get after so I'd better get going." She thanked him and Sarita again. At the door, she paused, then turned to Ken, "You know, Ken, I have more peace inside my heart now than at any time since we lost Nadine. Somehow I get the feeling she has been instrumental in bringing you and my mother together. I feel that she is helping us all to heal and... it gives me renewed hope, I guess I'm saying."

"I could not agree with you more, Angie," Ken smiled warmly at her. He found her wiser than her years.

They hugged once more and he saw her to her car. He watched her back from the driveway and then wave to him. When he returned to Sarita, she was removing her apron and her black eyes shined with happiness.

"My amigo, you are blessed by all the saints. That Angie, she is one so fine, so gracioso (gracious). That is one dear little señorita."

Ken smiled his pleasure at Sarita, having known she would be as enchanted with Angie as he was himself since meeting her. They chatted awhile and then Ken excused himself to call Muriel.

"Muriel, that little daughter of yours was a big hit with Sarita, but then I knew she would be. Sarita has asked her to come over any time, 'even when the señor is not home.'" He chuckled.

"Oh, Ken, I am so happy. It does sound as though you all three enjoyed your visit."

"Only thing that could have made it perfect is if you had been here too, pretty lady," he said huskily, missing her with a sudden intensity.

"I thank you for that, hon. I miss you but it won't be long before you will be here. By the way, it finally came to me where I have seen that old green Jeep, if it was the same one. It was parked in front of Pace Allard's office. Of course, part of that building is also an insurance office, as you know."

"Muriel, do you happen to remember the time of day you saw it there?"

"Now that you mention it, I do. One time was when I was coming in to work so businesses were starting to open their doors. But then, one night, it was there long everyone else was closed except us and Bailey's Lounge. I had closed up at Dolly's and was driving past when I happened to see this man coming out the main entrance door. I didn't think too much about it really because sometimes Pace might have a client late. In Rosewood, people tend to be flexible about business hours. Anyway, I noticed that he got in that Jeep and floored it down the street."

"You ever get a good look at the guy, hon?" Ken prompted.

"Not really. He looked like a hundred other guys around here, sort of nondescript. You know, Western hat and boots, and I would say average build."

"Well, if it is Catlin Willard, do you think that you would have known him if he had come into Dolly's?" Ken ventured.

"I just don't know but I rather doubt it. For some reason, I suspect his appearance has changed a lot from eighteen to age fifty."

"I think you are probably right, however, some people really don't change their overall appearance that much. Muriel, have you talked to Angie recently?"

"No. As a matter of fact, she is to give me a call tomorrow evening. Why?"

"It's nothing to be concerned about, sweetheart, it's just that I think she will have something of interest to share with you. Since I feel that she will want to tell you, I am not going to say any more."

"Darn it now, Ken. I am going to call her tonight because I won't rest until I know what it is," and her throaty laugh coursed through him.

They whispered softly of their love and the urgency of needing each other again and then said goodnight. Ken returned to find Sarita watching her evening news. He suggested that he take her to an old family restaurant the next evening for supper. She started to protest but he raised his hand and shook his head.

"Dear lady, you will have insulted me if I am refused your presence at Chico's." Ken knew it was her favorite and she had gone there many times with their family over the years.

"Oh, all right, señor Ken. You have twisted my arm," and her eyes shown with pleasure.

"Good night, Sarita. Have a good night."

"A good night to you, my amigo," she smiled.

Ken was making his way down the hall to enter his bedroom when the phone rang. "It's all right, Sarita, I will take it in my room."

"Si," she answered as he strode quickly to answer it.

"Ken Ferries," spoke a familiar male voice.

"Speaking," and Ken felt a prickle like an icy shaft run up his back. It was the voice of the man who had threatened him at Larkin's Motel.

"Just listen now. I know that you and the cops have been looking for me and I want to tell you there is more than meets the eye here. Don't count on everything being cut and dried. Before I am found, I intend to line all my ducks in a row and cut a deal, so you and the 'fuzz' just hang loose." He hung up before Ken could respond.

Ken noted the time on the small ornate boudoir clock on the night stand —it was just after ten o'clock. He rose from the bed and walked into his bathroom, got a glass of water and returned to sit in the overstuffed chair. His mind was whirling and he took a long drink from the glass. Now he relaxed, going over in his mind every detailed word from the caller.

"What did he mean, he was lining up all his ducks in a row first before the cops would find him? That he was then going to cut a deal? That the 'fuzz' should just hang loose?"

He would get hold of Sheriff Bruster first thing in the morning, he decided as he removed his shoes. He slept fitfully and dreamed strange dreams that seemed to parallel, then intermingle a strange interior like a jumbled mess of facts, facts with no beginning and no end. A pale white horse with a beautiful blonde woman astride it seemed to beckon him. She whispered that she was the dream weaver and he should follow her to seek the truth. She pointed skyward and he saw a giant red-tailed hawk circling overhead in a dusky blue sky.

Then, just as his sleeping mind tried to grasp the meaning of this, the scene suddenly changed. He saw a pale blue carpet, at first seeming to be a patch of milky blue sky. Then a deepening color of bright red spread and spread upon the blue, saturating it. Beyond, he saw two closed doors, one directly in front of him and one just to the side of him. He saw himself reaching for the one to the side, slowly turning the knob. Even in his sleep, he could felt the icy fear coursing through his body, stabbing his senses. Still, he felt the need to open this door, regardless of what he was to encounter.

He opened the door and beheld an arm holding a long-handled poker with a sharp spur on it. He glimpsed a monster momentarily that was spattered with the same bright red he had seen on the carpet. He stared into the wild eyes of a maniac, poised and ready to strike him down. He fled to the door that was in front of him. Inside that door, was what looked like an over-sized bedroom with a large four-poster bed in the middle of the room with the headrest against the wall. Wide French doors dominated one whole side of the room and he flew toward them as the monster pursued him. He flung the doors wide and ran to a patio that offered escape. He awoke gasping for air, while the fear still clutched his throat like a vice.

"Oh, God," he gasped as he switched on the lamp by his bed. He noted that the time was 3:30. He settled back after fluffing his pillows, leaving on the light and pondering the nightmare. He thought about the details and could still see the eyes, those wild maniac eyes, once more. They were almost silver gray but the pupils were so enlarged that he could not be fully certain. His throat felt very constricted suddenly and he got up for another glass of water. He drank it down and decided he must be reacting to something he ate plus the unsettling phone call which had combined to send him into this weird dream world.

Finally he switched off the light and, after awhile, was able to drift once more into sleep. When he awoke again, sunlight was filtering through the drapes and he could smell fresh coffee. He got up and took a refreshing shower. As he briskly toweled himself off, he thought of the dream again. Suddenly he knew that he had to see the inside of the Rogers home when he returned to Rosewood. He quickly dressed and then called Sheriff Hernado.

Katie answered the phone and Ken greeted her cheerily. "Say, Miss Katie, how are you today, you young-looking grandma?"

"Why Ken Ferries, you do make a lady feel so good. I am just fine, and yourself?" she asked brightly.

"Never better, Katie and thank you. Now, is that Sheriff man around?"

"Yes, he is. He just went into his office. I'll advise him that he has a call."

"Thank you, Katie. You have a good day now."

"Oh, I will and the same to you, Ken."

After a few seconds, Bruster's good-natured voice came on the line. "Well, good morning, Ken. How are you?"

"I'm right as rain, thanks Bruster. But I have some news that I think you are going to find interesting."

"All right. Go ahead, I am all ears."

Ken related the phone call he had received the night before and Bruster did not speak for a moment. Then he whistled low into the phone. "Well, it does seem that we got our boy a might shook up, eh Ken?"

"It certainly looks that way, but what do you think it all means?"

"Don't rightly know just now but, I tell you one thing, I bet he isn't in the Rosewood area right now because he figures he is being sought out. Another thing, Ken— it's a strong possibility that he didn't do this crime but he knows who did but thinks he might take the heat for it. Now mind, that is just possible. I learned quite awhile back not to get seduced by any one idea but just kick it around awhile and chew on it."

"That's sound judgment, I'd say," Ken agreed.

"Now, I do think that maybe, if I give this fella the idea that we are taking his advice and cooling it, then he will show when he thinks the heat is off."

"Well, Bruster, you know how to operate something like this far better than I would so you no doubt have a workable plan. He may just get reckless and show up when he thinks the coast is clear enough."

"Sometimes it is the prudent thing to do even when you feel like you want to pull out all the stops. Especially in a sour situation like this, there are three mens' lives on the line here and that keeps clutching at my throat."

"I know, Bruster. Mine too."

They mulled things over some more before finally bringing their conversation to a close and hanging up. Just as Ken got up, the phone rang again. He sat down once more and picked it up to find Muriel's husky voice on the other end.

"Why, Muriel honey, this is a pleasant surprise."

"Ken, I gotta run or I will be late to work but I wanted to tell you that I talked to Angie last night. She told me about those snapshopts we had taken the night of the dance. Be sure to bring them with you when you come back, okay hon?" Her voice sounded as though she was on the verge of tears.

"Oh, pretty lady, you bet I will. Now, honey, I want to tell you that I got this weird phone call last night shortly after 10." He told her about it and cautioned her not to mention it to anyone, not even Angie. She assured him she would not as she had not told Angie anything about the investigation or Ken's powerful experiences. She was concerned that Angie would be afraid.

"Ken, you handled that so well with Angie. She told me she had been frightened before she talked to you."

"That is quite a girl you have there, Muriel. She is intelligent as well as a great beauty, a very classy young woman and, I bet, a wise old soul."

"Yes, I have always thought so even when she was a tiny baby."

"Say, while I am at it, I want to tell you about this wild dream I had, a real bearcat. It woke me at 3:30 and I had to take awhile to settle back down. Finally did though and got a fair night's sleep." He related the dream and heard Muriel gasp in shock at the details.

"Ken, did you know that you described the inside of the Rogers' house to a T?"

"No, of course I have never been inside their house but now I would like to go in and see what happens to me once I am there, what I pick up on."

"Ken, listen, Will is being released form the hospital on Monday. Do you think that you come back here Monday instead of Tuesday so we can go out there?"

"How about if I leave here Sunday and then I can be with you that much longer, pretty lady?"

Oh, Ken, that would be great because I didn't think I could handle much more of you being away from me." The passion was clear in her deepened voice.

"Well, sweetheart, it is the same with me, you know. Besides, I have got a lot of this book put together now and I will pen more notes after I get there."

Chapter_____12

"Oh, honey, I've got to run or I will be late. See you Sunday and I love you, Ken Ferries," and she smacked a good kiss over the phone. He returned the endearment and they hung up.

Ken remembered that he had told Mr. Chan he would need a room at the motel and decided to call him and cancel. "I'll do that after breakfast," he murmured aloud to himself as he made his way to the kitchen. Sarita was taking a tray of muffins out of the oven and the wonderful aroma of fresh blueberry muffins filled the kitchen.

"Ah, the wondrous delights from Sarita's kitchen," he smiled at Sarita, who was carrying the tray to a place on the table.

"Good morning, señor Ken. Please sit down and I have for you scrambled eggs and ham to go with these muffins." She winked at him happily.

"My dear lady, I am truly indebted to you, not only as a wonderful cook and caretaker, but as a friend. I have not found another who could equal you."

"You do know, my amigo, that is the same that comes from here," and she touched her heart while her eyes shone with emotion.

Ken sat down and just savored his surroundings. Once again, he wondered if Muriel would come to love this home as much as he did and if she would be willing to move here to Waco. He reasoned that she had been a busy lady all of her life, with much of it spent raising a daughter on her own, but he thought that the two of them could travel. He had the financial means to do so. They needed to talk about so many plans. Everything between them was still so shining and new and they had been so caught up in their adoration for each other that they had not discussed the future. Mundane things had taken a back seat for their concentration was on each other and the Rogers case.

"You are deep in thought, my amigo," Sarita said and Ken realized how caught up he had been.

"Oh, just thinking about Muriel and wondering if she will love this home and be willing to move here."

"Mr. Ken, this lady will love it here. I know these things, my dear amigo. She is a woman who will fill her time when you are busy in your office writing." She held up her finger and shook it, "Now you please mark my words and so not to worry."

They finished breakfast and Ken was pouring a refill of coffee when the phone rang at the counter bar. When he picked it up, Holly's sweet voice spoke, "Hi Daddy. What's happening? We haven't heard from you in quite awhile."

"Well, Holly girl, how's my sweetheart?" Ken brightened to hear her soft drawl.

"Oh, Bart and I are both fine, busy all the time but doing great. I just wanted to call you because we have some news to share with you."

Ken knew instantly that Holly and Bart were expecting and he said, "The stork is on its way, right?"

"Oh, Daddy, you are so intuitive. I am always in shock even though I have known it for years. Why, Carter and I could never get by with one thing," and she laughed merrily.

"Well, you were good kiddos, honey so I didn't have to get out the yardstick often," he teased.

"Daddy, you never did punish us that often, let alone use a yardstick. Why, I just hope that Bart and I will be half as good as you and Mama were."

"Honey, trust me. You are going to be super parents, both of you."

"Well, we will find out. We were both so elated that we can't contain ourselves. I couldn't stand it another moment and just had to call you this morning. I am a little over six weeks gestation so it looks like we will have a winter baby, Daddy. Are you up to being a grandpa?"

"As a matter of fact, I can't wait, sweet child," he assured her.

"Daddy, have you been real busy with your writing?" Holly asked. Ken thought she must have spoken to Carter recently and was wondering what was taking up his time, or who.

"Yes, I have been on a murder case that maybe you recall happened almost a year ago now." He related some of the details to Holly and then asked, "Have you talked to Carter lately?"

"Yes, just last night. He tells me you are going to come see him in a few days...." She hesitated then and Ken knew she was getting ready to broach the question about who was going to Houston with him. He was amused and decided that he would toy with this spunky daughter who couldn't stand secrets.

"Oh, did Carter mention that I was coming to visit?" he asked innocently.

"Daddy, you know full well what I am getting at, darn it. Now who is going with you?"

"Well, sweet Holly, let me pose a question to you. What are you and Bart doing next weekend?"

"Nothing that I am aware of. Bart has that weekend free so another doctor will be on call at the hospital. Why?"

"I was wondering if you and Bart could possibly join me at your brother's?"

"Say, that would be super, Daddy. Listen, I will call you back and let you know by this evening, okay?"

'Honey, I haven't seen you two kids and Bart for so long and I miss you a lot."

"Oh, Daddy, I know it gets lonely for you but we miss you like crazy too. Now I can see that you are not going to let me worm any information out of you, right?"

"That is correct, little mama to be. You will just have to hang tight for now," he chuckled at Holly's exaggerated deep sigh.

"Oh, I know I won't be able to stand it but so be it. How's Sarita?"

"She is right here and I know you would like to talk to her. She is anxious to talk to you." He handed the phone to Sarita.

"Ah, my little chick, how are you and that fine young doctor man? Now, Miss Holly, I do not know, big mystery, you see," and she crossed her ample bosom to offer penitence for the little white lie. They hung up after a brief exchange and Sarita turned to Ken with a wide grin. "Well, I see, Señor Ken, you sidestepped the family sleuth."

"Yes, I did Sarita. I don't know how. You know, she would have made a great interrogator, that little busybody," Ken laughed and Sarita pursed her lips with a half grin and nodded her agreement.

"I am going to be a grandpappy, Sarita. How about that?" His face was alight with that announcement.

"I, for one, am so happy. It is wonderful that I have lived this many years with this family and to see you finally become abuelo (grandfather)."She clasped her brown hands together and bit down on her lip to contain her emotions. Ken felt strong emotions well up in him too and he thought of Gloria, who would have been so proud. But, somehow, he felt that she knew.

"Sarita, I had a dream while I was gone and I saw this little girl who called me grandpapa. Maybe she was letting me know beforehand that she was on the way."

"Knowing you, my amigo, I think by all the saints in heaven that you were given second sight and you know these things." Sarita spoke softly and regarded Ken with a kind of awe and deep esteem.

"Yes, I have been having some extraordinary visions that have become stronger and more intense these last several weeks. At first, it was quite overwhelming."

"You have been given a gift from God. There are no mistakes."

Ken nodded, then picked up his coffee mug to take it to his office so he could call Larkins Motel in private. He sat at his desk and poured over all of this morning's events and smiled. "A grandfather— wow!" He thought about the conversation he had had with Bruster awhile back regarding the esteemed position of grandparent and his smile deepened.

"Mr. Chan, good morning. This is Ken Ferries. I wanted to advise you that I won't be needing the room since I will be staying with friends in Rosewood." On an impulse, he asked Mr. Chan if he had noted any other strange events since he had left.

The man answered that someone had asked about him early one morning, which surprised Ken.

"Mr. Chan, could you give me a description of him, please?" Ken felt the prickly of goose bumps as Mr. Chan described the man he had seen in Bailey's on his first visit to the town. "Did you happen to notice what he was driving, Mr. Chan?"

"Let me think." Mr. Chan paused for a moment. "Why, yes sir, it was an older green Jeep, quite faded in color."

"What did he want to know about me, Mr. Chan, do you recall?"

"He asked me if you were still here in Rosewood and I told him I thought you were gone. Then he asked when you would return as he said he had a business matter to discuss with you."

"What did you tell him, Mr. Chan?"

"Sir, I do hope that it was all right but I did tell him that you would be returning next week. I do hope that was all right."

"Oh, of course, Mr. Chan, no problem."

"Well, Mr. Ferries, after all that occurred that one night, I was concerned that I should not have given this stranger any information at all."

"It is quite all right, sir. Please advise me if he does return, however." He gave Mr. Chan his home phone number and Muriel's number but cautioned him not to give these to the man if he showed up again.

"Well, Ken, sit tight. It does appear more and more that his mystery man is going to soon present himself," Ken mused as he sipped his coffee and then turned to work at his computer.

"Oh, heck, I hope that Holly will call before Sarita and I go out to dine this evening." He decided to call and leave her a message instead with a time to call and then resumed work at the computer. He worked on until the time that Sarita called him to lunch and he was surprised that he had hunger pangs after the well-rounded breakfast he had enjoyed earlier.

"Sarita, I think I will give Maggie another run this afternoon because I have decided that I will leave again Sunday for Rosewood instead of waiting until Tuesday."

"Well, Maggie and I will miss you but I am so happy that you are going to meet with your Carter and I pray that Holly and Bart will be there as well."

"Oh, I called and left word on Holly and Bart's recorder as to the time to call tonight since I forgot to tell her that we were going to Chico's this evening. As for the trip, I am first flying to Huntsville late on Wednesday afternoon and I will speak with those three men at the prison there. Muriel and I will rent a car and drive on to Houston on Friday afternoon. Now, my dear lady, I will share something with you that I am going to surprise Muriel with," and his blue eyes were full of great joy thinking of the future event. "When we get to Houston, I plan to take Muriel to a jewelry store that handles the best and most exquisite gems and then out to dinner at one of Houston's finest where we can set a date for our wedding. Now what do you think of our having it here in this home, Sarita?"

"Oh, Señor Ken," and she was dabbing at her soft brown eyes with the corner of her apron. "Such a lucky lady and si, a wedding here is so perfect if she agrees to it. Now, you must make certain that she will want the same plans."

"Oh, of course because that is what will please me most is for Muriel to have her day too. It is for both of us."

"Please now sit down. I have here a cold pitcher of lemonade and fresh melon and a sandwich. I hope that is not too filling because I have chocolate cake for dessert. I think maybe, with the big feast at Chico's tonight, we need room, you know?" and she laughed as she rubbed her ample tummy.

"Of course, Sarita, that is a wise decision because this is a festive celebration for us this evening at our favorite restaurant. I am looking forward to it with my very special friend, always good company." He winked at her.

"He knew that Sarita's birthday was this day but she had carefully avoided mentioning it. He had a surprise for her that he would present this evening at supper. They finished their lunch and cleared away the dishes.

Then Ken rounded up Maggie from under the lilac bush. "Come on, girl, we have places to go and squirrels to chase." Maggie whirled and whirled in her excitement and eagerly followed him through the kitchen to the garage.

They made their way to Brazor's Lake and walked to the area of picnic tables. There they noticed a short squat man with an equally squat English bulldog on a leash. The man was at least seventy years old and it was obvious that it was ponderous for him to walk. The bulldog puffed as much as his owner as they lumbered toward Ken and Maggie.

"Fine day," the man said with a British accent. Ken agreed. The man paused now to rest, removing a handkerchief to wipe his flushed cheeks and brow. The bulldog was interested in Maggie, who promptly sat down and tolerated the other dog's sniffing, drooling and grunting.

"Aw, now Rex, she is a fine lady but out of your class," the man chuckled. The bulldog sat down finally to lick noisily at his chops.

"There's a good lad, Rex, you old fart," and he laughed in a har, har method that rolled from his belly like a crashing wave.

"Come on, Maggie, We best be heading up the trail," Ken smiled at her as she looked up at him, obviously grateful to be moving on.

"Maggie, is it," the man said. "Well now, Maggie, the top of the day to you."

"The same to you, sir, and to Rex. He is a fine fellow, too."

"Well, he is that now, aren't you, Rex?" The man agreed as he pulled the dog aside and closer to him so Ken and Maggie could pass by.

Ken noticed that more people were in the picnic area than before and many of them were young families with children. A tow-headed boy of about five came up to Maggie to pet her as his slightly older red-haired sister called sharply to him.

"Billy Dale Meeker, you know what Mama told you about petting strange dogs," she scolded.

"Aw, Sally Anne, go eat a fat worm," the boy sassed.

"Now, kids, it's all right because Maggie here is a good dog but, son, your sister is right. You need to be careful because some dogs aren't as friendly as Maggie."

A pretty young woman approached them and began to apologize.

"It's all right, ma'am. I just cautioned Billy Dale here to be careful and explained that not all dogs are like Maggie with her nice disposition."

She thanked Ken and led her children back to their picnic table.

Deeper on up the trail where it was less populated, Maggie found two chattering squirrels in pursuit of each other and she joined the fracas. Quickly enough, both squirrels leapt for the security of a large pine tree, finding shelter together from the more ominous foe. Ken laughed aloud at their antics while Maggie ended up, as usual, at the bottom of the tree looking mystified about where they had gone. The squirrels set up a noisy chatter above her until she looked up and gave one sharp bark. They then proceeded to climb higher and reach a branch where they could keep their vigil. At last, in disgust, Maggie strode away as proud as a queen, not bothering to give them a second glance.

They walked on and just ahead, Ken was surprised to see a wild mother duck with a number of fuzzy ducklings following her in a line. "Maggie, come," Ken commanded. "Let Mrs. Mallard and her young brood pass by. There's a good girl," he spoke softly to her as she came to his side, sitting patiently as the duck family disappeared one by one into the marsh area by the lake.

"Well, now, that was a treat, wasn't it girl? You are such a good Maggie," he crooned down to her as he petted her glossy coat. He thought of how he had almost decided not to take her and once again was so grateful that he had. She was a wonderful friend and, Ken reasoned, true friends are most valuable, whether from the animal or human kingdom.

He breathed the air and caught the full flavor of the pines and the marshy areas. He noticed the small wildflowers dotting the landscape and the birds sending information as they flitted from bushes to trees. From somewhere on the lake, he heard the call of ducks and noticed a great heron on his spider legs carefully approaching the lake's edge. It dropped its long neck with rapid speed and gathered up what appeared to be a big frog which had not been fast enough to escape the long beak of the heron.

"Nature is great, isn't it, Maggie?" and she swished her silky tail in agreement.

The day was uneventful, just a nice one, he determined as he sat down on the log he had found the day before. He thought of the visitation he'd had while sitting there as he watched Maggie investigating every nook and cranny.

"I have had every conceivable evidence of the mastery of God and his power," he thought, and wondered how anyone could doubt God for one moment. He knew that, when Gloria died, his faith was briefly shaken, but not in God really, just a feeling of being dis-spirited for a time.

"I know that you understood, Father. You always have and you always will," and he breathed deeply inhaling the sensitivity of this inner knowledge.

"You have angels at your back and they look after you and guide you in to the safest harbors," and he momentarily wondered where that came from but it settled into his heart like a greater peace.

"Maggie," he called, "come on, girl. Let's travel on up the trail a bit more." She came to him in a few short bounds. They walked on and came to a clearing where he could look for some distance over the lake. He spotted a lone fisherman on the other side. They continued on awhile and Ken saw movement in the brush just ahead. He was concerned that they had encountered more peccaries so he called sharply to Maggie. She whined but came to his side. Quickly, from the brush, two cottontails appeared and raced on up the winding trail ahead of them.

"Look at them, Maggie. Aren't they cute? I suspect they have a den close by and maybe little ones they are hoping to lead us away from." They walked on about a mile and at least half of another, then Ken checked his watch and was surprised to see that it was getting close to four thirty.

"Hey, girl, we'll do this again one day when I come back but I do believe we had best be heading home now. Sarita and I have a date at her favorite restaurant for her birthday this evening. We will be serenaded by the strolling mariachi while I present her a gift which will overwhelm her." Maggie cocked her head as though she fully understood Ken's every word. They made their way back down the trail and it was almost five when they got settled and on the road home.

"Sarita, we're home," he called out as he and Maggie made their way into the kitchen. When she didn't answer, he surmised that she was in her room getting ready for their evening out. As he opened the sliding glass door to let Maggie out back, Sarita came into the kitchen.

"Ah, Señor Ken, you are home."

"Sarita, you look wonderful. That color blue is most flattering for you." Her brown eyes sparkled as she twirled around to show off her elegance.

"Now, señor, I do hope that I am presentable to be escorted by a fine gentleman out to dine this evening."

"You most certainly are, my dear lady. I only hope that I too will look worthy of your fine company," he said caught up in the gaiety of Sarita's happiness.

He excused himself then and said, "Sarita, I had best be getting a shower. Please take the call if Holly should call while I'm in the shower."

"Oh, si," she agreed.

After he showered and dressed, he joined Sarita. "Good news, Señor Ken. Your daughter called and said that they will see you this coming weekend at Carter's."

"Say now, that is terrific, eh Sarita?" His spirits soared even higher.

'Well, my lady," he said and crooked his arm to lead her to the garage where he opened the car door for her. She settled in and they made their way to Chico's.

When they entered, Emanuel, the owner, greeted them himself. "Mr. Ferries, Sarita, it has been a long time since we have had the pleasure of your company. Come, come now, I have a special table just for you." He was a trim Mexican man in his early sixties with wavy steel gray hair, an extraordinarily handsome man. Ken remembered when he had no gray hair, but then neither did he at the time. Emanuel led them to a table and seated Sarita first, then Ken. He motioned to a slim Mexican youth with a white bar towel draped over one arm.

"Raul, please bring the lady and gentleman the best vino in the house. This is my treat."

Ken started to protest but Emanuel raised his hand and shook his head. "No, no señor, I insist."

"Well, gracias, Emanuel," Sarita said in response, "mucho gracias, my amigo."

Emanuel held both hands up and splayed his fingers wide. "Is nothing. You are long-time friends and this is a special occasion."

Sarita pretended that she hadn't heard his remark. Ken found it humorous because she probably thought that he had not known it was her birthday and that Emanuel did since this was where they usually came for her celebration. Emanuel motioned for a pretty young Mexican woman to bring the menus. Raul did the honors and poured the wine, then bowed a brief bow, giving them a flash of perfect teeth.

"Señor, señora, if there is anything I may do for you, please let me know."

"No thank you, Raul. I think we are fine for now," Ken said.

The young Mexican woman retreated and then later returned to take their orders. After she had done that, Ken raised his glass and looked at Sarita. Then he announced, "Sarita, a joyous birthday and God bless you with many more, dear lady. You thought that I forgot, didn't you?" His eyes were teasing. She dropped her head and said something in Spanish, then put two fingers to her lips to hide a shy grin.

At that moment, the strains of a soft Mexican tune accompanied by two Mexican vocalists could be heard. The pair walked to Sarita, one on each side of her, and serenaded her. Ken knew she was blushing, yet he could see the great smile of pleasure in spite of her head being tilted down. Finally, she looked at Ken who was smiling at her and he met her great dark eyes and winked broadly. She propped her arm on the table top and covered her mouth to hide a sudden giggle. Finally, the two vocalists drifted to another table, serenading a young blushing couple nearby.

"You, amigo, are such a good man," she said and her eyes were bright with the feelings she felt for him.

"Well, my dear señora, I am blessed by the company of an especially dear person." He pulled an envelope from the inside breast pocket of his jacket. "Happy birthday, precious lady" and he laid the envelope in front of her plate. She opened it and he heard her gasp as she looked first at the sizable check and then the round trip airline ticket to Mexico City. She sat speechless for a few moments and then looked up at Ken, her dark eyes filled with unchecked tears.

"Oh, no señor, this is too generous. I cannot accept all of this."

"Yes you can, Sarita. And you must because, not only is it highly deserved, but you will hurt my feelings if you don't accept it." He knew it was dishonorable in her culture for her not to accept after he put it that way.

"Well, my dear amigo, then gracias is too little to say but it comes from my heart, my very soul." She dabbed at her eyes with the handkerchief Ken handed her. She said something then that Ken had not heard her mention and it surprised him.

"You know, my madre, she reaches ninety-five years in two weeks and my sister Petera and my brother Roberto, they say to me, can you please join us for our madre's celebration. All of the grand-grand-children and the grand and the children— the list is many," and she grew more excited as she spoke. Her face was radiant.

"Sarita, I have heard you mention your family very little in all the years I have known you. I didn't know that your mother was still living."

"Si, but my father died a long time ago." She crossed herself. She went on to surprise him even more when she told him of her late husband who had died at an early age. "I lost my Juan when he was thirty-two years old," and she swallowed hard. "I did not want to marry again and the bambino we had, she passed too early in our marriage. We could not have more children, though we tried." Her eyes showed the pain clearly and Ken realized that was why she did not speak of it before this.

"My Juan was blessed with a family who was able to send him to law school so we had a better income than so many of our countrymen. So, when he passed away, I felt that the one way I could help my loved ones was to leave Mexico, you see. Besides, Señor Ken, so many— how you say?, memories of Juan and our daughter Tinea…" Her voice was husky with restrained emotion. She went on, "I work hard, it helps me through my pain." She put her hand to her heart. "And I go to school where I learn the English and then I finally come to the state of Texas. I am so very blessed then ever more, for you see I get to share with you and Gloria your beautiful children and your so special friendship." She paused, then said, "My Father has been so good to me, dear señor."

Ken was overcome and couldn't speak. He reached across the table and squeezed Sarita's hand. Finally he spoke, "Thank you for sharing this with me, Sarita. We all love you, dear lady."

The waitress came with their order and Sarita breathed deep. "Ah, is heaven, is it not, Señor Ken?"

"I certainly agree all the way, Sarita," he smiled tenderly at this lady for whom he held such deep love.

"Oh, but Señor Ken, what of the home if I leave and Maggie, that sassy ball of fluff the high and mighty Milky who forgets she is a cat?" She chuckled lightly.

"It is all covered because I am going to ask Angie if she will house-sit."

Sarita brightened and agreed that was a great idea. Then she said, "But señor, what of your wedding? I do not wish to miss that."

"Oh, Sarita, not to worry. We would not get married without you being there. I would not feel as though it was complete if you weren't there."

"Then, amigo, I feel at peace and now I am so happy. It is all perfecto. You have covered all the big bases." Her joy was a pleasure to behold and Ken's heart sang.

They dined and talked of all the upcoming events and just savored the good meal. At the closed of it, the pretty Mexican woman brought a small cake alight with candles. The mariachi group followed behind her and they sang happy birthday in Sarita's native tongue. Ken joined the gaiety and blended his voice, singing happy birthday in English. Sarita's smile shown brightly. The whole establishment sang to her and, at the finish, she served them each a slice of cake.

They departed for home feeling high with the bliss of a perfect evening.

"I will call Angie first thing in the morning, Sarita. Listen, you may want her to come over here before you leave to go over things, all right?"

"Si, señor, and mucho gracias for a wonderful birthday celebration."

"Good night, sweet señora, and once again, happy birthday. Sleep well and I will see you in the morning."

Ken went to his room and packed his things in preparation for leaving early the next morning. He took a look at the time and realized it was still early enough that he could go add more to the book. He seated himself at the computer and worked for an hour when the phone rang. It was quarter after nine, he noticed as he picked up the receiver.

"Hi Ken, it's Angie. Sorry I called you so late."

"Oh, Angie hon, it's not late but you must be a mind-reader because I was going to call you first thing in the morning to pose a question to you."

"All right," she agreed.

"Well, later I will but you must have something to say so you first."

"All right. I just talked to Mom and she told me about the plans you all have. I think it is super and I am happy she is going to meet your son."

"Well now, Angie, she is going to get to meet my daughter Holly and her husband Bart too. They will meet us at Carter's. I have to tell you that my Holly is expecting so I am about to pop my buttons." He gave a happy laugh and Angie responded with a cheery "Wow!"

"Ken, you are just being blessed from many directions. Congratulations on all counts to both you and Mom."

"Thank you, honey, and you are one more of the blessings I get too."

"Me too," she giggled. "I feel like I am blessed and about to get a sister and brother in the bargain. Ken, now what did you want to ask me?"

"How would you like to house-sit here for me while I'm away working in Rosewood for a couple weeks. Sarita will be gone to see her family in Mexico and I need someone to see after Maggie and one very independent cat."

"Of course, Ken, but when?"

"Well, I'm going to leave for Rosewood in the morning and Sarita would like to have you come over so she can show you around. Then by Monday, she will be leaving so it would be like right away. I probably won't see you but Sarita will be here getting things together for her trip."

"Does she have a way to the airport, Ken?"

"Oh, yes, I have covered all the bases for her, so not to worry. A neighbor friend of ours will take her."

"Well, Ken, shouldn't I come over and just stay tomorrow evening?"

"Yes, that would be great if you could come in the afternoon and then plan to stay. This won't present a problem for you, will it?"

"Not at all and I'm so pleased that you asked me."

"Angie, I am grateful that you will do this." They said good evening and Ken returned to his computer for almost two hours. He was happy with his progress when he finally retired for the night.

Morning looked like the start of a beautiful day and Sarita was especially charged with high spirits. She was humming a tune while she cooked one of her tasty omelets.

"Good morning, Sarita. You sound like you are on top of the world, my amigo." He got out the dog food to place outside for Maggie.

"Ah, Señor Ken, I am up there on top of the world. I called Roberto, my brother, and told him I am leaving tomorrow and he should come pick me up. I said not to tell our dear mama so she will be most surprised."

"That is great, Sarita. Now listen, Angie called last night and all of that is taken care of. She will come over this afternoon and stay tonight. And Mrs. Archer will take you to the airport."

"Well, are you not one hombre with perfect orders. My Juan was the same. Is a good way to be, no?"

"A good way to be, si," he laughed, "but alas, I am getting more credit than I deserved, Sarita."

"I know you, amigo, many years. And si, you deserve mucho credit." She came to place the omelet onto his plate. "Now you sit down and eat a good morning meal. It is a big drive you have."

With breakfast out of the way, Ken retrieved his luggage to put in the car and then returned to bid Sarita goodbye. He told her not to be concerned about anything but just to have a wonderful time and to give his blessings to her family, especially her madre. He handed her an envelope and asked her to give it to Angie, then hugged her quickly. He was surprised when she hugged him back warmly.

"God be with you, dear amigo," and he departed.

He searched his stereo cassettes and found a Lou Rawls favorite and eased out of the driveway with a satisfied feeling of accomplishment.

"Well, Ken Ferries, you are going in all these directions, it would seem. Getting a wife and following up with a first grandchild," and he began to hum along with the tune coming from the stereo.

Chapter____13

He breezed along easily, noticing that the traffic was minimal. He was glad that it was because he could go over some of the events that had happened at home without having to be on extra alert.

He went over the phone call from the man who had suggested that he and the cops just keep it cool until he was ready to "cut a deal". Plus the statement that everything wasn't as it appeared was really baffling to Ken. He thought back to the vision of a man running across a pasture and reaching a near concealed Jeep in the grove of trees. "Had he almost been caught in the act of murder by the three men now in prison? Or had he himself witnessed someone else killing Nadine and ran to protect himself? It was a mystery but one that Ken hoped was nearing a close. What of the incidents at the Conways? Did that tie in with this murder?" he mused.

His mind traveled to the dream he had of the flight from a beastly predator. He remembered the wild insane eyes, the weapon with the spur on it waiting to club him down as he ran for that door. He could still feel his heart pound just thinking about trying to find another escape door. It had to be Nadine's feelings of horror that had come to him and he gulped at the enormity of it all. Sometimes, he was so deeply overcome the savage death of this lovely woman that he could not check his tears. He wiped angrily at the tears with the back of his hand and swore softly, "Dammit all to hell anyway. Get hold of yourself, Ken Ferries, and concentrate on helping to get this whole sad affair closed. At least then people can start healing. And wherever you are Nadine, you will then have peace, full peace."

He drove on with a renewed determination, his mind set on accomplishing this soon. Too many lives had been shattered by this senseless act of violence and vindication would bear out. He vowed he would see it come and pounded on the steering wheel with one big solid fist.

"Guess I need a coffee break," he said aloud as he spotted a small café ahead. He pulled off and parked in front of "Carl and Ellen's Café". He seated himself at the counter and was greeted by a lady about mid-fifties with hot cherry pepper red hair. "Surely not her own," Ken deduced and was glad for the diversion.

"What will it be, mister," she greeted him. He ordered a black coffee. She turned to reach for the coffee pot and Ken noticed the hoop earrings adorning her ears. Surely, they were large enough that she could have worn them for bracelets. But her smile was radiant and he sensed that she housed a good soul.

"Can't interest you in some of our special now?" she drawled and motioned toward the man in the kitchen. "Carl there can put together the best catfish and hushpuppies you ever ate this side of the Mississippi."

Ken looked at his watch and noted it was close to the noon hour. He made the decision he would try Carl's specialty. He wasn't sorry, for after the first bite, he assured her he had eaten none better.

"Be sure to stop in again, mister. And tell folks about us, won't you?"

"Certainly will. Ellen, is it?" He smiled up into her wide blue eyes.

"Yes, sir, I am Ellen. Now Carl and me, we got the kids sent off to college and decided to open this little café last year and not just sit around and get fat." She laughed at her own humor.

"I reckon if Carl keeps cooking catfish and the fixings like that, you will be drawing in a lot of customers," he assured her. He paid his bill, put a sizable tip on the counter, and bid her good day. On the way to his car, he stopped short and stared at the incredible number of butterflies covering his car windshield. They flew to him and encircled him, then a few at a time, flew off on a gentle breeze which appeared. Suddenly, they were all gone. He stood for a moment before he opened the car door. He closed his eyes and could hear a voice, the ancient strange voice of Nathan Tom.

"You are the wind and, where you travel, there will follow the colors of the rainbow. You will plant the quiet of peace within the hearts of many."

Some force seemed to compel him to look up into a crystal clear blue sky. There he saw an impressive red-tailed hawk circling over him. He watched it sail around several times and then it simply disappeared. He slid behind the wheel and closed the car door. As he reached to turn on the ignition, the fragrance of roses was undeniable. He knew that she was here and he closed his eyes, laying his head back.

"You will find the way and know that all is well. Go to the source of the demise and know the answer will speak to you. I leave you now in the Light of Love." He knew it was Nadine who spoke. The fragrance began to disappear and still he sat there with his head resting back. It was almost overwhelming but he knew that a power from the Highest was making him aware of all of this magnificence.

"Mister, are you all right?" He opened his eyes and saw Ellen peering in anxiously at him. He smiled to reassure her and said, "Oh, yes. Just resting a bit before I head on to Rosewood."

"Well, by golly, you're going there? I have a sister who lives in Rosewood," she drawled. "Has for years. Guess it is a small world, as they say," Her face crinkled up ever more with the deep smile.

"Yes, ma'am, it does seem so, all right,"

"Well now, you have a safe trip and be sure to come see us again."

Ken told her he would and she went back inside the café. He made his way out to the highway and settled in comfortably for the next few miles to Rosewood.

The messages were clear— he knew he had to get out to the Rogers ranch and get into that home of Will's. He was certain a powerful message of truth awaited him there.

He drove to Dolly's and parked almost in front of the café. Churchgoers were still there having lunch and he knew Muriel would be busy serving customers. She didn't see him when he came in as she was waiting on a large group of three tables joined together.

He sat down at the counter and a girl who appeared to be about sixteen asked him if he wanted coffee. She laid a menu in front of him.

"Yes, black coffee, and a piece of that cherry pie to go with it would do fine."

He wondered how long it would be before Muriel noticed him and it amused him to play this little waiting game.

"Say, Della Ann, how about a refill on this coffee?" The young man sitting next to Ken called out while the girl was slicing a piece of pie.

She turned around and pointed the pie knife at him. "Raymond Billings, you just keep your shirt on now. Reckon I'll get there when I have the notion."

The youth laughed as Della turned back to her task and neatly sat the pie on a serving dish. She turned with the dessert in one hand and picked up the coffee pot with the other. She carefully sat the pie in front of Ken, then stood looking at the youth Raymond with disdain.

"Will that be all, your lordship," she said with a quick curtsy, and she proceeded to fill his coffee cup.

"Now, one more thing— I just wanted to ask you if you know where they send orphaned chickens." When she didn't answer and merely rolled her amber eyes, he went on. "I heard they send them to Foster Farms." He chuckled and the girl stood back with her hands on her slim hips.

She appraised him with a look of scorn. "That's dumb, Raymond, really dumb." But Ken noticed she had a flicker of amusement spark briefly in her eyes.

"Well, I'll make up for it, Dell, if you will go to the movies with me tonight. There's a real rip snorter playing with Tommy Lee Jones over at The Flicker Shack."

"Well, maybe, if you'll promise to lay off the corny jokes, Raymond." Her voice softened. "But you know I won't get out of here until after seven o'clock most likely."

"We'll catch the second flick then. I'll be here and pick you up."

She nodded and then went on down to the end of the counter to refresh someone's coffee. Ken was concentrating on his pie and didn't see Muriel when she walked up behind him.

She placed her hand on his shoulder and whispered in his ear, "Why don't you come up and see me sometime, big boy," in her sexiest Mae West drawl.

He turned to look into her teasing cat-green eyes and took her hand. "Hi baby. I've missed you."

"Me too," she said, and then, "How long you been here, Ken? I didn't see you come in."

He laughed. "I know. You were mighty busy so I didn't want to bother you. Besides, I wanted to see how long it would be before you noticed I was in here."

She swatted him playfully and then kissed him quickly. Ken could see the love for him in her eyes and knew his own expression conveyed the same feelings for her.

She reached into her apron pocket and slipped her house key into his hand then winked at him. "Gotta run. This place is wild on Sundays but come have supper here this evening, okay? Then later, I will see you at home."

"All right, pretty lady. I think I'll take a drive around and then see you later."

He finished his dessert and laid some money on the counter. Della Ann smiled happily at the tip he left and thanked him as he stood to leave.

He walked to his car and decided he would drive out to Sage Murdock's to help pass the time. Besides, he had taken a special liking to that plucky old gent. He moved along the country road and soon arrived at the entrance road to Sage's ranch. He noted the name Murdock on the mailbox and just beyond up the lane, he could clearly see the older ranch home with a barn to the left. He drove up the lane and into the wide yard in front of the house with a wraparound porch. A boarder collie came bounding off the porch to greet him. He knew the dog was friendly and happened to recall that Sage had called him Tatters. He got out of the car and called the dog by name.

"Well, Tatters, is Sage home?" He stroked the dog's silky coat and walked toward the porch. The front door opened and Sage stepped out.

"Well, sir, come on in. It's mighty fine to see you. I just finished up with some chow but I'd be rightly pleasured to fix you some too."

"Why, thank you, Sage, but I already ate. But I'd take a cup of coffee with you."

"Come on in here now 'cause I sure enough got a fresh pot readied up for us."

Ken felt like he had stepped back in time to his parents' farmhouse and his boyhood. He was completely at ease in these surroundings. Sage motioned to an old-fashioned oak table and chairs close by a wide kitchen window. He went to get two coffee mugs from the tall cupboards. "Sit down over there, Ken, and take a load off ya," he offered.

"So, how's the world been treating you, Sage?"

"Why, Ken, just doing fine but then I mostly am. You know, at my age, I don't reckon I got a lot of time to be spending on down times," and he laughed good-naturedly.

"You got a point, Sage. It is sure enough a good way to be looking at it too," Ken agreed.

"Say now, are you still sportin' that pretty woman, Miss Muriel?" the elderly man smiled.

421

"Sure am, Sage. If she hadn't been working today, I would have brought her out here for a visit too."

"Well, there's another day. Now, don't let me forget, I got to give you some of them eggs I mentioned before. Got way more than I can handle, even selling some."

"You will let me pay you for them, Sage."

"Nope. They are not for sale, sir, but you can have them," he said briskly.

"All right then, the pleasure's mine. I will sure help Muriel get rid of them."

"Sage, have you remembered anything more about that time you and Tatters scared someone out of your barn?"

"You know, Ken," the elderly man said as he set down the mugs and seated himself, "Seemed that something kept wanting to come to me. It was lying there in the back of my mind. Kept troubling me— you know how a thing can ride at you. Well, I just swore to clear it away and not think on it so hard and, then one day whilst I was puttering around in the barn, it comes to me." Ken could feel his heart skip with hopeful anticipation. "Just felt for some reason that I ought to know that feller that took off like the hounds o' hell was hot on his tail but I didn't get a long enough look at him 'cause I was rightly startled myself."

"Who did he look like, Sage?" Ken pressed.

"Well, I ain't right sure but he looked like somebody I've seen. And you know what really chilled my old hide when this come to me— it looked like he had blood on him. Well, I reckoned maybe he injured himself somehow but, you know, what with it havin' been the same morning Will's Mrs. was found, it really gave me a fright."

422

"Now, I can see that it would," Ken agreed.

"You know something I can't figure," Sage said thoughtfully, "I know that Gomez boy, have all of his life. Know the family and they are good folks. Now, Larry, he was a tad wild but not a bad kid, hard-working lad. I've had him and his Pa work for me and I tell you, they know how to put in a day's work. Something just don't feel right to me that Larry Gomez would've been party to the idea of robbing folks, let alone an act of murder. No, sirree." He shook his head and then took a long swallow from his coffee mug.

"Well, did you know the other two men, Sage? And what's your feeling about them?"

"Now I know old Jyp and again, a hard-workin' old scudder. No indication of any other than a good man. Sorta quiet-like, tended to his own kind, and I never heard the man say a mean thing about anyone, nor even a cuss word. Now, the other feller, I just knew him in passin'. Guess he was a bit of a dandy, you know, and had an eye for the ladies, but some way or another, I didn't get the feeling he was a lady killer. I kinda figured him for a love 'em and leave 'em sort."

"Sage, if you do happen to remember where you saw the man that exited your barn so fast, would you do me a favor and either get hold of me or Sheriff Hernado?"

"Why sure will, Ken. Now, tell me, is there some new development on the Rogers case that wasn't uncovered before?"

"Sage, there just might be and I am going to ask you not to mention to anyone what you've recalled about that morning, not to anyone but the sheriff."

"You can rest assured I surely won't say a word to anyone else. But how is it you are involved?"

"You know I worked as a reporter and did some investigating on a number of crimes over the years. I noticed several things about this crime that I felt had not been resolved. But again, I would prefer you not to discuss my researching this case for the time being."

"Sure enough, Ken. But I want to tell you I am glad you may be surfacing some more things 'cause I got me a hunch about this whole shootin' match. I ain't said much 'cause folks round here's been so riled up and it's a mighty sore subject."

"Yes, I know. It is one of the reasons I have gone as low key as possible myself. Then too, it is pretty touchy another way with the family, all of whom I have come to know and have the highest regard for."

"That's some of the best folks you could ever know, Ken," Sage agreed.

Ken nodded and took another sip of coffee. He noticed the jars of honey lined up on a shelf above the kitchen sink with country-checked material covering the tops. "Sage, are you in the honey business? I see you have several jars of it put up?"

"Yes, I sure am. Got me some beehives and my sister Dorothy duddies 'em up all fancy-like. Seems it makes them more appealing."

"Say now, I'd take a couple of them but only if you allow me to pay you for them," Ken was implicit.

"All right, sir, it's a deal." The sturdy old gentleman got up to bring the jars of honey to the table. "Whilst I'm up, I'll fetch them cackleberries." He opened the refrigerator and retrieved the cartons of eggs, then sacked them up and brought another bag for the honey jars.

"Good thing Dot brings me all her pokes 'cause I sure make the use outta them." He walked back to the table and sacked up the honey. Ken noted the stickers with prices neatly applied to the jars and placed more than the amount on the table. Sage protested.

"Let's just say it is my way of saying thank you for your help, Sage, and for a mighty fine cup of java and good company to boot."

"Well, I reckon any time you can head out this way, you know you're sure enough welcome. I've taken a likin' to you. Now, for the record, I'm mighty pleased about you and that pretty lady of yours. The best to both of you."

Ken stood up and firmly shook hands with him. The handshake from Sage's rock-hard hand was as firm as Ken's own.

"I sure appreciate that, Sage. I hope that you will attend our wedding because there is going to be one soon enough."

"Well, by danged, Ken, you and Miss Muriel can count on that. That's the best news I've heard in a coon's age." And his dark eyes sparked with pleasure.

"Once again, thank you, Sage. Now guess I better be heading on. Maybe I'll stop by to see some other folks if they are home and look over the area.

The older man opened the door for Ken and stepped out to the porch with him. He waved farewell as Ken got into his car. Ken smiled at the scene of the old rancher and his dog Tatters standing on the porch and he thought of the elderly man who had shown him and his brother Tommy the art of frying frog legs. Where did

425

all those years go? He mused that he often felt as though he had lived four life cycles in one lifetime. "They have all been good, too, for the most part and, God willing, they will keep being so," he said aloud, announcing it to the pristine landscape passing by.

"Well, where to now?" he thought as he came to the main road. He decided to take a left turn and go up the country road to acquaint himself with the area. He passed the mailbox and lane that led to the Rogers ranch and, on the other side, the rough road that wound its way to Nathan Tom's. He drove on another couple miles and came to a mailbox that read Wilson. Then driving on another four miles, he passed a mailbox with the name Webber lettered on it. He reached the foothills shortly after that and, as he made the incline, he could see the whole panorama of ranch country spread out before him. He decided to pull over and take a better look from this vantage point.

He climbed from the car and took a deep breath of the fresh air full of the scent of clover and wildflowers. "Ah, the country," he sighed and stretched his arms wide as he bent his head back. He breathed more deeply and then slowly expelled his breath. Looking down, he noticed that the Webber property seemed to parallel a fair portion of the Rogers property. "Must be a big spread like the Rogers ranch," he concluded aloud.

He noticed cattle off in the distance and large sprawling fields of alfalfa. It was a truly beautiful setting and he paused, understanding why Catlin Willard might want this ranch, if indeed it was Cat who had approached Nadine. Surely this was very prosperous land. He felt that he had arrived at a near conclusion on that issue.

He got in his car and drove a ways farther up the road, moving slowly along. He noticed a water hole for the Conway cattle with a few trees around it. The setting was pretty with lush grass and good grazing for cattle.

"I hope that no more trouble befalls that family," Ken thought soberly. He remembered the young bull Bud had found shot and the prowling incident. Yet, he reasoned that if this man was one and the same who had been calling him and leaving him threatening notes, he was probably hidden somewhere away from this area. Apparently he knew things were closing in on him. Ken wondered again, as Bruster had, if this man did know something but hadn't been the one who killed Nadine. He no doubt was a shady character but perhaps he had stumbled upon the crime scene minutes after it happened and ran away to avoid a murder wrap. Yet, why was he so eager to keep research from being done on this case? All of this was coursing through Ken's mind like a tumbling current of water while he drove along. He was hoping he could sort through it enough that a possible answer might surface, one that made a pattern of good reasoning. He was eager to go to the Rogers home and was certain that he would pick up on more just being in the crime setting.

He checked his watch and was surprised at the time but felt he needed to linger awhile in this peaceful place. A soft breeze seemed to come, rippling the grass. He watched a bird sailing across the sky and imagined how wonderful it would be to do that. He envied the bird. Something compelled him to pull over at a wide area on the roadside. From this vantage point, he could just make out the little community of Rosewood looking like a miniature village. A hush seemed to surround him and, as he looked out at the wide spectrum before him, a knowingness came over him that seemed inexplicable. He felt that he knew all that is and all that ever will be. He closed his eyes and saw an old man from some ancient time with long gray hair and a white beard. A breeze lifted his hair slightly. The old man pointed a knarled finger and a flash of pictures appeared on a wide screen in his vision. He saw past, present, and future including climatic events. He understood "life" and "death" more fully than before. Suddenly the vision left and he felt more at peace in his core than he had ever imagined was possible.

He made his way back in the direction he'd come, driving slowly and taking in the pleasant countryside. For some reason he didn't understand, he felt compelled to turn in at the Webber ranch. He drove up the gravel lane to the sprawling ranch home to be greeted by a massive dog in the yard. The dog was a St. Bernard and stood like a sentry at attention watching Ken. Ken sat looking back at the animal.

"Hm, should I get out or would it be wise to sit here?" He thought it over and decided not to be foolhardy. He had not pondered long when the screen door opened and a silver-haired woman in her sixties called out to him. "It's all right. Buck here won't hurt you. His size is just intimidating to folks who don't know him." She came out and walked down the porch steps.

Ken got out of the car and said, "Hello, ma'am," and introduced himself.

"Howdy, Mr. Ferries. I'm Fern Webber. Have you come by to see Tom, my husband?"

By now, Ken was almost at a loss for words. He was wondering what on earth had made him decide to turn in here. As though he had clearly thought it out, a question came out of his mouth and it shocked him when he asked this friendly smiling woman if she knew Catlin Willard.

"Well now, as a matter of fact, I do. He was working here for us awhile but, about a week ago, he came to Tom and said he had to leave as he had some unexpected business had come up."

Ken was so surprised that he hoped the shock hadn't registered on his face. "Mrs. Weber, how long did he work here for you folks?"

She reached up and scratched her head for a moment and frowned. 'Why, so many of these drifters come and go that I don't remember unless I look at the payroll slips. Seems to me it was sometime early last spring."

"Did he say he was coming back here by chance?" Ken hoped that he sounded low key when he asked her but he could feel his heart surge.

"Why, he didn't really indicate. Sorta left it where you could take it that yes maybe but then again perhaps not. He was a good worker but not the friendliest sort of guy. I'd say a real loner, that one. Is he a friend of yours, Mr. Ferries?"

"Oh, sort of, you might say," Ken said, trying not to sound evasive. "I just heard he was in these parts, Mrs. Webber, and thought I would stop by and say hello."

"Well, Tom and me, we've been here on this spread going on twenty two years, and over that time, we've had lots of folks that has worked here. They have come from all over, I reckon. Never did know where Cat came from, since he was short on conversing, like I said. He prefers to be called Cat. That seemed a little different to me but whatever floats one's boat, I reckon."

"Mrs. Webber, here is my card. In the event that you should have Catlin get in touch or should he return, please call me at this number." He wrote Muriel's phone number on the back of the card. "If you don't reach me at this number, just call me at my home here in Waco," and he pointed at the number on the other side. "Please call me collect at the Waco number. I will be in this area until Wednesday and return on Monday the following week. I do plan to be in Rosewood awhile."

"I will certainly be glad to, Mr. Ferries, but somehow I doubt that he will come back here or call."

"You're probably correct on that but, nonetheless, there is that slim possibility. Ma'am, I do appreciate your time but I had better be getting back to Rosewood. It is a pleasure to have met you and I must say you folks have a wonderful ranch here. It is a pretty setting too."

"Why, thank you, Mr. Ferries. You're welcome any time. I will call you if Cat should get in touch with us." She extended her hand and said, "It has been my pleasure, sir."

He bid her good day and got back in his car. As he turned around to leave, he saw the big dog Buck follow Mrs. Webber back to the porch and lay down at his post. Ken sensed that the dog was all right but he knew that he was watchful and would take on anyone who offered the least threat toward his mistress. "He is the kind of fellow you would want in your corner," he deduced.

He was still surprised that, for no apparent reason, he had stumbled onto the ranch where Cat had worked. And, he had established that Cat was the one they suspected of the threatening phone calls and notes. Very likely, he was the one who shot the Conway's bull and prowled their ranch, as well. He decided he should call Bruster at home with this information as soon as he could since he wouldn't be in his office now. He would rather talk personally to Bruster that to the deputy on duty.

He went straight to Muriel's home and unloaded his luggage and the items from Sage, and then settled down to call Bruster. Bruster answered on the first ring.

"Well, hello Sheriff. You must have been sitting by the phone," Ken greeted him cheerfully.

"Howdy, Ken. As a matter of fact, I was. What's going on?"

"You won't believe what I happened onto today. I got to Rosewood early this afternoon and, after stopping in at the café to see Muriel, I drove out to visit Sage Murdock. He seems to have gotten a flash or recall about that man who was hiding in his barn. He had gone to see what had stirred up his dog. Sage said that, as he was puttering around in the barn, it came to him that the man he had seen that morning Nadine died looked like he had some blood on him. Now, here is the strangest part. Sage felt that this man looked like someone he had seen before but he couldn't place him. He did say he would know him if he saw him again."

Bruster hadn't said anything but then Ken heard him suck in his breath. Then he exclaimed, "Jeez and Mother Mary, I got a chill clean through to my toes, Ken."

"There's more, Bruster. After I left Sage's, I decided to take a drive on up the country road and do some sightseeing. I passed by the ranches and got out a couple times to admire the panorama. I noticed then the Webber ranch appeared to border the back of the Rogers property."

"Yes, it does, if I recall rightly," Bruster agreed.

"After admiring the landscape some more, I headed back toward town. For some reason I still don't understand, I pulled into the Webber ranch. Now, they have a mighty impressive dog so I didn't get out of the car right away. I was thinking of turning around to leave since I didn't really know why I was there but then a lady came out of the house and greeted me. I got out, feeling sort of foolish, but then blurted out a question, asking Mrs. Webber if she knew Catlin Willard. I still don't know why. Now, imagine my shock when she said that he had worked there for a year and had just left about a week ago because he said some business came up."

"Well now, don't that beat all. Why, I'd darn near be tempted to say you're about half psychic. Danged if that sure don't beat all," he exclaimed again.

Ken suppressed a laugh and thought, "My Lord, Bruster, if you only knew the half of it."

"Bruster, I didn't let on to Mrs. Webber why I was inquiring of Catlin. She arrived at the conclusion that he was a friend of mine and I just left it at that. But I did tell her to call me if he returned. I left my home number and Muriel's. Now, Wednesday, after Muriel and I stop in at the art show, we are leaving for Huntsville and then on to Houston to visit my son. My daughter and her husband are flying in to be with us too. I want them all to meet Muriel."

"Now, Ken, that sounds to me like some pretty serious intentions. I want to be the first to say I am wishing you and Muriel the best."

"Thank you, Bruster. I truly appreciate that."

432

"You're mighty welcome. Say, those reports on the handwriting ought to be here by Monday or at least Tuesday. I'll bet it is Cat Willard's too. It is still kind of a jigsaw puzzle at this stage, but I have a feeling it is all about to come together pretty darned quick now."

"You know, Bruster, I think maybe I ought to call Mrs. Webber and ask her not to tell Catlin I was asking after him if he does show up or call."

"Yes, I would, Ken. You could just say you are a friend from a long time ago and want to surprise him."

"I guess it surprised me so much I hadn't thought it out. But I will give her a call as soon as we hang up. Meanwhile, if I have anything more to report, I sure will right away."

"Good enough. By the way, there is an alert out statewide for Catlin Willard but it is hush, hush because we hope he will come forward. I suspect that, before long, he will be getting in touch with me and asking for clemency."

"That sounds like a possibility because I am beginning to feel like he dug in too deep and over his head. Maybe he didn't kill Nadine but he probably knows something and is being wary. He had been trying to feather his own nest, it would appear, but maybe now feeling that a trap is set up. He's trying to figure something out so he isn't set up for murder one."

"That's crossed my mind too."

"Well, all right, Bruster. I will see you before Muriel and I leave. A good evening to you."

"Same to you, Ken." They both hung up.

Ken checked Muriel's phone directory and called the Webber residence. Mrs. Webber was agreeable to Ken's proposal. Ken saw that it was close to 6 so he decided he had better head back into town for supper at Dolly's.

Muriel greeted him with "Hey, big guy, what have you been up to today? I tried to call you a couple times."

"Oh, went for a drive. First I stopped and had coffee and a chat with Sage Murdock. Honey, I uncovered a lot of new developments today. It will keep until you are off work, though." He looked around the café at the several customers having Sunday supper.

"I just hope it is all good events."

"It's good, honey. I know this— things are about to blow wide open. I just have one of those hunches." He winked at her. He saw the hope and excitement fill her eyes and she swallowed hard.

"Well, sweetheart, you come on over here and sit right down. By the way, our special roast beef dinner with all the trimmings is really good this evening."

"That sounds good to me, pretty lady," he smiled down into her eyes, seeing that special teasing look she reserved just for him.

He slid into the booth and she went to get him coffee. He picked up the newspaper someone had left and scanned it, noting the headlines. Then he laid it down again when Muriel returned with his water and the coffee pot.

"Say, Muriel, that is such a magnificent view up there in the foothills area past Sage's ranch. You can see for some miles from that vantage point."

"Yes, it is. I haven't been out that way for some time but I used to drive up there every so often just for woolgathering. I guess I was really meditating. I seemed to focus on things better for days afterwards."

"I think it must be a power spot and, when you come home, I will tell you why I feel that it is."

She smiled at him. "Ken Ferries, with the gift you have, I believe you are a power spot. It gives me power when I just look at you." She gave him a naughty wink.

Ken chuckled. "Well, all I have to do is think of you and I am literally alive with power spots." The suggestive remark was clear and Muriel bit down on her lower lip trying to suppress a giggle.

"Ken, I gotta go. I just saw some more folks coming in. Love you." She walked over to the table where the group was just settling down. He heard her take their orders for coffee and she walked back to the counter to get them menus.

"God, girl, I am so in love with you," he thought as he followed her cat-like movements. He picked up the newspaper again while sipping his coffee, and within a few minutes, Muriel returned with his order.

"Mmm, that smells good and looks good too. And it was served by my favorite little waitress," he teased.

"Listen, you handsome hunk, I better be your only favorite waitress," she said saucily, but her eyes sparked with a teasing glow. "Oh, Ken, did you remember to bring those snapshots that Angie took?" she asked hopefully.

"Sure did, honey. That is just one of the things we'll get to tonight," he assured her with winsome appeal in his eyes.

Chapter____14

She raised her eyebrows with mock surprise. "Why, Mr. Ken Ferries," she whispered as she bent down to look him squarely in the eyes, "I do believe you are attempting to make out with me."

"No!" he said with exaggeration and surprise, then smiled at her.

She put her hands on her hips and smiled tenderly at him. She turned then as Jeff walked up behind her and put his arm around her waist.

"Hi Jeff. How are you? Right sharp looking you are, Mr. Colter, all dressed up. Been some place special?'

"Howdy, Ken. Good to see you. And yes to all your questions, lady Muriel." He chuckled low. "Reckon with that kind of response, I ought to get duded up more often." The silver gray Western suit and gray Stetson set off Jeff's eyes to great advantage. Ken thought he was a very good-looking man as he slid into the booth across from him. He had a manly aura that was certain to appeal to women and a solid trusting persona that made it easy for people to like him.

"I had better be moving on, fellas. Jeff, good to see you. Do you need a menu?"

"No, Muriel. I just thought I would have a cup of coffee. I saw Ken's car outside and wanted to talk to him a few minutes."

"Good enough then. You two visit and I will bring that coffee over here for you," and she left to retrieve the coffee pot. After filling a mug for him and refilling Ken's, she whisked away to another table.

"Say, Ken, guess I'll just get right to the point. I know you talked to me about this and well, I reckon it's an investigation on Nadine's..." and his throat constricted, "well, on her case." He visibly struggled to avoid saying her death or murder. He picked up a piece of silverware and toyed with it, then proceeded. "I was out to Webber's ranch about a week ago. We do some business together, Tom Webber and me. I swear that I knew this ranch hand they had working there. I couldn't rightly place him but he looked familiar. He seemed to want to avoid me and took off toward the cattle grazing area in an old dull green Jeep. I asked Tom who that was that just took off, that he wasn't too sociable. Tom laughed and said it was Cat Willard and he sure wasn't sociable but he was a good worker. He had been here about a year. I didn't say anything to Tom but, sure fire Ken, that is the same Catlin Willard I went to school with. Now, I know you have been harassed, Ken. I talked to Muriel for some time when I went out to her place to discuss another matter. She told me some guy in an older model green Jeep might be the one who has been calling you with threats and putting notes on your car. You showed me one at the hospital, remember?

Ken took a drink from his glass of water and looked level at the man before him. He knew he could trust him and decided to tell him the events of his own day, how he too had "stumbled" onto the ranch where Cat had been working. "He's left though, Jeff, and it seems the Webbers have no idea as to where he went. All he told them was that some business came up."

"Do you think he is the one responsible regarding Nadine?" Ken could see Jeff's jaw line harden and a flash like fire sparked his steel gray eyes.

"Jeff, I don't know yet, but there's reason to think more and more that those three men in prison are not the ones who took Nadine's life."

Jeff slumped his shoulders and Ken knew he was fighting for control. "Ken, I've come to like and respect you. There's few people I feel comfortable enough to level my feelings to but you are one of them. I was in love with Nadine Rogers but Will was my friend, more of a brother really. They were in love the minute they set eyes on each other and there was no way I would have tried to come between them. I reckon I went around a big part of my life like I was sleep-walking, carrying a torch too big to put out. Now I am finally coming alive, waking up from a long sleep. I know this life has to go on, we owe that much to ourselves." Ken didn't interrupt as Jeff sat in silence a few moments before continuing. "The monster who did this to Nadine and her family and to all her friends and to those men in prison has got to be taken out, Ken. I don't understand all this but I know you've felt right off that something wasn't right with this whole thing. I want to apologize to you 'cause I reckon I was pretty short when you tried to discuss this earlier."

"Jeff, you are a good man and you don't owe me an apology. I knew you were hurt and angry and why wouldn't you be, man? My God, man, you are human and this had been horrific."

"Been all that," Jeff answered somberly, stirring his coffee.

Muriel returned with the coffee pot and filled both of their mugs. She asked Ken if he would like some dessert and he declined with a hint of smile just for her.

She winked knowingly at him and Jeff showed a faintly visible smile. After Muriel left to wait on other tables, Ken engaged him in further conversation.

"Jeff, you know another strange piece of information I heard today has set me more to giving some thought to another possibility. I decided to stop and visit Sage

Murdock and he gave me some information about a strange occurrence at his place the day Nadine lost her life." He could see Jeff wince slightly at that but he prompted Ken to continue with a nod. "Well, when Muriel and I went to the dance, Sage told me that he and his dog had scared some man out of the barn. It startled Sage the way the guy took off but he did say he was dressed like a jogger. Said he didn't know at the time about Nadine as it was still fairly early morning. Seems he's pondered that day over and over in his mind because there was something else that wanted to come to him. Finally he just put it aside figuring it would come. Then one day, while he was puttering in the barn, he could see the man with clarity and saw what appeared to be blood on him. He thought at first that maybe the guy had hurt himself."

Jeff's eyes narrowed and Ken noticed that he shook as he picked up his coffee mug to sip. "Go on," he prompted Ken. His voice had an edge to it.

"Sage felt he had seen the man somewhere before but can't place him. He did tell me that he would know him if he saw him again."

"Well, I just got a big hunch that there is more here than meets the eye. I think one or both of these men are in some way responsible for what happened out there at Will and Nadine's home."

"I'm near convinced on that score, Jeff."

"I wish there was a way that it would happen, that old Sage would see this man and be able to clear up as to his identity. Then he could be picked up for questioning."

"That would be a real slam dunk, wouldn't it? I did caution Sage to keep all of this to himself except to me and Bruster so I am hoping he will come across this man and get in touch with one of us."

"Ya, because if that got around, I've got a feeling that the old man's life might be in jeopardy. It's safe with me, Ken."

"I know it is, Jeff," and Ken reached across the table with his hand extended and Jeff responded with a firm handshake.

"I'll be damned glad to have this thing resolved and those men out of the pen because those guys are living on a tightrope every day."

"Not only that, the stuff that is bound to be done to them is horrible, especially to a kid like Larry Gomez." Ken shook his head sadly.

Jeff just nodded his head in agreement and then stood up. "Well, I will see you around. And if I happen onto anything at all, I will sure let you know. You have a good evening now," and his eyes held a glint of mischief as he turned to look at Muriel waiting on a nearby customer.

"Good enough. Thank you for the information and a good evening to you. Say, listen, I do appreciate your sharing things with me and the best to you. I've got a feeling that life is coming around for you."

Jeff's roughly handsome face transformed with a wide grin. "It rightly has, I reckon," and he strode off after first giving Muriel a quick kiss on the cheek. She reached up and patted his face in response and told him good evening.

"Whew," Ken said as he breathed outwardly, releasing all of the energy he had picked up discussing everything with Jeff. He watched Jeff's tall frame stride to the door and once again saw the figure of a slender woman enfolded in his arms. He bent down and lifted her up to him, searching her lips with his own. "He's fallen hopelessly in love with this woman and she with him." But Ken felt a fear surrounding the woman and he wondered about it. An icy chill coursed throughout him as though he had stepped within the very essence of this woman's being. He stood up and put a large tip on the table, then walked to the cashier counter with his bill. The bright-eyed teen who had waited on him earlier greeted him there.

"Hi. Did you enjoy your supper, sir?"

"Oh, yes miss, I surely did, thank you." Ken smiled warmly at Della Ann.

Muriel walked up to them. "Sweetie, listen, I should be out of here at least by 9, if not before," she said and kissed him quickly.

"Good, then I will see you in a couple hours or less," and he made his way out of the café for his car.

The evening felt like fresh spring should be, Ken felt as he opened his car door. The first hint of summer was in the air because it was warmer than it had been lately. "Maybe Muriel and I can take off for the north coast and get out of the Texas heat on our honeymoon," he thought as he slid into the car and started the engine.

His mind was on that as he drove along, mapping out all of the scenic spots along the coast of California, when he had to slam on the brakes to avoid a coyote which had risked crossing the road.

"Well, old fella, you just about bought it, didn't you?" he spoke aloud.

He pulled up to Muriel's house and parked on the side, not wanting to block her from the garage. He made his way to the front door, hoping the key worked there as well as the laundry door. It opened first try and Ken decided to leave the door ajar while going back out to retrieve his luggage after catching the strong odor of skunk.

"I don't think Muriel would appreciate your visit to her residence, Mr. Skunk," he chuckled as he looked warily about. After getting his luggage, he placed it just inside the door and walked into the living room where Muriel had thoughtfully left on a lamp. He took his luggage to her bedroom, then sat down in the hefty chair that had become his favorite. He opened his briefcase to go over some notes and add more. He had worked for the better part of an hour when his head started to nod and he slipped into sleep.

His dreams took him to a band of primitive peoples who were performing a war dance in celebration of a recent victory. One warrior stood aside with arms clasped, adorned in a war bonnet. As Ken stared at this formalized figure, he realized it was Nathan Tom. He raised his hand with the palm outward and spoke in his ancient tongue— and yet Ken understood his meaning.

"The trail of the rainbow is nearing an end and peace of the hearts will follow. The spirit of the one so wronged will reside in peace."

Ken woke then with a start and grabbed for a pad in his briefcase to write the words he had just heard. He wanted to record them while they were still fresh in his mind.

He heard a car drive into the driveway and knew Muriel was home. Checking his watch, he saw that it was nearing 9:30. He sat the briefcase on the floor beside the chair and she came to him. She slid down onto his lap and kissed him with passion. Then she stood up and smiled, "Be right back after a shower. Say, if you want, you can go use Angie's shower."

Ken nodded and smiled as she whisked away. Then she turned back, "I'll meet you in the bedroom," and she gave a seductive wink.

Ken went to the other shower, noting all of the girl's finery there— bath soaps, lotions, perfumed oils lined up on the shelves and in the corners of the tub. It took him back to sweet Holly with all of her girl paraphernalia crammed into every nook and cranny until finally Gloria beseeched Ken to add an additional bathroom next to Holly's bedroom. That spared the family a morning scramble getting ready for the day ahead.

He finished his shower and walked to the bedroom where Muriel was propped up in bed by a large satin pillow. She got out of bed and stood facing him, slipping out of the clingy black lace gown.

"Muriel, you are so beautiful," he whispered as he walked to her and engulfed her in his arms. Together they lay across the bed. Their lovemaking stretched into the dawn hours until at last they slept holding each other close.

The jangle of the phone awoke them and Muriel sleepily reached for the receiver. "Hello. Yes, he's here, just a minute," and she handed the phone to Ken.

Ken took the phone and looked at Muriel questioningly.

"It's Bruster," she whispered and slid off the bed to head to the bathroom.

"Hello," Ken said, hoping his voice didn't sound too sleep-fogged.

"Hello there, Ken. Hope I didn't disturb you," he spoke in a voice of high excitement. "Say, got the statement back from the handwriting analyst and it seems that Catlin Willard is our boy for sure. He definitely wrote those notes."

"That is great to have that confirmed, Bruster. Now, seems that Jeff Colter also happened across Catlin one day awhile back out at the Webber ranch. He talked to me at the café last night. Catlin took off out toward the pasture when he saw Jeff so Jeff asked Tom Webber who it was. He never let on to Tom about knowing him from years before."

"Well, hot damn, I surely do wish we had caught up to him before he skipped town but I got a strong hunch he will get in touch, like I mentioned before."

"In all likelihood he will, from what he said to me when he called my home. Meantime, he may be picked up before he decides to get in touch with you."

"I just hope that it happens soon, one way or the other."

"It will, Bruster. I just got one of your hunches," he laughed, thinking with some humor what a pun that was.

"Maybe before you take off for Huntsville, you can swing by the office?"

"Sure will. Listen, call here and if Muriel and I aren't here, just leave a message and I will get in touch with you."

'That's fine, Ken. We will keep in touch. Give my regards to Muriel."

"Sure will. We'll see you before we leave Wednesday."

Ken could hear the shower running so he got out of bed and went to Angie's shower. He dressed quickly and made his way to the kitchen. He found an opened can of coffee and made some, then remembered the eggs and honey from Sage that he had forgotten to bring in. He went to his car to get them when a woman drove by in a well-maintained older car. She craned her neck as she saw Ken. He waved flamboyantly and smiled broadly as she passed by. She appeared startled by this and could only respond with an open gaping mouth. She shot down the road faster then and Ken could see that she adjusted the rearview mirror to observe him further. He shook his head and chuckled as he reached for his bags and made his way back to the house.

Muriel was pouring coffee into two mugs and set them on the table. "Well, sweet man, thanks for making the java. What have you got there?"

"When I went to see Sage yesterday, he gave us these eggs and honey."

"Well, that was sweet of that old cowboy. Tell you what, why don't I just whip up some scrambled eggs. Do we need to regain our strength?" Her green eyes held a teasing note.

"Sounds great, honey girl but I think we are in deep muck," he smiled broadly at her.

"Whatever for?" she quipped and frowned.

"Well, I believe your neighbor lady will have it around soon that you are a soiled dove. She saw me at my car fetching these things that I forgot to bring in."

Muriel's eyes took on a startled look at first and then she doubled over in laughter. She finally collapsed into a chair at the table. Her laughter struck Ken as funny and he joined her. After some time, they were wiping their eyes. But just when they thought they had recovered, they would look at each other and start laughing hysterically again. The irony of the event won out.

"Oh, Ken, this is what a small community has done to me," she finally gasped after striving for composure.

"How's that, honey girl?"

"You know, at my age, I should give a fat rip what Mrs. Busybody has to say. It just hit me what a ridiculous colorless matter this is, especially when everyone already knows that you and I are two grown consenting adults."

"Well, pretty lady, I wouldn't go so far as to say it is colorless. I tend to see it as pretty darned spicy and hot. And no doubt, that lady has got to be green with envy," he chuckled.

"Ken Ferries, it is time to fix those scrambled eggs and get some coffee down us before we fall over in a heap. This is a bit much to handle on an empty stomach. After all, we put in a lengthy night." She bit down on her lower lip but her eyes were teasing.

Ken came to her, lifted her from her chair into his husky arms and kissed her soundly. "Is that colorless?" he grinned, looking into her cat-green eyes.

She breathed huskily and placed both hands alongside his head. "Baby, you know what I meant. Who but my nosey neighbor would care what we are doing? But if she gets satisfaction carrying around stuff like the National Enquirer, why should I care?"

"Now, my little country girl, you have arrived at a valid point." He raised her hand to his lips and kissed her fingertips, still holding her eyes with his own. She smiled with the passion of a woman deeply in love, and after another lingering kiss, left his arms to get a bowl to mix the eggs. They ate their breakfast and made plans for the day.

"I know what would be great. Why don't we prepare a picnic lunch and then, later on this afternoon, go out to Will's," Muriel suggested.

"That sounds like a good idea, Muriel. Say, let me go fetch those pictures Angie gave me."

"Oh, yes I almost forgot."

He spread them out on the table for her to view. She put her hand over her mouth and looked at Ken, her eyes wide with shock. Finally, she clasped her arms around herself and visibly shivered.

"Ken, my God, it's Nadine. Oh….oh…" she gasped and continued to shiver as though an arctic wind had blown through. Ken stood up and went to her, bending down over her shivering body and clasping her in his arms. He kissed the top of her soft fragrant hair, still slightly damp from the shower.

"I know, baby, I know," he crooned.

"I want to cry or shout or… I don't know what. I'm, well, I guess I'm stunned."

"Honey, you are in shock. Listen now, just breathe deep and let it go," he whispered in her ear. He stayed in the same position for some moments until he could feel her body start to relax. He picked up her coffee mug and went to fill it after she stopped shaking. She started laughing but rather hysterically and her eyes held a sort of wild glee mingled with tears which now ran freely down her cheeks. She swallowed hard several times and then wiped the tears away with the back of her hand.

"Ken," she said with a raspy voice.

He reached across the table and held her hand tightly in his own.

"Ken," she repeated, "if ever anyone has doubts about life after death and they could see these pictures, they would have to believe it." Her lower lip trembled.

Ken just nodded but held her eyes, communicating the deep love he felt for her. She sat silent now and resumed her study of the snapshots in more depth. When she spoke again, she said, "Ken, I am going to take these with us to show them to Will today."

"Muriel, do you think that he is up to seeing these?" Ken nodded to indicate the photos spread out on the table.

"Probably not, but you know something has got to bring that man back to the living. He can't keep going on like this, honey." She scooped them up and placed them back in the photo envelope with a kind of determined expression on her face. Then she began preparing the picnic lunch, moving quickly around the kitchen gathering items from the cupboards and refrigerator.

"I say, pretty lady, that when you have made up your mind on a thing, it is darn well settled," He chuckled as he bent to kiss the back of her neck as she made sandwiches. He tucked his head down on her shoulder, then she turned to look up at him as she locked her arms around his waist.

"I love you, Ken," and her voice was husky with emotion.

"I love you, lady," he said with shared emotion and kissed her upturned lips with passion, welling ever strong from the depths of his being.

449

"Say now, we'd better stop or else we will never get out of here today," he teased, giving her a playful swat on her curvy bottom. She grinned like an impish little girl and swatted him back, then gave him a small shove.

"Yes, sir, you are right. Now, please, my loving man, go out to the laundry room and fetch the picnic basket from the cupboard above the washer and dryer."

"Yes, ma'am." He gave her a boyish grin and saluted her smartly, then made his way to the laundry room.

They eventually made their way to the car, loading the picnic basket in the back. Muriel had donned a wide-brimmed straw hat with yellow daisies around the brim and clad herself in a pair of jeans that made clear the curvy body housed in them. She wore a cheerful yellow blouse with an appliquéd scatter of honeybees on the pocket. Ken noticed the same bees on the hip pockets of her jeans.

"Honey bee, you are sweet enough to eat," Ken grinned as he appraised her and took the wine bottle she handed him.

"Why, thank you, prince charming," she winked before putting on a pair of shaded glasses. "Darn near forgot that wine but I did put a couple wine glasses in the picnic basket."

"Good, then we are all set." He opened the car door for her and off they headed for Rosewood.

"Do you want to go to the area you drove through yesterday, Ken? If we go a bit farther, there is a lake. That's one of the places Angie and I used to go a lot with Nadine and her children. It's cool there under the trees, and so peaceful."

"It sounds great," Ken agreed. When they got to Rosewood, he made his way through and found the country road he had traveled the day before.

They passed by the ranch lands and Muriel pointed out a couple of catfish ponds she knew to be stocked with some of the biggest catfish in the county. "Some day we will bring fishing poles with us. Do you like to fish, Ken? By the way, I can fry up the best fish dinner you could ever dream of eating." She poked him in the ribs and grinned invitingly.

"I don't doubt that for a minute, pretty lady. Cooking is just one more of your many highly esteemed talents," he said and held her eyes with a flirty look. She nestled in closer to him and put her head on his shoulder, breathing deeply.

"It is so perfect, Ken, everywhere you look. The flowers seem to have a special radiance of color and I haven't noticed for a long time how many different brightly colored birds there are around."

"Honey girl, it is because you haven't had much free time for just you. It is so easy to get oneself in a rut and not take time to smell the flowers, to quote that old cliché. And not only that, sweet lady, you may be taking a different perspective since you have fallen in love," and he pulled her closer to him.

"I know," she murmured softly, "isn't it wonderful?" For an answer, he brought her hand to his lips and kissed it.

They climbed up some rolling hills past the area Ken had visited the day before. At last, from a higher rise, a lake came into view. They could see a wide area from this vantage point. It wasn't a large lake but pristine with the sun shining down on the water and a soft breeze creating little ripples on the surface. In one area, some cattails stood at attention along the shoreline. Ken noticed some picnic tables with the portable bathrooms nearby.

They selected a place with some trees giving ample shade and carried the picnic basket and wine to the table. Muriel produced a red-checked tablecloth and began to cover the table.

"Oh, oh, hon," Ken said, brushing a large beetle off the tabletop. "I don't think we need him joining us for lunch," Ken chuckled.

"Maybe I better put this picnic basket back in the car for now," Muriel suggested, "because we just finished breakfast a little while ago. Besides, I think it would be fun to walk a ways first."

"Good idea, lady. We will hold the tablecloth down with the wine bottle. I don't believe any little four-legged critters will want to drink while we're gone but I wouldn't bet on the lunch. They would chew through the wicker basket if they had to!"

"My assumption exactly," Muriel grinned. She started to take the basket to the car but Ken took it from her and put it in the trunk.

"Let's go exploring," he said and they set off to walk around an area of the lake. They listened to the various birdcalls and identified many varieties. Numerous black and orange winged blackbirds flitted around the marshy shoreline. Some of them hung suspended off the cattails, waving in the breeze. Muriel suddenly began to laugh as she viewed this scene.

Ken looked at her quizzically and her laughter heightened. She finally choked out, "I'm sorry, Ken. I was just remembering a time Bill and I came here on a picnic. I asked him if he could get some of those cattails for me so I could use them to make a wreath or floral arrangement. Well, bless that dear man, out he strides and gets stuck ankle-deep in mud and water. He fell on his kiester and was flopping around like a hog in mud. I ran out to help him and then we were both wallowing in the mudhole." She was giggling hard and Ken started to laugh picturing the two of them thrashing around.

"Well, I hope you are not still into the floral and wreath-making activities because there's no way I'm going to retrieve cattails for you after hearing that story." He feigned a stern look and then chuckled when she gave him a playful shove toward the edge of the lake. He looped his arm around her waist and they walked on, breathing in the smells of wet vegetation made more pungent by the warm spring day.

"Muriel," he said, stopping her after walking quietly for a time. He turned her chin up and gazed into her green eyes.

"What is it, honey?"

"Well, you recall that I mentioned we have a lot to discuss." She nodded and waited for him to go on. "How would you feel about living in Waco? I mean, would it bother you to move there and live in the same home that Gloria and I lived in? You don't have to give me an answer right now, and if you would rather not, please know that I will understand. I don't want you ever to say something just because you feel it is what I want." He explored her face carefully looking for a sign.

"Ken," she said as she took a step back from him, "guess what? I had already decided that I would be fine with that in the event that you should ask. I thought you probably would. Listen, my love, why not? I'm all grown up and I know it is practical for you. It suits me fine. I am not all that hung up and insecure about the fact that it was yours and Gloria's home. Your time with Gloria was ever sweet and wonderful, just as mine was with Bill, but they are both gone. I just know they would want us to move on and be happy. What difference does it make where we make our home together?"

"Oh, baby," he moaned and reached for her, crushing her to his broad chest. The emotion that welled up made it hard for him to speak. After clearing his throat, he looked down at this woman he loved. She was smiling up at him with such a touching look. Her shining hair had a deep pink aura surrounding it which darkened to indigo at the edges. Her heart, he knew, was pouring out love to him as his was to her. The air seemed charged with a special electrical energy. Their kiss was filled with that same wild yet gentle energy.

She had pushed her wide-brimmed hat down onto her back, held fast by a silky yellow cord at her throat. The sun created soft highlights of color in her hair.

"Oh, Muriel, I am so in love with you. I just didn't think I could ever possibly be in love once more, at least not like this," he whispered passionately.

"I know, I know, me too," and her voice was throaty and deep.

Finally they turned to make their way back to the table. Ken got the picnic basket and Muriel opened it to pull out the wine glasses. She handed Ken the bottle opener and he opened the wine for them. She poured their glasses half full and they made a toast, proclaiming their love forever.

After that, they set out the picnic plates, chicken salad sandwiches, more wine, some fruit and homemade cookies. They were surprised at their hunger. Ken told Muriel it must be the country air.

The day stretched into mid-afternoon and still they sat and talked, making plans for their future.

"What would you think of taking off right after our wedding for the coast of California or maybe Oregon for an extended honeymoon? Or maybe the East coast?"

"Honey, I do believe we will have an extended honeymoon the rest of our lives together." Her smile was sweet and she put her hand on the back of her neck and rubbed it, the gesture Ken so cherished. She seemed caught up in thought and then finally spoke. "I would love to go to the West coast. I have always wanted to and never got to. They say it would be so much cooler than the hot Texas summer, wouldn't it?"

Ken nodded his agreement and reached across the table to cup her hand. She was perspiring slightly across her smooth forehead and it gave her even more radiance and such a youthful look. She was truly beautiful and would grow more so with age. Ken raised his hand in mid-sentence and turned his head to listen while Muriel frowned in question.

"Do you hear that?" he prompted.

"Yes, it sounds like a large gathering of waterfowl has arrived to feed on the lake," she answered.

He nodded and smiled at her lovingly. "Those are sounds I love to hear, another sound of the season. When you listen closely, it is like nature's acoustics combine to make one memorable sonata after another."

"You, my sweet man, are a romantic. Is it any wonder I fell so hopelessly in love with you?" Her voice was extra husky with emotion.

"Come with me, fair lady. Let's go watch them." He took her hand and they walked to the lake's edge. There, indeed, were a multitude of waterfowl noisily feeding on the insects and plants of the lake. A rumble sounded off in the distance and they noticed a darkening of clouds in the east.

"I think we had better retrieve our picnic basket and head out, pretty lady, because it appears we are about to get a late spring dowsing."

"The birds out there will love it, but they probably knew it was coming before we did. It is rather incredulous the way animals seem to know things before people do, isn't it?" she pondered thoughtfully.

"I suppose it is, in part, because we have lost the ability to perceive as readily due to our own inner clamoring."

The next rumble of thunder seemed closer and Ken took Muriel's hand pulling her swiftly toward the picnic area. Ahead of them, a cottontail made haste to a refuge in a cluster of overgrowth at the side of the trail.

"Aren't those little fellas the cutest? They look like children's plush toys," Muriel said.

"Sure do," Ken replied.

They scooped up the picnic basket just as the first light spatters of rain fell. The air was already fresh with that clean smell rain always brings. Ken reached for Muriel who was holding her hat on with one hand. He kissed her with intensity similar to the brewing rainstorm.

"Thank you, pretty lady, for a perfect day," he whispered as he looked down at her after the passion-filled kiss. Little spatters of rain fell on her upturned face and she closed her eyes, breathing in deeply.

"Ah, yes my darling, thank you too for a perfect day and for just being you," she said as she expelled her breath.

After a brief look around to make certain that they had not left anything, they joined hands and scampered to the car. Ken climbed in after he had seated Muriel and placed the picnic basket on the floor in back. He had just gotten in when loud thunder boomed overhead followed by a sheet of lightning over the lake.

"Looks like we made it just in the nick of time," Muriel laughed. "Say, that last kiss out there could have been the hottest one we ever had," she giggled.

Ken chuckled at her salty remark and started the car. They made their way to the main road, noticing that the wind had picked up and the grasses waved topsy turvy at the road's edges.

"We are stopping in to see Will, aren't we, Muriel?" Ken questioned.

She looked at her watch and then gave a deciding nod. "Yes, it is only a few minutes after 4. It's early enough that we won't interrupt supper. They don't eat as a rule until late. You know how ranchers are."

"Sure do, having grown up on a ranch. The folks always tried to make the Sunday meal early with us all together and whoever happened to be there. It was a well-known fact that my Mother had a superior talent with chuck roast so I'm sure it was no accident that we usually had one or two extra at the table. Plus, there were my Dad's colorful stories," Ken reminisced.

"I am looking forward to meeting your parents, Ken, and tomorrow would be a great time for you to meet mine. I have told them about you and Mom asked me why I hadn't brought you over. She is spunky, my sweet Mom. I told her they had met you before I did. She didn't remember until Dad reminded her of 'that reporter fellow inquiring after the Rogers family'. Then she had a flash of recall," Muriel chuckled.

"Daddy said you seemed like a right nice fellow and Mom just sniffed and said, 'Nice enough, I guess, but we'll see.'" Muriel giggled at that.

Ken laughed and thought that it was probably why Muriel was a bit salty and outspoken herself. He determined that she had probably inherited more of her Mother's attributes than her Dad's, that earthy quality he was drawn to.

As they moved along, the thunder shower seemed to be abating. The country road was not too muddied, for which Ken was grateful.

"Oh, honey girl, I suspect that I will win your Mother over in short order," he suggested.

"Somehow I don't for a minute doubt that," she affirmed and snuggled closer.

They drove the rest of the way in silence, just enjoying the comfort of being together. Then they reached the turn-off to the Rogers ranch. The sky was a blaze of blue now and it seemed to take on an intensity of color as they came closer to the Rogers home.

"This is impressive. What a beautiful place," and then he almost wished he hadn't said that because no doubt it seemed tainted to Muriel since her best friend died here.

"Yes, it is," Muriel mused. "It is always going to be a part of Nadine regardless. There are some beautiful memories here."

Ken parked the car in the ample driveway and turned to Muriel. He reached for her hand and drew it to his lips for a kiss while his eyes sought hers.

"It will be all right, darling. I am right here for you," he assured her.

"I know, Ken. Thank you. I will be all right, I promise."

Chapter_____15

He got out and helped Muriel out. She held his hand all the way to the massive Santa Fe style front doors. Ken could even now feel that this home held the expression of a couple's warmth and love. Muriel rang the bell and they were greeted by a smiling Ty who pulled her into his arms.

"Auntie Muriel, Ken, come on in. Reckon this will sure be a bonus plus for Dad, finally getting out of the hospital and then seeing you both. He is in his bedroom and we've been trying to figure out how to get him fixed up to sleep there with that cast clear up his leg," Ty said, shaking his blond head and chuckling.

"Well, maybe Ken and I can help you with that, Ty, and anything else you need help with."

"No, no, I appreciate it but I believe we've got it figured out. He isn't going to be comfortable for awhile, no matter what we do, at least until he can be relieved of that cast."

"Tyler, you're certain now we can't help with something," Muriel pressed.

"Nope, got it all covered. Mrs. Muñoz has cooked up a storm and all we gotta do is pop things in the oven to heat them up. Then she's over here often too and so is Carmen sometimes. So, between them and Will Earl and myself, we've got it all down to a gnat's eyebrows." His good-looking face spread into a kind-hearted smile. "Well now, Dad's just sitting in his room watching TV so why don't you just come with me to see him. He's gonna be right pleased you are here."

Ken couldn't help but shudder when they walked past the sprawling fireplace in the large living room, which he knew the Rogers family called the Texas room. The home was so pleasant and tastefully decorated that it was obvious only an artist like Nadine would have possessed the cleverness to accentuate and balance a home like this. A large wing-backed chair sat a few feet from the fireplace and, though it was facing in a different direction, Ken knew it was the chair Nadine had often sat in doing her crafts. She liked to face the large window and watch outside. The scene was so prominent in Ken's mind, it seemed that it was happening this very moment, a tiny beautiful woman with golden hair concentrating on a huge paper flower. Her thoughts had lingered here at that time and Ken could hear them as a whisper now— "I bet Phyl and Bree will be here soon but running late, as always. Bless that girl of mine. I love her so."

Ken could feel his heart pound and almost hear it as well. He noticed the carpet under his feet was thick and luxurious in a shade of icy pale blue, just as he had seen in one of his visions. Muriel looked up at him now imploringly, concern clearly etched on her face. He mouthed, "It's okay," to her and managed a reassuring smile.

They made their way to a wide hallway leaving the expansive Texas room and Ken could feel his throat constrict more. He found it was hard to breathe and felt an icy chill of terror invading his whole being. "God, man, get ahold of yourself," he silently chastened. But still he could not shake the wringing terror and felt an overpowering urge to run.

He noticed a door to his left which they passed by and then Tyler stopped at the next door. He knocked on that one and called out, "Dad, you've got company. May we come in?"

"Sure, come on in," Will answered.

He was sitting in a reclining chair a few feet from a large four-poster bed. Above the bed was a beautiful large painting of a man and a woman, of Will and his wife Nadine. Ken fought to maintain his control with every ounce he could muster. He knew he was well on the verge of total anguish.

Then he saw the wide French doors that led from the right side of the room out onto a sprawling patio. This was why Nadine's body was found in the hallway leading to the bedroom. She had been trying to reach her bedroom and escape to the patio. Whoever had killed her had almost been caught by those three men. Ken knew with a sick certainty that the killer had hidden in that enclosure just off the hallway, the one they had just now passed by.

"Well, look who's here, by golly," Will smiled, and again Ken was struck by his handsome features. He was even more so now that Ken was seeing him clearly for the first time. At Windom Hall, he had been so intoxicated and sick.

"You remember Ken, don't you Will?"

"Howdy, Ken," Will said holding out his hand. "Yes, I do but I was in sorry shape that night," and his face colored slightly.

"Oh now, Will, there are times when we have all been that way." Ken worked at putting in a note of joviality for Will's benefit as well as his own.

"Ty, pull up a couple of those chairs over there for Muriel and Ken, would you, son?" He indicated another area of the vast bedroom. Ken went to help Ty, glad to have the diversion while still trying to quiet himself. Pictures of every personal association which had taken place in this room were flashing through his mind, of

Nadine and Will and their children. Three small children scampered onto the same four poster bed, pouncing on top of their mother and father, giggling and shrieking with merriment.

"Look out, mother, we've been invaded," a tousled young father was saying as he laughed. He caught one child then another to his broad chest. Ken could see a golden-haired woman looking not much bigger than the oldest boy almost concealed by the tangle of squirming children. A black puppy was at the side of the bed, whining to join in the melee.

Scenes of lovemaking also came clearly to Ken and then scenes of sorrow came in flashes and torrents like crashing waves. Every ghost from a distant past and present rolled out in front of him, showing a family sharing every emotion of life playing out like a melodrama. It was overwhelming and incredulous to him, yet from all that came the realization that he was witnessing reality from another realm.

"Dad, why don't I go get us some refreshments," Ty suggested.

"Good idea, son," Will agreed as Ty departed.

"Will, I have some recent pictures I want to show you," Muriel said as she opened her purse to pull out the photo envelope. "Now listen, Will, this may shock you but I feel that you need to see these," Muriel said as she opened the envelope.

Will looked at her with questioning eyes. "All right, Muriel, but don't see why they would shock me," he drawled.

She reached for his hand and held his eyes with her own as she handed him the photos. Ken and Muriel watched as he looked at the first photo. Will's jaw dropped and his eyes widened. His voice was strangled when he did speak. "My God,

Muriel, how can this be? This can't be," he gasped. He looked at still another and then the cry that emitted from him was like that of a wounded animal. His head went back, he clutched at his chest, and tears came along with wracking sobs.

As Muriel rose in a crouched position from her chair, she reached for him, putting her arms around his chest. She began to rock him to her as though comforting a small child. Ken touched Muriel on her arm to get her attention.

"Honey, listen, I'm just going to step out while you and Will talk. You both need this time alone." Muriel nodded her head, understanding etched in her eyes.

When he left the room, he paused in front of the door. Ty came into the hallway with a tray containing a plate of cookies and a carafe of coffee with mugs.

"Ken, hi, is there something wrong? I thought I heard Dad cry out."

'Yeah, Ty, there is but it's going to be all right, son. Muriel and your father are fine but they need some privacy right now. I will take this tray in to them and then be right back. You can show me around then, okay?"

"Sure, you bet. I understand and yeah, I'll show you around."

Ken knocked on the door and took in the tray. Will was wiping away tears and his body was still shaking. Muriel looked up and her lips were quivering while her eyes held unshed tears.

"Ty is going to show me around while you and Will talk. You all just take the time you need, there's no hurry." He placed the tray on the night table and then put a comforting hand on Will's shoulder. He bent to kiss Muriel's cheek and gave her hand a reassuring pat. Then he went back to the hall where Ty was waiting.

"Say, Ty, what's this door? Does it lead to another bedroom?" He tried to sound off-handed about it.

'No, it's a large storage area. Dad keeps old records and files in there. Then there's a portion where we store winter clothes or summer clothes, depending on what we need. Mom used to call it her Fibber McGee and Molly closet." He opened the door to reveal a sizable area with shelves and a length of file cabinets. At the end of the room were paneled doors of Philipine mahogany which extended across the whole wall. Ken knew that had to be a closet.

"Do you mind if I step inside, Ty? By golly, this gives me an idea for a system to put in at my home."

"Go ahead, Ken, and look it over. Be my guest."

Ken could feel the panic and dreaded apprehension clutching him as he stepped inside the room. He needed every last drop of sheer willpower to remain calm while he looked around. He kept admiring the order of the room to Ty. He was praying that Ty didn't notice anything amiss in his demeanor.

His eyes fell on a smudge of brownish color on the carpet just inside the doorway that would be easily overlooked if one didn't observe with close scrutiny. On closer inspection, Ken saw yet another slight spatter on the carpet. He knew it was blood and felt an icy chill shake him from head to foot. He turned his face away so Tyler couldn't see him and he closed his eyes tightly.

Clear vision came to him, of a man dressed in white jogging clothes and white tennis shoes with a sweatband around his head. His clothes were covered with red spatters. He held a long-handled fireplace poker as though ready to strike anyone who opened the door. The man was of medium build but well-muscled. He appeared to be listening. Something about the man looked alarmingly familiar but Ken's mind couldn't zero in on it. A voice spoke to him within, "Soon the time will come. It is not yet the time."

"Is everything all right, Ken?" Ty questioned, breaking through the labyrinth of visions.

"Yes, yes, fine, Tyler. I was just trying to mentally calculate how many square feet are in this room."

"Let me fetch a tape measure and we'll find out."

"All right, Ty, that would be good of you." Ken was glad for the short time Ty would be gone as it would allow him to better view the brown spatters. The moment Tyler departed, he knelt down. He assured himself it had to be dried blood. The man had hoped to avoid stepping in the blood of Nadine's body but reason told him that it had been overlooked by the police. After the quick arrest of the three men, Ken knew that no further investigating had been done. The case had been taken out of Bruster's hands and that in itself was sad. Bruster had clearly expressed that he had doubts about the guilt of the three men but had not been given free rein to explore the case.

"Here is the tape measure. I'll help you measure it off. I brought paper and pencil too."

"Great. You hold down the tape for me, Ty, and I will just take it down this way first." They measured it off and then walked quickly down the hallway with

Tyler pointing out his bedroom and Will Earl's. The closed room at the very end had been his sister's room until she got married.

"Our Mother made it into her studio then because it is all so open with perfect light. She told us it was just right for an artist studio. She did some fine work in there." And he swallowed hard.

"You don't need to show me in there, it's fine, son."

"No, I'm okay with it. Somehow I feel that my Mother would have wanted you to see it. I don't know why but something just tells me she would.'

He opened the door and stood aside for Ken to enter. The first thing he saw was a full-length window with an artist easel set up by it. What stood out were the numerous paintings that hung around the room, mostly scenes of Texas but some of Nadine and Will and the children too. One showed Will astride a beautiful proud black horse. Another had scenes of cowhands rounding up cattle.

"She was in her element here. When things get to me big time, I come in here. At first, I just couldn't and I had to get away from here, you know?" He hesitated a moment. "But then I sometimes felt I could hear her calling to me and telling me I needed to come back home. It would happen when I was sleeping or when I was awake. Never knew when it might be that I was going to hear her." He met Ken's level gaze. "Do you reckon that was just all in my head, Ken?"

"No, son, I don't believe you simply imagined it. A lot of people might dismiss it as being one's imagination but I don't buy that. I have experienced enough things of this nature myself so I am open to the possibility of your mother coming to you. Those we love never do really leave us after they pass away."

The young man's face expressed relief. Ken turned to look at a painting of a small child, walking closer to inspect it.

"That's my niece, Bree. Cute little monkey, isn't she?"

"Yes, she sure is. Now your sis has another little girl, doesn't she?"

"Yeah, and she is named after Mom," he smiled softly.

The sweet fragrance of roses suddenly permeated the air and Ken knew that Tyler's mother was there with them. He looked at Ty to see if his expression would indicate that he too had caught the scent. Tyler's eyes widened and he looked at Ken with surprise on his face.

"Ken, do you smell the fragrance of roses? That was the perfume my mother always wore."

Ken just nodded, feeling greatly overcome at the look of pure joy on this handsome youth's face. "Oh, Mom," Ty whispered, his voice heavy with emotion. "I know you are here." Then he breathed deeply, savoring the heady scent.

They stood motionless and silent for at least two minutes until finally the perfume scent began to fade away. Tyler was the first to break the silence and Ken noticed that his eyes were bright with tears.

"Ken, let's go outside now, okay?" His voice was husky with emotion.

"Sure, Ty, you lead the way." Ken agreed with a note of solemnity.

They made their way out to a cheerful kitchen and on out through a screen door to yet another patio area. Several planter boxes bordered the patio with an array of cheery flowers. Beyond the patio, Ken could see a section of pasture land with a border of trees on the east side. He knew it was the area in his vision where the man ran toward his green Jeep partially concealed in the trees. They moved in the direction of the large red barn several yards west of the house. Ty paused when he heard the phone ring shrilly in the house.

"You go ahead to the barn and I'll meet you out there. I better get the phone so Dad won't have to."

Ken nodded as Ty ran back to the house. He reached the barn and noted the fine stallion standing at erect attention in the holding corral. He made his way to the wide open doors of the building. The horse appeared to be the one in Nadine's painting of Will. "Beautiful animal," Ken expressed aloud, noting that he was several hands high. He made his way on into the barn and shook his head at the perfection of the well-tended surroundings. This barn had every convenience, making it a rancher's dream. The smells of hay and horses assailed him. He picked up on the fresh mash smell that came from a mixture of ground feed for livestock. All this brought back his days as a youth growing up on a ranch.

The sound of a girl's teasing giggles made him pause to figure out where it came from. He reasoned that it was here inside this building. He moved in the direction of the sound and heard the girls laughing now. He also heard a man's voice as he quietly moved forward.

"Damn it, Carmen, what are you trying to pull now? Jeez cripes, woman, get something on before somebody shows up. What do you think it's gonna look like?"

"I don't really care what anyone thinks, but Will Earl, I know you are not made out of iron. Just take a good look at these goodies, my sweet hombre. This is only the half of it. Think what you can do with this," she taunted. Her voice held a husky note. "You want me too. I can see it. You are shaking, Will Earl."

Ken stood at a distance but, due to his height, he could easily see over into the horse stall where the big gray horse stood. He was mildly shocked at the sight of Carmen Muñoz at the side of the big gray, her ample breasts exposed. Ken noted that they were perfection, creamy white with tiny pink nipples. Her breasts heaved with unrestrained passion and her sultry full lips were parted as she reached out to pull Will Earl's hand to one breast.

Will Earl suddenly came into view and Ken heard him gasp and moan as Carmen pulled him toward her. She clutched his hair, brought his mouth down to her parted lips, and twisted her ripe young body toward him. Ken stepped up onto a bale of hay and could clearly see now that Carmen was totally naked. He watched her pull Will Earl's hand down between her legs and saw her sway and rotate her rounded little bottom. Will Earl pulled his hand away but he was gasping loudly.

"Please, Will Earl, take me now. I want it and so do you."

Ken felt his face grow hot at the scene before him. A mixture of emotions stirred within him, giving way to his own arousal. Yet he felt a kind of sad sickness coursing through him thinking of Angie.

"No, Jesus, no," Will Earl shouted in a strangled harsh voice. He pushed the girl away from him and hastily exited the stall.

Carmen called after him, "You are a coward, Will Earl Rogers, but we will finish this, hombre. You'll see." Her laughter was taunting. She slowly pulled up her jeans over slender shapely legs. He heard her low chuckle, then she reached for a plaid cotton shirt which she tied in a knot beneath her breasts. No bra or panties, Ken noted.

"Well, this old fella better be moving on before Ty gets in here and sees one Miss Carmen Muñoz in the all together." He quietly stepped away from his place and began making his way out of the barn where he met Ty.

"Oh, Ken, sorry. I got tied up on the phone. Angie called and we got to talking awhile. I just met Will Earl who came roaring out of the barn, darn near knocking me down. But I got him stopped long enough to tell him Angie was on the phone. What's got his pants on fire?"

Ken was hoping that he displayed innocence when he shrugged his shoulders and shook his head. He couldn't quite meet the young man's gaze.

"Let's just mosey on out to take a look at those beef over there, Ty. I saw the barn and that is one mighty fine barn. Can't say as I've ever seen one better." He felt the back of his neck redden. They made their way to the pasture where several head of fine cattle grazed.

"I'd guess there's a hundred and fifty right here but that's just a few of what's out in the pastures north of here. Dad's got these here to go to market in a couple days."

Ken turned when he heard Muriel calling him. "Say, you two, don't get too far away. We have some lemonade and cookies waiting. Will wants the boys to join us in his room too."

"Sounds good to me. I'm feeling thirsty, aren't you, Ty?"

"Good plan. Now, if Bro can tear himself away from the phone, we will join you all in Dad's room. But give us about 5 minutes because I know Will Earl and Ang when they get on the phone." He chuckled.

They reached Muriel and Ty made his way to the side entrance and the kitchen while Ken and Muriel made their way through the main entrance.

"Ken, Will has decided that he would like the boys to see those snapshots while we are here. He feels he needs our moral support."

"Well, he certainly has that, honey girl. Lead the way." Ken tucked her around the waist, lending her a measure of support. She looked up at him and kissed his neck. He brought her smooth hand to his lips and kissed it as they made their way to Will's room.

"Love you, baby, so much," she whispered huskily before she knocked on Will's door.

Will drawled, "It's open, you all. Come on in."

"Howdy, Ken. I haven't meant to keep this lovely lady from you so long," and his voice deepened more as he smiled at them with a gentle sad look. Ken also noted a sort of peace there that he hadn't seen before.

"No problem, Will. I'm glad that you and Muriel have the kind of special friendship where you can discuss anything. Besides, Tyler was gracious enough to show me around your place. I truly enjoyed that. You do have a wonderful ranch and quite a picturesque setting too. Quite peaceful here."

"Thank you, Ken. Yes, we've known some happy times here. Now that Muriel's talked to me and I've seen those snapshots of my beautiful wife reaching out to us, maybe we can know a measure of peace here again."

"You will," Ken assured him.

"Ken, Muriel tells me that you have a gift and I believe it. Frankly, if I hadn't seen these photos, I may not have been as receptive to the information. However, that is a problem with so many of us because, if we can't see it or touch it, most of us tend to think it isn't real."

Ken's broad face spread into an easy smile and he merely nodded his response to Will's observation. There came a soft knock on the bedroom door.

Will called out, "Come on in, boys."

Ty entered first followed by Will Earl. They both had questioning looks, glancing first toward their father, then toward Muriel and Ken.

"You boys help yourself to some lemonade and some of those fresh lemon cookies Mrs. Muñoz made this morning."

At the name Muñoz, Will Earl's face slightly colored. They settled back in their chairs and enjoyed their refreshments. Will watched them closely before he spoke. The boys were looking intently at their father.

"Listen, boys, first I want to begin with an apology to you both. When I call your sister and have her stop by this evening, I want to do the same with her. You all know I wasn't here for any of you for some time now but that's all going to change now. Reckon I have been plum loco and, well, dammit, pretty selfish."

Both young men started to protest but Will raised his hand and cocked his head to one side. He continued. "Nope, now you both hear me out. If it wasn't for your Auntie Muriel here and Ken, God only knows where we all might have ended up. I know I was making additional sorrows on you all and myself too." His voice caught but he held strong. "Now, I don't reckon I would have never believed this but it helps to see it with my own eyes. A fella gets mighty hard-headed sometimes, you know, gets in his own way too often." His handsome face took on a serious sorrowful expression for just a moment.

He reached over to the serving table beside him, picked up the snapshots and handed them to Tyler. Will Earl leaned over to see the photos his brother held. They both gasped at the same time as they stared down at the first picture. Ty quickly shuffled through the rest of them, his jaw hanging slack. Will Earl's dark tan had gone ashen. Both young men appeared to be in total shock and they slumped back in their chairs. They met their father's gaze wide-eyed. Finally Will Earl seemed to find his voice but it came out in a sputter and he had to swallow several times.

"Why, why, what does this mean? Oh, is this some kind of mean joke? I don't get it. Why, it looks like Mom but, God almighty, how can that be?"

Tyler's mouth was wide open and tears were clearly visible on his face. A kind of fear showed in his eyes and his nose began to drip. Will reached for his own handkerchief in his hip pocket and handed it to his son.

"Yes, it is your Mother in these pictures. She wants us to know she isn't far away. She knows that we need to heal because we were all drifting apart and that's the last thing she would want. So God let her come to us in a manner that would speak louder than words."

"Then I didn't imagine it when Ken and I were in Mom's studio earlier. I could smell the rose perfume she always wore and I have felt her presence before too," Ty's voice came out in a ragged whisper.

"No son, I am certain you didn't imagine it," Will assured the young man who now looked even more like his mother in the painting above the bed.

Will Earl's shoulders were heaving and his body shook but no sound came from him. His head was hanging to his chest when a sudden deep moan sounded that seemed to originate in the depths of his soul. "Oh, Mama, why did we have to lose you. It's so hard to bear." His young voice rose to an anguished pitch followed by heavy racking sobs.

Tyler reached for his brother and held him close while Will struggled and shifted to reach his sons. Ken went behind his chair and pushed it closer to the boys. When he looked at Muriel, her face was awash with tears, as was his own.

"Will, you and these boys need this time alone now, so Muriel and I are going to leave. But if you need anything, anything at all, you just call please. We are going to leave for a few days so Muriel can meet my children but we will stay in touch."

Muriel rose to her feet and put her arms around Will's chest from behind. He clasped her arms and turned his head to kiss her cheek. She touched her cheek to his.

"Thank you. You are the best friends a man could ever have. God love you both." He reached for Ken's hand and held it firmly for several seconds before releasing it. Muriel then went to the two younger men and knelt at their feet to kiss each one of them as if she were their mother. She held them both together in her arms for at least a minute before she arose. She and Ken soundlessly left the bedroom and made their way to the front entrance to depart.

Ken heard Muriel sigh when they got outdoors and then she gasped for air on the note of a sob. He pulled her close and just held her as though she were a child needing comfort.

"Oh, Ken, it is going to get a lot better for this family now, isn't it?" she whispered.

"Yes, it will, with some tough moments for awhile but better day by day."

After he helped Muriel into the car and got in himself, he followed the circle of the ample driveway toward the main road. He noted that the day was still bright but it was getting toward the shadow of evening.

"Muriel, let's go to Dolly's and have some supper. Is that all right with you?"

"Yes, it is. I would like that, to unwind over a light meal would be so good. And with the man I love, who is my fortress of strength." She sighed deeply once more and moved closer to him to lay her head on his shoulder. His heart felt light with the outpouring of love he had for this beautiful sensuous woman.

"Love you, pretty lady," and he brought her hand to his lips and kissed it on top, then on her palm. She snuggled even closer and her breathing deepened. They had not driven a mile when he noticed that she was asleep.

He saw the unusually large red-tailed hawk sitting on a fence post up ahead. Just as he was slowing down to get a better look, the hawk suddenly lifted with an enormous spread of wings and alighted on the hood of the car. He came to a full stop and Muriel stirred, then spoke.

"Is everything all right, Ken?" she said and sat up straight.

The hawk did not move for several seconds but peered intently at them before he swept like a prehistoric creature into the sky.

"My God, Ken, can you believe what we just saw?" Her eyes were like great green orbs as she turned to look at him.

"Yes, I saw it. I have before too and it seems to come when something has been confirmed or is about to be," Ken spoke softly as though in a trance.

"Are you all right, Ken?" Her voice held a note of alarm.

"Yes, yes I am, honey. I'm fine," and he drove on slowly. He hadn't told Muriel that a scene had played out before him while the hawk watched them. He had seen a man who looked like a bird of prey and Ken knew him to be a substance of evil. When that creature had focused on him, all he could see were cold hate-filled eyes of a strange shade of gray. He knew them to be the eyes of someone he knew but who? And why did it elude him again?

"Ken, hon, are you sure you are all right?" Muriel implored again.

"You bet I am." To reassure her, he squeezed her hand lightly and looked down at her with a smile. The strange trance continued to lift.

"What in the world would make a red-tailed hawk become the size of an eagle, Ken? Well, darn near as large anyway."

"Maybe he isn't really a hawk, Muriel, but gives the illusion of being one. You know there are some strange things that are not readily explained."

"Yes, that is certainly true. After being exposed to them since meeting a powerful psychic, I can accept just about anything now, " she smiled, relaxing more.

They made their way to Dolly's. He noted that they walked in a little after 6 pm.

"Hi, you all," Della greeted them, her teen face all smiles.

"Guess what, Muriel. Dolly says that she thinks I can handle working out on the floor now so I will be your server this evening."

Muriel gave her a warm hug and smile. "Why, of course you're ready, Della honey. You will do just fine."

The girl picked up two menus from the counter and led them to a booth, still smiling proudly. She handed them the menus and made certain that she mentioned the specials posted on the mirror behind the counter. Then she returned with a pitcher of ice water and two mugs of coffee. She took their orders and retreated once again.

"She is going to be a good waitress but I hope she goes on to college in the fall. I hate to see kids shorten their education because it is so vital to have more than a high school diploma these days," Muriel observed while she watched Della walk away.

"Yes, that is the truth, at least technical school if not college. It's not like it used to be when you could get a good job just out of high school."

When Della returned with two bowls of soup and two small loaves of bread, Muriel engaged her in light conversation.

"What are your plans after you graduate, Della?"

The girl shrugged and smiled. "Well, I plan on working here and saving all the money I can, then I'm going to college in Tyler. You know, Mom has it pretty hard with two kids still at home but I am willing to work to get through school."

"Atta girl," Muriel said as her face brightened with relief.

Della smiled back, pleased with the approval. She filled their coffee mugs, then turned away when another customer walked in.

Muriel still looked pleased. "You know, Ken, Della's Mom had to raise her 3 kiddies alone because their father took off shortly after the youngest one was born. But she has done a darned good job, even holding down two jobs, and folks around here have helped some. God bless her."

"I can see just by meeting Della. She is a fine young lady. You might mention that, in case she isn't aware of it, grants may be available to her."

"I will call her Mom and talk to them about it." Muriel smiled then as she saw who had just walked into the café.

"Oh boy, Ken, look who just walked in— Mr. High and Mighty himself." Ken followed her gaze to see Pace Allard turn his pearly whites onto Della. She indicated a table at the window just right for two people.

"Will someone be joining you, Mr. Allard? Would you prefer a booth?" She left the question hanging, waiting for his response.

"Yes, someone will be coming soon," and he checked his watch, then turned a dazzling smile once again on Della. "I believe the table will be just fine."

"Very good then, sir. I will be your server this evening," and she gave him a composed smile. Ken thought that this young woman was going to be able to handle anything in her life and it made him smile with appreciation at her confidence.

Pace hadn't noticed Ken and Muriel as he seated himself. He thanked Della for the menu as she turned away to get him a beverage. He appeared to be in troubled thought for a frown creased his forehead and he hunched forward, with his elbows on the table and his fists planted under his chin. His eyes were downcast and he was not aware of anyone else in the place.

Ken reached out to read the man's thoughts and found a jumble of everything stirring within him. There was an area that seemed to elude him, as though it was such a dark deep hole that Pace's own mind could not engage it. Ken wondered why. He knew Pace was extremely bright, yet very cunning. He regarded himself with higher esteem than his fellow beings did but it was more than that. For some reason, Ken could not grasp what it was.

Pace only lifted his hands and folded them in his lap when Della returned with a glass of iced tea. He flashed his dazzling smile at her again. He must have suggested that he wait to order until his dinner companion had arrived as Della nodded and walked away.

"He is certainly caught up in some heavy thoughts, isn't he," Muriel mused, lifting a spoon full of soup to her lips. She blew slightly on it to cool it.

"So it would appear," Ken agreed. "He hasn't really been aware of anyone since he walked in."

The door opened and a woman in her mid-thirties walked in. She was tall, leggy, and strikingly attractive, with shoulder-length black hair and a stylishly tailored suit. She appeared to be a businesswoman from her appearance and her dark briefcase. As she stood there, she took off her sunglasses and looked around the café. Della approached her and, as she spoke, the girl indicated Pace at the table by the window. Pace, still deep in thought, had not seen the woman enter but he arose, smiling now, as Della and the woman came to his table.

"Well, Arlene, good you are here. My but you are looking lovely, as always," and Pace was appraising her with a flirtatious smile as he seated her. Then he returned to his seat across from her.

Ken suddenly realized who she was, though he had only met her one time a few years ago just before Gloria became ill. They had attended a social gathering at an attorney friend's home and Arlene LaRue was the man's niece. She had not been out of law school long then, as Ken recalled.

Arlene held Pace with a deep clear-eyed gaze and Ken read the look immediately: she was in love with the man. He saw her breathe deeply the way a woman does when she is overcome with emotion and fighting to maintain a casual attitude.

"Whew," Muriel said, her voice low. "There's some hot sparks flying there, huh?"

"You noticed," Ken chuckled lightly.

"Now I suspected the good prosecutor for some time because Marilyn has not been happy, almost from the time she married him. I just never saw him in action before. He sure has played it cool. After all, the Falzones are monied people and Pace is one ambitious sort of guy."

Ken said nothing for a moment but then, in response to Muriel's statement, said, "Well, it doesn't surprise me because he sure fits the bill for that type of guy."

The couple across from them were so engaged in deep conversation that they were oblivious to anything but each other. The woman looked up at Della in a daze when the girl returned to take their order and bring her a glass of iced tea. She shook her head as though to clear it and Ken could hear her give Della an order for a chef salad. She had elevated her voice as one would to regain their thoughts. Then Della asked Pace for his order. He spoke more softly and then Della left to place their orders.

Muriel and Ken finished their meals and Ken put a hearty tip down on the table for Della who had returned to ask if they wanted dessert. They both declined and she thanked them several times, her eyes alight at the sizable tip.

The couple were so oblivious to everyone that they appeared startled as Muriel and Ken stopped at their table. Ken noticed the tight smile form on Pace Allard's face but he maintained it with extreme effort. "Now, if it isn't my favorite waitress and the famous case-cracking journalist. Meet Arlene LaRue. Perhaps you've heard of her uncle, the well-known trial attorney, Neil LaRue. Arlene has followed in her uncle's footsteps as an attorney."

It appeared to Ken as though Pace was prattling on like a man who had been caught with his pants down but he gave no indication of this as he extended his hand to Arlene.

"Perhaps you don't remember me, Ms. LaRue, but I have been a friend of your uncle's for years. By the way, how is Neil? I haven't seen him in some time? Oh, and please forgive me, this lovely lady is my fiancé, Muriel Jacob."

Ken turned to look at Pace who seemed to be at a loss for words for a moment. Total surprise was clearly etched on his face at both of Ken's announcements. Arlene's eyes registered a flicker of recognition now but Ken knew she was struggling to place him.

"It is so nice to meet you, Muriel, and good to see you again, Mr...?" She paused and Ken smiled down at her, noting that her eyes were dark blue with long black lashes. They only added to her perfect creamy white skin and Barbie doll looks.

"Ken Ferries. I met you at a social gathering at your uncle's home. I believe you had just finished the bar at that time so, of course, that has been at least 6 years. My wife Gloria, who has since passed away, was with me. As I recall, you asked her to autograph a recently published book of hers."

"Oh yes, but of course I remember you now. You are the well-known Ken Ferries who was with the Waco Centennial. How foolish of me not to know right away. My uncle always speaks highly of you."

"Well, thank you, Ms. LaRue."

"Please, call me Arlene. I will be sure to tell Uncle Neil hello for you. He is doing very well, thank you."

"That would please me. I know your uncle has many successful trials to his credit. He developed a reputation for career excellence known far and wide." Arlene smiled her approval and appreciation.

"Wonders never cease, do they," Pace noted with a condescending tone. "Here our famous Ken Ferries has gone and stolen away little old humble Rosewood's favorite waitress. And he is just full of surprises about the varied circles he travels in."

Ken felt Muriel stiffen, and when he looked at her, her face appeared cold. But she smiled down at Pace in a way that let him know he had more than met his match and to be prepared for a quick comeback.

"Yes, it is too bad that I won't be your favorite waitress from now on, but you know how it is, climbing the social ladder and all. Say, how is your lovely wife, Marilyn? I haven't gotten to chat with her for some time. I must tell her how fortunate it was that we ran across you and your lovely companion…er, business associate."

Muriel's retort was well-placed and Pace's face colored ever so slightly. He shifted a bit in his chair and his pearl gray eyes flashed anger, even though he put on his most dazzling smile. Muriel chose to ignore him and turned her attention to Arlene now. In that husky tone of hers, she said, "You and your uncle must attend our wedding. Do bring a fine good-looking man to escort you, dear, one who is as attractive as you are." She reached out and shook Arlene's hand and then boldly winked at Pace. "I just happen to know a fine gentleman who would be perfect for Arlene. Well, it has been nice to meet you, dear. I hope we will meet again soon."

Arlene looked from Pace to Muriel and back again. Muriel smiled warmly down at her with complete composure.

"Yes, Muriel, I would enjoy attending your wedding. My uncle wouldn't want to miss it. Thank you."

"Wonderful," Ken interjected before anyone else could say another word. Silently he was saluting her for the way she had "cut the pant legs off" Pace Allard. Smiling down at Arlene, he asked in his most congenial tone, "Arlene, are you still . in the Waco area?"

"As a matter of fact, no. I was asked two months ago to come and join Arvis Cline's law firm. He has accepted me as full partner." She reached for her handbag and handed Ken her card. He scanned it quickly and noted "Cline and LaRue Associates" with a list of their specialties. He noted that the address was in Longview, which was probably how Pace had come to know her.

"Let me congratulate you, Arlene. Now we know where to send the invitation, my dear."

"Have you set a date for your wedding?" She looked quickly at Pace, who by now seemed to have regained a measure of composure.

"No, we haven't but it will be soon. Muriel and I are leaving Wednesday for Houston to make plans with my children."

Arlene smiled, revealing a warmth that came from a truly sincere person. He hoped that she was wise enough to walk away from the situation with Pace.

"Well, I wish you both every happiness. Please do call on me and perhaps we can get together over lunch soon?" She left it hanging and Pace shifted slightly, flashing disapproval quickly across his face.

"We'd enjoy that a great deal," Muriel smiled at her and reached for her hand, shaking it. "It has been a pleasure to meet you, Arlene."

"The pleasure has been mine."

Ken reached to shake her hand next. "Yes, we will get together for lunch and soon, Arlene," he assured her. "Now we must go but it has been nice to see you again."

They departed and by now the evening stars shone brightly. When they reached Ken's car, Muriel expelled her breath heavily. "Pray tell me, Ken, how can that lovely woman be so taken with that conceited ass?"

"That one's easy, honey, because he has never shown that side of himself before. I suspect that, since she appears to be a savvy woman, she will have had her senses sharpened by our little encounter with Pace and his ungracious attitude."

"Well, I certainly hope so," she said as she slid into the car.

As Ken walked around to the other side of the car, he chuckled at how Muriel hadn't missed a beat with pace. She went straight for his jugular and he was proud that she didn't let anyone walk over her, no matter who they were. That was one of the things he had sensed about her from the beginning.

When he slid in beside her, he pulled her to him and kissed her soundly.

"Wow, what brought that on? Mind you, I am not complaining," she laughed.

"You are one feisty and gutsy lady, Muriel Jacob, and that is one of the reasons I love you, pretty lady."

"Well, growing up in a household with wall-to-wall kids, I had to learn how not to be a wimp if I valued survival." She chuckled light-heartedly.

Ken started up the car and they headed out of town toward Muriel's house.

"It's been a good day, hasn't it Ken?" she said softly. He nodded his head in agreement.

They reached the driveway and pulled in. Ken noticed a note stuck on the side entrance door but said nothing about it. When they got to the door, Muriel found it. She unlocked the door and stepped inside to turn on the light in the laundry room.

"Oh, hon, we forgot to bring in the picnic basket," and she started out to get it. Ken suggested that he get it while she read the note to see who had visited her. When Ken returned with the basket, Muriel was seated at the kitchen table and she handed him the note.

"You're not going to believe who this is from, Ken."

He took the note but kept his eyes on Muriel, giving her a questioning look as he sat down at the table. When he finished reading it, he looked at her and felt shock and surprise moving through him. For a moment, he said nothing. They just stared at each other.

"Well now, this really puts the icing on the cake, doesn't it," he said softly.

"Yes, it really does but what are you going to do? This scares the hell out of me because I think Catlin Willard is a dangerous man, even more so because he is scared and feeling desperate."

Muriel, I think he is scared, yes, but I also feel that he is trying to reach out to someone for help. In some weird way, he has decided that I am safe even though he has tried to intimidate me. I don't get the sense that he is a cold-blooded killer."

"Then just tell me why he was trying to enter your motel room until he got the crap scared out of him by that hawk. My hair still stands on end thinking about it."

"Who knows? Maybe he thought I would chicken and run back to Waco and just forget the whole thing. The man is probably in pretty good shape after the kind of work he was doing so he thought he could rough me up a little. Let me tell you another thing— when he realized that the sentence of murder might be put on him, you'll notice that the whole theme of things changed."

"So then you plan to meet him next week as he's asking in this note? He wants you to go to some remote area where anything can happen. Dammit, Ken, I just think you had better at least advise Sheriff Hernado and have some protection somehow."

"I have got to think about this, because the last thing I want is for Willard to scat and leave this case hanging even longer. Those three men in prison don't deserve any more time there than necessary. For them, every day there is like living on the edge of a cliff with somebody ready to push you off for any small slight."

"I know that but God, I would die if something happened to you. I lost one fine man and I don't want to lose another one."

He went to her and lifted her from her chair. He held her close to his chest and buried his face on top of her hair, breathing in the soft fragrance of it. Finally, he held her by her arms away from him and held her eyes deeply with his. "Listen, pretty lady, I have far too much at stake here to be a fool and risk my life. I'm no hero but I am not a coward either. Yes, I do know there are risks, there always are when you are dealing with desperate people and situations, but we have got to get to the bottom of this thing. It's clear that I have been led here. I know that and so do you. I for one feel that there is a protective force that surrounds me on this mission. Now I just need to think about this and figure out what the best measures will be for the best outcome. Frankly, I think Catlin Willard is using this for some kind of trade-off because he is certainly not lily white after those earlier threats and shooting that bull at the Conways."

Only the sound of the kitchen clock could be heard as Ken looked into the troubled green eyes of his love. His heart turned over at the fear in them.

"All right, Ken Ferries. Do what you feel that you must but, by damn, you come back to me all in one piece." She stretched her body up high and brought his lips down onto hers in a crushing kiss. Ken could feel a rush of emotions course through her. Muriel broke away to take Ken by his hand and lead him from the kitchen. She switched off the light, led him through the living room and on down the hall to the bedroom. When they reached the side of the bed, she switched on the lamp with the soft pink light.

"Ken," she whispered as she began to unbutton his shirt. Next she unbuttoned her own blouse, pulled off her bra, and stooped slightly to pull off her jeans. "Finish undressing, honey, then we will go get in my shower." Then she rained kisses on his bare chest while he slid out of his jeans, pushing his shoes off at the same time.

He watched her firm hips, smooth like a sleek tiger moving effortlessly and seductively ahead of him. She switched on the night light and turned on the shower. That done, she stepped easily into the tub, allowing the water to flow over her and into her mouth. Her eyes were sexy and taunting as she turned to look at Ken. Then she blew water onto him and giggled like a girl when he reached for her, laughing lightly and joining her in the tub.

Their bodies swayed and heaved as they made love under the flowing shower. Their lovemaking was particularly intense after the upsetting note. They both felt as if they couldn't get enough of the other. After they had made love for several minutes, they took turns bathing each other, then finally stepped from the tub to towel each other dry. Muriel toweled her hair and combed it before going into the bedroom.

"I love you, Muriel. I know that everything will be all right. You must trust that, darling."

"Ken, I love you and yes, I believe that it will be all right. Perhaps I accept that from you more easily since you have the abilities that you do. I don't know that I would otherwise."

They turned to each other to kiss but this time with a tender sweetness. Afterwards, they snuggled close and drifted away into sleep.

When Ken awoke, he could smell fresh coffee. He clasped his hands behind his head and stretched, then stretched his arms out above his head, stretching his fingers wide too. The bedroom door opened slightly and Ken saw Muriel peek in, then she opened it wider, greeting him with a happy smile. She made a dive for the bed in one quick motion, putting the upper half of her body onto his chest.

'Howdy, pardner," she drawled, her eyes holding a spark of mischief which he found so refreshing and youthful. He appreciated her vigor for life and all that spunk to boot. She brought magic back into his life that he knew he had been missing for far too long.

"You, my dear, are the spice of my life and the nectar of the Gods, just in case you don't know it." Her lips were sweet and yielding on his own.

"I had better get into that bathroom like now," he said. As she rolled over and stood, he arose from the bed. She whistled as he made a dash for the bathroom. When he returned, he dressed quickly and went to the kitchen to find Muriel at the stove making pancakes. She turned with the spatula in her hand. The radiance on her face was just beautiful to him. Nadine was beautiful, Ken thought, but at this moment, Muriel had an inner glowing beauty that was clear to everyone. He felt more and more like he had known her forever.

"You are so beautiful," he sang.

"Ken, you have a great singing voice. Did anyone ever tell you that? And, by the way, thank you, sweetie." Her smile, as always, reached inside him, touching his heart in a beautiful way that he could never explain. "All right, my favorite crooner, sit right down and sample Muriel's specialty pancakes made from scratch. I would be less than honest if I didn't fess up and tell you that my Mother has made these as · far back as I can recall." She brought him a plate of pancakes and pointed out the various homemade jams along with syrup and butter already on the table.

"Come on, lady, join me. There's enough on my plate for two."

"All right, will do." She poured two mugs of coffee and seated herself. Ken put two of the cakes on her plate.

"Uh, no can do, sweetie, else you will have a chubby tubby," and she put one of them back on his plate.

"I would love you even if you were a chubby tubby," he said and grinned, then winked at her playfully. He decided on strawberry preserves, then closed his eyes to savor the first bite. When he opened his eyes, Muriel was watching him, her elbows propped on either side of her place and her hands cupped under her chin.

"Well, what's the verdict?" she drawled. Her lips were slightly curved into a smile.

"Need you ask? You undoubtedly have inherited your Mother's talent. These are delectable and so are the preserves, which I presume you made?"

"Sure did, along with Angie's help last summer. And right out of our own little strawberry patch." Her smile was pleased.

"In case I forgot to ask, if you haven't been spoken for already, would you marry me?"

"What, just because I make good potato pancakes and know how to put up preserves?" She feigned a pretty pout.

"Well, there might be a few other reasons too," he chuckled.

She reached behind her neck and rubbed it, pressing her lips together suppressing a smile. Her eyes were bright with a mischievous spark.

"Well, I think I get it," and she looked as if she was pondering a moment. Then, she chuckled in that husky voice and gave him a slow sexy wink.

While they finished breakfast, Ken mentioned that they should go in to see the Sheriff soon. Ken went to call him while Muriel went to her bedroom to finish getting ready for the day.

Bruster's good-natured voice came on the line after the second ring. "Morning, Bruster. Ken Ferries here."

"Hey, Ken, I was just thinking about you and hoping we could get together this morning."

"Do you have some more information for me since we last talked?"

"Well, yes. I know for a certainty that it was Cat Willard who wrote those threatening notes you got. And, of course, it's a bet that he was calling you with threats too. By the way, I have Muriel's high school yearbook for her. Say, another thing, when you get in here, I've got another piece of news regarding our Cat man. This one about puts the topping on the cake but it also says how scared our man is now."

"I believe he is right enough, Bruster. When I see you this morning, I'll tell you something that happened last evening while Muriel and I were out. But I'll save it until we get there to your office."

"That will be fine. So, I'll be seeing you about what time this morning?"

"Well, looks like Muriel is ready now," Ken said as she came into the living room, her head bent to the side as she put on an earring.

"Very well then, I will see you in a few minutes." Bruster hung up.

493

"Are we ready to head in and see Bruster, pretty lady? Seems he has some information for us too.'

"Yes, you bet. Let me just grab my purse and we are out the door. This day is going to be a pretty one, it would seem," Muriel observed as they made their way to the car.

"I agree. Did you get a whiff of those sweetpeas as we passed by? Nothing more wonderful than the sweetness of flowers, except for the sweetness of my fair and lovely lady." Ken smiled at her while he held the door open.

She leaned over the door to kiss him quickly before getting in. "Thank you, dear gallant sir. I do feel like Lady Guinivere."

He felt the warmth of his deep feelings coursing through him like an inner melody. He thought that this was surely a gift one receives in life when two people feel as complete as they did together. Nothing would dampen his spirits, he vowed as he walked around the car and slid in beside Muriel.

They pulled up in front of the Sheriff's office and walked in to be greeted by Katie. "Good morning, Muriel, Ken. The Sheriff says for you both to go right into his office. He is expecting you."

"Thank you, Katie. We will then," and Ken took Muriel's arm to lead her back to the office, pausing to knock on the door.

"Come in," Bruster drawled in his good-natured voice.

Muriel went in, followed by Ken who had his hand outstretched to greet Bruster. They shook hands and Bruster indicated the two chairs in front of his desk.

"Good to see you both. May I get you some coffee?" They both thanked him but declined. "First, before I forget, here is your yearbook, Muriel. I certainly want to thank you for it proved invaluable."

"I am so pleased that it helped, Bruster," Muriel said, taking the book from him and placing it on her lap.

"Now, Ken, Bud Conway was in here earlier this morning and showed me this. I asked him if I could hang onto it for awhile for evidence and he was only too happy to comply. I figure it is just one more thing that kinda sweetens the coffee on this whole thing."

Ken took the envelope with Bud's name written on the outside and opened it to find a money order made out to Bud for a sizable amount. Ken looked up at Bruster after studying the money order and recognized the handwriting of Cat Willard.

"There is a note you overlooked in there too, brief but a note." Bruster leaned back in his chair and clasped his hands behind his head. Ken found the note and unfolded it to read it. It said, "Sorry, but hope this covers it for that bull."

"Well, Bruster, I would have to agree that this indicates even more that Cat Willard is running scared of being sent to prison. He's afraid of being pinned with a murder he didn't commit but wants to be in a better light by sending this money order to Bud. He's hoping for a break on that one anyway."

"Sure would appear like it. Reckon he's smart enough to figure that he will have some jail time at best but is willing to work out something for leniency."

Ken looked over at Muriel, her face sober. She knew that he was about to reach into his shirt pocket and hand Bruster the note from her door the night before.

"Bruster, Muriel found this note on her door when we got to her place last evening. As you see, it's made out to me."

Bruster's heavy eyebrows shot up as he read the contents of it and he pursed his lips, whistling softly. "Ken, this is a very ticklish situation and one that I am perplexed over. I don't want to risk a citizen getting hurt because this is something the authorities should handle."

"Yes, it would be but I would imagine that you will come up with something since we have a few days to think on it. We don't want to risk scaring Catlin away again because I suspect he is right around here within a few miles."

"Things like this have been done before and I tell you, one way would be to hide an officer in the car with you and have you both wired." Ken could hear Muriel shift uneasily in her chair. He reached across the space between them and took her hand.

"Now, Muriel, there is no way that we will allow Ken to be put in jeopardy but we may have to use this method to get Catlin Willard to come forward. As long as Ken has some protection, I don't feel that there is any imminent danger."

Muriel sank back into her chair and looked at Bruster a moment before she spoke. Her voice was low and halting. "Can you readily guarantee that? Because, let me tell you, Cat is a desperate man. If Ken does this, is Cat going to be arrested on the spot or what?"

Bruster looked at her thoughtfully before he spoke. "I've got a hunch that he wants to talk this out first with Ken here and see if Ken will go to bat for him with the law. Then he will give his cooperation when he feels he "has all his ducks lined up in a row."

'Well, all of the 'what ifs' scare me because we don't know for certain what Cat has in that mind of his. And Ken is really sticking his neck out if something goes wrong." Ken could clearly hear the fear in her voice and he wanted to hold her and reassure her but he just squeezed her hand.

"I do understand your concerns, Muriel, but we've reached a point now where this whole thing is ready to reach a climax. This solution will get those men out of prison and Ken here, thank God, has been made the instrument for justice to prevail. They have already lost close to a year of their lives for something they didn't do."

"Oh, Bruster, I know that. I hate to say it, but you're right. It just scares me to death for Ken." She sounded perplexed.

"Muriel, I sure promise you that we will be there for him all the way. Now, Ken, are you willing to do this?"

"Yes, Bruster, I am. I don't see any other way. By the way, I think you might check out something I discovered in the Rogers home while Muriel and I were visiting Will yesterday." Bruster looked quizzical. "I had Tyler show me around the house while Muriel was talking to Will. Well, the place where Nadine's body was found in the hallway is right outside a large storage area. On the pretence of being interested in the storage room, I asked Tyler to get a measuring tape to get the dimensions. While he was gone, I quickly inspected some brown stains by the inside of the door. They weren't immediately visible—I just happened to spot them."

"Oh jeez, Ken, this just shows how sloppily this case has been handled. Ten to one it is blood and probably Nadine's because whoever killed her probably hid in there until the coast was clear. Undoubtedly that person was spattered with her blood and, God willing, we can still get some palm or finger prints in there. Hate to put Will and his family through any more— they have been through so much— but we need that evidence to help fit more pieces together."

Ken just nodded, his throat tightening. He met Muriel's sorrow-filled eyes but she squeezed his hand firmly to reassure him that she was bearing up. They left the Sheriff's office without speaking, each deep in their own thoughts.

Ken spoke first as he was helping her into the car. "Let's go to Dolly's and just relax over a cup of coffee. I think we could use some space to talk for awhile."

"I am certainly open to that. I just hope we don't meet Pace again because I don't think I can be responsible for my actions right now." Her face was grim.

"All right. I say that we just go drive and find a place for coffee. I am agreeable to anything you would like to do. Don't be so gloomy," he said as he tipped her chin up to meet his eyes. "I have one of my hunches that everything is going to be just fine."

She brightened. "I know where we could go— this little quick food place. The coffee is fair but they have soft drinks and lemonade too. Would that be all right?"

"Sure honey, I told you wherever is fine with me."

Steve's Coney Island came into view after they turned onto the main highway and traveled about three miles out of town. When they entered, Ken smiled at the 50's flavor of the place.

"Kinda neat, huh Ken? Angie had her first job here when she turned 16." Muriel's eyes twinkled up at him. He could see she was enjoying the moment of recall and he could picture pert little Angie dressed up in a 50's waitress uniform like the two waitresses now buzzing around the little café. The young man with a cook's hat was behind the counter to take their orders. His thin youthful face spread into a wide grin when he saw Muriel.

"Hi there, Muriel. How's it going? And how's Miss Toots these days?"

"She's just fine and about ready to come home for the summer."

'Well, if she wants a part-time job when she comes home, be sure to tell her to stop by. Sure miss that little gal. Good worker like her Mama, too."

"Thank you, Steve. I will tell her when I call her this evening. Steve, this is Ken Ferries, a friend of mine from Waco. Ken, meet Steve Autry."

"Pleased to meet you, sir," Steve smiled at Ken, reaching for his hand and giving it a firm shake. Ken at first figured him to be in his early twenties but then decided he was probably late twenties or possibly thirty. He had the looks of a man not much older than his waitresses with his upturned nose sprinkled with golden freckles, his crisp red-blond hair and generally scrubbed clean appearance.

"What are you going to have? By the way, it's on the house today. My treat for you and Mr. Ferries here."

"Aw no, Steve, now you can't make any money that way," Muriel protested.

"Now, I insist. It's my congratulations present to you both. In case you are wondering, I am privy to all the local gossip in this place," he chuckled lightly.

"So, tell me, who was this tale carrier?" Muriel's voice purred but she had a slight amused smile playing at the corners of her mouth.

"Let me see, I believe the first time I heard it was from Melinda Peters, that girl Ty Rogers takes out fairly often. Then a couple others too but it escapes me who they were now."

"That is something that never changes now, does it Steve. One just had to expect it from these little communities where everyone knows everyone. There are no secrets to be had," but her voice was cheerful and she smiled again warmly at Steve and added, "I believe I will have a lemonade." Ken agreed that he would have the same.

"You aren't getting away from here without the specialty, my coney dogs with all the trimmings," and he flashed his boyish grin at them.

"Oh, all right Steve. We would be honored to say the least. Thanks for your thoughtfulness. You're always so nice."

Steve winked, "Well, Muriel, you and little Toots are two of my favorite people. Now, just pick a spot and I will have Patty bring your orders in about two shakes of a lamb's tail."

They slid into a booth of bright yellow naughahyde with a lipstick red table top. Posters of various entertainers and movie stars of the 50's decorated the walls as well as records. "Yeah, this takes me back," Ken chuckled, "right down memory lane to the bobbie socks days."

"I thought you might enjoy this, Ken. I always feel like a kid again myself when I come in here. Maybe that was Steve's idea for he does a good business, if you notice."

Ken nodded and checked out the juke box at their table. He selected one of the popular 50's tunes after inserting a coin. "Now, my lovely woman, if I had a dime for every time I danced to that number, I would be as rich as Rockefeller. In fact, if we could, I would twirl you around like I used to, with my famous little dipsy doodle. You would love it. All the girls did," and he gave her a teasing wink.

"I bet you had the girls' heads in a whirl, Mr. Twinkle Toes. I don't doubt it for a minute."

He chuckled, "Well, maybe a few of them." He gave her a modest smile.

"Uh huh, I am certain it was just a few. It couldn't possibly have been more than that, especially because you are not at all smooth as silk on the dance floor or all that good-looking or charming either," and she rolled her eyes heavenward. Then her lips curved into an impish grin.

"Well, there was a time, especially in the forties, when ladies were desperate. Then any man who could dance, regardless of his looks, was an instant hit. Then, of course, Gloria came into my life and, well, she was the only girl I could see after that. But I never regretted that meeting, or the meeting of one lovely Muriel Jacob," and he reached for her hand and kissed the palm while looking into those cool green eyes, eyes that had a sparkle for life and unconcealed happiness. He could read into her soul and he knew he would never regret a day spent with this beautiful woman either.

"Hello, Muriel," a sweet young voice spoke. They looked up to see one of the waitresses with two of Steve's specials which she placed before each of them.

"Hello, Patty. How are you and your family doing?"

"Really well. Eddie is graduating college pretty soon and then I am going this fall." The girl's young face was alight with a sweet smile and Ken thought she didn't look much over fourteen with her pixie features and the twinkle in her deep chocolate brown eyes.

"Well, honey, that is just great. I am so proud of you and of your brother Eddie too. I hear he's going places, that lad, and that he tried out for the Dallas Cowboys. Now that is the big time and you all gotta be mighty proud."

"Well, Mom sort of got her dander up at first because she thought he would go on into the retail business in management. But Dad got her calmed down and pointed out that that can still be an option for him later on."

"Always comes out all right in the wash now, don't it, hon?" Her voice held that husky drawl that always made Ken quiver all through him. He smiled at his own private thoughts.

"Oh, Patty, meet my dear friend Ken Ferries. He's here visiting from Waco." Ken smiled at the girl. "Pleased to meet you, Patty."

"Pleased to meet you too, sir. I hope you are enjoying your visit to Rosewood,"the girl said, turning her dark friendly eyes onto Ken. He noted that her eyelashes were long and curled, giving her a wide-eyed look, almost like a doll.

"Yes, Patty, I am enjoying my stay but mainly because of the people here. I find them so pleasant and now I have been privileged to meet yet another one." He took her small slender hand and shook it.

"Why, thank you, Mr. Ferries. I hope we will be seeing you often, sir."

"Just call me Ken. What are you planning in the way of a major?" he inquired.

"Well, I thought quite a bit about designing, fashions you know. But I haven't fully decided yet. That seems to be the one that keeps pulling at me though."

"Then check it out because you are getting a message from your deepest inner self. After you have, you will certainly know if that is the vocation you are meant to follow."

The girl looked extremely pleased at this informative advice and smiled gratefully at Ken.

"I do thank you, Ken. You know, that is just what my Daddy said too so I do think that I should follow up on this."

"Well, you do know that the information was already present within yourself and you just wanted some validation. It appears that your Father had already given it to you." Ken's face spread into a warm smile at this youngster whose face shown with a bright light for her future.

"So good to meet you, Ken, and great to see you, Muriel. Guess I'd better get back to work. I see several people coming in and Steve will be overloaded if I don't carry out my end of it here."

They smiled after she had walked away and then Muriel looked at Ken with open appraisal. "You saw that girl's future, didn't you?"

He grinned with amusement playing at the corners of his mouth. "Well now ma'am, I reckon as how I did," he said with an exaggerated drawl.

"Well, don't keep me in suspense here. Is she going to make it as a fashion designer or what?"

"You really want to know then, I take it."

. "Ken Ferries, you tell me this instant and stop teasing me. I can't stand not knowing and you know it," she feigned a pout.

He leaned forward with one arm laying across in front of him on the table and the other one with his elbow resting on the tabletop. He covered his mouth with his hand to hide the teasing smile there. "Oh, all right. Guess I will never be allowed secrets around a willful lady like you. I can see it now, between you and Sarita I am a dead duck. She too is always hep to everything. So, yes I could see the minute Patty began to talk about it. And when she walked up to our table, I saw her as the grown woman she will be in a few years. She will get into fashion design and become quite financially well off once she has established herself. One reason, of course, is that she is very talented but another is because she is not afraid to work hard for what she wants."

Muriel took a bite of her coney dog and a sip of lemonade. Then she just shook her head after swallowing. "Know what? You are a total wonder. I would say it is the other way around though, that I could never keep a secret from you," she laughed lightly and Ken winked at her.

As they ate their coney dogs, Ken couldn't help but see Muriel as a teenager. She momentarily transformed into a girl with longer hair pulled up high in a pony tail with a green bow that matched her letter sweater in green and white. She was watching everyone who came in the door. The only difference was that the room took on a drugstore appearance with a soda fountain and high stools but Muriel was seated at a table by herself.

"What?" she said suddenly as she realized that Ken was looking intently at her.

"Well, I've just been seeing you in the past at, oh say, sixteen with a ponytail and green bow and a green and white letter sweater. Looks like you are sitting in the local drugstore waiting for a date. How am I doing so far?"

"Ken, this just floors me. I can't believe this. I mean, I know it's true but it simply overwhelms me. Yes, that was me to a gnat's eyebrows. It was, of all things, the time I went out with Cat Willard." She blushed slightly and then looked at Ken with a guilty little smile. "I was meeting him at Fay's Drugstore and Soda Fountain because Mom would have tanned my hide if she had known I had a date with Cat. She thought he was way too wild for a good girl. Well, she was right and she found out anyway. And the talking to we got I won't go into but, trust me, I never tried to pull anything over on her again." Her chuckle was husky and she shook her head at the recall.

"That is probably why I picked up on that particular time frame of your life, because it was a little something that kept hanging there in your mind. Then it surfaced lately because of the circumstances with Cat now."

"Yes, I can see how that would be true because I have thought about it a lot with all of the things going on. Cat was sort of wild but I can't accept that he would do such a terrible thing."

"Nor I, Muriel. That is partly why I don't think we have a lot to be worried about with my meeting him next week."

"I have to tell you that I still feel better the way Bruster is setting it up though."

Ken nodded agreement and they finished their lunch. They told Steve goodbye and waved to Patty on their way out.

"Say, why don't we go visit Sage awhile if he isn't too busy? I told him we would the next time that you were free."

"I would enjoy that. I love that old character. He has always been one of my favorite people and was so good to Angie when Bill died. But then, lots of these folks are so good-hearted. In retrospect, I have to say I have been blessed in many ways."

Ken hugged her to him as he opened the car door for her. He felt good, an on-top-of-the-world feeling warming him. "I am so blessed myself, dear lady." They smiled deeply into each other's eyes.

They made their way out to Sage's ranch and drove into his yard where they were greeted by Tatters. He stood wagging his tail at them as they got out of the car. Sage came out onto the porch and opened the screen door, holding a dish towel which he tossed up onto his shoulder.

"Well, howdy folks. By danged, if you didn't bring this pretty woman out here to visit. That pert near makes my whole day." His smile was mellow and full of good cheer.

"So, Sage, how's the world been treating you?" Muriel said, giving him a warm hug. Ken followed with his hand outstretched. They shook hands warmly and Sage ushered then into his kitchen where Ken could smell freshly perked coffee.

"You just grab you a seat over there at the table, Muriel, and I will pour you a cup of this coffee. I just brewed it up and Dot dropped by this morning with fresh apple pies. Shucks, she fears I ain't eatin' good enough but a man my age don't need the chuck he used to. Ken, now you park yourself too and let me just slice us all some of this pie." Muriel got up to help Sage serve the pie, getting plates from the cupboard.

"So, Sage, how have things been going for you since I was out here last?" Ken asked while he watched Muriel put the pie on the small plates.

"It's a funny thing, Ken, but you know I was just fixin' to call Sheriff Hernado in a few minutes. Now you remember that little subject we discussed when you was here. Well, darned if I didn't see that feller out trotting up the road early this morning. I am about certain it is one and the same— you know, one of them joggers. I was heading out to feed my old hens and check on some calves and their mammas. Then there he was on a dog trot but I knowed it was the same feller I seen that morning in my barn."

"Sage, you never mentioned this to anyone else, did you?" Ken asked as Sage came over to the table with two steaming mugs of coffee.

"Nope, nary a word, even when Dot came whirling in about that time grumbling about them fools tearing up the road like race horses. She says they wouldn't be needing to do that if they put in an honest days work." He guffawed his agreement. Ken chuckled and gave Muriel a sly knowing wink, giggling over Sage's descriptive way with words. Muriel brought over the slices of pie and Sage asked her to fetch the rest of it and just park it on the table, certain they would want more than one slice of his sister's pie.

"Sage, that man has to be a local because you wouldn't have seen him again otherwise. And you felt that you knew him from some place," Ken suggested.

"That's what I figure, Ken. Now it does sound strange, I reckon, but I think it was that Pace Allard fellow, you know, the big shot lawyer. But then I would just be accused of being an addled old fool if I was to swear that he was the same man that I seen in the barn and trotting on the country road this morning."

Ken looked sharply over at Muriel and she appeared close to fainting. He heard her suck in her breath deeply. He felt the hairs on his arms and back of his neck tingle while an icy chill coursed through him. He was aware that Sage was looking keenly from one to the other.

With concentrated effort, Ken finally spoke. "Well, Sage, it probably was unless Pace has a twin," and he tried to laugh to lighten the shock.

Undaunted, Sage went on. "Well, I take a liking to most folks on the spot but never was very taken with that man. Seemed to me there was always way too much sticking out of him even when he flashed all that charm some folks are so taken by."

Muriel had still not fully recovered but she looked at Ken when Sage turned his attention to his pie plate. Her eyes were full of shock and fear. Ken reached across the table and squeezed her hand, holding her eyes with his own. He felt her relax some.

"Now, it's mighty plain to see you two folks are pretty serious. Would you indulge an old man?" He turned a flirty teasing look on them both. "When's those wedding bells supposed to ring or haven't you got a date set fer that?"

Ken was glad for the lighter moment and Muriel smiled at Sage. "Sage, we sure would be happy to have you join our celebration when we get that date set up. It wouldn't be the same for us if you weren't there, you know."

Chapter____16

Girl, that's one shindig you couldn't keep this old cowboy away from. I been hopin' for years that a fine man like Ken here would come sweep you off your feet— well, since I knew I didn't have a chance." He winked broadly at Ken. Muriel chuckled, glad for Sage's light humor.

"You know, Sage, just in case I never told you before, I just had the biggest admiration going for you starting about age seven. I have never seen anyone handle a horse better than you. You broke some of the orneriest ones there ever was." Muriel smiled at this salty old rancher with open fondness.

"By cracky, sweet child, I did tame down a fair share of them critters in my day. But that strong-headed sister of mine got her spurs into me and laid down the law awhile back, tellin' me I was a danged fool to bust them wild critters at my age. She didn't want me ending up an old cripple. So when she put it to me short and sassy, I figured I better be playing her tune." His dark eyes filled with a sparkle which showed his soft heart.

"Sage, were you ever married?" Ken asked feeling comfortable to talk openly with him. He was obviously the kind of person one could trust.

"Yep, sure was for a brief time," the elderly man said with a far away look in his eyes. He seemed to be caught up in his private thoughts for a few moments but then spoke again. "Not many folks around here knows it," and he paused again. "I was young, not even twenty, and she was seventeen, an Indian girl. One of the prettiest I ever set my eyes on. At that time, there was a lot of caterwalling if a white married an Indian but we was so gone on each other that we just didn't pay any mind to it. One day we sneaks off and got ourselves hitched." He paused again and Muriel was sitting on the edge of her seat, her face showing great interest.

"Lordy, I loved that girl and she did me. I used to trade horses with her Pa— that was how I met her off up into the territory. We'd sneak off come night fall and pitch and woo. Her Pa didn't take too kindly when he found out. But I asked him one evening if he would let me marry her and he flat out refused, even though I offered him a whole string of fine horses." He took a bite of his pie and chewed slowly, looking far away again.

"Now, if you happen to know much about Indian folks back in them days, it's purely a fact that once they got their mind set, it's a waste of yer time to try to dicker with them. So me and Little Fawn waits until we are certain everyone is asleep and then she meets me at one of our sparkin' spots and we high-tailed it out of there for the border. That girl could match me for riding any day and she had a good mount. I can still see her sitting astride that paint, her long black hair flying behind her and those brown legs tucked tight into that horse."

He suddenly stood and said, "Come on into my parlor. I want you to see a treasure of mine. Not many folks have seen it, and if they have, they just think it's real pretty. But I don't tell many about it." They got up and followed Sage into a room furnished with what would be an antique collector's dream of old Tiffany lamps and heavy furniture that had been treated with care. The arms of the chairs and the red velvet settee were covered with lace doilies. Sage opened the heavy red velvet drapes allowing the sun to stream into the room. As they looked at the large painting on the wall, Muriel drew in her breath sharply. The painting showed a girl smiling down at them, dressed in the ceremonial white leather wedding dress. She was smiling faintly but her dark eyes held a note of sultry teasing in them. Ken thought she was without doubt one of the most beautiful women he had ever seen.

Muriel turned to Sage and spoke. "Sage, she is so beautiful." Her voice was barely above a whisper.

"Now, she surely is that," Sage said, shaking his head in agreement. "I lost her and our son at the same time. She died in childbirth, she did, and the boy went with her." His voice was husky with emotion. He continued, "She was just coming twenty years old and this was the only child we had. When I sent one of the hands to get the Doc because she was having trouble with the birth, he didn't want to come. So Chet, my ranch hand, managed to get the elderly widow lady midwife to come over. She was well up into her eighties but, bless her, she came. But by that time, my brave little wife had lost so much blood that she died. The little boy went soon after even though Mrs. Clayborn worked hard to save the little feller." Muriel went to Sage and put her arms around his lean body still as hard as flint.

"Now little lady, don't you be frettin' 'cause I tell you, one of these days, I will be meeting up with both of them up yonder. I come in here every evening and just sit right over there and talk to her. I ask her how she's doing, which might sound like an old man's gone clean out of his head but I swear by all that's holy that she speaks to me in that sweet voice of hers that sounds like a soft running brook. She says that she and that young man of ours will see me one of these days."

'Sage, thank you for caring enough to share this with us, "Muriel said softly. Ken nodded in agreement. Sage smiled warmly.

"I found out that one of my ranch hands had a talent for art. He was sort of a mystery man from back East some place, never exactly said where. But he was a bit different than the usual hand from around these parts. He spoke all fancy like. So, to make a long story short, I got him to paint this picture of my wife. I reckon the · Maker never makes any mistakes so this feller drifted in here for a mighty good reason."

"I don't doubt that for a minute, Sage." Ken agreed with him and turned back to look at the painting again.

Muriel and Ken admired the setting of the parlor too and Sage related that most of the furniture had been in his family dating back to his parents wedding. Some of it was actually from his grandparents. Ken could feel the presence of these "ghosts" which was not at all eerie to him. He could hear their whispers and it felt comfortable and commonplace. They made their way back into the kitchen after Sage presented them with a bonbon dish that had belonged to his mother. It did no good to protest such generosity.

"Nope, at my age you just get at it while the getting' is there. You don't know when that time is about to roll around. This is your wedding gift a might early is all."

They had one more slice of pie and another cup of coffee at Sage's insistence, while listening to more accounts of days gone by. Ken mentally took notes to put on paper later. They left after another hour, and in spite of Sage's sinister news, they felt they had received the greatest gifts of a long life. They turned to wave and promised to return soon. Ken marveled at what he saw. Standing beside the elderly man was his beloved boarder collie. And beside Tatters was a beautiful Indian maiden dressed in a white doeskin ceremonial wedding dress, her black hair hanging below her waist. She held her palm out in the farewell gesture of the native peoples. Ken was overcome with a strange mixture of joy and sadness. He knew that Sage would be all right and he would not need to be concerned for his safety.

As they pulled away, Muriel turned to Ken, "Shouldn't we be concerned for Sage if what he saw that day in his barn is the person he says it was?"

"No, because Sage is a man fully of his word and he will not divulge this story to anyone. It was good that he told me and not anyone else or he could very well have been in a deadly situation— if Pace Allard is the person who was responsible for Nadine's death."

"You're probably right. Undoubtedly, something would have happened to Sage if the man in his barn thought that he was a threat. Now, another thing I'm wondering, how was Catlin involved then?"

"Good question. I have a theory on that. It could be that Catlin Willard was blackmailing Pace. Didn't you say you had seen his Jeep outside Pace's office a few time and rather late?"

"Yes, and not only did I see the Jeep there, but I saw Pace standing outside the office with the man who drove the Jeep. I had thought it a bit odd at the time but then decided it was not really that uncommon in Rosewood to work after hours. I decided that, from the look of the man, he might have been a ranch hand who couldn't conduct his business until after normal office hours."

'At any rate," Ken went on, "it would explain a lot of this and why Cat feels like he might have a trap snared and waiting for him. He had to realize that Pace is certainly no fool and would be glad to have him take the murder rap. Pace probably figures that people would more likely pin it on a man like Cat Willard than a high-powered attorney like himself."

"Of course, we just don't know for certain that it was Pace in that barn, do we. It would only be Sage's word on it."

"Well, I don't think we will find out much more, at least for a few days. I imagine that Sheriff Hernado has already contacted Will about checking out the house more thoroughly."

"Ken, do you think that Pace Allard is the kind of person who would do such a horrible thing? I mean, granted I don't like the man because he is a totally puffed up ass, but wouldn't he be smarter than that? Doesn't it take a certain type of person to commit an act like that?"

Ken parked the car a ways from the sheriff's office and pressed the buttons to allow the electric windows to roll down before he turned to Muriel. He steadied her for a few moments before he said anything. "Honey, I have tried to understand the human psyche for many years and I still don't get it, even after being exposed to so many different crimes. I can offer some summations about this situation. Number one, he was no doubt obsessed over Nadine and she wasn't aware of it nor was anyone else. When he finally came forth with his feelings for her and no doubt made advances, she pulled away and perhaps told him she was going to tell Will. He likely turned violent then, going completely out of control. When she broke and ran, he grabbed the fireplace poker and may well not have been aware that he had a weapon. By this time, he was over the edge and likely panicked. Here he was, a man with a weighty position in the community and married into a wealthy family and just couldn't have this out in the open. Can you see how it may have developed?"

Muriel's eyes widened with unshed tears and she swallowed hard before she spoke. "I just think that Pace Allard is used to having what he wants and has no scruples when it comes to getting it. So really, when I think about it, I should not be so surprised that it was him because, deep down, I have always had an awareness of the person he truly is. Just look at the way Marilyn changed over the years. I believe he mistook the Nadine's kindness and wonderful friendly spirit as something more than it really was. Then when he was told no, it was the trigger that turned him into a mad dog, especially if he had been obsessed for so many years." Her voice cracked in a sob.

"We don't know for certain that it was Pace but I think we had better go talk to Bruster and tell him what Sage told us." He held her close, smelling the sweet floral fragrance of her hair. "You all right, pretty lady?"

She nodded and smiled at him faintly as he pulled away. "Let's go talk to the Sheriff, if he is in." He reached to open the car door. "It's going to be all right, Muriel."

As he slid out of the car, his attention was drawn to a figure standing just beyond the entrance to the sheriff's office. The figure was standing in the shade of a large tree in a small grove planted in a grassy island between sidewalk and street. He felt the same chill he had experienced before and the figure moved into plain view. Nathan Tom was staring at him. Ken could feel, even from this distance, those penetrating black eyes that seemed never to blink. They were conveying a message to him even as he helped Muriel from the car. When Muriel stood on the sidewalk, he realized that she had been speaking to him.

"Ken, what is it?" And she turned to look where Ken's eyes seemed to be staring.

He shook his head as though coming out of a trance. "What?" he said, still shaking his head and frowning.

"Ken, what do you see?" Her voice rose slightly with concern.

"It's Nathan Tom, standing just beyond us in the shade of that closest tree. Don't you see him?"

She looked again and then turned to him. "Honey, I don't see anyone there now. How could he disappear so fast?"

"I don't know. It seems that he shows up just to spook me and get my attention when there is some message he wants me to get."

"Well, I have witnessed more of the mystic in the past several weeks than many people do in a lifetime and I'm not even psychic," she tried to laugh lightly. Ken could hear the stress in her voice though and put his arm around her waist. They walked to Bruster's office.

"Muriel, most people just see the obvious until something happens that triggers a deeper awareness. One could liken it to a river. We just see the surface but, if we step closer, we see other things as well. Just because we choose not to see it, doesn't mean it isn't always there."

Muriel just nodded her understanding while Ken held the door open for her.

Katie greeted them, "Muriel, Ken, good to see you again. Are you looking for the sheriff?" Katie came around the dispatch desk where she had just completed a call.

"Hello, Katie. Is the sheriff in?" Ken greeted her.

"As a matter of fact, he just arrived back here to the station but he is on the phone right now. I will let him know you are here. Just take a seat over there, you folks, and it won't be long, I'm sure."

When they were seated, Katie went to advise Bruster that they were waiting. Ken looked again to see if he might catch sight of the elusive Nathan from the large window near their seats. Katie hurried back to her desk to answer an incoming call.

"Bruster said for you all to come on into his office now."

Bruster gave them a short wave and indicated the seats in front of his desk. He was still on the phone. "Well, yes, Brice, I just got back from the Rogers and it has been hell on those fine folks. But I do think the info I have given you needs to be followed up on today. The sooner, the better. Yes, that is fine. And would you have Royal Parker get that information back to me as soon as you know? Yes, Brice, I certainly do appreciate it. Have a good day now and give my regards to Vivian."

Bruster turned his attention to them after hanging up the phone. "Muriel, Ken, I'm glad you stopped by. As you probably gathered, I just got back from the Rogers ranch. Talked awhile to Will because I didn't want to barge in there checking all that out without talking to him first. God knows that family has been to hell and back but he was very cooperative."

"Bruster, I didn't tell Will what I had seen in that storage room when we were out there because I felt it was something I shouldn't mention."

"Ken, Will understands that and told me that, if those three men are not responsible, then there was a terrible injustice committee. The one who is really responsible needs to be where those men are now." Bruster continued to gaze at Ken's face. "Reckon you got something you need to tell me, else we wouldn't be visiting again so soon, right?"

Muriel shifted in her chair but kept her eyes averted. She was engrossed in inspecting her nails and Ken knew she was uneasy with what he was about to say.

"What I am about to tell you, Bruster, makes an even better reason for you to sit down. This will probably seem pretty enormous to grasp. It was to Muriel and probably will be to the local people here too."

Bruster leaned back in his chair and seemed to brace himself for what was about to come.

"Muriel and I went out to visit Sage Murdock today and he told us he had been about ready to call you. He related the following to us when I asked him about that incident in his barn the morning of Nadine's murder. You know I cautioned him not to tell anyone other than you or me and he hasn't. Well, he said the same man had been out there jogging up the country road this morning early and it dawned on him that it looked just like Pace Allard. He said he figured anyone who heard that would think he was an addled old man."

Ken watched Bruster's eyes widen in surprise and shock. For a moment, his jaw hung slack and he sat stupefied for a few moments. Then he expelled his breath heavily and leaned forward, placing a closed fist near to his mouth. His shoulders hunched forward as he peered down at his desktop. At last, he regained enough composure to speak and his voice came out raggedly. "God almighty, Ken, this just sends shivers clean through me. I just don't know what to say." He slumped back heavily in his chair as though the wind had been knocked out of him. " I sure enough did hear right. I did hear you tell me that Sage said it was Pace Allard that morning in his barn?" He looked imploringly at Ken.

Ken just nodded and then glanced at Muriel who was now quietly looking at Bruster. He knew she shared Bruster's shock. Bruster shook his head as if to clear it.

"Of course this still doesn't mean for certain that he was out to the Rogers' home that morning but it does seem strange that he would take off like he did when Sage went out into the barn. And that Sage saw what appeared to be blood on the man."

"That is my contention, too," Ken agreed.

"Now, here is another fly in the ointment, too. Sage is right about this because some slick-a-bob attorney could blast what Sage said to kingdom come but nonetheless I would like to have him stop in here on the QT and get a closer look at Allard for a positive I.D."

He reached for his phone and punched in a series of numbers. "Hello, Sage, Sheriff Hernado here. How are you anyway? Well, now that's good. Uh huh, yes, I certainly will Sage. Oh yes, she'd be glad to come out there if you have extra eggs. We'd rightly appreciate that. That's good of you, thanks. Now I was calling about the matter you and Ken discussed today. I'm wondering if I might impose on you to come in here and talk to me some— say, within the hour? I would really like to talk to you more, if you could spare the time. Well, say now, that's right good of you. I'll be seeing you this afternoon then. I'll be here until about six this evening. Very good. See you then."

He hung up and turned back to Ken and Muriel. "Well, if this don't about blast me out of the saddle. But then, I just got a hunch we are about to find a berry patch clean full of information when you and Mr. Willard meet next week. If what he has to say sheds some light on this piece of news, we will have it sewed up, I have a feeling. Then we can get those three fellows out of the pen."

Bruster seemed to have collected himself from the initial shock but he sat there now as though pondering it all. Finally he spoke again. "You know, this is taking a form here to me, now that my head has cleared a bit," and he picked up a pen, toying with it on a notepad. All these pieces are trying to fit together for me. Just let's suppose that Pace did that horrible deed and this Catlin Willard happened in on it while it was going on. But Pace never saw him, being so caught up in the frenzy. Then Catlin sees him take off all covered in blood and, being no prize himself, thought he may just be able to profit off this and blackmail Pace. Then when you show up in town, Ken, and start to quiz people, Catlin and Pace try to scare you off. I just wonder then if Catlin didn't smarten up and see how he might take the murder rap himself, realizing that Pace is no fool."

"Catlin undoubtedly got himself involved way over his head or he wouldn't have felt the urgency for me to stop my research on the Rogers' case. All that you've said certainly appears to point to that scenario."

521

Bruster looked at Muriel who had not spoken the whole time. "Muriel, you seem pretty thoughtful. Is there anything you would like to say?"

"Well, I know this won't go any farther because I have never liked tale carriers. I have to say that some things I have heard from some good honest sources I won't divulge have made me feel that Pace Allard does have a vicious streak." She halted for a moment, obviously struggling because she had sworn not to discuss this with anyone. She twisted her hands in her lap and bit down on her lower lip before going on. "Bruster, Marilyn Allard is scared of her husband. Yes, it's been covered up and few people know that because Pace has that surface charm. Marilyn won't say anything because of her fear of the bastard. I have seen her depressed for many years and I knew something had to be wrong. She used to be such a sweet sunny girl before she married him. I saw the decline, especially after their first child was born."

Bruster listened quietly to Muriel and then turned away to watch a bird who had perched on the window ledge. Ken noticed it was a bluebird who appeared to be watching the three of them inside the room. Bruster then turned back to focus on Muriel fully and Ken knew that this man had already figured this out before Muriel had ever spoken of it. He was never one to be deceived about a person's true character.

"You do know, Muriel, that this does not make Pace a certainty in this murder, don't you," Bruster drawled, watching her closely.

"Of course I do, Bruster, but I felt you should have this information for what it may or may not mean later on," and her voice was deeper and hushed in tone.

"All right. Yes, I live here and I have come to know these folks around here pretty well. When you study people enough, you don't miss much. Muriel, you work in the café and I would say you are exposed to folks on a daily basis just as I am. So you catch the clues from people after awhile and figure out what makes them tick. That's one of the reasons that you and Ken make such a right good match," and he grinned broadly, breaking the tension of the subject. Muriel smiled at him and then at Ken.

"So, now you two will be leaving tomorrow afternoon for Huntsville, then heading on to Houston the next day. Now, Ken, when you see those three men in the prison, just don't reveal too much to them. It won't hurt to give them some moral support and let them know there is a possibility of new evidence on their behalf but not more than that."

"Why certainly, Bruster. I do understand and don't want anything to leak out to anyone at this point. But don't you think maybe old Judge Bullard and Con Womack should be made aware of the latest information? After all, I did tell them I would let them know of any new developments."

"Sure, go ahead. Tell you what, I will give both of them a call today, if you'd like," Bruster agreed.

"That would be good. I think both Con and Judge Bullard took quite a bit of heat for their positions on this case. But they are a pair of insightful old pros, in my estimation. They are truly vets from the old guard put under siege but fully capable of shedding excessive opinions like snakes shed their skins," Ken smiled as Bruster chuckled loudly.

"You summed it up right to a gnat's eyebrow, Ken," and he stood up at the same time Ken did and reached out his hand to clasp Ken's. Muriel stood up and reached across the desk after Ken and took Bruster's arm. "We want you and Sadie to come to our wedding, Bruster. You'll certainly get an invitation."

Bruster came around the desk and put his arm around Muriel, giving her a quick hug. Then he stepped back to smile happily at her, saying, "I was hoping you would be asking because Sadie and I have always been mighty fond of you and that little Angie. I was telling Sadie last evening that it was high time this pretty woman found herself a proper match here with Ken." He smiled warmly at Ken and took his hand once more. "Congratulations, just in case I haven't said it before. You are a lucky son of a gun. You're getting quite a lady here but then I do believe I clued you in to that before, didn't I."

"As a matter of fact, you sure did. And you were right on target, I have to tell you," Ken smiled warmly back at Bruster.

Muriel's eyes shone with pleasure and she hugged Bruster again.

"Now, just in case something develops more on this while you are gone, would you keep in touch with me?"

"You bet, Bruster. I do have your home phone too, in case you aren't in your office this Saturday while we are in Houston."

'Good, then you two have a grand visit with your family, Ken, and I will be hearing from you. Again, thank you for this information today." He checked the clock on the wall. "I imagine that Sage is due any time and, with luck, maybe Pace will mosey over to Dolly's for coffee about the same time. He likes to circulate about this time. I will have Sage go over first for coffee and then pop in like I am taking my break. Sage doesn't know Pace on a personal level but he knows who he is and would recognize him from living in this town for so many years."

"Sage strikes me as having keen eyesight and to be in top physical condition for a man of his years," Ken suggested.

"That old scudder is as tough as a boot heel and he was breaking broncos until fairly recently until his sister put her foot down. Why, he would stand up even now up to any man but Dot is another matter," Bruster chuckled and shook his head.

Ken and Muriel smiled and bid Bruster good day once again. On the way out, Katie waved from her stations at the dispatch desk.

When they reached their car, Sage drove by in his ancient old Ford pickup and parked it a fair distance from the sheriff's office. He steeped from his truck and looked around for a moment. Ken thought he was using good judgment. Finally, he proceeded on foot to the sheriff's office and quickly went inside. Ken started up his car.

"It's better that Sage went right into the station because I really don't believe he needs to be seen going into the sheriff's office at this point in time," Ken observed aloud. Muriel murmured her agreement.

"Ken, is there a chance that Sage could be in danger?" Muriel said thoughtfully.

"It's not likely at this point because several months have gone by since Sage saw that man in his barn. He didn't mention it to anyone because he thought it was just a jogger who needed a rest. He figured the blood on the man's clothing came from hurting himself and he was just nursing his wounds in the barn. You know, sometimes, when things occur quickly, we have a jolt, a setback if you will, until something sparks that whole memory. Obviously, Sage got some recall when he saw Pace this morning. Maybe, for Sage's own safety, it's better that he didn't remember sooner."

Muriel slumped back in her seat as though heavily fatigued.

"Listen, pretty lady, I want to make a suggestion. We have both had a big day so let's go home and take a nap. Then I will be the chef tonight and you aren't going to do anything but let me baby you. You can go soak in a bubble bath while I fix dinner. It's my surprise. I get to prowl your cupboards for all the fixings for the Ferries gourmet dinner, my fair lady."

"I am either dreaming or else have become a fairy princess," Muriel's voice was a sexy whisper and she snuggled up to Ken. She was almost asleep when they pulled into the driveway of her home.

"Say, sleepyhead, let's go in and just unwind, let things go where they want to go. IF the phone rings, we are not here. I think we deserve that. If it's something important, they can call back."

"Well, there is the recorder so we are in good shape," and she rolled her eyes, arching her eyebrows high and giving a suggestive laugh.

"So, we've got that all covered," Ken said as he slid from the car. They entered the laundry area and the phone was ringing. Muriel looked at Ken and grinned impishly. Ken swatted her trim buttocks and reached for the phone. When he answered, Bruster's heavy drawl greeted him.

"Hey, Ken, we got a positive on that ID. Sage tells me for certain it was Pace Allard he saw in his barn and that he was the one out jogging this morning. He was dressed in the same attire he had on the morning in the barn. Now, that other matter, we ought to have the results back from the Rogers home sometime the first of next week. I didn't get hold of the judge or Con so I will try them in the morning."

"Thanks for calling, Bruster. Looks like we are heading in the right direction here, doesn't it?"

"I got one of them hunches and it has seldom failed me so stay in touch. I'll be talking to you as things develop." They hung up.

Muriel was leaning against the kitchen sink with a glass of water in her hand. She had an expectant look as she waited for Ken to tell her what Bruster said. Ken filled her in on the conversation.

"Ken, I just don't know how to feel about this. Nadine was totally devoted to her marriage and her children. How could somebody who knew her as long as Pace did even begin to dream that he could have her. It makes my skin crawl to think of it. Frankly, I am filled with this terrible rage and it wouldn't bother me to blow him away myself." She was shaking as she spoke and Ken went to take the glass from her hand.

"Muriel, listen, a sick mind is hard to figure out. You know that Pace has many faces and that is the way of a sociopathic personality. Often they go over the edge and become violent."

Muriel didn't say anything but finally nodded her head while Ken watched her. Then he kissed her softly. "You go in now and take that bubble bath while I search your kitchen. We'll eat when you're ready, pretty lady, then we are going to retire early after I clean up the kitchen. You know we have another big day tomorrow."

"All right then, captain, I am heading for the tub." Her face broke into a wide smile and she gave him a smart salute. Then she dodged under his arm after whacking him playfully on the backside. At the doorway, she turned back to remark, "You'd better be careful, sugar, because I could easily get used to this princess role."

"I certainly hope so," and he gave her a suggestive wink. He turned around to search the refrigerator after she slipped away, then he heard the bath water running. He found the eggs from Sage and then some cheese and the extras he would need for an omelet. He carried on a conversation with himself as he often did when he was pondering a subject. Then he set the table and, as an afterthought, went out to the sweetpea vines to trim some and put them in water. Their abundant splendor and heady sweet fragrance made the table festive.

When Muriel came in, she stood there watching him for several moments before he noticed. "Well, my princess, do come dine with me," and he bowed low, then pulled out a chair for her. With a wide sweep of his hand, he gestured to the chair while holding a dish towel draped over his arm.

Muriel's heart was in her eyes as she came to the table. She bent first to smell the sweetpeas and then turned to kiss him. "Ken, I can't express to you all that is in my heart."

"You don't have to, darling. I already know," he whispered low as he turned her around and seated her.

"You are an excellent omelet maker, Mr. Ferries. Would you marry me?" she said coyly after her first bite. Then she took a bite of toast as Ken placed some preserves in front of her.

"Oh, I think perhaps I am available, but I do have this little black book with all these lovely ladies who have their caps set for me. So you know, I had better set things right with all of them first." Muriel reached over and softly swatted his hand, smiling at his teasing remark.

They finished their meal and lingered over a cup of coffee, making small talk and discussing points of interest they would like to see on the West coast during their honeymoon. Finally, Ken shooed her out of the kitchen so he could clean up. When he checked on her, she was breathing deeply and he knew she was asleep.

He stood at the foot of the bed looking at her for awhile. She appeared almost child-like in her sleep. His love for her felt overpowering and once more he gave thanks for their coming together. His heart was happily full. He showered and slid into bed beside her so as not to disturb her sleep. She stirred slightly and murmured his name. He watched her in the moonlight and could smell the fragrance of her hair. He breathed it all in deeply before closing his eyes and drifting away into sleep.

He awoke with a start and stared in disbelief at the misty figure of a woman at the foot of the bed. He could hear Muriel's even breathing as she slept on. The woman spoke and yet her mouth did not move but Ken could hear every word.

"You are coming to the close of this chapter. You will ever walk in the light of love. No harm will befall you, Ken. Your mission has cleared a path to right what was taken away and to filled all with everlasting life again." The fragrance of rose perfume filled the room and she was gone.

He lay there and saw in his mind again Nathan Tom standing in the shade of the tree near Bruster's office. "I always know that a message is coming my way when I see you, Nathan," he said in a quiet whisper. He lay awake the better part of an hour as he pictured the scene of the beautiful woman in his mind again. Her white-blond hair looked even lighter in the moonlight streaming into the room. Her gown appeared to be glowing gossamer of pure white and he had watched while everything about her seemed to glow brighter and brighter before she was suddenly gone. He knew with a powerful inner assurance that everything was closing and that this spirit had come to tell him of it. And new life for all concerned was to be spent in joy with far greater awareness.

"Nadine, your life has not been in vain. You are still, as you did here, giving all that is true love," he whispered, then fell into a deep sleep.

He dreamed of the red-tailed hawk that took him on a journey to places they had been many times before but only in his dreams did he recall them. An ancient soul greeted him as he came to a massive hall and the hawk soared away, leaving him to walk behind this old soul he felt he'd known forever. They came to a hall of records and a large book lay open on a table before them. The ancient one, dressed in a long robe, pointed to it and indicated that he should go to read all that was there. Ken had a feeling that the records in this hall recorded everything that was and ever would be.

He saw a soul he knew to be himself from other times and places and the lives unfolded before him. Each life he witnessed as he read became the sum total of all he knew he had become.

When he awoke, he could hear Muriel stirring about in the kitchen. He felt a peace course through him, holding the assurance for all the reasons of life. He knew the reasons he had reached this stage at this time to become all that he was. All of the pains he'd felt he could not bear were like a wellspring to deeper understanding. He had survived and gone on. He was now grateful that he had not given way to total despair and stumbled on half alive. The meaning of life in its entirety seemed conscious to him, a greater awareness than he had ever perceived before. He got up with a light heart and knew that his life would never be quite the same. At least, he would never see it the same way.

Muriel opened the door. "Good morning, honey. Breakfast is ready when you are, so just take your time." She was so delightful to look at, so whole and lovely.

"I'll be there in a few minutes. Love you, honey." When she left, he finished preparations to meet the day. While he shaved, he thought about the messages he had received and about the meetings with the three men he knew would be released from prison. He prayed silently that this would not forever taint their lives. Thoughts of his children filled him with joy and he was eager to have them meet Muriel. His whole life felt complete and rounded.

"To everything there is a season." He had heard this somewhere before but it impacted him fully now as he dressed for the day. He carefully selected a pair of slacks in a summer weight material which he remembered feeling frivolous for buying because of their high price. He put on the shirt he bought at the same time, one of a deep royal blue that intensified his eye color and gave a deep glisten to his dark hair. The silver at his temples in no way detracted from this man of sixty who did not look it. Later, for the art show, he would put on the single-breasted silver gray sports jacket but, for now, he just tried it on to see the effect. Just then, Muriel opened the door.

"Wow, you handsome man. You do almost leave a girl breathless. And, honey man, you are all mine." She playfully pinched herself on her extended arm. "There now, I am really not dreaming." Her green eyes sparked with a sexy smile and she stepped aside and pointed out of the room. "Come, my handsome prince, before I changed my mind and we don't leave this house today."

He chuckled, pleased that she found him good-looking and that she approved of his clothing selections. A lady's approval always helped one look their best, he reasoned. "Guess I had better dress like this more often," he said, pulling her close for a soft kiss and then following her to the kitchen.

"You made pancakes again, didn't you, sugar. You have pure instinct for what I love. It's one of my favorite breakfasts. In fact, I remember my mother used to fix them sometimes for supper. Tommy and I were as happy as if she had made a gourmet meal."

They sat down and Muriel poured coffee from the carafe in the middle of the table. The placemats and napkins were a tea rose pattern with eggshell colored plates rimmed in gold. More sweetpeas were added to the ones Ken had arranged the night before and they added to his warmth and grandiose feelings this morning.

His mood must have shown brighter than usual because he suddenly noticed Muriel watching him closely. He was opening the cover that held golden pancakes and crisp bacon slices.

"Um, fit for a king," he said and smacked his lips.

"Well now, " she drawled and her cat green eyes sparkled.

"What's up?' Ken questioned, looking at her with a half smile and one eyebrow raised.

"You tell me, because there is something different about you. I don't quite know but you seem to have an extra glow around you this morning," she said putting her fork down beside her plate and waiting expectantly for him to share.

"Didn't realize it showed but yes, something did happen that has just made everything come full circle, like a sentence needing a period at the end. I was in a deep sleep when all of a sudden I awoke with a start. I just stared in surprise while trying to get my bearings. A lady was standing at the foot of the bed with light blond hair, at least it looked very light. She was wearing a filmy flowing white gown and, while I stared at her, the mist around her deepened into such a beautiful glowing light. I just can't describe it to you but it was so pristine and glorious to behold. She seemed to speak to me but her mouth never moved. Still I heard what she said very plainly. She said, 'You are coming to a close in this chapter and you will ever walk in the light of love. No harm will befall you.' And she said my name. Then she said, 'Your mission has cleared a path to right what was taken away to become now what is to be filled with everlasting life again.' Then the fragrance of rose perfume filled the room and she was suddenly gone but the perfume lingered."

Muriel swallowed hard and her eyes were wet with tears but there was a settling of peace filling them too. "My sweet Nadine," she whispered, barely audible as she reached to take Ken's hand. "Let's pray, Ken. I will lead us, all right?"

He nodded and put his head down as Muriel softly gave thanks for Nadine being able to come to Ken and to give the messages she had, especially this one. She gave thanks for all the blessings they had and offered praise for the beauty of this beloved friend who had blessed their lives so richly. Her voice broke twice as she prayed and Ken lightly squeezed her hand in support. "Ken, she was letting you know that it will be all right now. You will be safe when you meet Catlin next week."

"Yes," he agreed, "that was part of it, honey. But she was also saying to go on with life and that life is everlasting so embrace it all and ever walk in the light of love. I feel she has even forgiven this horrible transgression committed upon her. We are not to stumble throughout life being bitter or full of rage. She brought me a deeper understanding about— well, about the whole meaning of life. Some people just haven't gone far enough to have reached that but I tell you, it certainly is freeing to one's spirit to come closer to that knowingness."

"Well, it shows on you, beautiful man. I can even see a light around you. In fact, it is a pink light and the blue violet above the pink. I read once that pink is the heart showing and the other color shows a high level of awareness. I would definitely state that you are one of those deeply advanced souls, Mr. Ken Ferries."

"Thank you, my lady, but I believe you are also a deeply advanced soul, much more than you are aware of." He leaned over to kiss her soft yielding lips.

They finished breakfast and, while Muriel finished packing, Ken took their luggage to the car. When he returned, the phone was ringing.

"Do you have that, Ken?" Muriel called out to him.

"Got it, hon," he said as he picked up the receiver in the kitchen. "Good morning. Jacob residence," he said, and though he knew someone was on the line, he could only hear breathing.

"Hello, is anyone there?" but still no response. He could suddenly "see" the person on the other end of the line and chills ran up his back. The first thing he saw were the coldest eyes he had ever seen and he knew they were the eyes of the person he had seen in his vision in the Rogers home. They were cold, gray, and consumed with pure hate. The form of a man came into focus, getting plainer. He was sitting at a desk and was dressed in white jogging attire. Perspiration was running down the face of Pace Allard—then the picture faded away as he hung up. Ken carefully replaced the phone and Muriel called, "Who was it, Ken?"

"Oh, just a wrong number," he said, hoping the on edge feeling he had didn't sound in his voice. He knew with a pure certainty that Pace was capable of doing whatever he deemed necessary. He could sense that the man "knew", with some kind of cunning like an animal, that he was being hunted. He was a force of evil and one to be reckoned with carefully. Ken poured himself some more coffee and sat down to ponder this when once again, the phone rang. It was Bruster.

"Good morning, Bruster," Ken greeted him after he had answered with a cautious hello.

"Good morning there, Ken. Say now, I just got off the phone with Judge Bullard and then Connie Womack. Old Sam Bullard, I reckon, is just about right with his response, and, only as the Judge could be, colorful and all. Says to me, 'What do you expect for Christ sake? Nothing surprises me at my age. Besides, a puffed up peafowl never did sit good with me. Rightly enough, the bastard was smart to a point but he had this major ego and a twisted mentality that got to hell in his own way. You know, there's bigger men than this end of a horse's backside that's fell by the wayside. Reckon they get to thinking they are mightier than God and they get knocked to the ground one way or the other.' With that, he thanked me and asked me to keep him abreast of any and all future developments. He asked about you and said to give you his best. He says you are one of the few among the general establishment he respects at all. Then he hung up before I could respond."

Ken chuckled, as did Bruster. "How about that? I am truly honored."

"You ought to be because that old man is not known for being flowery in the least," and he chuckled again. "I told him that they were hoping to find more evidence at the Roger's home and gave him what we know so far in regards to that and the part you are playing with Catlin next week."

"That's good, Bruster. I am glad that he is aware of all these developments. Now, how did Con Womack receive all of this?"

"Why, I think there for a few minutes the man was speechless, Ken, because he didn't say anything. Then he said, 'I'll be damned. Why that piker son of a bitch. If this is really the case and he killed that woman, then put those three men in prison, I hope by God he gets life. When those cons in there know who he is, he won't last long anyway. I'll tell you, he'd wished he got a death sentence. For sure, it would be more humane than what he'll get in there, by a long shot.' So, anyway, Ken, he wants me to keep him on the alert too. He told me to tell you to be careful and to give you his regards. I assured him we would be damned sure you are protected. He also said he had the highest esteem for you."

"The sad part of it regarding Pace is the fact that he does have a family. But there have been men before him who never took that into account."

"Yes, I'm afraid so. It is a tragic thing all the way around. You see that it ever comes back to the fact that no man is an island because what we do touches all life in one way or another."

"You couldn't be more right. I've lived long enough to attest to that."

"Well, reckon I'll tell you adios but I will hear from you after you see those boys down there in Huntsville."

"Sure will, Bruster. Now you take care and hope you get some sound results from those tests done at Will's home."

"Count on it. Good day to you."

He hung up the phone to see Muriel standing there smiling at him. She winked when he looked at her wide-eyed. She was a vision of loveliness in a light lemon yellow skirt with a kick pleat and a silver concho belt at her slender waist. The silk blouse of the same color draped perfectly to show off her high-set breasts. Her hair glistened with highlights. The silver hoop earrings completed the picture of a tastefully dressed woman.

"Muriel, you are a glamour girl and heads will turn when you walk into that art show today. And, pretty woman, you are all mine," he said huskily. He walked over to her and kissed her with the passion he was feeling. "Let's go now before I carry you to that bedroom," he murmured softly while kissing her throat.

"Yes, we have to drive out to Rosie's and pick her up, remember?" Her voice was throaty and lower, the way it always got when she was full of emotion.

"Let's go. I've already got the luggage loaded so off we go to fetch Mrs. Rosie Wilson." They made their way out to the country road and pulled off on the lane to the Wilson's sprawling yard. Their well-tended ranch home had a long porch with morning glories climbing up the posts. Down from the porch roof hung lavender wisteria hanging like grape clusters.

"Pretty, isn't it, Ken?"

"Yes, it sure is," he agreed.

A dog came slowly from the porch to greet them, wagging it's tail in slow motion. "This is Princess, Ken. She is a grand old lady now and retired, Rosie and Ham tell me, but she still brings the milk cows in like clockwork," and she patted the black and white shepherd on her glossy-coated back.

"Hello, Princess. Good to meet you." He patted her head as she followed them toward the porch.

"Here you are," Rosie greeted them as she swung open the door. "Come on in, the two of you. Come now and I will give you a quick tour of the premises, Ken, since you've not been here before. Allow an old lady to show off a bit, would ya now?"

Muriel hugged the older lady and Ken followed behind her into a sunshine kind of kitchen that clearly bespoke of the warmth of the two people sharing this home.

"You know, I dabble just a wee bit with painting and you must see my latest still life," she said with her sweet Irish brogue. Ken had appreciated that from the first meeting with Rosie. They followed her into the living room furnished with a homespun flair of early American furniture and out through French doors onto a screened porch. There on the easel was a lovely oil painting of a profusion of colorful flowers in a china blue vase. Ken noted the many potted flowers perched on built-in shelves around the porch, mostly African violets in a variety of hues. A pair of white wicker chairs were stationed in the area with a white wicker coffee table in front of them. A ceiling fan made it cool and Ken enjoyed the lightness of this small cheery and cozy enclosure.

"You have a lovely home, Rosie, and it looks to me like you are quite an artist," Ken said stepping closer to inspect the painting.

"Well, now 'tis sweet of you to humor me, Mr. Ken, but I have some way to go to join the ranks of fine artists such as dear precious Nadine, God rest her darlin' soul." She sniffed quickly and dabbed her eyes. "Ah well, if we had the time I would show off a bit more and bore the dickens out of you with more of my attempts but anyway, it amuses me in my spare time."

"Why, Rosie, I love this painting. It is one of the best ones you've done," Muriel said as she looked at it with great appreciation.

"It is lovely and you are far too modest. You should have your work displayed in a section of the gallery where you work and then the next art show, you need to enter yours too. You really should have this time."

"I fully agree with Ken, Rosie. You simply must," Muriel complied.

"Now you two, go on with you. You're setting this old woman's head awhirl. Why Ham won't be able to be living under the same roof with me at all," she chuckled but her merry blue eyes expressed her pleasure.

"Rosie, speaking of Ham, where is he? I thought maybe he would join us. Isn't he going to the art showing?" Ken asked.

'Ah no, I am feared not. He would be truly stressed with me if that dear man knew I had breathed a word of this but he cannot bring himself to see a picture of our darlin' Nadine even now. And sure there will be herself there in a lovely framed photograph on the display table. That darlin' man wouldn't be able to control the tears and he can't abide anyone should see him dissolve into that." Ken nodded and patted Rosie's ample arm with understanding. Rosie sniffed again as Muriel hugged her once more.

Rosie continued, "So there now, himself found he had a great hurry this morning to see about matters that could not wait here on the ranch. I'm sure the capable hands of the two Gunnason brothers could deal with anything, both of them strong as oxen, just like my Ham." She chuckled in an attempt to lighten the moment.

"Let me just grab a few things on the way out the door and we had better be going. Don't want Phyllis to think Rosie forgot her," and they walked back through the living room where Ken saw a picture he hadn't noticed earlier. It was of Rosie dressed in bridal white with curly long hair and, next to her, Ham in full military uniform with a heavy thatch of wavy black hair. In the background, a red sun was rising over the Irish coastline. Rosie had a demure smile on her lips but that same spark of mischief in her eyes that was still visible years later. Ken took great pleasure in seeing this photo taken so long ago and seeing a couple still so devoted to each other after all that life had given them.

They made their way out with Princess following along behind. Rosie instructed her to look after the place and to see after Ham. That done, she climbed into the back seat and Princess returned to her post on the porch. They chatted as they drove, with Ken carefully following Rosie's directions to the show. They entered the building and Ken noticed it had a special avant-garde attitude of posh surroundings. He let Rosie lead them to a table bedecked with tapered candles in long silver candlestick holders. Next to that was a tidy display of beautiful flowers.

A pretty woman in her mid-fifties greeted them from where she was seated by the guest book. She asked them to register their names and addresses as she handed them a feather plumed pen. After signing, Rosie led them to yet another table where several people stood chatting. Many of them turned to see who had just arrived.

This table held glassware and drinks— wine glasses and brandy. The host was a dignified man probably in his seventies with silver hair and eyes as blue as the Mediterranean sea. His tanned complexion looked as though he could have basked on its shores. Ken had visited the Mediterranean for a time during his military stint and he recalled the men and women he had seen at the coast, all tanned and healthy looking. The war had seemed a million miles away to him at that time. He was a fresh-faced young kid then, not out of his teens when he served his country.

"Penny for your thoughts, good-looking," Muriel quipped, bringing him back to the present.

"Oh, sorry, honey. I was wool-gathering," he said as Muriel handed him a glass of wine. Rosie was already talking to Phyllis who had just approached them.

"Phyllis honey, you are totally stunning," Ken said and his heart lurched because he knew she was a picture of her mother. The gown of emerald green was of a flowing material and her golden blond hair encircled her beautiful face like spun gold. She came to Ken and hugged him close, then stepped back and took his big hand in her own.

"Ken, thank you for all you have done for all of us. It has helped us to go on when we didn't think we could. You and Auntie Muriel have both given us more than you can know. I just want you to know we all love you. And, by the way, congratulations are in order, I hear."

"Well Phyllis, bless you, honey. Now you are going to attend our wedding, you and that good-looking cowboy husband of yours. We will be sending invitations before too long." He smiled down at this fairy princess of a woman, so delicate and full of sparkle that filled the room.

"Wild horses wouldn't keep us away. You can trust that we will be there," and she hugged Muriel, then said, "Come on. I want you to come see Grandpa and Grandma." Carolyn and Will Sr. were a striking pair. Carolyn looked regal with her lovely white hair arranged in a stylish chignon. Will Sr. stood tall and trim, fit for his age and still impressively handsome.

"Look who's here?" Phyllis said as she ushered Muriel and Ken into their presence.

"Well, by golly now, Carolyn, here are two fine folks we haven't seen since that son of ours got himself tangled up with that bull and landed in the hospital." He hugged Muriel and shook Ken's hand in a bear handshake. Carolyn hugged Muriel and then did the same with Ken, smiling happily at seeing them again.

"Congratulations, you two dear people," Carolyn smiled at first one, then the other of them.

"Yes, it's about high time someone like you put your brand on this beautiful woman. We were mighty glad to hear that you will be getting married. When's the date?" Will Sr. gave Ken a resounding pat on the back, laughing good-naturedly.

"Well, we haven't set it yet but we will very soon. Of course, you are both going to receive an invitation," Muriel smiled at them.

"Oh yes, we wouldn't miss it," Carolyn assured them. Then her eyes looked past them and grew excited. "Why, it's our two handsome grandsons and their equally handsome Dad." They all noted Will Earl pushing his father along in a wheelchair with Tyler at his side.

"Now, hot damn, if that isn't a sight to warm the cockles of an old man's heart," Will Sr.'s big voice boomed out happily. Will and his sons were all smiles and they joked about getting Will pulled together in decent attire to attend this event. Everyone was overcome with a mixture of joy about being together. Phyllis bent down to kiss her Father followed by Carolyn. Will Sr. noisily cleared his throat and then clasped his son's hands in his own.

Muriel and Ken made their exit politely and moved on to view the work of the various artists. They took their time to linger over each and every piece and marvel at the gift of every artist. They made a point of expressing their appreciation to the artist for the special flair they possessed. Finally, they entered the room where Nadine's work was displayed and the first thing they saw was the photograph of her on the round table covered in deep blue velvet. She was without question one of the most beautiful women Ken had ever seen, not just outer beauty but an inner radiance that emitted from her soul. That face could easily create poetry, he thought. He looked at Muriel and saw her throat working. He cupped her hand in his and kissed it.

"It's all right, pretty lady. She's not far away, you know."

"I know. I feel her around me a lot. I do right now." She drew herself up straight, then expelled her breath.

A guest book was placed on an adjoining table along with information about Nadine. The display included works from her early years as a painter, before she became a public artist. Ken and Muriel lingered lovingly over her work and imprinted each piece into their minds. Not one painting was austere, even the old downtrodden cowboy sitting astride his horse in a drenching rainstorm.

Muriel suddenly tugged at Ken's sleeve and inclined her head toward a woman standing nearby. She was so intent on the painting that she didn't notice them standing less than two feet away. It had to be Marilyn Allard, Ken sensed. She looked like the woman he had seen in the vision with Jeff. She was extremely attractive, with dark shoulder-length hair that had copper highlights. She was about the same height as Muriel with a very fine bone structure. She seemed to hold great intensity and depth of feeling. Ken knew she had suffered more than anyone knew because she was skillful at hiding her emotions. He reasoned that she had not always been thus but had learned to shut down in an effort to hide how afraid she really was, afraid of going over the edge.

"Marilyn, hi," Muriel said after she and Ken had stood there for some moments. Only then did she turn sharply and Ken sucked in his breath at what he saw. She had carefully concealed a purplish bruise under one eye but not so well that one standing close couldn't detect it.

"Oh, Muriel, hello. I'm sorry I didn't see you," she said and put her hand out to take Muriel's. She looked at Ken and then back at Muriel.

Muriel then turned and said, "Ken, this is Marilyn Allard. Marilyn, meet Ken Ferries."

Ken took her slender hand and noticed that her eyes weren't just brown, as he had surmised, but had olive green in them. She was impeccably dressed in a stunning white silk suit that only heightened her classy looks and set off her olive complexion. She seemed a bit flustered when Ken and Muriel turned to look at the painting she had been viewing so intently. The painting showed Jeff Colter dressed in Western apparel, his long legs in chaps. He leaned against a corral fence with his arms resting on the top rail and his Stetson pushed back on his head. The painting gave a close view of his ruggedly handsome features.

"Wow, that is a great painting of Jeff. I hadn't seen this one before. It looks like it was done just a short while ago, before…" and Muriel's voice trailed off.

"Yes, I imagine it was," Marilyn added quickly.

Ken noticed that she had a large wide silver bracelet on each wrist. When she absentmindedly reached up to point out some detail in the painting, the bracelet slipped back to reveal a deep bruise, as though someone had grabbed her wrist in a twisting motion while pinching it hard. He could then suddenly "see" a vision of this woman in a bedroom with white Priscilla curtains. She was looking out from an upstairs window at a large yard carpeted with a lush green lawn. Her thoughts were heavy, tormented, full of an overwhelming sorrow. Then the bedroom door flew open and he saw her whirl around startled, then cringe at the rage in the face of the man advancing toward her. He grabbed her wrists and began to twist hard as she cried out in pain and shock, trying to pull away. His eyes were the same ones Ken had seen in the storage area of the Rogers' home, the ones full of madness. Ken got one icy chill after another. His throat tightened and constricted as he felt Marilyn's fear as she stared into the eyes of her husband Pace.

He could hear the deadly retort of this evil man, "Get this, you scandalous bitch tramp, if I hear one more even slight suggestion from these scandalmonger lowcast sons of bitches, you can count on being six feet under. Now listen," and he tightened her wrists even more and she sobbed in pain, "you know there are ways. Make no mistake that it wouldn't be the easiest thing in the world to make this one tragic accident. Do you have that straight?" His voice was barely a whisper and Ken could feel Marilyn's body shaking. Pace suddenly stepped back from her, still holding one wrist in a torturous grip. He hit her under one eye as he swung her body toward the bed, knocking her head back and sending her almost over onto the floor. She was close to unconscious from the blow and she lay there for some minutes after he left the room. Finally, she arose and staggered to the bathroom, almost falling. She clutched at the doorknob to steady herself. He saw her reach for a washcloth wet it with cold water, then apply it under her eye. Her mind was so jumbled and distraught, fear had taken over and she could no longer think rationally. The vision left him as abruptly as it came.

He appeared to still be staring at the painting of Jeff, not fully aware that Muriel and Marilyn had moved on to the next painting. They were discussing it when Muriel's voice broke his attention, "Ken, Marilyn and I were just saying how the colors in this one are so perfect. Just look at this sunset. Isn't it beautiful?"

Ken brought himself around and stepped over to the painting. He was also struck by the brilliant orange glow over the landscape. "Yes, it is. You two ladies have excellent taste but most lovely ladies do," he said in an effort to lighten up the terrible scene still clouding his mind. Muriel smiled her thanks and Marilyn's face gently smiled but still the sadness was present in her deep olive eyes.

The trio moved on, still looking and appreciating the paintings. When they reached the painting that took mastery over all the others, they stood silently viewing it. Finally, Marilyn spoke, "You know, every time I have seen this painting, something happens to me that I can't explain. I just feel this peace."

Muriel nodded agreement and added, "It has a mystical quietude."

They stood for some time looking into the face of Nathan Tom just as Ken had seen him on the hill, with the rainbow trailing above him and surrounded by butterflies.

"Ken, you bought a print of this one, didn't you?" Muriel turned to him now.

"Yes, and I asked about purchasing this beautiful work but Phyl said she couldn't sell it. I can certainly appreciate that but I am pleased with the print. And I'm glad the original is in the gallery so all of Rosewood can enjoy it."

Suddenly the fragrance of rose perfume became apparent and Muriel looked sharply at Ken. Marilyn turned to them, "Why, that perfume! Do you smell it? Didn't Nadine wear that rose fragrance?"

"Yes, she did, Marilyn." Muriel's voice was hushed.

"Well, isn't that strange because it doesn't smell like what I am wearing nor like the fragrance you have on." Her face showed puzzlement.

"Oh, well look who's here," Ken said as he turned to welcome Jeff who was standing a few feet away looking at them. He flicked a glance at Marilyn and her face had paled under the olive coloring yet her love for this man shown plainly as well. Jeff was turning his Stetson in his big rough hands, never taking his eyes off the woman he obviously loved. He made no motion to approach them so Ken walked over to him with his hand extended. "Hello, Jeff. Good to see you here."

"Tell you what, I didn't intend to come here today, Ken. I'm not big on these kinds of shindigs but I reckon I just needed to rub elbows with the jet set today," he drawled. He shifted his tall frame from one booted leg to the other, still turning his hat by the brim nervously. "Say, Ken, you don't reckon the ladies would excuse us for a few minutes. I got a matter I need to talk to you about."

"Why certainly, Jeff. I will just tell Muriel we will be back in a few minutes. She can talk with Marilyn. They are having a great time and won't miss us a bit." He chuckled lightly yet knowing that something was pressing heavily on Jeff. He could see the urgency in his demeanor.

Ken went over to the ladies and let them know they would be back in a few minutes. Muriel looked at Ken, her face full of questions but she didn't say anything except to sweetly agree. Marilyn pretended to be absorbed in the painting.

"I won't be gone long," he assured Muriel and gave her a quick hug.

"Ken, let's go outside— too many people in here. I need to get this said before you and Muriel leave."

Ken pointed the way and they proceeded out the doors. "Let's go to my car, Jeff and I will turn on the air. All right?" Jeff just nodded agreement, looking grave. Ken knew he was not a man who showed inflamed intensity but he looked close to it.

Ken opened both car doors and slid in to start the engine. He sat there a moment while the air conditioner began to cool down the inside.

"All right, Jeff, get in. It's cool enough now." Jeff complied, sliding his tall frame easily into the passenger side. They shut the doors and rolled up the windows. Ken turned to look at him but he was staring straight ahead, his jaws clenched tight. He looked like he was fighting hard to maintain control.

"Ken, do you believe in ghosts?" he said and Ken looked at him in surprise, taken aback so much that he was unsure how to respond.

"Now, Jeff, why do you ask that?" he countered.

"Ken, last night I had an experience that rattled the hell out of me. I have never in my life experienced anything like that." He paused and swallowed hard before going on. "I didn't turn in very early last night, had some paperwork I'd been putting off. I just figured I would dig in and get it done so it was after midnight before I hit the hay. Now I was beat and it didn't take me long to get to sleep. I'd been working out on my spread all day and really zonked out like a light. Now this is the weird part— I woke up with a start for some reason and looked at the clock on my nightstand. It was only a half hour after I'd gone to bed. I had not turned on the light, just looked at the clock and settled down again. Next thing I knew, someone called my name. I raised my head from the pillow and, as God is my judge, standing at the foot of my bed was Nadine."

Ken still hadn't said anything and waited for Jeff to go on. But he looked beseechingly at Ken now as though for a sign that he hadn't gone mad. "Go on, Jeff," he prompted, looking at him straight away. He remained in listening mode.

"I guess I was frozen in shock and didn't say anything but just stared. Then she talked to me, only her mouth never moved. But she did speak and I know I was not dreaming. I swear to God I was wide awake." Ken nodded but still said nothing.

"She said, 'You must take Marilyn and leave with her for a time, telling your friend Ken but no other or her fate is sealed as was mine. Do this before the night falls another day. God is with you and your love, who was ever there for you.'" He sat there looking at Ken now and waiting for his response with a kind of fear in his steel gray eyes. Ken knew that a man such as Jeff would be greatly unsettled by such an event and he hoped he would be able to give him the assurance he needed.

"Jeff, you asked me if I believe in ghosts. Well, I have had numerous experiences of what I suppose you could call the supernatural. That is why the spirit of Nadine told you to come to me. I may never have mentioned this to you otherwise but I have had Nadine's spirit present itself to me at different times." He could see relief on Jeff's face.

"Then I haven't gone clean out of my head, thank God. But why did she tell me to take Marilyn and leave here for a time?"

"Jeff, you're in love with Marilyn, aren't you? And she with you?"

Jeff looked at Ken for a moment and Ken reached to shut off the engine. He turned to face Jeff once again. "Well?"

"Yeah, yeah, I'm in love with her and she is in love with me." He turned his face away to stare out the window. "It started several weeks ago. I never told anyone but Muriel because I needed a friend to confide in. I didn't know what to do because Marilyn is terrified of that bastard and well she should be. It started when I was driving in to town from the ranch and Marilyn was sitting in her car out there on the country road. I live just about a mile and a half off of it. She was slumped over the steering wheel and I was so alarmed that I parked my truck to see if something had happened. She didn't even raise her head and I thought she might have suffered a heart attack. Anyway, I reached through the open window and she was really startled. She had a mark across her cheek, a hand print as red as a firebrand. She wasn't sobbing but tears just kept rolling down her cheeks. I got in her car and sat there until she finally admitted that she suffered from abuse." He stopped and clenched his teeth, his jaw jutting out angrily.

"She begged me not to say anything, Ken, but I wanted to go smash his phoney damn face in. It just went from there, from her confiding in me, and one day I took her in my arms and we just came together. Now, when this vision came and told me to take Marilyn away, I was just shook in every direction. That's why I came here today because I knew she would be here and you would be here too."

Ken finally spoke. "First of all, Jeff, just for the record, I want you to know that Muriel never broke your confidence, even to me. But I knew you were in love with Marilyn when you talked to me at Dolly's that evening. Do you recall?" Jeff nodded and Ken went on. "Now, I want to tell you to heed what the spirit of Nadine said if you want to have a life with that lovely woman. Leave right away. I can't stress this to you enough. I can't divulge to you right now all that I know but Pace is extremely dangerous and Marilyn's life is in great danger."

Jeff was nodding his head and then he looked at Ken. The man's heart was showing on his face as a deeply gentle composure. "Ken, you know I was in love with Nadine though I fought it. I got over it but I love her still and always will. I feel like she is the one who brought Marilyn to me." Ken nodded his agreement. "So, I set things up with my foreman, Ed Price. Good man, Ed, but I didn't tell him where I was going or who with, just said to hold it together for me and I would be back in a few weeks."

"So your instinct to follow Nadine's advice was strong enough that you came here so why do you doubt it?" Ken asked him, watching the expression on his face as he bit his upper lip and shook his head slowly.

"Yeah, Ken, I see where you are driving," he drawled, nodding his head.

"So, now you take that lady and hit the road with her, far enough away that Pace isn't going to track you down. She may put up some resistance at first but listen, I will help you with that. I will go in there and bring her out here with Muriel so no one will notice anything amiss. All right, fella?" He reached for Jeff's hand and clasped it.

"Ken, I got an uncle up in Montana, haven't seen him for a long time. He has a big ranch up in that cattle country close to Dillon. I gave him a call this morning and he told me to get up there and bring that 'someone' with me. He kinda chuckled then and said he didn't need to know who it was but we were welcome to stay as long as we wanted to."

"You see, Jeff. All the signs point to go. Now you go for it and Godspeed to both of you. Listen, write that address and phone number down where I can reach you because I will probably be calling before long," and he reached into the glove compartment for a notebook and pen. Jeff complied and Ken put it in his pocket. He started up the car again and told Jeff to wait there while he brought the women out, giving him another reassuring pat on the shoulder.

"Ken, thanks. I don't know what else to say."

"Thanks will do it," and he slid out of the car to walk briskly back inside the art center building. He made his way through the throngs of people, smiling at all and giving the appearance of being completely absorbed in enjoying the art show. Muriel and Marilyn were engaged in conversation when he reached them. They were standing in front of a picture of Nadine's children.

"Hi, Ken. Where is Jeff?" Muriel smiled her welcome and Marilyn looked wistful.

"Listen, both of you. While there is no one close by to overhear, listen because we don't have a lot of time."

They both gave him a puzzled look and Muriel said, "Well not right now but someone may come. Why don't we go outside?"

"You're right. Ladies, please come with me. I think it would be best if all three of us go outdoors. I noticed a flower garden on one side of this building with some wrought iron benches. Just trust me now. I am not at liberty to tell you more here."

Marilyn's forehead was creased with a frown while she stared at Ken. Finally she spoke, "I don't understand. Has something happened that I need to know?"

Chapter____17

Ken made a spur of the moment decision. "Yes, Marilyn, it has. I would very well say it could be a life or death matter."

Muriel took Marilyn's arm then because she visibly paled. "Come on, Marilyn. We need to go with Ken right now." She started walking with her out of the room and toward the garden with Ken following closely behind. Ken directed the two women to sit on the bench while he stood before them, holding his gaze steady on Marilyn.

"Marilyn, what I am about to impart to you is gravely serious. I cannot impress upon you enough how serious this matter is. You know that Jeff was here." Marilyn's eyes flicked briefly and she nodded. "He came here for you." He raised his hand when she looked startled. "Now, hear me out before you say anything, please. You are in danger, Marilyn, and Jeff wants to take you away for awhile. I know some things that I can't explain right now but you have got to trust me and certainly trust Jeff. You don't know me but you certainly know Jeff and Muriel here. I know that they trust my judgment. If you haven't heard," and he smiled, "Muriel and I are going to be married soon. You know she is mighty selective so you can relax with the fact that I am an honorable chap."

She smiled faintly and took Muriel's hand to squeeze it, expressing her feelings for her but still not speaking.

"Marilyn, we are your friends, yours and Jeff's. Now, Jeff never told me this until a few minutes ago but he didn't have to. I can see what has happened to you. I did when I first saw you in there," and he nodded toward the art center.

Finally she stood up, face to face with Ken. "I can't leave. I'm afraid for Jeff. Yes, I am obviously in love with him and he is with me. But Pace is capable of anything— I've known that for a long time. I have been afraid to leave him." She stopped, choking back tears. When she regained control, she continued, "I should never have gotten involved with Jeff knowing how much danger it could put him in." Now the tears scalded her cheeks and Ken reached into his pocket for a handkerchief which he handed her.

Muriel finally spoke. "Marilyn, your staying and breaking away from Jeff would still leave you in grave danger. Even if you had never met Jeff, you would still be in extreme danger now. Please listen to Ken and leave with Jeff."

"Where is Jeff?" Marilyn asked as Muriel steadied her.

"He is waiting in my car for us. Let's go before he wonders what has happened to us," Ken urged. As they started to leave the garden area, Marilyn drew in her breath sharply at the sight of Pace walking into the art center. He had not seen them so Ken took one arm and Muriel the other, guiding her to the parking lot where Jeff awaited.

Jeff got out of the car and handed Ken his keys. He took Marilyn in his arms. "Baby, you are coming with me." He kissed her and she pulled back.

"Jeff, oh God, Pace just walked into the art center. He may ask someone if they have seen me. Several people saw the three of us come outside." She was shaking so hard that Jeff lifted her in his arms and began to walk away with her.

He turned briefly to say, "We're out of here. You know where to reach me, Ken. Thanks, buddy." Jeff was almost running with Marilyn in his arms. Ken saw him put her down long enough to open the door of his pickup, a newer model than the one he usually drove. He helped her get in on the driver's side and scooted her over so he could slide in. She slid down out of sight as they drove quickly past. Jeff waved and then accelerated when they reached the street.

"Oh, boy, now the crap will hit the fan, won't it." Muriel let her breath out heavily, as though she had been holding it for some time.

"Yes, I imagine it will but there for a while I thought we weren't going to get Marilyn to go with Jeff. I don't know if she would have if Pace hadn't shown up."

"Well, thank God she did see him, if that's what it took to get her out of here!" Muriel slumped against the car and then looked at her watch. "Ken, Rosie will be looking for us to take us to the airport pretty soon so we'd better get back in there."

"Yes, but honey, if Pace is still in there and he asks us about Marilyn, we will tell him she said she wasn't feeling well and was going home."

"That sounds good to me. I am relieved that we are leaving soon. The air will be too heavy to breathe around Pace Allard," Muriel quipped.

They went back into the Art Center and scanned the crowd for Rosie when Pace approached them.

"Well now, look who the cat's dragged in," Muriel drawled. Ken watched her face, seeing a pasted smile but eyes that looked like a cat watching a foe with guarded fear and intense dislike.

"Muriel, Ken, you wouldn't have seen my wife, would you?" He was flashing an extremely pearly white smile but the cold look in his eyes prevailed.

"Yes, as a matter of fact, Muriel and I went outside with her for a few minutes. She said she wasn't feeling well and was going home." Ken held his gaze with a level of his own.

"Well, I hate to depart from this lovely gathering but I really need to attend to my wife," and then quickly added, "to make certain she is all right. So, if you will excuse me. Oh, and thank you. Enjoy the art show." Ken noticed a nerve jerk in his cheek and saw the veiled hate course through those cold pearly gray eyes.

Muriel hadn't said another word to him and Ken knew she had avoided speaking for fear of what she would say. She could be spicy with her retorts, as she was with the cowboys who teased her in the café. But, if it was someone like Pace Allard who was unwisely condescending, she could not hold back her well-placed suggestions or kissing her pretty derriere. Ken smiled down at her while she watched him leave with a loathing on her face.

"What?" she said as she looked up at him.

"Oh, nothing, honey. I was just thinking that I wouldn't want to tangle with you in hand to hand combat." He chuckled.

"Whatever do you mean, Ken Ferries?" she purred in that low sexy voice, looking as though she didn't understand what he meant.

"Come on, kitten. Don't try to pull the wool over this old snoop's eyes. I have been around the horn several times and made an extensive study of my fellow beings' nature. Let's just say I am happy you are in my corner." He chuckled again and took her arm. "Let's go now and find that spunky Irish lady." They started moving toward more of the crowd.

"Ah, here you be. I had my sights out for you and Polly, my sweet lass, said she saw you two and Mrs. Allard going outdoors. I was on me way to fetch you when here you be." Her round happy face was warming to Ken, like a breath of fresh air.

"Yes, Marilyn said she wasn't feeling well, so we walked outside with her. Then she told us she was going home," Muriel imparted.

"Oh, that poor darlin'," Rosie said. "Now that husband of hers was asking Phyllis if we had seen her." Her voice held a distinct edge of dislike but she covered it quickly with a cheerful, "well, we had better be getting underway to the airport."

"Yes, all right, Rosie. We are in good shape now. How far is the airport?" Ken asked and then checked his watch.

"Oh, roughly ten miles, Mr. Ken. You be leadin' the way." Rosie sparkled up at him and took his arm while Muriel took the other one. They made their way out of the art center to his car.

"Now, tis a hot Texas chili day, isn't it folks?" she said as she reached in her dress to fetch a hankie which she used to dab at her brow.

"It is that, Rosie," Ken agreed. He took out his handkerchief to grasp the door handle after unlocking it. "Now you ladies wait a minute while I turn on the air conditioner and clear out some of this heat."

Rosie was fanning herself now and chatting to Muriel until the car was cool enough for them. They settled in comfortably and Ken reached for a bottle of water between the seats and offered it to Muriel.

"Are you all right now, Rosie?" Her face was flushed and she was still fanning.

"Oh, now surely be I do tend to sweat like an old mare running her last race at the track. Not to worry though." She drank some water from the bottle.

"Sorry it was so warm, Rosie," Ken commented.

"Ah now, water is water, Mr. Ken and God bless you. We had better be moving then and getting the pair of you to that airport." She waved her hand at them both, smiling, then took another drink.

"It's so good of you to take us," Ken said, looking at her in the mirror.

They arrived at the airport and unloaded their luggage from the trunk. He handed Rosie the car keys and bade her farewell.

"Now, I will just see you into the terminal and make sure everything is in order before I take your car away," she said as she started inside. Ken winked at Muriel as they followed behind. Muriel's face lit up with an amused smile. Rosie was obviously a mother hen and Ken smiled with growing fondness for this brisk take-charge good soul. After their tickets were confirmed and luggage checked, Rosie felt it was safe to leave them on their own. After once again checking on their return flight, she hugged them. With the swish of her blue taffeta slip, she departed.

"For a minute or two, I thought maybe that sweet lady was going to get on the plane with us and see that we were strapped into our seats before take-off," Muriel chuckled. Then she added, "Don't you just adore her though?" She shook her head, smiling and watching the figure of Rosie leaving through the glass doors.

"She reminds me a lot of Sarita and I do adore them both, those wonderful bossy fuss-budgets," he agreed. "They always snap a person back to the present somehow, with their down-to-earth attitudes."

"That is exactly why Sarita was a Godsend to you after Gloria died, just as Rosie was for the Rogers family." She sounded more serious now. Ken nodded his agreement and then listened as a woman's voice announced the flights and gate numbers.

"All right, pretty lady, off we go for Huntsville," and he hefted the carry-on luggage and took Muriel by her hand to lead her to the departure gate.

"You have the window seat, sugar, so slide right in there," he instructed while he stowed the two small bags above the seats. Soon after that, they taxied out on the airstrip and were soon airborn.

"Do you enjoy flying, hon?" Ken took her slender hand in his own.

"Well, I haven't much but yes, I think so. It's an adventure to me, probably because I haven't done it much." She turned to look out the window.

The flight was uneventful. While Muriel looked out the window, Ken drifted · into a light sleep. He awoke to Muriel's kiss on his cheek and the pilot announcing that they were ready to prepare for landing. After they landed, Ken retrieved their carry-on bags and they made their way to the baggage area, then on to the shuttle to their rental car.

"I didn't even realize I was drifting away like that until you kissed me. I hadn't realized I was quite so sleepy. Must have been the wine I drank at the art show."

"I am certain that added to it, hon, and the heat too. I am looking forward to those ocean breezes on the coast of California." She smiled up at him and brushed a stray lock of her hair back from her cheek.

"You're so lovely, my soon to be Mrs. Muriel Ferries. I can't wait for that and for our extended honeymoon." He raised her hand to his lips for a kiss.

They picked up their car at the rental agency and got comfortable in their large sedan, then drove to the resort where they were staying in Huntsville.

"Now, honey, there are boutiques, a beauty salon, and pools with saunas for you to enjoy while I am over at the prison. I want only the best for you, my pretty lady. Then we will have a nice supper when I get back. If you want, we will go into the ballroom and dance after dinner.

"Ken, do you know what? It was worth all those years of waiting for you. I was without a man for so long because you were coming along the pathway in my direction. Thank God, I waited for you."

"Life is sweet, like a good blend of fine wine now and again, Muriel. I do believe we will have a bountiful harvest for the rest of our lives," he said with certainty. That settled peacefully into his heart as they pulled into the resort driveway.

When he stopped the car and raised the trunk, a doorman came to assist them. He loaded their luggage onto a cart while another man helped Muriel out of the car. Ken gave him the car keys and they walked into the lobby. The doorman pulled the cart with their luggage to the registration desk, a counter of shiny copper and limed oak that glistened with high polish. Everywhere they looked were flowers artfully placed or potted greenery. Ken smiled at the look on Muriel's face as she took in the richness of their surroundings.

An exotic, strikingly attractive Asian woman greeted them at the desk with a welcome. Ken gave her his name and she said, "Oh, of course, Mr. and Mrs. Ferries." She rang a bell and the bellhop appeared. Before they followed the bellhop to their room, the woman produced a map showing the resort's various attractions.

When they entered their suite, Muriel gasped at the total beauty of it all. The apricot and shell pinks contrasted with the bright bursts of azure blue.

"Jeez, pinch me, Ken. I must be dreaming. This is sheer elegance." She twirled around with her arms outstretched. Ken had given a tip to the bellhop and he departed with a wide smile on his face. She ran to grab him and pull him from room to room, exclaiming over every piece of decorating genius. He laughed happily over her enthusiasm and acknowledged how her joy and appreciation gave him joy too. He thought she was even lovelier than ever.

"Muriel, do you know that, when you are excited, your eyes turn to a deeper shade of green?" He met her mouth and parted her lips, kissing her with the passion stirring in him. He lifted her in his arms and carried her to the bed. He undressed her and then himself and they made love hungrily. After slowing to a more gentle pace, they finally slept.

Ken awoke and looked at the clock. It was close to 6 p.m. Muriel was already up because he heard the bath water running. He lay there a moment more and then made his way to the other bathroom to take a warm shower, then cooled off before stopping.

When he returned, Muriel was dressed in a sleek black evening dress of street length. She was arranging her hair at the dressing table. She gave herself a final look in the mirror, then picked up an earring of silver and black onyx. As she reached for the second one, she saw Ken standing behind her smiling.

'Say, pretty lady, you are a dish," and he bent down to lift her silky hair and kiss the back of her neck.

'Well, thank you, sweet man," she purred and lifted her shoulder, smiling up at him in the mirror. After fastening the other earring, she handed Ken the matching bracelet. "Hon, would you?" She extended her wrist to him. He fastened the clasp in place and then she stood up to twirl around for him.

"So, do you think I will pass in this swanky place?" she asked with a sparkly of mischief in her eyes.

"Well, I should say so but I am a bit concerned," and he looked serious but suppressed a grin at her sudden concern.

"What is it, Ken?" Her voice held a note of alarm.

"Oh, it's just that some of these well-to-do local boys might want to horn in on this old guy's glamour girl and steal you away."

'Oh, you are as full of it as a creek full of crawdaddies," she drawled low and sexy. Then she swatted his bottom playfully and kissed him warmly. "Now, you handsome hunk, I am hungry so get your dudes on and take this starving lady out to dine."

"I do believe that, after all that hot passion, we are in need of some sustenance. I will be ready in five minutes. Can you hold up that long?" he teased.

"Just barely but I think so," she chuckled huskily.

He went to put on a smart suit of off-white linen, greatly suitable for evening, then reached for a red rose bud in the vase on the vanity and pinned it to his lapel.

Before they entered the dining room, Muriel paused for a moment. "Ken, is my slip showing?" He stepped back to look and assured her it wasn't. She swallowed hard while she smoothed nervously at her dress.

"Honey, you are perfect. Now, come on." He tucked her arm through his. A hostess appeared and led them to a candlelit table and placed menus before them, smiling pleasantly at them. Ken could see Muriel starting to relax.

"Some of this is in French. I can't speak French, let alone read it." She looked at him with total dismay.

"Sweetheart, will you relax?" He chuckled and gestured around the room. "I am willing to wager that more than half of them don't know French either and the rest of us marginally remember a bit from high school French class."

"Well, since I never took French in high school, you will have to help me along here. Or I will settle for braised lamb, the one item I can read but has never been a favorite of mine," she said in all seriousness.

Ken grinned a mile wide, then raised his hand to summon the waiter who was passing by. He stopped at their table.

"Good evening, sir, madam," he bowed slightly, nodding to Muriel as he did so.

"Yes, would you be so good as to suggest your specialty this evening?" Ken said in his most dignified tone.

"Most certainly, sir. I would highly recommend the Bouillabaisse to start. And for the main course, the Spanakopita is..." and he made a kissing sound as he placed his fingers to his mouth. Then he quickly flipped his hand back in an exaggerated expression of highly rewarded praise. He gave another slight bow, once again smiling. "May I advise Gaston, your server, that you are ready to place your orders?"

Ken looked at Muriel who was shaking her head yes. "Yes, please. Thank you," he agreed. The waiter gave another brisk bow and departed.

"Now, what is that whatever he just said?" Muriel asked in a hushed voice.

"Well, the first one is a seafood soup and I believe the second is a Greek dish with spinach as the main ingredient. I should imagine it is like a quiche."

"I do declare, they've snuck in a Greek culinary artist here among all these Frenchmen." Ken laughed heartily as she created the most haughty expression she could muster and extended her fingers daintily around the long-stemmed water glass, sipping carefully of its contents.

Suddenly, Gaston was at their table smiling and bowing crisply. He gave them another choice, Chicken Livers au Vin, which made Muriel wrinkle her nose. They decided on the first waiter's suggestions and added Blintz Torte for dessert. While they waited, they enjoyed a bottle of the house wine. Ken was certain that Muriel would be fully relaxed after that.

Muriel's cheeks began to flush and Ken knew the richness of the wine had mellowed her out. She began to giggle and tried to suppress it by placing her hand to her mouth. He smiled across the table at her with a teasing note in his eyes.

"What is it, pretty lady?"

"You taste every minute of life, don't you, Ken? Good food, good conversation. You love the fine things and because of that, you communicate well with people."

"Yes, I believe you could say that. I happen to have one of the best things of all right across the table from me and I'm looking at her right now. She's my lady," he said reaching for her hand. He held it while he looked deeply into her eyes.

He suddenly saw a Muriel of about six years old, without front teeth and with a ponytail. Her face was crinkled up tight and she was lamenting, "Mommy, I don't wanna. It's a dumb play and I don't want to be that dumb old Goldilocks."

"Ken, what is it? What are you thinking?"

"About you, pretty lady. Have you always been afraid to be put in the limelight?"

"I don't really know what you mean," she said looking unsettled.

He still held her hand. "Then I will focus it in for you because on a conscious level, you probably don't know what I mean. But everything about us is inside intact and we do know it but we bury it. We never really forget anything, we are the sum total of all of our experiences. We gather information daily and record it all. It crops up in many ways and every so often we pause and think, 'Wonder where that came from!' So your fear of looking foolish and feeling unworthy either came from something in your childhood or at some other time. Am I making myself clear, sweetheart?"

"I feel worthy enough," she protested.

"Do you? Do you know as we sit here and look around, I see attractive ladies, yes, but none of them is as strikingly pretty as you are. Maybe you don't realize it but heads turned when you walked in here tonight."

"Well, one of the things my parents, especially my Mother, stressed was not to blow your own horn, not to get too big for your britches. I was the youngest kid out of that big family and I guess some of my older siblings got sort of jealous of me because they thought I got more attention." She shrugged. "Maybe I did, being the little one coming along after the folks thought they were done having rugrats." She laughed nervously.

"How did they express that jealousy?" Ken prompted her.

Her face took on a slightly sad look but she went on after thinking for a moment. "Well, I was six years old and, because I had blonde hair, I was selected to be Goldilocks in the class play. I told my sister Ann and brother Frank first thing when they got home from school. I was all smiles, of course, but Frank pulled my ponytail and said I would look stupid being Goldilocks without front teeth. And Ann said that my straight stringy hair wasn't right because Goldilocks had curly hair. That was a long time ago though and we were just kids." Her voice held a sort of wistfulness. "Anyway, I didn't have to be Goldilocks," and her laugh came out in a broken pitch. "Oh, hell it was a lifetime ago," and she shrugged.

"Yes, but it doesn't matter if it was or even several lifetimes past. These things still react in us because they have become an integral part of us, do you see?"

"Yeah, sort of, I guess so but you don't have to go around like a wounded duck with a broken wing because of a mishap. We all have those." She followed behind that statement with a question. "Are you saying that, because my twin sis and brother ganged up on me out of some sibling rivalry, I'm marked for life?"

"Sweetheart, you have certainly not gone through life like a wounded duck but what I am suggesting is that everything affects us in some way, even if we don't realize it all the time. You made up your mind that you weren't going to be in that play, didn't you?" She nodded slowly and he went on. "Can you recall how you felt about it and what you were thinking?"

Muriel closed her eyes for a minute and then related, "I felt sad and I guess I thought I wasn't pretty enough, that I would look dumb if I got up in front of people. At the time, I thought Frank and Ann knew so much more than me because they were older."

Ken reached for her hand again and held her gaze. "Darling, pretty baby, do you realize that even if you were only six, you did carry that into your life as an adult?"

"I guess she never really left, just went underground is all." She laughed huskily. "So maybe that is why I am somewhat uncomfortable in settings like this." She waved her hand around briefly. "Maybe that's why I felt like I had swallowed a toad when we came into this posh dining room. I was afraid that I couldn't present a perfect picture." She put her hand under her hair to rub the back of her neck.

"Now do you see what I was saying, pretty lady?" Ken smiled tenderly at her.

She smiled and nodded at him.

"This kind of moment is like taking a nice cleansing bath or shower. It begins to wash away all the baggage we don't need to carry with us any more."

"Gotcha, sweet man. I really do get it." Her smile was radiant like a light had blazed its way into a shining clarity.

"Now look at this. Isn't this marvelous?" Ken said as the waiter placed the rich soup in front of them.

"Yes it is and it smells wonderful. I am starved. You know, it just dawned on me that we haven't eaten since breakfast. You are probably ravished by now."

"I had not thought about it but you are right, I am famished. I guess we just had a lot going on and completely forgot to eat." He winked at her suggestively.

Muriel bit down on her lower lip, leaving her teeth exposed, and grinned impishly at him. "This is simply excellent. Good choice," she exclaimed between spoons full of the tasty soup.

"Yes, it is. I wasn't certain about my selection but I hit a bullseye on this. Now, if the main course is this good..." Ken alluded.

They both exclaimed several times throughout the meal how delicious it was. They both managed to eat it all with relish, right down to the dessert. Ken suggested that they go dance, so after the meal, they did for a couple hours, then made their way to their suite.

"Ken, you are going to be too tired to go to the prison in the morning," Muriel said when they entered their suite.

"Not this old fellow. I have had a wonderful time with the most beautiful woman in this resort," he grinned, feeling a little tipsy from the effects of the wine they had drunk in the ballroom.

"I will personally attest that you are not an old fellow," and her voice was slightly slurred. She giggled like a high-spirited girl and kicked off her shoes, walking barefoot into the bedroom. Ken laughed and bent over to pick them up. She was trying to unzip her dress but he stopped her and pulled it down for her. She wiggled her trim bottom and the dress dropped to the floor in a heap. She giggled again and stepped out of it. He picked it up. By now they had reached the bed and she was struggling to get out of her slip. Ken pulled it over her head and she fell backwards onto the bed. She was asleep almost instantly so he pulled the covers back and lifted her under them. Her rich shining hair fanned out across the pillow and he smiled down at this woman he loved. She looked so peaceful and utterly lovely that his heart filled with love. He disrobed and slid in beside her, quickly drifting into a deep sleep.

The ringing of the snooze alarm awoke him but Muriel was still fast asleep. He slipped quietly from the bed and went to shower, hoping she would sleep as long as she needed. After his shower, he shaved and dressed, choosing a cool light shirt and pair of slacks. He left her a sizable amount of cash and a note saying, "Go and enjoy, pretty lady. Celebrate you because you are prettier than Goldilocks ever was. I LOVE YOU! Me—you know, that fellow who wants to marry you."

He eased out of the suite carrying a briefcase with papers to take notes while talking to one or more of the men. He was hoping that all three of them had agreed to see him but he had a gut feeling that they would out of curiosity more than anything else. He was at least a diversion for them.

He decided on a light breakfast in the coffee shop at the resort and then asked the desk clerk for his car. The chauffeur brought his car to the resort entrance. As he made his way to the prison, he said a quiet prayer that all three men would see him.

When he reached the prison, he was escorted to the warden's office. After a brief exchange, he was told that all three men would see him, the first being Galin Harmond. In the afternoon, he would see Franklin Donahue and Larry Gomez the next morning. Ken breathed a sigh of relief as he followed the husky guard to the visitor's quarters. He had been in prisons before and the oppressiveness never failed to course through him. He picked up on every emotion know to man, especially the most powerful ones such as despair, rage, apathy.

He was seated at a counter with a thick screen secured between him and the other side. On the other side was a similar chair for the prisoner with a phone device on each side of the screen for their communication. The heavy door on the prisoner's side opened and a guard stepped into a room followed by a tall man dressed in prison clothing and another guard. The guards took their posts by the door after directing the man to be seated.

Ken knew he would have recognized Galin Harmond even if he hadn't been told who the first man would be. He picked up the phone and spoke to Galin, who sat watching him with a quizzical expression. He was a handsome man, well built though lean and muscular. His eyes never wavered from Ken's, eyes that held a deep look of despair, as if he had given up on life.

"Galin, I am Ken Ferries. How do you do?"

"Howdy," Galin's deep male voice resonated in Ken's ear. "Now, I can't shake your hand but I reckon you understand," he drawled somewhat trite.

Ken just smiled and nodded. "Galin, I was a reporter for several years with The Waco Centennial where I did investigative reporting as well as other journalism. While I was still a reporter there, your case came to my attention. Since I felt there were some discrepancies in the Rogers case, I began to investigate as a freelance journalist since I recently retired from the newspaper."

Galin didn't say anything, just watched Ken almost warily. He noticed the knife wound across his cheek that Galin had received some years ago and he watched the man's jaw harden.

"Galin, would you go through that morning with me exactly as you remember it?"

"Well now," he drawled, "they didn't seem to accept the truth of it in that kangaroo court session with that smart-assed prosecutor screaming for our blood and all them folks hatin' our guts. Reckon they would have liked to get rid of that old judge too because he didn't give us the death sentence. He threatened to clear the courtroom, but then hell's fire, we got life so we might as well be dead." His voice was bitter with suppressed rage. He leveled a stern look at Ken now and his brown eyes had a gold cast in them that deepened with his emotions.

"So, what the hell good would it do to tell some former reporter gone freelance who already knows what happened that morning? If you have followed that case from day one like you say, do you just need some gory details to fill up your book?"

"Listen to me, Galin. I am not here to waste my time. I came here because you need to know that there have been some recent developments in the Rogers case. They could very well be in your interest. I am not at liberty to say more at this point but, hell, man, you need to trust someone at this time. Frankly, what have you got to lose?"

That drew Galin's attention and he appeared to relax.

"Now, that's a fact," he said, his voice less tense. He began to relate to Ken a step by step account of the morning he and Franklin and Larry had gone to the Rogers home and found Nadine's body. "Larry acted like he was home, you know, having known the Rogers family all of his life. He just knocks at the door and calls out Mrs. Rogers name and then goes on into the kitchen. Me and old Jyp tagged along behind. We had taken up with Mr. Rogers the night before about some extra wages due the three of us for some work we'd done. He said his missus would have our checks made out early the next morning on account of her leaving early to go into town.

"Larry is thinking that Mrs. Rogers must be in her studio so he just walks through the kitchen. So Jyp and me just stay in the kitchen to wait. Meanwhile, I see this long-handled fireplace poker laying on the floor, kind of concealed under some low cabinets. So I reached down and picked it up and says to Jyp I wonder what it's doing there. Then we heard Larry scream. I still get shivers clean through me when I think about how that boy screamed. 'Course, Jyp and me run into the living room and Larry, he is staggering towards us, his eyes just crazed with horror. He is about to fall and old Jyp is sayin' what's wrong. The kid can't even talk."

Ken made notes as Galin gave his account of the events.

"Jeez, all the kid could do was motion toward the hallway so Jyp and me, we still got the boy between us. Hell, man, he's in such shock that we're havin' to drag him toward the hall. Well, I see this woman laying face down there in the hallway." He swallowed hard and went on. "Blood was all over and here is this woman laying face down there. I thought I was going to lose it right there. I never fainted in my life but I damn near did then. We're staring down at this person and, Christ, she's got her head bashed in. Man, I just bolted. Anyone could have told she was dead. I couldn't even think, all I wanted was to get the hell out of there.

It would have been the same story if we had stayed there, you know, but who wouldn't want to get out of there? Man, we were all in shock and, I guess, scared out of our wits. So, yes, we ran. My mind was racing around like a caged monkey that had gone nuts. I hear old Jyp yelling at me all of a sudden that we'd better go to the sheriff's office and tell them what happened. I was scared, man. With my former record, I knew that my ass was grass but old Jyp kept pleading with me. And Larry, he's just sitting between us, frozen and staring straight ahead. Well, all of a sudden, here comes this pickup and these guys start shooting at us, then they ram us and run us off the road. IF the sheriff hadn't roared up when he did, they would have peppered us right there. But I tell you this, I could never have the stomach to kill somebody, let alone a beautiful woman like that lady was. I had my youthful stupidness after I left my folk's ranch but I learned my lesson after a while in the slammer. I'm not perfect but I stayed straight with the law."

"Listen, Galin, I believe you. I don't think you three men had anything to do with that murder." Ken watched the man's face and could see he was fighting for control, his throat moving up and down. His eyes were bright with tears he was fighting hard to keep from falling. "Listen, Galin, just hang tight now and you will be hearing from me again. All right? I just want to thank you for talking to me."

Galin began to regain control but when he spoke, his voice was still husky with deep emotion. "You know, when you're really young, you think you are bullet proof, but I tell you, I learned a long time ago how vulnerable we all are. If a miracle ever happens that clears us of this thing, I got a whole scope set for the life I fully intend to apply. A man's got a lot of time to think in this place, you know."

"Well, Galin, thank you again. I want you to know that I have tracked down a lot of things in the several weeks I have been investigating this case. I will get to the bottom of this, trust me."

"I do, for some reason. I just feel like I do. I guess I'm like a drowning man reaching for a life raft," he smiled for the first time as Ken motioned to the guard in the room with him. He watched as the two guards on the other side led Galin away.

Ken followed the husky guard out of the visitor's section and checked his watch as he walked to his car. He made the decision to go back to the resort since he could not see Jyp until later in the afternoon. He would have lunch with Muriel and relax awhile before heading back to the prison. When he reached the resort, he decided he would call Bruster to see if he had a report back regarding the spots in the Rogers home. He stepped into the elevator and wondered if Muriel would be in the suite. He hoped she had rested and then gone to treat herself to whatever took her fancy.

She wasn't in their suite so Ken made the call to Bruster. Katie took the call and in a moment, Bruster came on the phone.

"Well, Ken, how did it go in Huntsville so far?"

"I've seen Galin Harmond so far and will interview Franklin Donahue later this afternoon. Tomorrow morning I'll talk to Larry Gomez. I was received all right by Galin after we got past a few things."

"Well, Ken, I know you must be anxious to find out about the report I received. Yes, it was blood that you saw on the carpet and the door. Hardly enough to show but, with that chemical they use in forensics, it showed up right enough. It was Nadine's blood. So now we know that someone hid in that storage area with her blood dripping from that fire poker. I would certainly attest that it wasn't those three men who are in Huntsville now. There weren't any fingerprints in that storage room other than the family's though."

"All the same, this is one of the breaks we've been needing, Bruster. It does prove that Nadine's killer was hiding in that storage room. He was probably there a short time and he probably almost got caught by someone, like maybe seen by Cat Willard taking off from the residence after the murder. I guess the light will dawn on that one way or the other after I get back from meeting Cat."

"Yeah, and I got a strong hunch that the direction we are heading lays on the doorstep of Pace Allard, but I wouldn't say that with much certainty yet to anyone but you."

"I can appreciate what you mean under the circumstances but I really do believe that he fits the profile from all we have uncovered so far. I guess I had better be finding a place for lunch so I can get back to the prison. Thanks for the information, Bruster."

They said goodbye after Ken said he would check back in a day or two. He wished after he hung up that he had asked Bruster if he had called Judge Bullard and Con Womack with these new developments. Knowing Bruster, he probably had.

He checked his watch and noted that it was close to noon. He decided he would check out the coffee shop and see if Muriel was there. He left the suite and did find her sitting close to the entrance in a booth. She was engrossed in the contents of her coffee cup, looking down while she stirred it. He made his way over to her and only then did she become aware of his presence. He slid into the booth and she looked up surprised.

"Hey, I didn't expect you back this soon."

"I thought I would have enough time to come over here and enjoy lunch with my pretty lady," he smiled engagingly at her.

"Why, that is just great. I was sitting here pondering how to start spending your money this afternoon." And she grinned with a flirty little wink.

"Well, I hope that you do because I want you to enjoy every moment of this, honey."

"I am, but just being with you is the most enjoyable part of it for me. Now, I haven't ordered yet— I just got here. I was thinking I would have that corned beef on rye. Here, take a look," and she handed him the menu. He scanned it quickly and decided he would order the same.

"So, how did it go, Ken? Did you see one of those men?"

"I did. Galin Harmond was first, then at three, I see Jyp Donahue.

"At first, Galin didn't receive me but came out of curiosity. Finally I started getting through to him and he related well."

"I'm glad. Now, are you going to see Larry too?"

"Yes, but that will be tomorrow morning. I went up to the suite when I got back here and called Bruster. He told me that it was Nadine's blood in the storage room but no fingerprints. It does prove that someone hid in there after," and he let the latter hang. Muriel nodded her head, not saying anything. The waitress arrived then to take their orders.

"Muriel, are you all right, hon?" He touched her hand that was laying on the table.

"I'm all right. I just suppose the rest of my life I will go over this. I wonder why anyone can take another person's life, just snuff it out. You might have to in self-defense but not be a cold-blooded killer. I can't understand that."

"No sane balanced person would do that. I guess that sums it up."

She just nodded again but her eyes held such a sad note. He smiled brightly at her. "Say, what did you think of the note I left for you this morning?"

She brightened and then chuckled. "You have this wondrous way, Ken Ferries. I will never again think of Goldilocks in the same way."

579

Ken winked at her. "Now, listen, lady. You get whatever suits your fancy. There are all kinds of wonderful treats here for a lovely lady to have and enjoy."

Her smile was happy again and she took a sip of coffee. "I have already started treating myself," she said. "This coffee is wonderful— I have added one of the flavorings to it. I usually never do but decided to be different today."

"See there? Doesn't it make you feel good to break the mold and let yourself drift down the river sometimes? Just go with the flow and see where it takes you." His smile was happy.

"Yes, it does, as a matter of fact. Since I have met you, I have been doing that a lot. I love it, by the way. You are so good for me."

"That, my love, is a two way street, you know," he smiled. He took her hand and kissed it. The waitress brought their orders. Ken remarked that the potato salad was great along with the sandwich. "Good choice. I am sticking with you on your food selections, my lady."

"Well, unless it's in French and then I will go along with you," she drawled.

He laughed and realized how this lady always put him in high spirits. He felt so comforted, such a sense of well-being just being with her. They finished their lunch and Ken suggested that she go treat herself while he went to make some notes and maybe sneak a twenty minute nap.

"I believe I will just do that. I saw this cute little boutique before I came in here for lunch so I'll go check it out."

Chapter____18

He gave her a kiss and said he would see her before dinner. She blew him a kiss as he stepped onto the elevator.

He sorted his notes and put them in order, adding bits and pieces as he did, He had known from the beginning that this would end up being a book, a legacy to a beautiful woman who had so cherished life. After some time on the paperwork, he went into the bedroom and removed the spread so he could stretch out. He dozed off quickly, seeing in his dream a woman in a white flowing gown with golden hair that seemed to lift as in a slight breeze. She danced and twirled while, above her, a colorful rainbow formed and showered prisms of colored lights everywhere. When he awoke a few minutes later, he lay there for a moment and smiled at the sweet message of the dream.

"Nadine," he whispered, "you know that you can be fully at peace very soon. Bless you, lovely spirit. You have given so much and I will make certain that everyone I can reach will always know you and never forget you. That is my promise to you." He found that his cheeks were wet and knew he had wept in his sleep. But he knew it was in joy and not in sorrow for this golden lady of his dream.

He arose and prepared to leave. He went to the desk to get his car and glanced around to see if Muriel was nearby but didn't see her. He hoped she was having fun.

He wondered about Franklin Donahue as he made his way to the prison, how being in this place had affected him. He knew he was a mild-mannered man from what others had said. Would he retreat farther inward now, away from people? Who could blame him, Ken thought? Yet the human spirit can and often does suffer from many conditions and then go forth to the greatest triumphs. Not all of the triumphs are widely known but they often develop the soul.

The prison loomed in front of him and he showed his pass at the entrance again. The guard waved him on. He parked and then gained entrance to the building, being escorted by another guard to the visitor's room. Jyp Donahue was soon ushered in by his own guards and Ken noted that this man was about as tall as Galin but a bit stooped. He reasoned that it undoubtedly came from hard work as a ranch hand. He still looked lean and sinewy. What clutched at Ken's heart was the man's great owl-like eyes. They held such sorrow and grief that it was almost unbearable to look at them.

Ken knew that this man had never been an intrusive person, just quietly made his way through life, offering what he could to others. He had never been one to make waves. And now he was a man in total despair. His hair was whiter than Ken recalled from the TV coverage of the trial and he seemed to slump more.

"Franklin Donahue, hello, sir. I am Ken Ferries. It is good of you to see me."

"Yes, sir," the man said. "It is my pleasure." He dropped his eyes from Ken.

Ken thought, "This might prove to be a hard interview due to the apathy of this poor man." He hoped he could gain something in the nature of hope in this poor man.

"Is it all right if I call you Jyp or would you prefer your given name?"

"Reckon it don't rightly matter. Jyp's fine. Most folks call me that."

"Well then, if that is comfortable for you, then it works fine with me too, Jyp." He smiled warmly at him, hoping to see a glimmer of life stirring. "You know, Jyp,

I am a former investigative reporter with the Waco Centennial and I have been working on you r case since before my retirement from that paper."

Jyp politely nodded, waiting for Ken to proceed. He watched him with a dispassionate expression. Ken wondered why he had agreed to see him so he decided to ask.

"Jyp, what made you decide to speak with me?"

That question seemed to take him off guard and he looked at Ken closely for the first time. For the first time, Ken saw a flicker of something in the man's eyes. Jyp was obviously searching for words, weighing them carefully before answering.

"Well, most likely, I was figuring why a man like yourself would take time to bother with a convict." His voice was low and filled with shame.

"Jyp, what if I was to tell you that I don't believe you belong in here and that I have been trying to get to the truth of what really happened that morning?"

"Well, I reckon that I would have to say I'm grateful to have at least one person who does believe us, sir. But, no offense, there's a passel of folks that don't believe like you do, else we wouldn't be here."

"Jyp, sometimes the majority can be wrong. It has happened before, you know. I have worked for many years on a lot of crime cases and I've gained some instincts about these things. Peoples' emotions often cloud their realities. In this case, I've felt from the start that not enough investigating was done." Ken leaned back and looked closely at Jyp, waiting for him to speak. When he didn't, Ken went on. "Now, Jyp, could you please go over with me what you remember about that morning you went to the Rogers home?"

Ken could see that the man had started to trust him and he slowly began to speak. "Well now, it's mighty hard for me to speak of it. I've known the Rogers' family for years, sorta thought of them like my own family. I reckon my own have passed on years ago and all. Saw them three young 'uns grow up and I even took them boys out to learn to ride when they was sprouts. Now, little Phyl, she was as frisky as a colt and she was right out there with me and the boys. By golly that child could ride like the wind was pushing her, especially on that big bay she took claim on," and for the first time he laughed. His face suddenly went sorrowful again.

He told his version of the story, often clearing his throat or shaking his head. His story was very similar to the one Galin had told earlier, with a few additional details added about their activities. "If I live to be over a hundred, I will never forget seeing that lady, so small she was and beaten down to lifelessness like a broken doll. Oh God, her blood was everywhere!" His eyes filled with tears and he choked as he wiped them away but more followed.

"Jyp, it's okay if you don't feel like going on," Ken said in an effort to comfort him. His eyes showed profound grief.

"Guess we just panicked and hustled out of there. I reckon not one of us was right in our heads. I told Galin we'd better get to the sheriff's office and report what we saw." And he continued with the story of their run-in on the road and how the sheriff saved them from certain injury or worse.

"You know, mister, I never was big on words and I never spoke of this," he drawled, "but it seems to me it ought to be spoken of before I have hung up my spurs and taken my final ride to meet my Maker."

"Yes sir," Ken said, "go right ahead, Jyp. What you say will remain with me if it is personal in nature."

"Fair enough," Jyp said, nodding his head. "Well, the first time this came about, I through I was going plum loco so I just pushed it aside. I can't take much claim to sleepin' good and I got plenty of time to think here so I'm layin' in my bunk when I see this lady. The lights had been shut down long before but I see this bright light shining in my cell, starting kind of dim but growing brighter. Now, mister, I do swear by all that is Holy, it was Mrs. Rogers and she called me by name. She told me not to give up my faith, than an earth angel would help me."

Ken could feel his skin prickle.

"It happened again a couple nights ago. The lady said to keep trusting and to hold my faith. She said the earth angel would set me free."

"Jyp, listen, what more powerful message do you need? You did get one and yes, you are of sound mind. You can trust it. I have had experiences like that myself," Ken shared and watched the man transform before him. His eyes took on radiance and suddenly he didn't look so old.

"Mr. Ferries, if I could, I would shake your hand. I am much obliged."

"That truly is all right, Jyp. Please call me Ken. Now, you will be hearing from me but is there anything else you want to tell me before I leave?"

"Yes, there is. That lad Larry Gomez is...well, I'm concerned about him. I think he may be getting in too deep with some of these bad news cons that he may go over the edge. We took him under our wings as much as we could but that boy is so bitter and filled with rage. He is either gonna be killed or kill somebody. Guess I was hopin' you could bring him some hope too." His eyes held a pleading note.

"Jyp, Larry agreed to see me in the morning. Hopefully I can give him some encouragement then. I believe that things are about to break so just keep that thought. And do hang on to your trust and faith." He smiled warmly at him.

"Yes, sir, Ken, I'm gonna do that." Jyp's expression showed that a great weight had lifted.

Ken motioned to the guard on his side to be escorted out. "Oh God, let this be over soon for these men," Ken thought as he left.

It was after four o'clock and he was anxious to return to the resort and find Muriel. He knew if she wasn't in the suite, that she would be by six so they could get ready for dinner. Then maybe he could work on his notes for a while. He hoped she had been enjoying herself.

When he reached the resort and turned in his car keys, the desk clerk told him he had a message and handed him a note. He read it as he walked to the elevator. It was from Bruster, asking him to call as soon as possible. He scanned the lobby as he walked through but didn't see Muriel. "Wonder what Bruster has to tell me?" he thought.

He opened the suite door and found that Muriel was not there. He sat down to call Bruster. Katie didn't answer this time but Bruster did.

"Bruster, hello. Just got your message. What's up?"

'Well, Ken, we've got a situation here and I just wanted to know if you could shed some light on it."

"I will if I can."

"I will get right to the heart of it. Pace Allard was in here today to file a missing person report on his wife. It seems that her car was still at that art center building today. Did you see her yesterday at the art show?"

"Yes, Muriel and I did see Marilyn at the art show. And I want to confide in you that she had been beaten— she had a black eye she had tried to conceal and some badly bruised wrists. Bruster, the woman is terrified of her husband."

"Oh, God Ken. You're not telling me that you think Pace did something to Marilyn and came in here to cover it up?"

"No, thankfully, but if she hadn't left, he would have eventually killed her. I do know where she went but I promised not to reveal that."

"Well, as long as it was her choice to leave and she is all right, I will not pursue this. She has a right to leave that man but, I want to tell you, this guy is a persistent SOB. I just hope he doesn't get someone to track her down."

"I really think she will be all right. She will be now that she has left him."

"I do hope so. We've had enough trouble with murder here and don't need another tragedy. How is Franklin Donahue holding up? I have been concerned about him and Larry Gomez.'

"I won't be seeing Larry until morning. I saw Franklin this afternoon and I think he is holding more peace now. But when they brought him into the visiting room, you never saw a more broken man. I don't think he would have lasted much longer. He is extremely concerned about Larry. He says Larry is full of rage and asking for trouble."

"Oh Lord, Ken,, I pray that boy can put this behind him once he gets out. He will need some therapy but I'm going to do what I can to help them all out. The older fellows will probably adjust faster than Larry does."

'If he can survive this thing until we get him out, I just believe he will level out. It will probably take some help but I think he can make it."

"That boy's always been a free-wheeler and kinda thumbed his nose at rules but basically he is a good kid. I just never figured him for a killer though. Well, I'll let you go now. Just enjoy getting together with your family and we'll keep in touch."

'Wait, Bruster, I darn near forgot to ask you again. Did you happen to give the Judge and Con another update?"

"Sure did, Ken. I told them about the blood being the victim's in that storage area. They thanked me, which is certainly not the Judge's usual style," he chuckled.

Ken laughed and they said their good-bys. Then he worked on his notes, putting them in order and adding to them as needed. As he was storing them in his briefcase, Muriel entered the suite with some shopping bags. He noticed that she had on a smart looking new sundress of soft pastel colors and her hair was swept up in a cluster of soft curls. Her long tanned legs were housed in smart sandals.

"You are a vision of loveliness, pretty lady, like a perfect spring day," he smiled. He held his arms out to her. She put her packages on a chair and twirled around once before landing in his arms.

"Then I meet with your approval?" she smiled sweetly at him.

"You always meet my approval. You are so totally lovely in every way."

"I've got to show you what all I bought, sweetheart. And, by the way, I had the works right down to a pedicure in the salon. Never had a pedicure in my life. If I had know what it does for feet, I would have treated myself to it before." Her smile was shining, showing the inner joy she felt.

"Let's just have a look," he prompted, sharing her enthusiasm.

She produced an assortment of silky lingerie while Ken gave a wolf whistle. She slapped him playfully while he ducked. After she had shown off her other treats, she gave him a gift and watched excitedly as he opened it, protesting.

"Honey, this was to be your special day to treat yourself," he said.

"I did but part of that treat is treating you, big man," she said sexily.

He winked at her suggestive statement. The small velvet box he unwrapped held a man's ring with a beautiful emerald stone setting. Ken gasped at this precious stone, knowing that Muriel had purchased it herself because he had not given her enough for such an expensive piece of jewelry. He was speechless, just staring down at this gift and then back at Muriel.

"Happy birthday, baby," her voice was extra husky with emotion.

Ken finally found his voice. "But, Muriel honey, you can't afford this. I mean…" and he flushed as his voice trailed off.

"Don't you like it, Ken?"

"It's beautiful. Oh, honey, of course I love it but it is such a generous gift. I even forgot it is my birthday."

"Well, I didn't and yes, I can afford it. I have set some money aside for a rainy day and it was a fairly nice amount."

"Come here, kitten. I just love you so much and didn't mean to offend you."

"You didn't. You just want to take care of me and you need to learn to allow me the same privilege of taking care of you. Now, let's make sure it fits. I've had this in mind for a while so I took the measurement of your ring finger one morning while you were sleeping." Her eyes sparked with a little amusement.

"Muriel, you just surprise the heck out of me with all these little tricks up your sleeve." He kissed her and put the ring on, then held his hand up for her to see. "Look, it fits perfectly. Now listen you little minx, maybe a certain lady needs to help an old man celebrate his sixty-first birthday with an evening on the town."

She looked around with a vague stare.

"What is it, hon? Is something wrong?" he asked concerned.

"I was looking around for that old man we are going to celebrate with," she said innocently.

"Come over here, pretty lady, before my heart swells so big that I cry like a little kid." They kissed with sweetness, expressing their tenderness. Then Ken smiled, "Shall we go someplace away from the resort this evening?"

"You're the birthday boy so it's your choice. I am ready if you will just let me touch up my lipstick." She slipped away while Ken checked his appearance.

When they were both ready, they made their way to the lobby and called for the car. After settling in, Ken decided to go where they danced to country music. HE knew the restaurant was good there too.

The place was in the style of a large red barn with wagon wheels and hay bales strategically placed at the entrance. They entered the restaurant and were greeted by a young dark-eyed Hispanic woman with a pretty smile. Her attire consisted of snug blue jeans with rivets at the pockets and a Western shirt in the design of the Texas flag, the Lone Star just above her shoulder.

"Good evening, folks. Welcome to Bucky's Corral. Would you prefer smoking or non-smoking?" They selected a booth in the non-smoking area and another waitress dressed in Western attire came to hand them menus and take their drink orders.

"This is neat, Ken. You didn't decide on this because of me, though, did you?" Muriel posed to him.

"No, no, honey. We both like this kind of setting. You are forgetting that I am basically an old country boy." He chuckled at her look of concern.

They studied the menu and then Ken asked, "Are you game for those hickory smoked spare ribs or are they too messy?"

"Let's go for it. We can get messy— it's your birthday and I'm open to anything that paddles your canoe, babe," and she gave him a broad sexy wink.

"Say now, is that a double-barreled answer or what?" he grinned at her.

"Oh, take it in the best context. Whatever makes you happy," she said, still flirting with him.

They were chuckling still when the waitress came to take their orders. When she returned, she handed them each a large bib with a Lone Star design on the front and Bucky's sprawling signature under the star. In a few minutes, she was back with their ribs along with side dishes of Western style beans and golden corn on the cob.

"Whew, girl, is this living or what?" Ken's handsome broad features spread into a wide grin. "I do believe I can get around all of this very nicely." He suddenly realized he was quite hungry.

Muriel looked a little overwhelmed with the amount of food but then she gamely dug in after tying the bib in place and placing the huge napkin on her lap. Ken was grinning at her as she ate, her lips covered with hickory sauce. She was concentrating so heavily on her ribs that she was unaware that Ken had stopped eating to watch her. She reminded him of a little girl at a watermelon-eating contest. Finally she looked up, still holding a rib in her hand. "What?" she said with a smear of sauce on the end of her nose.

"You, that's what. Did you know that you are as cute as a little pup sitting there with hickory sauce on the end of your nose? I adore you, pretty lady."

"Well, I am glad you find such favor with me, even with a face smeared with sauce," she said, reaching for a towelette to wipe her hands and face. "Good thing I came prepared to touch up my makeup," she giggled.

"I wouldn't care if you were covered in sauce. I would still find you irresistible," he quipped sweetly.

They finished the meal and made their way to the dance hall, entering from the restaurant into a bar. The large dance hall had a stage at one end, with tables and chairs surrounding the outside edges. A hoedown was in progress so they found an available table and sat down to watch the square dancers twirl around the room.

"You want to give that a try when they break?" he spoke loudly, leaning across the table in order for her to hear above the square dance caller and two fiddlers.

"Sure but I won't promise much. I'm pretty rusty on all this since it's been a lot of years since I've square-danced," she yelled, leaning close to him.

"That makes two of us, honey, so let's go for it." They clasped hands across the table.

When they swung into the next call, it felt natural to Ken and he could tell it was for Muriel too. They were having a grand time and formed quick friendships with other couples dancing. Their elation gave their spirits wings. The evening passed too soon and they left for the car giggling like two teens on a date.

"Ken, wasn't that fun?"

"Yes, but mostly because we were together and together we match like cheese and crackers." He hugged her close.

"Or like peanut butter and jam," she giggled.

"Or maybe like oil and vinegar," he countered.

"I got another one. Wait a minute— like toast and butter," she added.

"How about sardines and crackers?" he returned.

'Ugh," she grinned and then giggled. "You win."

They got in the car and Ken turned to her and kissed her. "How would you like to round this up with a dip in the pool at the resort?"

"If you're game, baby, so am I," she whispered seductively.

They arrived at the resort and the clerk called for an attendant to put the car in the garage.

"Is it too late to use the pool?" Ken asked the desk clerk.

"Oh no, sir. The pool is available at any time for our guests," he politely replied.

They went to their suite to change and wrapped terry cloth jackets over their suits. At the pool, Muriel dropped her robe on a chair, then walked to the end of the diving board. Before diving, she said, "Last one in is a rotten egg." She dove, her slender body cleanly breaking the water. When she surfaced, she said, "Say there, handsome, why don't you join me?"

Ken dove into the water and swam to her. "Muriel, my girl, you are so perfectly lovely." They kissed long and passionately. They swam until they grew tired and then returned to the suite. Once they retired, they were both fast asleep within minutes.

When Ken awoke, he frantically looked at the clock on the nightstand and felt relief that he hadn't overslept. He turned to look at Muriel but she wasn't in bed. At that moment, she walked in, carrying a cup of coffee and smiling softly at him.

"You were sleeping so soundly, my sweet, so I got up and took the liberty of requesting that room service bring us breakfast." She handed him the cup and saucer.

"Oh, honey girl, bless you. It will save some time this way since I slept in." He sipped at the coffee, then set it on the nightstand. "Listen, I will get presentable and then we will eat after a shower."

"Great," she smiled sweetly at him and picked up the cup and saucer. "I will just wait for you until you are ready."

After showering and dressing, he made his way into the living room. Everything was in readiness— a white tablecloth covering the table set for two, plates with silver domes covering the food. A vase with pink and white rosebuds sat in the center.

"Now, this is royalty," he bent to kiss Muriel before sitting down. She was wearing one of the sleepwear sets she had purchased the day before, a soft aqua that intensified the depth of color in her eyes.

Ken lifted one of the domed lids to see what kind of breakfast awaited them. HE winked at Muriel as he spotted Eggs Benedict. He knew it was her favorite and it looked very tasty. "This really is perfect, isn't it pretty lady?" He took a bite of eggs.

They also enjoyed a melon assortment and sticky buns which tasted great with the coffee.

"I am so pleased to make you happy," she smiled at him, looking radiant with her pretty hair shining in the sunlight filtering through the sheer panels of drapes.

"I believe it is an on-going contest between us, girl, pleasing each other. That is the way I feel about you, darling. I just want to give you happiness the rest of our lives."

"Well, Ken, you do. Just to think of you gives me such joy and happiness. I couldn't even describe it if I tried." Her voice was deeply husky.

They finished breakfast and Ken gathered his things. Muriel turned on the television and told him to dress cool since it would be 100 degrees that day.

"Yes, I suspected it might be. It has been heading that way for a few days now. As soon as we can, we will go enjoy those cool ocean breezes on the north coast."

"I am looking forward to it, Mr. Ferries," she winked at him.

"Me too, soon to be Mrs. Ferries." They kissed and Ken picked up his briefcase, went to the door and blew her a kiss before he left. She returned the kiss.

He knew he would have just enough time to get to the prison. He could already see the heat waves rising from the pavement. "Weather like this makes one appreciate air conditioning," he thought as he drove along. He hoped that tomorrow would bring a break in the heat.

The same guard waved him in as he showed his pass at the gate. A different guard escorted him to the visitor's room. Larry Gomez soon arrived and sat in the chair opposite Ken.

"God, he is so young," Ken thought looking at him. He had deep hazel eyes and skin lighter than most Hispanics. His hair glistened a deep crisp black. His movements showed a cat-like vigor and he regarded Ken with a cold suspicious manner. He reached for the phone device as soon as Ken did and waited for him to speak.

"Larry, I am Ken Ferries. I came here yesterday and interview both Galin and Franklin. Have you had a chance to speak with either of these men since they saw me yesterday?"

"Yeah, what about it?" he answered sullenly.

Ken thought, "Oh, boy, this kid is going to be hard to reach." HE could see that the youth's trust had been shattered.

He spoke to Larry, "Then you know that I have been investigating this case for some time now and have uncovered some things we feel may help you all."

Larry asked with suspicion, "You said we. Who is we?" His voice was flat with a sneering overtone.

Ken held his cold stare evenly and decided to tell him something that might jolt him enough to be responsive.

"Well, Sheriff Hernado for one and Muriel Jacob for another and another Rosewood resident I can't reveal at this time."

He was caught off guard with this information and Ken saw his jaw go slack with surprise. Now that the mean look had eased, Ken could see he was an exceptionally handsome youth. He was at a loss for words. Then something else showed in his eyes, perhaps a flicker of hope.

"This isn't some kind of rotten joke just so you can get an interesting story, now is it, mister?" His voice held that icy edge again.

"Larry, I wouldn't waste my time on it one speck if I didn't believe that important new evidence was being uncovered. I did investigative reporting when you were just a twinkle in your Mama's eyes. And speaking of which, I had the pleasure of meeting her and you are mighty blessed to have such a lady for your mother."

Larry swallowed hard and Ken knew without question that he adored his mother. He sensed that she would be a main factor in bringing the boy around when he was released.

"You met my Mom?" he said and his voice had softened. "How is she? Did she say how my Pop is and my little sister?"

"She is wonderful and prays all the time for you. She believes in you, Larry, so don't let her down." He looked straight into Larry's eyes somewhat sternly. "Now, your father has not been too well and your little sister is depressed, your mother told Muriel. But, you listen to me, Larry, that will all change once you are free. Several of us are working toward that goal."

From that point on, things smoothed between them. That allowed Ken to lead him to the time when he discovered Nadine's body.

"Guess you have been told how it was and all," Larry began and it was difficult to see the deep sorrow on his face. Ken could see that he held the deepest respect for the Rogers' family and thought of the Rogers' boys as his brothers.

'Yes, I have but I want you to tell me what it was like for you, Larry. What you remember is important."

He told the same story of going to the house to pick up their checks after changing clothes at the bunkhouse. Then they had planned to go into town to spend their day off. Larry struggled to tell of finding Nadine and then he remembered very little until the guys in the other pickup started shooting at them.

"I couldn't believe we were accused of killing Nadine, much less being sent to prison for it. If anybody had tried to hurt her with me around, they wouldn't have gotten far. Mr. Ferries, I used to scrap with some fellas my age but hurting people is not my style. I would never be violent to a woman," and his eyes filled with tears.

"Larry, I believe you. Like I said, there are other who know you and don't believe you would do that."

Larry angrily wiped the tears from his eyes and said in a ragged voice, "Well, man, thank you for that. Tell folks I do appreciate it and would you tell my family that I love them?"

"You bet I will, Larry. Now, son, just know that I am getting the wheels rolling here so just hang on. I got a feeling it won't be long before we see you in Rosewood." He smiled warmly at him.

"I do aim to hang on now. I didn't care about anything until today so thanks. I got something to keep breathing for now." He smiled, exposing his perfect white teeth.

Ken watched as the guards led this young man away. His body language expressed a different countenance than when he came in and Ken was glad. He said a silent prayer that it wouldn't take long to free these men, then he stood up and followed the guard out.

When he reached his car, he opened the door and a blast of heat assailed him. So he started the engine and the air conditioning, then opened the windows to let the heat out. After standing outside a few moments, he climbed in, rolled up the windows and started back toward the resort.

Since it was still a while before check-out time, he thought perhaps he and Muriel could go to the coffee shop for an early lunch. That way they wouldn't have to stop in the heat of the day for lunch. And they would be in Houston by suppertime at another resort Ken had reserved for them.

When he reached their suite, he found that Muriel had packed all of their belongings. Ken asked her if she would like to have an early, unhurried lunch.

"Sure would but I only need a light one after that man-sized breakfast we put away," and she kissed him. She stood back, holding his hands and asked, "Ken, how was Larry?"

"At first he reeked of anger and suspicion but, when I was able to get him to hear that there were people who didn't believe he was guilty, he softened. I also told him I had met his mother. He asked me to tell you and the sheriff and anyone else who believed in him that it is appreciated. He also asked me to tell his family that he loves them. It was a different young man who returned with those guards to his cell."

"I am so sad that these men have spent almost a year of their lives in prison for a crime they were never guilty of. That is bound to leave some terrible scars."

"That's one reason I hope they will all get some therapy. I do believe that the human spirit can heal from bad experiences if it is allowed to. I suspect that these men have the capacity to heal. Frankly, I think Jyp and Larry were both at a dangerous crossroads and wouldn't survive safely much longer. Galin was already jail-wise from his previous trouble but even so, prison is a dangerous place to be."

Muriel retrieved her purse from a nearby table and they made their way to the coffee shop. They both ordered generous fruit salads on crisp lettuce and raspberry iced tea. After lunch, they returned to their suite and called the bellhop to come for their luggage. That done, they returned to the lobby to check out.

The ride to Houston was filled with talk and plans for their wedding. They also became more and more excited about surprising Ken's children with his bride-to-be.

The resort was as beautiful as the previous one and housed a jewelry store, as the other one had. When they settled in, Ken suggested that Muriel rest a bit before supper. He was relieved when she agreed to a long relaxing bath and a cat nap.

He waited until he knew she was in the tub and then quietly left to go to the jewelry store. The set that he selected was an exquisite matching engagement and wedding ring. The man's wedding band was a harmonious match to Muriel's set.

Ken let himself back into the room, hoping she had not realized he was gone. It had been close to a half hour but he knew ladies had a tendency to linger over a good tub soak when they could.

He checked the bedroom and found her curled up like a sleeping kitten. Soundlessly, he closed the door and decided to go over his notes some more. He thought he would wait to present Muriel with the rings over a candlelight supper.

Before starting on the notes, he picked up the phone and called Carter. Carter's voice, so like his own, answered with a greeting that never failed to warm him. He thought again how much he missed his children.

"Carter, son, I am here in Houston."

"Dad," his voice sounded pleased. "When did you get here?"

"Oh, about an hour ago." He had been careful not to say "we". He explained that he was tired from the drive and decided to get a good night's rest. "So, listen son, I will be there first thing in the morning. What time are Holly and Bart arriving?"

"Holly called to say they will arrive about 10 so I will get them at the airport. Dad, she has been almost tormenting me to death with questions about you. She won't believe that I don't know anything." He laughed lightly then went on. "You know, I really think she should have been the sleuth in the family."

They both chuckled at that and Ken wondered how many times she had called Carter. "Yes, she has always been a topnotch interrogator and not at all able to contain herself when Christmas or birthdays rolled around."

"I sure do remember. She would try to bribe me in every way she could devise and with all the goodies Mom and Sarita could provide. I don't know how any package could survive her shaking, even the ones that weren't hers. Ah well, nobody has a sister sweeter than Holly."

"Yes, we are so blessed. But then, I am double-blessed with children." His voice was husky with emotion.

'We are too, Dad, because we truly lucked out to get you for a father." Carter's voice also held a husky note. "Now, do you think you could get here about 8am and I could take the family out for breakfast? I know this great restaurant close by my apartment complex."

"Sure, Carter, that sounds great. I am looking forward to it. Is Lila coming too? I hope so. She is a lovely young woman. I took to her and so did the rest of the family."

"Well, she did to all of you too. Yes, she will be there," he assured Ken.

"Great. Then, son, I will see you all in the morning."

"Can't wait, Dad. I miss you all so much. This is going to be a great weekend together."

Carter seemed lighter to Ken, happier than he remembered him to be in quite a while. He suspected it had to do with the beautiful and spirited Lila. After all, he hadn't been that old when Gloria died. Holly had also just been a young adult. He reasoned that usually people expect their parents to have a longer life expectancy.

As he spread his notes on the table, he wondered about Marilyn and Jeff. He hoped they had reached Jeff's uncle's ranch in Montana. The thought struck him that Marilyn's parents might have started their own search by now. He decided he would try reaching Bruster at his office or at home to ask him to inform them about their daughter. They had no way of knowing that their daughter had been in danger, that Pace had been abusive to her. She had been so careful to conceal the abuse, as is so often the case with battered women. The logic of an abused person is not often sound due to their extreme stress and feelings of low self-worth.

He called the sheriff's office and was just about to hang up when Bruster answered. "Bruster, Ken here. I am so glad I was able to reach you."

"I'm glad you called when you did. I was just heading out of here to go home. I had been working a little late to catch up on paperwork. I sent Katie away for a week to her daughter's. She's been needing some time off. Bless her, she is my gal Friday. I can see already how invaluable that lady is. Now, what's going on, Ken? Where are you at by now?"

"We got into Houston about two hours ago and checked in at this resort. Tomorrow morning we will be over at my son's. The daughter and her husband are due in tonight and Carter is picking them up at the airport. Everything is going

along well. Now, Bruster, a thought hit me a while ago and I don't rightly know

why it didn't occur to me before. You see, the Falzone's are no doubt frantic over

Marilyn. Have they contacted you?"

Chapter____19

"Yes, they were in here earlier and were both scared to death over their daughter. It is Marilyn's habit to stop over to their home fairly regularly or she calls them every day. Seems that Pace went out there and wanted to know if they had heard from her. He told them she may have been kidnapped since her car was left at the art center and she had been gone all night. I had to explain to them that she had left Pace for her own safety but that she would call them. I told them that she was all right but under no circumstances should they tell Pace that she had left of her own accord. I had to calm Mr. Falzone down when I told them that Marilyn was terrified of Pace. He demanded to know why she had stayed, that he would have protected her. Mrs. Falzone sat there quietly with tears running down her face, but finally said she had asked Marilyn if she was abused because she seemed so unhappy, but Marilyn denied it."

"You can see how that comes about but a surprising number of people don't understand it. A woman can get so traumatized by an evil person like Pace that they can't think. So many women end up murdered by these nuts. Thank heaven more light is being shed on this area all the time but many are still in a cloud of ignorance."

"I couldn't agree with you more, Ken. Maybe you had better call Marilyn and have her get hold of her parents. They are not about to tell Pace they have heard from her but it will rest their minds knowing she is all right."

He called Jeff's uncle right away on the off chance that they had arrived there. A man's voice answered and Ken supposed it was the uncle.

"Mr. Colter, this is Ken Ferries. I think that Jeff may have told you I would be calling. Is he there by chance?"

"No, sir, they haven't got here just yet. But Jeff called me this evening to say they will be here in the morning. You can leave a message if you want and I will relay it to them when they get here."

Ken told the man why he had called and the man was agreeable to pass it on. When he hung up, Ken felt a sense of relief, knowing that all would go well from this point on. He was glad they were almost there, knowing they had traveled quickly to get there as soon as possible. Jeff would undoubtedly know that Pace would find her absent soon and jump to some conclusions, especially after he found out Jeff was gone.

Ken just hope he would not find them but he knew there had been no choice but to get Marilyn away from there. Hopefully, a Montana ranch was remote enough to hide them as long as necessary.

He had worked on his notes close to twenty minutes when Muriel came into the room. He didn't notice her until she put her arms around his shoulders and kissed the back of his neck. He clasped her arms for a moment. Then she stepped around in front of him, striking a pose. She was dressed in an elegant evening gown of street length in a deep shade of plum. Matching heels accented her shapely legs.

"Wow, luscious lady, you are a knock-out!" He gave a low wolf whistle while taking in every bit of this alluring woman. She smiled teasingly at him.

"I wanted to surprise you with this so I waited until this evening to put it on. I thought you might like it," and her eyes sparkled with pleasure.

"Muriel, you are one lovely woman and I haven't seen one thing about you yet that I wouldn't love. You are definitely sensational in that dress." He stood up and kissed her, holding her close to him, knowing that he had better not give way to the rising passion he felt.

"Well, pretty lady, I had better get going and shower so I can take my love out for a wonderful candlelight supper. Let's see, it's seven o'clock so I won't be long, honey." He departed for the bathroom.

After a cool shower and shave, he selected an appropriate suit for the evening, a silver gray with a very pale pink shirt that Sarita had literally begged him to purchase. He topped it off with a silver gray tie and then stood back to inspect himself in the full length mirror. He deduced that Sarita had been right about the shirt— the colors were stunning together. Ken was appreciative of the way he looked and hoped that Muriel would find him so. He gave his hair a final inspection and then pocketed the rings in the inside jacket pocket. He returned to the living area and Muriel's eyes widened, then she whistled at him as he had whistled at her earlier.

"Wow, do I get to go stepping out with this big handsome man? I will be the envy of every woman around." She came to him and put her arms around his waist. "Mmm, you smell so fine. What is that you have on, Mr. Ferries?"

"You like that? It's called Fendi for men. I decided to try it and hoped you would like it. There is some for ladies too so maybe we should get you some. What do you think of this shirt Sarita insisted I buy? When she gets her mind set, she most often wins." He laughed good-naturedly.

"She was completely correct because it is a perfect compliment for you. You look great. And by the way, the two of us go together with our colors, don't you think?"

"Yes, we do, but honey, we go good together without a stitch on too," he teased and lifted her off the floor to swing her around. When he stopped, she swatted his behind playfully. "Let's go before I get ideas. Besides, I'm hungry. The salad we had at lunch waned some time ago."

They made their way to the elegant dining area and Ken requested a table that would be more private. He ordered champagne as the waiter handed them menus. Massive chandeliers hung from the ceiling, making the crystal candle-holders sparkle. The soft light from the candles gave a flickering glow to their faces. When the waiter returned with the champagne, he filled their glasses and retreated. Ken held his glass aloft and Muriel did the same.

"To the soon-to-be Mrs. Ferries, my lovely counterpart, who was joined with me by the force of a beautiful presence who would not be stilled and who will live on to bring peace to hearts and joy to lives". His voice was heavy with the emotion he felt. They each took a sip of the wine after lightly clinking their glasses.

"All right, it's my turn." Her voice was low and her eyes were bright with the love she felt for this man. "Ken, you are my beloved and I am honored to be your wife. And since I do not believe in happenstance, I know that Nadine, my dearest friend, is waiting in the wings to bless this beautiful marriage. I thank you with all my heart for bringing him to me." Her eyes became a dazzle of lights from unshed tears. They repeated the clinking of glasses and took another sip.

Ken reached inside the pocket of his suit and produced the gold lame ring box. He placed it in front of her dinner plate. She looked from the jewelry box to Ken with some surprise etched on her face. "Well, Ken Ferries, what have you done here?" she said while a slow delighted smiled formed.

"Just open it up, pretty lady. It is for you and I hope you like it," he grinned at her and then winked. She reached for it and her eyes held his until she looked down and opened the box. She gasped at the brilliance and beauty of the set of rings inside.

"Oh, Ken, they are just beautiful. Oh, honey, this is too generous. I mean, these are a fortune," she said still stunned. She looked at him wide-eyed, her jaw hanging slack.

"Listen, you are the girl I love and cherish beyond anything. I would give you the stars and the moon if I could, all wrapped up in silver and gold. Now, hand me that box and allow me to put this engagement ring on your pretty finger."

She did and he held her hand, kissing it after inspecting the ring that was a perfect fit. When she looked down to stare lovingly at the ring, she whispered, "Ken, I love you, my darling. Thank you."

"You're welcome, sweetheart, but I thank you too," he answered back softly. He looked at her across the table, seeing the candlelight flicker across her face. He suddenly saw her from another time. They were in an elegant room something like this, at a table with soft candlelight. She was probably less than twenty years old and he was not much more. They were dressed in beautiful ballroom clothing and · were deeply in love. She was extracting a promise from him that he would return to her safely. He was promising that he would while he reached across the table to take her hand. He stood up and bowed in a courtly manner. She followed him as he led her to the dance floor where they joined others in a minuet. The scene faded and he smiled at her. He was unaware that the waiter had asked to take their orders.

"Please, sir, could we have a few more minutes to go over the menu?" Ken addressed him.

"Oh, but of course. Allow me, please," and he refilled their glasses. He stepped back, still smiling and said, "If I may suggest, madam, sir, the orange duck is excellent and a specialty of the house."

Ken looked inquiringly at Muriel and she nodded.

"Well, yes, that sounds wonderful. The lady and I are both in agreement."

"Very good, sir. And our chef creates his own special Cherries Jubilee with a flaming liqueur," he said, smiling temptingly.

"Oh, my, but that does sound heavenly," Muriel smiled at the waiter.

"You will not be sorry, madam. A wise choice, and for you, sir?" he turned to Ken again.

"I wouldn't miss out on such a treat," he assured the waiter politely. "Thank you, sir." The waiter, still smiling, bowed and departed.

"Muriel, do you remember at the dance at Windom Hall, you mentioned to me that you had seen us in another time and place?"

"Yes, yes, I do. I told you then that I could see it was us and we were dancing," she answered.

"Well, tell me, hon, what do you recall about that vision you had?"

She looked around the room and then back to Ken. "It was all very posh like this and we were dressed in clothing of that time period, which seemed to be the Revolutionary War era. Oh, we were having a fine time and yet we were both sad because you were going away. I was afraid I would never see you again. I felt like you had been called away to the war."

"I am certain that you saw an accurate account of it because I saw it too, just a few minutes ago. I was so caught up with seeing you at that other time, I was not even aware that the waiter had come to our table," he chuckled. "We were younger, you were hardly more than a girl. I was probably an old man of twenty one or two." He shook his head and laughed lightly. "I do know that we were as deeply in love then as we are now," and he smiled, looking into her eyes with such tenderness.

"I think that love that is real carries on forever, Ken. It knows no limits or boundaries." He nodded his agreement.

Their meal came and they exclaimed that it was every bit the gourmet wonder their waiter had claimed. Muriel was enchanted when, after the main entrée, the waiter skillfully produced a flaming dessert. She fully enjoyed the spectacle. She had relaxed this evening and a new assurance shone in her.

After dinner, they went to dance in the resort's ballroom until midnight and then returned to their suite. They whispered their love and came together in tender lovemaking. The consistent hum of the bedside alarm awoke Ken and he easily slipped out of bed trying not to disturb Muriel. He reached for his robe and slipped it on. When he turned to look at Muriel, she was watching him, a little smile playing on her lips.

"Oh, hon, I guess, with the excitement of our official engagement, I forgot to tell you that I called Carter while you were napping yesterday. He wants to take all the family out to breakfast this morning."

She got out of bed and looked at Ken evenly. "You do know that this is going to be a large shock to them since you haven't said a word about us to them."

He came to her, putting his hands on her shoulders and looking her in the eyes. "Muriel, how well do you know Angie?"

"Why, I feel that I know her as well as I do myself," she said and her eyes never wavered from his.

"Well, then, my green-eyed kitten, I want to tell you that I feel the same about Carter and Holly so please trust me on this." He turned her around by her shoulders. "Now, you go in that bathroom and get ready to meet the kids."

She turned to him just before she walked away, smiling, "All right, big daddy. I will just let you lead this parade." He swatted her firm bottom and gave her a gentle shove toward the bathroom.

He only waited a short time in the living room before she came in looking fresh and cool in an iridescent lilac pants set with a white embroidered tee and white sandals. The color set off her tan and made her a vision of loveliness.

"Muriel, you are so beautiful. You are my goddess," his voice was full of emotion as he looked at her.

She came over to him and bent down to kiss him softly. "You are not so bad yourself, my handsome hunk. Just in case you don't know it, you manage to take my breath away just thinking of you." She pulled on both of his hands and said,

"Come on, now. Let's go so I can meet those children of yours. I just know I will love them because, after all, they are part of you. How can I miss?" Her eyes were twinkling.

As they drove, Ken thought how nice it was that traffic was light early on this Saturday. He knew it would be intense later.

"Honey, you know that Carter was in the service a while and, when he came home, he decided to come here to Houston for college. He just wasn't sure what he wanted to do career-wise. Then, one day, he called me and said he had decided on police science. It did surprise me because he had leaned toward journalism earlier. But I felt that whatever he decided on was fine. I have always been supportive of whatever my children choose. So, now he is about to graduate from the academy. You will have to come back with me in a couple weeks for his graduation?" He left it hanging as a question.

"Oh, Ken, honey, you bet. We will both be here. That is a special event we will not miss."

The apartment complex was in a nice setting, a semi-suburban type with a private gate one had to enter. They parked in the guest area and then walked to a nearby section of apartments. Ken pressed the doorbell on a lower floor apartment and the door swung open. A young man around mid-twenties stood there and Muriel caught her breath at this image of Ken in front of her.

"Dad," he greeted him and the two embraced. Then he stepped back and smiled quizzically at Muriel.

Ken said, "Carter, meet Muriel Jacob. Muriel, my son Carter."

Carter took Muriel's hand and looked keenly at her, still smiling. "Well, Dad, Muriel, come on in here. Muriel, it is a pleasure to meet you."

"My pleasure to meet you too, Carter. You certainly look like your father," she smiled warmly at him.

"So I have been told." Then he chuckled, "Just better looking, that's all." And he hugged Ken, who was nodding his agreement.

They were standing in a foyer when suddenly a small pretty woman flew to Ken from an adjoining room. She was squealing with joy as she jumped into Ken's arms, her arms encircling his neck. She hugged him hard. "Oh, Daddy, you look so good. I just couldn't wait until you got here." She hadn't seen Muriel yet in her excitement. She was chattering ceaselessly and Ken was smiling down at her.

Finally he said, "Where is the other part of this family? Didn't Bart come too?"

"Oh, sure, he just didn't want to get trampled in the stampede," Carter drawled. "He is in the living room."

Suddenly Holly became aware of Muriel standing back smiling. Holly's eyes widened in surprise and Ken had the amusing thought that for once his pert little daughter was at a loss for words.

"Holly, this is Muriel. Muriel, my daughter, Holly."

"Why, why, it is a pleasure to meet you, Muriel," Holly sputtered.

"It is my pleasure, Holly," Muriel greeted her back warmly.

"Well, come on in the living room. Bart and Lila are waiting to greet you all too." Carter directed them and took Holly's arm to hold her back so Muriel and Ken could go first. Ken knew without seeing Holly that she was making a questioning gesture to Carter, her eyes wide with wonder. He decided that he would let this sit a while before he would explain that Muriel was his bride-to-be. He fought to suppress a chuckle at this endurance test for his daughter's insatiable curiosity.

A tall blond man greeted them when they came into the living room. "Well, Ken, it's been a while." He came to him for a hug, followed by a strong handshake. With a warm smile still on his face, he extended his hand to Muriel. "Hello, I am Holly's other half, Bart. And you are?" he asked as he shook her hand.

Before Muriel could speak, Ken said, "This is Muriel Jacob from Rosewood, Texas."

"So, it is good to meet you, Muriel," he said with a friendliness that Ken could see put Muriel at immediate ease. Bart had that way with people.

Lila came into the living room then, smiling broadly. When she saw Ken, she came over to him and gave him a hug and a kiss on the cheek. "Ken, you look great. It has been some time since we've seen you personally. I've missed you. I was just in the kitchen making coffee for later." She turned to Muriel waiting for an introduction.

"Lila, this is Muriel Jacob. Muriel, meet Carter's friend Lila Quinn." Ken noted that Lila's eyes still held that spark of mischief he had admired before. That vibrancy and quick wit were part of her good nature. Ken could see that she had already surmised that he was teasing his daughter with the surprise of his companion and she found it amusing.

Ken could see that Muriel was wondering when he was going to tell all of them who this lovely woman really was, that she was going to be Mrs. Ken Ferries shortly. But she was leaving it all up to him, knowing he was waiting for the right time.

"Well, now that is all done," Carter said, in high spirits. He came over to put his arm around Lila's waist and suggested that they all follow his car over to the nearby restaurant. "Why don't you and Bart come with us, Holly? Dad and Muriel can follow."

Holly looked perplexed and gave her brother a meaningful look, which he received with a wide grin of amusement. Ken was straining to maintain a "poker" face as they all trooped outside. Carter went to the garage to retrieve his car and Ken and Muriel went to get settled in theirs. They followed along behind Carter to the restaurant.

Finally Muriel couldn't stand it. "All right, Mr. Ferries. What is going on or would you care to share it with me?"

Ken finally let out the chuckles he had been holding back. He reached for Muriel's hand and squeezed it lightly. "You know, I told you that Holly girl cant' stand secrets. We jokingly call her the family sleuth. Well, we are having fun with her, testing her to see how long she can hold out before she starts the major interrogations," and he chuckled again.

"Ken, are you sure you are doing the right thing? Won't you hurt Holly's feelings?" Muriel held a note of concern.

"Holly? No way, not that little minx. She enjoys the pursuit of the digging and the sorting out. The interrogation is part of the fun for her." He chuckled again.

"Well, I see you know all of the family dynamics so I am just going to relax and watch the interaction," she added on a husky note and grinned.

"I love you so, my pretty lady and I can tell you this. My whole family will too so just relax there, pardner, and enjoy it all."

"Oh, you bet I will. Listen, while I think about it, let's give Angie a call this evening. I haven't talked to her in a while and I want to be certain she is doing all right. I would like to update her too," and she held up her engagement ring and flipped her fingers around.

"You bet we will. I would like to talk with Angie too. I have grown deeply fond of that sweet daughter that I want to be my daughter too."

'Well, one thing I believe is that all of them will like Angie because I know she will like them," Muriel said contentedly.

"You will see shortly just how happy this family will be to welcome you. They will be happy about us and they will love Angie. Trust me on this, sweetheart."

Carter pulled into a parking lot and Ken found a place near his. They all walked into the restaurant. They were escorted to a sizable table and Ken noticed that Holly slid quickly into the chair next to Muriel ahead of Lila who was just ready to sit there. Lila winked at Ken and moved to the seat on the other side of him. Carter sat across from Lila and Bart sat next to him. The waitress took their beverage orders and Carter opened the conversation with a question to Ken.

"So, Dad, how is the situation in Rosewood? You told me that you have been checking it out. By the way, is that how you and Muriel met?" He smiled warmly at Muriel.

"As a matter of fact, that is how I met Muriel. I've been researching this case because it was just not well investigated before. I believe strongly that three innocent men went to prison. We expect that this case will break wide open soon. Muriel has been one of the people who have helped with this investigation." Everyone turned to smile appreciatively at Muriel.

"Soooo," Holly said, smiling at Muriel, "that is how you met my Pops. Well, Muriel, are you a reporter?"

"No, as a matter of fact, I was a long-time friend of the woman who was killed," and her voice broke. Holly reached over to clasp her hand.

"Oh, Muriel, I am so sorry. I do have this habit of prying and my motor mouth gets going when it shouldn't."

"No, no, I took no offense, Holly. It is natural that you would wonder how I was involved in the investigation. Thank heavens your father has done this because it is helping so many people with closure."

Holly then noticed the sizable engagement ring on Muriel's finger. "Why, Muriel, what a beautiful ring. Gee whiz, somebody really loves you! Who is the lucky man? You must be very lucky too, from the looks of that ring." Muriel didn't know what to say.

Ken chuckled. "Well, I guess it's time to lay our cards on the table." He stood up and then took Muriel's hand to have her stand beside him. "I want you all to meet my bride-to-be and we hope you will give us your blessings."

Everyone sat still for a few seconds staring up at them, then Bart stood up clapping and saying, "Hear, hear, way to go. Let me be the first to congratulate you two." His warm brown eyes were filled with pleasure.

"Oh, Daddy, Muriel, how great," Holly said as she reached for Muriel and hugged her. Then she came around to her father and clasped him in her arms. He gave Muriel a happy wink. Muriel was smiling happily with tears in her eyes. Lila came to hug Muriel too, and then Ken. When Carter could get to Muriel and his father, he had a more serious look on his face. As he spoke, Ken could feel his son's heavy emotion. He noticed that Muriel held her breath anxiously.

"Dad, Muriel, you cannot know how long I have prayed for our father to meet a lovely lady and not be alone. Now, let me hug our second mother here." He walked up to Muriel and put his arms around her. "Hello, Mom Muriel, welcome to the family," he said and stepped back. He took her hand in his and kissed it. Then he turned to his father and held him close for some time. "Dad, I love you," he said huskily.

"I love you, son," Ken said to him.

Then the waitress came to take their orders. Everyone was in a jovial mood.

Holly inquired, "Have you two set a date for your wedding yet?"

"We haven't arrived at an exact date but we will be married in June," Muriel said, more relaxed now and smiling warmly.

"Yes, and then we are leaving soon after for our honeymoon on the West coast. We plan to be out there a while," Ken announced happily.

"Muriel, do you have children too?" Lila leaned forward a bit to address her.

"Yes, I do. She is twenty years old and attends college in Waco. Her name is Angie," Muriel said proudly.

"And she is a wonderful young lady. In fact, she is house-sitting for me now while Sarita is away visiting her family."

"Oh, good, then Carter and I gain a sister too," Holly said, delighted.

Bart smiled over at Muriel and asked, "What is your daughter's major in college, Muriel?"

"She wants to be an elementary teacher," Muriel replied.

"Do you have a picture of her with you?" Holly prompted.

"Yes, of course. Like all Moms, I carry around my little brag book," she laughed lightly and opened her handbag to produce a book of photos.

"Wow, this girl is a beauty, but then so is her mother," she added. She handed the photo book to Bart as Muriel thanked them for the compliments. Carter leaned towards Bart to see the photos too and they agreed she was a beauty.

"Who is the handsome young guy in this one?" Bart asked, holding the photo book up for Muriel to see.

"Oh, that is a friend, Will Earl Rogers. We have known him and his family all of our lives. I grew up with his Dad. Their mother was my best friend. She and I met when we were in our twenties. Will Earl has a brother and sister too." Carter studied the photos more and then handed them across the table to Lila.

"Oh, my yes, she is darling, just a real beauty," Lila said as she looked over the pictures. "Now, is Will Earl her sweetheart?"

"Well, yes they are sweethearts. I am certain he will be my son-in-law some day. I might add, he is a wonderful young man," Muriel said with pride.

Ken looked at Carter and knew that his son had picked up on the Rogers name. Carter only indicated his knowledge with a quick fleeting glance.

"So, are you all going to make it for my graduation?" Carter said, deliberately swinging the conversation in a new direction.

The group chatted and exchanged until it was time to return to Carter's apartment. Ken knew there would be a lively exchange in Carter's car on the way back. Everyone planned to return in two weeks for the graduation and they agreed on some sightseeing in and around Houston then too.

Ken teased Muriel about being right on in regards to his family's acceptance. Lila engaged Muriel in further conversation regarding Angie's college major since that was the one she had also chosen. Lila was due to graduate shortly as well and Ken made a mental note to bring something special for her from the two of them when they returned. He was reasonably sure that their wedding would not be the only one to take place in the near future, he mused as he watched this vivacious red-haired young woman. He noted his son staring at her with complete adoration.

"Now the time has come for Bart and I to make our announcement," Holly said as Bart reached for her hand. "You tell them, Bart. Okay?" She snuggled closer to him and he smiled down tenderly at his wife.

"All right. I am honored to tell you all that Holly and I are expecting in about six months," and his boylike features spread into a joyous wide grin. Carter and Ken went to the couple who were still beaming. Carter pulled his sister to her feet and kissed her while Ken shook his son-in-law's hand. He then scooped Holly up into his arms and kissed her.

"Aw, honey girl, this is wonderful. Isn't this just wonderful?" he said to Muriel who was now standing beside him, smiling with pleasure.

"Oh, it certainly is. Congratulations to you both, Holly, Bart. I am so happy for you."

Lila took Holly in a warm embrace when Ken released her and then in turn did the same to Bart while murmuring congratulations.

'Well, sis, do you have names picked out yet?"

"Yes, if it is a girl, we have agreed to call her Gloria and a boy will be Frank after Grandpa, Mom's father who passed away a few years before Mom did."

"That is great," Ken said and hugged Muriel to him. He could sense that Muriel felt that way too.

"Holly, that is a wonderful tribute to your mother. How good it is that you two lovely people have agreed on it."

Ken knew that nothing could have endeared this lovely woman to his children more than that expression she had just bestowed.

"Oh, thank you for that, Muriel," Holly said and brushed tears from her eyes.

They all sat down and chatted until Lila checked her watch. "Say, it is time for lunch and we are going to have it right here. Carter and I have put together one of our specialties so we want to surprise you. This does seem to be a day for some great surprises. Now we get to present one too, right Carter?"

"Right, so you all just sit tight and visit while Lila and I go into the kitchen. Soon we will have lunch." Carter got up and followed Lila into the kitchen area. The conversation flowed easily until Lila poked her head out.

"Lunch is ready so come on into the kitchen of Carter Ferries, Incorporated," and she giggled happily.

The kitchen was snug but ample and pleasant, with cheerful yellow and white curtains at the wide window where the table sat. It had been pulled out to make room for everyone. At each place sat an artfully decorated shrimp salad in a clear glass dish.

"Say now, this is great. You two have outdone yourselves," Ken assured them appreciatively. They also served a chunky beef and bean soup with garlic bread followed by the salad, all of which was excellent.

"Carter, now you hang on to this girl," Holly admonished, "because she is teaching you to be a valuable whiz as a cook."

"Well, it was a joint effort," Lila winked at Carter and then smiled tenderly. "Oh, but now come the best," she said and got up to open the refrigerator. She produced a 3-layer cake with coconut smothering the thick icing and a lone candle centered on top. Carter got up to fetch matches and light it.

"Happy birthday, dear Ken," she sang with the others joining in. She placed the cake in front of him.

"Now, make a wish before you blow out the candle," they all chorused.

Ken felt overcome with emotion as he looked from one dear face to the other. He closed his eyes for a moment, then blew the lone candle out. Everyone clapped their approval. Then Lila took the cake to slice it as Carter removed ice cream from the freezer. While they sat enjoying their dessert, Carter excused himself, then returned shortly with a gift-wrapped package.

"Dad, this is from all of us." Carter grinned at Holly, then winked at Bart while Ken went about the task of untying the ribbon and removing the paper. When he looked up after reaching into the box and pulling out an expensive pair of field glasses, his eyes were twinkling with amusement.

"Yes, Daddy dear, we knew you were still hanging onto those ancient relics you have had all our lives and then some," Holly chided him. "You know, the ones that make you goggle-eyed and you vainly try to adjust," she tittered, then got up to go hug her Dad. "Anyway, happy birthday, sweet Father. We love you so."

"It is so very mutual, my dear ones. Thank you," Ken said huskily. "This cake literally melts in your mouth, by the way. It is so good!" Ken complimented the bakers.

"It is an old family favorite and has lots of ingredients so not one I make often. But with Carter helping me, it was— no pun intended— a piece of cake," Lila chuckled happily. Ken once again thought how much he liked this girl. He thought his children had done well in choosing their mates.

"So, Dad, I hope to eventually move along with this police career and get into investigating. My instructors tell me I have a good chance with my military background and good test scores." Carter waited for a response from his Father.

"Carter, that is great. I have always told you and Holly that you can do anything you want to do badly enough. At the risk of bragging, I believe I've helped to raise two pretty sharp folks. Bottom line, however, is the fact that you were both diligent enough to want good lives."

The day passed pleasantly and Ken suggested that he take them all out for dinner as that time approached. They returned to the same restaurant and Ken felt completely at peace as he looked around at his family. He had such a joyous feeling that Gloria was there too and expressing her approval. He "knew" she was sending her love through her beautiful essence.

"Holly, have you and Bart called Connie to give her the wonderful news that she will be a Grandma soon?" Ken smiled at them.

"Not yet, but tonight we plan on calling her and Grandma and Grandpa Ferries too. We wanted to tell you and Carter first. Bart called his parents just before we came to Houston." Holly looked up at Bart, both of them passing that certain look that says "I adore you" reserved just for couples. They returned to Carter's apartment until Ken suggested that, since traffic had probably cleared, they needed to return to the resort.

"Have to get to the airport in the morning and return the rental car. Then we fly out of Houston shortly after that and get to Longview where friends will pick us up in my car," Ken said.

"Oh, we have to leave in the morning too, Daddy," Holly said, "but we are all getting together again in two weeks to see this big good-looking brother of mine graduate." She smiled fondly at Carter.

After long embraces, Ken and Muriel departed.

"Well, what did you think of the crew?" Ken asked as they drove back.

"In this short time, I felt like I have known those wonderful people forever. I just fit right in," she said softly.

"That is the way I felt when I met Angie. That just shows that we are supposed to unite and all the signals are saying so."

"I do believe you could not be any more correct," she sighed and nestled closer to him. A feeling of shared joy and peace lay between them.

Later that evening, they showered and nestled into bed, falling blissfully into sleep in no time.

"Good morning, Grandpa-to-be," Muriel greeted him smiling. She held out a cup of coffee as she looked down at him.

"Well, I never heard the alarm. What time is it?"

"I shut it off just before it was to go off so it is early yet. We have time to relax and enjoy our coffee." She sat down on the edge of the bed and reached for another cup of coffee while Ken fluffed up his pillows and leaned back. He reached for the cup Muriel had put on his nightstand.

"Ken, I called Angie this morning and I received some news I don't quite know how to digest at this point."

Ken reached for her hand. "What is it, pretty lady?" He was concerned by the grave tone of her voice. She looked down into her cup before she went on.

"Well, it seems that Will Earl showed up Saturday night and he was there this morning when I talked to Angie."

"Go on, hon. What is this all about? You seem rather grave," Ken prompted her.

"Well, she said that Will Earl wants them to be married very soon and not wait until next year when she is out of college."

Ken just nodded but waited for her to go on. Given what he knew of Carmen Munoz, he was not at all surprised. She was putting heavy pressure on this young healthy man. He had no intention of telling this to Muriel, though.

"It isn't that I have not felt they would be married in due time. But isn't this a bit premature, especially since Angie is established in Waco at the university?"

"Well, Muriel, how does Angie feel about getting married now?" Ken asked.

"She says it has hit her unexpectedly and all but Will Earl even brought her an engagement ring. Angie said he just begged her not to wait another year, that they could work it all out so she could finish her last year at a nearby college and stay in Rosewood. Angie even brought up the possibility of them living in my house. I told her that part would be great. Angie has always been such a level-headed girl and I respect her judgment. I think those two were meant for each other so I'm not opposed to her marrying Will Earl."

"Listen, Muriel, I don't see any problem myself. It sounds like they have talked it all out. You know they are both level-headed and that young man is deeply in love with your pretty daughter. I think that is a two way street. I would say that they are going to be just great, whether they get married sooner or later. How soon are they thinking of getting married?"

"Angie said that she doesn't want to interfere with our plans and knows that we are going to the West coast after our wedding. They thought the first week of August might be possible but they wanted to discuss it with us first."

Chapter____20

"Frankly, I just can't see why that wouldn't work. Now don't you agree? Angie is planning to go right ahead and graduate with a teaching degree so really, on the whole this is just great in every way," Ken said cheerfully.

"Oh, all right then. Let's call Angie when we get back to Rosewood and tell her we think it is wonderful." Her face relaxed into a happy smile.

Ken reached for the phone on the nightstand. "Let's call now and that way we can talk to both of them."

Her smile widened and she breathed deeply, closing her eyes momentarily while Ken dialed the number. When Angie answered, he handed the phone to Muriel.

"Hi, Angie. It's Mom. Ken and I have been talking about you and Will Earl. And well, honey, we just want you to know that we both feel it is a good plan. Ken says that August would be just fine if that is when you kids want to be married."

Muriel listened to her daughter's response and then chuckled and shook her head. "Well, honey girl, when a man is in love, he can be very persistent, you know." She gave Ken a cheery wink. "Now, put that long-legged cowboy on the phone to talk to his future ma-in-law," she drawled huskily.

"Will Earl, you are twisting the arm of that pretty little daughter of mine," she said on a teasing note. "No, no, honey child. I am not upset. Of course, I had to mull it over a bit after I talked to Angie earlier this morning. It sounds like you young folks are thinking ahead and Angie is going to finish college. That is sound judgment. Here, I am putting Ken on the phone. He wants to talk to both of you."

"Say, there, how is it going, Will Earl? Now, that is fine. I just want to be the first to congratulate you two fine young people. Oh, you bet and I sure do thank you."

"Angie, honey, I got a feeling that you need to be with that young cowboy. Honey girl, I want you to know your mother and I are very happy for you both. Oh, you bet and I am so honored that you want me to be. Now, honey, here is your mother. Yes, we will see you soon."

Muriel and Angie talked a few more minutes and Ken left her alone for that. He went into the bathroom to prepare for the day. They needed to get to the coffee shop for breakfast soon and then leave for the airport. When he returned to the bedroom, Muriel was in the other bathroom getting ready.

"Muriel, honey, I will call the bellhop to come take our luggage down to the lobby as soon as you are ready. Then let's go have some breakfast."

"Great. I'll be ready in about five more minutes." She came out of the bedroom smiling with her eyes full of mischief. She was dressed in a summer white dress and a yellow daisy garland necklace, looking cool and fresh.

"What, may I ask, is that impish little look in your eyes all about, young woman?" He grinned at her.

"Oh, I just couldn't help thinking how everything is moving along. Here I am going to be a grandmother and the mother of the bride all in one year, of course not in that order. And, I am about to become a bride myself," she chuckled.

"Yes, isn't it just super?" Ken said, laughing with high spirits. "Now, I will call the desk and have the bellhop come up, then we are on our way to breakfast. Come on, Grandma," he said and gave her a playful swat on her bottom. "I must say you are a sexy-looking grandma."

The bellhop came and they departed for the coffee shop. After being seated and giving the waitress their orders, Ken said, "Angie asked me to give her away, Muriel. Of course, I told her I would be honored to do it."

"I was certain she would ask you, Ken. She has really taken you as a father."

"Well, she is another daughter to me. I really love that girl and Will Earl is a very special young man. I just see a wonderful life for those two."

"Don't you think that Carter and Lila will be getting married soon too?"

"Yes, I suspect that they have already discussed that but are just waiting to graduate. They are both finished soon so I expect that announcement right soon."

"Wow, then we just may have two weddings to attend this year within a few months of each other, not counting our own," she smiled, self-satisfied. She picked up her cup for a sip of coffee.

Ken nodded and then turned his attention to the waitress who was placing their food on the table. After asking if they needed anything else, she departed. While they sat there eating, another vision suddenly appeared to Ken. He put down his fork and reached for his coffee, holding the cup suspended in front of him. Muriel was concentrating on her own breakfast and was not aware of Ken.

He appeared deep in thought but was actually seeing Will Earl walk into the kitchen of the Rogers home. Standing at the sink preparing vegetables was Carmen Muñoz. The two were alone. Carmen lay down the knife on the countertop and turned to face Will Earl, wiping her hands on the apron. She walked over to him and pressed her body snug against him, then locked her arms around his neck, kissing him in a fury of passion. Will Earl was vainly trying to pull her arms down while the girl's hips rotated in a sexually rhythmic motion against him. Finally, trembling, Will Earl pushed her away.

"What the hell is wrong with you, Carmen? What part of no don't you · understand?" He then turned and walked out of the kitchen with Carmen smiling tauntingly after him.

"Ken, you haven't touched your breakfast, honey. What are you thinking about? You are a million miles away?" Muriel's voice brought him back to center.

He smiled at her. "Just wool gathering, I guess. I was just going to say that, the more I think about it, the more I am certain that Angie and Will Earl marrying soon is an excellent idea."

"Well, not that it has seeped into my head, I am getting used to the idea. I do believe you are right," she smiled at him and patted his hand. "Now, honey, eat your food before it gets all cold."

They finished breakfast and made their way to check out. The attendant brought their car to the doorway and they started for the airport.

"Hm, people on their way to church," Ken observed aloud.

They reached the rental agency and turned in the car, then took the shuttle to the terminal.

"Now it won't be long until we see Rosie and Ham waiting for us. It has been a great few days away, hasn't it, pretty lady?"

"One of the best trips ever and one I won't forget. It goes down as extra special in my book of memories," she said, hugging him around his waist. They checked their luggage and made their way to the gate. As they waited to board, they watched the antics of two small Asian children jabbing at each other while their mother was blissfully unaware. When she looked at them, the little girl and boy feigned innocence.

"That is the way that Angie and Ty used to carry on," Muriel chuckled. "They had this contest going on that Nadine called one-uppance."

"He was more a brother to her, wasn't he, Muriel?"

"Yes, he was. They both tagged after Phyllis and Will Earl like two adoring puppies." She smiled softly. "I just believe that Angie and Will Earl had a special feeling for each other from the beginning, even though they dated other people in their teens. Nadine used to say that they seemed destined to be together and she was right," Muriel said, her voice husky with emotion.

Ken smiled and took her hand. "You see, people usually know these things if they just listen with their hearts."

She nodded agreement. Then the announcer called their flight number and they boarded. They had to change planes and wait a couple hours on the way back. During the layover, they had enjoyed a refreshing glass of lemonade in the lounge while talking about where they would go first on their honeymoon. The next plane they boarded was a small one and Ken watched Muriel's curiosity and delight in the whole experience. Life was an interesting unfolding for her.

The Wilsons greeted them joyfully and Ham insisted on carrying their suitcases.

"Say, hope you are carrying good appetites because Ham and I know about this darlin' little place that serves up the best food you ever tasted. It's just like me Mum used to serve up when I was a lassie."

"Oh, yes, Rosie, I have heard about Maggie McGuire's. Is that the place you are speaking of?" Muriel asked.

"One and the same. It has just been open a short while so the mister and me thought one day we would try it. I tell you now, you'll not be disappointed."

"It sounds very good, Rosie. I am agreeable. Aren't you, Muriel?"

"Sure am. You two lead the way. And yes, we brought along good appetites." Muriel assured Rosie, taking her arm and walking ahead of Ken and Ham to the parking lot.

They reached the restaurant with Ham's clear directions. The temperature had cooled off several degrees since the last time they were in Longview and he was grateful for the change.

When they were settled at a table, a young lady approached them with four-leaf clovers tucked into her bobbing ponytail. Rosie gave them suggestions from the menu and the waitress wrote down their selections.

"So, now, how was the trip and the meeting with your children?" Ham asked, addressing both Muriel and Ken.

"It was wonderful. Ken has a delightful family," Muriel said affirmatively.

"Yes, and they fell in love with Muriel, which I knew they would," Ken said. He took Muriel's hand and held it up.

"Well, that is the biggest goat's eye I ever did see. Ham, would you be lookin' at the ring on this girl's finger?" Rosie gushed excitedly. That brought a round of laughter from everyone at the table.

"Now we are truly blessed. Not only has this lady agreed to become my wife, but my daughter Holly and her husband Bart are expecting their first child in six months," Ken said with a wide smile.

"Now indeed the pair of you are blessed by the Almighty," Rosie sniffed and used her dinner napkin to blot away at her eyes. She patted Muriel's hand fondly.

Ham reached over to shake Ken's hand and then clasped Muriel's in a warm expression of friendship. "This is just tiptop, the best news ever," he proclaimed gruffly but his eyes held deep emotion as he smiled at them both.

"You are indeed the dearest of folk and the mister here and I surely do give you our deepest congratulations from the bottom of our hearts. We wish you a wonderful life and all the best for that wee one soon to be arriving," Rosie said between sniffs.

They chatted in high spirits until their meals arrived. The waitress spoke to Rosie in Gaelic and Rosie answered her, nodding and smiling.

The meal was a hearty Irish stew with tasty soda bread and a medley of greens for salad. The meal was served with a good Irish beer and topped off with a mouth-watering dessert. Ken noticed that, after her second mug, Rosie's cheeks turned florid and her brogue a bit thicker. He suppressed a smile as Muriel lightly tapped his ankle with her foot.

"Oh, for all the saints in heaven, I near forgot to mention the latest news. What with seeing you all and the grand news you have, I forgot. But, did you know that Mrs. Allard has been missin' and nobody's seen her since the art show?" Her car was found the parking lot but it's like the earth swallowed her up," Rosie gestured excitedly. "Now, that husband of hers, I don't care for the likes of him, but the Falzones are near out of their wits, God bless them."

Ken spoke up because he knew that Muriel didn't know what to say under the circumstances. "Well, Rosie, perhaps she left of her own accord, leaving her car behind to throw her husband off the track."

"Yes, because we all know that Marilyn wasn't happy in that marriage," Muriel interjected.

Ham thoughtfully added, "Then hopefully that is the case, but someone had to have taken her away in their car. I hope it wasn't an act of foul play but a friend who wanted to help her."

"Well, I pray also that is the case, Ham," Ken said to encourage that idea.

"Of course, Pace has probably contacted their children by now," Muriel extended.

"Ah, well now, who knows about that man? If he hasn't done so, then the Falzones surely have," Rosie slurred. "Well, I have been lightin' a candle for the poor darlin's safety ever since we first heard of it. Lord knows, we do not need another tragedy," and her kindly face took on a grave look.

Ham changed the conversation to a happier vein. "So now, do you two have a date set for your wedding?"

"We haven't exactly but we are planning a June wedding so we have a lot of preparations to do," Muriel said.

"Well, whatever I can do to give you a hand, do not hesitate to call on me, my darlins'," Rosie smiled with a good flush spreading across her cheeks.

"You know, Rosie, I just had an idea. You are so talented, would it be too much to have you do the invitations? I think you would create such a beautiful theme. Don't you agree, Ken?" Muriel turned to look at him.

"That is an outstanding idea, if Rosie is agreeable to it. But I will only agree if she will arrive at a sizable amount for her work. After all, that is a lot of work," Ken smiled at Rosie.

"Why, I am honored that you are askin'. Go on with you now. It would be no trouble at all." Rosie sat up tall and smiled proudly at them.

Ham turned his attention to Ken. "Say, Ken, do you know if they ever found out who shot that young bull out there at the Conway's? It just faded away to nothing after that one piece in the local paper."

"Well, I don't believe there has been any further evidence on it or else someone would have heard by this time." Ken hoped he sounded convincing.

The company of the Wilsons was always uplifting to Ken and he could see why Muriel and so many others had such fondness for them. Rosie excused her self after another mug of beer and Ham winked broadly at Ken, his eyes full of merriment as he watched his wife walk stiffly in the direction of the restroom. Upon her return, they all chatted a while, then got up to leave. Ken motioned to the waitress for the check.

"Ah, no sir, t has been cared for," she said in a thick Irish brogue. She thanked them and bid them good evening.

"Rosie, you are a sly fox,' Ken said, casting his head down at her and pointing a finger. A smiling Rosie leaned against Ham for support. "We thank you both, not only for a wonderful meal but for the company of two dear friends."

Muriel embraced them both and thanked them herself. "We love you two special people so much."

"Go along with you now, before you have the mister and me blubbering all over you," Rosie sniffed. Ham cleared his throat while patting Muriel on her back with his large work-worn hand.

They drove leisurely to Rosewood, then took the country road to the Wilson's ranch with Rosie sharing a few of her witty Irish stories on the way.

Ken reminded her that they were going to write those stories down. "Have you started to compile some of those for me? Remember our book project."

"Ah, well, yes I have done that but don't you worry about that for a time. You will be needin' to attend to more important matters than the prattling of an old Irish folklorist," she giggled.

"Rosie, you would be surprised at how quickly I am able to write it up on the keyboard. Whenever you have it ready, you just give it to me and we will get it done pronto," he assured her.

"Then I will be getting after it pronto. Now, would the two of you like to come in and sit with the mister and me for a spell?" Rosie invited.

"Oh, thank you but it has been a long day, sweet Rosie. I believe we must take a rain check this time," Muriel said, "but we will come out here and visit soon."

"Then do because Rosie still wants to fix a good supper for the two of you," Ham said cordially.

"Yes, how about this coming week? Would you be open to that one evening?" Rosie prompted.

"Just let me check what is going on, Rosie. There are some matters coming along next week that I need to be involved in," Ken said prudently. "Muriel will call you soon and see what we can work out." He gave Rosie a big hug and shook hands warmly with Ham.

They thanked the Wilsons again. It was twilight by now and the first star was out, which Muriel pointed out to Ken. "Aren't they just the sweetest couple? I don't believe a person would ever find two more caring and sincere people."

"They certainly are but I have been privy to meeting several wonderful people like the Wilsons since I arrived in Rosewood. One of them happens to be in my company right now," and he raised her hand to his lips to kiss it.

Muriel got out of the car when they reached her driveway and went to open the side door. Then, after turning on the yard light, she returned to help Ken unload their luggage. Ken then switched off the headlights but paused for a moment, thinking he had seen something at the corner of the garage. He decided it must have been a critter of some sort since he knew they were plentiful there. The horses nickered while he and Muriel carried their luggage in.

"Who tends to your horses when you and Angie are gone, Muriel?"

"Oh, Sam Scholts has always been great if I needed someone to help out. He is a retired veterinarian of about seventy and lives a short way from here. After you have left town and turned down this road, you see his home sitting back off the road. You've seen that place back in there with all the trees around it?"

Ken nodded and she went on. "He and his wife Marion are so nice. They have always just loved Angie. I expect Angie learned more from Sam about horses than any kid around here when she was growing up. The little twerp used to tell me how it was done, and by golly, she knew what they needed too. When she was a tyke, she would ride over to their place and she knew she could count on them for cookies and lemonade." She laughed.

"She is a plucky young lady, Muriel. You have done a good job raising her."

"Thank you, Ken. I guess it shows how proud I am of her, huh?"

"That's all right, pretty lady. You should be. Now let's just put all of this luggage in the bedroom and tend to it in the morning."

"Fine with me. I am ready for a shower and bed, aren't you?"

They took their separate showers and returned to the bedroom. Muriel was in bed first and threw back the covers. "Hop right in here, you handsome man," she teased with an exaggerated sexy implication. Ken slid in beside her. They held each other and drifted into sleep. He noticed Muriel falling asleep before him, listening to her even breathing.

He awoke with a start, having to focus his eyes to read the clock. It was 3 am. "What's this all about?" he thought, laying there fully awake. Muriel had not stirred but he felt compelled to get out of bed. He carefully reached for his robe and realized he was thirsty so he headed for the kitchen. He wondered if that was why he had awakened so suddenly. Yet there was a nagging inside his head that told him otherwise. He knew he had been overly tired when he had retired earlier.

He made his way to the kitchen, feeling grateful for the nightlight in the living room. He knew that saved him from fumbling and waking Muriel. He opened the refrigerator and sat the pitcher on top of the counter. He knew he could find a water tumbler by the sink.

"Probably that Irish ale," he thought and smiled thinking of Rosie walking ramrod stiff after she had polished off three hearty mugs of the potent ale.

He drank down a full glass of chilled water and then went to relieve himself in the bathroom. Wide awake now, he didn't feel like returning to bed as he knew he would just lay there. He put the pitcher back in the refrigerator, then stood at the kitchen sink staring out the window at a silver moon slipping from behind a cloud. It gave a pristine illumination to everything visible outside. A sudden movement from underneath a large willow tree made Ken freeze in his position. He frowned and remained at his vigil, hoping to see it again. Then he could determine if it was an animal. "Perhaps a stray dog," he reasoned until it moved again. As his eyes adjusted, he could see that it was someone standing under the tree, apparently leaning against the trunk. The sight startled him and he felt an icy chill course through him. The figure suddenly squatted down on the ground and a light flared from a cigarette lighter. The flash illuminated a portion of the man's face. He wore a Western hat, Ken could see before the light went out. Now the glow of the cigarette was visible.

Chapter_____21

He pondered what he should do and made a decision after running through a few ideas. He decided not to call the sheriff's office because it would take them too long to arrive. Quietly, he stole into the living room and went to the fireplace to get the long-handled fire poker. Taking the front door entrance to the porch, he made his way around the house. His mind was churning as he noiselessly tiptoed toward the back. He hoped that the man did not have a firearm on him. He knew that was a risk he was taking and he could be getting in over his head. Yet, something propelled him to make this contact.

Ken crept carefully toward the tree and he could tell that the man was still unaware of his presence. He silently asked for protection in case the man was armed. He took refuge behind a tall flowering bush and spoke to the man.

"What are you doing here, mister?" he called out. The man froze but then slowly stood up. Ken tightened his grip on the poker.

"Ken Ferries, would that be you?" the man drawled.

"Who wants to know?" Ken answered him.

"Well, if you are him, I need to talk to you about a matter on that case you've been investigating."

"You Catlin Willard?" Ken asked, still staying out of sight but he could see the man's leg still standing under the drape of the willow tree.

"One and the same. I been out here thinking on how I was gonna talk to you before the time we had set up. I don't rightly want any cops around right now."

"Catlin, you just ease on out from under that tree with your hands where I can see them, arms in front of you and palms up," Ken commanded, keeping his voice low enough that he wouldn't chance waking Muriel.

Catlin complied, walking out from under the tree with his arms out. Ken could see that he held no weapon.

"Now, you just slide yourself down at that picnic table ahead of you there, nice and easy. Don't try anything because, I tell you, I won't hesitate to defend myself if I have to."

"Well, you don't need to figure I'll be trying a fracas, Ferries, because I ain't wanting any more trouble than I already got. I just need to talk to you and figure out what to do. Right now, I ain't hankerin' to have no third party. That will come soon enough." Something about Catlin's attitude gave Ken rise to believe that the man was not trying to mislead him so he stepped from behind the tall shrub but continued to hold the fire poker tightly at his side.

"Can't we just sit down here together and talk? Hell, I guess rightly I can't blame you but lots has changed since I screwed up and sent you them threats."

"Yes, well, not only that but you intended to break into my motel room and attack me too. So just tell me something, why would I trust you?"

"I was kinda loco about then and obsessed with trying to get Mrs. Rogers to sell me the ranch that used to be ours. Then that damned maniac killed her and I got scared that it was gonna get pinned on me. It sure as hellfire looks like it has ended up that way. Now that's why I didn't want no cops around when I talked to you. I figured you would be more apt to listen if I give it to you straight and all."

643

"All right, Catlin, maybe you are shooting square with me so I will hear you out." He walked to the picnic table and sat across from the man. He still kept the fire poker close in case he had entered a trap.

"Okay, Catlin, you start this ball rolling. I will listen and will only interrupt if I need to get something cleared up."

"That's fair enough," Catlin ventured. Ken noted that he had not lost any of his Texas drawl even after leaving the state at a young age.

"First of all, I don't rightly claim to be a choir boy but murder is another story. I got older, you know, and looked back on some damned stupid stuff my old man tried to get through my head. He told me I was headed for trouble but I reckon I was a wrong way seed from the start." He paused then, long enough to reach into his shirt pocket for another cigarette. "You mind?" he asked.

"Go ahead," Ken said and watched while he lit the cigarette. The man had strong features that reminded him of Charles Bronson. He was dark complexioned, probably from working outside so many years. Ken wondered if he might be part Indian.

Catlin took a drag and then turned his head slightly to blow smoke away from Ken. He then studied the end of the cigarette, as though trying to think how to proceed. "Reckon when all was said and done, I was getting close to 50 and started thinking I got no roots. I thought I would come back to Texas and make it right with Pa. I figured I could at least help him out on the homestead. Well now, that hit hard when I got back here and found out he had died. And I hadn't done right by him after Ma died and all. I couldn't handle losing my Ma so I just took off. A damned fool of a wild kid, I was. Then I got myself in trouble down in Louisiana and got put in the klink for a year. I didn't have the guts to get in touch with Pa then so I started drifting and finally got into something in California that paid good. Busting my hump, I reckon, but the money was good doing stunts for them Hollywood folks."

He paused again and took another drag from the cigarette. "Well, I get back here to Rosewood and head out to the ranch, thinking on how I will just surprise my Pa. When I seen the place, I figured he had done well all these years. I get out and go to the door this one morning and a boy about sixteen come to the door. I asked him if Mr. Willard is there, the owner of that spread, and he tells me the Conways live there now and he don't know any Willards at all. I just got a real sinkin' feeling in the middle of my gut and I just knew then that my Pa was gone too. I went into Rosewood and found a café open so I figured I would get some breakfast, then nose around about the ranch. I was thinking maybe Pa had retired and leased it out, then moved into town like a lot of folks do. Figured it wasn't the case but I was still hoping."

"I got up to the counter and there is an old man I recognize from when I was a kid. He don't know me so I just start visiting with him, leading him into conversation. He confirmed that my Pa had died several years back and that Bud Conway was leasing the ranch from Mrs. Rogers. I just left half my breakfast and drove kinda aimless like. I figured I was going to settle here and get Mrs. Rogers to deal with me on that ranch. Hell, I knew within reason that if she was Will's wife, they were probably damned well-heeled for money but I had set aside a hefty sum over the years and was prepared to offer top dollar. I drive around, looking at the countryside and familiarizing myself with it again. Then, I see this law office later when I come back into town. I went in to make an appointment to see Pace Allard. He tells me that Nadine is sole owner of that ranch and that he handled all the Rogers business transactions. Well, my head is churning and I am thinking I will contact Mrs. Rogers to make her an offer."

"I got myself a job as a ranch hand not far from the old Willard place the next day and then went over to the Rogers ranch to talk with Will's missus. When I get there, this young man comes to the door and I figure he was probably a Rogers 'cause he looked like Will did as a kid, only real blond. Then I see his mother and I know where he got that blond hair. God, man, she was a beautiful lady," he drawled and shook his head. "Go figure how anyone could hurt her."

"I don't know how, Catlin, but I am glad for your sake that you weren't the one. But I tell you, you didn't help yourself with the shenanigans you pulled after the fact," Ken admonished him.

"Yeah, you are sure as hell scoring right on that fact. Nobody knows it better than me. But I didn't kill that woman. I know I am looking at some time but I don't want to be in there for murder one." He continued, "You see, I got dug in there up over my head with wanting to buy that property. After Mrs. Rogers murder, I got into trying to scare the Conways, killed that young bull and then scared the hell out of those two kids that night. Started getting sick then at the fool thing I had done and I tried to right at least some of it by paying Bud for that bull. I found out you had been an investigating reporter and I tried to run you off because, by then, I had come up against a big gun like Pace Allard. Now, who was the law likely to believe done that murder, Ferries? You get my drift?"

"Well, man, you didn't come forward about it and three men have spent nearly a year in the pen on account of it," Ken said in a level voice.

Catlin dropped his head then and it was awhile before he spoke. "And for that, I am ashamed. Hell man, I am ashamed of my whole sorry life but I can't change that now."

"So, let's make a stab at doing the right thing, Catlin. Did you see who killed Nadine Rogers?"

"I didn't see it but I heard it, least ways I guess it was while it was happening. I was out on this section working for the rancher and it borders the Rogers spread. You can see their big ranch home from the back where I was. I parked my old Jeep under a grove of trees and figured while I was that close, I would just go talk to Mrs. Rogers one more time and offer a bigger price. I had hopes she could work something out with the Conways too. Well, I walked up to the side entrance of the house and looked in through the screen door into the kitchen. I knocked and was just about ready to call out when I heard a commotion from inside. I heard a man's voice and he was damned near screaming like a raging bull."

"What was he saying, Catlin?"

"He said, 'Don't turn me away, you bitch. I'm gonna have you. You have driven me crazy for years now. Come here, woman.' I could hear a woman sobbing. God, it sounded like she was scared to death and then I didn't hear any more. I knocked again several times but nobody came to the door. I thought maybe it was just the television so I stepped just inside the kitchen and called out, 'Is anybody home?' Then I called out again. For some reason, the hair on my whole body stood up and I wondered again if it had been the television. So I walked on into the living room real careful like and then towards the hallway. And my God, I have never seen anything that shook me like that. Oh, jeez, there she was and it looked like her head had been bashed in but she was so covered in blood and so was the hallway. I felt like I couldn't breathe and I knew she had to be dead.

"Then my legs just took over and I started to run out of that house. I literally fell down over that bank that drops down in the backyard. I got up, pawing my way out of the sticker patch and then dropped down again. Then I see this guy I recognize come slamming out of the screen door. He was wearing white jogging shorts and a white matching shirt all splattered with blood. He slid on his hind end a few feet from me and, how he kept from seeing me, I don't know. But I can tell you this much and no mistaking, it was Pace Allard, that attorney. He took off like a wild man and ran faster than hell clean out of sight in nothing flat. Now, I didn't hang around, let me tell you. I got to hell out of there and back to my Jeep. I just couldn't think, Ken, and I knew with my record, I could very well be pigeon for it. I was just plain in shock."

"So, after that, what did you do, Catlin?" Ken pressed, feeling his stomach heave.

"Well, I kept a very low profile and then decided I would make an appointment with Allard. I knew the case was moving along then. I didn't go to town from the ranch where I worked until I heard my boss talking about the three men who had been arrested for that woman's murder."

"Did you blackmail Allard, Catlin?" Ken asked, keeping his voice emotionless.

"Naw, hell no, but I just wanted to make sure once more if it was him I saw. I knew it was but I reasoned I had been so scared that morning, not to mention sick to my guts. So I trumped up this plan to go talk like Mrs. Rogers and I had discussed that property. And too, I could be interested in some other land and needed a good attorney to handle my business. He asked me to come in after hours due to his case load and of course that was agreeable to me. But, I tell you, I was certain the first time I saw him that it was the same guy. Then I saw him out jogging some weeks later when I came down that country road. I was making a delivery for my boss, a truckload of young heifers. Here comes that Allard fellow and he was dressed like I saw him at the Rogers place, same white jogging clothes."

"Catlin, is that all or do you have something else you want to tell me?"

"Only thing I reckon was how the guy really gave me the creeps. I was even more certain that he was a full-fledged cold manipulator. And I could see how he could set up a situation for someone else to take the heat for him too. And then, it was sorta like something was scoring in on me too, after I came to your motel room to try and scare you that one night." He stopped for a moment and Ken saw him visibly shake.

"Go on, Catlin. What is it?"

"I experienced something that was right out of a Hollywood horror movie and, man, I still get the chills clean through me thinking about it. I was fumbling around with the door of your room and I heard something whirring above me. All of a sudden, and this is unbelievable, Ferries, a hell of a big bird clawed my back to shreds. Ripped my shirt off and I was covered in blood. I know you had to have heard me screaming. Christ, I expect the whole town heard me but I ran to my Jeep and took off. I mean, I guess it was a bird of some sort. It's the only thing it could have been. Jeez, man, you did hear me, didn't you?" he beseeched Ken.

"Catlin, I will be straight with you since you have been straight with me. Yes, I saw the whole thing and so did the Chans who run the motel. I don't claim to know as a certainty but it looked like a red-tailed hawk, the biggest one I ever saw."

Under the circumstances, it does pale in comparison but, I tell you, it was one of the most bizarre and frightening things I have ever encountered. It had to be a supernatural event because a red-tailed hawk ain't that big and doesn't attack a man like that unless he was cornered."

"Well, Catlin, I grew up as a country kid myself and I agree with you that a hawk doesn't usually do that. So, maybe you are not far off when you say it was a supernatural event," Ken agreed with him.

"I know one thing for certain, it snapped me back into reality after I calmed down. That powerful force put a warning onto me."

"Then, that's good." Ken said, looking toward the house and hoping that Muriel was still asleep. "Now, listen, Catlin, this is a loaded question but it may be of help to you in the long run. And, by the way, I do not intend to press charges." Ken heard the man sigh.

"Oh Lord, man, that is white of you. Just tell me what I need to do because I am agreeable to get the truth out and be cleared of the possible sentence for that murder I swear I didn't do." His voice held a desperate pitch and Ken felt a stirring of compassion for him.

"Well, Catlin, you felt that you could trust me. Now I want to tell you that Bruster Hernado, the sheriff, has been working diligently with me and you can trust this man. I want you to let me call him and have him come out here so you can tell him what you just told me."

"Then I will be put under arrest on the spot, but I reckon I don't have a choice," Catlin said shaking his head. "But, what the hell,, I don't really have a whole bag of choices anyway."

"Yes, you do. Because you have come forward and you are cooperating, you will be needed as a witness. Just don't get discouraged." He paused. "I need you to come on in the house now so we can call Bruster. I don't know what time it is but we will call him before he goes to his office. Are you agreeable to this?"

"Yeah, man, at this point I am. I have thought on this for a long time and I figured you were about my best bet," he said shaking his head.

"Where have you been hanging out, Catlin?"

He gave a short sardonic laugh. "Here, there, and everywhere, even a cave I used to play in when I was a kid."

"You won't have to do that any more."

"Nope, I will probably have a free stay at the crow bar hotel," he laughed in an attempt at some glib humor.

"Come on, let's go in the house now."

"Well, what is Muriel going to think of finding the likes of me in her home?"

"She has been following along with me on this and all she wants is for it to be resolved. Don't worry about Muriel."

"All right, I will just take your word for it," he agreed.

Ken led him into the house by the front entrance since the other door was still locked. Ken asked him to be quiet since Muriel was still sleeping. They stood in the semi-dark kitchen and Ken said he would close the bedroom door and then make some coffee. He noted that Muriel still slept peacefully. He turned on the kitchen light and directed Catlin to sit at the table.

"You hungry?" Ken turned to him after filling the coffeepot. "I believe we have some breakfast rolls. We might as well enjoy them with the coffee."

"That would go real good," Catlin agreed. "I just drink my java black. I am obliged to you."

"It's fine. I figure that we both ought to have a little wake-up power because it may be a long day. How did you know where to find me?"

"Well, I reasoned that you and Muriel were an item because I saw you together often enough. Then I drove by here and saw your car now and again," he smiled knowingly. Ken thought how much a pleasant smile improved the man's bearing.

"Yes, she is quite a lady and going to be my wife in a few weeks."

"Congratulations to you, Ferries. I might add that I do agree she is quite a lady. I had a major crush on her when we were kids but, like most everything, I goofed up on that too."

"Catlin, just some advice to you. It is not too late to empower yourself from this moment on. You will be surprised to find how many great things will start to show up for you. I believe you have already started with this so just hang in there."

"Damn it, the thing I regret the most is the way I hurt my folks and now being the reason that those three men have been in the pen, just because I turned yellow," and his voice held a note of shame.

"Well, I won't reference any quotes on that, Catlin. I think for certain that your parents know everything that is going on with you, including your remorse. From where they are, they have forgiven you all your transgressions. Now you have to start forgiving yourself. I believe you have reached a turning point today."

The man just slowly nodded, looking down thoughtfully at the table while Ken got the mugs ready for their coffee. Then he took the package of rolls and the butter from the refrigerator and some small plates from the cupboard. He heated the rolls quickly in the microwave, careful to catch it before the buzz sounded. With all in readiness, he sat down with Catlin.

"Let's just go ahead and enjoy this. It's too early to call the sheriff so we may as well just talk a while and get to know each other, all right?"

"Suits me," he drawled.

"You ever been married?" Ken studied the man's face for response.

"Naw, but I figured no woman would ever have wanted me. Hell, I have probably talked more to you this morning than I have to any other human being. Been a loner all my life and reckon that has been a major portion of my troubles. Never knew how to talk to anybody, just bottled things up, acted stuff out, and dummied up, you know. Maybe talking would have helped but I just didn't trust anybody. I don't know why either."

Ken measured the man for a moment, letting himself absorb Catlin in depth.

"Did you know that we are all seekers, even if some of us don't realize that?" He paused searching for the appropriate words. "It's like we are all trying to experience life in various ways for whatever growth we each need in order to be perfect. Do you follow me?"

"So some of us pick a hell of a collisions course for ourselves in other words," Catlin offered.

Ken nodded and took a sip of coffee. "However, since we all have free will, we can change our course any time. We are paddling our own canoes, so to speak. Human beings are so complex that sometimes we don't even know ourselves what prompts us to do and say certain things. That's why there are so many personalities of people."

"It is all pretty damned deep to me but I have pondered some of it, especially these past weeks. I had a lot of time on my hands," he said and took a bite of roll. "I can't rightly see getting perfect but I do have a hankerin' to make peace with a lot of folks if I can."

"Start with yourself, Catlin, and then you'll find out it won't be so hard to do."

They had just finished their rolls and coffee and Ken got up to refill their mugs when Muriel came into the kitchen. She looked surprised to find that Ken wasn't alone and stared at Catlin while she tightened the belt of her robe.

"Hello, Muriel. Long time no see," Catlin drawled.

Her eyes widened in shock as she recognized the man sitting at her kitchen table. Ken went to her and put his arm around her waist in a protective gesture.

"It's all right, Muriel honey. Catlin just came here to talk to me so that no law would be present. But he has agreed that we will call Bruster pretty soon. The two of us have been talking, a while outside and now here so we could have coffee and rolls. I hope we didn't wake you up."

She shook her head and frowned, still looking confused, staring from one to the other.

"Here, let me pour you some coffee and I will explain what is going on," Ken said, having her sit at the head of the table where he had been. "Catlin knows that it was Pace Allard who took Nadine's life. He saw him run out of the Rogers home early that morning and he was covered in blood. He has told me that since he was so close in the section that borders the Rogers ranch, that he was going to talk to Nadine about selling that ranch of hers. When he got to the kitchen door, he heard a commotion inside and first thought it was the television."

"Ken, I will try and explain it to Muriel here and I am not gonna whitewash what I did, because it was purely wrong. But, Muriel, I saw that poor lady and I just went loco and wanted out of there fast. I knew somebody was home on account of that TV, or what I thought it was. So I kept calling out to Mrs. Rogers when I went into the kitchen. I told Ken here that I knew something was wrong because I didn't hear the TV any more. I went into the living room and then headed toward the hallway and, God almighty, there she was. I couldn't move for a minute and then complete horror took over. I ran out of that house and fell over that bank head first!"

He went on and Muriel kept staring at him, not uttering a word. "You see, Muriel, I got myself in trouble when I took off from here and was in jail for a year. I just felt like nobody would take my word for it. I had met this guy Allard when I came back here to Rosewood because I wanted an attorney for some business of mine. So, you see, I knew him enough that I could recognize him come tearing out of the house. I went to his office a couple times after that to get a real good gander at him again. Then, one morning, I was driving some heifers on that country road and here he comes jogging, dressed the same way I saw him that morning."

"You should have come forward with this," Muriel's voice was lower than usual. She was struggling to hang on to her emotions.

"Girl, I reckon nobody knows that better than me. I can't excuse myself. I just got scared, even though it purely sickened me. I got so hung up on the fear that it was going to be pinned on me that I really went haywire for a while. So now I gotta pay the piper and I reckon that is the right thing. Can't see letting this sorry mess get by with what he done. I figured Ken was the best bet I had to listen to me and I got that right— he has been."

Ken looked at the wall clock and suggested that he call Bruster. Catlin leveled a steady gaze at him. "Yeah, it's time to get this show on the road, I reckon."

Ken picked up the phone and dialed Bruster's home. A woman answered.

"Mrs. Hernado, this is Ken Ferries, a friend of your husband's. I do apologize for calling so early but there is an important matter I need to talk to Bruster about before he leaves for his office. Why, yes ma'am, that would be fine. He can reach me at Muriel's," and he gave her the number.

Ken then sat down and said, "Bruster was in the shower so he will call in a few minutes. Now, Catlin, I don't rightly know how the sheriff will handle all of this but I tell you we have had some reason to connect Pace Allard with that murder. I can't elaborate on that now because it is under investigation and has to be kept confidential. I will say that you have chosen a good time to come forth."

"Maybe, but it would have been better to come forward to start with, but spilt milk is spilt milk. I reckon I can just fix it now, least ways I hope so," and Catlin looked at Muriel with shame on his face.

"Cat," Muriel said with a low husky voice, "I want you to know something for the record. I could not feel that you had done this brutal killing. It was wrong that you didn't come forward earlier but you are doing the right thing now."

For the first time, Ken saw naked grief on the man's face and knew that his eyes were ready to fill with tears. The phone rang at that moment and yet Ken was glad to see that Muriel had been able to bring this honest sorrow up for Catlin. He suspected that Cat had rarely ever given in to these feelings and he knew it was a real beginning for this man.

"Hi, Bruster, I didn't want to call you so early but something has developed. I believe you will be relieved to know that Catlin Willard is right here with Muriel and I. What's that? Oh, everything is fine. Catlin has talked at length with me and he is very agreeable to talk with you now. We were hoping you could swing by here before you went into your office. That's fine, Bruster. We will see you right away."

Ken hung up the phone and turned to Cat, who had by now collected himself but still looked sad. "Cat, it's going to be all right. I am just going to let you and Muriel talk while I go get some clothes on. I won't be long."

When he came back, Catlin and Muriel were talking. She was telling him about her husband Bill, that he had died several years earlier. Ken could tell that they had both relaxed.

"Always thought he was an all right guy. You got any children?"

"Yes, she was very little when Bill died. She is in college now, all grown up and getting married this summer. She and Will's oldest son Will Earl are getting married."

"The heck you say. Is that the blond fellow I met the first time I stopped by there?"

"No, that is Tyler, the youngest boy. He is the same age as my Angie. The oldest is Will's daughter Phyllis."

"A lot of time has passed, hasn't it," he said wistfully.

"Yes, yes it has, Catlin. Now, what were you doing right before you came back here?"

"Well, I got into stunt work for films out there in Hollywood. Of course, that involved some traveling too, on location a fair piece of the time so I was pretty rootless. Reckon that didn't bother me none for a long time but then I guess life started catching up to me after enough broken bones. I was heading toward fifty and just getting tired." He shook his head as he reflected.

Ken watched him and thought that he was really talking about being heart-tired. That kind of realization often comes about at his age. It was a soul longing.

A knock came at the front door and Muriel started to get up and answer it.

"It's all right, Muriel. I will get it," Ken told her.

Bruster stood there, hat in his hand. Ken greeted him.

"Bruster, come on in. We are all out in the kitchen. I will pour you a cup of coffee."

Bruster followed Ken out to the kitchen and, upon seeing Muriel, he said, "Good morning to you." He nodded to Catlin and Ken went to get his coffee.

"Bruster, you sit down here and you three men can talk while I go get dressed. By the way, there are more of those breakfast rolls if Ken will do the honors for you," she smiled warmly.

"Thank you, Muriel. I just believe I'll take you up on that offer." Bruster smiled at her and took her seat as she left the kitchen.

"Well, Catlin, it's been a lot of years since we've crossed paths," Bruster drawled.

"Yeah, I reckon so. How's Sadie doing?"

"Well now, she is mighty fine. Keeps busy helping out with the grandkids and anyone else who needs a helping hand." He smiled fondly just mentioning his wife.

Ken was busy heating up more rolls and pouring coffee when Bruster said, "Now Catlin, tell me, how did you happen to get hold of Ken here. Just come in the night and wake him and Muriel up?"

"Well, I must of woke Ken somehow because I was out in the back yard standing under a willow tree and all of a sudden, there he was. Now I wanted to talk to Ken before I got arrested, which I figured would be in a short time, but I was pondering how I was gonna manage it. I just figured I would wait until somebody got up and started stirring around the house."

"What was wrong with just coming to the sheriff's office?" Bruster prompted.

"I don't rightly know, other than I just felt like I needed that time to converse with Ken here first, just one on one. Then the law could do with me what they deemed fit, not that I am looking forward to going to the slammer. Been there a couple times in life and it's not my favorite rooming place."

"Well, we'll see about that later but I am glad that you stopped by here to talk to Ken. So now, let's just get to the meat of this thing and tell me what you have to," Bruster urged.

Catllin related the story to Bruster as he had to Ken, while Bruster made some note, interrupting him from time to time to clarify certain points.

"You do know, Catlin, that if this all checks out, and I believe it does, that you will undoubtedly be getting a much lighter sentence or perhaps none at all, other than for the threats to Ken here."

"Listen, Bruster, I told Catlin that I am willing to drop the charges against him since he has come forward with this other information," Ken said.

"Well, then I believe that Catlin here has got a pretty damned good break, considering everything. I hope that you see for yourself how square that is of Ken,"

Bruster fixed a penetrating sharp look onto Catlin, who was looking down at his hands.

Catlin raised his eyes to look fully at Bruster. "Sheriff, I reckon there's been little in my life that has been worth a tinker's dam but I am mighty obliged to this man here," and he motioned his head to Ken. "And if there is anything I can do for Ken, I am more than mighty glad to. All he has to do is say the word," he added.

"Well, Cat, I would say you can't do any better than that, other than just sailing straight and true the rest of the way," Bruster drawled, then reached for the sugar bowl and put three spoonfuls in his coffee.

"Well, I aim to do that," Catlin agreed.

"All right, now the way I see it," Bruster paused to scratch the back of his head, "Seems we got us a little situation here. Reckon I am going to have to think on this some because it's a fact that Pace Allard is a wily fox. Seems to me, we need to devise a plan to ensnare our fox. Meanwhile, Cat, you've gotta have a place to stay out of sight. Need to keep you low for a while. How about you stay in my old bunkhouse 'til we get this figured out."

"That's agreeable to me if your missus don't mind. I am right handy so if you got some chores that needs doing, I would pitch right in," Catlin added.

"Good, then I believe I will just have you come with me after we finish up our coffee. You got a rig some place Catlin?"

"Yeah, I parked it down from here a ways. It's an old white truck."

"Did you get rid of your Jeep?"

"Yeah, a while back because I figured the law had a make on it."

Muriel returned to the kitchen and suggested she fix breakfast for all of them. Bruster thanked her and declined. "We've imposed on you two good folks long enough. Now I reckon Sadie lady will do that for us and then I need to be heading in to the office to start devising this plan."

"Bruster, you give me a call if there is anything at all I can do," Ken suggested.

"I will do that, Ken. Listen, as soon as I come up with an idea on this thing, I will have you come into the office and we can talk on it. I think I already know the way it is going to be but I gotta call somebody first."

"All right, then I will just wait for you to give me a call," Ken said and watched Bruster put on his hat.

He stood up and turned to Catlin. "Come on, Cat, let's go. We'll stop so you can get your truck, then follow me out to my place. Thank you, Muriel, Ken, for the refreshments."

"That goes double for me. I do appreciate your listening to me, Ken and Muriel. I am ready to face whatever music I need to, 'cause like the sheriff said, you have been mighty square with me." Catlin stood there clutching his battered old Stetson.

"All we want is justice for the murder of that lady, Catlin, and those three men set free," Ken assured him.

"Yes, and I'd like to add that we'd like to see you get into a life, a real life for you, and realize that people want to be your friends if you give them a chance. Start to trust, like you did with us," Muriel said with an emotional tone in her voice.

"Aw, Muriel girl, I hear you. I want to tell you I will do that. And, by the way, I still think you are the prettiest girl I ever knew," and he tried to smile while his throat worked with emotion. "Thanks again," he said gruffly.

Ken saw them out and, when he returned, Muriel was wiping her eyes. "What is it, pretty lady?" he said, putting his arms around her waist.

"Oh, just so much going on, a mixed bag of feelings, I guess. Like Catlin wasting a lot of his life and just all of it, you know. Then wondering why someone couldn't have been there earlier to save Nadine's life. And those men spending nearly a year of their lives behind bars," her voice cracked.

"I know, honey, I know," he crooned, pulling her closer to him. She put her head on his chest while he rocked her lightly as though she was a child. "Listen, love of my life," he whispered, "you sit down over there and I am going to fix us breakfast." He kissed her gently.

Ken made a quick breakfast of scrambled eggs and toast. At one point, Muriel got up to help but he pointed the spatula at her and teasingly told her not to move from her chair or he would soundly spank her. He twirled it for a moment for emphasis and she saluted him and sat down. Her eyes shown amusement though she tried to control her smile.

"Ken, do you think that Catlin has begun to change?"

"Oh, definitely. I got it that the real change began when he experienced the event that scared the daylights out of him. Then he had a lot of time to think things out."

"Well, I guess a person is never really too old to learn," she agreed.

They ate breakfast and Muriel suggested that she clean up the kitchen while he go rest. "You didn't get much sleep so before Bruster calls you, just slip in there and catch some shuteye. It will give me a chance to make out a list of the people I want to attend our wedding. Then later you can do yours and we can tell Rosie how many invitations we will need."

"All right then, pretty lady, I will take you up on that since I do feel a little weary," and he got up, then bent down to kiss her before going on to the bedroom.

It didn't take him long to drift into a sound sleep. The dreams he had were a mixture of seeming realities that drifted into fragmented and segmented incompleteness. When the phone rang, he looked at the clock on the nightstand and saw that he had slept nearly three hours. He felt more rested.

Muriel opened the door to say that Bruster wanted to speak with him. He reached for the phone. "Say, Ken, would you care to come on into my office, oh say, within the next hour?" Ken agreed that he would.

Bruster continued, "Now, you know the plan I spoke about. Well, I got hold of some people who think we had better be putting it into action soon. I got a go ahead on it and just want to discuss it with you. Oh, and Pace Allard's daddy-in-law, Abe Falzone just left here. He said that Pace had called his son and daughter, checking to see if Marilyn had gone to see them. Abe asked my advice on what he ought to do and I told him to do nothing at this point. They can't know where she is yet. It's too bad for those young folks but it has to be that way for now. Abe agreed with me."

"I agree too, Bruster. It has to be done this way for Marilyn's safety."

"That's another reason that some action has to be taken soon. Those two young folks are coming here. Then Abe also tells me that Pace has hired an investigator, a private snoop. I have heard that he is real talented in his field so I don't imagine it will take him long to figure out where she is. I reckon that's even more reason for expediency on this."

"Okay, Bruster, I will see you shortly."

Ken decided on a quick shower, then hastily dressed. When he went into the living room, Muriel was working on her list of names for the wedding. "Honey girl, do you want to go to the sheriff's office with me?"

"How about if I stay here and you go ahead? I will wind up on this list while you are gone and get some laundry done too."

"Are you sure? I can help with that when we return. After we see Bruster, we could go eat lunch at Dolly's."

"No, sweetie, you go have lunch there and I'll go ahead and get some things done here. We have a lot to plan for and I may as well get some of it out of the way." She stood up and came over to him, kissing him. "Now scoot, I know you and Bruster have a lot to go over. When you come home, you can tell me about it."

"All right, pretty lady. I love you and will see you later."

He drove to Rosewood and parked by the sheriff's office. As he was going in, Bruster's son, Tony was coming out the door. He was struck again by the resemblance between father and son. Tony greeted him warmly.

"Well, hello, Mr. Ferries. How are you? Looks like it may be another cooler day. Week before it was a real scorcher," he went on before Ken could reply.

"Yes, it is pleasant and I am glad for the break from that intense heat. How are you, Tony?"

"Aw, keeping busy here with the job and the family too. Then I got involved coaching little league again. Said I wasn't taking it on this time since I figured I had done my share, but then you know those little guys said they would feel bad if I didn't. So I guess I am solid into it," he chuckled.

"Yes, your father said he tried to get other activities going here for the older youth but without success. I think that's a darned shame."

"Well, I do believe that is going to change because we hit onto it with some of the folks in the area at a recent town council meeting. After Dad and I talked, they kinda took a different view on it and talked about raising funds to build a community center with an indoor pool, gym, and a host of other entertainments."

"Now, that would be great. When you can get people to go along with a plan of action, that will draw the community together better than ever," Ken said smiling.

"Yes. Well, good to see you. Nice talking to you, Mr. Ferries." Tony smiled warmly.

Ken bid him good day and entered the office. He noted the absence of Katie so he knocked lightly on Bruster's door himself.

"Howdy, Ken. Come on in and draw up one of them chairs. I will get right to it and tell you what we got here. I devised this plan and ran it by the guys in special forces, since they are working side by side with me on this case. They okayed it to have a wire on Catlin Willard. Old Judge Bullard is backing it up too and has expedited things. Now I know Cat will gladly cooperate with us on this whole thing. He is anxious to get it over. I believe he has truly had a change of heart myself."

"Yes, I do believe you can count on Catlin now, Bruster. So, how is this going to be set up—with Catlin wearing a wire to talk to Allard?"

"I'm going to head out to home and see if Cat can set up an appointment this evening with Pace. He can tell him he found some property and needs some legal items taken care of first. Anyway, I am hoping that he'll agree to this evening appointment. Then Catlin is going to have to cut right into it, that he saw him come out of the Rogers home with blood smeared all over him, that he heard the commotion going on inside when he knocked on the door, and that he found Nadine on the floor. Now he can let Pace think what he wants to. I don't suggest that he tell him he is going to blackmail him but I reckon that is what Pace will think."

"Catlin is going to be in a lot of possible danger, isn't he Bruster?" Ken leveled at him.

"Well, no more than we can help. That is why we want it this evening, before anyone else is hurt. You know, Catlin has been around and I just figure he can handle himself. Then too, that place is going ot have some cops there undercover and a van sitting close by where every word will be heard. You know as well as I do that there are always risks with these things but it is the only recourse we have open for us. Thank God Catlin has come forward with this."

"You bet. Then there is Sage Murdock too, who can also substantiate what Catlin says. I know that isn't a recourse you want to take but I know it may be needed sometimes."

"Well, it is going to be twice as difficult if we can't get it done before the son and daughter arrive. Matter of fact, I wouldn't be greatly surprised if his son isn't here by this evening. Be a while before the daughter arrives because she is overseas." Bruster looked somewhat perplexed and scratched the back of his head. Then he frowned, looking down at the top of his desk.

Ken hadn't seen him before when he wasn't laid back. He knew that people often mistakenly saw that but that he was actually ever watchful.

"May I suggest that this is going to work and also that you join me for lunch at Dolly's. It's just about that time," Ken said checking his watch.

"Ah well," he sighed, "I know and I guess it shows that I am overwrought at the moment. Your suggestion for lunch is good. I need to get out of here a while and relax. I'm feeling just plain tension because I want everything to go well. I had a big breakfast and would settle for a light lunch. Then I need to get out to my place and talk to Catlin. Allard will be back in his office about two o'clock so I need time to go over this with Cat before that."

"It's eleven thirty right now so we have plenty of time. Come on now, I am buying," Ken urged him, grinning.

Bruster grinned back his wide, gold-toothed smile. He took his hat from the rack and placed it on his head. "Don't ever let it be said that Bruster Hernado turned down a free lunch," he laughed with the good nature Ken had come to know.

"It's all coming down to an end, Bruster, then we can all breathe easier. Trust me, I have one of my hunches." Ken winked at him. "Talked to your son Tony this morning. Met him as I came into the office. He is a fine man. He tells me that the two of you finally got the town council to think about a community center."

"They are good folks but sometimes a bit staid and slow to move on anything new but then the wheels of progress... You know," he chuckled.

They reached Dolly's Café and took a table the waitress directed them to. Ken watched Bruster casually survey the café.

"Yes, Tony is a fine man. I feel like he was instrumental in getting these folks to agree to see about funding for a center," Bruster related.

"How's that?"

"Well, Tony has a lot of charisma and folks are drawn to him. Always were. I tell you, I think he would make a fine sheriff one of these days. I'm hoping he will run because I'm thinking I won't be running again after this term. Sadie and me need to have some time to relax and do what we want, maybe some traveling."

"I agree with you and can see that Tony does have a lot of charm but, I tell you, he is a chip off the old block. Now I retired a little earlier than I had planned but you know I wanted to do freelancing. So I think if you and your wife can do what you want after retirement, then go for it. I believe Tony would be a fine sheriff, just like his Dad has been."

"Thanks for your support. Uh oh, would you look at what the cat's drug in that the dogs won't eat?" Ken saw a momentary flash of total dislike and disgust in Bruster's eyes.

Pace Allard made his way to their table and Ken braced himself for the usual onslaught of barbs from this sawtoothed blade of a man. Just his presence was foreboding to Ken, let alone a verbal exchange.

"Well, the good sheriff and the esteemed Mr. Ferries," Pace emphasized the latter as though he were in the presence of high nobility.

"Pace," Bruster addressed him while Ken merely nodded and leveled a steady gaze at him.

"Have you by chance heard anything regarding Marilyn's disappearance since I spoke with you last, Bruster?" Pace asked. Ken noted that those pearl gray eyes were devoid of feeling.

Ken turned his attention to the coffee the waitress had set down in front of him. He picked up his mug for a sip while Bruster related that he had no further news. A downdraft of a chill filled Ken suddenly and he was unaware of anything further in their conversation. He looked around the café feeling that presence he knew so well. He saw no one other than the usual assortment of customers but, for a reason he could not comprehend, he looked at the large window near their table. Regarding him was Nathan Tom, but the old man was dressed in ceremonial fashion, the likes of which Ken had not seen before on this ancient man. Ken knew that once more he had stepped into the spirit world and "saw" Nathan ready to celebrate this righted wrong.

"Ken, are you all right?" Bruster was saying. It snapped him back and he noticed that Pace had moved on to a seat at the counter. He was talking to a man Ken had not recalled seeing before.

"Guess I was wool-gathering while you were talking to Pace. Sorry. I didn't even see him leave."

"Well, he saw Lars Olsen, that private investigator, come in here so he excused himself. He didn't even notice that you never responded to his goodbye. He said he would see me later," Bruster said watching the pair at the counter.

"You really dislike the man, don't you, Bruster," Ken asked, watching his expression.

"Which one?" Bruster chuckled. "Frankly, I never cared for either of them. Had a few run-ins with Lars over there when he tried to get in my way. I had to let him know I wasn't open for his brand of interference."

Ken laughed at Bruster's description as the waitress brought their soups and sandwiches.

"They are both a couple of chafing boors and in a category all their own. Honest to Mother Mary, I never could figure how a lovely woman like Marilyn ever got tangled up with the likes of that Allard. But then, I reckon she got sold a bill of goods as a sweet young thing when she was off at law school. She was always a gentle sweet girl and I just wish that it had been Jeff Colter and her at the start. I thought maybe it would be in high school and maybe it would have been if she hadn't gone off to Boston."

"Well, maybe the time just wasn't right for them but I feel it is now." Ken took a spoon of soup, enjoying the flavor.

"And after all they have gone through, I suspect they can hold up to anything now. I know Marilyn's daughter is like her and will be accepting but her son has shades of his dad, I am afraid." Bruster shook his head.

"Well, he will either come around or he won't. Sometimes a tragedy will snap a person into some deeper level mindset. Look at Catlin."

"That's a pure fact, Ken. I just hope it is the case because, I tell you, this is going to be mighty hard on that family, finding out just how terrible and ruthless that man was, and here they've known him all their lives."

"Yes, I have thought about that, how a thing like this affects a family. On the flip side, look what it's done to the Rogers family. This shattered so many lives. People like Pace apparently come into the world the way he is, devoid of feelings for anyone but himself, sadly enough."

"I agree with that. Then you've got the fence straddlers who can go either way, like Cat was for so long. I hope that Marilyn's son has enough of her in his veins that he will wake up."

"Guess time will tell," and he watched Bruster take his usual three spoons of sugar and add them to his coffee.

Pace and Lars left the café together and Ken wondered if the investigator had managed to track down Marilyn's location. They appeared to be in heavy discussion. Ken and Bruster finished their lunch and walked back to the sheriff's office. They bid each other goodbye and went their separate ways. Bruster promised to inform him of the plans for later.

Ken drove back to Muriel's, thinking about his vision of Nathan Tom. He knew that the ghostly figure of the ancient one had gone unnoticed by everyone at the café but him. Nathan was a mystic with the power to transform and appear and it was a warning or message he brought.

When he arrived at Muriel's and came into the kitchen, she was on the phone. "Yes, yes, he is here now. He just came in. Oh, yes it does look very favorable. Well, sweetie, so good to talk to you. Keep your faith now, dear. It's Mrs. Gomez, Ken." She handed the phone to him.

"Hello, Mrs. Gomez. Yes, I did see Larry and I want you and your family to know that he sends you all love. Yes I was able to talk with him for some time and, when I left, he was much more at peace with the news I gave him. I know, I do know, Mrs. Gomez, but please trust as you have been doing. I know that your Larry and the other two men are going to come home. Just hang on a while longer and it will happen. Things are moving swiftly now but, please, just keep it in your family for now. I cannot relate all that has developed but, be assured, it is all in favor of your son and those other two men. Yes, Mrs. Gomez, thank you too and have a good day now."

He hung up and turned to Muriel who was seated at the table. "Now I do believe that dear lady's hopes are high and she has good reason. I wish I could have told her more but I can't. However, soon it will be a fact and those men will be released."

Muriel's eyes brightened and she sighed heavily. "So, Ken, how did it go with Bruster?"

"Well, Bruster is on his way home to present Catlin with a plan that will hopefully transpire tonight. He feels that Catlin has reached a place where he will fully cooperate and try to get Pace Allard to break tonight."

"What are they going to do, Ken?"

He outlined the plan as Bruster had told him. And he assured her that the police would be there to protect Catlin the best they could.

"He is going to tell Pace that he saw him after he killed Nadine?" Muriel's voice was raised in alarm.

"Honey, it is the only thing they can do. Yes, it is dangerous because a man who figures the jig is up may do anything, especially a guy like Pace." He knew she was concerned for Catlin and he tried to ease her worry. "You just have to do as I told Larry's mother, to keep the faith and hang on. That applies here too."

"Oh, I know and I just pray it won't turn into another tragedy."

"I do too, pretty lady, but listen, Catlin has been around and you can bet he will be able to handle himself."

Chapter_____22

"I am going to light a candle this evening anyway and say some prayers," she said and got up to kiss him. They held each other with a gentle lovingness for some time.

Then Ken finished up his invitation list for their wedding. He then put together more notes for his book, knowing that this was coming to a close. It felt like a part of himself was ending a chapter, but also that he had graduated to a new level. Wasn't that what it was really all about, that tasting life and moving on with reflections of every pathway taken? Some maybe weren't so good but each one is a step of life and soul development. Does every human being espouse a cause, each one creating life in their own design? He thought so.

He remembered back to his youth when "natural" events would come to him like bolts out of the blue. It had often seemed strange to him when others regarded him with surprise or, worse yet, like he was different. Thus, he had closed it off more often than not.

But now, in his sixties, he had reached a centering finally, more polished and less concerned about the opinions of the general populace. He was on his own pathway now, as they were on their own. A deepening peace settled over him and he glanced up at Muriel, who was smiling warmly at him, holding a mug of coffee.

"A penny for your thoughts, big man," and she winked. She put her mug down on the writing table in front of the swivel rocker.

"Oh, just some more wool-gathering, pretty lady. Look here, I have that wedding list finished and made more notes for my book. I can boast that it will be ready shortly, just have to get the rest on the computer. Say, Sarita will be home shortly and then I would love to have you go to Waco with me to meet her. While we are there, I will just get this done," and he indicated the notes.

"In fact, we could fly out of Waco to Houston for Carter's graduation. That would be easier than from here," he suggested.

"Yes, I am sure it would be, Ken. I am looking forward to meeting Sarita and also seeing Angie there." The idea appealed to her, Ken could tell. She had gotten past that initial family meeting and now was at ease.

"Where is your coffee, Muriel. Aren't you joining me?"

"Only if you are finished, honey. I didn't want to disturb you."

"You aren't— I am finished for now so I will join you at the kitchen table." He brought the wedding list with him as he picked up the mug.

"Now, I think we need to count up these names and perhaps have Rosie make up some extras, just in case we have overlooked someone."

"Angie will be out of school soon so she can help with the preparations."

"That's great. Sarita is always eager to help too," Ken mused.

"Well, we won't be lacking for help with Rosie either, I can tell you. I do believe we are going to manage to sail along. Now, what do you think about a reception here in Rosewood, maybe at Dolly's Café?"

"I think that is a great idea, for maybe a couple days after the wedding, for folks who couldn't attend in Waco."

"I thought it would be a good plan."

Ken nodded his agreement, basking in these plans with this lady. He was happy and feeling tranquil.

They made a count of all the people to attend their wedding and, afterwards, Muriel sat back in her chair and tapped her pencil lightly on her closed lips.

"You know, Ken, I really think we should consider doing the reception at Jillie's Steak House because Dolly's will never hold all these people."

"Honey, that sounds great to me," Ken agreed.

"They have a large banquet room that would certainly work well. People have receptions there all the time. I will set it up as soon as we have a date for our wedding. Maybe things will be more normal around here soon." She looked at Ken for support.

"Yes, it will. I'm thinking the first week in June. Don't you agree that would be a good time, pretty lady?" He took her hand and kissed her fingertips.

"Let me get a calendar and you set the date, okay?"

"What about the wedding on Saturday, June 8th. Then we can have the reception here the following Saturday, because we are going to need a break after the wedding to unwind a little. Is that agreeable?"

"Sounds perfect, sweet man. I know we are going to have a lot to do to get this all to come together." She sighed with relief that she could now get things underway.

"This has all been so hard on us, hasn't it? Especially for you. It is going to be good when it is time to turn the page."

"Yes, it has been extremely hard at times but I know, thankfully, that we will have a good life together. And I just feel that Nadine brought us together. I know she will be watching over us that day, Ken. I just feel it in every sense of my being."

He held her eyes with his own. "You can count on her being there, my love."

She bit down on her lower lip and Ken felt the heavy emotion surging through her. "Say," she said brightly, "I have some spaghetti to put on and have already made the sauce. How does that sound, my husband-to-be?"

"That is appealing to me and will hit the spot. How about if I make a green salad to go with that spaghetti? I am a terrific salad master," and he blew on his closed fingers and polished them in a comic gesture on his chest. This helped to lighten Muriel's mood.

"Now, handsome, I have always wanted a man who can turn me on with a good salad," and she smiled seductively at him. The lightness and flirting made their dinner preparations go smoothly, taking their minds off the events coming later in the evening. They sat down to the meal and Muriel produced a good blend of wine to go with it.

"Ah, yes, I have hit the jackpot for certain, finding the man that truly is a master salad maker. Now, are you already spoken for, you sexy man?" Muriel purred and batted her lashes at him.

"No, I am the one who hit the jackpot, pretty lady, because I have not only found a beautiful lady to share my life but a mighty good cook too, in the bargain." Ken winked over his glass of wine as he tipped it in salute to her.

They finished dinner, and after cleaning the kitchen, Muriel suggested watching a program on television. Ken knew that she was trying to stay in control and not become overly concerned but waiting for the phone to ring was difficult for them both. They sat watching the screen and Ken wondered if Muriel was seeing any more of this than he was. He had several passing thoughts, most of them being that he would be glad when this evening was over.

During a commercial break, Muriel turned to Ken. "Say, would you like some coffeecake and a cup of coffee?"

"Yes, honey, that does sound good," he agreed, glad for this diversion.

Muriel got up and went into the kitchen. Ken stared at pictures on the screen but saw none of them. The picture that began to form was not on the TV but he sat transfixed by it.

He watched a nervous Catlin Willard pause at the office building entrance, breathe deeply before entering. He watched him pause again before he entered · Pace's office. He knocked lightly on the door. Catlin seemed constrained as he opened the door to a smiling Pace Allard. He followed Pace into his inner office.

Ken watched as one observes a dream as Catlin seated himself in a leather chair in front of the desk. Pace seated himself behind the desk, reclining into a massive swivel leather chair. They exchanged pleasantries, then Catlin leaned forward in an anxious pose. Ken watched Pace as his face constricted into one of hatred. The pearl gray eyes were the cold ones Ken had seen in the hallway of the Rogers home, the eyes of a demented and terrifying mad man. He watched in fascinated horror as hands thrust into a drawer to pull something out, then there was a large explosion and the vision began to fade.

Ken's body thrust backward and he experienced a searing pain in his left side, leaving him gasping in pain with the impact. When the phone rang, the hurtful pain had disappeared, as though it had never been. He had been heavily jarred and realized he was perspiring heavily. HE reached for his handkerchief just as Muriel came into the room to say that Bruster was on the phone. HE stood up but his legs felt weak as he mopped his face.

"Ken, are you all right? You are white as a sheet!" her voice registered alarm.

"Yes, I'm fine," he lied but was visibly shaking as he picked up the receiver.

"Bruster, what has happened?" he asked, holding his breath.

"Well, Ken, Pace is dead and Catlin's been shot." Bruster's voice was heavy and ragged.

"How bad is it, Bruster?"

"At this point, we don't know but they took him to the hospital maybe five minutes ago."

"Where was he shot, Bruster?"

"His left side. But he was talking to the police when they got to him so he was conscious. Said he moved just right or he would have been hit in the chest or stomach." Bruster paused. "I guess when Pace aimed at him, Catlin moved to one side fast enough that the bullet didn't hit where Pace wanted it to."

"Where were the cops, Bruster? This should never have reached the point that it did?"

"One of them was right outside that office door and reckon if he hadn't moved as fast as he did, Cat wouldn't be here at all. I don't know what else them boys could have done. I hate it bad that Cat took a slug but I just pray he isn't in serious condition. I'm taking off for the hospital when I get through talking to you."

"Listen, Bruster, I do know the risks are high in these situations and I don't mean to fault those officers. They had a mean tiger by the tail. After I call Jeff, I will meet you at the hospital."

"Good enough then, Ken. I just figure maybe that boy of Pace's will be there too. It's gonna take a hell of a lot of explaining and I'm dreading that so I could use some support."

"Hang on, Bruster. I will be there soon. All right?"

They hung up and Ken turned to see Muriel standing there with an anxious look on her face. "What happened, Ken?" He could see that she was dreading the answer.

"Muriel, Pace Allard is dead and Catlin is in the hospital. He took a bullet to his side."

Muriel seemed to swoon and he reached to steady her. "How bad is it, Ken?" Her eyes were wide with fear and concern.

"I don't know but Bruster said he was talking to the officers when they took him to the hospital."

"So much has happened, I only pray that Catlin is all right," Muriel's voice held a shaky edge to it. "Pace shot him, didn't he, and then the police killed him?" She looked searchingly at Ken.

"Yes, He was fast apparently, pulling that gun on Catlin. No one had much time to react before Pace fired and hit him. Bruster told me he was struck in his side but, if Catlin hadn't reacted, it could have been worse."

Muriel slid down into a chair at the kitchen table and bent her head low, her elbows bracing her as she held her head.

"It's going to be all right now, honey. Listen, I am going to call Jeff and then I told Bruster I would meet him up at the hospital. I'd better be getting that done and scoot up there."

Muriel just nodded in agreement, not able to speak. Ken dialed the number of Jeff's uncle and Jeff's voice answered the phone.

"Jeff, Ken here. Is Marilyn there with you?"

"Yeah," Jeff drawled. "What's up, Ken?"

"Jeff, don't let on while I am talking to you since Marilyn is right there. What I am about to tell you I believe you need to pass on to her when you can sit down together and talk. Okay?"

"All right, let's have it. I'm listening," Jeff drawled slowly.

"I'm just going to tell you straight out. Pace Allard was shot and killed this evening." Ken heard Jeff take in a deep breath before he spoke. It seemed longer than normal before he asked for more.

"What, what happened?"

"A witness agreed to be wired and confront Pace in his office this evening. When confronted, Pace drew a gun and shot this man. Now the fellow is in the hospital with a bullet wound but he is alive."

"Jeez, Ken, what the hell is going on? What did he do to have all this happen? I don't understand." Jeff's voice rose slightly.

"Well, he committed a murder and the guy who witnessed it got scared to say anything. He just came forth recently."

"God, Ken, this is overwhelming. I mean, who did he kill?" Suddenly he heard Jeff gasp before he could answer. "Oh, jeez, oh God, it was Nadine, wasn't it?" He struggled with horror at this realization. His breath came in gasps.

"Jeff, are you all right?" Ken prompted.

Finally Jeff answered him and the man's voice was thick. Ken knew he was still reeling with shock.

"Yeah, I'm all right. Just tell me, did he kill Nadine?"

"Yes, Jeff, he did," Ken said, his voice almost a whisper. He heard a strangled sound like a wounded animal.

After several moments, Jeff spoke again. "Ken, I need to go now but I reckon we may fly out there. I can't think right now. I just need to talk to Marilyn but I will call you in the morning early before we leave."

"That's fine, Jeff. I'll be waiting to hear from you." The phone went dead and Ken stood there holding the receiver. Muriel could see the sorrow and grief that he had picked up from Jeff. His own heart was heavy. Muriel came over to put the receiver back in its cradle and pulled him into her arms. They stood there together for several minutes saying nothing, just holding each other. He knew that Jeff was reliving the horror and sorrow of that beautiful life that had been ended too soon. He felt tears course down his cheeks.

The weeks of it all had taken a toll on all of them and yet Nadine's ever-present spirit had prevailed. He knew that life really has no ending and he hoped all those who loved her had fully received this message. He suspected that they did. When he and Muriel finally drew back, he kissed her softly and took her arms.

"Pretty lady, I will be back soon. You go on to bed and don't wait up. Honey, if anything comes up, I will call you from the hospital."

"All right, Ken. See you after while," and she reached up to kiss him again.

He made his way from the driveway and noticed a full moon casting it's silver shadows. The radiance seemed to promise brighter days of life ahead. When he arrived at the hospital, he parked next to Bruster's cruiser by the hospital entrance. He proceeded to the first nurse's station since no one was at the front desk.

"Yes, may I help you?" a nurse with salt and pepper hair sternly addressed him. She looked over the top of her glasses, appraising him.

"Yes, ma'am. A man by the name of Catlin Willard was just brought in here within the hour. Perhaps you can tell me how he is."

She scanned a sheet before her. "Yes, that patient is in surgery and at this time we don't know his condition. Are you a relative?"

"No, ma'am, I am not but I am a friend of Mr. Willard's."

"Well, I can suggest that you go up to the surgery floor waiting room there and wait," she said crisply.

"Yes, ma'am and thank you."

She gave him a brisk nod, saying nothing and resuming her paperwork. Ken turned in the direction of the elevator, remembering its location from his previous trip here. He made his way to the waiting room where Bruster stood staring out the picture window. He had not realized that Ken had arrived until Ken spoke his name.

"Oh, say, I was really caught up and a couple light years away up there somewhere, I reckon." He smiled at Ken, the two gold teeth briefly catching the soft lamp light. He looked weary and sad. Ken knew this whole evening had taken its toll on him as it had on himself.

"Bruster, I was told that Catlin is in surgery so I assume you haven't heard anything yet."

"No, sure haven't. Still don't know how bad it is."

"Well, listen, why don't I go get us some coffee and we will just talk until they come let us know how things are for Catlin."

"I could handle some coffee, I tell you. I will just take it black. Sadie's been after me to cut back on the sugar. Thanks." He sat down wearily on the couch and Ken went to get the coffee from a nearby vending machine. When he returned, Bruster was absently leafing through a magazine but he reached up smiling when Ken handed him the coffee. He thanked him again.

"I expect you're wondering how everything went so I will get right to it. When Catlin went in to Pace's office, an officer wasn't far behind him but, of course, kept out of sight until he had to go in. Cat had that wire on him and everything was clearly heard out in the van. Cat didn't waste much time when he got into Pace's office. He told him he had seen him cut out of the Rogers home that morning and saw Nadine's blood on him. Right off Pace told him he could never prove anything. And if he thought he could blackmail him, he was dumber than he looked. He added some stout obscenities to that. He told him that this time it would look like an attempted robbery, where upon he pulled that gun and you know the rest. The officer shot Pace because he fired on him too when he came into the office."

Bruster took a sip of coffee and carefully placed it back on the table next to him. He stared thoughtfully at his watch and then compared it to the clock on the wall. "Did you get hold of Jeff? How did he receive the news?"

"Yes, I did, Bruster and, needless to say, he was shocked. But he figured out almost immediately that Pace had killed Nadine when I said he had murdered someone. I didn't tell him about Catlin being the witness. I believe he was still trying to absorb the fact that Pace was dead. I did tell him that the witness had been afraid to come forward until very recently."

"Of course, he will have many questions, as will Marilyn, when they get back here. I hope they come back soon because her son and daughter will be here. I bet Thor already is." Bruster put his hand wearily to his forehead and rubbed it lightly.

"Jeff said something about them flying out in the morning but he said he needed to talk to Marilyn first. He cut the conversation short but said he would check in early tomorrow morning and let me know."

"I do rightly hope that is the case because that family is going to need to support each other. I just hope that son of Marilyn's has grown up a tad more than he was. He tended to be a bit puffed up and full of himself. I reckon, if he hasn't, something like this may just create a man out of him. Depends on how much inner grit he has. I am hoping he has enough of his mother's genes to gear him in the right direction. Any way you look at it, it's a hell of a blow to find out your father has done a thing like he did. It would take every bit of flint in your spirit to make yourself move on," he shook his head sadly.

Ken nodded solemnly and then looked startled at a man who could very well have been a younger Pace Allard. Ken could feel Bruster start as he made his way toward them. Bruster stood up heavily, holding his breath. The young man's pearl gray eyes held a bewildered expression and extreme pain. "Thorton," Bruster greeted him.

"Would you tell me what is going on and what happened? I can't understand what has happened except that you were at the hospital." The young man's breath was coming out in short gasps.

"Thorton, son, you come over here and sit down. Who told you to come here?" Bruster said and took the young man's arm to lead him to a chair.

"Well, there was a delay in my flight so I had a little bit of a layover. Dad wasn't there to meet me at the airport. He said if he wasn't there, to just wait and he would come soon. I tried to call both the house and office and got some guy on the office phone who wanted to know who I was. He wouldn't tell me anything. He just told me to come here and not wait for someone to pick me up."

As Ken looked at the young man, he could see some of Marilyn's olive coloring in him and his mouth and nose were shaped like hers. He was perhaps two inches taller than his father had been but his presence was very much the same.

"Is my Dad here in the hospital, Bruster? Has there been an accident?" His adam's apple noticeably moved up and down as he swallowed with a worried frown.

Bruster was leaning forward in his chair. He looked at Ken sharply and a brief exchange passed between them. A sad task lay before him but Ken also knew that, if anyone could handle it, this unassuming yet assertive man could. Ken felt like a helpless bystander at this point but he reasoned that his best recourse was to be ready for whatever support he could provide Bruster.

Bruster cleared his throat and then plunged ahead. Thor was looking at him with a look of impending dread, sensing the unbearable message that was coming. "Thor, first of all, I want to tell you that your Mother is all right."

"Oh, God," Thor exclaimed and sank back heavily in his chair. "I have been sick to my stomach. I thought you were going to tell me that something terrible had happened to her." His voice was shaking. "Where is she, sheriff?"

"She is with some friends and I expect her back here in Rosewood very shortly," Bruster answered him and then went on. "Now, Thor, your Father has met with…well, son, your Father was killed tonight."

Ken could tell that the man could not assimilate what Bruster had just told him. His face paled and his jaw went slack while his eyes held a stupefied look. He appeared to be in complete shock. Suddenly, he doubled over and clasped his stomach, emitting a hoarse scream. He began to thrash around in an effort to raise to his feet just as Dr. Ellis came in. He looked at the scene before him with alarm as Bruster and Ken were restraining Thor.

"Dr. Ellis, please, this man needs something to calm him down," Ken said while still holding onto Thor.

The doctor paged a nurse who appeared quickly while the doctor came to assist the other men. The nurse came back and the doctor asked her to administer the injection while the others continued to hold Thor. Within a short time, Thor slowed his movements and then his body slumped. Ken looked at Bruster whose eyes were bright with unshed tears. He was shaking his head and looking at Ken. His eyes held the look of a man in total despair for this young man now sobbing like a baby in his arms. Two attendants came with a cart bed and lifted Thor onto it. Dr. Ellis indicated that he would return soon.

Bruster wiped at his eyes and then sat down heavily. He was still greatly overcome. Bruster reached for his handkerchief and blew his nose noisily, then coughed.

"Bruster, are you all right?" Ken asked. Bruster looked solemnly at Ken and shook his head sadly. He swallowed hard before he spoke.

"God, Ken, the horror for that young man and his family has just begun. When they find out that Pace was a murderer…" He hung his head with yet more sorrow.

"Bruster, grief has its own rhythm and pace for all of us. It's part of every one of us but we grow from it even when we aren't aware of it. I'm not trying to be cavalier or clinical because naked grief and anguish are a terrible shock, like that young man is experiencing now. Frankly, I believe that is hell, right here on this earth."

Bruster leveled a look at Ken and then nodded after some reflection. "You know, Ken, I just get a real awareness about what you've just said. I've arrived at a speculation myself because I reckon I've lived long enough now and seen the good and the damned adversities of humans to throw in with your observations." He paused before continuing. "Regardless of the fact that Pace was a ruthless man, I suppose his children saw another side to him, just like some folks around here did. You know, too, that some people aren't as keen on picking up manipulative personalities in such a clever man as Pace. Rightly now, I never liked the man but I didn't realize the extent of his coldness until now."

"Well, Bruster, he was part of the establishment, a citizen people would naturally look up to. Don't be too hard on yourself, my friend, because no one can be a hundred percent all the time. Besides, Pace was a very cunning man."

"Yeah, I know but what a waste all the way around," he murmured.

Dr. Ellis returned and sat down on the couch facing the two men. "Now, officer, perhaps you will fill me in regarding the man we just sedated. By the way, he is now completely under from that drug."

Doctor, his Father is the one who shot Catlin Willard, the man who was just in surgery. The man you just sedated is Thorton Allard. Thorton just found out that his Father was killed this evening. I did not give that young man details because he went completely into shock, as you noticed." Bruster filled the doctor in on more details of the evening with a professional demeanor, even though his heartsickness was in his eyes.

"Does Mr. Allard have any family close by?" Dr. Ellis pressed as he measured Bruster and Ken.

"Yes, yes, he does, Doc and I will be glad to call his grandparents, the Falzones. I am certain they will arrive shortly once they are aware that their grandson is here. Now, Doc, how is Catlin?"

"Well, that is the one bright spot of the evening. Catlin is an extremely lucky man, although he will be pretty sore for a while. He just got a rib fracture from that bullet but it missed all his vital organs narrowly. It was more of a flesh wound fortunately."

Ken felt himself go awash with relief and the same showed on Bruster's face. Dr. Ellis suggested that Bruster go to the nurses' station and call the Falzones, then bid them both good evening. He mentioned, before he departed, that Mr. Willard would be sleeping for quite a while in recovery.

Two weary men walked outside of the hospital and Ken waited with Bruster until the Falzones showed up. They had needed the fresh air. A night bird's lilting call told them that the promise of life beyond sorrow was coming.

Ken made his way to his car, surprised by the time when he climbed inside. The clock read 10:30. He hoped that Muriel would not have waited up for him but he suspected that she had. His mind listed all the events of this evening and he prayed that, in time, healing would come to all involved. At the same time, he asked that those who had not known Nadine personally would come to know her and her message in his book. He prayed aloud that they would glean a brighter awareness for what life truly meant and follow the beautiful trail of the rainbow.

Helen Makinster

About the Author

Helen Makinster was born in the rural farming and ranching country of western Nebraska during the "dust bowl" era. In the early '30s when Helen was less than two years old, her family left Nebraska for the Sacramento valley in California. Life for Helen and her family proved to be little better than it had been in Nebraska. Clean air free of dust was at least noteworthy, her mother observed years later. A wide range of experiences was to follow for this child of the "dirty thirties." As she got older, she held a growing desire to write, thus providing release and escape from an often harsh existence. Helen was a sensitive shy girl who did not easily express herself due to her difficult childhood. It would be years later that she finally realized the value of what she had to say. While Helen wrote her first novel, she felt guidance bringing an inner awareness that, even in fiction, there is an element of truth.

Helen now resides in northern Arizona with her husband Robert.